The New Confessions

The New Confessions

by
WILLIAM BOYD

Hamish Hamilton · London

HAMISH HAMILTON LTD

Penguin Books Ltd, 27 Wrights Lane, London W8 5TZ (Publishing & Editorial)
and Harmondsworth, Middlesex, England (Distribution & Warehouse)
Viking Penguin Inc., 40 West 23rd Street, New York, New York 10010, U.S.A.
Penguin Books Australia Ltd, Ringwood, Victoria, Australia
Penguin Books Canada Limited, 2801 John Street, Markham, Ontario, Canada L3R 1B4
Penguin Books (N.Z.) Ltd, 182–190 Wairau Road, Auckland 10, New Zealand

First published in Great Britain 1987 by
Hamish Hamilton Ltd
Copyright © 1987 by William Boyd

British Library Cataloguing-in-Publication Data:
Boyd, William, 1952–
The new confessions.
I. Title
823'.914[F]   PR6052.09192
ISBN 0–241–12383–6

Printed in Great Britain by
Richard Clay (The Chaucer Press) Ltd
Bungay, Suffolk

For Susan

Contents

Monsieur Rousseau embraced me. He kissed me several times, and held me in his arms with elegant cordiality. Oh, I shall never forget that I have been thus. ROUSSEAU: 'Goodbye, you are a fine fellow.' BOSWELL: 'You have shown me great goodness. But I deserved it.' ROUSSEAU: 'Yes, you are malicious, but 'tis a pleasant malice, a malice I don't dislike. Write and tell me how you are.' BOSWELL: 'And you will write to me?' ... ROUSSEAU: 'Yes.' BOSWELL: 'Goodbye. If you are still living in seven years I shall return to Switzerland from Scotland to see you.' ROUSSEAU: 'Do so. We shall be old acquaintances.' BOSWELL: 'One word more. Can I feel sure that I am held to you by a thread, even if of the finest? By a hair?' (*Seizing a hair of my head.*) ROUSSEAU: 'Yes. Remember always that there are points at which our souls are bound.' BOSWELL: 'It is enough. I, with my melancholy, I, who often look upon myself as a despicable being, a good for nothing creature who should make his exit from life—I shall be upheld for ever by the thought that I am bound to Rousseau. Goodbye. Bravo! I shall *live* to the end of my days.' ROUSSEAU: 'That is undoubtedly a thing one must do. Goodbye.'

The Private Papers of James Boswell

Beginnings

My first act on entering this world was to kill my mother. I was heaved—a healthy eight pounds—lacquered and ruddy from her womb one cold March day in Edinburgh, 1899. I like to think that for a few hours she knew she had another son but I have no evidence for the fact. The date of my birth is the date of her death, and thus began all my misfortunes. My father? My father was lecturing to his anatomy students at the University. Word of my mother's confinement was sent to him at once but the messenger—a dim porter called McPhail—could not gain admittance to the lecture theatre. My father's habit was to lock the doors from the inside and refuse to be interrupted. I believe that day he even had a cadaver on a marble slab before his lectern. The messenger, McPhail, having tried the door, peered through the portholed glass, saw the corpse and queasily decided to wait until the lecture was over. My father later emerged to learn the good and bad news. By the time he arrived at the infirmary I was alive and his wife was dead.

How did he feel? I can almost see his bloodless bony face, the thick tufts of unshaved bristle on his cheekbones as he looms over the cot. No emotion would be registered there—neither joy nor desperation. There might be a thin reek of camphor and formaldehyde overlaying the smell of tobacco that normally clung to his clothes (he was a sixty-a-day man). And his hands, firm on the cot-frame, would be perfumed too, with carbolic, and the nails would be edged white with residues of the talcum powder that preserved the rubber of his dun, transparent operating gloves.

My father was normally a clean man, almost obsessively so, and I could never understand why he did not take the end of a match or the point of a penknife to his cuticles and scrape away the small talcum beach deposited there. It was one of two personal features that I found continually aggravating. The other was his refusal to shave those bristles from his cheeks. Twin dense sickles of beard grew there, beneath his eyes. It is an affectation I have observed frequently among Englishmen, particularly in army officers, yet I would say that my father was a man almost bereft of affectations—so why did he persist with such an obtrusive one? As I grew older it sometimes drove me almost insane with irritation.

On those rare occasions when I came across my father asleep, I would stand and gaze at his waxy features—at once smooth (because of the paleness of his skin) and crude (because of the sharp angularities of his facial bones) and be genuinely tempted to attempt a clandestine razoring. I might at least remove or so seriously damage one that he would be obliged to shave off the other. Of course, I never dared, and the cheek-fuzz remained.

Why do I go on about it so? you might ask, with perfect reasonableness ... let me put it this way. When you live with someone, when you see their face every day, and you do not love them, the banal traffic of social intercourse is only tolerable when there is nothing on that face or about that person that attracts your eye. It could be a scar, a squint, a tic, a mole—whatever—the gaze is irresistibly drawn there. You know how sometimes in the cinema a hair or a piece of fluff will get trapped in the projector's lens and flicker and twitch maddeningly at the edge of the frame until freed. When that happens have you ever been able to pay full attention to what is on screen? Never. An irritating blemish on the face of a constant companion has the same effect: a large portion of your mind is always claimed by it. So it was with me and my father. He was usually irked by me, and I was needled by him.

Ergo, I did not love my father ... I do not know. Perhaps I did, in my own way. Certainly, it was a complicated enough relationship to do duty as Love's understudy. I know he never loved *me*, but that, as far as I am concerned, is of little importance. He did not love me because, quite simply, I was a constant reminder of his loss. As I grew older the correlation paradoxically reasserted itself. One of the last times I saw him—he an octogenarian, I in my fifties—I caught his image reflected in the slightly ajar door of a glass and mahogany cabinet (I had turned my head to call for tea). There was a detectable flare to his nostrils, a quiet disgusted shake of his head. And I remember being particularly pleasant to him that afternoon, in spite of his appalling testiness. But at that stage of my life nothing—not even he—could disturb my own misanthropic calm. His last words to me that day were, 'Why don't you get your bloody hair cut'. Hair. Very apt. Full circle. I almost told him I would if he would shave off his sodding cheek-bristles; said I would have seen a hell of a lot more of him in the last thirty-odd years if he had, but I kept my peace. I can see his pale blue eyes, hard and clear, sandwiched between their hoary brows, upper and lower, and still hear his strong metallic precise Scottish accent (I had lost mine by then, another source of scorn). 'Yes, Dad,' I said, 'right you are.' Fifty-two years of age and still trying to please the old bastard. God help me.

Anyway, I digress. Let me tell you something about this enterprise upon which we have both—you and I—embarked. Here is the story of a life. My life. One man's life in the twentieth century. This is what I have done and this is what has been done to me. If on occasion I have used some innocent embellishment it has been only to fill the odd defect of memory. Sometimes I may have taken for a fact what was no more than a probability, but—and this is crucial—I have never put down as true what I knew to be false. I present myself as I was—vile and contemptible when I behaved in that fashion; and kind, generous and selfless when I was so. I have always looked closely at those around me and have not spared myself that same scrutiny. I am not a cynic; I am not prejudiced. I am simply a realist. I do not judge. I note. So, here I am. You may groan at my unbelievable blunders, berate me for my numberless imbecilities and blush to the whites of your eyes at my confessions, but—but—can you, I wonder, can you really put your hand on your heart and say 'I am better than he'?

My name is John James Todd. My father was Innes McNeil Todd, senior consultant surgeon at the Royal Infirmary and Professor of clinical anatomy at the University. When I was born he was thirty-seven years old, astonishingly young for a man in his eminent position, a rapid promotion brought on by his eagerness for experiment and innovation. He was a 'modern' in the world of medicine, striving earnestly to free it from the tenacious hold of its medieval past (still alarmingly prevalent in the late nineteenth century). He sensed a lightning in the east and he wanted to be there to welcome the new dawn. He would try anything to advance its progress, such was his zeal, and some of his efforts paid off.

My darling mother was Emmeline Dale, the daughter of Sir Hector Dale, of Drumlarish, Argyllshire, a laird of vast acreage, little means and less intellect. My parents married in 1891. My mother was the fifth child of Sir Hector (his wife, her mother, died when she was five). She had four older brothers and a younger sister, Faye, who lived in England. My mother was by all accounts much in love with my father. They met when he came to cauterise an inflamed goitre

3

on Sir Hector's throat. In those days Sir Hector possessed an Edinburgh town house, in the New Town, Ann Street (which was shortly
sold, alas) where the Dale family spent the worst winter months,
returning to the big house at Drumlarish in the spring. Innes Todd
married Emmeline Dale in St Mungo's parish church in Barnton,
then a village outside Edinburgh whence the Todds originally hailed.
Sir Hector conferred on his daughter a modest dowry and the young
couple moved into the enormous apartment my father had taken—
for reasons best known to himself—in the unfashionable High Street
where, again by all accounts, they lived in blameless happiness—until
I arrived.

In 1892, some sixteen months after the marriage, my mother gave
birth to her first child, a boy, my brother. Prior to his conception my
mother had miscarried when five months pregnant. (A girl, I later
learned. Ah, my lost sister, what a difference you would have made!)
The new child was thus doubly anticipated and the anxiety attending
his birth also multiplied. Not uncalled for, as it turned out. My
brother's proved to be a difficult painful parturition and, although he
was robust and healthy enough, my mother required several months'
convalescence. He was called Thompson Hector Dale Todd. Curiously, he was Sir Hector's first grandchild (his four sons were all
bachelors and deficient in all manner of areas) and this fact, and
the suppliant nomenclature, earned my brother a lucky financial
settlement from his grandfather's dwindling estate (I was some years
too late).

T. H. D. Todd, my brother. Thompson Todd. I believe some of
his friends actually call him 'Tommy', but, even since earliest childhood, I swear, I have been unable to call him anything else but
Thompson. Names are important to me, almost talismanic. As a
christian name Thompson seemed (and seems, he still flourishes, the
miserable bastard) absolutely perfect for him. The stolidity, the
solidity, the thick consonants, the—from my point of view—utter
impossibility of imbuing it with any tones of affection.

Go to Edinburgh. Stand on the esplanade of the tremendous castle,
the gatehouse at your back. You are looking down the Royal Mile,
the ancient High Street of the city, the spine of the Old Town. Ignore,
if you can, today's scrubbed stone and loving restoration, the bright
tat and crass bustle. When I was born the Old Town was in a state
of severe decay, the buildings black and scrofulous, dark already but
darkened further by the smoke and cinders of a million chimney pots
and the belching soot from the railway station in the valley below.

The street itself was erratically cobbled, some of the stones were two hundred years old, round and worn like pebbles on a beach. In other places they had crumbled or subsided and the holes in the pavement were filled with sand and dirt. Here and there were pale grey new cobbles of Aberdeen granite. On either side stood dark misshapen terraces of shops and houses.

Turn now and look north towards the firth of Forth. All of Edinburgh's dignity and decorum has moved across the steep valley of Waverley Gardens to the neat elegant grid of the New Town. Its sunny leafy squares, its classical assurance, its perfect Georgian symmetry stood in potent contrast to the narrowing foul descent from the castle on its crag to the palace of Holyrood and its modest park.

Now leave the castle's esplanade and walk down the High Street towards St Giles' Cathedral. Stay on the left hand side. Through the Lawnmarket and on. As you go, you pass low doorways, squat dark tunnels that lead down to chill terraced canyons. Let four or five of these doorways go by and you will come to an entranceway named Kelpie's Wynd. Enter. Those of you taller than five foot eight inches will have to duck your head. Pass through the tunnel and you emerge in Kelpie's Court. Look up. The tall, stepped gables crowd in above, revealing a hedged, mean patch of sky. Only in mid-summer are the old heavy flags of the courtyard warmed by the sun. This is where the Todd family lived. Second door on the left. Number three.

These are curious buildings on each side of the Royal Mile. Imagine the street as being set on top of a vast sloping ridge. On the south side the buildings clutter and tumble haphazardly to the Grassmarket and Victoria Street below. But on the other side, the north, there is an abrupt steep descent to the railway lines at the bottom of the valley. On the north side of the High Street a house with four storeys at the front can have, because of the angle of the slope, nine or ten at the back. From Princes Street, across the valley gardens, these vast strict blocks face you like masonry cliffs seamed with narrow chasms. In those days they seemed prodigious edifices, embryonic skyscrapers, still growing.

Some of these old buildings contained up to twenty apartments, some small, some grand. Ours was one of the latter; I think at one stage two had been knocked into one. There was a large drawing room, a library, a dining room, six bedrooms and a bathroom. A large kitchen with a pantry, a scullery, and a sleeping closet constituted the servants' quarters. There had been buildings on this site since the fifteenth century. From time to time they had fallen or burnt down and new dwellings had been constructed on the ruins. The architecture on the High Street had the character of an antiquated, stone, shanty town. Houses had grown piecemeal, by accretion and alteration. Windows were all sizes—actually a pleasing diversity—and installing water closets and modern plumbing required real ingenuity.

The oldest part of the building was invariably the stairs and stairwell. Stone and spiral, they survived the periodic destructions. The steps were smooth, concaved by the stigmata of a million boots. The doors off were small—easier to defend, I suppose—or built for smaller, earlier Scotsmen. The well was always dark. A faint light drained down from a high window at the roof. Here and there a gas mantle hissed. There was a musty vegetable dampness about these stairways—like an old gloomy cellar: earthy, mossy, feculent.

Our apartment was on the first floor. Through the tiny doorway was a hall with wooden boards, empty, save for a fireplace with a coal fire always burning there winter and summer, as if to shield our home from the stair's chill grip. To the right a door led to the kitchen; to the left the living rooms. It was as if one moved not only from one climate to another but also from another era. From a world of stone and steel (the pocked handrail) to wood, panelling, paper, rugs and pictures. The drawing room had a fine moulded ceiling, the library an oriental silk carpet. The corridors were panelled in fumed oak, the bedrooms lined with hand-blocked printed papers. This was a legacy of my mother's last, fatal confinement. After her death, the character of the apartment—which had been tasteful, soft and comfortable—changed, so I was told. The house I grew up in was comfortable enough, but in a severe way. Few traces remained of my mother's presence. Or rather, by the time I was old enough to notice them, they had been transformed by time: sunfaded platinotypes, dampstained wallpaper, worn-flat rugs. My father did not believe in change for change's sake. Thank God my mother had installed a water closet—at least we could shit in a civilised manner. There were still not a few apartments in the 'lands' (as these great tenements were known in Edinburgh) further down the High Street where a housemaid collected chamber pots from every bedroom and emptied them down some infernal funnel set in the corner of the kitchen floor, where the excrement dropped a hundred feet into a communal septic tank, emptied once or twice a week by corporation night soil workers.

We had an inspiring view from our drawing room windows. Princes Street, with its department stores and hotels, dense with pedestrians, omnibuses, tramcars and motors; the National Gallery, the Scott Monument, the Calton hill; and below us the lush greenness and always busy pathways of the Waverley Gardens. They never seemed to be empty, these gardens; they were always populated by strolling families of Edinburgh folk, staring at the fountains, listening to brass bands, gaping at the humdrum flowerbeds. You would have thought they had never seen grass and trees before, so assiduously did they frequent the place. And yet the city is overwhelmed with views of the countryside, wherever you look. Stand on George Street and you have an unobstructed panorama of the Forth and across the wide water to the farmlands of Fife. Arthur's Seat and Salisbury Crags form a backdrop to the east. To the west the gentle Pentland Hills . . .

I used to be annoyed by the seemly traffic of the gardens. I always, from my earliest memories, preferred the Old Town—the uneven, black, friable descent of the High Street, dirty and reeking as it might have been. The most modest fall of rain had the gutters overflowing with mud. Further down the hill, past the North Bridge, the grey water would foam past the haggard derelict lands, the grim pubs, the foetid coffee houses and 'residential hotels'. Here the drunks, itinerants and prostitutes lived, plied their trade and whiled away their time. A castle at one end, a palace at the other and a cathedral in the middle. It was the spine of the city but also its large intestine, as it were, stretched out, coiled around the linked vertebrae—bile mixed with bone.

*   *   *

The child accepts his environment, however bizarre, as a norm, unaware of alternatives. It was a long time before I thought of my upbringing as anything out of the ordinary. Was I happy at no. 3 Kelpie's Court? I suppose I was, in that I never thought of posing myself the question. Thompson and my father were irregular companions, Thompson at school, my father at work. I grew up, almost entirely, in the care and charge of our housekeeper, Oonagh McPhie. She had a succession of scullery maids who helped in the kitchen, made the fires, swept and cleaned, and Oonagh's husband, Alfred, looked in every day to bring up coal if the bunker needed replenishing. But everything was controlled by Oonagh. During the day between breakfast and supper it was her demesne and answered to her sway.

She must have been in her mid-twenties when I was born. She was a braw, buxom girl from the Isle of Lewis. She had dull fair hair, always worn up in a bun, and big strange protruding eyes with heavy lids. She was illiterate but had a tough, sharp mind. Alfred, her husband, was a French-polisher and they lived not far away in the Grassmarket. She had three children, two boys and a girl, all school age, but they were never in our house. Oonagh would arrive at six in the morning and leave after dinner at eight. How did she run her own household? What happened to her children? We never inquired. I did, from time to time, but she always deflected my questioning. 'Oh, they're fine. They can look after themselves,' or 'Why do you want to see my tiny place when you've got this lovely home all to yourself?' I did not persist. I was not really concerned, to tell the truth, all that was important was that Oonagh should be there, at home with me. I never remember her taking a holiday.

Of course, I loved her desperately, with an aching violent passion that even now can make my eyes smart. Can you blame me? I never called anyone mother in my life. By the time I was old enough to discover the truth it was too late. I assumed everyone had an 'Oonagh' who arrived in the morning and went home at night. What else could I do? My mother's death wreaked its baleful consequences on me before I even knew it had occurred.

First memories. The rot setting in. Oonagh, holding me, saying something, crooning in her foreign Gaelic tongue. Oonagh looking at me. 'Poor wee man. Who's got no mammy? I'll be your mammy, Johnny.' Did she unbutton her coarse blouse, heft out a breast for me to nuzzle, tug and kiss? From where do these imaginings come? Infant memories, buried deep? Did she ever ... Did I ever press my small hot head to those cool, pale breasts?

One day—I am sure of this—I must have been seven, in the kitchen, Oonagh pinning up the flap of her apron, glowing white, new-starched, to her blouse. The thrust of her big bosom. Her raw hands smoothing the crispness round it. My huge eyes.

'John James Todd! What're ye staring at?'

'Nothing, Oonagh ... I mean—'

'Cannae take your eyes off my bobbies, eh?' Her hands unpinning. 'D'you want a keek?'

I fled, burning-eared, breathless with embarrassment, Oonagh's delighted laughter chasing me from the room.

My God, Oonagh had a lot to answer for—along with everybody else in that household. I look back now and understand that the prime function of a mother is to protect and shelter the unformed malleable character of her child. A mother's constant unquestioning love gives the child a bland but fertile mulch of normality and ordinariness in which to grow and flourish. What chance did I have in that house? My strange father, cruel plump Thompson, and Oonagh.... I *had* to turn to Oonagh. She loved me, after a fashion, but I was the child of her employer. She cared, but she established limits to her caring. So the need flowed one way, from me to her. Fortunately, I seemed

8

genuinely to amuse her; my presence, my personality was somehow diverting, and if I could gain her attention she would happily pre-occupy herself with me.

At first, I made the child's mistake of thinking that I only needed to behave badly to achieve this, but Oonagh had powerfully deterrent penalties. She would flick my ears with her short hard nails—my ears would glow hot for hours. She would pinch me under the arm, squeezing the soft flesh below the armpit between blunt forefinger and sharp knuckle of her thumb. She would lead me from room to room by the volute of one nostril. She would crack me on the head with a particular wooden spoon—and my skull rang with a deep bass bell—and once, once only (once was enough), after a truly heinous offence (what on earth did I do?) she put washing soda on my penis. Three days of boiling, flaming agony that no water could quench (how *could* I tell my father?)

So my transgressions were few. I took to winning her attention by the idiosyncratic direction of my conversation, by making up stories. Once engaged, she would chat away herself and then, sometimes, would come the endearments—a kiss, a Gaelic pet name, a hug, the soft yielding crackle of a starched apron in my ear, my nose full of the mild oniony smell of sweat from her armpit. The embraces diminished as I grew older, but my need for her love never waned.

Because her affection was so disinterested at first I experienced no jealousy when she became pregnant with her fourth child. I was six when it was born, a boy—Gregor. She would bring him with her when she came to work and prop him in an empty log basket in the corner of the kitchen. Did she breast-feed Gregor? Was that the source of my own false memories? (He was a large, ugly, though mercifully quiet child.) Did I mentally transpose positions with him? Was that where I saw those round stretched blue-veined breasts, Gregor's snotty button nose against their gooseberry tightness? ... Quite possibly. I was a jealous child. I still have that abrupt and destructive jealousy within me. It has cost me dearly, once, as you shall see. My neutrality towards Gregor swiftly disappeared. I hated him. He was the first person I hated.

I have said he was a quiet baby, he was, almost suspiciously mute, in fact. But one week he was colicky, or teething. He squealed and girned all day, his wretched noise even keeping me from the kitchen. Oonagh would pick him up, sing to him, swing him around, pat his back. She did other things to quiet him too—strange Highland customs, I suppose—like blow on his face or dip his feet in bloodwarm water. I came into the kitchen for my tea—cocoa, herring and turnips.

9

Gregor wailed in the corner, a grinding costive yell, his fat face livid with effort, fat little fists hammering in the air. Oonagh handed me the plate.

'Little devil,' she said. 'There's nothing for it.' To me: 'Go ahead, eat up.'

She lifted Gregor from his basket, unwrapped the swaddling from around him and laid him naked on the kitchen table. I looked on in some astonishment. He bellowed.

'Angry wee man,' she said. To me: 'It'll go cold.' I loaded my fork with herring.

Oonagh bent over Gregor and took his tiny penis in her mouth. He stopped crying instantly. He gurgled. One hand beat the air. His wall eyes turned sightless towards me. He shook his head to and fro as if resisting some powerful narcoleptic force. His eyes closed. He slept. Oonagh sucked on for a minute, rhythmically. At one moment our gaze met. I was immobile, fork in hand, drythroated. Oonagh rolled her eyes, as if to say, 'here we go again'.

She stopped.

'Right. That's you seen to.' Gregor's small rigid penis glistened, a thin pink cone.

To me: 'Sssh. Don't make a noise, whatever you do. Come on now, finish your tea.'

Oonagh, Oonagh ... Did you ever do that to me? Was I ever so fractious that you had to quiet me with similar ministrations? ... My God, those are dangerous years. When I look back on my childhood her influence is in many ways the most powerful and long-lasting. If the child is father of the man, then Oonagh shaped me. She educated me. She was the first woman I ever loved, unreservedly, whole-heartedly, unconsciously. From one point of view Oonagh made me.

But that is unfair ... It was not her fault that my mother died, that my father employed her, or that I turned out the kind of person I am. It just did not help. And the ticking time bombs she placed in my psyche have been detonating ever since.*

I never really liked my brother, Thompson Todd. He was a plump

---

* I met an anthropologist at some later juncture of my life (Paris, 1932, I think) and told him about Oonagh's patent baby-quietener. He was not astonished. He said he knew of many primitive tribes and societies where such practices were very common. In fact, *his* mother, he volunteered, used to masturbate him as a child—every night in his bath—up to the age of eight. Jesus Christ, I thought, the poor man! What sort of snake pit seethes in that brain?

child, with an oddly mature, jowly, sullen face. He never lost that corpulence. He had pale brown hair and pale eyelashes. In the summer, when the weather was fine, Oonagh would take us sea-bathing at Portobello, along the coast from Edinburgh. My first, fixed memory of Thompson—he was twelve, I was six, I suppose—is of being pinioned on the beach, my small shoulders beneath his fat knees, as he gleefully washed my face with sand. I had grit in my teeth all day. I have no idea why he did not like me. Normally, with an age gap of six years an older brother will treat a younger with a fond enthusiasm—a favourite sidekick, an instant fan, almost like a pet—but Thompson's attitudes then, as far as I remember, were either indifference or irritation. Perhaps, unconsciously, he sensed our enmity growing already; sensed the divergent nature of our personalities.

Unlike Thompson, I was an attractive child in my pre-pubertal years. I was small, dark and dark-skinned, slim with an unusually large, almost out of proportion, head with a shock of glossy black hair cut straight-across my forehead in an uncompromising fringe by Oonagh. There is a photograph of me, age seven, standing with Thompson on the beach at Gullane. Beside his bulk (his almost girlish breasts swelling beneath the horizontal stripes of his bathing costume) I look stick-like and frail against the bright sand. We are holding hands, untypically. I have just emerged from the water and my hair is wet and slicked back from my forehead. The altered hairstyle causes me to resemble my older self, in my twenties, in Berlin—gaunt, ascetic, cold, ill-used. A stiff breeze flattens the grass on the dunes, sand grains sting the backs of my legs as I gaze fascinated, innocent, into that neutral enticing lens.

The camera was held by Donald Verulam, an acquaintance and sometime colleague of my father at the University. Donald was in his thirties, an Englishman, a bachelor and a lecturer in classics. He sat on some University committee with my father and a reserved form of friendship had grown up over several years and had strengthened since my mother's death. Donald had a professional interest in medical history and had edited Vesalius's *De Humani Corporis* and had published monographs on classical theories of reproduction and of circulation of the blood. He was very tall, well over six feet, and had the slight self-conscious stoop common to many shy, tall men. He had a bony handsome look about him, marred only by his long neck and a rather prominent adam's apple. His balding hair grew long at the back. He was a kind diffident man who came to dinner once a month and played golf with my father during the summer on the many links courses around Edinburgh and the Fife coast. These were the only 'family' excursions I can recall from my early years. Oonagh, my father, Donald Verulam, Thompson and me. We went to Long Niddry, Aberlady, Gullane and Musselburgh, and sometimes across the Forth railway bridge to Crail, Anstruther and Elie. We must have made a curious group: the two earnest men, strong Oonagh, effortlessly lugging a picnic basket (sometimes Gregor too), moody Thompson, with a catapult or a kite, and me, fervent with anticipated pleasure. And yet my merriment was always shadowed by a distant sadness, as if I sensed the disparity in this amalgam of personalities, realised that its very existence hinted at another life, one that I should have been living, had my mother survived the fatal day of my birth.

Donald was an accomplished amateur photographer. He had a new Houghton's Folding Reflex camera and after he and my father had played their round of golf they would return to the beach where we had had our picnic to collect us for the return journey. Then, more often than not, Donald would have us pose for his camera. Thompson could never really be bothered; Oonagh declined—suddenly super-stitious—but I would obligingly stand on rocks, practise a swing with one of my father's golf clubs, or feed sugar lumps to donkeys—anything to aid Donald's compositions.

The only photograph of my mother that we possessed (in a black ebony and silver frame kept on my father's bedside table) had been taken by Donald. It was only later that I discovered that he had taken many more.

I was not a clever child, academically speaking. I was alert, bright, chatty and energetic but by the age of seven I could barely read. Thompson was by then attending the Royal High School, where my father hoped eventually to send me. However, it soon became clear that my difficulties in reading and writing were going to make entry into that strict establishment uncertain. Thompson had been taught to read, had been read to nightly, by my mother. Oonagh, as I have said, was illiterate. I spent my days with her as an infant and it was she who put me to bed at night. Without fail, I would ask for a story and she would tell me one. She spoke to me in Gaelic—old folk tales, I like to think—but I was completely entranced. The room dark, one lamp glowing, Oonagh's haunch warming my side, and her soft lilting accent with its sonorous, soft gutterals. Oonagh's square face crudely mimicking the effects of shock, surprise, horror, fabulous joy ... It was more than enough. I am sure, too, that here lies the key to my development as an artist, that this was why my personality took the maverick course it did. In those crucial, early days my imagination was not formed by any orthodox literary or pedagogical tradition. Oonagh's entrancing, meaningless tales and her big expressive face were sufficient fuel. I am convinced that it is this factor that separates me from my fellow artists, and it is this that makes my vision unique. Inchoate sound and dramatic expression were the foundations of my creative being. Sense, logic, cohesion played no part. Oonagh's mysterious voice and the bold analogues of her grimaces set my mind working independently. I owe nothing to any precursor, I had no tradition to guide me. What I saw in my mind's eye was mine alone.

Of course, my father was convinced he had a backward child— another burden I had imposed on him—and he sought to resolve the problem by sending me, aged seven, to his own elementary school in Barnton. He was on the board of governors of the Barnton village school. As its most celebrated former pupil, he had no difficulty placing me there. For some reason he had a perverse faith in its ability to reproduce in me the same rigid self-discipline and unwavering ambition that had secured his own swift elevation to academic heights. He was wrong. I failed as dismally there (in all but one subject) as I would have elsewhere.

His truculent conviction that Barnton village school held the answer had the irritating side-effect of a long daily journey there and back by train. Every morning I would catch the 6.42 from Waverley station to Barnton (whence I had a fifteen minute walk to the school) and in the evening, if I was lucky, I would catch the 4.30 train back. Thompson had a ten minute ride on a cable tram to handy Regent Road, while I spent up to two hours a day commuting to and fro from school. I was a lonely commuter too, moving against the tidal flow in and out of the city. More often than not I sat solitary in smoky third class compartments as the train puffed slowly through the banal suburbs, on its meandering branch line.

Donald Verulam lived in Barnton and, once or twice a month, if he had been working at home and was going into town to dine at his club, or attend a University Photographic Society meeting, we would encounter each other on the station platform in the afternoon. It was Donald—not my father, not Oonagh—who told me about my mother.

'You have your mother's nose and eyes,' he said once, a singular expression on his face. He pushed my fringe back. 'Yes ... She always wore her hair back.' He made a slight pursing movement of his lips, his adam's apple bobbed.

'A gentle spirit, Johnny ... A terrible, terrible tragedy. You'd have—' He broke off and looked suddenly out of the window.

He often had his camera with him, in its stout brown leather, velvet lined box, and sometimes buff envelopes of photographs and plates. He would tell me of the elementary principles of photography, of the carefully registered exposure of light to light-sensitive paper. And one summer evening as we rattled through Blackhall, he unpacked his camera, extended the lens on its leather bellows and allowed me to look through the view finder. I stood by the window, the bulky instrument heavy in my hands and looked at the world through a camera for the first time. It was only the back gardens and allotments of Blackhall, a view I had observed innumerable times but something about the mediation of the lens, the constriction of the frame, changed all that. It no longer seemed the same. It looked strangely different, somehow special, instinct with some potential ... The gardens and houses chased past before my eyes.

'Go on, press,' Donald said. 'It's easy.'

Which moment would I choose? I hesitated. Click. That instant frozen in time. My fate decided.

A week later when he came to dinner he gave me the print. A skidding blur of houses, light and shade, a tepee of runner beans, a diamond spangle from a greenhouse.

'Not bad,' he said. 'Good impression of speed. You'd think we were going fifty miles an hour.'

I showed the photograph to Oonagh. She turned it over, her tongue bulged her cheek.

'What is it?' she said.

'It's my first photograph. I call it "Houses at Speed".'

'It's no very good. Cannae see much.'

For my tenth birthday I asked for a camera. I was given a tiny Watson's Bebe, a hand or detective camera, as they were known. My father, happy to see some kind of interest growing in his son, gladly purchased it. I took very few pictures, from choice, not necessity (Donald's darkroom was always available). This parsimony of image-making seemed to suit me. I would go out and about in Edinburgh with my camera and often return home without having removed it from its box. So, what pictures did I take? I photographed a cabman's shelter in Balcarres Street, decorated with two stuffed marionettes. I photographed the lugubrious, mangy camel in Corstorphine Zoo. I took a picture of my father, in full academic dress, shaking hands with Queen Mary when she and George V visited Edinburgh in 1911. I caught Thompson dozing on a sofa in a sunny room, his mouth gormlessly open, one hand cupping his balls. I took a portrait of Sandy Malcolm, a blind man who sold bootlaces on the Waverley

Market railings. Round his neck hung a placard: 'Please buy. Am blind from dynamite explosion in Nobles works Falkirk 1879.' I snapped Oonagh with four other women and their children in the Canongate one day as they gossiped outside a milliner's. They all wore tartan shawls, even Gregor, five years old and barefoot. I was not interested in landscapes, streets or panoramas. I took living things.

Our shared hobby brought me closer to Donald Verulam. In 1912 he showed two of my photographs (Sandy Malcolm and a stonemason at work) in the University Photographic Society exhibition in the Trade Hall on Leith Walk. On the evening after the exhibition closed, a Friday, and as a kind of reward, I spent a night at his home in Barnton. We planned to go out to Swanston the next day with our cameras to watch the haymaking.

Donald lived in a large stone semi-detached house with a long neat garden at the back. I remember it as dark inside, with walls the colour of brown paper and with hard carpets of deep maroon and navy blue. After his housekeeper had cleared away our dinner dishes we went into the library. Donald smoked a pipe. I examined his new Ross Panross stand camera with its patent lens tilt. Donald seemed thoughtful, vaguely melancholy.

'How old are you now, Johnny?'

'Nearly thirteen.'

'My God. Thirteen years. Is that right?'

My father never mentioned my age. I knew what Donald was thinking. He looked at me. He had not changed much in the six years I had come to know him, except that he was now almost completely bald.

'I should've shown you these ages ago,' he said. He got up and went to a glass bookcase and took down an indigo leather album. He handed it over. I opened it.

Pictures of my mother. Close-ups, studio portraits, casual snapshots. I looked at her as if for the first time, as if I were a groom in an arranged marriage contemplating his distant bride. I saw wavy fairish hair, a slim small-breasted woman with eyes and eyebrows like mine. She had a hesitant smile in the portraits, her top lip tensed rather over her teeth. The reason for this was revealed in a snapshot where one saw small white teeth set in a wide gummy smile as she leapt down from a pony and trap into my father's arms. It was strange too to see my father with a woman, his face somehow decades younger, his posture more supple and limber.

Donald explained that my father had asked him to take my mother's

15

portrait. They had had several sessions, which explained the number of studio shots (he used an empty upstairs bedroom as a makeshift studio, he said).

'You mean she came here, was in this house?'

'Many times.'

I felt an odd tautening of my spine. I looked over my shoulder. I tried to see my mother in this room. I felt strange. I turned back to the album. The other pictures came from excursions and jaunts they all three had taken as friends. There must have been fifty or sixty photographs in all. (Donald gave the album to me. It became one of my most treasured possessions and I kept it with me through all my travels and ordeals over the years until a thief stole the suitcase in which it was contained from my hotel room in Washington DC 1954.)

'I offered the album to your father after she . . .' Donald said. 'But he didn't—said he couldn't bear to have it.' He smiled sadly.

I looked at him. I thought: *Why did you make and keep an album full of photographs of my mother?* Why? And how did I know then, aged nearly thirteen, that darkening summer evening in Barnton, that Donald Verulam had been in love with my mother? What made me sense that? How do children intuit these things? I have no idea. But I remind you I was no ordinary child. Already in those days my mind was working in distinctly personal ways. I cannot explain, though, why this conclusion presented itself to me with such particular force, but as I flicked through the pages, contemplating this pretty young stranger who had given birth to me the day she died, I felt myself brimful of a new liberating certainty. I had divined something; I possessed my first adult secret. I nourished it and let it grow inside me, warm and exquisite.

This realisation allowed me to cope with my father's strange coldness towards me, of which I became more aware as I grew older. He was never unkind or cruel. His attitude towards me was one of irritated bafflement rather than antagonism. He saw his second son, somewhat small of stature to be sure, but fit, personable, polite, the thick black hair now neatly parted on the left, the face, before the imminent ravages of adolescence, agreeable, open, apparently intelligent and, from some angles, distressingly reminiscent of his dead wife. Yet this boy's intellectual development seemed insuperably retarded. By age thirteen I could read and write, though my spelling was vile, but I appeared incapable of making any real progress with my other school subjects. 'Bad', 'lazy', 'stubborn', 'plain stupid' were the epithets that figured on my school report. Except for one: arithmetic.

'It says "excellent" here,' my father addressed me across the dining table. 'Why?'

'I don't know. I just find it easy.'

'Well, why don't you find anything else easy, for heaven's sake!'

'I don't know.'

'Latin: "no progress". Compositions: "unsatisfactory, makes no effort". Then I read "excellent". What am I meant to think?'

'I don't know.'

'*Stop saying "I don't know" idiot child!*'

'Sorry. But—'

'You're clearly not an imbecile. An imbecile wouldn't get an "excellent" for arithmetic.' He looked at me. 'Spell "Simpleton".'

Ah. This I knew was a trick.

'C. I—'

'*No!*' His eyes thinned above his cheek tufts. He looked at me with what I can only describe as despair.

'If you don't improve, John, I shall have to take steps to see that you do. I'll not allow a boy of your age to bamboozle me.'

These 'steps' had been referred to with increasing regularity over the last two years. I was not sure what he had in mind; I feared a private tutor or some sort of crammer. I hung my head with a suitable display of filial humbleness and left the room. I was not as perturbed as I looked. Since my discovery of Donald's love for my mother other complications had suggested themselves to me that made my father's ire and hostility more comprehensible. What if Donald's love had been reciprocated? In terms of attractiveness there was no comparison between the two men. I hugged my secret to me like a hot water bottle. It protected me; it set a distance between me and my father. Donald Verulam and Emmeline Todd ... it seemed entirely natural and likely.

Fancifully, I contemplated my face in the mirror. My mother's eyes, her brows. In the looking glass I thought I began to see traces of Donald's high forehead. I stretched my neck and swallowed trying to make my adam's apple bob like his. Could there have been something more?

I tried to elicit more information from Oonagh.

'Oonagh, did my mother have many friends?'

'Aye, surely. She was a very popular woman. Much loved.'

'By who, exactly.'

'All sorts. Everyone. Family—brothers, cousins—always busy, always visiting, out and about.'

'Did my father go with her on these visits?'

'Well, he's a busy man, ye ken.'

'I see.'

She was giving away nothing. But her reticence convinced me she knew or suspected more.

My father was still a busy man. His work at the infirmary kept him away from home almost all week. At weekends he often returned to the wards for a few hours to see how his patients were progressing. He kept a journal—a professional journal—and wrote up his observations every night.

He was always experimenting with new techniques of treatment, and these experiments were the only thing that formed a bond between us. It all started when I was about ten. One evening he came into my bedroom, a rare event.

'Johnny,' he said stiffly. 'Would you like to help me with something?'

I could hardly say no.

'This weekend, would you do me a favour? Eat nothing but apples and drink nothing but water ... I'll give you half a crown.'

He explained what he was on about. He was alarmed at how many of his patients died after surgery. He felt sure that the key to their survival lay in the purification of their diet. A 'complete cleansing of the system' was his aim. You have to give him some credit. Working in the days before sulphonamides, penicillin and our modern antibiotics, and in the earliest days of sterilisation, he had come across something that later generations would endorse. But he was working in the dark.

'It's the sepsis, you see, Johnny, I'm sure. Somehow we've got to keep the system unadulterated.'

He had been most distressed by a recent case, a little girl who had pricked her finger on a rose thorn. The tiny puncture had become inflamed, poultices had been applied but to no avail. When she was brought in to see father her finger—middle right—was swollen twice its size and a nasty plum colour. Father was a follower of Pasteur and Lister. Scrupulous cleanliness was his watchword. Over the next few weeks, in such an environment, he first lanced the finger, re-lanced it, amputated it, then removed the girl's hand, then her arm up to her elbow. He was contemplating whether to take her arm off up to the shoulder when she died.

'And all because she pricked her finger on a thorn. A tiny thorn ...' There was a look of stunned incomprehension in his eyes as he told me this story. It was a real affront, cruelly illustrating his basic powerlessness, and questioning his calling as healer. Hence this new obsession and my role in it as guinea pig.

At first I was happy to comply. He had never taken such a close interest in me. I ate apples and drank water all weekend. My pulse and blood pressure were taken hourly, my urine analysed and my stool examined.

'How do you feel?' he asked on Sunday night.

'Fine.'

'Any different from normal? Do you maybe feel a wee bit better than you did on Friday?'

I looked at him. His pale, clear blue eyes. Dad, I said to myself, I want to help.

'Yeeees . . .' I drew it out. 'I think I do feel a wee bit better.'

'Good lad. There's your half-crown.'

And so, once every two or three months I would be called on to help with the great system-cleansing experiment. There was the bread and milk diet. The root vegetable diet. The meat diet. The salted fish diet. I went on a week-long rice-pudding diet—rice pudding for breakfast, lunch and supper—during the holidays which earned me a guinea.

'How do you feel? Bit more strength?'

'I think I do . . . I feel . . . I feel a bit more lively.'

'Grand! Well done, Johnny, there's your quid.'

During my regime I would let myself out surreptitiously and wander round to the Grassmarket and buy a couple of sticky buns from the baker. I felt no guilt. I made father happy and it distracted him from my case, as it were, for a time. I feel very sorry now for those patients—the frail amputees, the feeble inmates of the isolation wards—upon whom I conferred the added discomforts of thrice-daily boiled turnips or constant salted fish as they struggled fitfully to convalesce.

By some standards I must have been quite a lonely child. Periodically, my father made an effort to integrate me into the social lives of his colleagues' families, but none of the friendships that ensued seemed to last very long. I recall twin boys with whom I played fairly regularly for a year or two until one died of diphtheria. And there was a girl—Lucretia Leslie—to whose house I was often invited. I cannot remember much of Lucretia (a violet dress, a cute chubby face) even though we were fast friends for a good while, except that we definitely did not expose our private parts to each other. At school I was reasonably popular, but because I did not live in Barnton I was unable to extend my acquaintance with my school chums beyond classroom hours.

For a while I hung around Thompson, while he was in his mid-teens and I was approaching double figures. I was not welcome. He tolerated me, no more. Anyway, as he entered his final year at school his extra-curricular activities took up much of his time. He was captain of his school debating society and was prominent in one of the quasi-religious, paramilitary organisations for boys (I forget which) that seem to proliferate in Scottish cities. He was a sedulous church-goer for some years (my father was not) and I remember him going on trips to convocations or rallies. Once to Birmingham and once, I think, to Antwerp.

Looking back on Thompson's indifference I wonder if it was a subconscious resentment of me, like my father's. Thompson was six when his adoring mother was taken away and replaced by a bawling baby brother. Did he, somewhere in his being, blame me for this crucial deprivation? My mother's death was the start of all my misfortunes. Possibly it made Thompson what he was, and what he is today: a cold, selfish, conceited philistine without a drop of fraternal affection in his body. And very rich.

So I was left largely to my own devices: Oonagh, my rare friends, my hobby. I wonder what I did before I got my camera? Played with Oonagh, I suppose. She always seemed to be there with young Gregor—her last child, as it turned out. Should I tell you anything more about Gregor? ... I treated him rather as Thompson treated me. In fact, Oonagh showed me more kindness than she did her own child. She called Gregor 'snotty-beak'—he seemed always to be in the grip of a ferocious cold, summer and winter, his top lip glossy with phlegm. Gregor ... It seems hardly worth it. He drifted out of my life shortly after. Later I heard he married, joined the merchant navy. Is he still alive? Are you out there, Gregor? ... Gregor need not concern us; he was around then, that was all, and he is one of the few people in my life to whom I bear no ill-will.

Oonagh. Oonagh was the tender nexus of my universe although I never reflected on it at the time. When I arrived home from school, breathless from the hike up from the station, it was into the kitchen that I turned.

'Here he is,' she would say and that would be it. I would sit down, my plate would be set in front of me and we would take up our conversation from where it had been left off.

Around the time I learnt about Donald Verulam and my mother— the summer of 1912—there was a slight but discernible shift in the relationship between me and Oonagh. By then she must have been in her mid-thirties, still a handsome strong woman, her protruding eyes as restless and shrewd as ever. She moaned with more regularity about the cold, her back, the doings of her offspring. We had had the electric light installed in the apartment now and what with Thompson and my father more often out than in her duties were not onerous.

What brought on this change? One day, one week, one month something was different, that is all I can say. She was more guarded, that is the best I can express it. Our easy discourse continued but now I seemed to sense a watchfulness behind it that had not been present before. Why? It was my growing older, I am sure. She missed nothing, and perhaps she sensed one moment the first adult glance I bestowed upon her, felt in my love for her the undertow of carnality. At thirteen I was counting every pubic hair as it appeared, scrutinising my chin and armpits. I was a rapt participant in the usual trade of smut and sniggers at school. I once barged into Thompson's room one morning to find his bed a small thrumming tent, Thompson's eyes firmly shut, an ardent pout of pleasure on his lips. I knew what he was doing. I had been trying it avidly, vainly, myself. So was it the shadow of the adult that fell between Oonagh and myself? In any event, things were never entirely unreflectingly the same between us again.

'Oonagh?'
  'Aye?'
'Do you know Mr Verulam?'
  'Aye.'
'What do you think of him?'
  'Well . . . I don't think much of him.'
'Why not?'
  'He's English, isn't he? Do I need another reason? Daft laddie.'
'Did, ah, did my mother like him?'
  'I haven't a notion. Now, get out of here, 'fore I dot you.'
I did not believe her for a moment, and her evasiveness confirmed my now burgeoning suspicions. She disliked him because she knew something had gone on. I was aware too that I would get nothing further from her. I needed another source of information and I had a good idea where I could get it—Mrs Faye Hobhouse, my mother's younger sister.

Faye was two years younger than my mother but had married earlier. Her husband was an Englishman, Vincent Hobhouse, a solicitor and magistrate, who lived and practised in Charlbury, a small

21

town near Oxford in the Evenlode valley. Faye had a look of my mother, but was taller, with a slightly ungainly pear-shaped figure. She had a pretty, even-featured face which was given a further louche attractiveness by her heavily shadowed eyes. She always looked as if she had not slept for three days, no matter how bright and alert her demeanour. It seemed to indicate another, covert side to her personality: a latent promise of depravity beneath the veneer of dutiful wife and mother. In due time I came to find almost everything about her—her heavy hips, her small breasts, her dun curly hair—almost overpoweringly attractive.

We did not see much of her and Vincent Hobhouse, or her three children, my cousins—Peter, Alceste and Gilda. I remember only two visits before this summer of 1912. They came in early August. Vincent Hobhouse had taken a lodge near Fort William for a shooting party. Vincent had one of the fattest faces I have ever seen, a prodigious jowl making his head quite round. From the front you could not see his collar, not even the knot of his tie. I often found myself wondering how he tied it in the morning, imagining him having to lie on his back across a bed, his head lolling over the edge like a corpse's to allow his fingers unimpeded access to his throat. He was a quiet, charming man, prone to melancholy. He had always been stout but apparently after his wedding he had blown up like an abbot. I could never understand why he ate and drank as much as he did; it seemed quite contrary to his nature. He and Faye were an oddly matched couple but they seemed ideally content.

Faye took a genuine affectionate interest in my welfare, rather spoiling me in fact, and, unlike the other members of my family, never giving rise to any suspicion that she blamed me for my mother's death. Indeed, I heard later that she had offered to adopt me, but my father had declined, averring that he and Oonagh could be trusted with my upbringing.

One evening, while they were staying with us, I showed Faye my camera and some of my photographs.

'They're splendid, John. Look at them, Vincent, they're extraordinary!'

'Good Lord,' Vincent Hobhouse said, quite astonished. He looked at me with new respect. 'Why don't you take up something like that?' he said to his son, Peter (two years older than me, a perfect snob, I thought). They occupied themselves with the prints. I turned back to Faye, watching closely.

'I was taught by Donald Verulam,' I said quietly.

A perceptible flinch.

'Oh ... Donald Verulam?'

'You've met him, Faye, I'm sure,' my father said. Faye glanced over at her husband. 'Colleague of mine. Known him for years.'

'Yes, I think I must have,' she said quickly. 'I ... I think with Emmeline once.'

My mother's name occasioned the usual subliminal tremor. It was more than I could have hoped for.

The next day we saw them off on the train for Fort William. Vincent supervised the porters loading their luggage, guns and hampers. I stood by Faye.

'Why don't you write to me, John,' she said. 'I'd love to hear how you're getting on.'

'I'm afraid my spelling's useless.'

'So's mine. Doesn't matter a jot.'

'Well ... all right.' I paused. 'Aunt Faye ... about Donald Verulam. You met him with my mother.'

'Yes ...' Odd expression. 'They were good friends, now I remember. She often mentioned him.'

'When?'

'In her letters mostly. She wrote to me every week, you know, Emmeline and I—for years.' She looked round. 'I think we're off.' She bent down and looked me in the eye.

'Why don't you come and see us, Johnny? I'd love to get to know you better.' She cupped my cheeks with her hands. 'Have you ever been to England?'

'Not yet.'

I looked into that kind face, those bruised, hinting eyes. She kissed my cheek. Her own cheek brushed mine, a powdery softness, a scent of some wild flower—musky, dry, promiscuous.

*   *   *

Donald Verulam and I sit in a tea room on the High Street in Newhaven. We have spent the afternoon taking photographs of the fishermen and the fishwives around the little harbour. We drink tea, eat large slabs of bread and butter, potato scones and jam, waiting for the charabanc to take us back to Edinburgh.

Donald fills his cup from a heavy brown teapot. He has a slight frown— he seems to be thinking about something. He runs his hand over his head, smoothing down the few strands of hair on his pate. His face looks thinner, more ascetic than usual. He takes out his pipe, fills it with shag and lights it. Plumy smoke snorts from his nostrils.

On the chair beside us sit our cameras in their boxes (I have a new

Sanderson) the leather already much dulled and scarred from constant use, the corners bumped and softened. I spread raspberry jam on my bread and butter. The ligaments in my jaw crack audibly as I take a huge bite. Donald eases back in his chair, his pipe going well, crosses one corduroyed leg over the other, and loosens his tie at his throat. One booted foot taps slightly to a hidden personal rhythm.

The lady who runs the tea shop approaches. She has a thin aristocratic face, her hair folded up on her head in an old-fashioned style. An agate brooch at her throat winks light as she passes through a wand of afternoon sun. Outside a dog-cart clops by, a slow rumble of iron wheels on the cobbles. From the back garden comes the contented gurgling of hens.

'Will you be having any more tea, Sir?' A nice voice—educated, soft.

'Thank you, no,' Donald says.

She glances at me.

'No thanks.'

We all smile at each other. Donald goes, 'Hmmmm ...' I look out of the window. Opposite a sign reads: 'W & J Anderson's Smithy. Ironmongery.' Someone walks by wheeling two empty milk churns in a barrow. A kind of buzzing tranquillity seems to fill my ears. I realise, consciously, for the first time ever, that I am happy. This moment is a watershed in anyone's life. It is the beginning of responsibility.

'Mr Verulam,' I say. 'Did you ever meet my mother's sister, my aunt, Faye Hobhouse?'

'Faye Hobhouse? ... Oh yes, Faye Dale. In fact I met her before I met your mother. Vincent was in my college at Oxford.'

The buzzing in my ears seems to have developed into a roar.

'When I got my job up here Faye introduced me to your mother and father.'

I needed no more evidence. Here was a web of falsehood and duplicity. They were old friends. Why had Faye pretended not to know who he was? To spare my father's blushes? There seemed, moreover, to be some complicity between the two sisters. I was confused. At the time, I was being led by instinct, only half recognising adult evasions. Had I been more worldly I might have asked if Donald Verulam had met my mother at Oxford? Maybe the two sisters had made trips there together to visit Faye's beau? Or, conceivably, if Donald and Vincent were so thick, perhaps Donald had met my mother at Faye's wedding? But all I knew for sure then was that certain charges seemed to flow through the air whenever the conjunction of my mother's name and Donald's occurred. My adolescent antennae picked them up and they reinforced the romantic fantasy I entertained about myself. A stranger in his own home, out of step with his family, the profound reluctance—I had to admit to this now—of acknowledging Innes Todd to be my natural parent.

I felt strengthened by what I had discovered. Things had been unknowingly divulged which allowed me to face my future with more composure and self-esteem. I began to see myself as trammelled up in a great doomed love affair. Perhaps the only two people who knew or guessed at the real truth were my mother and myself. The knowledge I possessed electrified me. For decorum's sake the masquerade continued, and would continue for a while yet, but as we drove back to Edinburgh that hot windless August evening I felt convinced for the first time of my own uniqueness. I could live the lie of being John James Todd a little longer.

Does that seem unduly precocious? of course it is, expressed in that way, but the sensations I experienced that evening were those exactly, if unarticulated.

I felt different from those around me. I felt I *thought* differently too. Different things affected me from those that affected others. My chancing upon the traces of Donald Verulam's love affair with my mother merely explained the source of those feelings. It brought a certain calm, allowed me to face my troubled future with some equanimity.

My father and Thompson faced me across the dining table. Thompson was going up to the University and in anticipation had grown a moustache, a sorry, soft thing that he kept touching and stroking as if it were a pet. Paradoxically, it made him look younger.

We had eaten soup—mulligatawny—and Oonagh had just cleared away the fish—breaded mackerel—and was now bringing in the neck of veal when my father said, 'We'll have that in fifteen minutes, please, Oonagh.'

Oonagh glanced at me and backed out of the dining room. She could read the signs as well as I. I had thought something was wrong from the moment we sat down. My father gave nothing away, but Thompson kept looking expectantly at him and his remarks to me were untypically solicitous.

'How are we today, John James? Fighting fit?'

'*We're* fine, thank you, Thompson. How's our moustache?'

My bravado would normally have stung him. He just smiled

complacently and needlessly smoothed the tablecloth.

I knew what father was going to address me about. My entrance examination for the Royal High School, taken a week previously. I said nothing. We ate our first two courses in almost total silence. Then Oonagh was banished with the neck of veal. My father took a piece of paper from his waistcoat pocket.

'Scripture—2 out of 20. Geography—4 out of 20. Spelling—0 out of 20. Latin—5 out of 20. French—4 out of 20. Arithmetic—20 out of 20 . . . "Dear Professor Todd, we regret that with results like these, notwithstanding your son's remarkable achievement in arithmetic, the examining board is unable to consider him a candidate for admission . . . etc. etc. . . . perhaps next year . . . further tuition . . . high calibre of other candidates, and so on."' He looked at me. His expression was more puzzled than angry.

'What's wrong with you, boy? You don't have to excel. Mediocrity would be sufficient. Aspire to that mundane level.'

'I don't want to be mediocre.'

'He'd rather be totally inept.' Shrill, pleased laugh.

'Thank you, Thompson.' To me: 'Don't you *try*?'

'I do,' I lied.

'Why, how, do you get 100 percent in mathematics? Explain that!' He was shouting.

'It's easy. I can see what I'm meant to be doing.'

'My God . . . *Right!* I'll tell you what I'm doing with you. The straw we must clutch at is your unaccountable talent for arithmetic. I spoke to a colleague in the maths department. There is a man, a Mr Archibald Minto, who runs a school for such wayward talents as your own. You will start there this September.'

This was not such bad news. 'What's the school called?' I asked.

'Minto Academy.'

'Can I get there by train?'

The one blessing would be an end to my constant commuting. My father smiled.

'Alas, no. You will be boarding. It is some thirty miles away. Near Galashiels.' He looked seriously at me. 'You have brought this upon yourself, John. I didn't want to have to send you away, but I refuse to allow you to indulge yourself any further.' He turned. 'Oonagh! We'll have that veal now.'

The next day I took the train out to Barnton. I had to talk to Donald. I have no idea what I thought this might achieve but I felt a strong need to see him, and I knew he would want to be aware of this decisive change about to affect my life.

I turned down the green avenue to his house. The blinds were half lowered in the upstairs windows. In the front room I could see a housemaid dusting. I rang the doorbell.

'Is Mr Verulam in, please? I've come to see him.'

'Sorry, sonny, Mr Verulam's away on his holidays. He's gone to England.'

The rest of the summer passed with distressing speed. Minto Academy, I learnt, had no uniform apart from the kilt, a garment I had never worn. Oonagh took me to Jenner's in Princes Street where I was measured for three kilts and chose the tartans. Two kilts were of a coarse heavy cloth for daily wear. The third was finer, a dress kilt for formal occasions. I had two sporrans bought for me, two short tweed coats with tweed waistcoats and a black velvet jacket with silver buttons. We also purchased oiled wool knee socks, stout ankle boots and delicate pointed lace-up dress shoes. For the first time I came face to face with the paraphernalia of my national costume.

'You look grand,' Oonagh said, when I tried the dress outfit on. I was not convinced. I was a city child, I felt I was being suborned by some primitive tribe.

Three days remained before I had to catch the train to Thornielee near Galashiels. From there the school trap would deliver me to the Academy, a few miles up the Tweed near a village called Laidlaw. As seems to be the norm with disaster, the baleful day was heralded by a spell of brilliant weather.

I sat in my bedroom looking at my already packed travelling trunk, fingering my camera and wondering if I should risk taking it and my album to school. More darkly, I swore obscure revenge on my father and felt strangely betrayed by Donald Verulam's untimely absence. I thought of leaving the apartment and Oonagh and my sense of self-pity overwhelmed me. I felt full of tears, like a sodden sponge—one slight squeeze and water would flow.

I think Oonagh sensed this separation as keenly. For all her irony and judicious affection I had been her charge for thirteen years. I wandered in and out of the kitchen smiling weakly, morose, pondering my future.

'Here,' she said. 'Let's go bathing tomorrow. We'll take the bairn to Canty Bay. Just like we used to.'

Oonagh, Gregor and I caught an early train from Waverley. On arrival at North Berwick we walked through the village and along the stony cliff path towards the bay. The sky was a pale ice blue. A few plump tough clouds hung up above, their shadows obligingly distant over the Forth. Coming over a rise I could see the uneven dome of the Bass Rock clear in the hazeless air. A very faint breeze rose up from the firth and below us stretched the bay. A few bathers and children congregated at the town end around the striped canvas bathing machines and a duckboard jetty where a long thin steam launch advertised 'circumnavigation of the Bass Rock—6*d*.' A small gnarled gypsy tended three dusty donkeys for those who fancied a trot up and down the strand.

We trudged up the beach to the far end away from the crowd. We were surprised by a hale old man—elbows and knees a lurid pink— who emerged from the sea quite naked and who, with a blithe 'Fine day', strode fitly across our path towards his clothes. We found our picnic spot hidden in a gully between two high dunes. Paths wound in and out of the sand hills fringed with coarse grass and disappeared into the gorse and whin bushes beyond. We spread a travelling rug, unpacked the picnic and found a cool spot for the ginger beer bottles. Gregor was stripped, hauled into a bathing costume and despatched with bucket and spade to the water's edge. I went behind a dune and undressed slowly. The radiant day could not lift my spirits. The excursion was so evidently an attempted antidote that I could not see beyond its ulterior motives. I tramped back to the picnic site enjoying the way the sharp dune grass cut at my bare legs.

Oonagh was halfway through changing. Her skirt and petticoat lay on the rug. Her swimming costume—a coarse woollen thing—was pulled up to her waist and she was now trying to work its bodice up beneath her blouse and camisole. I sat down with a histrionic sigh and picked moodily at a scab on my knee.

'Cheer up,' Oonagh said, impatiently removing her blouse. 'It's no the end of the world.'

'That's all right for you to say.'

She dropped her blouse on the rug and came and knelt in front of me.

'Come on, Johnny,' she said quietly. 'If you don't like it tell your faither, an' he'll fetch you home.'

'That's what you think.'

She made an exasperated face. 'Well, I'm not going to waste my good time feeling sorry for you if you're so set on doing it all yourself.'

As she talked she undid the buttons down the front of her camisole and shrugged it off. I looked up and for an instant saw her big white breasts with their brown nipples before she slipped her arms into the sleeves of her bathing costume and tugged the bodice up and over them. She pulled on her bathing cap and started stuffing stray tendrils of hair beneath it.

'Are you too sad to go for a swim?' She got to her feet.

I ran down to the surf beside her.

I have a photograph of Oonagh taken later that day as she stood knee-high in the green and spumy water. She is in mid-stride heading towards a wailing wave-doused Gregor. Her arms are raised to clear the next incoming breaker which is about to crash against her canted hip. The sodden wool serge of her costume clings to her strong thighs and heavy breasts. Her mouth is open—part smile, part shocked anticipation of the cold wave. But she is not sufficiently preoccupied to forget the photographer and her big bulbous eyes are caught—bright and knowing—just at the moment she glances obliquely at me. The pose is at once guileless and natural but the glance, the posture, the full curves of her body exude a robust coquettishness. As we swam and played in the surf I looked at Oonagh anew, touching myself, fast in the grip of her bracing carnality. For the first time I felt the rapt exhilaration of a pure sexual excitement. It seemed to catch at my chest as if my lungs were held by powerful hands. That perfect day at Canty Bay Oonagh exerted an influence that has dominated me ever since. My God, Oonagh, when I think of you now ... The terrible thing you did to me. But how were you to know? How is anyone to know? From that day on what excited me in the women I met and loved (except one, except you) was whatever element of Oonagh they seemed to echo and evoke.

We ran up the beach from the water, grasping Gregor between us. Oonagh wrapped him in a towel and started to dry him but he shook her off and went in search of other seaside diversions. Oonagh turned with the towel to me as I stood there, fists clenched, arms held out from my body, allowing my teeth to chatter, an idiot grin on my face. She hung the towel around me and began to rub my back and shoulders vigorously, warming herself through the effort. I looked at her wide face, her jaw undershot, her nostrils red-rimmed from the cold, the absurd cerise frills on her bathing cap.

'There you go, Johnny,' she said. 'There you go.'

Was it the word 'go'? Or the way she said my name? I wept. She held me to her, kissed my forehead, pounded my back, found me a handkerchief, fed me a stream of impossible reassurances. But I saw the swift knuckle at the corner of your eye, Oonagh, my darling, my downfall. You knew I was going away and nothing would ever be the same again.

VILLA LUXE 12 May 1972

On this island where I have made my home for the last nine years we are in the grip of an unusual unseasonal drought. The April rains just simply did not happen this year and the brute sun has been blazing at August temperatures.

I rent this old villa from Eddie Simmonette. It's comfortable, if somewhat dilapidated, but it has the advantage of a swimming pool. It sits there before me: blue, enticing, empty. In March a crack developed in one of the sides and it had to be drained for repairs. Believe it or not the roots of a fig tree, some thirty yards distant, had somehow managed to fracture the foot-thick concrete casing. And now, thanks to the drought, there isn't enough water to fill it again, without a special dispensation from the mayor. I've applied and still wait for a decision. I stand on my pool terrace and look into that perfect dry rectangle of nicely variegated blue tiles and the heat seems to roar up palpably out of it. At my age the only exercise I take is a gentle swim at midday before I mix my first dry martini. There is a beach which belongs to the villa but it's a good twenty minute walk away, down a winding path through the pine woods, then zig-zagging down to the sea where the cliff face allows it. The Villa Luxe is set high on the edge of the cliff looking out over the Mediterranean towards Africa. It has a large garden with mature trees—mainly pine and carob—and rather too many cacti for my taste. The villa is quite remote, a half mile walk from the village, down an unpaved track, which is why I like it and why I stay here.

I wake early, breakfast, then I write letters and devote the rest of the morning to the organisation of my papers. I work steadily through my archive each day—my many diaries, multitude of notebooks and memoranda, box upon box of correspondence and some fragments of memoir. I sift, I file, I collate. I'm trying to set them in some form of order, trying to discern some underlying pattern or theme amidst all that insignificance and muddle. It's a good job for an old man with time on his hands. (Whatever wretched biblical sage decided to plump for three score years and ten did none of us a favour. It is the most arbitrary watershed—why not four score years?—but once you pass it a fear is unleashed into your life like a ferret in a rabbit warren. It's like being out in a war-torn city after curfew. You are out of bounds and it's a good time to set your house in order, to pick through the fragments.)

Around noon I break for my swim then have a drink. Emilia arrives shortly after to prepare a simple lunch and clean the house. On her day off I wander up to the small café-bar in the village. On that day I usually take the local bus to a larger village some miles away where there is a bank and a post office. I post and collect the week's mail. I try and deal with my dwindling resources and the increasing complications of my financial affairs. Once a month—maybe—I venture into our island's main town, but less frequently in the summer because of the tourists. There are one or two people whom I know there—a journalist, a fellow Scotsman who runs a car-hire firm. Sometimes Eddie visits and sends a car to fetch me (he doesn't come to the villa at my request). I enjoy these reunions, we are old friends and he amuses me—and I him.

It's a quiet solitary life but I have no complaints after all that has gone before. A long way from Edinburgh in 1899. I look back on my childhood with the usual mixture of incredulity, pleasure and regret. In the context of this sad chronicle my life here presents some aspects of an Edenic paradise. I have a routine, a home, no enemies, no persecution, no real worries.

Outside the cicada's metallic shirring reaches its noontide peak. I hear the gentle farting noise of Emilia's mobylette. I wish the pool were filled.

2

A Sentimental Education

Archibald Minto welcomed me and the other two newboys with a genuine smile.

'I'm a fair man,' he said at the end of his speech. He had a soft, cheery voice. 'Some may say too fair ... But when I'm crossed, I flog. I rarely flog. I've flogged only five boys in the last two years. But when I do,' he was still smiling, 'I'll welt the hell out of you. Do I make myself plain?'

'Yessir,' we said. My fellow newboys were three or four years older than me. They looked like men, and one of them wore a beard.

'You're welcome to Minto Academy and you're all damned lucky to be here. Be sure and thank your parents.' He looked at the bearded boy. 'I'll allow a 'tache, Fraser, but I can't abide a beard on a boy. I think only of the filth it hides. Get it off at once.'

'Sir,' Fraser said, looking surprised. I shared his reaction as Minto himself was bearded. No one made any comment.

I do not know why it should have been so but Minto's genial threat worked. He only flogged half a dozen boys in the years I was at school. By and large we behaved ourselves and when we transgressed so arranged it that Minto remained in complete ignorance. In this we had the connivance of the senior boys. For all its strangeness it was a happy school.

Minto Academy had once been a moderately large private house. It stood in its own grounds on a rise overlooking the Tweed. From the main door terraced gardens—now grassed over—descended to a rugby pitch. The house itself was of a purplish brown sandstone that turned a dull murky mauve when wet with rain. There was a classical pedimented porch at the front with four fluted pillars, in the centre of an elongated but elegant two-storey façade. The top floor consisted of Mr Minto's apartments and those of the three masters the school employed. On the ground floor was an assembly room, a dining room, kitchens, locker and washrooms and three large dormitories where the boys slept. It was a small school with never more than sixty pupils. Behind the house was a square stable block with a courtyard and clocktower. Two sides of the square had been converted to classrooms; the other two were still occupied with horses. To this day I associate school with the smell of horse shit. Above the classrooms and loose-boxes lived the school maids and Minto's handyman and factotum, Angus.

The school had been founded by Minto's father in 1865, specifically established to 'cater for children gifted in mathematics and music'. After the Scottish Education Act of 1892 Mr Minto senior refused to relinquish control to the Galashiels Burgh Council and struggled thereafter to remain independent. In 1898 Archibald Minto returned from the University of Göttingen—where he was studying mathematics under Hilbert—to take over the running of the school after his father had suffered a severe stroke. Under him the school prospered modestly. He sold off some land and advertised its special facilities further afield implying that it not only welcomed mathematical and musical talents, but also anyone, so the brochure hinted, who could not fit into orthodox scholastic environments.

Minto was a passionate rugby football enthusiast and he determined that the Minto Academy first XV should excel in this also. Accordingly, he granted 'scholarships' to any strapping lad or nippy sprinter he fancied for his team. The school regularly triumphed in the local leagues, held up and down the Tweeddale valley. This obsession explained the presence of the bearded Fraser—he was required for the second row of the scrum.

We were a curious student body. There were genuine mathematical and musical talents but while I was there there was only one prodigy. Then there were people like me whose vague gifts seemed only to lie in one or other of these directions and whose parents were despairing of getting them educated. Then there were the misfits, encouraged by Minto's all-embracing manifesto. Boys who could draw well; boys who 'were good with their hands', boys who could run fast. Some of these types verged on the freakish. There was a brilliant juggler. There was one boy with exceptional eyesight who could read a printed page at eight feet. There was another, a thin long armed fellow who could hurl a cricket ball well over a hundred yards. There was a prodigious high-jumper. And so on. This category was the smallest in the school, seldom more than a dozen all told at any one time. They made up a sullen edgy population (we called them 'black buns' for some reason) who often lasted no more than a term or two. Outside the orthodox curriculum they were encouraged to develop their speciality under Minto's eye. He believed passionately in excellence and if that happened in an individual case to confine itself to cricket-ball throwing, then so be it. And then there was the rugby team. Local lads plucked from farm or mill (rumour had it Minto actually paid their parents), provided with board and lodging, offered the notional gloss of secondary education and throughout winter and spring as much rugby football as they could take.

Most of us were averagely good mathematicians or musicians. Minto took us for maths; Mr Leadbetter taught the musicians. The school orchestra was quite proficient and played regular concerts in council chambers and corn exchanges in the Tweed valley, incidentally providing the Academy with another source of income. Two other teachers, forlorn-looking bachelors, a Mr Fry and a Mr Handasyde, made a stab at the other subjects necessary to have the Academy accredited by the regional school board. These two glum, wistful men seemed more fearful of Minto than us boys and we wondered what duress kept them at the school.

Minto himself was a smallish man in his late forties. He had dark ginger hair—close-cropped on cheeks and chin, dry and wispy on his head. He wore round horn spectacles and had a friendly light voice with a trace of rhotacismus: 'weally vey good,' he used to say in approbation. Ostensibly there was nothing threatening about him. Any member of the rugby team could have knocked him flat, for example, but his discipline was unquestioned and would have done credit to an army barracks.

After one of his rare vicious floggings I asked the victim (a twenty year old wheelwright from Kelso) why he had not retaliated. His crime had been to give cheek to Mrs Leadbetter. He looked at me as if I were an idiot.

'D'ye no ken aboot that Angus?'

Angus was a big stupid man with pronounced pidgeon-toes. It was his job to control the beefier pupils. He had killed a man with his bare hands in a public house brawl, so local legend had it. After his prison sentence (manslaughter) Minto had taken him on. From time to time, I was told, Angus had administered savage beatings to any member of the rugby team who questioned Minto's authority.

In spite of these deterrents—perhaps because of them—the school was a tolerant, tolerable place. Only once did I suffer at the hands of other boys but it was an initiation rite that everyone underwent.

This was a bonding ritual known as the 'wax-bogey plate'. On his first night in the dormitory a newboy was obliged to consume a symbolic meal consisting of small balls—the size of shot—made up of earwax and phlegm. The other boys mined their orifices for the raw material which they then diligently rolled into little balls. Collected on a plate, these were then presented to the initiate. It looked like a loose beige caviar. You had the choice of eating them individually or all at once. I selected the latter course. It was not so unpleasant. A swallow, a quick swill round the mouth with your tongue. Only the sour taste of earwax lingered for an hour or two.

I was reasonably happy at Minto Academy, and I owe it two great debts. I learnt as much about mathematics as I was going to learn in a classroom, and I met there the truest friend anyone could have.

Hamish Malahide was the school's only bona fide prodigy. He was a year older than me and had been at the Academy for two years. He was so good at maths that Minto gave him private tuition. I encountered him shortly after I arrived.

One dark Sunday evening before chapel a senior boy sent me over to the classroom block to fetch something or other. On my way back I saw a group of boys—six or seven—gathered round the railings at the rear of the house. Here there was a small basement well that led to the coal cellars and the boiler house—Angus's responsibility and strictly out of bounds. As I approached I recognised the boys were all 'black buns'. They were laughing with enjoyment and pleasure, holding their kilt fronts up and urinating into the basement well. I looked down and saw a figure trying to dodge the spraying streams with little success. Then he tripped and the arcs of piss zeroed in, pattering loudly on his clothes until he scrambled up again. The ordeal lasted only as long as the tormentor's bladders held out. Soon the urinators gave up and wandered away. In the well the figure tugged fitfully at his damp clothes. I was struck by the fact that he had made no sound of complaint. He looked up at me.

'I suppose you want to have a shot now.'

'No,' I said. 'Not at all.'

'Give us a hand,' he said as he climbed the steps.

I grabbed his moist hand and helped him over the high railings. The gate was padlocked.

'Thanks.' He explained how he had been caught by the 'black buns' and had been hustled into the well.

'Why did they do it?'

'Who knows?'

We walked in the back door. A maid came out of the kitchen and glanced at us curiously before walking away. In the light from the gas mantle in the corridor I took a closer look at the victim. At that stage I did not know his name but I knew his face. Hamish Malahide had the worst acne I had ever seen, or have ever seen since. He had spots everywhere, from his forehead to his chin. They clustered thickly round his nose and below his bottom lip. His neck and jawbone were rashed with them. He even seemed to have spots in his hair. His face looked so angry and sore, not to say repellent, that one wanted to flinch. I saw later the boils on his back, the large red buttons, the hard pink wens of incipient pustules.

I did not flinch, in fact, but he would not have noticed anyway, preoccupied as he was with the state of his clothes.

'I'll have to change,' he said. 'Bastards.'

'Why don't you tell Minto? He said we should report bullying.'

He looked at me. 'New rat?'

'Yes.'

'Minto would flog them, I suppose, but he always flogs the fellow who clypes as well.'

'Oh.'

'It's not worth it. You'll understand when you see how Minto flogs.'

'Why does he flog the victim?'

'Makes sense. He has a quieter life. He knows that when someone does complain it's really serious.'

He smiled. He had large uneven teeth. He had fair hair and a pale skin that somehow made his acne seem worse. He was an ugly boy.

'What's your name?'

'Todd.'

'I'm Malahide. Thanks for not slashing on me, Todd.' He paused. 'I won't forget it. Ever.'

It was a strange thing to say. He smiled again and walked off. So began the most important friendship of my life.

Mathematics. Why was I good at it and indifferent-to-poor in my other subjects? I believe that sort of skill or talent is something to do with the cast of the individual mind, innate, *a priori*. How could I, whose imagination was first stimulated by unknown stories in an incomprehensible tongue, have a talent for mathematics? The only answer I can supply is precisely *because* my imagination is stimulated in that way. I went to school clear-eyed, unformed. I remember my first arithmetic class. The rear wall was covered with charts of the multiplication tables.

'Right, Todd. Six times table.'

'What table, sir?'

Uproar in the class. I was put at a separate desk to learn my tables. The numbers crowded before my eyes. I looked at the nine times table. I saw at once, with the clarity of instinct, that the integers in the answers to each calculation themselves added up to nine. $9 \times 2 = 18$. $1 + 8 = 9$. $9 \times 3 = 27$. $2 + 7 = 9$. And so on up to ten. I drew my teacher's attention to this and received my first words of praise.

What made me notice this? What made me see the pattern? And what kind of conjuring trick in that most abstract of worlds is being played here? I am not saying that I felt in some way blessed but I do consider that some sort of inkling was being offered to me here. Since that first day at school and since that discovery the realm of mathematics was, for me, teeming with promise. What other secrets would I find? What other insights?

It is said that there are two types of mathematician. 90 percent see in figures. 10 percent see in pictures. The most brilliant, the most profound come from that 10 percent. In my own case I think that for a few early years I saw the world of numbers in pictures, that I had the gift up to the age of ten and then, for some reason, it faded into mere proficient numeracy. But the great mathematicians never lose that facility. Perhaps that is why infant prodigies only occur in the world of maths, music and chess. These regions can be surveyed pictorially, patterns and shapes can be perceived there. Order can be discerned among randomness, sense separated from contingency. Or at least that is what I used to think. I have abandoned explanations now. Mathematics and physics have led me to greater more disturbing truths than these, as I shall reveal to you. Sense, order, pattern, meaning . . . they are all illusions.

Hamish Malahide, of course, was one of those 10 percent. I like to think we all are at birth, but the *tabula rasa* is quickly scored with confusing hieroglyphics which we never manage to erase again. I was lucky. I had that guileless vision for a few extra years. Hamish never lost it. He was extraordinary. Mathematicians, like artists, tend to have their peak periods. Hamish did also and as a young man produced the celebrated Malahide Paradoxes I and II. There was a brief refulgence in the '40s with the discovery of the Malahide Number but after his twenties the creative power waned, almost like a form of ageing. But his perception remained ever vigorous and acute, right to the end of his desperately unhappy life.

At Minto Academy it took me some time to realise his qualities. At school he was a reviled and unpopular figure because of his appalling acne. Even Mrs Leadbetter, the matron, gave up any pretence of medical impassivity in her vain attempts to keep it under control. She wore cotton gloves when she dabbed the goo and patent lotions on his face, her nostrils tight with disgust. Some of the school wits called him Job and the name stuck. In summer we often went to the Tweed to bathe and Hamish had to swim downstream from the rest of us. Even I, his only friend, had to admit that unclothed he did look repulsive. Consequently I often found myself divided in that role. There were things about him that I found potently intriguing, but if I looked too closely at those vivid encrusted spots my scalp literally began to crawl and my eyes water. But Hamish, with his typical sensitivity, sensed my dilemma. One day he showed me a small pot of ointment.

'What's that?'

'My mother sent it to me: "Dr Keith Harvey's Emulsion. Cures Warts, Acne, Lupus, Locomotor-Ataxy and St Vitus's Dance". She sends me these things once a month.' He smiled. 'For my rotten plooks.'

'Oh yes,' I said, as if I had just noticed them. 'It must be a ...' I could not think of a word—nuisance seemed such a grotesque understatement.

'A curse,' he said. 'I've been cursed, I know.'

The candour was sufficient to remove the awkwardness between us. After that we often spoke about his spots. I even read the book of Job in the Bible.

'They'll go,' I said. 'My brother had spots, they all went.'

'But what'll I look like underneath?' he said with a weird grin. 'I can't imagine what my face'll be like, clean.'

'Normal ... won't it?'

'I'm not so sure.'

My friendship with Hamish grew as that first term passed. Although we were both maths specialists he was so far advanced he might have been doing another subject altogether. To take an architectural analogy: while the rest of us were designing cab shelters and public lavatories Hamish was building Gothic cathedrals. From time to time he spoke about mathematics and I began to gain some insight into the strange and beautiful workings of his mind.

In our class Minto had set us a project to discover all the prime numbers up to one million. (A prime number, for those of you who do not know, is a number which is not divisible by any other counting number—apart from itself and one. 11 is a prime number, so is 19, so is 37.) The project was a long-term one and had been going on for years. Successive generations of schoolboys had been like Minto's researchers, scrabbling away amongst the numbers from 1 to 1,000,000, and coming up, like gold prospectors with the occasional nugget—a prime. As we discovered them we wrote them on a vast wall chart. We were systematically organised by Minto, each one having a few thousand numbers to sift. The project was completed shortly after I arrived. We counted up and had a total of 41,539 primes. Then Minto, with the air of a conjuror producing a rabbit from a hat, showed us a calculation for estimating the amount of primes between any two given numbers. But, interestingly, the figure the calculation produced was 67 numbers out. Checks established that the calculation, while close, was never exactly right.

'Why is it only approximate, sir?' Hamish asked. 'Why can't we get it right?'

'Because we can't.' Minto seemed irritated. 'That's the nature of primes.'

On his own Hamish tried to improve the accuracy of the calculation, but with no success.

'I can't get any more accurate. Just can't,' he said to me one day as we watched a rugby match.

'Never mind.'

'It bothers me ... There must be something significant about primes—the way they exist in the way they do. It must be telling us something.'

'Do you think so?'

'Numbers are infinite, so there must be an infinite number of primes.'

I had no idea what he was talking about.

'But there's no pattern. They don't crop up in any order. That calculation we did—it's never exact. Why? Why can't we pin them down? What are they trying to tell us?'

'Are you feeling all right?'

'Why is there no pattern? There *should* be.'

'Did prime numbers exist before we thought about them?' I was surprised at my own question, unsure of its implications. But Hamish seemed to know.

'Exactly, Todd, exactly. Think of the first man who started counting, started adding up ... Look where it's got to now.'

It made no sense to me. Now, I understand more of what Hamish saw as a fourteen year old. For him the world of abstract mathematical explanation was like an entrancing, enchanted forest to an avid explorer. He was already far down a jungle path beckoning me to follow.

*   *   *

I soon settled into the routine at Minto Academy, but because of my friendship with Hamish it was a little difficult to establish any closer aquaintance with the other boys. It did not perturb me. There was little bullying. The dormitories were segregated by age with one senior boy appointed dormitory leader and responsible for discipline. These were in fact the only ranks in the school, off the sportsfield. There were eighteen in our dormitory. We slept on iron beds separated by thin wooden wardrobes. Hamish's bed was four away from mine (yes, I had eaten his wax-bogey). Apart from vigorous masturbation there was little vice. A few boys chose to creep into each other's beds but no-one objected or thought it unduly strange. Food was plentiful but unimaginative. Porridge, milk and bread in the morning. A joint of meat—mutton, nine times out of ten—at lunch, and the same joint cold in the evening with vegetables, and cocoa to drink.

At weekends, the Saturday was spent watching the rugby team win at home or away. And on Sunday the entire school was taken on an immensely long walk by a drab Mr Fry or a sad Mr Handasyde. Time passed, and not so slowly. I found that my homesickness had left me after a week. My only regret was that I received few letters. Oonagh could not write, my father was too busy and Thompson could not be bothered. I thought about taking up my Aunt Faye's offer but could not summon up the courage. I received the occasional post card from my father. I still possess one. I reproduce it in full.

> 3, Kelpie's Court,
> Edinburgh,
> 21, October 1913
>
> Dear John James,
>   Thank you for your letter. Yes, your friend Malahide may consult me if you wish but it sounds as if a dermatologist might be more efficacious. I regret to say that the rice diet had no significant effect on my patients. Thank you for asking.
>   Thompson is well, Oonagh sends her cordial greetings.
> > > Your affect. father
> > > I. M. Todd

I wrote once to Donald Verulam, on the pretext of some photographic business, and he replied promptly and fully asking me to write again. I meant to, but never got round to it. The school was not what I had feared; and in it, to my vague surprise, I felt I had discovered a kind of freedom. As my friendship with Hamish cemented I found I had all the companionship and stimulation I required. I was not a gregarious child and tolerance by my fellows was all that I asked.

At the end of my first term something peculiar occurred. One night, long after lights out, Hamish woke me. Everyone was asleep, the house absolutely still.

'Come with me,' he whispered.

I got out of bed and followed him out of the dormitory.

'What is it?'

'Ssh.'

He led me down the corridor to the locker-room. I went through the door after him. Suddenly he turned and clamped a damp rag over my mouth. My head filled with rank chemical smell. Before I blacked out the room went bright yellow, then scarlet, then purple. I thought I saw my father's face.

I came round, so Hamish told me later after half an hour. I opened my eyes. I was nauseous and cold. He was squatting beside me. My head boomed with a headache. Feebly, I punched him in the ribs.

'Steady!' he said.

'Shagging Job!' It was the first time I had used his nickname. 'Shagging maniac!' I sat on the floor, head banging. My brain seemed to steep in some alchemical brew. I suddenly felt uneasy.

'What did you do to me?'

'Chloroform. I chloroformed you.'

'Great. You didn't do anything while—'

'No, no. I just watched. Checked your pulse from time to time.'

'For heaven's sake, Malahide, you can't just chloroform someone when you feel like it!'

'I had to test it. I knew you'd never volunteer. It has to be a secret.'

'Test it? What for?'

'Something we're going to do next year. I'll tell you after the holidays.'

There was a science lab at the school where elementary chemistry and physics were taught. Hamish had lately been spending a lot of time there. He told me he had made up the chloroform himself. An unsuspecting Minto had ordered the chemicals himself. His ambush of me was to test the strength of the potion.

I sulked for a couple of days, but Hamish's insouciance confirmed that my role as guinea-pig had been solely in the interests of science. Besides, I was by now intensely curious to know what plan he had in mind. But he would not tell me, said merely that all would be revealed next term.

We had a quiet Christmas that year. Thompson was away, for some reason, and my father seemed even more preoccupied with his patients. I went with Oonagh to a tedious pantomime at the King's Theatre and, with more enthusiasm, to a noisy variety show at the Pavilion in Leith. The dark winter nights and the low grey days seemed to hold Edinburgh in a hunched frozen posture, as though pinioned by the cloud blanket. A scouthering east wind lashed the streets at all hours of the day and night, numbing your face in seconds. Now that I had been away from it for a few months I discovered a strange affection for my home and was content to stay indoors. Oonagh disguised her pleasure at seeing me again and said she was sure I had grown. My Christmas present (was my father guilty?) was a developing equipment and an enlarger and I converted one of the spare bedrooms into a temporary darkroom. From time to time I ventured out in search of pictures.

Hamish wrote to me from Perth, where his family lived. We had made plans about a visit but in the end nothing materialised.

The new year—1913—arrived and we were first-footed by Donald Verulam. We had quite a jolly party that night when various of my father's colleagues and their wives appeared. My father drank more than I had ever seen him do before. At the bells he sought me out. I was the only member of his family present (Thompson was still away—in Birmingham, I think—on church business).

'Happy New Year, Father.'

He shook my hand and would not let it go. I remember vividly the texture of his grasp: his palm cool, dry, oddly farinaceous. He looked at me, his eyes a little glazed, maudlin. Did he see his wife in my face?

'How are you, boy?'

'Fine.'

'How's school? It's not so bad is it?'

'It's fine.'

'That's the spirit. My son the mathematician, eh?'

Then he did something I can only describe as an attempt at an embrace, though from my point of view it resembled more a cross between a cuff and a shoulder charge. In the event he managed to brush roughly against portions of my body with certain portions of his. It was odd—I remember thinking even at the time—for we never touched each other, except to shake hands. He moved off, and I was taken up by the wife of one of his colleagues and made a fuss of. People allowed themselves to feel sorry for me at occasions like these—I became a legitimate catalyst for selfless fellow-feeling. I was kissed, had my hair ruffled, was praised and flattered. I wondered if, had I looked like Hamish, I would have received the same treatment. I felt a sudden intense liking for my curious friend and for an instant experienced vicariously what his life must be like. At this very hour people would be avoiding him as industriously as they sought me out. I could not imagine any professor's wife pressing her lips to his livid cheeks.

After a while I went through to the kitchen. Oonagh sat on one chair, her legs stretched out upon another. She was drinking whisky from a sherry glass and munching on a square of shortbread.

'C'mere, darlin',' she said. 'Happy New Year, Johnny.'

Without getting up she pulled me to her. I smelt her whisky sweet breath, felt her strong grip around me, heard the starch crackle on her pinny. She kissed me again and again on my left temple muttering Gaelic endearments. I hugged her in return, my forearm innocently squashing her breasts. My face was crushed against her cheek. I pouted my lips. My first kiss freely given. That gentle pressure made her turn her head and as she did I kissed her again, quickly, full on the mouth.

'Happy New Year, Oonagh,' I said. 'Let's hope it's better than the last one.'

There was the briefest knowing pause before she spoke.

'Aye,' she said. 'Let's.'

*   *   *

If anything, Hamish's spots looked worse in cold weather: something to do with the skin tightening making the knobbled quality of the pustules more evident. In the oblique washed-out afternoon light his skin looked more like bark or a section of wall from a pebble-dashed villa.

It was four in the afternoon, night coming on fast. We were crouched behind some bushes, shivering slightly as we waited for the light in the art rooms to go out. The art rooms were in a small cottage some distance beyond the stable block. Hamish held some rag wadding in one hand and a small bottle of his home-made chloroform in the other. We were waiting for the object of his revenge.

This was a boy named Radipole. He was one of the 'black buns' possessing both a talent for drawing and the ability to run very fast. He was a tall, fit youth with reddish hair and curious slanted eyes—almost Eastern in configuration. He was known, imaginatively, as 'Chink'. Apparently he had been the chief instigator of the urine soaking Hamish had received the previous term. It was he who had encouraged the mob to bundle Hamish over the railings and he had been the first to lift up his kilt and let fly. Hamish had never forgotten, never forgiven. But his mind worked with its own cool logic. Hamish decided to postpone his getting even for many months. So he presented to Radipole a face of resigned amusement, a grudging acceptance of the rag—sure, it had not been very pleasant, but still, no point in making a fuss over a bit of good-natured horseplay. Radipole duly forgot all about it. He and Hamish were not friends but there was no animosity between them. The whole point of this, Hamish reasoned, was that when he did eventually strike he would be one of the last people Radipole would suspect. No-one could recall a four-month-old slight, and Radipole, being a boisterous unfeeling lout, had made many enemies since.

'He's coming,' Hamish said. A light had gone out in the art room. 'Remember,' he said to me. 'Count to three after he goes past.' Hamish crept off.

By now the light was almost gone. The evening meal and evening roll-call were an hour away. The gloomy pines and ash trees that lined the path to the school house made it even darker here. I saw Radipole coming down the path. He was whistling through his teeth, kicking at fir cones as he went. I crouched behind a tree. He passed by. One, two, three.

'Hey, you!' I called in a deep voice.

Radipole stopped and turned, looking back curiously. Hamish stepped up behind him and clamped the rag over his mouth and nose. Radipole gave a shudder, an arm flailed and he went down. We dragged him off the path and further into the small grove of trees. We heaved him upright against a trunk and with Hamish holding him fast I ran a length of washing line several times around him and the bole of the tree and tied it secure. We stepped back and looked at him. He was semi-upright his head lolling, making small snoring sounds. He had all the inert limpness of someone shot by a firing squad. A long string of drool hung from his bottom lip.

'Well,' I said. 'What do we do now? Piss on him?'

'No. We don't want to remind him of that.' Hamish looked at Radipole. 'I'm going to hit him a few times, then cut his hair.'

Hamish slapped Radipole's face with some brutality, making the drool jerk into the grass and punched him in the torso. Then he took a small pair of nail scissors from his pocket and swiftly cut—transversely—half of Radipole's hair away, leaving an uneven gingery stubble.

'Let's go,' he said.

45

At roll-call that night Radipole's absence was discovered. Minto sent Angus in the trap to Galashiels and Thornielee stations to determine whether any boy answering Radipole's description had been seen boarding a train. During the evening meal Hamish initiated a rumour (which he attributed to somebody else) that boys from the Innerleithen orphanage had been seen in the school grounds. Later that night, at about nine o'clock, one of the maids in the stable block heard Radipole's desperate bellows and he was released. By this time Angus had returned from Galashiels, irritated by his fruitless journey.

For some reason, Minto decided to flog Radipole: he was offended by his bizarre appearance and maddened by his inability to remember anything more than a bass shout of 'Hey, you!' I suppose Minto thought he was lying and, on the principle that everyone involved in a misdemeanour was punished, considered that he might as well thrash Radipole forthwith than wait for the eventual truth of his culpability to emerge. Which it never did, of course. By this time, the orphan gang rumour was rife. Minto sent a rude letter to the principal of the orphanage and received a ruder rebuttal in reply (he was accused, I later learnt, of being 'unchristian'). Both Hamish and I commiserated with Radipole about his torment and the flogging (an unforeseen bonus, Hamish admitted) and the fact that he was gated until his hair grew back. I know he never suspected us. He rounded on a few people but the hysterical veracity of their innocent protestations convinced him. He ended up believing in Hamish's rumour and swore vicious revenge on all orphans.

I was, I confess, mightily impressed by Hamish's subterfuge. Not so much by the audacity and neatness of its execution but by his sinister patience. From that day on I stopped worrying about him. I only wish he could have shown as much confidence in himself as I did. Later in life when he was at his lowest I would remind him of the Radipole incident, hoping it would cheer him up, offering it to him as a sign of his own self-composure. 'But I was a child then,' he would say. 'It's a different world, the adult one—I was never cut out for it.'

In any event, the besting of Radipole made Hamish a kind of hero in my eyes. He was not just a brilliant mathematician, I felt he had it in him to be something great.

'Wait 'til your spots go,' I said. 'It'll be different then.'

'No. Not me. *You*. You'll be the one.'

He had his own faith in me, I now realise, although I have no idea of the evidence he based it on. Perhaps he was biased by our friendship—that I was not repelled by his pustular mask. After

Radipole a real bond formed. It survived many years and many separations.

*   *   *

The school terms passed with no significant upheavals. In the spring of 1914 Minto flogged three boys in one week and for a while we thought we might be on the brink of a reign of terror. Minto bought a motor car, a Siddley-Deasey, on the profits—we whispered—of the Minto Academy orchestra's tour of six Scottish cities. Angus severed two fingers from his left hand while chopping kindling. One boy died of meningitis. Mrs Leadbetter produced twins.

And at home Oonagh became pregnant and miscarried—'The Good Lord's Will,' she said with a beaming smile. My father developed and patented an antiseptic spray pump for operating theatres that blew a fine mist over the general area that was to be operated on. I spent many hours as a docile 'patient' while my father perfected the smooth functioning of the mechanism. By now he had abandoned his faith in diet as the key factor in the fight against sepsis and had become convinced that a nostrum would be found in a distillate of pine resin. In the summer of 1913 and '14 we rented a house on Sir Hector's estate at Drumlarish where I was impressed as chief resin gatherer in the copious pine woods that grew round about. Our apartment in Edinburgh became suffused with the smell of brewing vats of resin. Even today the scent of certain soaps and deodorants brings on an attack of nausea. Miraculously, father managed to produce a resinous solution that was at once non-adhesive and easily vaporised. He published an article in *The Lancet* and a chemical company in Peterborough purchased a licence from him to produce Todd's Antiseptic Resin commercially. I believe at one time its use was fairly widespread in the North-East of England. I once got a nasty shock in a field dressing station near Dickebusch when I saw a shelf-ful of Todd's Antiseptic Resin bottles. As far as I know the resin spray had no adverse side effects and may even have been of some benefit. While it was being developed no-one in our household ever suffered from a cold. The major advantage accrued to father: he made rather a lot of money.

Hamish visited us twice. Once at Drumlarish, once at Edinburgh where my father sent him, vainly as it turned out, to eminent dermatologists. To Hamish's intense pleasure one specialist had him photographed for a medical textbook. Donald, too, visited us on the west coast during the summer of 1913. We went walking together many times, visiting remote crofts where we took pictures of vanishing

aspects of Highland life. It was like the old days of Barnton village
school and our intimacy soon re-established itself. He said I could
call him 'Uncle Donald' if I wished (he had asked my father's
permission) and I said I would. But I preferred not to, and consequently called him nothing. 'Mr Verulam' would have been too
formal after such an invitation, so I simply stopped using his name.
He seemed not to notice. Several times that summer I considered
asking him directly about my mother but I was restrained—by my
youth and shyness. I sensed that I would know instinctively when
the right moment would occur.

Sometime during that summer I passed through puberty. I do not
remember my voice breaking; it seemed to deepen gradually. The
fine hair on my groin curled and thickened and, one warm afternoon,
masturbating *al fresco*, lying on a bed of springy heather, my imagination making breasts out of the clouds above, I was rewarded with a
meagre spurt of semen.

That September, when we returned to Edinburgh prior to the start
of the school term, Thompson said to me across the breakfast table
one day, 'Get that disgusting bum-fluff off your face, will you? Makes
me sick.'

Oonagh came with me when I went to buy shaving soap, brush,
safety razor and a supply of double edged blades.

'Quite the young man,' she said trying not to laugh. But she could
not help herself when I emerged from the bathroom oozing blood
from a dozen nicks and grazes. I looked as if I had shaved with a
nutmeg grater. Thus began a lifetime's torment. I have always hated
shaving and yet because of the density of my beard I am obliged to
shave twice a day if I am to look presentable in the evening. From
time to time I have grown a beard but I have never managed to get
it to stop itching. I am condemned to be clean shaven.

My father had brown hair. So too had Thompson. My mother was
fair. I, on the other hand, was exceptionally dark in colouring. My
skin is not olive but it has a curious dun whiteness to it. It's not the
translucent pallor of the classic blue-eyed, dark haired Celt. There is
a hint of sludge about it. Also, as a boy, I was aware of the fine down
of black hair that covered my body. Even my spine was furred in this
way and when I was wet you could see a sharp line of matted hair
running from the nape of my neck to my coccyx. Once past puberty
these hairs began to grow: on my chest, stomach, legs—but also on
my shoulders, shoulder blades and buttocks. I looked at my father
and Thompson and noticed the difference. (I deliberately barged in
on Thompson in his bath once and saw his plump girl's breasts and

shiny folds of hairless belly, and his surprisingly long, surprisingly thin penis. I got my ears boxed, two dead legs and a chinese burn for my indecorum.) Then I looked at Donald Verulam, at what hair he had on his head, and noted its darkness. He never bathed, or at least I never saw him, not even on the hottest days at Drumlarish, but when he removed his cuffs and rolled up his sleeves in the darkroom I saw the dense black hair on his forearms, glossy and springy.

*   *   *

We were on holiday at Drumlarish when war began in August 1914. Donald and I were returning from a photographic expedition to Loch Morar. My father had walked out along the Glenfinnan road to meet us.

From a distance I saw him waving the telegram at us and suddenly became convinced that he bore bad news, destined for me in particular. I felt sure that Hamish had been killed and never stopped to ask myself why his parents would have taken the trouble to telegram me. We rode up to him and dismounted.

'It's the European war,' my father said. 'We've declared war. Telegram from Thompson.'

'My God!' Donald said.

'Thank goodness,' I said, vastly relieved.

'What do you mean by that?' my father said.

'I thought it was Hamish.'

'What's it got to do with Hamish? Stupid boy!'

He was genuinely irritated and I could not convince him I was not being flippant. There was a discussion about whether we should abandon the holiday and return home, but after due consideration it was decided that nothing would be gained by this course of action. So we stayed on at Drumlarish until the end of August as planned. I do not recall feeling apprehensive or troubled but it took some time for my father and Donald to relax. They both went into Fort William to make unnecessary telephone calls and speculated endlessly about what was to come.

At school matters were somewhat different. Minto, a staunch Germanophile who had studied in Germany for many years, addressed us with uncharacteristic emotion. This was a great tragedy, he said, the worst to afflict Europe since the French Revolution. The whole thing was a conspiracy between the Russians and the French. The Russians wanted war to distract the population from thoughts of insurrection and they were being encouraged in this by the French because, if there was revolution in Russia, she would renege on her massive debts to France. Germany and Britain, Minto said, were the natural allies in all Europe. To find two such countries at war was a travesty.

It was rather over our heads, and indeed not what we wanted to hear, as we boys were virulently anti-German and highly bellicose. Minto's futile propaganda diminished as the year progressed. He entered a profound depression from which he never recovered. He cut his throat in 1919.

War all too easily becomes remote to those not engaged in or suffering from it, and in 1914 and '15 the Tweed valley was particularly conducive to that point of view. Thompson tried to enlist, was refused and returned to his studies. Donald Verulam left the University for some undisclosed job in the War Office. At school the most obvious effect was the decline in our numbers. By the summer of 1915 most of the rugby team had joined the army or had been recalled to their now essential jobs in the mills and on the farms. The student body dwindled to just over thirty and economies began to be introduced. The Siddley-Deasey was sold. The hot water heating was more often off than on. We got joints of mutton every other day and then only at weekends. Our diet was supplemented by black pudding, an increase in root vegetables and a regular mincemeat stew of dubious provenance, with a coarse texture and a gamey smell.

As far as Hamish and myself were concerned the worst consequence of the war was that we were drafted into the rugby team. We were not keen sportsmen, though neither of us was weak or frail, but preference or inclination had no influence on Minto. I was instructed to play centre three-quarter, where I was relatively content. I kept out of the scrum, could run quite fast and got rid of the ball as soon as I received it. Hamish was on the wing at first but then after one match Minto switched him to hooker. He had no aptitude for the position at all but his shocking acne proved to be a potent disinclination to the opposing front row. Nobody wanted to rub cheeks with Hamish and as a result the binding in the rival scrum was dangerously loose. We got a lot of possession from set play and with the various talents of the 'black buns' we actually won a few matches.

Hamish and I did not enjoy this extra rugby (regular coaching, a match every Saturday and extra coaching on Sunday if we lost), as it cut heavily into our free time. Normally on a Saturday we would sneak away from the compulsory spectating of the school game and climb Paulton Law, the hill behind the house. There we would sit in the shelter of a dry-stone wall, smoke cigarettes and talk. We talked about everything but, inevitably, Hamish would bring up the subject of mathematics. He did most of the talking. He was already at home in conceptual worlds I would never penetrate. In fact, I sensed the end of my tether once we started doing quadratic equations. The maths gift was dying on me fast. The terrain ahead seemed shrouded in an opaque mist. By this time Hamish was aged seventeen. I could no longer understand him but I was beguiled by the way his mind worked. Mathematics was for him an entrancing playground. On one of our last Saturday afternoons, I remember, he had become obsessed with the idea that numbers were infinite. He was always fascinated by immensely large numbers. It was a sign of the gulf between us. My brain seemed to seize up at anything over a million.

It was October 1915, I think. The Saturday match had been cancelled due to heavy frost. It was a fissile, sharp day. A blue, washed-out sky and hard clear views of the Tweed up as far as Thornielee and down river to the smoke from the mill chimneys in Galashiels. We sat huddled in our usual spot smoking Turkish cigarettes and taking sips from a flask of rum that Hamish had smuggled into school.

'Do you remember that time,' he said, apropos of nothing, 'when you said did prime numbers exist before anyone had thought of them?'

'Did I say that?'

'Yes ... Well, I was thinking. Is maths something we invented or something we discovered? And I thought: we couldn't have invented something as complicated as maths. The history of maths is a history of exploration. As we go we find out more. It is all there—' he waved at the general scene, 'waiting to be found.'

'I suppose so.'

'And what does that tell you about the world?'

I said nothing.

'If maths in some way is already *there*. Who created it?'

'I don't know ... God?'

'Yes. Maybe. Maybe maths proves God exists.' He looked at me. The cold air was having its usual unfortunate effect on his face, but his eyes were wide with the intensity of his thought. To my astonishment, I suddenly felt a little frightened.

'What I think is,' he began slowly, 'is that maths is the key to everything.' He paused. 'If you go far enough, perhaps you'll discover the meaning of life.'

I was going to scoff but I saw that he was caught in a strange fervent mood. He drank from the flask. He was intoxicated, but not as a result of any spiritous liquor. That afternoon he went on to tell me about a mathematician called Georg Cantor, a man, he said, who had organised the infinite. He talked about set theory, transfinite and irrational numbers, π and the square root of two, and the mysteriously potent designation alef-null that Cantor had devised. He told me many things most of which I understood not at all, or which promptly slipped my mind, but I will never forget the passion of his monologue. It had a quality which was rare, and, although it may be bizarre to talk about it in association with an abstract academic subject, I can find no better word to describe it than 'faith'.

*   *   *

It was shortly after that day on Paulton Law that my uncle Vincent Hobhouse died, not from apoplexy or heart failure as one might reasonably have supposed, but from being run over by a motor bus in Charlbury High Street. I wrote a clumsy but sincere letter of condolence to Aunt Faye. She replied at once saying how 'touched' and 'moved' she had been by my sympathy and concern. Perhaps her own bereavement reminded her of mine, but whatever the reason she began to write to me regularly once a week. At first I thought this a little strange but gradually I grew to look forward to her letters with impatience. I started writing back too, and our correspondence was soon in full spate.

You will understand that the average seventeen-year-old boy has little or no power over his affections. In my case this impotence was singular. I live under the sway of my emotions. Even as an adult the struggle to resist is exhausting. I possessed no resilience then. This sort of nature is both a curse and a blessing. Try to understand me as I was and do not judge too harshly when you hear what happened next.

I have always felt vividly and instantly with no mediating influence of reflection or logic. My nature gives an impulse and a motive to all my work which, however the critics may have carped, they have never denied is my prime and most valuable asset. It is a propensity which has brought me the happiest moments of my life and wreaked terrible devastation. Oonagh was the first to receive my love, and my Aunt Faye was the next. She initiated my first adult, equal discourse. I fell in love with her through print. I had not seen her since that day in Waverley station when she kissed my cheek. Now, those seconds of contact returned—and with what transforming force. I saw her dark, bruised eyes, humid and alive; smelt the odour of her perfume; felt the soft contact of her cheek with mine. I realised, with thrilling hindsight, that I had in fact loved her, unknowingly, since that moment. When the post arrived and was distributed, I held the letter unopened for minutes, my heart clubbing my ribs, my breath painfully constricted. 'All my love, Faye.' I derived a hundred nuances from those four bland monosyllables. This was my first blind passion and I celebrated it nightly with physical release.

I began to take more care over the composition of my letters, expanding them from tedious itemisation of the school news into what I hoped were stylish intimations of my own character and personality. I told her of Minto's deepening gloom about the war; of Hamish's speculations about mathematics as the key to all nature; I whimsically embellished and exaggerated our own roles in the rugby team, as if we were a couple of knowing aesthetes pretending to be bloods for a dare. I presented her with myself stripped of any secondary defining role—child, pupil, nephew. It was a test, in its way, and I took the increasing candour and intimacy of Faye's replies as a sign that I had passed.

In the spring of 1916 I asked her for a photograph. It required some courage, and until it arrived, I was in a constant sweat of trepidation that I had gone too far. But it came, a snapshot. Faye, in the country, leaning on a five-barred gate, her curly hair in a loose bun, her smudged, debauched eyes narrowed by her smile. One hand held the top of a dog's leash and the other the knuckly end of a blackthorn walking stick. On the back she had scribbled, 'Shipton-Under-Wychwood. March '16'. Who had taken it, I wondered? Probably Peter, her son. It was too well composed to be little Gilda or Alceste's work. I opened the accompanying letter and began to read.

Dear John,
   Photograph duly enclosed. I hope you like it. Donald took it for me. He comes down most weekends from London. I cannot tell you what a support and kindness he has been since Vincent died. He is sorting out all the dreary problems to do with the will and estate. He sends his best wishes.

There was more stuff about Donald, sweet Donald, but I could not read on. I felt as if I were about to burst into tears. I experienced a sense of such towering injustice that I could hardly speak. What gave Donald Verulam the right, I demanded, to occupy a place in my Aunt Faye's good favour? For what possible reason could he have taken on these responsibilities? On what conceivable grounds did he ingratiate himself with a member of *my* family, whom he hardly knew? I was outraged, brimming with hurt and disappointment. I, who could only write to her, had to accept that Faye's life was not centred on my weekly letters as mine was on her's. I was in the grip of an irrational jealousy so intense it made me want to vomit.

We like to laugh—do we not?—at the baroque passions of high adolescence, but we cannot deny that they control and guide us during those few hot palpitating years. It is an unsettling, overwhelming power and one that most people will never feel so vehemently again, indeed, will never want to be so ruthlessly led. Adult life, if it is to function at all, demands a moderation of these extremes. From time to time, however, they break out—lava cracking the pumice—and dominate with the same rampaging potency. What is lust, adult lust, after all, but the desire to recapture the heady sensations of adolescent sexuality?

Personally, I have never lost that youthful capacity to *feel*, in its raw vital state. Thank God. This is what sets me apart from the many, hamstrung by decorum and convention, stifled by notions of respect and status. Even today, I can re-experience my seventeen-year-old jealousy, feel its grip at my throat, its claw in my guts. It was unfocused and indiscriminate. I did not see Donald Verulam as a rival, more as an interloper, destroying an ideal duality. But it would not let me go. I could not forget my love for Faye; could only think that he was there with her, and I was apart. One idea came to dominate my thoughts: I had to see her, if only for a few hours. I had to run away.

'What do you expect's going to happen?' Hamish said unsympathetically, when I told him my plan. 'Do you think she'll want to marry you the instant she claps eyes on you?' This was what I did not want to hear. I knew he was right. Faye Hobhouse, attractive widow, was being comforted through her period of mourning by Donald Verulam. They were two adults. I was a seventeen-year-old boy. But a darker fear, a more profound dismay tugged at me, unarticulated. All I knew was that I had to see her; present myself to her as I now was, erase the image of the child she kissed on Waverley station. I tried to make Hamish see this.

'But then what?'

I did not know and confessed as much. All I knew was that I had to interpose myself between Faye and Donald Verulam. I had to see her and let her see me.

Hamish agreed to help, even though he thought I was a complete fool. In fact I think he admired my singlemindedness, however crazily motivated. We made plans for my escape. We pooled our financial resources, which proved more than adequate. The subterfuge was simple. Before dinner on Sunday there was a roll-call, as there was at every meal. After dinner I would cycle not to Galashiels or Thornielee but in the other direction to more distant Innerleithen. There I would buy a ticket to London and board a 10.30 train which, after a couple of changes, would get me to Reston, arriving there in plenty of time to meet the 11.55 overnight express from Edinburgh to London, King's Cross. I chose Innerleithen to forestall for as long as possible any information emerging about my destination. People buying tickets to London were rare enough events as it was on that Tweed valley branch line. I would be easily remembered. Minto would send Angus immediately to Thornielee and Galashiels as soon as my absence was discovered. I might get a day or two's start before they thought of asking further up or down the line.

There lay between us the unspoken knowledge that Hamish would become implicated. He would do his best to cover up my absence in the dormitory. A simple lie—that I had been taken ill and put to bed in the small sanitorium upstairs would be sufficient. Our dormitory leader, a simple lad called Corcoran, would think nothing untoward, especially if Hamish made the pretence of taking my toothbrush and pyjamas upstairs. Such complicity would inevitably result in a flogging from Minto. As we discussed the details of the escape (where to hide a bicycle, where to get enough carbide for the lamp—it was a fourteen mile journey to Innerleithen) I became more upset at the price Hamish would have to pay.

'He'll flog you,' I blurted out.

'Bound to happen one day.'

'Look, just promise me, don't let him flog you twice. Tell him everything straight away.'

'Don't worry. I'm not that brave.'

I wanted to touch him in some way—show my immense gratitude—but I knew it was out of the question.

'I won't forget this, Malahide,' I said, my voice cracking slightly.

'You helped me once,' he said. 'Just paying you back.'

A fortnight after Faye had sent me her photograph I left school to join her. It was May 24th 1916. That night for dinner we had mutton broth and rabbit and onions. Hamish gave me most of his portion. After dinner we had an hour of free time before we were required to be in the school house. Lights out was at 9.00 p.m.

Hamish and I met by the side of the stable block and walked through the small wood, past the art rooms, and on to a spinney of trees where we had hidden the bicycle. It was a fresh cool evening with high, heavy cloud. There was a smell of honey in the air from the sycamores and a circling wood-lark whispered high above us. A dull, bluey light lay over everything.

I was going to cycle along a dirt track that led to the home farm, skirt that and its noisy dogs on foot, then freewheel down the steep lane that led to the Galashiels–Innerleithen road. If all went well I should arrive at the station just after ten. The one obstacle we had not managed to overcome was my apparel. I still wore my kilt (hunting Stewart) and my short coat. We arrived at school in our uniforms and departed thus: our own clothes were forbidden. I was by now quite unselfconscious in my kilt but for the first time in my life was leaving Scotland for England. Somehow, the thought of being kilted in London unsettled me. But there was nothing to be done. I had a long overcoat and with a bit of luck anyone catching sight of my stockinged legs beneath it might think I was wearing plus-fours.

I pulled the bicycle out from a clump of bracken. We debated whether to ignite the carbide but I decided to wait until it got darker. I felt a sudden foreboding: my reason belatedly asserting itself. Fool, it seemed to say, abandon this mad idea . . . But it was too late now.

'You'd better get going,' Hamish said. 'Good luck.'

'Right.' I said. I got on the bicycle. 'Now, remember—'

'On you go.' He grinned, showing his large teeth. I felt hot-eyed with inarticulate gratitude. He gave me a shove, and I bumped off down the track towards the home farm. I would not see him again for four years.

Everything went as planned, at least on my side. The ride to Inner-leithen was actually quite entrancing. The road followed the Tweed, and to my excited eyes the slow river and its fragrant meadows grew ever more hauntingly beautiful in the darkening, dusky light. I bought my ticket to London, one way, third class, price one pound fifteen shillings, and made my connection successfully at Reston.

Sometime after midnight sharing a smoky, blurry compartment with two sailors and someone who looked like a commercial traveller we crossed the border into England. I left Scotland behind me and along with it my youth. Even at the time it seemed epochal enough. I knew somehow that nothing would be the same after this particular adventure. I did not think of the future, of my meeting with Faye. I was happy in the present moment, and there was nothing in my past, I felt, to make me want to cherish it. I hunched into my overcoat collar and tried to go to sleep. It took me an hour or so to achieve it.

The sailors talked (they were rejoining a dreadnaught in South-ampton) and drank something from a bottle. The commercial traveller tried to engage me in conversation but my taciturnity proved too much for him. I looked out at the dark countryside and tried to memorise—as if taking a talismanic inventory—the strange names of the stations we flashed past—Pegswood, Morpeth, Croft and Northallerton—as we travelled down England.

*　　　*　　　*

I recount the following events exactly as I recall them happening. I make no excuses for myself or my bizarre behaviour. I was seventeen. Please remember.

The sun shone in London. I was astonished at how much warmer it was than Scotland. I felt I had entered another climate. I was not overawed by the city; if anything, the traffic in Edinburgh seemed heavier, though here the noise was more concentrated and the streets were distinctly less clean. I took an underground train from King's Cross to Paddington. My kilt drew few curious glances. I realised at Paddington, where I saw a battalion of the Highland Light Infantry disembarking, that kilts had become reasonably commonplace south of the border since 1914.

But on the train to Charlbury my neutral composure began to desert me. I looked out of the window at the bland and innocuous countryside and told myself to calm down. Faye would be surprised but glad to see me, I reassured myself. Everything would be fine.

At Charlbury station I secured directions to the Hobhouses' address from a cabby. I walked up the hill through the small town, its dull ochre buildings looking quite peculiar to me, I recall. It was just after luncheon and the shops were being reopened. I had not eaten since the evening before and as I passed a baker's almost swooned from hunger. I bought a slice of veal and ham pie and checked I was going in the right direction. Everyone appeared to know where Vincent Hobhouse had lived.

I walked on up through the town eating my pie. It was too warm for my overcoat. I took it off. The sky was milky, the sun invisible. The dust on the verge was white. My heavy boots crunched on the gravel of the unpaved road. At one point two small barefoot urchins chased after me, laughing at my kilt and shouting insults at me in their incomprehensible dialect. I shied a couple of stones at them and they ran away.

The Hobhouse home was a large solid late-Georgian building set on a hill overlooking the town and the Evenlode valley. It had a spacious garden with many mature trees—a gloomy cedar, two monkey puzzles, elms and limes—and was surrounded by a tall beech hedge. Further down the hill was a small nursing home, past which I walked, and beyond it a row of cottages. The house was set back from what I later learnt was the Oxford road, and beyond it lay open fields and countryside.

I walked up the drive. Two lolloping spaniels, followed by a little girl in a sailor suit ran to intercept me. I stopped. I felt myself perceptibly weaken. I was suddenly appalled by the full audacity of what I had done.

'Hello,' I said, with fake bonhomie. 'Is your mother in? . . . You must be Alceste.'

'I'm Gilda. This is Ned and this is Ted.' She introduced the dogs. 'My father's gone to heaven.'

I felt sick. 'I know. I'm your cousin. John James Todd. Come to see you.'

Gilda took me indoors. We went through an entrance hall and an inner hall. I was left in a cool pale drawing room, heavy with the scent of pot-pourri and encumbered with the ornaments and collectibles of long inhabitation. On a round table was a group of leather- and tortoiseshell-framed photographs. I saw my mother's face. I closed my eyes.

'Johnny?'

I turned round, blood booming like surf in my ears. *Faye.* I felt my stomach rotate with stupid love. She wore a green apron over her dress and I found myself wondering—absurdly—if she had been cleaning silver. Her hair was tied loosely at the back with a velvet bow. She looked younger even than her photograph. I felt like laughing. I had never seen anyone more beautiful. Instantly, all my doubts disappeared. I had done the right thing.

'What are you doing here?' Her tone was puzzled. Her eyes took in my kilt, my socks, my boots. All my doubts returned. I had made a ghastly mistake.

'I've run away from school.'

'But why?'

Because I love you, I wanted to shout.

'Because . . . I want to join the army.'

*   *   *

What in God's good name made me say that? What malign fate put those words in my mouth? If I had only told the truth, think what I would have avoided. I am not sure how the subconscious mind works but this was no long repressed ambition: nothing could have been further from my wishes. After the first flush of war-fever, Minto Academy's aggressive instincts faded rapidly, partly as a result of waning interest, partly encouraged by Minto's passionate neutrality. Every Old Mintonian who died prompted another melancholy pane-gyric in favour of peace. Tones of 'I told you so' seemed to hang in the air for days after every futile battle. By the end of 1915 everyone's enthusiasm was at a low ebb. I must have blurted out my 'reason' as a consequence of an instinctive association of ideas. My embarrassment, Faye's eyes on my kilt, the Highland Light Infantry at Paddington—*ergo*, soldiering.

At first, as it turned out, it did its job admirably. All Faye's suspicions and surprise were allayed. To my vague disappointment she did not try to dissuade me. She reminded me I was too young, but perhaps I could join up next year. Possibly, her zeal arose from the fact that I was her nephew and not her son. In fact she told me that Peter had volunteered immediately on leaving school in the summer of 1915 and he had joined a public schools battalion. Faye thought this might be just the place for me. Peter would be able to supply all the right information and advice—might even get me into the same battalion. I found myself agreeing with diminishing enthusiasm. Peter, it transpired, was coming home on leave that very weekend. I should wait in Charlbury at least until then, Faye counselled, when I could ask him anything I wanted.

Four days. Four days alone with Faye (if one excluded the servants and Gilda and Alceste). I experienced a temporary relief. Problems and decisions could be postponed for a while. I was here, I was with her, living under the same roof. That had been the immediate aim of my running away and I had achieved it. I allowed myself to sink into the warm pool of her welcome.

The first thing Faye did was to telegram my father and the school. I felt curiously invulnerable and only wondered vaguely how Minto would react upon receipt of the news. I did not reflect too long on my father's response either. I was here in England; they seemed a continent away. This was, I now realise, the first indication of a dangerous tendency in my character: the long view, the long term, rarely attracts me. It is the here-and-now I find alluring. When I act it is because I am impelled by something irresistible within me and seldom as a result of some well-plotted strategy. This happened again and again in my life and usually brought swift satisfaction followed by disastrous remorse. Suppose I had stayed out my course at the Academy and completed my certificate exams? Who knows what would have happened? ... But this is futile. *How we live reflects our own natures.* The prudent, cautious, sensible approach would never be the one I chose.

So here I was in the large comfortable house. Did Faye ask herself why, if I wished to join the army, I had to run away to Charlbury to do so? She must have. But she would forgive me anything, Faye, as I was the son of her beloved, late sister, motherless since the day of his birth, bereft of a maternal guiding hand and illimitable source of love. It was only natural in such a confused moment that I should turn somewhere for solace and advice. (In fact this was the first question her son Peter asked me. I told him I had originally planned to enlist in London, as far away from my father's influence as possible. A sudden failure of nerve had drawn me to Charlbury. He understood completely.)

I was served up a late lunch that day (to supplement my veal and ham pie) of cold meat, bread and pickle and then Faye called the gardener (I cannot recall his name—an old man with a limp) to drive us in the family motor to Oxford to buy some clothes for me (a light flannel suit, two shirts, collars, a tie and, my suggestion this, a flat tweed cap). Faye took a real pleasure in our jaunt. It was a mild, hazy day. The drive to and from Oxford was taken up with a chatter of reminiscence. I am sure, too, that Faye secretly rather admired my resolve. When you meet people like myself who act foolhardily or spontaneously it is easy, from a haven of routine and security, to mock or deplore us. But at the same time, in your hearts, there is a profound and unsettling envy of the freedom that is expressed in our careless actions. And Faye, I thought that day, was in fact rather like me. We shared the same spirit, but she had confined hers to a life of provincial worthiness when she married Vincent Hobhouse. I sensed too that, after the grief and mourning an invigorating suspense and ignorance had begun to pervade her life. What now? Where next? With whom?

Two terse telegrams arrived early that evening to undermine my intoxicated mood. Minto's forbade me to return to the Academy and instructed me to consider myself expelled. My father's simply ordered me to come home at once. Faye advised me to ignore this last injunction. She felt that nothing would be gained by turning round and heading back so swiftly. She suggested I write explaining my motives in more detail and she would enclose a letter saying words to the effect that I was confused and upset and a few days unofficial holiday in Charlbury would be highly beneficial. The letters were written, sealed, stamped and taken down to the post box. At the very least, Faye said, we had a week's grace.

You can imagine what effect her complicity had on me. I felt she was behaving more like a game and spirited older sister rather than my aunt. I was sure it was significant. We were co-conspirators, it drew us closer.

That first evening, the two of us at dinner, adjacent, the corner of the table between us. The limping gardener doubling as a butler (the real one had been killed at Loos). Sherry, oxtail soup, whitebait in cream sauce, claret, lamb cutlets, bercy potatoes, apple charlotte, Welsh rarebit, port. Me in my new suit (I had shaved with Vincent's blunt cutthroat), my back warm against the dining room fire, my face hot, two red highlights on my cheeks like coins. I seemed to be breathing deeper, as if my lung capacity had doubled and the circumference of my nostrils had mysteriously expanded. Faye, in three-quarter profile. Smudged eyes, winking cameo on a velvet choker, a dusting of powder on the downy hair in front of her ears, the finest lines on her face and top lip. A dress of aquamarine. Silk? It shone and shifted in the candleglow. I was bold with wine. I felt ten years older and talked to her as an equal, another adult. The game and spirited older sister had quietly stolen away. I put my fork down and smiled. This could be my house, my wife, even. I felt brimful of a strange, cocksure composure.

'You know, you look so like Emmeline when you smile.'

Blood-ties crept between us like chaperones. I felt both sad and irritated for a moment. But it was a useful prompt.

'I was going to ask you ... that is if you don't mind. I was wondering—you said you had a lot of letters from her, from my mother. Could I—if it's all right—see them?'

'Of course.' Touch on my arm. I thought the flannel would smoulder. 'I'll look them out for you. Are you terribly hot, John?'

'Me? No, no. Fine, perfect.'

That night I left my own room and walked across the upstairs landing and along the corridor towards her bedroom. I stood outside the door, a faint luminescence from a nearby window highlighting the graining of the oak door and the metalwork of the latch. I sent my restless presence into her room and waited for it to be noticed. Was she lying awake, stirring beneath the sheet and blankets, thinking about me, wishing I had the courage to creep quietly into her bed? I stared at the mute and neutral door as if expecting it to become miraculously transparent ... It is at instants like these that believers

in the existence of telepathic communication either win or lose
disciples. If it worked at all then it would work tonight. I stood
outside and concentrated. All she had to do was call my name. I felt
a pounding in my frontal lobes. My brain power could have driven
an electric motor. But I heard nothing, just the creaks and settlings
of an old house.

That was my moment. I should have taken it. A year or two later,
I believe, I would have gone in, perhaps with some useful fabrication
to hand (a moment's grief, a night terror) to allow a plausible embrace.
I cannot blame myself; it asks a lot of a person to possess that
conviction and worldliness at seventeen. And yet I had run away
from school, my life was already set on that frenzied precipitous
course from which it never subsequently deviated. But for some
reason I was stalled by inertia. After God knows how many breathless
minutes I realised I was shivering vigorously and slunk back to my
room and my cold solitary bed.

The atmosphere was different the next day. Not significantly so, but
definitely altered. Faye, it seemed to me, had realised that the licence
of the previous night was too heady and distracting. The prosaic older
sister returned. I came down to breakfast and found her on the point
of leaving—'visiting'. On her way out she showed me two box files
full of my mother's letters.

I took them into the drawing room and began to read them through.
I ate my lunch alone and read on into the afternoon. I felt exhausted,
having run gauntlets of harrowing emotions.

It is bizarre, to say the least, to read about a familiar world as yet
unaltered by, and indeed indifferent to, your presence. Here was our
apartment, Kelpie's Court, Edinburgh, the High Street, my father,
Thompson, Oonagh ... Thompson proved the biggest strain. Here
was the little plump boy, doted on, drenched in his mother's love. I
have rarely envied Thompson. Sometimes I envied his money, but
only fleetingly. But that day in Charlbury I felt the writhing vicious
force of envy squirm into every corner of my body. I could have
killed him, then, it was so all-powerful. Killed him with glee, so
consumed was I by acid resentment of his good fortune. He had
known Emmeline Todd, and been loved by her.

Calmness returned gradually.

They were loving candid letters between sisters who were close
friends. My mother—sweet, good natured, generous—fully aware of
all life's pleasures ... The letters were fascinating; I heard a voice,
encountered a person of whom I was only dimly aware—and then

only in some gaudy, sentimental idealisation—but they provided me with no hard facts. They were chatty and inconsequential.

And then, quite unheralded, in September 1897.

... Donald has arrived. He seems well, all things considered. We had him to dinner last Tuesday. He is temporarily staying in rooms in Hanover St. but plans shortly to move ...

The unremarked arrival suggested mutual knowledge. Both sisters knew him. From then on Donald's name made regular appearances: what he was doing; where he was thinking of buying a house; his disdainful reflections on the academic calibre of his colleagues ...

Then: 14th March 1898.

... My dear Faye, I wish I could confide in you all that Donald says to me. I will say but this, whenever we are alone he speaks only in tones of tender moving respect. What am I to say to him? It is indeed a ghastly dilemma and I am powerless to respond in any way that will satisfy him, even though my feelings, as you will understand, are as equally engaged upon the matter ...

I noted the date. This seemed to be the moment when ordinary friendship developed into something more passionate.

7th April 1898:
... Donald and I talk and talk of what might have been if things had only been otherwise. Oh Faye, I try to stop him but he seems so full of emotion that if I do not let him the Lord alone knows what effect continued restraint might have. Sometimes I fear for his health ...

13th June 1898:
... Donald came with us to the Trossachs. He seemed in good spirits. I had made him promise not to unburden himself. Innes knows nothing, suspects nothing. Professor and Mrs McNair were our companions and it was essential that Donald should remain composed.

But yesterday I stayed behind while the others went walking. Then Donald returned early and of course, the two of us being quite alone, he could not hold himself back. I cannot tell you what an afternoon it was, Faye. Let me say only that in the end he wept. It was terribly sad and yet strangely uplifting to see what power true passion has over a spirit at once so strong, civilised and intelligent as Donald. I wept too, of course, you know what I am like, and we comforted each other ...

I stopped there, my mouth dry and rank, hands visibly shaking.
'... we comforted each other.' How easy it was to penetrate the
opaque euphemism. I read on. That afternoon during the walking
tour of the Trossachs seemed to have been cathartic. Donald appeared
to shake off his feverish melancholy. There was no more talk of
weeping. The letters became full of '... a splendid, heartwarming
day with Donald ...', '... Donald was in fine form ...', '... at dinner
Donald's old warmth and humour seemed to return as he told us
of ...'

Sometimes there were further hints: 'Donald now seems to understand the impossibility of changing anything, knows that all must
continue as it is. He is resigned and says he can find a form of
contentment ...' And: '... we talk often of that wild, mad day last
month and see it now as a final railing against frustration and heart-
break ...'

I went back through the letters and slowly charted the course of
their love affair, how they were condemned by the dignity and honour
of their own positions, and the impossibility of ever requiting their
love. My mother never referred adversely to my father, never com-
plained or criticised. It was clearly one of those passionate relation-
ships not so much doomed as stillborn, both parties knowing in
their hearts that nothing can come of it, but seizing a moment's
consummation as some sort of futile symbol of what might have been.

Then, 21st July 1898.

Dear Faye,
    I am with child again. I do not need to tell you how fear
mingles with joy. Innes is delighted, but I have not said anything
to anyone else but you, not even Donald ...

Not even Donald. Why not? I watched the process of my own
prenatal growth with a horrid fascination. My mother's joyful anticipation (she prayed I would be a girl ...) and her prescient fears for
her own health, after the narrow escape she had had with Thompson,
made ghoulish reading. But I could not finish her last letter, dated
two weeks before my birth. It started:

Darling Faye,
    I feel a little fitter today. Perhaps everything will be fine after
all ...

I knew I could not stand the strain of those terrible, fatal ironies.
I put the letters back in the box file. I felt I should cry, but I was
too exhausted for tears. I had learnt too much and my brain jabbered

with argument and supposition. I was too preoccupied with new knowledge to weep over my dead mother. Unless I was very much mistaken, all the evidence seemed to point to one conclusion. I knew it all now—although, deep in myself, I had half-known it for years. My true father, it seemed, if the letters were to be believed, was Donald Verulam ... I rubbed my face. This needed further confirmation. It was too much to handle at this juncture.

Faye returned.

'Sorry I stayed away, I wanted you to have a chance to read them on your own.'

She glanced at me, clear eyed and, I thought, interrogatively.

'I'm very grateful,' I said slowly. 'I know they're private ... but I had to find out about her. I hope you don't mind.'

'No. Not at all. I don't really have the right to keep them from you. Even if ...'

She did not know what to say. Now she would not meet my eye.

'It's all right,' I said, still with some caution. 'I always half-suspected, funnily enough. Just from talking to Donald.'

She visibly relaxed, then blushed. 'I'm glad,' she said.

'But I completely understand. Now. And I don't think anything was wrong,' I said boldly. It was my turn to touch her arm. 'Thank you. It was very important for me to read them.'

She looked me in the eye, seized my shoulders and kissed me on the cheek.

'You're a special boy, John James Todd. Donald told me. Very special. I'm glad you read them. I ... I telephoned Donald this morning. He's coming down this weekend.'

I was not sure quite how to take this. I saw what she was trying to do, but it was both good and bad news. I knew at once that the weekend would hold a necessary confrontation and possible recognition, but it also meant the end of my brief sojourn with Faye. After the tense conversation about the letters a relaxed amiability settled upon us again. But as the week passed I became more agitated at the thought of Donald's arrival because I knew from the way Faye spoke about him that she and Donald were now more than friends. And this bothered me. Can you understand it? I felt proprietorial. Foolishly (I knew this), I was still fascinated by her. The letters had brought us even closer. I regarded her as *my* legitimate interest. Donald belonged to another area of my life, with which I also had to come to terms. Having the two overlap was most unwelcome.

65

Perhaps, perhaps I might have got through everything—Donald, Faye, my future—if I had not let myself down once again. Another crass error of judgement.

I was looking forward to my last day alone with Faye. The weather was still warm and we had planned a picnic the night before (we would have to take the little girls but I did not regard them, properly speaking, as people). The intention was to motor to Oxford, hire a punt and punt up the Cherwell to find an isolated stretch of river bank. We were sitting at breakfast contemplating the pleasures of the day ahead when through the door came Peter Hobhouse, a day early.

My cousin was a year or so older than me, but he looked considerably more in his uniform—khaki jacket, jodhpurs, high laced boots, peaked cap. Peter was a big bland fair-haired fellow, with round unformed features and permanently rosy cheeks. We made a strong contrast side by side—almost two different ethnic types—prototypical Celt and pink and ruddy Anglo-Saxon. He was perfectly friendly but I instinctively disliked him, despite all the help he later gave me. I have no idea why, it was an honest—or rather, a simple prejudice. Perhaps it was just his soft burliness, his unwarranted easy manner, as if to say 'life holds no surprises for me'. However, we shook hands and exchanged pleasantries. Faye told him I wanted to join a public school battalion and, to my vague embarrassment, he energetically shook my hand again and said, 'congratulations'.

Thank God, he declined to come on the picnic, despite his mother's entreaties. But I should have recognised that his arrival altered everything. Here was her son; my role as 'nephew' was firmly re-established, just as hers was as 'aunt' and 'mother'. All this was lost on me: that is the kind of person I am.

We hired our punts at the boathouse at the bottom of Bardwell Lane. The sky was cloudy but the air was sweet and cool. There was a faint breeze. Thrushes and blackbirds sang in the horse chestnuts, great green continents of leaves.

It took me about ten minutes and about the same number of collisions with both banks of the river to gain some sort of insight into the dynamics of punting. Eventually we made our way cautiously but not too erratically upstream. My clumsiness had afforded Faye and the girls much amusement and our mood as we set off was, I thought, ideally merry. They laughed again, but more circumspectly, when we were overtaken by a punt energetically and skilfully propelled by a one-armed soldier (Oxford was one large convalescent home).

We punted for half an hour up the placid Cherwell as it wound through the fields and water-meadows of Kidlington. Presently, we found a suitable spot and moored the punt. We spread two travelling rugs on the bank and unpacked the wicker picnic basket. We ate cold chicken and game pie, stilton and apples. The girls drank fizzy lemonade, Faye and I a cider cup. The weather improved, grew milder, we got some sun. The day seemed summery but there was a latent spring coolness that made it invigorating and kept away the flies and wasps. I drank too much cider cup deliberately.

After lunch I played a furious game of tag with Alceste and Gilda while Faye read a book. I ran and shouted, twisted and turned, tiring myself and them. Soon I felt flushed and sticky with sweat. I persuaded the girls to wander some way down the bank to feed a family of ducks that were swimming there. I went back to Faye. She had erected a small ivory-coloured parasol with a long fringe and sat beneath it, her back resting against a pollarded willow. She was wearing a flared sand-coloured golfing skirt and a coral blouse with a scalloped collar. A wide straw hat lay on the rug beside her. She looked cool and serene. I looked at her. The dark shadows beneath her eyes. I gulped cider cup. A mild fire of alcohol flared in my body. Now or never.

'Isn't it lovely?' she said. 'It's ages since I've done this. I'm so glad we came.'

I sat down beside her panting slightly.

'You look hot,' she said.

'I think I'm going to have a dip. Coming?'

'No fear!' she laughed. 'Brave you. Are you sure?'

'Yes.'

We had brought swimming costumes as more of a gesture than indication of serious intent. Faye half-heartedly tried to dissuade me, but I snatched up my costume (Peter's) and went further down the bank, away from the girls. Behind a clump of hawthorn I slipped off my clothes and pulled on the costume. It was a little large, the shoulder straps kept slipping off. I thought about diving, but I did not want to distract the girls from their duck-feeding, so I waded in. The water was icy, it seemed to drive the breath from my body. Here the Cherwell flowed torpidly, there was barely a perceptible current, I sank beneath the brown water up to my chin and felt the cold band my skull like steel. Out in midstream I looked over to Faye. She was watching. I waved.

'What's it like?'

'Freezing!'

'Told you!'

I felt my throat contract in shocking anticipation of what I was about to do. I gave it no thought; there was only one path I could take. I swam to the side and hauled myself out. Behind the hawthorn I stripped off my costume. I looked down at myself. The black hair on my chest and stomach were slicked into a flat wet pelt. I could hardly see my cock and balls so shrunken were they from the cold. My head was entirely empty of thoughts. I was a creature of guts and glands.

I heard a bird call, the distant quack of ducks, Gilda and Alceste's thin cries of pleasure. I massaged myself back into some approximation of virility, feeling the warm blood surge. I still kept all thought at bay. I had to show her I was no longer a boy.

'Aunt Faye? Could you bring me a towel, please?'

Through the screen of leaves I saw her get to her feet, take a towel from a canvas bag and saunter over, smiling. I held the sodden costume in front of me. She came round the bush. Her face instantly tightened with surprise. She offered me the towel.

'There you are.'

As I took it I let the swimming costume drop. Just for an instant there was nothing there. She saw. I wrapped the towel around me.

'Faye, I—'

She slapped my face. Once, very hard, jerking my head round.

'Foolish ... *stupid* ...' she said in a clenched trembling voice, and walked away.

I tasted the vomit in my throat. Game pie, cider cup. I actually retched once or twice. I threw away the towel and dressed, hauling my clothes over my damp body. I tried desperately to draw up from my numb shocked brain something that would stand as a plausible explanation. I walked over, towelling my hair to hide my face. The cheek she had slapped felt pulsing and scorched. I was shivering, but not from cold.

'I'm sorry,' I said. 'I ... I just wasn't thinking. It was a terrible mistake. You see at school we ... It just fell from my fingers. I was cold. It was a mistake Aunt Faye. Honest, I swear.'

She would not look up from her book.

'Very well. Let us never talk about it again, John. It's forgotten. Nothing.'

But it was not forgotten. How could it be? Thank God for the girls. They allowed us a formal passage of communication; we could busy ourselves with them and their demands. Faye very quickly seemed as normal as ever, and so did I, I suppose, in an attempt to sustain the credibility of the excuse. But the incident stood between us like a wall. What was worse she contrived never to be alone with me again. I never had the opportunity to elaborate on that first feeble explanation. I could not apologise, could not explain.

Why did you do it? I hear you say. What in Heaven's name did you think would happen? I know, I know. It makes no sense. I put the ghastly blunder down to that dangerous flaw in my nature and my naïvety. All I wanted, desperately, was to make love to her and my time was running out. But I cannot condemn myself utterly. I may have been a fool but at least I was an honest one. I think I can safely say that this unhappy combination held true for the rest of my life.

I think now I would have survived the shame and indignity if I had had enough time to reimpose the original basis of my relationship with her. After all I was flesh and blood, her dead sister's son, and she was genuinely fond of me. I am sure that if only for her own peace of mind she would have come to accept my explanation uncritically. People do make mistakes. And adolescents are notoriously and spontaneously fallible when it comes to affairs of the heart. Perhaps— even—she might have allowed herself a quiet smile of pleasure, of female pride, at her nephew's evident infatuation? Perhaps she might even—in a private moment—have tried to recall the incident itself. My muscled, slim, glossy-haired body; dark glistening loins, the pale pendulous dripping genitals ... But I needed time. I needed days at least to engineer such a *rapprochement*, but that was exactly what I did not have. Donald Verulam was coming.

That evening Peter Hobhouse talked to me again about enlisting (Peter was a genuine bore of the first water—a good-natured one, granted, but a bore for all that, with, astonishingly for a nineteen-year-old, all the cataleptic powers of a whiskered clubman). I must confess my enthusiasm for the idea was now firmly on the wane. I was instead formulating vague notions about returning to Edinburgh. What with my embarrassment *vis à vis* Faye, the revelations about Donald Verulam and his impending arrival, Charlbury suddenly seemed a less welcome haven. I had an unfamiliar desire to get back home—home to Oonagh. But I half-listened to what Peter had to say. He seemed to have a dogged urge to get out to France, it was not so much fervent as dutiful; and besides, all his friends were going too and it would be a shame to miss out. He said that, really, one had to have a commission, but that meant going to OTC, if you were chosen. What he and his companions had done was to volunteer as private soldiers in one of the public school battalions. Basic training was shorter, you reached France more quickly and were almost guaranteed promotion to subaltern within months. The casualty rates being what they were, the public school battalions were constantly being drawn on to provide new officers for other regiments. His own case was typical. He had been promoted after two weeks and was now off to join the Loyal North Lancashire regiment as a second-lieutenant.

I asked some polite questions. Where should one go to enlist? Marlborough, he said, or Windsor. Ask for the 13th P.S. battalion of the South Oxfordshire Light Infantry, and mention Colonel O'Dell. He had been Peter's headmaster. Fine, I said, perhaps next year. In truth I had little desire to go to war. In 1914 it had seemed much more attractive; I thought it might be 'fun' or 'exciting', but I was no zealot. Several senior boys I had known vaguely at the Academy had been killed; Minto's melancholy scepticism, too, had got through to me, and moreover nothing or no-one in my upbringing had fostered an active sense of patriotism or selfless duty. To be honest I wanted to live for myself not die for my country. If I could go to war and subject myself to powerful new experiences *and* survive, unmaimed, then I was all for it. But I had no desire to risk my neck or any other part of my anatomy.

After dinner Faye left Peter and me with the port. Peter offered me a cigar which I accepted. We puffed away, Peter's weak eyes watering somewhat, and talked in a rather self-consciously manly fashion. Peter told a bad joke about an English curate who went to Paris and tried to shit standing up in a *pissoir*.

'I'm thinking about growing a moustache,' Peter said. 'What do you think?'

'Sounds like rather a good idea.'

'Makes you look years older, you know. You should grow one, for the recruiting officer. How old are you, anyway?'

'Seventeen . . . I was thinking of waiting 'til next year.'

'Wouldn't wait too long. Might miss out.'

'Good point.'

'Say you're nineteen. With a moustache you should have no trouble.'

He wittered on. Suddenly I wished I had grown a moustache at school. Imagine if I had arrived at Faye's door moustachioed! What an impression of maturity that would have conveyed . . . I resolved to start growing one the next day.

Donald Verulam arrived before luncheon. He wore a tweed suit. Somehow, I expected to see him in uniform. When I asked what he did at the War Office he said he was just a 'glorified civil servant'. He seemed glad to see me, and gently reprimanded me for running away from school. He advised me to go back home and promised to intercede with my father on my behalf. Instinctively, I was pleased to see him, but my own edginess, and the new information that my mother's letters seemed to contain, made me rather cool at first. I think he sensed this and was puzzled. Several times he asked me if I were all right. I reassured him.

I was in turmoil. Mettlesome theories and hypotheses kept thrusting themselves on me. I looked closely at his behaviour with Faye but I saw no evidence for anything more passionate than a friendship. He spent most of Saturday afternoon in town with the Hobhouse family solicitor sorting out Vincent Hobhouse's affairs. That evening there was a small dinner party with two dull couples, one of whom brought a tall myopic daughter—Nellie or Flossie—who, one sensed, was rather keen on Peter. To my relief, Faye was as good as her word. All after effects of the picnic incident seemed to have disappeared. Perhaps she believed it really was a mistake. She reverted to being nice Aunt Faye. So I turned my attention to the next relationship that concerned me. What was I to do about Donald Verulam?

Sunday. Church. At one point during an incomprehensible sermon (the vicar had a speech defect. His mouth sounded as if it were full of water. All I could hear was lapping and slurping—as of a subterranean stream) I turned my head and found Donald looking at me. He rolled his eyes, and I grinned back. It was like the old days at Barnton or Drumlarish. After luncheon (soup, fish, game, joint, sweet, savoury—war or no war one ate well chez Hobhouse) he asked me if I felt like going for a walk. I agreed.

We each took a stick from the umbrella stand in the hall and set out briskly along the Oxford road. We cut off it, climbed over a stile and walked along the edge of a field of green corn that led up to a small beech wood that crowned a hill. There we could see the modest valleys and ridges of Oxfordshire unfolding sedately to the horizon. It was a sullen coldish afternoon, the cloudy sky mouse-grey with only hints of yellow. We walked on briskly for a couple of miles. Normally on a jaunt like this we would each have had a camera; today, being without them, we amused ourselves by pointing out scenes we would have taken. I felt all my reservations and suspicions of Donald slip away, and as we walked on, talking occasionally, I sensed growing in me a sort of love which I could only describe as filial. A mixture of strong affection, respect and a happy subordination. The love that exists between a father and son is peculiar, possessing a clear

71

hierarchical structure, the son always, as it were, looking up. And the father, for his part, then voluntarily elevating his son to a position of equality. I never felt this with Innes Todd. But that day as we strode the hills above the Evenlode valley, I sensed unspoken in the air around us that fine, reciprocal interplay of feeling. Donald felt it too, I know, felt the intimacy between us which made him want to talk to me about Faye. We stopped at a gate and looked at the view.

'I'm very fond of your aunt, you know, Johnny.'

'Yes. Well . . . I could sort of see that.'

'She's a lovely person. Very like your mother.'

'Yes.' Now I could hardly speak.

He looked round at me and smiled.

'I'm going to ask her to marry me. What d'you think?'

I felt my tear ducts sting. I felt drowned in gratitude.

'I couldn't be happier.' I paused. 'Father.'

'What's that?'

'Father.'

'Sorry?'

'Father . . . You're my father.'

Edgy laugh. 'What do you mean?'

My eyes fogged with tears.

'I know about you and my mother,' I said slowly. 'I know. All about the love affair.'

'Hang on a second, Johnny old chap. You've lost me.'

'Everything. I read her letters to Faye. I know that you and she . . .' I began to grow a little desperate. 'You don't know this, but she became pregnant, after that afternoon in the Trossachs. 1898 . . . That was *me*. She never told you. But it's all there in the letter to Faye. You're my real father.'

I could not hold it in. I bawled. I blubbed and bellowed in my happiness.

He grabbed my arms and shook me silent.

'John! John! What're you saying? Where did you get this nonsense from?'

My head cleared. Miraculously. My tearwashed eyes dried. I wiped the snot from my nose and lips. I felt a nervous cold breeze: it seemed to blow only on my smarting eyeballs.

'I read it in the letter,' I repeated. 'To Faye. You had a love affair with my mother . . .'

Donald was twisting his body to and fro on the spot as if demented. He pressed his knuckles into his temples.

'John, listen. I did not. I never did.' He spoke calmly. 'Your mother was the best friend I ever had but I never had a love affair with her. Believe me, for God's sake.' He paused. 'It was Faye I loved. I always have. When she married Vincent Hobhouse I ran away to Edinburgh. If I hadn't had your mother's friendship and support I know I would have killed myself.'

He spoke on, urgently, eloquently, explaining everything, all my blind idiotic misconceptions. I felt as though something had split inside me, like black ink. A gloom filled me as I looked at his kind, excellent face. I owed nothing to that noble nature. My fate was settled, all hope of escape denied me. I was indeed the son of Innes McNeil Todd.

VILLA LUXE 16 May 1972

Good God, my heart goes out to my younger self. There's an almost tragic dignity about my sheer guts and audacity. Imagine it: if you want to attract somebody of the opposite sex expose your equipment. But I'm sure I never planned such a course of action precisely; I intended to do *something* that day, as or how the circumstances indicated. Perhaps I'd have touched her, or if she had joined in the tag, say, I might have caught her and held her against me for a moment. Anything to show her . . . But at the time I chose swimming. It was not to be.

What a fellow I was then! I must have been crazy, the things I did. Never a pause for thought. A creature of pure impulse and instinct—like an animal. Nothing seemed impossible or ill-advised. Sometimes I look back on the rawness of my youthful character with almost jealousy.

I can tell you now that those last days in Charlbury almost finished me off. I seriously contemplated suicide for a while. You may say I was being unduly sensitive but to experience first such rejection and then to learn the truth about Donald combined radically to undermine my confidence. People like me with an excess of self-esteem suffer proportionally once it is threatened. The fiction that I had so fancifully allowed myself to construct and cherish had been exposed as exactly that, and the hard truths about myself I had to fall back on were not comforting.

Everything changed for me that weekend when my delusions were exploded. A deep unhappiness settled on me. I felt an alien in that house, felt like a monoglot foreigner in that countryside. Another world, another identity waited for me to which I was condemned to belong forever. But my fantasies about Faye, and about Donald Verulam and my mother only indicated how urgently I had longed to escape from them. I couldn't go home to our dark empty flat and my dour father, at least not in my current state of mind. I was reduced to a Cartesian proposition: I couldn't be sure of anything and so chose to rely entirely on myself.

Growth and decay. Something had decayed in me and I had to grow again. Hamish said later that I should have applied the calculus to my problems. He was only half-joking. 'The calculus', he said, 'is the study of continual change.' But I wasn't quite ready for his theories in those days. The beautiful mysteries of mathematics and physics—their profound secrets—indicated no particular direction I should follow at that time. Hamish, I knew, sensed he was heading towards some illumination, but I was still a novitiate, untutored. I could *feel* that something was there, instinctively; I could sense the scope and potential, acknowledge the power of numbers, but as yet was blind to their truths. The next stage of my life was to educate me better to perceive them.

Had I thought about it I might have rebuked Hamish thus: the calculus deals with growth and decay, but it follows their elegant parabolic curves, exponentially rising or falling. It cannot deal with discontinuity, the sudden random change, which is the real currency of our lives. In due time Hamish supplied me with an answer to that. As for myself I was about to experience discontinuity in all its strict brutal force.

My villa is quite secluded, backed into the hill that separates me from the small nearby village. If I take a few paces up this hill and advance cautiously onto a large rock ledge that overhangs the sea, I can get a good oblique view down onto my neighbour's house. He has a large terrace with a swimming pool (filled).

The owner is a German—Herr Gunter. The villa had been empty for years. Then eighteen months ago he bought it and built a swimming pool. He has a sizeable grown-up family that visits him for several weeks during the summer. Two unmarried daughters, two married sons, daughters-in-law, boyfriends and four or five grandchildren.

From my rock ledge I can see them all quite clearly as they disport themselves around the pool—loud fit young people. The girls are attractive (the very word 'girl' is attractive to me these days) but, being German, they stir old uneasy memories. I managed to avoid them almost entirely last summer. They are curious about me. They have tried to talk to me when we met in the village but I find the past seems to crowd around, jostling at our backs, like a hostile crowd or a pack of pie-dogs ... It's all a bit of a strain. I mutter abrupt pleasantries and leave.

Around this villa there are many lizards. They are slim snake-like creatures, a dun olive-green with a chalk stripe. Some months ago, when my swimming pool had water in it, one of these lizards—a small one, four inches long—fell into the deep end. I saw it on the bottom and fished it out with the long-handled net I use for cleaning leaves and insects from the surface. To my surprise it was still alive, its mouth making tiny gaping movements. I put it on the pool surround and positioned a large leaf over it to provide some shade. It recovered fully in about half an hour and scurried off into the rocks.

In the lizard world, in the saurian scheme of things, that rescue and survival must have seemed like divine intervention of the most miraculous and inexplicable sort. Such fantastical things happen in our world too, I know. But at that stage of my life, in May 1916, I felt like that lizard. I had fallen in and was sinking to the bottom. I had some time to wait until my deliverance.

It's still insufferably hot. Yesterday Herr Gunter arrived with his family. I think I'll take my binoculars and go and watch them turning their strong white bodies brown.

3

'*L'homme de l'extrême gauche*'

I was the first man on the Western Front. Literally. By the time I arrived in France—August 1916—the line of trenches stretched from the English Channel to the Swiss border. The Western Front began at Nieuport-les-Bains in Belgium on the coast. There was the sea, the beach with its minefield and wire, and then in the dunes the trench-line started.

I was standing leaning against the revetted end of the allied line looking east towards the Germans. On my left was the beach and the sea and on my right a trench system six hundred miles long. I was at the very tip of an attenuated snake uncoiled limply across Europe. It provoked a curious sensation in me standing here, almost physical in its effects. The left side of my body, for example, felt unusually light— airy and untethered. But my right side felt burdened by the immense weight of this chain I started. All the armies of Belgium, France and Britain spread like the tail of a comet from my right side. The Belgians called this position *L'homme de l'extrême gauche*. It was more than mere description: it was like participating in a metaphor. I often found myself unconsciously massaging my right shoulder. And, strangely, my left side always felt cold, as if I stood in a strong draught blowing off the sea.

The German trenches were a thousand yards away at Lombartzyde, in the direction of Ostend. Between us lay pleasant dunes and strong barbed wire entanglements. It was a quiet sector; so quiet as to be almost inert. In fact this northern end of the Western Front was, strictly speaking, the responsibility of the Belgian Army but for some reason we had been sent here as replacements for one of their units. The fact was no-one really knew what to do with the 13th (Public School) service battalion of the Duke of Clarence's Own South Oxfordshire Light Infantry.

At the outbreak of the war a Universities and Public School Brigade was raised, entirely of volunteers. The four battalions became the

21st, 22nd, 23rd and 24th battalions of the Royal Fusiliers. However, keenness to enlist was such that the Army Council allowed other regiments to create privately funded service battalions similarly composed. The Middlesex Regiment, for example, had a battalion of ex-public schoolboys—the 16th. And so too did the Duke of Clarence's Own South Oxfordshire Light Infantry. Its 13th battalion was made up at the outbreak of war by boys from public schools in and around the Thames Valley—Eton, Marlborough, Radley, St Edwards—and overflow from the Public School Brigade. However, as the war advanced and as the casualty rates of officers soon outstripped supply, the ordinary rank and file of the battalion found themselves, as Peter Hobhouse had told me, in great demand as potential officer material. By 1916 there were few battalions left and those were very under strength as the initial flood of recruits died away. Back in England there were depot companies that went through the motion of recruiting but in reality the day of the public school battalions was over. Indeed, I think my intake was among the last. After that, any spirited public schoolboy could find a place in an established regiment without much difficulty.

A further problem was the constant poaching of our numbers. Our officers were the first to go, then the NCOs, and finally any moderately capable private found himself being offered a commission. The remainder found themselves obliged to occupy the roles of those who had left. Consequently our level of ability—as soldiers—remained consistently low. By the time I joined we were a depleted bunch of unintelligent initiative-less misfits, and all from minor public schools (the old school tie operated in the army too: connections were everything). We were not much in demand as soldiers.

I myself was graded as almost educationally subnormal. Minto Academy's bizarre curriculum let me down again. I lied about my age (19) and had no qualifications. I saw the ferrety sergeant at the recruiting office write NOM on my form. Not Officer Material. In fact it took some convincing of this loathsome man to accept that Minto Academy was even a public school. After he had searched vainly in the Public Schools' Yearbook I managed to persuade him that there was a separate Scottish edition in which the Academy was sure to be found.

I was ideal material for the 13th battalion as it was now composed. Minto refused to allow a corps at the school and so I did not even possess the most rudimentary military skills. Moreover my mood at the time was extremely depressed and I was generally sullen and unresponsive. It was only through Peter's recommendation to Colonel

O'Dell that I was passed through basic training.

I do not remember much about our camp. That it was near Oswestry is all I can bring to mind. It was a dismal featureless place where, along with a thousand other recruits, I learned to drill, fire a rifle, use a bayonet and gas mask. We spent many days simulating platoon attacks on trenches and strongpoints while instructors threw thunderflashes and shouted at us. I made no great efforts, or friendships, at that stage. I wanted merely to get through and get away, while I nursed my private griefs and shame.

It is hard for me to recall those dreadful hours after Donald Verulam told me the true explanation of those references in my mother's letters. At such moments of intense despair the brain does not function normally. Just as it is for the benefit of the organism as torment. We can summon up some old griefs, some shames, some envies—but not all. It would be too much to bear. There was nothing about those feverish, crawling, sweaty sensations I underwent then that I would ever want to retain. I became suddenly dull, that day, blandly smiling, making noncommittal remarks when required, while I furiously rejigged my perceptions of myself, rejecting fanciful romance for humdrum disappointing reality. Donald and I walked on, he troubled and concerned, I supplying false, unconvincing reassurances. Somehow I got through the evening. The night was devoted to ruthless self-castigation. The next morning I announced I was going back to Edinburgh. I packed, made my farewells and got devoted to ruthless self-castigation. The next morning I announced I was going back to Edinburgh. I packed, made my farewells and got on a train to London. I disembarked at Oxford, caught another train to Marlborough where I presented myself at the recruiting office. Some days later, at Oswestry, I wrote and told everyone where I was and about the change of plan.

My father, my true father, seemed not too perturbed. He wrote to me: '... it is not a course of action I would have advised but if you feel called to serve your country I will not stand in your way. There was no need to flee the Academy to achieve this. You might at least have thought to confide your plans to me. But let us put all this behind us. At the root of this unfortunate business it seems your motives are essentially fine ...' And so on, much in the same vein. I heard nothing from Donald Verulam or Aunt Faye.

*   *   *

Of the batch of new recruits that left Oswestry bound for the 13th (Public School) service battalion of the SOLI three of us found ourselves in the same platoon. We were notionally in the bombing section, two platoon, 'D' company. Prior to an attack this section would be issued with a supply of Mills bombs and we would find ourselves in the vanguard of any assault on the enemy lines. None of us was particularly skilled at bomb throwing. At Oswestry we had practised with potatoes. We had little specialised training apart from that. As I remember we spent most of our time fitting detonators into Mills bombs.

Our progress to the front was slow. At first the battalion was attached to a Naval Division regiment guarding Dunkirk where we acted as fatigues parties. Then, after two months, we were marched up the coast to Croxyde Bains where our fatigue duties continued, this time for the siege batteries of the Royal Marine artillery at La Panne. It was here that we were sent from time to time into the trenches at Nieuport. It was not testing or dangerous. The war here was an affair of long-range artillery duels. We heard the guns and sometimes saw the explosions—distant puffs of smoke—but it took place far above our heads. After a day or two the guns were no more alarming than distant thunder in another country: rain was falling on somebody else.

The 13th was considerably understrength. There were nine of us in the so-called bombing section and at Dunkirk and at Croxyde Bains we all slept in the same large bell-tent. The three new recruits to the bombers were myself, Julian Teague and Howard Pawsey. The fellow bombers we encountered were, clockwise round the tent (we three were on groundsheets near the entrance flap), on my left, Leo Druce, Tim Somerville-Start, Noel Kite, the Hon. Maitland Bookbinder and two others whose names I have forgotten. They made no impression on me. I remember one, I think, a dim fellow, always reading—Floyd, I think. Our company commander was an older man, a lieutenant, called Louis McNeice. He was grey-haired and worried-looking and known to everyone as 'Louise'. Louise had had a commission as a major in the Mashonaland Light Horse. He sailed promptly back from Africa to England at the outbreak of war, but the best position he could obtain was this company com-mandership in the 13th with a commensurate drop in rank. He had no hopes of promotion and was maniacally fearful of getting into trouble. His authority over his company was minimal, but he was looked on charitably by Colonel O'Dell who regarded him, however erroneously, as a regular soldier, as was the Colonel himself.

Indeed the battalion owed its very existence to O'Dell and to Noel Kite's father, Findlay. Both were rich men (Kite had made his fortune in dye) and in 1914 they had paid for the formation and upkeep of the battalion (food, uniforms, transport, pay) out of their own pockets for several months, until the Army Council recognised it officially as a New Army service battalion. Our first uniforms—navy blue serge— were made up at Selfridges. We even had our own pipe band.

Findlay Kite felt strongly that every battalion should have a band and had recruited and paid eight youths from Glasgow to join the battalion. The Army Council refused to take on this expense and it was still borne by the Kite family—much to Noel Kite's irritation. The pipers were fully cognisant of their privileged position and refused any other duties. They lived apart from the rest of us in well-tended billets (they received an extra allowance for food and clothing when overseas). The sight of the pipers lounging around their braziers in shirtsleeve order was the only thing that seemed to rile Noel, normally placid to the point of inertia. 'Workshy peasants!' he used to call them and regularly wrote to his father encouraging the band's dissolution. But his father and Colonel O'Dell always vetoed it. They liked the idea of an English battalion with a Scottish band. It gave the 13th a ready-made gloss of tradition, O'Dell argued.

A few days after my arrival at Dunkirk an orderly runner told me that I was wanted by the colonel. I went to battalion HQ worried that my father had changed his mind and was going to demand my return. But not at all. O'Dell was a bald cheerful man with a frizzy blond moustache.

'Welcome aboard, Todd. Peter Hobhouse's cousin, yes? He wrote to me.'

'Yes, sir.'

'Todd . . . Todd . . . You must have been in Fetter's then. George Armitage's house.'

'Sorry, Sir?'

'No, no. Got it now. Gallway's. Never forget a face. Grand you're here. Could do with a few more Stanburians, I can tell you.'

I did not correct him.

'Remember the motto? *Plutôt fort que piquant.* That's the spirit.'

'Yes sir.'

At Dunkirk apart from doing the Naval Division's fatigues we were sent on route marches with Louise around the warm and dusty countryside. 'Route strolls' as Maitland Bookbinder referred to them. We were relieved to march up to Croxyde Bains to take over the end of the Belgian line. The skirling music of the pipes led us through battered Belgian villages, gazed upon by the incurious eyes of the few

81

inhabitants who turned out to watch us pass. There was a discernible quickening of our spirits as we approached these hamlets. Our plod became a swagger; our caps were set at extravagant angles. Louise, on a bicycle, would cycle by and implore us to throw away our cigarettes. 'Nao ciggies, chips' he would say in his South African accent. 'Unsoldierly. Come on please, fags out.' We puffed on regardless. Louise gave up quickly. He had not been to public school—not that we cared—and I think he felt socially uneasy with us. It was strange, but every time we passed through a village we seemed to pick up an escort of four or five dogs that scampered alongside for a mile or so sniffing and tail wagging, before abandoning us.

The line at Nieuport is where I really date the start of my military career. At Dunkirk we were little more than servants and labourers in our working party duties for the disdainful Naval Division. At Croxyde in reserve, or in the trenches at Nieuport, at least we felt more like soldiers. We were facing the enemy after after all, albeit under reasonably pleasant circumstances. Here too I began to shed the integument of gloom and self-loathing that had enfolded me since that black weekend at Charlbury. I began to emerge. A fragile self-confidence established itself. I started to correspond with Hamish and learnt something of the events subsequent to my departure from school.

Our plan had worked well. I was not discovered absent until the next day. Angus was despatched to Galashiels station and then travelled up and down the line searching for traces of me. Hamish's role was discovered swiftly and he was duly flogged. He wrote: '... it was as bad as everyone had said. I do not think I have ever experienced such pain before. Still, it was a useful experience. Now I know what it is like to be mercilessly beaten. (Minto is quite batty, I am sure.) It all adds to one's store of knowledge.' He sounded almost grateful, as if I had opened a locked door in his life. But it made me feel guilty.

Our routine at Nieuport was straightforward. Two companies held the line for a week and were relieved by the other two. The resting companies occupied battalion reserve (an orchard) at Croxyde Bains and occasionally supplied fatigue parties for the Royal Marine siege gunners. After each company had spent a total of a month in the line we returned to Brigade reserve at Wormstroedt, some distance away, behind the British sector of the Western Front. Life at Croxyde Bains was pleasant, if boring. The town was out of bounds to us but not to Belgian troops. There was a sizeable detachment garrisoned here as King Albert had his HQ at nearby La Panne. There was a small closer village, St Idesbalde, which we were allowed to visit, with two cafés—one for officers, one for other ranks—but it did not offer much in terms of diversion. Our time was taken up with prettifying the reserve lines (creating ash-clinker paths with whitewashed stone borders, allotments, building a clay tennis court for the officers' mess) route marches, close order drill, musketry practice and endless sessions of battalion sports of every type. About two miles away, near St Idesbalde was a large Belgian field hospital. Once or twice we passed this, either marching or on a cross-country run, and we saw the off-duty nurses with red-crosses on their starched aprons and what I took to be an order of Belgian nuns with extravagant head-dresses, like stiff white linen sombreros, the vast brims complicatedly folded. This view excited some of our more sensual types—Leo Druce and Noel Kite in particular—who instantly planned to strike up acquaintances. Little was achieved beyond vain shouts of intro-duction as we jogged past—much to Louise's irritation.

My main pleasure at Croxyde Bains—when I had the chance—was to walk on the beach. If one left the orchard and walked down a lane past a farm one soon came to the dunes. They evoked for me memories of Scotland and, when the tide was out, the huge flat beach recalled the West Sands at St Andrews in Fife. Sometimes I would walk west towards Dunkirk, on other occasions I would walk east towards Nieuport and the front line. I would stop when I could just see the revetments and sandbags at the mouth of the Yser river at Nieuport that marked the position I so often occupied as *l'homme de l'extrême gauche*. At low tide the furthest extension of the wire was often exposed and I was often obscurely tempted to walk on and wade round the double entanglements, then traverse the mile of no-man's-land and perhaps by-pass the German line too. There I might meet my German counterpart: a young private, a little unhappy, uncertain of his future, whiling away his off-duty hours with a morose stroll on the sands at Ostende Bains. Perhaps we would simply nod 'Good morning' and saunter on? Perhaps I might ask him for a light: *Hast du Feuer?* It was a pleasing fantasy . . .

One day, I went down to the beach in just such a mood of contemplation. Hands in my pockets, collar up against the wind. Then I saw, slightly distorted by the reflections on the wet gleamy sand, what I took to be a man running along the water's edge. Absurdly, spontaneously, I thought: was this my German dop-pelgänger come to meet me? . . . I peered at the distorted black shape trying to separate bouncing solid from bouncing reflection. A man?

A small man? He was certainly moving in a curious gait. I seemed to see a cripple, terribly bent over, hunched, travelling along in a fast lolloping limp.

Then as I looked the enigma resolved itself. A dog, rather large, bounding along in a kind of easy half gallop, pausing occasionally to sniff at seaweed or piece of tide wrack before starting off again. I watched it approach. Then it saw me and changed course. The loose limbed canter became a pelting, ears-back gallop. I felt uneasy, then fearful. Bloody Hell, I thought crazily, what if this is some sort of Hun secret weapon? Killer dogs loosed behind the lines? Mad ... rabid.

I looked down at my heavy boots. I'll kick it in the throat, I said to myself, none too confidently. The dog was three hundred yards away and approaching fast. I threw away my cigarette, turned and ran for the dunes. I was seriously impeded by my greatcoat and heavy boots. I flashed a glance over my shoulder. *Christ!* It was coming at me like a cheetah—head down tail out. I could hear the skithering thump of its feet on the sand.

'*Help!*' I bellowed aimlessly at the tranquil dunes. '*Bastaaaaaard!*'

The dog was on me as I lumbered vainly along. Jumping up and down, barging into me, tongue lolling, darting forward and back, crouching down like a pseudo beast of prey in that irritating manner dogs have when they want some fun. I stopped, threw my head back and gulped air, hands on my hips.

The dog, I saw, was quite big, with untidy grey fur and a blunt stupid face. It looked like a cross between Irish wolfhound, setter and bull terrier. It came up to me, tail wagging and stuck its nose in my crutch.

'Get off! Dirty bugger!'

I slapped its face away. I felt hot, angry and itchy from my hectic run. I wiped sweat from my eyebrows and upper lip. My peaceful, contemplative stroll had been ruined by this idiot hound, who was now, as far as I could see, eating sand.

I trudged back through the dunes towards the company lines, the dog following. I spoke violently to it (it is strange how we address dumb animals so, is it not?)

'If you don't leave me alone, I'll go back to camp get my rifle and shoot you.'

*　　　*　　　*

The dog was adopted by the bombers as section mascot. Bookbinder and Pawsey made a great fuss of it giving it tins of MacConnachie stew several times a day. A name was chosen by lottery (I did not participate) and the dog became known as Ralph—Tim Somerville-Start's choice. I wanted nothing to do with the beast. In fact I was rather superstitious of it—it had come from the direction of the German lines after all. I refused to call it 'Ralph', never petted it, and every time it shat in the tent, pissed on someone's shoes, knocked over stands of rifles, coffee pots and mess tins my voice was loudly raised urging its peremptory execution. But the animal never left me alone. It came to me, it sat by me, it slept as near to me as it was allowed. This provoked considerable jealously amongst the others.

'Are you feeding Ralph secretly, Todd?' Pawsey demanded.

'Come here boy, here, here,' Teague would call. The dog never budged.

'I think Todd must have some special dog-smell,' Kite said. 'See how Ralph is always trying to snuffle at his balls.' Much laughter at this.

'Some sort of Scotch affinity with the beasts of the field,' Bookbinder said.

'Scots or Scottish. Scotch is whisky,' Druce said.

'Thank you, Druce,' I said. 'Look, I want to kill the damn thing. I hate it.'

'Och aye! The fury of the Pict when roused,' Somerville-Start said. 'Perhaps we should see how Ralph reacts to the pipe-band. Here, Ralph. Here, Ralphie-boy. Biscuit.'

Ralph went to him. He was always lured by food.

There was a certain amount of tedious, though good-natured mockery of my accent, which at that time was quite marked and in strong contrast to the others in the tent. I was something of the odd man out in more ways than this. Teague and Somerville-Start had been to the same school. Most people in the battalion came from schools in the south of England. Most knew of each other's schools, had friends at them, played sports against them. No-one had ever heard of Minto Academy. I kept my answers to their questions vague. Also, they were all older than me. Pawsey the next youngest was nineteen. Druce and Teague were the oldest, both twenty-four. They were all English too, and, at first, to my untutored ears they all seemed to speak with one voice, like a gang of Chinese.

Howard Pawsey was tall, thin, with straight hair parted in the middle. Every time he bent his head two wings would fall across his brow. To my increasing annoyance he had developed a habit of only sweeping one back and leaving the other dangling. He had a weak chin.

Tim Somerville-Start was fair, fresh-faced, broad shouldered and incredibly stupid. He and Julian Teague were longing to fight. They were the self-appointed warriors among us. Teague was more complex in his zeal, though. He had very curly hair forced back over his head to form regular waves, as if they had been created by curling tongs. He had a square face, a thick neck, a small moustache and small restless eyes. He was most unhappy that we had been posted to a quiet sector.

Noel Kite had blond thinning hair and a handsome lean face. He had the easy insouciance of the very rich. The material problems of his life having been taken care of, he cultivated a languid incuriosity about everything. Cynicism seemed to be the most vehement emotion in his repertoire.

Maitland Bookbinder was a curiosity: plump, lazy, genial, an Old Etonian—one felt he should have been in the Guards. When asked what he was doing in the 13th he said merely that he had wanted a change.

Leo Druce was the only one I instinctively liked, and at the same time was the most enigmatic. He wore his toffee-brown hair brushed straight back, glossy with a specially prepared, scented pomade. He had fine almost delicate features which sat oddly with his deep, bass voice. He was clever, cleverer than all of us, and this was why I was drawn to him. Druce was a lance-corporal, in charge of the section. The rest of us were privates. We were distinguished from all the other enlisted men in the British Army by possessing two letters in front of our army serial number. PS: Public School. I was PS 300712.

*   *   *

'Where are you going, Todd?'

It was Louise.

'Down to the beach.'

'Maike sure you're bick by six.'

'Could you hang on to Ralph for five minutes please, Louise? Just till I'm out of sight.'

Louise took hold of Ralph's collar.

'For God's sake, min, you mustn't call me Louise!'

He looked hurt, as he crouched holding a straining panting Ralph.

'What if the Colonel heard? Don't be so bliddy selfish.'

'Sorry, sir.'

'Right, that's bitter. Off you go. Ah've got the dog.'

It was the end of March 1917. It was a cold windy but clear day.

The trees were bare, only the hedges were in bud as I walked down the lane towards the dunes. We had been based at Croxyde Bains for over five months. Almost a year had passed since that dire weekend at Charlbury. My eighteenth birthday had come and gone, unacknowledged by everybody, a week since. The war seemed as if it would go on for ever, and as far as I was concerned it seemed we would be at Croxyde for ever too, guarding our stretch of dunes.

I had seen the enemy through binoculars, strolling around the parapets of their trenches in the evening. Nobody took cover in this quiet sector. Our trenches were immaculate: clean, strong with beautifully carpentered fire steps and panelled dugouts. At every firebay stood red buckets of sand and water, and all our equipment was oiled and greased against the corrosive effects of salt in the wind off the sea. We, the troops, were sleeked, well fed, and well rested. Only Teague and Somerville-Start fretted. Indeed, Teague seemed almost unhinged with frustration. He repeatedly asked Colonel O'Dell to put him up for a commission in another regiment but O'Dell always regretfully refused. He had seen the battalion's ranks casually plundered for years and was not prepared to allow further privations.

I myself was happy enough. I seemed to be in a kind of agreeable limbo, stuck in a society and a place that made few inconvenient demands on me. I had no idea what the future held and at the time I did not care. I had even seen my first dead man, a sergeant in 'A' company who had been run over by a Commer truck bringing in two tons of potatoes to the cookhouse. I had changed physically, too. I had reached what I later discovered was to be my full height—five feet nine inches—I had filled out and was now thickish set with a solid, well-muscled body. The moustache I had started growing the weekend I left Charlbury was a familiar feature in my shaving mirror each morning: thick, dense, neatly clipped, glossy. I looked older than my years. The main bugbear in my life was the dog, Ralph, who as the weeks passed seemed to become perversely more fond of me. Never had a man showed less feeling for an animal than I, but my very indifference seemed to act as a goad. Even while eating bread and jam from Teague's fingers the dog would pause—munching— and glance round to confirm I was in the company.

I walked down the lane towards the dunes. Behind me I heard a rattle of pebbles and a familiar hoarse panting. I looked round. That blunt terrier's snout, those moist idiot eyes. Louise must have let him go too soon. I picked up some stones and threw them at him. One hit his rump and he squealed. His tail wagged with masochistic pleasure. I set off. He trotted three yards behind me.

87

I climbed up a sand path that led to the crest of the dunes. It was a cloudy day, shadowless with a diffused silver light. The tide was out. I sat down, lit a cigarette and stared at the pewter sea. Life was settled, routine, ordered—but I was in turmoil. I was in love again. In love with a girl called Huguette.

In our first stint in the Nieuport trenches we had been called back twice to Brigade reserve at Wormstroedt. Wormstroedt was a large village, or a small town, some twenty miles behind the front line. Before the war it had enjoyed modest prosperity owing to the siting there of a tobacco factory. This was now empty, one wing of it destroyed by bombardment during the German advance of 1914. Here, we were billeted in tall airless rooms smelling strongly of tobacco. We slept in low wooden beds, sixty to a room like a vast dormitory. Leave in Wormstroedt was preferable to our off-duty hours in St Idesbalde if only because we were freer to roam around. There was a cinema set up in a tent in the shattered main square and a good dozen cafés and restaurants. Men of the 13th tended to patronise a large estaminet conveniently close to the factory. It was run by an extended Belgian family who were doing well out of the war. They had been swift to adapt to the tastes of the British soldier. Fried eggs and chipped potatoes were the staple diet, and it was not unusual for us to order up to six fried eggs at a time. You could also eat bread and pickled mackerel, or bacon, brawn, bread and margarine with jam or cheese, rice pudding or sponge pudding with jam. They even made tea—and this was Huguette's job. The tea was brewed in large copper vats and liberally sweetened. Milk was added by punching holes in several tins of condensed milk and dropping them into the stewing tea. The paper labels floated off the tins to form an unusual, brightly coloured scum on the surface.

Huguette was the daughter, or cousin, or niece of the owner. I think she was sixteen or seventeen. She was plump; even at that age a tender double chin hung damply below her jaw. She was dark haired and had a distinct moustache of tiny fine fairs on her top lip. But she was pretty in a sulky, spoilt way. I can see her now, impassively puncturing condensed milk tins with something that looked like a steel marlinspike and tossing them over her shoulder into the sandy pool of simmering tea without a backward glance.

The estaminet was capacious and always crowded. Over a hundred people could fit into it without difficulty. On my first visit I waited at the head of the queue while Huguette milked a new batch of tea. She had been working all day. Her shapeless lime-green dress, tight in the armpits, was damp with fresh sweat. I could smell it, clear and thin, through the strata of odours—smoke, grease, egg, tea—that suffused the atmosphere. I stood beside her, estimating the size of her breasts, inhaling it. Her sharp smell seemed to prod at my lungs like a stick. She stirred the tea vat with a three-foot wooden ladle. The condensed milk cans clanked dully in the dun liquid.

'*C'est formidable . . .*' I said. '*Le thé. Pour le soif.*'

She looked at me incredulously.

'*Vous pensez?*' she said. '*C'est pas vrai.*'

'Oh, yes—*oui*,' I said. '*Votre thé . . .*' I kissed my bunched fingertips, a parody gourmand.

She turned and said something to her father or uncle and they both laughed. I laughed with them. But as a result of that exchange she remembered me. I ate there every day—fried eggs and chipped potatoes washed down with gallons of her disgusting tea.

'*Oh, voilà monsieur Thé*,' she said as I came round for my third refill. 'Tea. Ver' good. You like,' she laughed.

'John. John James Todd. My name . . .' I paused. '*Votre nom?*'

'Huguette,' she said, turning the spigot on the vat. Tawny tea frothed into my enamel mug.

I thought of her now as I looked out over the tea-coloured sand. I would not be back in Wormstroedt for getting on two months. I wondered if I could last that long; if my carefully hoarded store of images would sustain me through two months of masturbation. Perhaps I could persuade Louise to send me to Brigade reserve on some specious mission . . . Perhaps . . . To my surprise I found I had my hand on the scruff of Ralph's neck and had been absent-mindedly scratching behind his ears for God knows how many minutes. His humid eyes gazed at me. A loop of saliva hung from his jowl. I gave him a mighty shove and he went tumbling down the dune slope onto the beach. He got to his feet and shook the sand from his coat.

'Bugger off!' I shouted. I slithered down to the beach and walked down towards the distant water's edge. I looked down at my boots and puttees, felt the rough serge of the khaki trousers chafe my inner thighs. I took a rather bent cigarette from one of my breast pockets and turned away from the wind to light it. I walked on. Flat sky, flat sand, flat sea. I was the only vertical thing in my universe. All very straightforward. I felt surprisingly good. I felt strong, all of a sudden. I was an adult at last, a soldier, with my big moustache, and dreams of my girl, Huguette. I grinned . . . Where was that bloody dog? I looked around for a pebble to throw.

Ralph was not his obligatory three paces behind me. I saw him two hundred yards off, loping towards the front and the German line, running along the water's edge, his reflection merging with and separating from his body, bounding back to wherever he had come from.

'Go on!' I shouted after him. '*Traitor!* I knew it. I bloody knew it!'

Good riddance, I muttered, finally got the message. I reached the sea's edge. It was a calm day, a small surf turned over on the ridged gleaming sand. I turned my back on Ralph and the east and headed west towards the tiny distant shapes of the ruined villas and bathing huts of Oost-Dunkirk.

I must have walked nearly a mile before I saw them. I was on the point of turning back, the evening was drawing in, when I noticed what at first looked like a cluster of smooth pale rocks upon which the waves were breaking. But then I saw that the waves moved and shifted them to and fro. I walked closer. A strange minatory weight seemed to press on me ... Some sort of cargo? Washed overboard in a storm? In the nacreous late afternoon light I approached full of dread curiosity.

There were eight drowned men, huddled together as if for comfort by the advancing tide. Most of them were naked, or almost so. One man wore a shirt; one man still had his boots on. I was struck by their inert tranquillity. I felt no lasting shock. I counted them. Eight. They looked like deep sleepers: expressionless, untouched, unblemished by whatever tremendous experience had washed them up on this shore. I saw a tattooed forearm, creases in a belly, the dark print of pubic hair on blue-white loins. The wavelets rolled one over, who flung an arm on the sand as if seeking purchase.

'Jesus,' I said out loud. I looked up and down the deserted beach. I was equidistant from the villas of Oost-Dunkirk and the mouth of the Yser. The packed greyness of the late afternoon seemed to thicken and condense around me. The tangle of bleached bodies surged as if one, and crept a few inches up the sand.

I ran for the dunes. A naval battle? A mine? A ship rent in two, a wardroom of sleeping men tossed into the North Sea? I felt a kind of clawing in my gorge. I raked my throat and spat.

There was wire on these dunes. I found the zig-zag path and stumbled up it to the dune-crest. I ran down through the gorse and broom bushes and along the muddy edge of a cabbage field. The kitchen smell of cabbage nauseated me. I suddenly associated the reek with those washed, clean, dead men ... Through a hawthorn hedge and onto a cart track. I ran on. An old man sat in the doorway of a half-demolished cottage. I stopped. What was the French for drowned?

'*Mort*,' I said, panting heavily. 'Eight, *huit morts.*'

'*L'hôpital.*' He gestured up the road. He had a lazy eye. It seemed to be trapped in the middle of an interminable wink.

I remembered. The field hospital at St Idesbalde. I turned and ran on.

I entered the hospital precincts from the side somewhere. I saw the back of what looked like a row of loose boxes, rounded them and came upon a neat square of a dozen large olive green tents. A nurse was coming out of the first one.

'*Huits morts . . . dans la mer!*'

'I speak English,' she said in a cool, perfect but somehow instantly foreign accent.

'Eight drowned men,' I said. 'On the sea shore.' It sounded like a nursery rhyme.

I led this nurse and three nuns back down to the beach. An ambulance was following with orderlies and stretchers. The tide was further in but our group still clung together. The evening light shone lemon through gaps in charcoal clouds. The sand seemed shot with blue and green. We walked down the beach, the nuns muttering some prayer or heavenly invocation.

'We'd better get them out,' the nurse said. She took off her watch. She had not brought her coat. 'Can you keep this dry for me?' she said. I put it in a pocket and watched with some astonishment as she waded strongly into the sea, the waves soaking her to the waist, and she began to haul a man out. The nuns joined in. I registered the incongruity of the dark surplices and the absurd meringue hats as they stooped and tugged at the naked men. Naked men . . . Nothing to what they saw in that field hospital. I sloshed into the water with them. The bodies shifted out of focus beneath my sensitive gaze. To grasp an ankle or a wrist. I saw a hand, limp, elegant—like something on a classical statue—and took hold of it. Very cold. But no more rebarbative than picking up a leg of lamb or a plucked chicken. I pulled him onto the beach. I took his other wrist. He was heavier on the sand, heels furrowing. The nuns were working two to a body. I heard shouts and saw the orderlies come running down the beach with their stretchers.

It was almost dark by the time the beach was clear. I stood with the nurse. She had a wide round face, a slightly large nose, covered in coarse prominent freckles. I could not see her hair as it was hidden beneath her neat head-dress.

'What do you think it was?' I asked.

'Who can say? At least they looked peaceful. They didn't seem to be hurt.' She looked at me. 'I didn't know there were English troops here.'

I explained about the Royal Marine gunners.

'Have you got a cigarette?'

I gave her one and lit it for her. She inhaled avidly.

'The nuns don't approve. I have to take my moments carefully.' She blew smoke through her nose. 'Wonderful. English tobacco!'

I suddenly remembered the time. 'God! I'm going to get merry hell. Look, can I give your name?'

'Of course. I'm a sister at the field hospital. Dagmar Fjermeros.' I got her to repeat it a couple of times.

'Can we give you a lift?'

'It'll be quicker along the beach.' I said goodbye and left her.

Louise was furious, and put me on company report. Two hours later my story was confirmed after a few telephone calls. I was perturbed and unsettled by the whole experience. It was the tangle of bodies that bothered me and their untroubled expressions. They seemed docile and compliant in death, perfectly at ease. But for the first time since joining the army I felt frightened. I feared for my skin. That day I resolved to do anything not to get hurt. Not to die like those men.

While my alarm deepened, and self-preservation occupied the key position in my mind, I found another image began slowly to claim my attention. Dagmar, the nurse ... Her round placid face highlit by the flare of the match I applied to her cigarette. The full pout of her lips as she inhaled ... I had written down her name on my return. Dagmar Fjermeros. A Scandinavian of some sort. I still had her wrist watch in my pocket.

After this excitement life returned to normal. The only event of note was a battalion parade where we were required to hand in our old phenate-hexane gas respirators. These were horrible objects, like a canvas sack with glass eye-holes, and which had to be tucked beneath the collar of one's jacket. New box respirators, we were informed, would be issued to us in the next few days. Meanwhile, in preparation, Captain Tuck, the adjutant, would give us a lecture later that morning on anti-gas precautions and the best use of the box respirator gas mask.

At half past twelve 'D' company was mustered for Captain Tuck's gas lecture. As we filed into the tent we were each handed what looked like a rectangular pad of lint with two cotton tapes, eighteen inches long, attached at either end, and a pair of rubber goggles.

Captain Tuck, a Wykehamist, was a brisk jolly man who spent most of his time looking at birds through his field glasses. He had an odd pursed look to his face, as if he were playing an invisible musical instrument—a spectral oboe or clarinet, say. First, he told us about the various types of gases—phosgene, chlorine and mustard—and their effects. Chlorine turned your face blue and you drowned in the water produced by your own tormented lungs. Phosgene caused your lungs to discharge four pints of yellow water every hour. Mustard made your eyelids swell and close, burned and blistered your skin, made you cough up your mucous membrane. Tuck read out other ghastly symptoms—congested larynx, collapsed lungs, swollen liver. I was very shocked.

A box respirator was circulated among us and we tried it on. Tuck explained how it worked. He informed us that the entire battalion would be issued with these in a matter of days.

'In the meantime,' he said, 'we will be relying on the temporary respirator handed to you as you came in.'

I looked at the lint pad in my hand. I wondered how it would stop me coughing up four pints of yellow liquid in an hour. Suddenly I felt an acute, rotting fear. I saw the dead men on the beach. I glanced right and left. Everyone seemed to be smiling; even Tuck had a grin on his face.

'In the very unlikely event of a gas attack in this sector, this is what—it says here—you must do.' He opened a pamphlet and read from it. ' "When the gas alarm goes, first put on the goggles. Then soak the cheese cloth pad, or a handkerchief or a sock in fresh urine before applying it to the face, making sure both mouth and nostrils are covered." '

He paused for effect. His audience took this in for a second in silence before baying hoots of sceptical laughter and cries of disgust erupted.

'Gentlemen, please!' Tuck shouted above the din. 'A final word of advice ... According to this document the urine of older men is particularly efficacious! Dismiss.' Tuck strode out of the tent very pleased with his performance. 'D' company was most amused.

The next day I went in search of Louise and asked if I might cycle over to the field hospital to return nurse Fjermeros's watch. He agreed reluctantly, signed a chit and I drew one bicycle from the quartermaster's stores. I pedalled off down the drab lanes in a fine drizzle. I noticed a curious fizzing sensation at the back of my head. I recognised the symptoms of mild euphoria.

It took me twenty minutes to get to St Idesbalde. A Belgian sentry directed me to an office in a wooden shack where I waited for Dagmar. She arrived wearing full uniform. I handed over the watch.

'It's very kind of you.'

'Not at all . . . I wondered if the men—if you knew?'

'We think they are Dutch. A fishing boat, perhaps hitting a mine.' She shrugged, then smiled. 'Can I offer you something to eat, Mr . . . ?'

'Todd. John James. Yes, please.'

We walked through the hospital. It had originally been a rather grand farmhouse with numerous outbuildings. Large tents had been pitched in every available space and duckboard walkways laid between them. Looking inside one tent I could see neat rows of patients in low camp-beds. We crossed the lawn of a small walled garden and emerged from it onto the gravelled driveway of the main house. Three motor ambulances were pulled up at the door. Some men, in filthy uniforms and stark, almost indecently white bandages were being helped inside.

'We're very quiet at the moment,' she said. 'Waiting for spring offensives.'

I nodded and followed her across the driveway and into a stable block. There was a row of loose-boxes and for an instant I was back in Minto Academy. I had paused involuntarily, and now Dagmar stood at the door of an old barn waiting for me. I followed her in.

The noise of conversation was colossal. The barn had been converted into a canteen and was filled with trestle tables around which sat dozens of injured soldiers, some in uniform, some in pyjamas and dressing gowns, eating, drinking, playing cards, and all—as far as I could hear—talking at the tops of their voices. Smoke from their cigarettes drifted up into the exposed rafters. A big fat iron stove stood in the centre of the room and at the far end was a makeshift kitchen and serving area staffed by nuns. There I was given a plate of stew, three slices of coarse greyish soda bread and a tin mug of coffee.

Dagmar and I found two unoccupied seats and sat down. Here and there amongst the groups of soldiers were nurses and nuns. I suddenly felt a shaft of envy for these wounded Belgians, with their loud conviviality, their plentiful food and their female company. I looked at Dagmar—she was tucking stray hair back under her cap. Her hair was a fine reddish blond.

'Not eating?'

'No,' she said. 'I already finished. Please, don't mind me.'

I ate the stew. A curious tasting meat—half pork, half venison (it was mule, I learnt later). We chatted about something or other. She told me she was Norwegian and had joined the Red Cross in 1915. I let her know something of my past, only lying blatantly when I said I had abandoned a place at university to enlist.

'I think you were better to stay at university.'

'I think you're right,' I said spontaneously, my new mood of apprehension prompting me. I smoothed my moustache with thumb and forefinger. I took out a tin of cigarettes—Trumpeters—offered her one and received a wry refusal. I lit mine and passed the tin across the table to her.

'Have it,' I said. 'I've got tons.'

She smiled and quickly slipped the tin into a pocket in her uniform. This mild illicit act joined us as fellow conspirators. I felt my face hot and a curious sense of disequilibrium afflicted me for an instant. I looked at her square face, her random freckles ... Her hands were on the table, one nail tapping gently. I saw fine red-gold hairs at her wrist. I wanted to ask her if we could meet again, but the words seemed to form in my stomach rather than my throat, as if only vomiting would release them.

'I keep thinking about those drowned men,' I blurted out. 'They're the first actual dead ... I mean, like that—casualties.'

'You should stay here for a day. We filled two cemeteries since I'm at St Idesbalde.'

'Of course. I see. It's just that, for the first time ...' I gave a weak smile. 'This quiet sector, it's very misleading.'

She met my gaze. 'I know you'll be all right,' she said seriously. 'I get these sensations about people.' She smiled. 'I'm almays right.'

'Sorry?'

'I'm almays right.'

'Oh. Good, good.'

That was what it sounded like to me. 'Almays'. Was it a speech defect? Did she think it was an actual English word: a conflation of 'almost always'? Did she mean 'almost' or 'always'? I decided to take it for the latter. I felt a benign sense of release spread upwards through my body from my bowels, a kind of erotic fatigue. I felt I had her word for it. I was going to come through.

'I hope you are,' I said. 'Right, I mean.'

95

She looked at her watch. 'I should go.'

She walked me to the camp gate. I put on my cap and climbed on my bicycle. She leant towards me.

'Thanks for the cigarettes,' she said in a low voice. Her sweet breath hit the side of my face.

'Do you ever go walking on the beach,' I said, 'at Croxyde Bains?'

'Me? No . . .'

'I do, as often as I can.'

'Maybe I'll see you one day.'

'Yes. Fine . . . Well, goodbye.'

It was the best I could do. I cycled back to camp in a dull, vexed mood; too dull even to be angry with myself. At the camp, teams from 'A' and 'D' companies were playing football with each other, thirty-a-side.

I went into our tent. Teague was there, his foot up—sockless—on a pile of blankets.

'Twisted my bloody ankle,' he said, 'playing bloody footer.' His thick face was red and sweaty. The normally immaculate ridges of his hair were mussed.

'Where the hell have you been?'

I told him. And recounted how I had met Dagmar.

'Bloody marvellous,' he said. 'Here we are, meant to be fighting the Hun. One lot plays football, another goes to have lunch with his girlfriend. "What did you do in the war, Daddy?" "Me? Oh, I twisted my ankle in a match against 'A' company." Makes me *sick*.'

He was genuinely angry. But I had seen him often enough in this mood not to be perturbed.

'You should visit that hospital. You wouldn't be quite so keen then.'

'What do you know, pictish lout?'

I was not frightened of Teague, especially as he was immobile.

'I know I'd watch my lip if I were you, Teague. Or I might just twist your other ankle.'

'Shag off.'

'Shag off yourself, fat-face.'

It carried on like this for a minute or so before I left to watch the end of the match. It sounds depressingly puerile, I know, but remember we were most of us just out of the sixth form and we often bickered this way. Our profanities coarsened steadily as time went by. We took our lead from the pipe band, cheerful foul-mouthed fellows, with a colourful line in invective.

Two days later we went up the line to relieve 'B' and 'C' companies. I looked at the immaculate trenches with different eyes. There was something sinister, almost insulting about their order and rectitude. My encounter with the drowned men made me preternaturally wary. I no longer strolled along the parapet at dusk, as I used to. I never even exposed my head above the sandbags. I surveyed the distant German lines through a periscope. I saw the small figures of the enemy quite clearly, as indifferent to our presence as we were to theirs. For the first time I completed the equation of myself, my rifle and the target a thousand yards away. Then I transposed it. Congruence. My alarm deepened.

One evening in the section dugout Teague and Somerville-Start asked Druce to persuade Louise to let them form a raiding party.

'What on earth for?' he said. We all listened intently.

'To *do* something for once,' Teague said.

'We're going mad with boredom. Let's take a prisoner. Interrogate him.' Somerville-Start grinned, showing his big teeth. 'Have some fun.'

'No,' I said, suddenly terrified. 'It's the most stupid idea I've ever heard.'

'Does sound a bit on the keen side,' Bookbinder said. 'I'm not complaining.'

'Anything for a quiet life,' Kite said. 'Who wants to go prowling around in the dark?'

'You might get hurt,' Bookbinder said.

'Bloody funk,' Teague said to me.

'It's not funk, it's sense.'

'Louise'll never agree, anyway,' Druce said calmly. 'He'll ask O'Dell and O'Dell will say no. This is Belgian line, you know, not ours.'

'They're mad,' I said to Druce when the others had gone. 'Raving mad.'

Druce smiled. 'Raiding party. Don't know what they're talking about.' He slapped me on the shoulder. 'Keep it up, Jock, you'll save our necks yet.'

I liked Druce for that. He seemed so much older than the rest of us; calmer, more sceptical, less ruffled by events.

However, despite Druce's presence, as our sixth month in the Nieuport sector wore on, my own worries steadily increased. The drowned men had thrown me off balance. The unreal routine and the tolerable nature of our life at the front had been exposed for the temporary haven it was. We would not be left in a quiet sector forever. As each day passed it brought a possible posting closer. I began to speculate about the nature of my death, all the horrible versions that were available. And behind this fear another deep disquiet was nurtured. I was still a virgin, and, Oonagh apart, I had never even kissed a girl. The thought of dying with life so unlived, so little experienced, seemed outrageously unfair. My encounter with Dagmar had naturally exacerbated this emptiness at the centre of myself. Dagmar or Huguette? Huguette or Dagmar? Which one would I choose? In such bouts of vain self-deception did I while away my time. It was doubly galling as it was difficult to masturbate discreetly in the trenches. I used to wait until I was on sentry duty in a small observation sap pushed forward some ten or fifteen yards into no-man's-land where for four futile hours I was meant to guard against a German attack. (As it happened, one did occur in July of that year—1917—but by then we were long gone.)

From my diary:

April 23rd 1917. Druce has just told me that I am on sentry duty from 2 a.m. to 6 a.m. Tried to sleep in dugout but had serious row with Teague and S.-Start about the 'thrill of battle'. Teague openly accused me of killing Ralph. Even Bookbinder and Kite seemed not to accept my story. Eight days to go and then back to Wormstroedt and Huguette.

I remember that date vividly. All through that night of sentry duty the German batteries at Wilskerke shelled the bridge across the canal at Wulpen. I could see across the sand hills the distant muzzle flash of the guns but I could not see or hear the shells land. The irregular flickering and the faint reports kept me alert and edgy. Around five o'clock I began to see the shape of the ruined lighthouse at the mouth of the Yser emerge from the darkness. It had been a warm night, the warmest of the year so far.

I had a piss in the corner of the sap. As I did so I looked up at the lightening sky and saw the faint stars still sparkling in an immense field of lightest bluey-grey. I rubbed my face and looked at my watch. Half an hour to go. A breakfast of tea, a tin of sardines and bread and margarine waited. I sniffed, spat, yawned, flexed my fingers and allowed my gaze to wander out over no-man's-land.

I saw the gas instantly, as it rolled thick, white and heavy down through the dunes from Lombartydze. A breeze on the seaward side swung a flank round faster on the left, hooking in towards me. It seemed dense and solid as smoke from burning green leaves, obliterating everything as it advanced. I turned and ran back down the sap to the trench. There a large highly polished section of girder hung from a bracket, and beside it an iron bar.

I seized the bar and beat furiously on the girder, numbing my fingers cruelly with the blows. The clear harsh sound of metal on metal clattered down the trench line.

'*GAS!*' I screamed. '*GAS ATTACK!*'

I heard other gas alarms being sounded—sirens, gongs and rattles—shouts of frantic inquiry. I tore my goggles from a pocket and put them on. I fumbled for my lint pad. *Not there!* I re-searched my pockets. Nothing. *Nothing.* I thought of pints of yellow fluid, foam-filled rotting lungs, searing mustard burns ... I hurled myself into the dugout. Blurred faces shouted nonsense at me.

'Gas!' I bellowed. 'Gas!'

I scrabbled amongst my kit, found my lint pad and stumbled back outside. The gas was fifty yards away. Our platoon crawled out of dugouts. The air was filled with alarms, loud with meaningless panic. I saw a baffled Noel Kite who had also been on sentry duty trying on his lint pad. Dry.

'Urine, Kite!' I yelled at him, and at the others who now piled haphazardly out of the dugout entrance, tin helmets on, rifles ready.

'Wet the pad. Quickly!'

Violent fear galvanised them. Full early-morning bladders were emptied steaming onto the lint. I laid my own pad on the firestep and snatched at the buttons of my fly with blunt agitated fingers. I saw Teague wrap a sopping mask around his face, saw the more fastidious Kite wring his out before applying it. Somerville-Start crouched behind the sandbagged parapet on the firestep, fixing his bayonet, his hanging cock luminously white against the knaki of his battledress. I strained desperately to urinate, but I had emptied my bladder minutes before. *Nothing.* Not a drop. I could smell the gas above the acid reek of urine which filled the trench. The whole section was now masked and ready except for me and Pawsey, who had raised his sodden pad to vomit. I saw Louise, half-dressed, stumbling along from his dugout.

'What's going on?' he shouted. 'Who gave that alarm?'

'*Gas, Louise!*' I shrieked at him.

'Don't call me Louise!' he bellowed back.

I remembered Tuck's lecture. *An old man's urine is particularly efficacious.*

'I can't piss!' I shouted. I grabbed at his fly buttons.

Louise saw his masked men and panicked. He laid his square of lint beside mine on the firestep, ripped open his trousers and sprayed the two pads with wild arcs of urine.

'Quickly,' I yelled, pounding his kidneys with my fists. 'Faster!'

It was too late. The gas was on us, sweeping thick and white over the breastwork of sandbags. Cool, moist, almost refreshing and faintly salt. The first sea mist of the spring.

Luckily, no one in real authority knew who started the panic. I myself claimed I had heard an earlier alarm from the Belgian lines to our right. We had many cuts and bruises among us but in 'A' company there were two broken arms and a fractured pelvis. Louise was furious and sent me back to Croxyde Bains on field punishment. Single-handedly I dug latrines for an entire company of amused Royal Marines at La Panne. Then I joined a working party from 'C' company filling sandbags for three days. My charge was unsoldierly conduct: unacceptable and unseemly behaviour which caused confusion and indiscipline in the ranks. You can imagine how popular I was with the bombers who had not welcomed the close contact with their own excreta. It was hard to convince them it was not a practical joke. Captain Tuck, who was orderly officer the day I reported back to Croxyde Bains, severely rebuked me for my behaviour, adding that I had not only let down the 13th battalion but also the public schoolboys of Britain.

'But what if it *had* been gas, sir?'

'But it wasn't, so your observation is irrelevant. What school did you go to, Todd? Harrow? Charterhouse?'

'Minto Academy.'

'Stands to reason then.' He dismissed me.

The only tangible result of my false larm was the prompt issuing of the new box respirators two days later. But I received no thanks for this.

One day during my field punishment I was walking back to Croxyde Bains—shovel and pick over my shoulder—with the orderly sergeant who had been supervising my latrine digging. He was an agreeable enough man, a short-sighted twenty-year-old who had done a term at Cambridge and who had an interest in photography. We were discussing the relative merits of plate over roll film, I rather listlessly—I was filthy and my back and shoulders ached. We walked through a tiny hamlet, quite ruined from the 1914 advance, on the La Panne—Oost Dunkirk road, when we passed a broken down Fiat lorry full of nurses. A driver busied himself with the engine while some of the nurses waited by the side of the road in the mild late-afternoon sun.

'Mr Todd.'

I turned. Dagmar. I introduced the orderly sergeant who discreetly, and decently, took himself off a few paces.

'Miss Fjermeros ...' I felt an irritating blush grow. I took off my trench cap, set down my clinking tools. The dim peasant greets lady of the manor.

'*Fjermeros*. The "j" is silent.'

'Sorry. Of course. How are you?'

'What're you doing? You're so dirty. Are you in trouble?'

'No, no. I've been digging latrines. Nothing serious.' I needlessly ran my fingers through my short hair, touched my moustache as if it were false and coming unstuck.

'Where are you going?' I said. The soft sun on her face at that moment made her almost unbearably beautiful. I felt like weeping. I wanted to lay my head on that starched apron and weep.

'We're being transferred.'

I nodded. She mentioned a name. I suppose I should have remembered it but my head was full of a drumming sound, like heavy rain on a tin roof.

'I'm sorry we didn't have our chance of a walk on the beach.'

'Yes,' I said.

'Thank you for bringing my watch that day. It was kind.'

'Don't mention it.' My sergeant cleared his throat. 'I'd better be off. I hope he fixes your lorry soon.'

'Oh it doesn't matter. It's agreeable to be in the sun.' She lifted her calm face to the oblique rays and closed her eyes. I saw the irridescent golden eyelashes, the fine blue veins pulsing on her lids.

'Isn't it ... Well, goodbye.'

She opened her eyes. 'Remember what I told you, Mr Todd.'

The walk back to camp at Croxyde Bains might have taken place underwater so blurred and streaming were my eyes. I sneezed and honked into my handkerchief all the way back, unable to control myself.

'Hay-fever,' I said to the sceptical sergeant.

That night I wrote in my diary:

Dagmar has gone, and with her, what wonderful opportunities? Living, it seems to me, is really no more than a long process of steady embitterment.

*   *   *

23rd May 1917. Back in Wormstroedt at Brigade reserve. All my lust for Huguette has returned, enhanced and fortified by the loss of Dagmar. I spend all my time in the estaminet.

It is curious how the enamoured eye transforms. Huguette now seemed to me the very image of pulchritude. Every detail contributed to the harmonious impact of the whole. The dark downy hairs on her lip, the thick fleshiness of her upper arms, her plump cheeks, the three or four creases round her neck. All this made me love her more.

She greeted me as always—curtly—but at least she knew who I was. She was manifestly fatter since our last time at Wormstroedt but in my inflamed state the idea of fat round soft thighs, round fat soft belly and fat soft round breasts seemed far more attractive than anything more svelte and lissom. And there is, is there not, something enticing about youthful obesity, where the extra weight has bounce and firmness and nothing has turned loose or slack?

In my preoccupation I only half-noticed the increased traffic in Wormstroedt. The big guns and their limber constantly moving through the town, the lines of lorries, the increase in staff officers in sputtering motors, the military police, the frequent arrival of new units. In the tobacco factory we had doubled up to provide space for others and for the first time the reek of tobacco was overwhelmed by the smells of hot, tightly pressed human bodies.

There was some talk of a transfer away from Nieuport. Teague and Somerville-Start indulged in eager speculation about potential postings. Such guesswork that reached my ears only turned my thoughts more towards Huguette. One fact now dominated my thinking: I must not die without the experience of sex. I played in a few football matches, I visited the bathhouses, drew new equipment, went on a bombing course, I drilled as if I were some sort of automaton. During off-duty hours I sat in the estaminet, drinking Huguette's abominable tea, eating eggs and chipped potatoes, watching her punch holes in condensed milk tins or move sullenly through the tables collecting plates and cutlery on a tray wedged against her yielding thigh.

On the 3rd June we received orders to return to Nieuport where the 13th was to await further instructions. Our days in the quiet sector were all but over. Teague's face was round with glee. I realised we might never be in Wormstroedt again. That last evening I stayed on as late as I could in the estaminet. Most of the 13th had left. There were three noisy tables of Australian engineers drinking beer. There was little demand for tea. Huguette stood by the dull copper urn, head down, preoccupied, as she picked at a callous on her finger. The late evening sun shone through the small windows turning the room's smokehaze milky, basting the chipped tables and curved chair backs with a rare polished gleam. I moved through a wand of light towards her. She looked up.

'*Voilà, Tommy; encore du thé?*'

'No, no thanks.' I gestured outside. '*Une minute. Parler?*'

She glanced at me quizzically. Then looked around the room, her top lip held between her teeth. It made her look faintly simian.

'*Pourquoi pas?*'

We went out through a side door into a small sad courtyard. Some lank hens scratched. We turned a corner and found ourselves in a narrow sunny lane, unused, weedy. Over a brick wall I could see the slab back of the tobacco factory and its rows of grimy windows. Huguette led me down the lane to a shed and we went in. I saw an old machine, a swede mincer, rusted and useless. A clean scythe hung on the wall. At the back was a dank hump of turnips. A pile of jute sacks was on the floor. An earthy root-vegetable smell in the air— wet, organic, dark.

Huguette leant against the wall. I tried to kiss her. I was trembling and sweating. She pushed me away.

'*Baiser, c'est dix francs!*'

I emptied my pockets and gave her ten francs. I held her big face between my hands. Slowly, tenderly, I touched my lips to hers.

Her squirming agile tongue almost made me shout with shock. It was like a live leaping eel in my mouth. I felt I had a piston in my chest compressing the air of my lungs. It was astonishing. Then she pushed me away again.

I had six francs and a few sous left. All my money gone on her filthy tea and eggs and chipped potatoes. I held the money out on a slick and jittery palm. She scooped the coins up.

'*C'est pas beaucoup*,' she said, counting, somewhat sulkily. She put the money in a pocket, shrugged, took my hand and thrust it up under her skirt. I felt her thighs—warm, soft—and moved my hand upwards. Fingertips touched hair—curled, springy, dry—just like my own. I gently cupped her groin. I seemed to have stopped breathing. I will show you fear in a handful of fuzz. My eyes were fixed on a knot in the wood of the plank wall before me. Huguette shifted slightly.

'*Finis?*'

'Yes. *Oui.*'

I stepped back. She looked faintly surprised.

'I love you, Huguette,' I said, hoarse.

'*Oh, poff, oui* ... "I loave you", *ça marche pas!*' She shook her finger grimly. '*C'est une question d'argent.*'

She opened the door. I walked out into the palpitating dusk. The sun hit the tall windows of the tobacco factory turning them to fabulous golden mirrors.

At last I had *said* it. A man to a woman. I had kissed, I had touched that secret place. I felt buoyant, strangely calm. On the train back to the railhead at Croxyde I sat on the floor of the truck beside Leo Druce. He had his cap off; it was sitting balanced on one of his knees. A faint sweet smell came from the oil on his hair. His kind delicate features seemed at odds with the crude cut and serge of his battledress coat. He twirled his cap on his knee.

'Where do you think we'll be going?' I asked.

'Don't know. The Somme? Arras? Louise hasn't told me.'

'Is there a push on?'

'Looks like it.'

I felt a stomach-churn of alarm.

'I shouldn't worry, Todd old fellow. They'll probably forget about us.'

I was grateful for his words of reassurance however unrealistic they might be. I wanted to tell him why I was so apprehensive, indicate the true nature of my fears.

'I'm just worried that I—you know—haven't *done* enough.' I smiled faintly. 'In life, as it were.' I paused. 'I mean I've never really even been in love. Properly.'

'Well, imagine if you were. You might feel worse.'

'I suppose so. I ...'

'What?'

'You know that girl in the estaminet?'

'The one that serves the tea or the one that washes up?'

'The tea one.'

'What about her?'

'What do you think of her?'

'I don't know ... obliging enough. Pretty cheap. Thirty francs isn't bad for a roger.'

'*Huguette?*'

'Is that her name?' He turned to Kite. 'Hey, Noel, that bint in the estaminet, Todd says she's called Huguette.'

'Ah ... Huguette,' Kite said, tasting the name. 'Did you shaft her, Todd?'

'Yes ... oh yes.'

'She's Bookbinder's favourite,' Druce said. 'Noel and I prefer the washer-up.'

'Ah.'

'I should give her a go if we ever get back there.'

'Good idea. I will.'

*　　*　　*

I think my health began to give way round about then. Suddenly I felt ill all the time, laden with apathy. It was not so much my health declining, perhaps, as my well-being. I held myself in low esteem, disgusted at my naïvety, not so much because I had made such a banal romantic error, but for what it revealed to me about my own conceit. This made me even less prepared for our transfer, and more fearful of this 'push' that everyone was discussing. I was determined somehow to get out of the front line ... If I could just get sent back to reserve, back to Dunkirk even. I would happily work in fatigue parties for the duration.

I began to think wildly of desertion, or even a self-inflicted wound, but I knew I had not the courage for such a course of action. This was the source of my apathy. I wanted to act but had no guts for the effort required.

It was Pawsey who gave me the idea. Ever since he had vomited during the false gas attack he had looked wan and peaky. The alarm had unsettled him. He claimed the urine made him sick, but it was the fear. He was generally regarded as a malingerer, especially by Teague and Somerville-Start. I watched Pawsey closely, and after a while I began to suspect that he was half-trying to poison himself. Whenever we were outside he chewed grass constantly and I never saw him spit out the pulp. He looked anaemic and thin and was never out of the latrines.

Then we heard that our move was to be three days hence—destination a secret. More importantly, for my purposes, the entire battalion was to parade in companies for an inspection by the brigade medical officer the day before our departure. From somewhere in the back of my mind I recalled an old leadswinger's trick (I cannot remember who told me this—possibly Hamish) the gist of which was that heavy smoking on an empty stomach forced the heartbeat up dangerously high. I reduced my eating to a minimum and started smoking as much as I could bear.

This regime did indeed have a curious effect on me. At first I experienced a palpable euphoria. I felt light-headed, strangely taller. After forty cigarettes a dull headache set in and I began to feel queasy. The morning of the inspection found me etiolated and bilious. I lit a cigarette immediately on waking and managed to smoke three more before my rising gorge demanded a cup of tea.

Druce remarked on my addiction to tobacco.

'Relax,' he said. 'I'm sure we'll be going back to reserve. We're quiet-sector material.'

I smiled weakly and set fire to another cigarette.

'D' company were called for inspection at 11 a.m. As we filed into the tent I noticed a sign saying 'FFI inspection'. I asked Druce what the letters stood for.

'Free From Infection,' he said.

'But what exactly does that mean?'

He said he had no idea.

A morose-looking, sallow-faced doctor confronted us. He had a swagger stick under one arm. I put my hand on my heart. It certainly seemed to be beating unusually fiercely. My headache keened thinly at my temples, too. I was pasty and a film of perspiration covered my face. My hair was damp on my brow. Surely, I said to myself, they cannot send a man in my condition into battle? Along the line I saw Pawsey, jade-green, his jaws working relentlessly.

'Right,' the doctor said. 'Drop your trousers. And your drawers.'

Baffled, hesitantly, some of us grinning lewdly, we complied. Our shirt tails, fore and aft, preserved our modesty. The doctor approached the first file of men. With his swagger stick he lifted the front of the first man's shirt, glanced down and said, 'Are you all right?'

'Yes, sir.'

He did this to everyone, moving quickly down the line. He reached me and lifted my shirt.

'Are you all right?'

'Well, sir, my heart—'

He was on to the next man. Louise, following, glared at me. I felt sharp tears of anger. I glanced at Pawsey. He looked shocked at my peremptory treatment.

The doctor reached him. Lifted his shirt.

'Are you all right?'

'No, sir,' Pawsey said boldly, swallowing his cud.

The doctor moved on to the next man.

*　　*　　*

It took him less than an hour to inspect the entire battalion and we were to a man passed Free From Infection. Free to go and get killed and not contaminate the battlefield, Pawsey said bitterly, when we compared our outrage later.

'I feel *dreadful*,' Pawsey said. 'Truly dreadful. I'm ill, for God's sake. That bloody quack ...' His chin buckled slightly as he tried to control his tears.

For my part I felt only sullen and resigned. I seemed to stand before a high looming cliff of despair. That afternoon, I slipped away from yet another football match and walked down the lane through the dunes towards the sea wall.

It was a day of high grey solid clouds, dense and packed like cobbles. There was a distant mist far out to sea that blended the water with the sky at the horizon. The light cast was even, drab, monochrome. The tide was going out and the vast beach gleamed with a dull wet iridescence.

I went through a gap in the wire and down the steps of the wall onto the sand, turned east and walked gloomily along for a good while, lost in my thoughts. I was trying to revive my innate, natural optimism, trying to regenerate a sense of my own special worth. Without self-esteem you can accomplish nothing, and I knew that I had to overcome the twin disappointments of Dagmar and Huguette ... Dagmar, I told myself; if only I had been bolder there. Remember her name: Dagmar Fjermeros. After the war you can go to Norway, find her, marry her, start a family. What had she said to me? 'You will survive. I'm always right.' Almays. If only she had said 'always' ...

I stopped. In the distance I could see Nieuport Bains and beyond its two piers I thought I could make out the shattered base of the lighthouse behind the trench line on the right bank of the Yser. I felt—surprisingly—suddenly proprietorial. That was my position— *L'homme de l'extrême gauche.* A special post. The first man on the Western Front. Others had occupied it; doubtless someone was occupying it now, but I felt as if I were leasing it to him. I remembered Teague's sneer: 'What did you do in the war?' It was quite a claim I could make. I turned and began to walk back. I was *l'homme de l'extrême gauche.* The more I thought about it the more pleased I was with the image. It seemed apt, portentous. That, I now saw, was to be my role in life.

A powerful blow in the small of my back knocked me heavily to the ground. Sand was kicked in my face. Winded, on all fours, I gasped for breath, trying to pick grains from my smarting, weeping eyes. I heard a depressingly familiar bark. Ralph.

The stupid brute capered and leapt about me like a lamb. He went into a semi-crouch, rump-up, tail wagging, front legs flat on the sand.

'Stop it!' I screamed. 'Leave me alone!'

I felt an irrational fear at the dog's return. Ralph was, to me at least, a bad omen: at best a powerful irritant, at worst some kind of malign harbinger. I walked back along the beach quickening my pace. I had not intended to come so far. Ahead the wet beach shone a lustrous scaly silver like a fish. I looked around. Ralph loped behind me.

'Go away!' I shouted. He pricked up his ears and came closer. I scooped a handful of sand and flung it at him. He barked with pleasure at this new game. I turned and started to run. I felt a sort of hot, mazy confusion descend on me. My self-imposed fast and huge intake of tobacco was still affecting my system. I stopped, suddenly exhausted, bile in my throat. I lowered myself to my haunches. Ralph panted idiotically beside me on the enormous beach. My solitude overwhelmed me—a reluctant actor on a vast deserted stage, giddy with fear and apprehension.

*   *   *

The happy return of Ralph prevented the others from noticing my distress. The movement order had come through. We were to entrain at Croxyde Bains at 0600 hours the next day.

'Where are we going?' I asked Leo Druce.

'A place called Ypres,' he said.

VILLA LUXE 27 May 1972

Emilia's day off. I wander up to the village for a bite of lunch. The café-bar is simple: crudely and entirely successful. A dark interior room, tiled and shuttered, with minimal lighting. Outside, a large L-shaped terrace. Vines and bougainvillaea grow above on trellises. Many well-watered pots boast flowers—zinnias and geraniums. If there's a breeze sit outside. If you seek cool shade sit indoors. Your eyes will soon grow accustomed to the limpid gloom.

The bar is owned by Ernesto, a swarthy amiable lout of a man, but it is run by his aged parents. Days can go by with no sign of Ernesto—he drives off to town in his ancient Simca whenever he feels like it. The old man, Feliz, and his wife, Concepcion, work on with placid patience. They greet me as a respected client. I have seen their son grow from an eager slim youth into this parody Lothario (he is always growing and shaving off a thin moustache). They know I know what they suffer. We smile and shrug. The children: what can we do? There is a benign freemasonry of old folk—we help each other get by.

I order a beer and a plate of olives. Feliz shuffles into the kitchen to cook me a tough steak. I look forward to an afternoon's pleasant mining of my dental cavities for meat fibres.

I am half way through my steak when the two German girls come in. These are the twins, Gunter's daughters. They must be in their early twenties. They wear shorts and T-shirts. Their legs are already pink with a few days suntanning. They are pretty girls, these twins, with square strong faces. They are well built, like swimmers, with broad shoulders and thick blondish hair. One twin, the slightly prettier, has streaked her hair with a whiter blond colour.

They sit outside with their drinks and a plate of pistachios and light up cigarettes. I munch on, chewing my steak—Feliz has excelled himself, my jaw aches with the effort of mastication.

The girls keep looking in at me. Then the less pretty one comes inside to buy more drinks. She puts on a pair of spectacles and pretends to look at one of the gaudy calendars Ernesto's suppliers have pressed upon him and with which he decorates the otherwise bare walls of the bar. I know she really wants to have a closer look at me.

Feliz's potatoes ooze oil. I mop it up with a piece of bread.

'*Guten Tag.*'

'*Tag,*' I say unreflectingly.

'Do you speak German?'

'A little ... I used to—that's to say a long time ago. But I'm forgetting it, ah ...'

'English?'

'Yes, that's easier.'

'We didn't know. We thought maybe you were Italian or Spanish.'

'I've lived here for years.'

'Are you English? ... May I sit down?'

'Scottish ... Please.'

'Would you like a cigarette?' She sits down. She has a crumpled soft pack tucked in the sleeve of her pea-green T-shirt. Her breasts shudder briefly beneath the verdant cotton as she sits.

'No thanks.'

She still has her spectacles on. Tortoise-shell. Modishly re-arranged rectangles ...

'My name is Ulrike Gunter,' she lights her cigarette. Her sister comes in. 'This is my sister Anneliese.'

We shake hands. 'Todd,' I say. 'John James Todd.'

Ulrike Gunter frowns. 'Todd?'

'Yes,' I say.

We talk about our villas, problems of water supply, staff, electricity. I tell them my pool is empty this summer. You must swim in ours, they insist. They talk good English, these fair strong girls. My irritation subsides, marginally.

Anneliese breaks a nail on a recalcitrant pistachio. I show her how to open the nuts using a discarded half shell as a lever. They are full of admiration. Did I invent this infallible method of opening pistachio nuts—the best nut in the world? You need never break another nail on them—you need never be frustrated by those nuts with their thin maddening smiles, never leave them unopened in the bottom of the bowl any longer.

Ulrike is enchanted by the simple efficiency of my device.

'Oh yes,' she says. 'It's like—how do you say? The same with *muskels*.'

'Mussels,' I say. 'The same word.'

'I should know,' she says. She tells me she is a marine biologist writing a thesis on molluscs.

After our drinks we walk back down the track to our villas, neighbours now. At their gate Ulrike pauses, frowning.

'Were you ever in Germany, Mr Todd?'

I'm already backing off—easy to pretend I didn't hear her.

'You must all come round for a drink. Very soon,' I call. 'Bye now.'

4

New Geometries, New Worlds

We missed the Battle of Messines Ridge by a few days. The huge mines were exploded beneath it on the 7th June, and thus was initiated the Third Battle of Ypres, which lasted, in fits and starts, until mid-November. In fact everything stopped shortly after Messines for a couple of months until the offensive was renewed again at the end of July. Meanwhile the 13th (public school) service battalion of the Duke of Clarence's own South Oxfordshire Light Infantry moved into the Ypres Salient.

We had hoped, indeed, Colonel O'Dell had assured us, that we were to be reunited with the regiment, but this was not to be. On June 17th we found ourselves posted to corps reserve behind Bailleul some dozen miles from Ypres. We were billeted in a farm across the road from a battalion of Australian pioneers. The bombing section of 'D' company pitched its tent and thus began the familiar round of equipment cleaning, fatigue parties and sports. My God, I was sick of sports by then! Football, badminton, rugby, cricket, everything— even battalion sized games of British Bulldog.

We could hear the guns on the front clearly. Somehow they sounded different from the long-range boom of the siege artillery at Nieuport—like the small thunder of a skittle ball, more sinister and dangerous, knocking things down. One week we laid a corduroy road of raw sappy elm planks for the use of a battery of heavy howitzers— squat, musclebound guns with fist-sized rivets—that fired a fat shell a foot in diameter. These guns were towed into place—hence the road—by traction engines. Standing back fifty yards, fingers in our ears, we watched their first salvo. The earth shivered, the guns disappeared in smoke. It took five minutes to load them; the shells were trundled up on light railways and then, with some difficulty, winched into the breech with primitive-looking block and tackle rigged beneath wooden tripods.

Boredom set in again, but it was of a slightly different order: beneath it lay a seam of excitement. An offensive was on; fairly soon, surely, it would be our turn for a 'stunt'. There was real enthusiasm in our tent, shared by everyone with the exception of Pawsey and myself. Even Noel Kite said he was keen to 'have a go at the Teutons'. Ralph the dog, whom we had brought from Nieuport, became the bombing section mascot. I have a photograph of us all, taken with Somerville-Start's box camera. There they sit—Kite, Bookbinder, Somerville-Start (Ralph panting between his knees), Druce, Teague, Pawsey and the others whose names I cannot recall—grinning, fags in mouths, caps pushed back, shirtsleeved, collars open, Teague clutching a Mills bomb in each hand. We look like a typically close bunch of 'mates', cheery and convivial. It is an entirely illusory impression. The months at Nieuport had forged few bonds. If truth be told we all rather grated on each other's nerves. We were like schoolboys at the end of term, needing some respite from the close proximity.

At the end of June we marched from Bailleul through Locre and Dickebusch to Ypres. The countryside had a look of certain parts of England. Gentle hills, red-tiled cottages and farms, scattered woods, and along the lanesides, a profusion of lilac, may and laburnum bushes. We skirted the shattered town and went into reserve trenches on the left bank of the Ypres canal. This was the first time the battalion came under fire from a few stray shells. We all thought we were blasé about shelling after the artillery duels at Nieuport but this was our first experience of real explosions. I remember seeing the puffs of dirt erupt and collapse in the fields across the canal and thought they possessed a fragile transient beauty—'*earth trees that live a split-second*'—I wrote in my diary. A few landed in the reserve lines, knocking down a couple of poplars, but I registered no alarm. There seemed nothing inherently dangerous in them—as threatening as the puffs of smoke that drifted harmlessly in the sunlit air after the clods of earth had thumped to the ground.

'A' and 'B' companies went into the front line to relieve a battalion of the Royal Sussex Regiment. Two days later I went up myself as part of a ration party, carrying four gallons of tea in a couple of petrol cans.

What can I tell you about the Ypres front in early July 1917? Later, I used to explain it to people like this:

Take an idealised image of the English countryside—I always think of the Cotswolds in this connection (in fact, to be precise, I always think of Oxfordshire around Charlbury, for obvious reasons). Imagine you are walking along a country road. You come to the crest of a gentle rise and there before you is a modest valley. You know exactly the sort of view it provides. A road, some hedgerowed lanes, a patchwork of fields, a couple of small villages—cottages, a post-office, a pub, a church—there a dovecot, there a farm and an old mill; here an embankment and a railway line; a wood to the left, copses and spinneys scattered randomly about. The eye sweeps over these benign and neutral features unquestioningly.

Now, place two armies on either side of this valley. Have them dig in and construct a trench system. Everything in between is suddenly invested with new sinister potential: that neat farm, the obliging drainage ditch, the village at the crossroads become key factors in strategy and survival. Imagine running across those intervening fields in an attempt to capture positions on that gentle slope opposite so that you may advance one step into the valley beyond. Which way will you go? What cover will you seek? How swiftly will your legs carry you up that sudden gradient? Will that culvert provide shelter from enfilading fire? Is there an observation post in that barn? Try it the next time you are on a country stroll and see how the most tranquil scene can become instinct with violence. It only requires a change in point of view.

Of course as the weeks go by the valley is slowly changed: the features disappear with the topsoil; buildings retreat to their foundations; trees become stumps. The colours fade beneath the battering until all you have is a homogeneous brown dip in the land between two ridges.

But I thought only of my idyllic prospect as I peered out through a thin embrasure in the sandbags as our tea was issued in the trenches. Admittedly the landscape in that part of Belgium is flatter and there are no real hedgerows, but as I looked out through our wire across a grassy meadow which ascended a gentle slope to the ridge opposite I thought I might as well be in a valley in Oxfordshire. There were hawthorn bushes and scrubby hedges marking the intersections of field boundaries. I saw an unpaved road, small clumps of trees (somewhat knocked about), a group of farm buildings (ditto), but essentially it was no more than a section of run-of-the-mill country-side. If it had not been for the enemy wire and the dark outline of the earthworks of their trench system, I might not have been able to stifle a yawn. The evening sun was pleasantly warm and I could see wisps of smoke rising from their lines. No-man's-land. It was unimpressive.

We spent a week on the canal bank during which we had two days and two nights in the line. There, I was gratified to discover—despite the occasional barrages—that I was not panic-stricken. It was still close enough to my experience of the trenches at Nieuport not to be too unnerving.

The most irritating consequence of our first visit to the trenches at the Salient was that we became lousy. I tried all the usual remedies: powder; hours of diligent nit-picking, like an ape; a candle-flame run up and down the seams, but nothing worked. Eventually I used to turn my shirt inside out, wear it that way for a couple of days, then turn it back again, and so on. It seemed to regulate the itching at least. I was always scratching but it no longer rose to peaks of intolerance.

After our time at the front we duly marched back to Bailleul and routine re-established itself. Cleaning, drilling, sports, working parties and occasional visits to cafés in the town. I gained a real impression, too, of the vast organism that is an army: all those separate units that allow the whole to function—ordnance, transport, clothing, feeding, animals, signals, engineering, roadbuilding, policing, communications, health and sanitation . . . There was an invisible city camped in the fields around Ypres and it required its civil servants, paymasters, administrators, labour force and undertakers to make it function. The part the 13th battalion played in its organisation was to dig cable ditches for the signallers, muck out open-air stables in the brigade transport lines, help lay tracks for light railways, stand guard over vast supply dumps, dig graves and latrines at a field hospital. We were no more than ants in an ant heap. But at the same time in those weeks of waiting I played atrociously in goal for the 'D' company football team (we lost 11–2 against the Australian pioneers); came down with a dose of influenza; wrote a letter to my father and three to Hamish; almost had a fist fight with Teague when he accused me of stealing; felt bored, sexually frustrated, tired and occasionally miserable and one night dreamt vividly of my death—eviscerated by a German with an entrenching tool. I oscillated between the roles of soulless functionary and uniquely precious individual human being; from the disposable to the *sine qua non*.

It all came to an end on July 16th when the guns started up again in earnest. Then the one week barrage preliminary to the attack was extended to two as the renewed offensive was continually delayed. For the first few nights the firework display on the horizon was tremendous but as it continued night after night it became only another source of grumbles. The 13th was not even in reserve for the big push of July 31st. The day the battle proper began we were marched to a sugar-beet factory near Locre for delousing.

We marched back to our billets that evening in heavy rain. It rained constantly for the next four days and nights. Suddenly the dark damp countryside seemed to ooze foreboding. Rumour abounded about the attack—all of it baleful. A company of the Australians—out rewiring one night—took heavy casualties ('heavy casualties'—a bland, soft phrase). I asked one man what it had been like. 'Fuckin' shambles,' he said.

On August 7th we were moved back up to brigade reserve on the canal bank. Before we occupied the trenches we were paraded in a field where Colonel O'Dell addressed us. The battalion, he said, had been ordered to provide reinforcements for other units in the brigade. I do not remember the details; two companies were going to the Royal Welch, I think. 'D' company was to be attached to a battalion of the Grampian Highlanders.

I already thought of us as the 'unlucky' 13th and this latest move seemed to me yet another turn for the worse. Teague and Somerville-Start, however, rejoiced. There was much excited talk about the 'Jocks' and their fighting spirit, and ill-informed speculation about this venerable regiment's battle honours.

The next night we set off, having left most of our kit at the battalion dump. Ralph was entrusted to the quartermaster. The 'bombers' made a great fuss of their farewells, you would have thought they were saying goodbye to their grandmothers. I had nothing to do with it—I was glad to be rid of the animal at last.

It took hours to join our new unit. There was immense toing and froing behind the front. We followed duckboard and fascine paths across black fields and were often redirected back down them. Once we eventually gained the trench system we were continually halted to allow a passage of ration and ordnance parties, engineers and signallers. Eventually we found the right communication trench. We toiled up this. Ahead I heard Louise reporting to an officer in the Grampians. Soon we were deployed in the support lines.

It was immediately clear that these trenches were not what we were used to: no dugouts, not even ledges cut for sleeping. I put my waterproof cape on the ground and sat down, my back against the rear wall. Druce passed among us checking all was well. I tipped my helmet forward and tried to sleep. My nostrils were full of the smell of wet earth and from the right came Bookbinder's body odour—truly appalling, a vile hogo. On my left Pawsey was having a shit in his helmet—he was too scared to go to the latrine sap.

*   *   *

From my diary:
*August 9th 1917. Our first morning with the Grampians. Woken
by random shelling. Stand to. Misty dawn. Up ahead, beyond our
wire, a low ridge and two obliterated farms. Over to our right,
according to Druce, the Frezenburg–Zonnebeck road. I can see no
sign of it.*

It is not very evocative, I admit. The biggest shock for me was not
the shelling but the transformation in the landscape. All the ground
as far up as the ridge looked as though it had been badly ploughed.
Almost all the long grass and shrubs that I had seen five weeks earlier
had disappeared. I could not see behind me, nor much to either side,
but the countryside we occupied was a more or less uniform dark
brown. It was hard to believe we were in high summer. I was also—
curiously, for I am not particularly fastidious—somewhat offended
at the mess everywhere. The trench was full of litter—empty tins,
discarded equipment, boxes and fragments of boxes—and through
slits in the parapet of sandbags no-man's-land seemed to be scattered
with heaps of burst mattresses. I swear it was five minutes before I
realised they were dead bodies.

Druce sent me, Kite and Somerville-Start into the Grampians'
trenches to draw our water ration for the section. We passed along
the support line through our company looking for the lead-off trench
to the battalion ration store. We turned the corners of a fire-bay.

'Where are the Grampians?' Kite asked.

'Another ten yards.'

We came out of the fire-bay. Five very small men—very small men
indeed—sat around a tommy-cooker brewing tea. They looked at us
with candid hostility. They wore kilts covered with canvas aprons.
Their faces were black with mud, grime and a five-day growth of
beard. Two of them stood up. The tops of their heads came up to
my chest. Neither of them could have been more than five feet tall.
Bantams ... These were the 17th/3 Grampians, a Bantam battalion,
every man under the army's minimum height of five foot three inches.
Kite and Somerville-Start were both taller than six feet.

'What the fuck are youse cunts looking at?' One of the men said
in a powerful Scottish accent.

'*What?*' Kite said, unable to conceal his astonishment.

'Rations,' I said. At least I could understand. He told me where
to go.

We made our way diffidently along the support trench until we
found the supplies' sap. There, a dozen Bantams were collecting

rations. We waited our turn uneasily, like lanky anthropologists amongst a pygmy tribe. We stood head and shoulders above these tiny dirty men. They seemed more like goblins or trolls than members of the same race as ourselves. The Bantams appeared indifferent to our presence, but we were all ill at ease, full of bogus smiles, as if we suspected some elaborate practical joke were being played on us and had not quite divined its ultimate purpose. We gladly picked up our petrol cans of water and headed back.

The Bantams did not like us. It cannot just have been because of our height, though it has to be said that as ex-public schoolboys we were on average taller than the other ranks in most regiments. I suspect it was a combination of our stature, our voices, our bearing and our Englishness that let us down. It did not help when on our way back that first day Kite said loudly 'I think they're rather sweet little chaps. Is it true they've been specially bred?' In any event, there swiftly grew up an invisible barrier between our company flanks and the Bantams on either side. It was so uncomfortable that we demanded our own ration parties which, somehow, Louise managed to arrange for us. The company's first deaths in action were sustained in this way. The pipe band were carrying up dixies of hot stew when they 'got a shell all to themselves', as the saying had it. Four were killed and three were wounded. It shocked us all profoundly: the pipe band had seemed indestructible. Louise, I recall, took it particularly badly.

Trench routine continued as normal for the next few days. My diary records the daily round:

> *Sentry duty 4 a.m.–6 a.m. Stand to. B'fast—tea, pickled mackerel, biscuit. Repaired trenches. Ration carrying. Lunch: beef stew, biscuits. Slept. Sentry duty 6 p.m.–8 p.m.*

It rained from time to time and I grew steadily dirtier. I watched my uniform take on that particular look common to heavily soiled clothes—one sees it on tramps and refugees, for example. The fibres of the material seem to become bulked out with dirt so that jacket and trousers look as if they have been cut from a thick coarse felt. Creases at armpits, elbows and backs of knees develop a permanent concertina-ed effect—rigid and fixed. Your hair dulls, then becomes oily, and then transforms into a matt, clotted rope-end. Finger nails are rimmed with earth; your hands hard and calloused as a peasant's. Your beard grows. Your head itches, itches all day long.

We knew our 'stunt' was approaching as the ridge in front of us steadily took more shelling. Tension increased, and the routine wariness that had characterised our waking moments was replaced by neurotic edgy alarm. We kept expecting to be pulled out of the line for a period of rest before the attack but we appeared to have been forgotten. Even Teague and Somerville-Start were subdued. As for myself, I had evolved a new approach. I decided to be logical. I was going, as far as possible, to *think* my way to survival, even if it meant disobeying orders.

We stood to at half past four, an hour before dawn. Our objectives were the two ruined farms. 'D' company was going for the right-hand one, along with the Bantams on our right flank. We were to capture the farm, secure it and repel any counter attack until the second wave passed us. All night the ridge had been pounded by our guns. As we lined up in the fire trench the bombardment was still going on. Louise passed among us, white-faced and muttering what I suppose were words of encouragement. I could not hear him above the noise of the shells. Beside me stood Pawsey. On the other side was Somerville-Start. He held a ladder, so did I. I was as ready as I would ever be.

But I had forgotten about the rum. The quartermaster-sergeant passed among us pouring out the tots from the big ceramic bottle. The rum looked black, evil, thick as molasses. I drank my allocation—half a wine glass, I suppose—in two gulps, and I was seriously drunk within a minute. I saw Pawsey vomit his issue and lean gagging against the trench wall. Somerville-Start's face wore a kind of fixed, zealous grimace—he was breathing fiercely through his nose, both hands on his ladder.

Then everyone urinated. I suppose an order must have been given. The trench filled with vinegary urine-steam. I was giddy. I felt the trench had acquired a steep, dipping gradient to the left, down which I might at any moment slide. I held onto my ladder, and adjusted the weight of my sack of bombs. I never heard the whistle go but suddenly I saw people begin to climb their ladders. Somerville-Start and I set off simultaneously.

I do not remember my first unprotected view of no-man's-land— that initial astonishing second—because Somerville-Start got shot in the mouth. The moment his face cleared the parapet I saw his teeth shatter as they were hit by the bullet and a plume of blood, like a pony tail, issued from the nape of his neck. Several teeth, or teeth fragments, hit me in the face, stinging me like thrown gravel, and one piece cut me badly above my right eye. My eye filled with warm blood and I blundered over the sandbags blindly, wiping my eye with my sleeve. I sensed Pawsey going by me. My vision cleared and I saw him running off in the direction of the ridge. There was no sign of the ridge itself—the creeping barrage some fifty yards in front of us obscured everything.

'Think!' I said out loud. I crouched down and scampered forward, almost on all fours, like a baboon.

'*Stand up, that man!*' somebody bellowed.

I ignored him.

We were now, I realised, being shelled in our turn and I suppose there must have been machine-gun fire from somewhere because I saw some Bantams on my right gently falling over. I scrabbled after the creeping barrage, dragging my rifle on the ground. As far as I was concerned the world was still canted over towards the left and I kept falling over heavily on my left side, bruising my left knee. I moved like some demented cripple.

Then a shell exploded near me and the blast of air snatched my rifle from my grasp and whipped my helmet from my head. Warm earth hit my face and I felt the weal of the chin strap hot on my throat. I was stunned immobile for some seconds. Then, crab-like, I scuttled into the fuming crater.

Kite was already there, on his back, wounded. He held up the stump of his right arm, fringed like a brush, not bleeding but clotted with earth.

'Somebody's gone and shot my bloody arm off!' he shouted.

I blinked. I screwed up my eyes to adjust focus.

'Damn nuisance,' Kite said. He seemed wholly unperturbed.

I wondered if I should help him.

'D'you want a hand?' I yelled, in all innocence.

'Very funny, Todd,' he said petulantly. 'Hardly the time or place.' He began to move. 'I can make it on my own.' He crawled back towards our lines.

I looked around. I could not see a soul. The din was so general it seemed quite normal, like the factory floor of an iron foundry ... I still had my sack of bombs. I wondered where I should throw them. I slithered forward, past some small dead Bantams. I saw what looked like a horrifically mangled side of beef, flayed by a maniac butcher with an axe. At the top there was an ear, some hair and part of a cheek. At the bottom, a bare knee with a smudge of dirt on it.

I crawled on until I reached some tangled wire. The German line? I glanced back. I could make out nothing. I turned: was that the farmhouse up ahead? It should have been easy for me to determine— we were meant to run uphill after all—but my dipping, left-biased world had made me immune to gradients. I had the disarming impression, all at once, that I was in fact moving parallel to our front line. So I turned, with some difficulty, right, leaning into the slope and felt I was falling. I immediately ran across Pawsey and Louise. Pawsey was shot through the chest. He had dry cherry foam on his lips. He was trying to speak but only pink bubbles formed and popped in his mouth. Louise, I guessed, had gone to help him and—so it seemed—had been caught by a concentrated burst of machine-gun fire in the throat, which was badly torn. He was quite dead. One bullet had taken off his nose with the neatness of a razor.

I looked up. The barrage had lifted. I could not hear the dreary clatter of machine-gun fire. I saw Bantams running back to our lines. More bubbles popped between Pawsey's lips. I grabbed him under the arms and began to drag him back to safety. I had not gone ten yards when he died. There is an unmistakable limpness about a dead person that no living being can imitate. Instinct tells you when it has arrived. But I needed no instinct, remember: I had dragged dead men from the surf at Croxyde Bains. Poor Pawsey felt the same.

I laid him down. There was no point in dragging back a dead man. Heavy firing was coming from further up the line, and a few shells were now bursting on the ridge, more an acknowledgement of the attack's failure than an attempt to silence the German guns. My section of no-man's-land was now strangely quiet. All the same I zig-zagged back to the lines moving carefully from shell hole to shell hole. In one particularly large hole I saw a couple of Bantams searching corpses for loot. I passed by on the other side.

I was helped into the trench by men I did not recognise. This must be the second wave of the attack, I guessed, whose presence had not been required. I was passed down the line into the support trenches. Eventually I found my bits and pieces and sat down. I felt terrible. My brain was tender and bruised. I was nauseous. My mouth was dry and rank. My legs were visibly shaking and my joints ached. So this is battle fatigue, I thought. I know now I was suffering from a massive hangover. My first.

After a while I managed to light a cigarette. I put my trench cap on and waited for the others. Then I began to remember, piecemeal. Kite, with no hand. Louise and Pawsey dead . . .

A corporal from another platoon came over. He looked very tired.

'Any sign of Lieutenant McNeice?'

I told him about Louise. And Kite and Pawsey. I wondered if the others were all right.

'I don't know,' he said. 'I can't find a soul from my platoon.'

'You haven't seen any of my lot, have you?'

'I saw someone . . . well, *explode*. Must have been a bomber. Whole sack of bombs went up. Took about five chaps with him.'

'Good God!'

'Are you all right?' he said. 'You've got blood all over your face.'

'Just a scratch,' I said reflexively, followed by a warm spurt of pride at my nonchalance. I put my hand up to my forehead. I felt a curious lump embedded above my eyebrow. It moved. I plucked it out with a wince. It was a tooth. One of Somerville-Start's incisors. I still have the scar.

*   *   *

The delayed shock arrived about an hour later. It was not so much what I had witnessed that overwhelmed me as the retrospective sense of awful peril I had been in. I saw myself running foolishly here and there about the battlefield, somehow avoiding the multitudinous trajectories of thousands of pieces of whizzing hot metal. I was not grateful for my luck. I was horrified, if you like, that I had used up so much. We all have narrow escapes in life, of some of which we are entirely unaware. What upset me was the hundreds of thousands of narrow escapes I must have had during my few hectic minutes in no-man's-land. I was convinced I had overdrawn my balance of good fortune; that whatever haphazard benevolence the impassive universe might hold towards me was all but gone.

We went back into reserve, were given something to eat and then paraded in a field for roll call. 'D' company's casualties were dreadful, well over fifty percent, and the Bantams had fared little better. Of the bombing section, only Teague and myself were present on parade. Louise was dead, so were Pawsey, Somerville-Start and Bookbinder. It was Bookbinder who had atomised when his sack of bombs exploded, and the blast had accounted for two other bombers dead and one wounded (Lloyd). Also wounded were Kite and, I learnt, Druce.

That evening I went down to the field dressing station to have the cut above my eye stitched. The dressing station was a bizarre place dominated by the twin emotions of intense relief and intense pain. It was established in a small quarry some four hundred yards behind the canal. To my surprise the ground was littered with discarded boots, and everywhere was the powerful contrast of filthy blackened men and new, very white bandages. Walking wounded sat in groups waiting to be driven to the field hospital. Rows of stretcher cases lay docilely in the soft evening sun. I had my cut dressed and went in search of Druce. I heard my name called. It was Kite.

He was sitting with a group of amputees and headwounds. A blunt club-shaped bandage covered his stump. He looked dark-eyed and his face was tense. I lit a cigarette and gave it to him. He seemed depressed, not nearly as jaunty as on the battlefield. I told him about our casualties.

'At least you'll be out of it,' I said.

He looked at his stump. 'I'm finding it a bit hard keeping the old famous unconcern going,' he said, his voice shaking. He started to cry. 'I just think it's a bloody shame. I *need* my hand.' His voice was raised, other men looked round.

'Steady Noel,' I said, and patted his shoulder. 'Here, have some fags.' I stuffed half a dozen into a pocket. 'Be back in a second. Have a word with Leo.'

Druce was lying some yards away, a leg bandaged. I told him the appalling news about the section.

'Kite's a bit shaken up,' I said. 'What happened to you?'

'I climbed up the ladder, took a couple of steps and got a piece of shrapnel through my calf muscle. I went down and was dragged back into the trench. Must have been out there for all of five seconds. Never saw a thing.' He paused. 'What about you? . . . I mean, what was it like?'

I thought. 'Very strange.' And then, 'horrible'. I told him in more detail about Pawsey and Louise. I tried to express myself better.

'It's like . . . nothing or nowhere else . . .' I had no vocabulary. 'It's just mad.'

*   *   *

'I'm not sure if I should have thrown the whole sackful down . . . I mean, in a dugout, you'd think one or two bombs would be enough. Damn! I should have held on to some. Think what—'

'Suffering Christ, shut up!' I said. We were stacking railway sleepers. During the attack Teague had in fact reached the German line. He had emptied his sack of bombs down a dugout stairwell and thrown in two after them. Apparently he had killed eighteen Germans and had been recommended for a decoration. On the way back to our lines he had sniped at a machine-gun crew and claimed to have hit two of them. He talked about the battle constantly to me. I was deeply bored.

'Where exactly did you get to? You said you got to the wire . . .'

'Yes. No . . . I think so. I got to some wire. Look, I don't know. I told you I hadn't a clue what was going on.'

'*Less fuckin' natter more work youse two English bastards!*'

These words came from platoon sergeant Tanqueray, a Bantam, supervising our working party. The top of his head reached my armpit. Teague and I had been seconded to a Grampian company in the reforming of the battalion after the attack on Frezenburg ridge. 'D' company could barely muster two full strength platoons so the rest of us were temporarily attached to the Bantams to fill gaps in their ranks. By this stage of the war the Bantam battalions had more than their fair share of half-grown lads and degenerates. My kit was pilfered almost daily. Anything precious I kept on my person.

Tanqueray watched us heft the sleepers. He hated me and Teague, as did the rest of his men. He was five feet two inches, just under the Army minimum. He was bitter enough as it was, missing out on the chance of a regular battalion by one inch, but having two tall ex-public schoolboys in his platoon seemed almost to have deranged him. Tanqueray had a weak chin, a ginger moustache and pink watery eyes. He was a fisherman from Stonehaven and I fancied he still smelt of fish. The fact that I was Scottish also incensed him, paradoxically. He insisted I was English and I was tired of remonstrating. I became a symbol of the dark genetic conspiracy that had contrived to render him small.

'You're dogshite, Todd,' he used to say to me. 'You and all your kind. Dogshite.'

I was not clear what he meant by 'my kind' but I did not care. My mood since the day of the attack on the ridge vacillated between taciturn depression and a brand of fretful neurotic terror which I could barely suppress.

My diary:

Monday. Btn. reserve Dickebusch. This morning I found three members of my platoon going through my kit. Two ran off. I attacked the third, a man called MacKanness, with a hare lip. He is barely five foot but quite strong. I held him down and punched his face. He says he will shoot me during the next attack. Tanqueray reported me to the orderly officer—who happened to be Lt. Stampe—who seemed sympathetic but had no alternative. I filled sandbags for two days. These are my fellow countrymen but I have nothing but contempt for them. Teague says you can expect nothing else from the labouring classes.

Since the attack on Frezenburg ridge we had had one other period, uneventful as it turned out, in the line. New drafts of recruits had come into the battalion and our rest periods were taken up with reorganisation and retraining. Teague and I, perforce, were thrust closer together. We tried to spend as much time as possible with the other members of 'D' company but as far as Tanqueray was concerned that was tantamount to fraternising with the enemy.

After a couple of weeks it was clear that the 13th was being brought up to full strength again and a new 'D' company beginning to take shape. Some of the original members were recalled from the Grampians but no movement order came for Teague or me. I began to worry that we had been forgotten. I spoke to Capt. Tuck, reminding him of our existence. He said matters were still in a state of disarray but assured me that when the battalion reformed Teague and I would be part of its number. Until then 'D' coy. of the 13th btn. SOLI was still attached to the Grampians. I should stop worrying and be patient.

We went back up to the front towards the end of August. Guns had been firing for days. It was clear we were about to enter a new phase of the offensive on the Salient. I felt ill with ghastly premonitions. I was so convinced of my impending death that the filthy squalor of the trenches and the sullen hate of my comrades in arms seemed mere irritants. But Teague—literally—had the light of battle in his eye. He seemed distant, preoccupied, as if inspired by some visionary impulse. I was baffled at his zeal. I felt meek and terrified; Teague looked forward to the prospect of fighting. I told him of MacKanness's threat (which was often repeated: 'Gonnae get youse, cunt, see'f ah doan't, right inna fuckin spine. Palaryse yu. Die in paaaaayne!' That sort of thing.) Teague was untroubled.

'Stick with me, Todd,' he said. 'We'll be all right. Look how we got through Frezenburg—barely a scratch.'

I looked at his square face and his small eyes. He was the second person, after Dagmar, who had assured me I would survive. We were sitting in support lines, the night before the attack.

'I'm going to die,' I said. 'I *know*. Just because I made it once doesn't mean a thing.'

'You'll be fine. You're like me, Todd. We're special, different.'

I could not think of anyone I was less like, except, perhaps Tanqueray and MacKanness.

'You *really* think you're not going to ...?' I left the question deliberately unfinished.

'I don't care. I'm just going to go in there and have the fight of my life.'

I looked away. For some reason Teague's attitude rather disgusted me. We had eaten well that evening: pea soup, fried corned beef, sardines. In my hand I had a piece of sponge cake covered in jam. I threw it over the parapet for the rats.

*　　*　　*

August 22nd 1917. I stand in the front line trench waiting for the barrage to lift. Teague is on my right by the ladder. Standing on its bottom step is Lt. Stampe, our company commander. Stampe is six months younger than me, just eighteen, a pleasant fair-haired person. Tanqueray refers to him as a 'pup'. Tanqueray himself comes down the trench issuing rum. I decline.

'I'll be watching you, Todd,' he says. 'Very closely.' I have a stupid song in my head. I can't rid myself of the tune.

> *Whiter than the snow, whiter than the snow*
> *Wash me in the water*
> *Where you wash your dirty daughter*
> *And I shall be whiter than the snow, holy Joe.*

The catchy tune keeps my mind off other subjects. This time we are to attack some long-ruined château, take the remains of a wood and advance through open country to the crossroads at S———. I have only the vaguest idea of our objectives. In any case, they will mean nothing once the whistle blows. There is no château, no wood, no open country, no crossroads at S———.

Teague turns towards me. Suddenly the barrage lifts for a second or two.

'Here we go, Todd,' he says. A whistle goes somewhere. Stampe puts his own to his mouth and blows fiercely. The pea jams. Silence. He smiles guiltily and climbs up the ladder onto the parapet waving us up and on. I go up the ladder, sober this time, the world flat and fixed. Ahead a cliff of smoke and explosions mark the German line. I crouch and head off, following backs of others through the gaps cleared in our wire. Within yards my boots are heavy with a thick rind of mud and clay. I have lost Teague. I keep my head down watching for mud pools. I walk in as straight a line as possible. Some shells start to burst around us. I skirt an icy lagoon forty feet across. I slip and fall. I look up; Stampe stands ahead.

'All right?' he yells.

I struggle to my feet. He moves on. Twenty yards to my left a British soldier levels his rifle at Stampe and shoots him in the back. Stampe falls. The soldier glances round. MacKanness. I crumple to the ground as if hit. I wait a minute, then (there is no sign of MacKanness) cautiously get up and go and look for Stampe. He is

face down in the mud. I pull him up and unplug the dirt from his
mouth and nose. He is still alive. Stampe is almost the same height
as me. To a Bantam all tall men must be indistinguishably high.

'Go on,' Stampe says. He pushes me away.

Teague is suddenly behind me. 'Come on,' he says. We run off.

'Where are we?' I shout.

'Nearly at the wood!'

Where was the château, I wonder? Through the drifting smoke I
see some stumps and shattered trunks of trees. Chunks of wood fly
up, spinning off them. Teague and I fall to the ground. Teague starts
firing his rifle. I do the same. I can see nothing. Teague takes a Mills
bomb from his bag and throws it. It explodes—yellow and orange,
white smoke, erupting earth. He takes out another and slithers forward
a few yards through the black trunks. He throws again. This time the
bomb seems to detonate almost immediately it has left his hand. I
hear him scream.

Then, seconds later. '*Todd! Todd!*'

I crawl over to him.

Teague has lost two fingers on his throwing hand and his face has
taken a lot of flash from the defective bomb. Most of his hair is burnt
away as is the first layer of skin, some of which hangs in long fragile
shreds from his cheeks like stiff rice paper. He has no top lip and, as
far as I can see, no eyelids left. His eyes are bleeding from the
perforated whites, filling the sockets.

I help him to his feet and we stumble off. Blood tears an inch wide
track his face. We are suddenly free of the black stumps, but I have
absolutely no idea which way to go. I seem to be in a circle of infernal
noise. Distant shapes of men scurry and creep in every possible
direction. I do not know if we are being shot at.

Teague sinks to his knees. He is moaning now. His face seems to
be effervescing, forming a creamy brown froth like the head on a glass
of stout. '*White than the snow, whiter than the snow*' hums in my head.

'I'll get a stretcher bearer,' I say faintly. I notice there are traces
of tangled grass amongst the mud and upturned clods of earth. We
must have come quite far.

I stand up. The noise of explosions has moved off a way. There is
still no-one firing at me. I lie Teague down and run off in what I
think is the right direction. Stretcher-bearers should be following the
second wave. I run on.

Then I hear the noise of an immense motor. To my left, bucking
and heaving through and over the tree stumps, is a tank, a huge three-
dimensional metal parallelogram, eight foot tall, its tracks hurling up

a heavy spray of clods and mud. There is a name painted on the front '*Oh I say!*'. The machine gun in the forward turret traverses and begins firing at me.

I fling up my arms, fall down and pretend to be dead for the second time that day. The tank churns on. I get up and, ridiculously, shake my fist and swear at it. Then I run off on my way again, looking for stretcher-bearers.

I stop suddenly, a horrifying image forming in my mind. I feel a bolus of acid nausea rise in my throat. I turn and run back towards Teague. I hear the engine of '*Oh I say!*' ahead in the drifting smoke, straining, grinding.

> *Wash me in the water*
> *where you wash your dirty daughter ...*

The tank has run over Teague's legs. He is alive but unconscious. His legs are oddly shapeless now, like partially filled kit bags. One boot is pointed delicately, like a ballet dancer.

I chase after the tank. I can see its tracks clearly in the muddy grass. I come over a small rise and stop, staring in astonishment. Ahead of me, fresh in the morning sun, stretches the Belgian country-side. Roads, trees, fields, villages, a steeple, smoke from chimneys. About a mile off I see the fortifications of the German third line and a column of troops being marched towards me. Reinforcements.

'Oi! You the British Army then?'

I turn round. The tank has stopped about fifty yards away. One of its crew is urinating against its side. I bite my bottom lip to stop myself from bursting into tears. I walk over. The man shudders and starts to do up his flies. He comes to meet me. He is small, almost as small as a Bantam.

'I reckons as we've gone a touch too far, mate.' He walks round the front of the tank. 'Right through the bloody middle, a hot knife through butter.'

I follow him round.

'No trenches here, see. Only blockhouses.'

On the other side of the tank the crew sit in the sun, in shirtsleeves. They are drinking whisky—Johnny Walker—from the bottle, and eating bread and ham. One man carves from a joint.

'Here's the British army,' my man says, introducing me. 'Better late than never.'

'Hello hello,' says another. 'Feeling peckish, I'll warrant.'

'You people,' I say, unable to control the tremble in my voice, 'you people have just run over my friend.'

'No chance,' says one. 'Not us, mate.'

'A wounded man,' I say slowly. 'You crushed his legs with your tracks.'

'No, no,' says the urinator. 'I'd have known. I'm the driver, see. You didn't spot no-one, did yah?' he says to another.

'Nah. Couldn't have been us, old son. We don't make that sort of mistake. We run over Huns. Not our lads.'

'His legs are flattened!'

'Ow . . . nasty. Probably a shell, though. Do funny things those shells.'

'Damn right. I saw this man once. Dead. Flat as a pancake. Could have rolled him up like a carpet.'

'Bound to be a shell, yeah.'

'*Bastards!* I'm going to report you. Bloody bastards!'

'Steady on, sunshine. George told you he didn't run over no-one.'

'And I should know as I'm the bloody driver, Jock.'

'Yeah, and watch who you're calling names, you Scottish berk.'

I leave them to their ham and Johnny Walker and run back. I see that, as the driver told me, there is no German trench-line here. Just mangled wire and ruined blockhouses. Somehow we have come through a temporary gap in their defences. Where I left Teague at the edge of the so-called 'wood' is a small group of men from the Durham Light Infantry, black, exhausted, making some attempt to dig in. They tell me Teague has been carried back, still alive but in a bad way. I ask them if they have seen the Grampians. No-one knows.

Shells begin to explode again in the wood. Large pieces of tree trunk are hurled tumbling into the air. A counter attack. I go back with a runner from the Durhams. He points me in the right direction and we separate. I come over the lip of a small rise and I see the undulating mess of no-man's-land in front of me and—just distinguishable—the thin humped sprawl of the British trench-line with its scribble of barbed wire three or four hundred yards away. I recognise nothing. I pause for a second. We must be in some kind of lull. The crash and rumble of guns continue and a ridge a mile away is being pelted with barrage after barrage. This strip of sodden clogged acres on either side of me is full of little figures crawling, hopping, shambling, being carried. Four-man teams of stretcher-bearers search the rims of foul mud pools for wounded. The sun still shines through gaps in the clouds and warms my back and shoulders. I sit down for a minute. Fifty yards away an officer limp-hops back to the lines, using a rifle as a stick. He pays me no attention.

I set off again, sticking to rough ploughed-field mud and avoiding the stuff that looks like runny porridge. I make slow progress. I pass a confetti of discarded equipment, a group of about twenty bloodless

dead men, people huddling miserably in shell craters waiting for
stretchers. I have lost sight of our trenches now. Your view changes
entirely in a ten-yard journey. I come across a well-organised machine-gun pit, ammunition boxes stacked tidily, a taut tarpaulin shelter
against possible rain. The men in it are alert, ready to repel a counter
attack. They look surprised to see me. I trudge past.

'Hoy!' the officer, a lieutenant, shouts. 'Where are you from?'

'German line.'

'Is it far away.'

'I should say so.'

'Drat! All right you men, pack up. Sorry chaps, wrong place.'

I leave them to dismantle their neat pit and slither down the
crumbled sides of a gully. A sunken track or road, pounded out of
recognition. I clamber up the other side and get a brief view of our
line again. Two hundred yards to go.

'Hey you! Help! Over here!'

It is a man, up to his armpits in a mud pool at the bottom of a
large deep shell crater. If he had not shouted I would never have
spotted him. His face is covered with dark red blood.

'You English? I can't see very well.' He has a strong Ulster accent.

'I'm Scottish, actually ... but it doesn't matter.'

'Get me out of here, pal, will you? I'm going down.' *Doyn*, he
pronounces it.

'Right you are.'

I slither carefully down the slope of the crater. The man is about
eight feet away. I sink in up to my ankles. The mud is thick like fudge.
I hold out my rifle. He stretches for it. There is still a two foot gap.

'I'm missing a fuckin' leg here, an' all. Blown up right into this
fuckin' bog.'

'I can't reach you. I'm sorry.'

'Sweet Jesus Christ ... Wade out a bit, pal. I'm going down.'

'I'll sink too.'

I can see he is going down. The muddy water is up to his neck.
He makes little fluttering movements with his fingers—as though his
hands were wings and he could fly out.

'God God God ... Well, put me out of me misery, pal. Will you
do that? I don't want to droyne in this shite.'

'*I can't do that!*'

'Sure Ay'd do the fuckin' same for yeu!'

He stretches his chin clear of the viscid surface. I make a final
futile stretch. I am up to my knees. He grabs. There is still an
insurmountable eighteen inches.

'Come *on*. Do us a favour.'

Suddenly, it seems the most reasonable request in the world. I put myself in his place. I would make the same plea. Of course.

'Look the other way,' I say.

He turns his head and I take aim. My fatigue makes my rifle sway. I fire. And miss. A gout of mud is thrown up behind his head.

'*For God's sake!*' he screams, his composure all gone.

'I'm sorry.' I pull the trigger again and my rifle jams.

'I'll get another,' I shout. I claw my way up the bank. I run here and there looking for a corpse with a rifle. At one moment I run back to the crater to check on my Ulsterman. But he has gone.

I shut my eyes and rub my face. I feel stupid and empty with tiredness. My back is sore, my leg mysteriously bruised. I trudge back towards the line of trenches. My shock and outrage steadily die as I slip and slither home.

I arrive at the British line and am directed to my sector. I seem to have wandered a mile over to the right. I try not to think about Teague or the man in the pool. I hum my tune, blotting out the images as I shuffle with the wounded along duckboards through communication trenches '... *whiter than the snow ... wash your dirty daughter ... whiter than the snow, Holy Joe.*'

I find the Bantams two hours later. It is midday. They sit on the banks of a sunken lane behind the Ypres–Commines canal, silent, morose, exhausted. We are all black, filthy, pasted with drying mud. I sit down, rest my arms on my knees and my head on my arms. A light drizzle falls and it gets cold. I hear short exchanges of conversation. The Bantams had a good day. One lot killed forty prisoners. It is their special pride that they kill everyone: the potent fury of small angry men. Tanqueray walks up and down checking who is missing. There is no sign of MacKanness. Stampe is alive and in a field hospital. Tanqueray rebukes me wrathfully and at length for losing my rifle. I hear his iron voice and a horrible fear invades me. Now Teague has gone and I am alone with the Bantams. I do not have the strength to cope with them any more. I know then that I have to run away.

I look up and offer my grimy face to the soft rain. I have had enough.

'*Johnny?* Good God, is that you, Johnny?'

I look round.

Standing there, tall, neat in a staff captain's uniform, is Donald Verulam.

VILLA LUXE 2 June 1972

My God. The Bantams. I used to have nightmares about them for years. Every time I went back to Scotland I was in a state of fearful suspense that I might run into my ex-comrades. Especially Tanqueray. I would go into pubs and have a good look round before I ordered a drink. I don't know if he survived the war, but those Bantams had a tenacious hold on life that was quite inhuman—given our species' particular vulnerability. They were more like some sort of insect—silver lice or cockroaches, a small tough well-armoured beetle.

I will only say this about that terrible day in the Salient. It changed me for ever. Not dramatically; in fact at the time I thought it had left me mentally as well as physically, unscathed. But it hadn't. It changed me for ever. You can't encounter such chaos and cruel absurdity on that scale and not have it affect your view of life. You never see anything else in quite the same way again.

This morning I moved my most comfortable chair from the poolside to the cliff edge. There's a small pine tree there that casts good shade until about 11 a.m. I used to sit facing the pool, never out to sea, but now I don't derive the same enjoyment looking at it empty. Now, on my new perch, 200 feet high, I have a superb view of the bay, and, when it blows, I can catch the breeze off the sea.

Below me the wide bay stretches out its arms, one long, one short. To the west, the long arm is a hilly promontory which in silhouette looks like a giant crocodile's head half submerged in the sea. You can quite clearly make out the twin bulges of its eyes, the long ramp of its jaw, the hump of its nostrils. I can see along its shoreline the new villas being constructed and the small public beach with its bright umbrellas, pedalos and restaurant shack.

To the east is the other, short arm. A smaller promontory this, ended by an almost perfectly conical hill. Nestled into the corner this hill makes with the isthmus of land that joins it to the shore is my beach. There's not much sand. The beach is composed largely of mounds of dry seaweed, regularly washed up here by some persistent current. Beneath your bare feet it feels soft, like shreds of old newspaper, a yard thick. I haven't been there for ages. There was no real need, while I had the pool. But now a sea bathe seems almost unbearably enticing. However, it can only be reached by an awkward twenty minute walk down a winding path through steep pine woods and along the cliff edge. And it takes me four times as long to return.

These days I find such hikes a real effort.

What else can I tell you about my property—Eddie's property? There is a small field to one side of the house filled with fine blond grass and dry clumps of camomile bushes. Along the cliff edge rosemary grows in profusion, like gorse. In the field, too, there are some bright green carob trees, two or three dying olives and the huge pestilential fig, its lazy boughs propped up by wooden crutches. The pines planted round the house exude an opaque spunky sap. It builds up like candle-wax on the trunks. The air is full of heady herby smells.

This morning as I sat on my new perch above the bay (I already refer to it mentally as the 'lookout') I watched a small motor boat putter out from the moorings by the public beach in my direction. It stopped almost below me. I went and fetched my binoculars.

It was Ulrike Gunter. The boat was a small vivid yellow four-seater with a powerful outboard motor which Gunter and his sons normally used for water-skiing. Ulrike was alone. She anchored the boat five or six yards from the cliff base and removed her T-shirt. She was wearing a dark heliotrope one-piece swimsuit. She fitted goggles, snorkel and a waistbag and dived in. She swam to the rocks and, as far as I could make out, started chipping away at them with a knife. She spent twenty minutes collecting specimens then returned to the boat.

As she climbed onto it and stood upright, her body and costume glossy with water, wringing out her hair, I felt in my viscera a lightening, an invigorating airiness that I recognised, quite unmistakably, as lust.

5

WOCC

Two weeks after that hellish day in the Salient Donald and I were driven in his staff car into the muddy courtyard of a small farm near the 5th Army HQ at Elverdinghe. An old woman looked impassively at us from the door of the farmhouse and did not acknowledge Donald's cheery wave. Another motor car, a clean Humber, was parked by a barn. A large pigsty, unused, and storehouse made up the other two sides of the square.

'Home,' Donald said and showed me inside the barn.

The big room had been divided into two. One half contained a table and chairs, a dresser and a stove. On a window ledge stood a gleaming walnut wind-up gramophone. In the other room were three iron beds, a vast wardrobe and numerous trunks and suitcases.

'I'm not far away,' Donald said. He was attached to the HQ staff and lived in a disused laundry at Château La Louvie. 'The other two'll be here before dark, I should say.' He smiled and handed me a key on a key ring.

'What's this?'

'It's for your motor. That's it outside. All your equipment's in the back. I'll pop back tomorrow to see how you're getting on.' He squeezed my shoulder. 'You look quite your old self, Johnny.'

In late 1915 Donald Verulam had been transferred from his duties in the War Office to 'Wellington House', the secret propaganda department of the Foreign Office, to aid in the establishment of a systematic filming programme of the war. Strange to relate, there had been no official filming or photography of the war at all during the first two years of its duration. Some independent film companies had sent cameramen out to the front, but they worked with French or Belgian forces as there was a complete ban on photography in the British sectors, such was the suspicion of the army staff. In 1915, the film trade, in the shape of the British Topical Committee for War Films, finally received permission to film from the War Office under

the guidance of Wellington House. This somewhat ad hoc arrange-
ment was reorganised in December 1916 when the War Office Cinema
Committee was created. It appointed official cameramen and it
became Donald's job to supervise their activities in the field. He had
also to ensure that the completed film survived its laborious journey
from France to the developing and editing labs in London; from there
to the Department of Information; thence back to France, and the
Chief Censor at General Headquarters. Only then could the approved
film be shown as a newsreel at home and abroad.

Donald had been in France and at work on this job since June
1917. He was in close contact with his immediate superior, John
Buchan, at the Department of Information in London. Still highly
cautious, GHQ had decreed that there were never to be more than
three film cameramen at the front at any one time. It was my good
fortune that one McMurdo had come down with pneumonia and had
been returned home to convalesce three days before Donald and I
met in that lane behind the Ypres–Commines canal.

I spent only one more day with the Bantams before my new posting
as official WOCC cameraman came through. I rested for a week
in Bailleul before the necessary documentation was approved and
authorised. I was deloused and consigned my old uniform to the
incinerator. I drew new clothes from Divisional stores: a shirt and
tie, a well-cut jacket, creamy khaki jodhpurs, glossy lace up riding
boots, a short, waisted overcoat, a peaked cap, an ashplant stick. I
became an 'honorary' officer.

And so now I strolled around my new billet, enjoying the strict
click of my boots on the cool flagged floor. The stove was lit; it was
warm inside. Two coloured calendars hung on the wall. The old
woman came in with an armful of firewood and brewed up some
coffee. Without asking, she fried me four eggs and served them up
with bread and margarine. I ate them, drank the coffee and smoked
a cigarette. My God, this was the life! A light rain had begun to fall
so I postponed the inspection of my motor. I looked at it through the
windows and wondered if I would be able to drive it properly. Donald
had elucidated the principles of motoring and it seemed simple
enough. As well as pretending to be able to drive, it had been
necessary—for Donald's plan to work—that I also claim to be intimate
with the operations of a moving film camera. He had shown me some
of the films the WOCC had produced and we had spent a couple of
afternoons practising with the standard Aeroscope camera. It was
more functional and robust than the alternative, a Moy-Bastie.

The Aeroscope looked like a small wooden attaché case with a rotating handle on one side and a hole in one end for the lens. A simple latched flap revealed its innards and it was a relatively straightforward process to load and unload. It was not particularly heavy to carry on its own but its tripod was a real burden. Sometimes, Donald told me, film cameramen could persuade battalions or companies who were being filmed to provide an orderly to lug equipment about, but most of the time we would have to carry it ourselves.

This was the most onerous aspect of what was otherwise to be a most pleasant existence. Indeed, after the Bantams it was like some paradisaical reverie. We dressed as officers—notional second-lieutenants—but we wore no rank or unit badges and carried no weapons. The old lady in the farm was paid (by the WOCC) to cook and care for us, and, twice a week, rations and fuel were delivered from the divisional QM stores. Our most important document was our pass. This allowed us access to all parts of the front and required individual commanders to facilitate us in every possible way. One would drive to a chosen area, present oneself to the adjutant, or whoever was orderly officer, inform them of what one wanted to film and set about it. According to Donald, the prospect of having a moving film made of their unit was irresistible. All doors were opened.

I had learnt all this during the two days I had spent with Donald in Bailleul. There was no embarrassment between us, I am glad to report. No mention was made of that hideous walk in the countryside around Charlbury. I even managed to ask after Faye without blushing. Donald was his usual courteous, caring self. I was the one who had changed. It was only just over a year since we had last seen each other, but the experiences I had lived through had transformed me from passionate, foolish schoolboy into a numb, prematurely disillusioned adult. I did not go into details about that last day with Teague and the attack on the mythical crossroads at S——, but Donald had clearly guessed from the state I was in that I could not have taken much more.

Anyway, such is the natural resilience of my character that I found I was no longer brooding on my unpleasant experience with the Bantams but was instead relishing the comforts I now found myself surrounded by. I visited the latrine (it was blissful not to be constipated, *the* fixture of trench life); I poured myself another cup of coffee. Then I heard a motor car arrive.

The first of my colleagues to return was Harold Faithfull—the celebrated Harold Faithfull. He had been one of the first film photographers on the Western Front, arriving just after the battle of the Somme in 1916. His greatest moment had come with the attack on

Messines Ridge a year later. Faithfull had been there and—by sheer luck, I am sure—had managed to record the explosion of one of the massive mines beneath the ridge. The resulting 50-minute film *The Battle of Messines* (Donald had shown it to me at Bailleul) had played to packed cinemas in Britain and America for over three months. Faithfull received all the plaudits (although I now know for a fact that it was also the work of one, if not two, other cinematographers); he delivered many lectures and he had just published a book—*How I Film War and Battle*—which was, Donald said, selling extremely well.

Faithfull greeted me in an affable and only marginally condescending manner—Donald had forewarned him of my arrival— but I instinctively disliked him. He was in his mid-twenties, and had a handsome, plump face and fine, thinning fair hair. His voice was surprisingly deep, full of sage gravitas. I was sure this was an affectation of maturity. The problem was that, to me, Faithfull reeked of deceit. I confess that at this stage my conclusion was based solely on prejudice (I am prepared to admit to some jealousy—already I envied his success with *The Battle of Messines*) but in spite of that there was something too glib about the man. He was always too conscious of himself and of the impression he was creating on others — an infallible sign of the vain and the fraudulent.

He was soon joined by his crony Almyr Nelson which completed our number. Nelson was an official stills photographer. He was known as 'Baby' Nelson, possibly because of his curly light brown hair. However, I could never bring myself to call him this. With Nelson I was on safer ground professionally, and I used to talk technical matters with him, preferably in Faithfull's hearing. Faithfull was suspicious of me and how I came to be in the WOCC unit—the most élite unit in the British army, as he dubbed it. I had not been an avid cinemagoer before the war and my few hours of instruction on the Aeroscope would not stand much interrogation. So whenever the subject turned to the subject of moving films I steered the conversation into general areas—composition, portraiture, the merits of the posed shot against the natural—and no-one, I think, guessed at my real ignorance. Faithfull possessed some wily intelligence. Nelson was more agreeable but as far as brains were concerned, he was—as Sgt. Tanqueray would have phrased it—'as thick as shit in a bottle'.

A routine soon established itself. Donald would arrive every other day with a list of potential subjects that the WOCC considered to be of newsworthy or propaganda value. Faithfull had first choice (he was very keen on visiting dignitaries—he claimed he had filmed the visits to the front of two Kings, three prime ministers and entire cabinets of politicians) and would set off after a leisurely breakfast, often accompanied by Nelson. Frequently, they stayed away the night. Faithfull seemed to receive a warm welcome at every regimental mess. Since *The Battle of Messines* he had become a celebrity. All his new films were very boring.

At the outset, Donald set me to work on a series entitled 'Great British Regiments', a simple enough job with the advantage that it allowed me to master the Aeroscope. I filmed a battalion of the King's Own Yorkshire Light Infantry, receiving victuals at a field kitchen, playing football, listening to a sing-song and marching up to the front along a road lined with shattered poplars. I shot four reels of film, sent it off to London and some nameless editor in the Topical Film Company's labs in Camden Town cut it up and patched it together.

A week later it was back, passed by the censor and we showed it to the KOYLI colonel and his officers in their battalion reserve billets.

I will never forget that evening. It was in November. We drove over at dusk. There was some sleet in the air melting like spit on the windscreen. A 'stunt' was on and a battery of 60-pounders in a field a mile away fired throughout our visit. We had a drink in the officer's mess and then went into a barn where a sheet had been tacked to a wall. I rigged up the projector, started the portable generator and the beam flickered, then sat—shivering slightly—but true-square on the makeshift screen.

I can bring it all back. The faint frowsty smell of old hay; the fragrant reek of pipe tobacco; the thrum of the generator; the rolling boom of the guns; the laughter and comments of the officers; the lanterns turned down, plump with oily light.

GREAT BRITISH REGIMENTS NO. 23
THE KING'S OWN YORKSHIRE LIGHT INFANTRY.

No other name, no credits (no sound of course) but it was mine. The opening monochrome shot of smiling marching men waving at the camera (I had been vainly shouting 'Don't wave! Don't look at the camera!'), then the inept jocularity of some War Office copy writer ... I watched it all pass before me, entranced. I cannot say I was in the grip of some artistic or aesthetic visitation, my mood was rather— what?—proprietorial. This was *mine*. John James Todd *fecit*. Donald stood beside me puffing on his pipe, and I thought back to that day on the train from Barnton when he had held me at the window and

I had taken my first photograph, 'Houses at Speed'. I felt a rush of affection for him and his constant generosity to me.

There was loud delighted applause at the end of the film. We returned to the mess for more drinks and much flattering appreciation was expressed. My first audience, my first acclaim. I felt enfolded in a radiant cloud of happiness and innocent pride.

I drove back with Donald, the two silver film canisters warm in my lap.

'Jolly good,' Donald said. 'Inniskilling Fusiliers the day after tomorrow.'

But I was not listening. 'I wonder why,' I said, 'they didn't use that shot of the sergeant-major in shirtsleeves—you know, feeding jam to his pet squirrel? . . . It was far and away the best.'

Prophetic words. Prophetic complaint. I knew then that what I wanted was control, total control. And it is from that moment—and not those first hesitant turnings of the Aeroscope's handle one morning in a village street on the Abeele–Poperinghe road—that I date the start of my career, my vocation, my work, my downfall.

*   *   *

In the next two weeks I filmed the Inniskilling Fusiliers and the Ox. and Bucks. Light Infantry. The finished films were virtually indistinguishable from the first. But all the while I was shooting them an idea was slowly forming in my mind. I decided, quite independently, to make my own film, one that was not just an assembly of loosely related fragments, but that had a distinct shape and form, that told a story. I think the title came to me almost before anything else: *Aftermath of Battle*. Already I could see it on advertisement posters, on hoardings above cinemas. This would be a film true to a soldier's experience of battle, an experience that the director himself had undergone.

From what Donald had shown me of WOCC material at Bailleul it was clear that most films of offensives dealt extensively with the build up to an attack. This was followed by a few shots of men leaving the trenches and, if you were lucky, a long view of the enemy trenches under fire. There was a final collage of glum German prisoners and smiling walking wounded at casualty clearing stations. The implicit message was that stalwart fortitude was the route to ultimate victory. The film I had in mind would be quite different.

I was not entirely candid about my ambitions with Donald. I suspected he would gently chide me for overreaching myself; running before I could walk. I told him only that I wanted to drop 'Great

British Regiments' and see if I could convey something more interesting about the immense range of activity that went on behind the
lines. He happily gave me permission to proceed.

One morning I left the farm well before dawn and drove up to the
northern sector of the Salient. I went to the battalion HQ of the 107th
Canadian pioneers and was given permission to film one of its wiring
parties coming out of the line. A sleepy orderly led me along a
duckboard track to the mouth of a communication trench. I set up
my tripod, mounted my Aeroscope on top and waited.

At about half past six the men appeared. There was just enough
light. I filmed their exhausted, haggard faces as they filed past me,
barely glancing at the camera. Some were wounded and leant on
other men for support. Stretcher-bearers ferried out the gravely
injured and three dead bodies.

With the orderly carrying the tripod I ran down the duckboard
track and overtook the shambling pioneers. I set up again on the far
bank of the canal by a pontoon bridge over the canal. Wisps of mist
rose from the torpid brown water. The men tramped across the
bridge, the pontoons dipped, ripples expanded through their bending
reflections, some early sun lit the water.

Later that morning I filmed them brewing tea and frying bread
and corned beef. I took long, long close-ups as they gazed without
expression into the lens. My last shot was of them sleeping, huddled
in bivouac sheets, still as corpses.

Then I cut to real corpses, two days later in a graveyard near a
field hospital. I had the Aeroscope focused on half a dozen bodies
and then directed the burial party to step into frame and dump the
contents of their stretchers beside them. Later, too, I filmed the bizarre
inflexible faces of a Chinese labour battalion digging graves for dead
Europeans. Then I caught the unhappy faces of the teenage boys in
the burial party pulling on long rubber gloves before hefting the dead
into their narrow holes.

In my naïvety I proceeded to film more or less chronologically,
shooting scenes in the order I wished them to appear, and in this
way, over the next week I put together my film, with an absolute,
almost uncanny confidence in the shape it was acquiring, absolutely
sure of its effectiveness. I filmed an officer writing letters to next of
kin; nurses bandaging wounds; carpenters making wooden crosses;
amputees receiving their new crutches; piles of bloodstained uniforms
being incinerated; and the calm, silent, sunlit rooms of the moribund
wards at a base hospital. The final image was the classic one: fresh

troops marching up to the front, grinning, waving their tin hats at the camera.

I wrote no script or outline for *Aftermath of Battle* but I had as clear a conception of its form as if it were all neatly plotted and laid out before me on paper. My next problem was how to ensure it was edited in the way I desired. I asked Faithfull how to resolve this problem.

'You've got this little chap back in Islington or Clerkenwell, see, editing miles of newsreel a week, bored stiff, mind on the pint of ale he's going to have at lunchtime, but he's got to stick all this stuff together. He'd be delighted if you'd help him out. Write it all down for him—words of one syllable mind—and make sure you've numbered your reels properly. Does it need captions?'

'No. I don't think so.'

'No captions?' He frowned at me. 'Even simpler ... What are you up to, Todd?'

'Oh, just "behind the lines" stuff.'

'I see ... Mmmm. Well, I'm going to put on a cigarette, I think. What about you? Chuck the tin over, Baby, there's a good fellow.'

Two interesting encounters occurred while I was filming *Aftermath*. First of all I met Teague again in the base hospital at St Omer. I had set up my camera in a moribund ward and shot my film. Then it suddenly struck me that Dagmar might conceivably be working in the place and I went in search of a matron to find out. I found her in another ward full of heavily bandaged men—burn cases. She informed me that she knew of no Dagmar Fjermeros on the nursing staff and as I turned to go I heard a voice from one of the beds.

'Hodd! Hodd!' it sounded like.

The top half of Teague's head was covered in a moist gauze bandage, thick with ointment, from which one wet, red eye peered. In place of his top lip there was a cotton wool moustache soaked in some camphor-smelling lotion. I felt my own head begin to ache in sympathy. Both his legs ended at the knee, the blanket tented by a basket work support. We shook hands gently—left-handed—his right was bandaged, a round white fist.

I had never really liked Teague but now I felt genuinely glad to see him. After all, we had shared most of that ghastly day. We talked of this and that—I explained my new job and uniform. As I looked at him, shattered and wasted, I sensed a sort of tickle in my brain, irresistible, like a cerebral sneeze forming.

I tried to resist it. 'I reported those swine in the tank, you know, but I'm not sure if anything happened.' I paused. 'How are you, all things considered?'

'All right, I suppose. Going to look a bit peculiar though. Not much left to work with. At least I've got an eye.'

I had to ask. 'How do you feel about it all—now?'

'Wouldn't have missed it for the world.'

'Seriously?' The scepticism in my voice made it go up a register. 'Sorry,' I added. 'It's just I never expected you to say that.'

'It's a risk you take and a price you have to pay. At least I'm still alive.'

I don't believe you, I said to myself. But I suppose you have to try and think like that. If you thought anything else, you'd go mad. Look at Kite, I thought, he cracked up and he only lost a hand. I'd be like that, like Kite, bitter and angry, full of resentment . . .

I filmed Teague later. I thought it might cheer him up. We had him being pushed in a wheelchair towards a camera down the length of a long airless corridor passing through shafts of autumn sunlight.

The second meeting was less eventful, but curiously more significant for me. The officer whom I filmed writing letters to next of kin was in fact Captain Tuck. The 13th had been reformed, rumours of a transfer to the Italian front had proved ungrounded, and the battalion was back in its usual role of furnishing working parties for the artillery. There were very few faces I recognised.

After Tuck had obliged me with a few scribbles and a suitably sombre face—he needed no persuading, the Aeroscope was an infallible seductress—he walked me back to my motor car.

'Half a mo',' he said. 'There's someone you should meet before you're off.'

He led me round behind a cow-byre to where the field kitchens were situated. On the ground, gnawing a bone, was Ralph, the dog. He got slowly to his feet and wandered over to Tuck. He was hugely fat.

'Quartermaster spoils him rather.'

I clicked my fingers. 'Here, Ralph, here boy.'

The dog did not budge. He looked at me, yawned and licked his chops.

'Doesn't remember you,' Tuck said. 'Strange.'

I felt my heart thump with joy and relief. 'It always was a rather stupid animal,' I said, and walked elatedly back to my motor. I never saw Ralph again.

*　　*　　*

'They've censored it,' Donald Verulam said. He looked serious.

'What?'

'*Aftermath of Battle.*'

'No! *Damn* . . . which bits?'

'The entire film. The whole thing. The chief censor is furious. You're lucky you're not cashiered. I had to tell him it was some sort of ghastly blunder. Fragments inadvertently edited together. It won't really wash. He wasn't convinced.'

I swallowed. 'Where is it?'

'I've got it back.'

'Thank God!' I paused. 'What do you think about it?'

He looked at me and gave a thin smile.

'Well . . . it's strong stuff. A bit grim and morbid for my taste. But I'm sure we can use bits of it. The early sections are good. We could cut them into Faithfull's film.' He looked at me. 'I wish you'd told me you were doing this, Johnny.'

'What's Faithfull's film?'

'It's called *Ypres*, or possibly *Wipers*. We need another battle film like *Messines*. Another Harold Faithfull battle film. Not yours.'

I thought quickly. 'Donald, will you give the film back to me. I'll tinker with it. Film some more scenes. Change its tone.'

We argued for a while but I knew he would give in eventually. I saw a miraculous opportunity ahead of me. The decision of the chief censor was a minor impediment. What I would do next would force him to change his mind.

I retrieved *Aftermath* and ran it privately for myself several times when Faithfull and Nelson were away. As I plotted what to do next I saw that the merits of the film were clear: this was *true*; this was what really happened after a battle. Whatever I did next I should not forget that fact. Unconsciously I was formulating a credo that would inform all my work. The truth was what mattered, unflinching verisimilitude. This was what made my film so different from all the others and this was what had to apply in the future.

One morning in the farmhouse, Nelson and I were breakfasting when an orderly runner arrived from Donald that I should take some extra reels of film to Faithfull as quickly as possible.

'You take them to him,' I said to Nelson. 'I don't know where he is.'

'No can do, old chap. I've got Marshall Foch handing out medals at noon. I can't go all the way to Étaples.'

'Étaples? What's he doing there?'

'Making his film.'

With bad grace I motored off to Étaples. I arrived there about eleven o'clock. Ahead of me lay the town and, from the crest of this hill, a distant grey glimpse of the channel. Nelson's directions led me to a camp—a vast trampled field enclosed by a wire perimeter fence. Inside were row upon row of tents and a dusty parade ground upon which squads of men were being drilled.

I had no difficulty finding Faithfull—everyone seemed to know of the film—and I was directed along a track leading towards the rifle butts. As I approached I could hear the noise of firing and other explosions. I stopped the motor and, lugging my reels of film in a couple of sandbags, went in search of the famous cameraman.

As I arrived everything went quiet. I passed two companies of men, standing easy. Ahead of me were gentle grassy hills and a hundred yard section of immaculate trench—revetted, zig-zagged, with precisely angled firebays, clean sandbags and taut wire in front—it reminded me strongly of Nieuport.

Faithfull was in the trench, camera pointed at a platoon of men with fixed bayonets.

'Ah, Todd, thank God you've come. I'm down to my last two reels.' He introduced me to a couple of beaming officers, then ran about conferring with various men and checking details in his notebook.

'What's going on?' I said.

'This is the Rifle Brigade attacking Glencorse wood in August . . . something like that,' Faithfull said. He turned. 'Captain Frearson? Smoke now please.' He crouched behind his camera. 'Remember your numbers, you men! Ready when you are Lieutenant Hobday . . . *Smoke*, Captain Frearson.'

Faithfull starting turning the handle on his Aeroscope. A small smoke canister was lit and white smoke began to drift over the top of the trench. Lt Hobday stepped forward and blew his whistle—'Don't look at the camera, Hobday!'—and the platoon went smartly up the trench ladders.

'One! Two!' Faithfull shouted. Two men flung up their arms and fell back. Hobday stood on the parapet, revolver drawn, and waved his men over the top.

'Three!' Faithfull yelled. '*Three!* Damn you!' Number three buckled and fell.

'Don't move!' Faithfull bawled. 'Absolutely still!' The dead men remained immobile while the rest of the platoon deployed and advanced in extended order through the uncoiling smoke, rifles waist high.

I stayed on long enough to see Faithfull mount the 'attack of the second wave'. Here he used his two companies of men, much more smoke and plenty of explosive charges. I had to concede that the battle was efficiently stage managed. My most grudging admiration was reserved for his final ploy when two men held up a tangle of barbed wire in front of his camera as he filmed the backs of the advancing men. I had covertly read *How I film War and Battle* and could imagine Faithfull's caption to the scene. 'From a shell-hole in no-man's-land I film the second wave attacking Glencorse wood under heavy fire.'

By this time I had removed myself away some distance. At first I felt a hot, angry incredulity at Faithfull's reconstruction and—I can think of no other way of expressing it—a sense of moral and aesthetic outrage. I knew how soon Faithfull's simple, tidy version of the attack on Glencorse wood would come to stand for the enormous chaotic horror of the real thing. It was not so much the gap between the film and the reality that offended me as the shock I felt when I saw how easy it was to falsify the truth. Only people who had actually fought in the trenches would recognise the grotesque fallacy of what Faithfull was producing—a tiny minority, whose protesting voices, in time, would dwindle and fade. But seeing Faithfull at work on *Wipers*, observing both the scale of the enterprise and its blatant factitiousness, had shown me what to do with *Aftermath*. The WOCC needed a battle film—well, they should have mine, and it would expose Faithfull and his film for the tawdry impostures that they were.

As it now stood, *Aftermath of Battle* was twenty-two minutes long. What I now planned to do was film an actual battle sequence of ten or fifteen minutes duration which would act as a sort of prologue. It would not only alter the tone of the existing sequences, it would justify them. I could not be accused of 'morbidity' in *Aftermath* if I had shown in all its raw potency just what had gone before.

It meant, too, I realised, a return to the front line, but now, for some reason, I seemed to have lost all my fear and apprehension at this prospect. I became wholly absorbed in the task in hand. I was going to film battle sequences that would make *Wipers* look like a stroll in the park.

And for this to happen I required above all more mobility. I wanted battle sequences unlike anything else that had appeared in WOCC newsreels. In a field near the farm I practised filming with the

Aeroscope balanced on my shoulder. I ran, cranking the handle as best I could from side to side. A tin of these experiments was returned to me marked 'defective', as indeed they were. I could not turn the handle at the requisite speed to ensure proper exposure. I would be obliged to use the camera from a static base.*

I made my plans carefully over a period of two weeks. I was still supplying film for the WOCC but I cannot recall what I shot at the time—it is of no interest, in any event (sometimes in old newsreels I experience a spasm of recognition when I see, say, an ammunition limber stuck in the mud, or a line of gassed men at a clearing station), all my attention was now focused on my battle film.

I was still misleading Donald, I am sorry to say. I told him I had broken my tripod and I needed another. Duly provided with one I cut its legs down to a length of eighteen inches. This way I could attach the Aeroscope to the tripod and carry them both together (it was heavy but manageable), and thus set it down and instantly begin filming from the necessary fixed and static base. The angle of all shots would be low, but this disadvantage would be outweighed by the stunning immediacy of the action.

The next task was to find a unit that would let me go forward with the advancing troops into no-man's-land. This had never been allowed—or suggested—before. Faithfull boasted that scenes in *The Battle of Messines* had been filmed from shell holes in front of our line, but this was a lie. His barbed wire trick more than confirmed this.

After some thought I attached myself to an Australian battalion. They were in reserve at Reninghelst, relatively fresh and expecting to be sent forward at any time. It was the beginning of October and the final assaults on the ruined villages of Poelcapelle and Passchendaele were imminent. (I had no idea of this at the time. My impression of the Third Battle of Ypres was extremely shadowy. It seemed merely that the fighting and shelling had been going on, with a few pauses and lulls, for weeks and weeks. It was true to say that at any given moment somewhere in the Salient somebody was under fire.)

I picked the Australians because their discipline was lax and easygoing. They did not salute their officers and on several occasions I had heard enlisted men swear openly and vilely at officers in English regiments. To ingratiate myself I filmed them for a few days at their usual rest area chores and diversions and got to know their officers,

* Note for film historians. I want to record this as the first use of a hand-held camera for deliberate dramatic effect.

particularly a young company commander called Colenso—a decent man, small faced but with strangely large nostrils, which gave him a look of always being about to laugh or sneeze. The weather at the time was miserably cold and wet, with driving rain and gusting winds. At the correct moment I asked the adjutant if I could accompany them to the front when the order came. He was delighted.

On the 10th or 11th of October I was informed that the Australians had gone up the line to relieve a battalion of the East Lancs on the Bellevue ridge. Directions how to find them were provided and I went up to join them at dusk that night.

I remember my emotions on my return to the front with vivid clarity. I drove into Ypres and parked my motor in the lee of a ruined church close to the transport lines of a Service Corps unit. Then I walked carrying my Aeroscope on its short tripod up the Ypres–Zonnebecke road. The light was fading and with the onset of darkness the traffic on the road increased. There was no sunset worth talking about. I walked east with an unwholesome sallow glow at my back. Apart from my camera, I was lightly burdened. I had a small haversack containing four rolls of film, a pack of fish paste sandwiches, two bars of chocolate, some malted milk tablets and two hundred Three Castles cigarettes—about a couple of days' supply for me then. I had a gas respirator in a leather case and a water bottle containing three parts Scotch whisky to one part water. I wore my double breasted greatcoat and had exchanged my lace up boots for a pair of thigh-length rubber waders. I had gloves, a scarf and a tin helmet on.

In that sulphurous light the Ypres–Zonnebecke road looked a drab and dismal place. On either side were gun batteries, with their usual litter scattered about. Here and there were supply dumps; here and there apprehensive groups of men lying on bivouac sheets waiting for orders. From time to time an exploratory shell would come over from the German lines and throw up a shower of mud. I walked on, past the occasional shattered bole of a tree. Thankfully, it was too gloomy to see much of the corpses. They were in the process of becoming part of the ground and had a vegetable or tuberous look to them, some fungoid growth or boletic excrescence. White tapes marked where the road had once been. It was muddy—say three inches deep—but beneath it one had a firm footing.

At Zonnebecke, captured a few days previously, I left the road at what I took to be the correct point and followed a winding duckboard path through the flattened rubble of ruined houses and then across what had once been fields. (What was it like? You know those corners of farmyards, or gateways to fields, where farm vehicles or herds of cattle have passed endlessly? It was like that, for mile after mile, with here and there the glimmer of water in the deep pools of the shell craters.) Ration parties were beginning to move now it was safer, and relief troops were being brought up as replacements. Squally showers of rain bothered us as we picked our way through the dark.

By a fritter of bricks I came across a large taped area which had been a jumping-off point two days earlier. I was on the right track. To the left was the shape of an old German blockhouse. It was unusual to see something solid and hard amidst so much soft organic fluidity. This was the Australians' battalion HQ.

I stayed there, getting a little sleep, until a runner took me up to the front line at four in the morning. There were no trenches. The Australians occupied a linked sequence of shell-hole rims and spade-scrapes lined with a few sodden sandbags. I found Lt Colenso and his company and explained my plan.

The barrage began at 5.15. I slithered out of my shell hole and crawled some twenty or thirty yards ahead into no-man's-land with the Aeroscope strapped to my back. My ears were stuffed with cotton wool. The noise of the shells bursting on the obliterated village somewhere in front of me was reduced to a dull manic roar. I moved with pedantic slowness in almost total gloom, feeling ahead of me with my fingers gauging the texture of the mud. After about twenty minutes I found a suitable hole, crawled carefully into it, found that the water in its base was only a foot deep and set up my camera—pointing back at our line.

At six o'clock, in a tarnished silver light, through the clamour of the barrage I heard the whistles blow and started filming. Through the lens I saw the men of Lt Colenso's company get to their feet with a geriatric sloth and squelch through the mud towards me. No-one attempted the impossible task of running. Machine-gun fire from the German strongpoints in the village began and a few men fell over. They did not collapse histrionically like the men in Faithfull's film. Most stopped abruptly, sank slowly to their knees and fell forward, dead, their heads resting on the ground like Mohammedans at prayer. The semblance of a line broke and people started slogging forward independently as best they could from cover to cover. A dozen men splashed by my hole. I picked up the Aeroscope and waded across the crater to the opposite lip. Here my truncated tripod served its purpose perfectly. Normally it takes five minutes to dismantle and set up but now I was filming again within seconds. Turning the handle I peered through the lens at the dark soldiers stumbling forward. I panoramed slowly right to left, left to right. Little men moving with almost drugged slowness, some upright, some crouched, some dropping down. An irregular flattish skyline, some puffs of white smoke. Here was battle. It was the best and most authentic battle sequence filmed in the entire First World War—search your archives for something superior—it was inglorious, entirely chaotic and, if it had not been true, incomprehensibly and indisputably dull.

Shortly after that I stopped filming. The handle of my Aeroscope was knocked off by a shell fragment. I received a second injury to add to that of Somerville-Start's tooth—a deep gash on the side of my hand. I wrapped a handkerchief round it and lugged the camera back to the line. But for this damage I would have filmed the second wave going over. As it was I made my way back to the battalion HQ blockhouse, caught my breath, drank some whisky, smoked half a dozen cigarettes and generally composed myself before attempting the risky journey back to Ypres.

I sent the new footage and the twenty-two minutes of *Aftermath* back to the Topical Film lab in Camden Town with precise instructions on how they be cut together. I told Donald that I had made significant alterations to the film and predicted that as it now stood there could be no possible objection from the chief censor.

Ten days later, one evening, I came back to the farmhouse to find Donald waiting for me.

'Is it back?'

'Yes.'

'Well? What d'you think?'

'I think it's splendid. Extraordinary piece of work.'

I felt pleasure drain through me.

'I've been ordered to destroy it.'

His face was taut, somehow both sad and stern. He spent a long time filling his pipe. Then he told me the rest of the news. Only with the greatest of difficulty had he been able to prevent me being sent back to the 13th. He had pleaded my youth and implied that I had been embittered by my own experiences of battle in the Salient, and that for me the film was a kind of expiation. Eventually, the chief censor had yielded somewhat. However, my pass was withdrawn. I was not to be allowed within one mile of the front line. All filming was to be vetted and supervised by Donald and must be strictly non-controversial. Any more 'seditious' film (the censor's word) and I would be court-martialled and disciplined.

'So what do I do?' I said, bitterly. 'Great British Regiments?'

'Out of the question. I can offer you the Army Veterinary Corps, or a balloon unit of the Signals regiment.'

Animals or balloons? I chose balloons.

Then I apologised sincerely to Donald. He accepted it and warned me that one more error would be impossible for him to cover up.

'By the way,' he shouted as he drove out of the courtyard. 'I've left something in the back of your motor.'

I walked over and looked in the boot. A sandbag filled with a cylindrical object. I looked—six silver film canisters. I felt my heart suddenly open to Donald, like a book. There was one copy of *Aftermath of Battle* extant in the world after all.

*   *   *

Faithfull and Nelson had learnt of my misdemeanour and that the censor's office at GHQ regarded me as highly suspect. Their manner towards me grew distinctly cooler, Faithfull in particular. I think he sensed I had been trying to outdo his *Wipers* film. I was suspicious of his motives, now, and hid the canisters of *Aftermath* separately about my kit.

On the 10th of November Passchendaele Ridge was finally captured and the Third Battle of Ypres was officially over, 156 days after it had begun with Faithfull's mines (as I always thought of them erupting under Messines Ridge, back in early summer).

I was, as ever, unaware of this a few days later as I stood in a sodden field behind Ypres watching the observers unroll and inflate their silvered canvas balloon. I did not resent my new assignments as much as I had anticipated. My balloon film, *Eyes in the Sky*, was almost complete. I filmed the balloon inflating, watching the bloated fish shape emerge and, with a billowing stirring, rise to the extent of its fore and aft tethers, until the roomy wicker basket slung beneath it just cleared the ground. The observers donned their parachutes and binoculars, connected their telephone lines and climbed in. With surprising speed the balloon rose up in the air to a height of round about a thousand feet.

I had everything I needed. I sat and drank tea with the winch operators, huddling in the lee of the lorry, sheltering from a keen wind that was blowing from the west. Our balloon was spotting for a 16 gun brigade of six-inch howitzers a quarter of a mile away in a ruined village. Every ten minutes or so we could hear the loud, drawn-out rip of the cannonade.

After a while the guns stopped firing and the balloon was winched down. We brewed up and had a surprisingly tasty lunch of cornbeef fritters and McConnachie stew, cooked over a primus stove. We sat and chatted, glancing from time to time at the balloon as it twitched and shrugged at its moorings.

I do not know what prompted me, but suddenly I said, 'Do you think I could pop up for five minutes with my camera? Not too high—just to get an artillery observer's view of the world.'

This was applauded as a marvellous notion by the observers. In truth, I was not thinking of *Eyes in the Sky*. I knew that here I would have my perfect opening shot for *Aftermath of Battle*.

I climbed into the creaking wicker basket and set up the Aeroscope on its tripod, which was lashed to the side. The simple operation of the field telephone was explained. I was offered a parachute and declined. I assured them I had no intention of jumping out. Soon all was ready. The mooring ropes were slipped and the balloon rose slowly up into the air.

For the first hundred feet or so I felt sensations of alarm, giddiness and faint nausea. I looked at the shrinking field where I had had my lunch, down the vertiginous arc of the balloon cable, watching the lorry, the crew, my motor car diminish in size. Over to the left was the battery surrounded by its usual mess. So this is what a bird sees, I thought naïvely, as the countryside was revealed to me like a map. The roads, the farms, the dumps, the billets, the motor pools and transport lines, the fields and copses ... From the air everything looked neater; had a context revealed which a ground view denied one. That bend in the road suddenly had a purpose—to avoid a stream. The jumble of shattered houses revealed the grid of streets and alleyways upon which they had been built. That distant straggle of trees edged a canal ... The banality of these observations only strikes the modern eye. This was the first time I could look down on the world from above. For me it was a kind of revelation, and never more so than when the front came into view.

At first glance it was like a vast path, stamped across Europe. I imagined a 600 mile thoroughfare for giants trudging from the Alps to the North Sea. On either side drab green wintry landscape bisected by this brown swathe stretched back into the haze of distance. I was astonished at just how localised it was. In the Salient the whole universe seems brown and mired. Up here you realised just how thin that mud-world was.

The green countryside browned gradually. There was a kind of bruised and trampled verge before the vermiculated lines of the old trench systems appeared—bay and traverse, bay and traverse—and beyond them the erratic spoor of duckboard and fascine tracks across the mud, the pools in the craters flat and opaque like pennies. From this range I could not see any men, but I knew they were down there, in their hundreds of thousands, hiding. It seemed like such a miserable attenuated strip of land to be fighting over, to have fought over for three years . . . A smear across the countryside. A giant snail, leaving its slime track across Europe. A messy point of impact between two colliding forces.

Different horizons, I thought, cranking the handle of the Aeroscope, different perspectives. I felt a curious privilege about having been allowed to witness both: exalted and abased. I swung my camera along the enormous furrow. What an opening shot, I thought; what a vision for my film. The Godlike view. And then the scrabbling, squabbling mortals in the mud pools.

I heard a strange noise, like '*pam pam pamperipam pam*'. I looked round. A small aeroplane was flying towards me through a cloud of black dust smudges. What happened next is hard to reconstruct. I retain certain distinct images. First, the aeroplane seemed to be flying so slowly. A puff of black dust would from time to time knock it comically off course. I felt a tug as the winch began to haul the balloon down. Then I remember an almost human gasp coming from the balloon itself. The field telephone started buzzing and as I reached automatically, chunks of wicker basket seemed to explode in the air around me. Then a great lurch, a tumbling in the pit of my stomach as the balloon and its basket soared up and away suddenly free. I hung on tenaciously as we swayed wildly to and fro. I caught a mad glimpse of Ypres turned on its side and then I was in the clouds— grey, damp, enfolding.

The clouds saved me, I suppose, and the fact that the wire cable had been fortuitously severed by a bullet or bullets from the aeroplane's guns. I floated in those clouds for three or four minutes, I would guess. When I descended from them I was above placid green countryside. Then I remembered the keen west wind and with a jolting heart, looked about me. Behind, retreating, was the brown stripe of the Western Front. Below was occupied Belgium.

VILLA LUXE *10 June 1972*

Emilia brings me my salad. How old is she, I wonder. She's worked for me for two years now. Her predecessor was an ancient crone who was eventually done for by sheer decrepitude. Emilia has five children and eleven grandchildren. Her youngest child is twenty-four, and yet she doesn't look much more than fifty. It's quite possible, girls often are married and bearing children at sixteen on this island ...

Emilia has thick curly chestnut hair shot with grey. She has a dark, strong and well-proportioned face and a lot of gold in her teeth. She exudes a mild but freshly acidic body odour. She is broad hipped and agile. Drives her little motorbike with élan. Covertly, as she places the salad before me, I examine the loose pale green folds of her faded green dress and try to estimate the size of her breasts ...

Why am I doing this? What's happening to me? For two years we have been fixed in an ideal, polite, respectful employer–employee relationship. I ruminate on a lettuce leaf. It was my spying on Ulrike that did it. And my dormant vanity was flattered by the obvious way the twins sought me out in the bar.

I watched Emilia saunter back to the kitchen. Heaven help me but I have a sudden powerful desire to spank her naked buttocks. Not hard, just in fun ... I have an image of Emilia across my lap. Those big pale buttocks, that deep dark cleft. Lots of joyous laughter.

This is quite bizarre! I have never had this fantasy before. What's going on? But, I remember. That isn't true. I *have* had these desires. In 1929, with ... I can't believe it. Good God, these things never leave you. After all these years, who would have thought it?

I get up and wander around, a palpable old man's erection beneath my trousers. How am I ever going to see her naked?

Off the kitchen there is a room where Emilia keeps the ironing board, brushes and the various tools and cleaning materials she requires for the housework. There is also a small WC for her personal use.

When she leaves I go and investigate. There is a window, bolted and shuttered. If I drilled a tiny hole through the frame at the precise angle I might just be able to see her as she raises her skirts to sit on the pan.

Five minutes' search of the villa's cupboards reveals a perfectly serviceable hand-powered drill.

6

The Confessions

I seemed fated to get tunes stuck in my head for days, weeks even. For five days I heard nothing but 'If you were the only girl in the world'. On and on, on and on. I tried to forget it, but that lilting melody would not leave me. It made my solitary confinement worse—perhaps this is one of the secret punishments of solitary? It was a sign, too, of just how impoverished my world was. I had heard a guard whistling it, a new guard, I suppose, none of the old ones made a sound, and since then it has played on in my echoing skull, an interminable gramophone record.

I turned to my only distraction. I pulled the chair over to the window, stood on it and looked out. The top two lights were plain glass, not frosted like the others. The view: a patch of longish grass leading to a steep ravine at whose bottom the river Lahn flowed. Beyond the ravine were the beech and elm-wooded hills of the Taunus forest. To the right, the palisaded square of the exercise yard where us 'solitary' prisoners were permitted to exercise, and beyond that the dull square buildings of the veterinary science college where one hundred and fifty Russian, twenty French and four Belgian officers were held prisoner. The four Belgians were all retired generals who were captured when the Germans took Brussels. They had had no time to change after their arrest and had never been issued with uniforms; consequently they still wore their civilian clothes—three in tweed suits, one in grey worsted.

The solitary cells were above the college's gymnasium. The gym was not used by the prisoners but sometimes the guards played volleyball there and I would hear the thumps of the ball and the shouts of encouragement rise up through the floorboards of my bare room. I had been kept here in the solitary cells for over two months. I was the only prisoner.

As far as cells went my room was not too uncomfortable. A pine table, a crude wooden chair that looked as though it belonged in a Van Gogh painting, a bed with a thin straw and woodshaving mattress, two grey blankets and a white enamel chamber pot with an un-matching powder-blue lid. There were bare floorboards and white-washed walls. It was cold.

My routine was invariable. I slept, if I could, until eight when I was roused by a guard with my breakfast of watery coffee and two slices of hard brown bread. At nine I was taken to a small washroom where I shaved and emptied my slops. From ten to eleven o'clock I was outside in the palisaded yard, weather permitting, where I could do whatever exercise I saw fit. Midday was lunch—soup and a plate of vegetables. Three p.m.—more coffee and bread. Four to five—exercise yard. Six o'clock—slop emptying. Eight o'clock—dinner: soup and a plate of vegetables sometimes augmented by saltfish or sauerkraut. Every two weeks I was given a brown paper cone of sugar.

I was not especially hungry and my day was one of constant interruption. I was not denied human company. The guards in the gymnasium were possibly as bored as their single prisoner. I spoke no German and we exchanged sign language or hopeful monosyllables. I am happy with my own company and the first weeks passed without undue strain. Into the second month, though, and the regime was proving more onerous. Nothing changed, and it was precisely this that began to worry me. Perhaps if conditions had worsened or improved I might not have begun to question them, but after forty days I became convinced that I had been forgotten. And this new worry suddenly made my reduced condition intolerable. I needed a sense of my incarceration being finite (I think we all need the finite—limits of some kind, it is locked into our human natures. We need to know that things will end.) Two months of this bland solitary confinement gave me an unwelcome hint of what eternity was like. Soon the only way I could distinguish one day from the other was by the kind of soup I was served. At least it always changed. Barley soup, cabbage soup, peawater soup, something called mango soup, oilcake soup, fish soup, rice soup, macaroni soup, turnip soup ... I began to think of the passage of time in terms of cabbage or peawater days. Had I not suffered a morning twinge of toothache last fish-soup-day? The weather on rice-soup-day had been unusually mild. Two turnip-days ago I had had diarrhoea ... and so on. As I shaved each morning I looked at my face and saw chronological time reckoned by the rate of my hair growth. On capture I had been showered and deloused, my clothes fumigated—quite unneccessary—and had had my head shaved. In those days my hair grew at a rate of two inches a month. After eight weeks I was tucking it behind my ears like an artist. As a matter of personal record my hair has never ever been as

long as it was in those months of captivity in 1917–18. I shaved off
my moustache too.

After two months of this unrelenting routine I was beginning to
fall apart. My mind was occupied by four things. One: 'If you were
the only girl in the world'. Two: the near-hysterical fear that my
'case' had been forgotten. Three: a frenzied craving for a cigarette.
And four: an overwhelming desire for mental diversion—anything,
something to occupy me other than those three obsessions listed
above. All my thoughts were quite overused by now—limp, soft and
transparent like an over-laundered shirt. I wanted new thoughts, new
stimulation. I wanted something to *read*. I suppose pencil and paper,
a source of music, lively conversation would have been equally
welcome but in my desperation I saw my salvation in a book. Any
book. I wanted to be entertained, beguiled, but above all to commune
with another mind, another imagination, than my own. I had stopped
dreaming; I had stopped masturbating. I was empty, a husk. I
required a little fertilisation. A drop of fuel to start the machine
running again.

*   *   *

My first flight, across the front and on into Belgium, was oddly
entrancing despite the danger of my predicament. My slowly deflating
grey sausage balloon appeared to possess the entire Belgian sky. The
wind drove me silently eastward, the only noises being the creaking
of wicker and the occasionally audible hiss of escaping hydrogen from
the balloon. I was descending very gradually and—so it seemed—
quite safely. At about two hundred feet I passed over a small market
town and caused consternation in the streets. Traffic halted, houses
and shops emptied as people ran out to stare and point at me. I
waved. The children waved back.

But of course as the air escaped the rate of descent increased. Soon
I was palpably aware of a dropping sensation. Fortunately, the wind
had increased and my lateral movement compensated for the vertical
fall. At under a hundred feet, or thereabouts, I was wondering how
best to brace myself for my eventual landing. I threw out the tripod
of my Aeroscope and lashed the camera to the basket side.

We cleared—just—a ghostly coppice of silver birch, the base of
the basket being scratched by the topmost twigs, and looked set to
land square in the middle of a ploughed field. As I perched on the
edge of the basket, waiting, I saw over to my right a man on a bicycle,
pedalling violently along a mud lane trying to keep up with me. The
balloon moved across the field, a tantalising ten or fifteen feet above

the ground. I contemplated jumping. Up ahead a drainage ditch with tall patchy hawthorn hedge on both banks and six or seven young poplars. The trees loomed as the wind gusted. I jumped at five feet and turned my ankle on the hard uneven furrows. Winded, I watched the soft collision of my wrinkled flying machine with the trees. Twigs and a few dead leaves fell to the ground. I got up and limped over to the basket, well snagged by the jaggy hawthorns, and with some difficulty retrieved the Aeroscope. I looked about me. Dismal flat wintry Belgian fields. The mad cyclist had abandoned his bicycle at the edge of the field and was now endeavouring to sprint across it. As he approached I saw he was wearing a uniform—navy blue with red piping and a tall cap with three brass buttons on it. We faced each other. I did not know what to say and was in any event astonished by the man's face, a hot pink flowing with perspiration, wordless mouth gaping for air. I assumed I was under arrest.

I should have taken the opportunity to hide or bury the Aeroscope, because with it I was immediately taken to be an agent in some sort of fiendish espionage exercise. My uniform, devoid of rank badges, was further cause for suspicion. In the series of patient interrogations I underwent as I was transported back towards Germany my story was universally and wearily regarded as the most blatant fabrication. For me the initial and most painful loss was the confiscation of my wonderful film of the two front lines. My strident demands that the film be kept safe were naturally ignored. Equally, the universal scepticism that greeted my account did not encourage people to check out the few details I gave them. I was playing for time, they told me, well, they were patient men. Gradually I began to find myself in a kind of administrative limbo: I was regarded as a spy, but spies do not wear uniform. I was dressed as an officer but wore no rank badges and was attached to no regiment. My pass and my documents were sitting in the briefcase I left in my Humber. The interrogations were protracted, tedious and civilised but could get no further because I was telling them the truth. They chose not to believe me and somewhere, somebody decided to let me stew. I claimed to be an officer so I was not to be sent to an 'other ranks' camp. But at the same time my suspicious circumstances (and, to be fair, I could see their point of view) dictated some more heedful form of confinement. I was to be kept apart from my own countrymen and held incommunicado until either I told the truth or the facts of my story were authenticated, or so the genial major interrogating me said.

And so, one damp early morning in February, with long tracts of mist hanging still in the Taunus forest I was marched off the train at Weilberg station and met by four guards from *Offizier-Kriegenstagenlager* 18, escorted through the near-deserted town and down the hill past terraced fields to the grey walls of the science college and my joyless cell above the gymnasium.

* * *

One morning before breakfast I lay beneath my blankets fretting about how I could get to see someone in authority. The guards—all middle-aged men—seemed to understand my repeated requests, nodded and grunted in acquiescence to my urgent demands that action be taken about me, but nothing ultimately happened. I was beginning to wonder if an act of disobedience would be necessary to attract some attention—an assault on a guard, an escape attempt, perhaps—when I heard quick footsteps in the corridor and somebody, a man, singing. The footsteps passed my door in an instant, but I heard enough to make out—

> *She looked so sweet and charming,*
> *When I beheld my darling,*
> *She looked so sweet and charming,*
> *In every high degree—*

As the tune dwindled I inevitably took it up in my head (it effectively banished 'If you were the only girl in the world') but it was not until some seconds later that I realised it had been sung in *English*. So when a guard (a dull fellow with a purple pickled nose) came with my breakfast, I sang a snatch of the tune at him—'Dashing away with a smoothing iron, she stole my heart away'—and said, '*Englander?*'

He looked puzzled, then gave a weak smile and said, '*Schön*', and applauded.

Two days later, none the wiser, I paced slowly round the exercise yard. It was a generous size for one prisoner, about thirty yards square, surrounded by a palisade about twelve feet high. On the other side of the wall was a raised boardwalk to allow a guard to supervise me. This practice was soon abandoned. Today, however, there was a guard watching. I glanced at him momentarily then carried on with my exercise. All I did was walk, but I tried to walk randomly round the enclosed square. The thought of beating out a path obscurely depressed me. I moved hither and thither, turned on my heel, with no system except to establish no system.

I had plucked a dandelion leaf absentmindedly from the ground and as I walked, still going through my futile options, I tore bits of it off. As one trajectory carried me beneath the guard on the boardwalk he spoke to me.

'She loves me, she loves me not ... ahhh.'

'Sorry?'

'Don't be inquiet, old fellow. She'll be waiting, I promise you, a fire burning in the window.'

He spoke English, with a marked but pleasant German accent. This must be my singer. He leant against the palisade top, rifle slung across his back, hands and forearms dangling over. He was young, much younger than the other guards, my age, possibly. His round forage cap was pushed back on his head revealing the short black fringe favoured by German army barbers. His face was long and thin, pale with a thin wide mouth. It was strongly characterised by his eyebrows, almost circumflex, dark and bushy, that met above his nose. It gave him a sharp Mephistophelean look. A mischief maker, but not necessarily malicious. Amoral, perhaps, but not necessarily malign.

'I like your hair,' he said. 'Mine it used to be so long. But now ...' He doffed his cap. I half expected his ears to be elvish, pointed, green-tipped. He rubbed his hands over his stubbly head.

'Little prickles, all over,' he said. 'I hate it.' He smiled. 'I shouldn't talk with you,' he said lowering his voice, 'but I can't speak bloody Russian, I can't speak bloody French, and these old fellows,' he gestured at the gymnasium, 'all they do is play cards, and talk about food and their disgusting illnesses.'

'You speak excellent English.'

'Listen, I live in London, 1912. For one year I'm painting, an artist. Camden Town. The Islington Angel. You know it?'

'No. I come from Scotland. Edinburgh.'

'Ah. Bonny Scotland.' He looked round. '*Scheiss*, here comes fat Otto. Seeing you anon.' He reslung his rifle and began ostentatiously to pace around the boardwalk.

I did not see him again for a couple of days. Then, one evening he brought me my eight o'clock dinner. Having only seen his head and shoulders I was surprised at how tall and thin he was—at least six foot two or three. His uniform fitted him badly and he looked very out of place in it. It was something to do with his posture. Everything about his attitude was the opposite of erect or stiff. He seemed permanently at ease, always in an attitude of total repose.

He put the tray down.

'Macaroni soup and—yes!—I see a bit of fish. A lucky day.'
He smiled, showing sharp-looking, uneven teeth. 'I hear you're a
dangerous spy. Very exciting.'

I told him my story. At first I was a little suspicious of his affability,
but I soon saw it was entirely disinterested. Over the next week or
so we had several short conversations. They never lasted more than
five minutes as, for all his insouciance, he seemed constantly alert to
the possibility of being discovered fraternising. He told me his name
was Karl-Heinz Kornfeld ('Charlie Cornfield' he translated badly).
He was twenty-two years old and he was serving as a prison camp
guard because he was unfit for the front. He pointed at his stomach.
'I have *magengeschwür*.' He mimed stomach cramps and swigging
from a bottle. 'Too much drinking,' he said, and smiled his thin rude
grin.

Steadily, over the next fortnight, a curious acquaintanceship grew
up between us. He told me he had abandoned painting and had
become an actor before being conscripted. He said he had a cousin
in Vienna, an eminent playwright who was going to write him a play.
I let him know something of my background but oddly it was he who
seemed to have the need to talk more than me. From him I learnt
more about the camp and its inhabitants—the generals in mufti,
the lugubrious Russian officers, now doubly pessimistic since the
revolution, who made delicate, beautiful wooden toys which they sold
to the Weilberg villagers to buy alcohol. They would drink anything,
Karl-Heinz said. From time to time he sold them turpentine when
they were desperate.

This last piece of information was casually dropped, to let me
know, I surmised, that he was corruptible. I had no money (my
panting florid captor had relieved me of my wallet) and had received
no Red Cross parcels. I let him know this.

'You have your sugar,' he said. 'You can exchange.'

And so the bartering began. For half my sugar ration I received
three cigarettes and a dozen matches. I cut them into inch-long
sections and smoked them at night, opening the window a crack and
exhaling through it into the night air. Suddenly, my life appeared
immeasurably rich. I had Karl-Heinz's irregular companionship and
I had my tobacco. I made the tiny cigarettes last three nights, rationing
my avid puffs, constructing a simple holder from the dry straw in my
mattress that allowed me to smoke down to the last shreds of tobacco.
Now I had something to plan for and look forward to, nightly, and
it was illicit. At last my life acquired some texture.

The next thing I asked for was meat. I said I had nothing to barter for it. Karl-Heinz thought for a moment. 'That's all right,' he said. 'You can pay me later.' I was not sure what he meant, but I had no complaints three days later when he brought me my breakfast and withdrew a saveloy from his jacket pocket. It was dry and shrivelled and full of gristle. I ate it with unreal pleasure.

Then I asked him to find out about my predicament. He screwed up his eyes. 'Difficult,' he said. 'I see what I can do.'

And so it continued for two weeks—three weeks? I do not know. Time was passing with slightly more variation but as much sloth as always. It was to counteract this that I asked him for one more favour.

'Karl-Heinz?' I said one day as he escorted me to the washroom. 'Do you think you could get me something to read?'

'My good God!' he said, feigning surprise. 'An English book? Where do you think I get that?'

'I don't know. But you seem to be able to get most things.'

'Difficult,' he said. He expounded further on the difficulties as I shaved. I wrapped the safety razor and bar of soap in the flannel and handed it back to him.

'There's a school teacher in Weilberg,' he said. 'Maybe I could borrow from him. No. Better to buy.' He made a sad face. 'But you got no money.' He looked at me. 'You give me something and I get an English book for you.'

'What do you want from me?' I said.

'A kiss.'

*   *   *

Kissing Karl-Heinz was not as unpleasant as I imagined. It was much more pleasant, for example, than eating my dorm-mates' wax-and-bogey balls at Minto Academy. Unlike Huguette, he did not open his mouth and use his tongue. We simply pressed our lips together and held them there for quite a long time, sometimes—I always counted—as long as a minute. We kissed four or five times, usually in the washroom, before the book arrived. I assume he expected things to go further. After our second kiss he asked me very politely if I would hold his penis but I declined. 'Fine,' he said, a little disappointed. 'Only kissing, then.'

The book was delivered to me in loose-leaf sections in the exercise yard. Karl-Heinz would tear some pages out—twenty or thirty—fold them up and stuff them in a crack in the palisade wall. It was easy for me to retrieve them, hide them on my person and take them back to my cell undiscovered. I will never forget my excitement that first day as I prised the folded wad of pages from between the planks.

Later, locked back in my cell I stuffed all but the first page into my mattress. If anyone came in I would have time to crumple up the page I was reading and pocket it.

I was ready to start. I sat down on my chair and spread the page flat before me on the table. The page was small, so was the type, as if it came from an octavo pocket edition. The paper was thin, like bible-paper. My hands were visibly trembling as I smoothed out the folds. I shut my eyes and paused before reading the first sentence. I felt humbled with gratitude. Karl-Heinz had given me only the text— I did not know the title, I did not know the author. I was ignorant of the book's subject or genre. Yet to me sitting there in that cell it felt as though I were on the brink of a fabulous adventure and that I held something immensely precious in my shaking hands. It was a divine moment. It was going to change my life.

'Chapter One'.

My heart beat vigorously with anticipation. The first sentences, the first paragraph . . . what would they be like? I read.

'I am now entering on a task which is without precedent and which when achieved will have no imitator. I am going to show my fellow creatures a man in all the integrity of nature; and that man shall be myself.

'Yes. Myself! I know my own heart and have studied mankind. I am not made like anyone I have seen. I do not believe there is another man like me in existence.'

I had to set the page down, such was my emotion. My heart clubbed, struggled violently in my chest. My God . . . I felt drugged, intoxicated, almost swooning.

I know I was in every possible way in reduced circumstances. Like a parched man in the desert coming across a spring of fresh water. But I have never read such an opening to a book, have never been so powerfully and immediately engaged. Who was this man? Whose was this voice that spoke to me so directly, whose brazen immodesty rang with such candid integrity? I read on, mesmerised. Ten pages were all Karl-Heinz had supplied this time. I read and re-read them. But the suspense was insufferable, agonising. I had to wait two restless days for the next instalment.

Karl-Heinz 'fed' me the entire book over the next seven weeks. The metaphor is exact. The thin wads of pages were like crucial scraps of nutrition. I devoured them. I masticated, swallowed and digested that book. I cracked its bones and sipped its marrow; every fibre of meat, every cartilaginous nodule of gristle was dined on with gourmandising fervour. I have never read before or since with such miserly love and profound concentration. I paid for half that book with lingering chaste kisses but the remaining portion was purchased more orthodoxly. I received my first Red Cross parcel. There had been some pilfering but I was left with a scarf, a pair of socks, a one-pound plum pudding and a bag of peppermints. Parcels began to arrive once a fortnight. I gave away my food for a book.

And the book? You will have recognised the unmistakable tones of Jean-Jacques Rousseau in *Les Confessions*. I was seized and captivated by this extraordinary autobiography—so intensely I could have been reading about myself. Read it, buy it, and you will see what I mean. I knew nothing of Rousseau, nothing of his life, his work, his ideas, and precious little about eighteenth-century Europe, but the voice was so fresh, the candour so moving and unusual, it made no difference. Here was the story of the first truly honest man. The first modern man. Here was the life of the individual spirit recounted in all its nobility and squalor for the first time in the history of the human race. When I set the dogeared stack of pages down at the end of my seven-week, fervid read I wept. Then I started reading it again. This man spoke for all of us suffering mortals, our vanities, our hopes, our moments of greatness and our base corrupted natures.

Pause. Stop. Reflect. We will come back to *The Confessions*. Suffice to say that at this juncture the book released me from prison, meta-phorically speaking. Rousseau and his autobiography delivered me. I never forgot that precious exceptional gift. The book, as you will see, was to become my life.

Karl-Heinz found it hard to understand my fervent gratitude.

'I can get another book if you like?'

'God, no! That's enough. I just need the one.'

'What's so special about this book?'

I tried to explain but I could see it made no sense to him. I think he thought I had become slightly demented by my imprisonment. Perhaps I was. I have to say that a kind of love had grown up in me for Karl-Heinz—not carnal in the least, but not simply fraternal either. I cared for him in an odd way and found his lazy corruption (I discovered later he had been pilfering my parcels), his casual attempt at seducing me surprisingly unreprehensible. I suppose our long dry kisses did bring us together. Even though he was some years older than me I felt as I imagine the father did for the Prodigal Son, say, a week after he had returned home and the remains of the fatted calf had finally been consumed. The passion had died and there was an odds-on chance that the boy would go to the bad again, but somehow he was still enfolded and protected by a blanket of tolerant paternal affection. I think this is about as close as I can get to expressing the way I felt about Karl-Heinz.

*   *   *

One day in May I was pacing erratically round the exercise yard when Karl-Heinz's head and shoulders appeared above the palisade.

'Good news,' he said. 'They have confirmed your story. You're going to transfer.'

I felt suddenly, strangely unsettled at this information.

'Where?' I said.

'A camp for British officers. In Mainz.'

Later that day this was officially confirmed by the camp commandant, a man whom I had only seen once before, on arrival, some six months earlier. He was thin and sickly looking, his collar loose around his scrawny neck. His tone was semi-apologetic; he used once or twice the adjective 'regrettable'.

I had one more meeting with Karl-Heinz before I left. He escorted me to the gymnasium washroom for my morning shave. He seemed entirely unaffected by my departure which rather irritated me (I suppose this was vanity. I was reluctant to accept that his sexual interest in me was simply opportunist.) I made him write my name and address on a piece of paper and promise to contact me once the war was over.

'Of course,' he said politely. 'That would be fun.'

'Give me your address.'

'I don't have one yet.'

'What do you mean?'

'All I know is that when I get out of this uniform I will be in Berlin.' He said this with unusual vehemence. Then he laughed. 'Go to Berlin and ask where is Karl-Heinz Kornfeld. They will tell you.'

I did not see him again. A day later I was marched back to the station. Up the hill to the town, through the cobbled streets, and put on the train for Mainz.

*   *   *

The new camp was in a barracks on a hill overlooking the city. From the window of our room we had a pleasant view of the cathedral and the Rhine. Compared to the gloom and deprivation of Weilberg the camp at Mainz was a hotel. Six hundred English officers were held there. We slept ten to a room in an atmosphere that was half boarding-school—hearty conviviality—and half boy scout camp—all ingenious make-do-and-mend. Officers were allowed to cash one £5 cheque a month at a Swiss bank in town and with that money we could modestly supplement our rations (almost the same as at Weilberg) with purchases from a small canteen: fish and liver pastes, plum jam, packets of dehydrated soup. With the usual relish that the British seem to exhibit when forcibly confined, the place boasted more educational possibilities than the average university. Classes, seminars and study groups existed in every subject from Aramaic to Zoroastrianism. There was a theatre club, a light opera society and a debating competition with dozens of teams that seemed to run for months. There was a well-stocked library and, of course, a literary society for those who wished to talk about what they had read.

I went to the library from time to time. On the advice of others I borrowed and tried to read Maupassant, Turgenev and Walter Pater. I read them listlessly and with no enthusiasm. Having been burned by the flame of *The Confessions* I found the alternatives pallid and lukewarm. I abandoned the library. My brain was still full of Rousseau's life and words. My memory was haunted by those last weeks in Weilberg and, oddly, with the image of Karl-Heinz. Was it there in Mainz in the tedious stuffy summer evenings when we were confined to our airless dormitories that first glimmerings of the enterprise that was later to dominate my life was conceived? ... In all honesty I do not think so. I had no idea what I was going to do. In my empty docile moods I did not even think of 'after the war', far less of a career or prospects. I lived monotonously in the present. I cashed my cheques, bartered the contents of my food parcels, played kabuki, dumb crambo and gin rummy and—a measure of how alien my mood was—I learnt to play the banjo quite proficiently. Eighteen months later, in London at a party someone had brought along a banjo. I picked it up, people gathered round expectantly (I had been loud about my accomplishments), but I discovered to my embarrassment I could not play a single tune. It was as if some twin or sibling had learnt the instrument, some ghostly edition of myself. The skill was fixed and localised both temporally and historically— Mainz 1919—beyond then it disappeared.

I was in the camp at Mainz for five months, and in a way I look on them as more dulling to the spirit than my time at Weilberg. In Mainz I became like the Russians—morose, pessimistic, unwilling to be plucky or cheerful. Nothing happened to me there to rival my experiences in my solitary room above the gymnasium. My fellow prisoners were affable enough, but to me—grown used to the exhilaration of my own company, Rousseau's and Karl-Heinz's—they seemed insufferably bland. In a funny way I came to feel nostalgic for Weilberg and its melancholic absurdities—the glum alcoholic Russians, the dotard generals in tweed. I felt left out here in beefy British Mainz (always *l'homme de l'extrême gauche*). I attracted no attention, my participation in the camp's social life was minimal, I was in no sense a character or personality. I would wager that none of my fellow inmates, a few years later, would be able even to recall the features of my face. 'Todd? ... Todd? ...' I can hear them say, faces screwed up to goad their memories. 'Was he the chap with the ginger hair and a wooden leg? ... No? Oh ... Can't help you I'm afraid.'

Perhaps it was a psychological problem? After Weilberg, to find myself in the society of men once more, in all its crude stinking intimacy, must have subdued me. Who can say? The war ended in November and within a month I was back in Edinburgh, just in time for Hogmanay.

VILLA LUXE 13 June 1972

This morning as I shave I catch myself wondering how often in my life I have performed this mundane operation. On average, say once a day since I was eighteen years old? Thousands upon thousands of times...

I rinse the bristles from my razor. All grey now. Whitebeard. My mind still works at the notion. Suppose, for the sake of argument, I shave off a quarter of an inch of bristle every week. That's one inch a month. A foot a year. That's a fifty-foot beard during a life, give or take a foot or two ... I try to imagine myself with a fifty-foot beard. Think of all the hair we men remove in a lifetime. Think of all the hair the human race cuts and shaves, plucks and depilates from heads, armpits, legs and groin. Think of all those locks and fuzz, whiskers and fluff building up through the history of recorded time. Where has it all gone? How astonishing that the world has been able to absorb it!

Later, Emilia arrives and sets about her cleaning. Ostentatiously, I pick up a book and go out to my lookout. I sit there half an hour and then, unobserved, I follow a circuitous route around the field, through a small clump of banana trees, to arrive at the back of the house. There, behind an obligingly thick jasmine creeper, is the small shuttered window of Emilia's WC.

I squinny through my tiny hole and settle down to wait. My heart beats with alarming strength, my breaths are deep and urgent. I reflect that this voyeuristic thrill seems hardly worth the strain it puts on the cardio-vascular system.

I wait, it seems, for hours. Hot, scratched by the jasmine, pestered by flies ... Finally, Emilia comes in. I breathe quietly through my mouth. The small hole is perfectly angled. I can see the top of the cistern and, where she is standing now, Emilia's legs from her ankles to her knees ... she doesn't move. She hums to herself. She must be looking in the mirror. Then she approaches the toilet bowl. She flips up her skirt, thumbs fit into her pants, and in one fast smooth action sits down.

Nothing. I didn't see a thing. I lean back against the wall. The toilet flushes and I hear the door close.

I feel the very opposite of aroused. I feel grimy, shameful, bothered. Suddenly I loathe my snouty old-man's craving. What has driven me to this sordid pastime? ... I know. The German girls. Ulrike. Old memories have crawled out like lizards from beneath their stones. The past is catching up with me.

7

Superb-Imperial

London. July. 1922. I kissed my pregnant wife goodbye and walked down the stairs to the front door. Sonia stood and watched me go.

'Remember. Be sensible. Use your head.'

'Don't worry.'

I stepped outside onto the Dawes Road, Fulham. A dray was delivering beer to the pub, the Salisbury, above which we lived. The weather was sultry, overcast but not too hot. I took off my hat and resettled it on my head. 10.30 in the morning—it was not such a bad time to be going to work. I felt in quite a good mood. I crossed the road to the newsagent and bought a copy of *The Morning Post*. I sauntered off down the road to Walham Green underground station. I worked in Islington and had a long journey to make across the city from Fulham. We lived in Fulham because Sonia had been born there and did not want to move far from her parents (a moderately pleasant couple: he was a retired salesman in pharmacological goods; we were never short of medicaments).

At Walham Green I bought a first class ticket to King's Cross. I was earning over £600 a year: I could afford to travel first class—which was one reason I preferred the underground to the more egalitarian 'tube' which had no first class carriages.

I smoked a cigarette as I waited for the train. I felt calm, pleasantly secure, as if my life had finally reached the plateau of stability it had always been striving for.

*   *   *

When I returned to Edinburgh from Mainz at the end of 1918 I possessed no such equilibrium. I have to say though that the side effects of my war experience and confinement had left no physical scars. My hands did not tremble, I did not start at every slamming door, I slept tolerably well with no nightmares. The immediate psychological effect, apart from the permanent one I mentioned earlier, was a curious disorientating lassitude. At first I lived reasonably happily with it, thankful that this was the sole consequence of those two traumatic years I would have to bear. But as 1919 wore on and I still found myself held in this lethargic stasis I began to grow more worried.

But I am jumping ahead.

Was there anyone to meet me at Waverley station in response to my telegram from London announcing my return home from the war? Answer: no. I walked across the bridge towards the High Street with a thin bitter smile on my face. It was a cold steel morning in Edinburgh with the usual frigid scouring wind. I wore a flat felt cap, a second-hand suit of clothes provided for me at a Portsmouth hospital, and an army greatcoat. Once again my unusual status as only an honorary officer had run me foul of established procedure. I did not look like a returning hero. I had imagined myself in my well-cut coat, my jodhpurs, my glossy boots, a jaunty cap. Now I looked as if I had just been turned out of a Salvation Army hostel.

I tramped up the worn spiral stairs to our apartment and beat on the door. Oonagh opened it. It was two and half years since I had last seen her. She was a little plumper but otherwise unchanged.

'Good God, it's you!' she said with some surprise. 'John James ... my, my.'

'Yes, it's me,' I said avidly, stepping inside.

'Your father said you'd be back today sometime. But there's no luncheon for you. You're too late.'

'*I don't want any fucking luncheon!*'

I threw my cap down on a hall chair.

'Dearie, dearie me. What a fuss!'

I had calmed down by the time my father returned. He looked older, the eyes more deeply set, the wrinkles on his face more emphatic, his cheekbone tufts more grizzled. His mood was one of faint embarrassment, clearly perceptible through his half-hearted attempts to go through the correct welcoming motions. For example, he put his hands on my shoulders and said with ghastly theatricality.

'Let me look at you!'

He looked.

'You're older,' he said at last.

'Well, it has been two and a half years. Of course I'm older,' I was exasperated. 'You're older, Oonagh's older. Everyone's older.'

'There's no need for sarcasm, John. It's a most unpleasant modern tone of voice.' He turned away. 'As young people we deplored sarcasm.'

I ignored the lie.

'Minto made me pay the fee for the whole term, you know.'

'What?'

'When you ran away. I had to pay the fee for the whole term. You might have timed it better.'

Later when I thought about his reaction I charitably decided that it was an attempt to cover up the real emotions he was feeling. Thompson, for his part, was entirely candid: he made no effort to disguise his edginess and unease. He had changed more than anyone. He was quite fat now, almost possessing a middle-aged portliness. His features had softened, his cheeks swelling over his jawbone into his chin. He was doing well at the bank and was snug in the pinstriped uniform of his trade.

No-one was especially curious about what had befallen me. Thompson had no desire to hear of my adventures—my presence alone was a sufficient rebuke to his sleek prosperity. My father was still too busy, and Oonagh, although a willing listener, was maddeningly unimpressed.

I spent a lot of time with her in the kitchen, as I had as a little boy. Then, she had been amused by my stories, now she nodded a lot and made remarks like 'Goodness me,' and 'well I never'. Prison camp made the only impact.

'Terrible thing for a family to have had a son in prison. Awful shame.'

Hamish was the only one who showed genuine curiosity. We met shortly into the new year when he returned to the university where he was doing postgraduate work in mathematics. He had completed his honours degree two years prematurely.

At his suggestion we arranged to meet in a pub in the Grassmarket. I arrived there a little late. It was dark outside and not much lighter within. There was a feeble smoky coal fire in the grate and the bar was crowded with men in greatcoats and still wearing their hats. It took me some minutes to spot Hamish. He wore a grey Homburg hat and stood at the farthest end of the bar looking up at the ceiling. He had a cigarette in his mouth and a pint of beer in his hand. I checked to see what he was staring at but the corner of the ceiling which attracted his gaze seemed unexceptionable.

'Malahide,' I said.

He removed his cigarette from his mouth, careful not to let the ash drop. Most of his spots had gone; a few lingered around his ears and at his collar edge. His face, cleared, was terribly scarred by the acne, as he had predicted, stippled with pocks and colour changes, the spectrum of pinks.

'Todd! Excellent . . . excellent!'

We shook hands warmly. He had grown taller; he had a couple of inches on me now. And thin. He smiled, showing his soft uneven teeth. At last, someone really pleased to see me. We found two seats not far from the fire and sat down. I told Hamish most of what had happened to me. He sat quietly and listened. He smoked constantly, keeping the cigarette in his mouth. He was scrupulous about ash falling and would ferry the cigarette to the ashtray—as if it were some fragile crystal phial—with a precautionary palm held beneath it, where it was gently and precisely tapped.

'I kept all your letters,' he said. 'Did you keep mine?'

'Yes. They were in my kit. Sent back when I—'

'Good.'

I smiled. 'How's it going? The maths?'

'Incredible,' he said simply. 'I can hardly go to sleep at night. The things that are happening.'

He started to explain what he was engaged on. Theories of relativity, I think he said. I could make nothing of it, but I was strangely affected by his passion. I was, for a brief moment, intensely jealous. I envied the strange world he was at home in. I said so, innocuously.

'It's not so difficult,' he said. 'You would understand the concepts. You were good at school.'

'I *was* good.'

'You started it all for me, you know.' He took the cigarette from his mouth and set it delicately down on the tin ashtray.

'I did?'

'Remember? Who invented prime numbers? I could do maths. But I never thought about it, what it all meant.' There was a clear subterranean glow in his sludge green eyes. I wondered briefly if he were slightly mad—or a kind of genius.

Then he said, shyly, 'Astonishing things are happening, John. The most amazing revelations. Everything is changing. Science is changing. We look at the world differently now. We thought we understood how it worked but we were wrong. So wrong.'

'I see.'

'I'll keep you posted.'

'Grand.' I did not know what to say. 'Another pint?'

'Yes, please.'

Hamish and I met once or twice a week, the only moments of interest in an otherwise dull and featureless four months. I mooched around

Edinburgh, sat in cheerless pubs, played the odd game of golf. Thompson, to his credit, introduced me to his set of friends—eager young Scots, crammed with ambition, full of getting and spending. I was poor company; after a month or two the invitations died away. For one week I developed a foolish passion for a girl who worked in the millinery department in Jenners and I took to following her discreetly in her lunch hour and on her journeys home to Davidson's Mains.

In the summer we spent our usual two months at Drumlarish. Old Sir Hector was now over eighty, distracted and drooling with impending senility. I spent long afternoons pushing him in his bath chair through the blown gardens, my head probably emptier than his, to and fro, up and down, the wooden wheels of his bath chair crunching the gravel on the garden paths.

During the last fortnight Donald and Faye Verulam arrived with Peter Hobhouse. Peter had been badly gassed at Arras and could barely get half a dozen words out between appalling glutinous wheezes. The noise from his lungs sounded like gumboots in a marsh. I tried to forget the details of Captain Tuck's gas lecture but I found the combination of Peter's brave smiles and cadaverous staring eyes too much to bear and I spent a lot of time away from the house with my camera on ostensible photographic excursions.

With Faye there was intense embarrassment, but only on my side. It did not last long. She kissed and hugged me when we met with what seemed like real affection. She and Donald were patently happy; they had been married just after the end of the war. And it was Donald, as ever, who came to my rescue. We were talking one day in the rose garden as I pushed Sir Hector around on his afternoon ramble. Donald asked me what I planned to do. I said I had not the faintest idea.

'Have you ever thought about the cinema?' he said. 'After all, you are a film cameraman.'

'No, I haven't.'

'I've got a lot of contacts,' he said, 'since WOCC I'll see what I can do.'

It took him some time. Summer passed. I sat on aimlessly in Edinburgh for the rest of 1919. My father and I began to fall out with irritating regularity. One day he offered me money to eat and drink nothing but pine kernels and goat's milk for a week. I refused.

'What on earth use are you, then?' he shouted.

'I'm not a bloody monkey!' I shouted back.

'Well stop sitting round on your backside with your mouth open and I might believe it!'

I strode out of the room at this point, properly outraged, reminding him of what I had suffered on his and the country's behalf. Peace was made, truculent apologies were exchanged, but it was ruptured a day or two later. Donald's news came—fortuitously—just over a year since my return home. There was an opening for a junior cameraman. I should present myself for interview at the Superb-Imperial Film Company studios in Islington, London, Monday next. The salary was £5 a week.

*   *   *

I changed trains at Earl's Court and waited for a non-stopper inner circle line to King's Cross. I was still with Superb-Imperial, now one of two senior cameramen and Raymond Maude had promised me that I should direct my first film 'soon'. As I recalled this assurance I frowned. This was one of the few irritants that was marring the banal placidity of my life. Maude had rejected my last four outlines for films. 'Simply not Superb-Imperial,' he had said regretfully. He meant it. I knew he was fond of me. 'Look what Harry's doing,' Maude always said. 'Take your lead from him.' And that was another irritant. Life did not seem so placid after all. 'Harry' was Harold Faithfull, Maude's—and Superb-Imperial's—most successful director . . .

I cracked open my paper. 'Viscount Curzon said that the government only had nine flying aeroplanes in contrast to eighty-five possessed by the United States government.' I was going to present Maude with another idea today, one of Sonia's. 'Be sensible,' she had said. She was right. Her idea, the film I was going to propose, was called—I could hardly bring myself to utter the title—*Wee MacGregor Wins the Sweepstake*.

Sonia . . . Sonia Todd, née Shorrold. I can see her now as she was then, with her short black hair held in place by clasps, parted like a curtain to reveal her oval face. The faintly puzzled expression that her round tortoiseshell spectacles gave her. The enigmatic expression was misleading. Sonia in those days had a certainty of intent and a clearness of purpose which I found immensely reassuring.

We had both started at Superb-Imperial in the same week. Her father sold chemicals to the film-developing labs there and managed to get her a job in the film perforating department. She was bright and dextrous and was shortly moved to the editing rooms where she became a film joiner. Our status as new employees brought us together. Soon, once or twice a week, we would go for a meal at the grill rooms round the corner from the studio.

Sonia was my age, a month or two younger. In those days she was quite a big girl, still soft, it seemed, with pubertal puppy fat. She was small breasted with heavy lips and legs, but was always neat and tidy and dressed thoughtfully in dark colours, greens and blues. Her central parting was white and straight, her hair fell away from it in glossy brown waves. She was not pretty, exactly, but there was a quality about her I found alluring. Perhaps it was the spectacles, which she was obliged to wear for her work and reading. She reminded me of a spruced up Huguette. And it was that association that encouraged me to ask her out one evening. We went to see *Secrets* at the Comedy Theatre, which she much enjoyed. I took her home to her parents' house in Fulham, and so our relationship progressed in its utterly conventional and inevitable way.

I left the train at King's Cross and took the Piccadilly line one stop to York Road. She loved the theatre, did Sonia, and the cinema. She was deeply affected by what she saw on stage and screen, wholly engrossed in the drama. I do not think I have ever observed such an eager, total, and committed suspension of disbelief. Which was why, I suppose, she became so good at her job. She quit the editing department and was appointed a title-writer for Superb-Imperial's two-reelers. She was very good. She had an instinctive feel for the exact clichéd expression which was unsurpassed. She had to leave her job when her pregnancy advanced but Maude told her she could have it back whenever she was ready.

Superb-Imperial's studios were off the Caledonian Road in a converted automobile engineering works. There were two large stages, where the old workshops had been, and where the corrugated asbestos roofing had been replaced by glass. In a mews lane at the back were the darkrooms, printing and chemical labs, carpenters' workshops, scenery docks, dressing rooms, a buffet, a greenroom, and the clerical and accounting offices. Everything required for the production of films.

I arrived at Superb-Imperial in its heyday. Raymond Maude had started making films before the war (backed by investments from his wife Rosita). He had made his money and reputation on a stream of two-reelers, two series of which proved inexhaustibly successful. These were the 'Anna' series—*Anna the Milkmaid, Anna Goes on Holiday, Anna Falls in Love*, etc. etc.—and the 'Fido' series, about, naturally, a dog—*Fido Saves Baby, Fido at Sea, Fido Falls in Love*, etc. etc. It is impossible for me to convey just how truly deplorable these films were. It seems to me now quite inconceivable that anyone should actually pay money to see them, but they did, in their droves, and Maude and Superb Films prospered. In 1918 he bought Imperial Films for its studio space and Superb-Imperial was born. Maude still churned out two-reelers but he had ambitions to make feature length films. He was a shrewd enough man, was Maude. After the war he hired Harold Faithfull (at £5,000 a year) and bought a lot of film stock from the WOCC—hence his connection with Donald Verulam—and produced a seven-reel action adventure war film called *Steady the Buffs*. Eighteen months later when I joined it was still playing in cinemas up and down the country. Emboldened by this success, Maude created a stock company of actors and started making longer versions of his two-reelers. Gertie Royston, who had played 'Anna' for years, became a real star. Faithfull directed her in *Summer Skies*, a ghastly sentimental tale about Anna on holiday saving some drowning lad who turns out to be Lord Fortescue's son and ... I cannot bear to go on. In any event, you will understand why my own suggestions were being turned down. Maude was not cynical: he was immensely proud of his company of actors (you will have heard of some of them: Warwick Sheffield, Alma Urban, Alec Neame and Flora de Solla were the most celebrated. There were others. For the record: Harry Bliss, Violet Scott-Brown, Ivo Keene, and a dreadful old soak called Elwin Hulcup, a has-been music hall comedian who was tolerated because he owned Fido, the famous dog.)

The first film I shot—Maude himself directing—was a Fido two-reeler called *Fido at the Wheel*. It was shamefully dire but I did not care. I was thrilled, excited, intensely grateful to be working. I loved the Islington studio. I was in awe of the actors and actresses. I gawped at Warwick Sheffield's sophistication, I thought Alma Urban the most sensuously beautiful woman I had ever seen. To be allowed to mingle with these luminaries was a fabulous privilege. It did not last. When I heard Harry Bliss's anecdotes for the third time it took a massive effort to keep the smile pasted on my face. It was not long before I detected a faint but unmistakable West Country burr beneath Flora de Solla's 'French' accent. Warwick Sheffield borrowed five pounds from me one evening after filming and never paid me back ... No matter. For a year or so I was entranced. I filmed *Anna Learns to Fly*, *Anna Triumphant!*, *Fido's Fortune* and many more. Then Maude teamed me up with Faithfull and we made two seven-reelers: *Sanctuary* with Alec Neame and Alma Urban and *Taboo* starring Reggie Fitzhamon, Flora de Solla and Ivy Pridelle. I learnt my trade. Panoramas, Akeley shots. How to deploy effectively the electric lights when London Fogs made daylight filming difficult: the mercury vapour lamps, the sunlight arcs, the tilts, toplights and spotlights. I was happy. Not even Faithfull could disturb me.

Of course Faithfull had not been pleased at my arrival. 'We wondered what had become of you, Todd,' he said. His attitude was always cool, though we worked well enough together as a team. But when I saw how complacently Faithfull directed (he was at the height of his renown in the years immediately following the war) I began to have ambitions to direct myself. I went regularly to the cinema, to American and European films, and I soon realised how deficient Superb-Imperial's product was in almost every area. I worked out a story about a young officer returning from a prisoner of war camp to find that his fiancée has married his best friend. He tries to be brave and cope with the shocking disappointment, but, to their dismay, the two ex-lovers find their passion renewing itself. The hero ends up with two choices: kill his best friend or himself. He opts for suicide to preserve his fiancée's happiness. I called it *Love's Sacrifice*.

I took my outline to Maude after I had been with Superb-Imperial for eighteen months. Maude was a diffident-looking man with a slack innocuous face and a soft grey toothbrush moustache. He wore light brown suede shoes and well-tailored suits. His wife, Rosita, was an overweight extravagant woman with vast breasts and a large mole on one cheek that, oddly, added a strange glamour to her. I think she was half Portuguese—or entirely Portuguese, I am not sure. The money behind Superb-Imperial came from sugar estates in Portuguese East Africa. I rather liked her. She spoke fast breathless English and smoked little black knobbled cheroots in a squat bone holder.

Maude called me into his office above the carpenters' shops a couple of days later. Rosita stood behind his chair. I was busy on *Taboo*. We had been filming a downpour in a jungle. I remember my hair was wet.

'About *Love's Sacrifice*,' he began. He looked doleful. 'I'm disappointed, John, very disappointed that you could suggest this to me.'

'Sorry?' I was baffled.

'Is not Superb film,' Rosita added loudly. 'Is no dram. Melodram yes, maybe. But dram, no. Not at a Superb.'

'Remember this, John, and you won't go off the rails. We want people to come out of our kinemas with a smile on their faces. Happy endings, please.'

There was more of the same platitudinous nonsense. It was possibly the most sustained bout of bad advice I had ever received, I went back to the dank jungles of *Taboo*.

Two more of my ideas were turned down for similar reasons. I told Sonia of my troubles on Saturday afternoon as we sat in a tea room on the New King's Road. It must have been October or November. *Taboo* was over. I was now working on *Fido Saves the Day*, or possibly *Anna Saves the Day*. Sonia was neat in an emerald green suit trimmed with black velvet. She had put her spectacles on to read the menu. I noticed that she was wearing a little lipstick. I liked to kiss her when she was wearing lipstick (we had progressed that far), I enjoyed the sweet waxy taste. She was going 'tum tum tum tum' as she read through the menu. I looked at her white parting, drilled across the crown of her head, and felt a sudden weakness in my lungs, as if breathing were an effort, and a curious spiralling sensation in my groin. The waitress came over.

'Pot of tea for two. Ceylon please. A slice of cherry cake and a rock cake. Wha' abou' you, Johnny?' She had a slight glottal stop in her London accent which she was taking pains to make more genteel. I knew I was in love with her there and then.

'Cheese bun, please.'

We were married on January 18th 1922 in St Peter's Church, Filmer Road, Fulham. No member of my family was present. My father sent £50, Oonagh her best wishes and Thompson a set of six silver-plated apostle spoons.

I now realise that I married Sonia for sex. I was almost twenty-three years old and still a virgin. Before I met Sonia my previous sexual contact with a human being (apart from myself) had been with Karl-Heinz back in Weilberg. And with a woman? Huguette in the dim shed behind the estaminet in 1917. I will not bore you with the details of Sonia's and my sexual apprenticeship, the gaffes and moist surprises of our wedding night (we honeymooned in Hove over a weekend—I was needed for filming on the Monday) but for two virgins we soon became quite proficient at the act. I was very fond of Sonia's plump friendly body. She had small firm breasts with odd domed nipples and remarkably luxuriant pudenda. She used depilatory creams on her armpits and on her legs below the knee. I pleaded vainly with her to let the hair grow again. I liked her too, I confess, because she was strange to me. English, a Londoner, almost as foreign as Huguette, and upper lower-class with an uneducated accent. She fell pregnant two months after the marriage. It seemed that after a twenty-three-year delay I was now racing headlong after maturity. I wanted a girl child. I felt I was not ready for a son and heir.

When Maude rejected my reworked version of *Love's Sacrifice*—the hero, about to commit suicide, learns of his rival's death in a motoring accident and is then reunited with his former fiancée—I was on the point of abandoning all my ambitions to direct. Superb-Imperial were making their most expensive film ever—a historical-romance-adventure called *The Blue Cockade* set in some Ruritanian never-never land. It was costing £18,000, Faithfull was to direct and I was to be cameraman. Maude, in another astute move on is a part, or possibly at Rosita's behest, went to America and hired Mary Mount at £1,000 a week to star. Faithfull had negotiated a bonus over his salary of £2,000. Out of the goodness of his heart Maude gave me one of £500. Suddenly I seemed preposterously well-off and secure. It was Sonia who urged me to try one more idea on the Maudes.

I do owe her this, I admit it. I would have done nothing more without her encouragement. Looking back on my hectic life, those early years in London now appear an island of bourgeois inertia and complacency. We had our flat above the pub (£3 a week), and I could send down for beer whenever I liked. I had a well-paid, stimulating and not too arduous job. I had a pretty, adoring wife. The fly feasting in the jam jar feels no need for a change of scene.

Maude and Rosita *loved* the idea of *Wee MacGregor Wins the Sweepstake* (I will not inflict the plot on you. It is all there in the title anyway.) They loved it so much they took me off *The Blue Cockade*. The film could start as soon as the script was written. I set to work immediately.

For some reason Harold Faithfull took my transferral from his film as a personal insult. Maude gave me a small office next to the sprocket punching department where I worked on the logistics of the production. Early one evening, as the girls next door were packing up, Faithfull confronted me.

Faithfull had grown sleeker since the war. He wore expensive clothes and that evening a ray of sun caused his yellow cashmere cardigan to blaze with arrogant wealth. His sulky handsome face gleamed. He was perspiring slightly, either from drink, choler, or the steepness of the stairs.

'What do you think you're playing at, Todd?' he demanded. He stood in the doorway and lit a cigarette. He glanced round my office. 'What are you trying to do with your poxy little film?'

'What are you talking about?'

'Either this is a misguided attempt to ruin me or you've got some nasty little back-street ambitions of your own.'

'You know I've always wanted to make my own films.'

'But you're a cameraman, Todd. Always will be. I'm the director.'

The patrician disdain in his voice made me angry.

'But you couldn't direct traffic in a one-way street, Faithfull,' I said calmly.

It was not such a brilliant riposte, I admit, but it did well in the heat of the moment. Faithfull lumbered forward and swung a punch at me across the desk. He missed, but his momentum knocked some papers and an inkwell to the floor. Ink spattered the cuffs of his pale mushroom trousers.

'You fucking Scottish cokehead!' He yelled. 'You make this film and you'll never make another!' He stomped out of the room. Some of the girls looked in, giggling, to see what all the fuss was about.

I was panting with excitement. I felt strangely invigorated. I knew why Faithfull was so upset: it was an oblique tribute to my crucial contribution to *Sanctuary* and *Taboo*. Faithfull needed me and he was worried about producing *The Blue Cockade* without me. I replaced the papers and inkwell on the desk and blotted up the stains. For the first time I had had my own confidence in my talent and ability confirmed—and by a hostile witness, no less. I wore a modest smile of satisfaction all the way back to Fulham.

*　　*　　*

It was Sonia's father, Vincent, who pointed out the advertisement to me. Every Sunday we had dinner chez Shorrold. They lived in a small brown terraced house with a good view of Fulham Palace football ground. The meal never changed—gravy soup, leg of mutton, fruit tart with custard—neither did the atmosphere of stifling boredom. After the meal, Sonia and her mother Noreen—a decent, dull, long-suffering woman—washed up, giving the men the opportunity for a smoke. Vincent Shorrold was a small spry chap with the impressive but ultimately fragile self-assurance of a travelling salesman. He would initiate conversations with remarks of what seemed at first adamantine authority

'No. No question. No, definitely. The allies should take over all of Germany's mines and forests. Every last tree.' He was reading about the reparation conference in his newspaper. 'It's the only way. The only justice.'

'But Vincent,' I said reasonably, 'what we need is cash. Seizing mines and forests won't provide any cash.'

He looked trapped, dismayed. 'Oh . . . Oh yes. Perhaps. I see what you mean.' He turned back to his newspaper.

Most of our discussions ran in this manner. Aggressive assertion, polite rebuttal on my part, wordless collapse. He smoked a pipe with a little perforated lid on the bowl. This attachment made me illogically irritated. I heard the clatter of cutlery on crockery from the kitchen and the indistinct noises of Sonia and her mother talking. I felt a profound inertia penetrate me; the air of the room seemed to brew with apathy. I gazed emptily ahead, a thin rope of smoke from my cigarette swaying and shimmying in front of me.

'This was your mob, wasn't it?' He read: '13th (public school) service battalion, South Oxfordshire Light Infantry . . .' He folded the paper open and handed it over. It was an advertisement for a reunion parade and dinner a month hence. Former members of the battalion were invited to foregather on Wandsworth Common at 4.30 p.m. for a brief parade and address by a Brigadier-General Pughe, followed by dinner in the function rooms of the Cape of Good Hope public house in Wandsworth High Street (price 5/6*d*.). Applications were to be sent to R. J. M. Tuck (major retd.).

I was a little late arriving at the common and I could see a group of several dozen suited men already lined up in front of a small dais equipped with loudspeakers and draped in Union Jack bunting. I walked across the grass towards them feeling a little nervous. I had been uncertain what to wear and in the end had dressed soberly, as if going to a funeral: a charcoal grey three-piece suit and black bowler hat. I even carried a macintosh. It was a mild September day, the chestnut trees on the common were beginning to turn. As I approached I saw that a lot of the men were carrying rolled umbrellas—surrogate rifles, I thought, and wished I had brought mine.

Someone I did not know crossed my name off a list and took my raincoat ('Can't march with one of those over your arm!') and I joined a column of men. I greeted a few people whom I recognised and asked myself why I had bothered to come.

We were marched off a hundred yards or so and stood easy. Then we saw three motor cars bump across the grass towards the dais. Some men got out, one of them in uniform. One man strode over to us. I recognised Major Tuck. He went to the head of the column, called us to attention, shouted, 'By the left, quick march!' We marched over to the dais, were halted, saluted and were inspected by the

Brigadier-General. Then we listened to him give a half-hearted speech about how we should not allow the iron bonds of comradeship forged in the bitter tempest of war wither and decay in the soothing balm of peace. We were assembled, I discovered, to celebrate the eighth anniversary of the founding of the battalion. The parade ended with the surviving member of the pipe band (the others killed, you will remember, carrying stew to the front line trenches in 1917) playing 'The bonnets of bonny Dundee'. We repaired to the function suite of the Cape of Good Hope.

Here the atmosphere was a little more convivial. At high table sat the General, Tuck, Colonel O'Dell and Noel Kite's father, Findlay, and beside him, Noel, with a crude wooden hand. We milled about looking for friends to sit beside. I heard my name called and looked round. It was Leo Druce in a chocolate brown pinstripe suit. He had four medals on his chest. We greeted each other with restrained but real enthusiasm.

'What's that lot?' I asked, pointing at his decorations.

'Campaign medals. Why aren't you wearing yours?'

'I didn't know I was entitled.'

'You were there, weren't you? Let's grab a pew.'

We ate rather well: clear mock turtle soup, boiled sole with a caper sauce, veal collops, roast ham, Coburg pudding and devilled herring roes (I thought we had done excellently for our 5/6d. During the speeches I learned that Findlay Kite was responsible for the purvey.) Druce looked prosperous. His thick toffee-coloured hair was brushed straight back from his forehead. His shirt looked to me like silk. He wore, I noticed, a large gold signet ring which I did not recall having seen before. We ate and talked and filled in the intervening years. I had more to relate than he. Druce's injury had kept him away from the front for months. Then he had been transferred to the Army Service Corps and had been commissioned a lieutenant in 1918. After the war he had tried various jobs and was thinking of going overseas before a modest legacy had allowed him to buy a small business in his home town, Coventry, hiring out motor cars and buses.

As the evening progressed and we drank more we became predictably maudlin and sentimental. We sought out Noel Kite, by now very drunk, and, with the inevitable nostalgia, began to reminisce about the 'good old days' at Croxyde Bains and Nieuport. We drank toasts to 'absent friends': Louise, Maitland Bookbinder, Tim Somerville-Start, Julian Teague—

'But Teague's here,' Noel Kite said.

'Where?'

Kite waved his wooden hand towards the end of the room. 'With the cripples.'

A trestle table with a generous overhang had been set up for men in wheelchairs. We made our way down towards it.

Teague's eyebrows had never grown back and his blunt burnt face had a stretched, sore, permanently surprised look to it. His terraced hair grew thick and curly as ever. His trouser legs were neatly pinned up—folded, I thought, like napkins. He was tackling his Coburg pudding with his one good hand. The damaged flesh on the other seemed to have fused the remaining fingers together into a strange arthritic point, like a carved beak. I heard Kite and Druce exchange *sotto voce* 'Good Gods' when they saw him. I sat down.

'Teague,' I said. 'It's me, Todd.'

He looked at me with his one good eye.

'My God,' he said. 'You made it.'

I ushered in Kite and Druce and the reminiscing continued. I told them about Teague's last day as a complete human being. Teague drank a toast to me: 'The man who saved my life.' I got rather drunk. I remember Teague whispering to me, 'I never told you, but I got MacKanness. Fixed him. Just before you and I met up.' Then Kite said,

'Here we are, all that's left of the "Bombers".' He looked at me with, I thought, real hostility. 'And only Todd came through without a scratch.'

I walked unsteadily back with Druce over Wandsworth Bridge, the coolish breeze off the Thames and memories of Kite's remark having sobered me up somewhat. Druce said he would pick up a taxi at Parson's Green. We had exchanged addresses, sworn to meet again at next year's reunion and in general had run the gamut of bibulous avowals. We stood under the electric light at Parson's Green and made our farewells. I felt a hard obstruction in my throat when I shook his hand and said goodbye. Of all the companions the war had forced on me Leo Druce was the one I liked the best. I thought back to my miserable weeks with the Bantams and felt sure that if I had been with Druce rather than Teague I would have borne up better.

'I'd like you to meet Sonia,' I said thickly. 'Must try and get up to Coventry. Once I've made this film.'

'I say, Todd,' Druce frowned. 'You couldn't see your way to lending me a tenner, could you?'

'Of course,' I took out my wallet. For some reason I had more than £30 in it. I handed two fivers over.

'Pleasure,' I said.

'Couldn't make it twenty, could you?'

I counted out another two. 'Pay me back when I come to Coventry,' I said cheerfully.

Druce smoothed his hair with both hands. He looked as if he had a dull but nagging ache somewhere inside him, deep.

'In fact . . .' he began. 'Everything I said tonight—to you and Kite and Teague—was a load of nonsense.' He did not smile. 'I'm broke. Stoney. Bailiffs have got my cars, my garage. I've got a couple of ten-seater charabancs in a friend's yard, but I can't afford the licence fee. I came here, tonight, to see if I could tap an "old comrade" or two.'

He told me more about his difficulties. I half-listened. I was moved by his candour. In the state I was in I would have emptied my wallet, no questions asked. I saw the essential decency of Leo Druce then, and I felt truly sorry for him. His appearance, his manner, his personality seemed to promise so much. But nothing in his life had lived up to his potential. I resolved to do what I could to help him.

That did not turn out to be much of a problem. At my instigation, Superb-Imperial hired Druce's two charabancs as cast and crew transportation for the filming of *Wee MacGregor Wins the Sweepstake*. He had to wait a couple of months and had to get the vehicles up to Edinburgh, but Maude paid him half his fee in advance which saw him over his initial difficulties and kept his creditors at bay.

We started filming in mid-November in and around Edinburgh (Harry Bliss was playing *Wee MacGregor* and we had to wait for him to finish his role in *The Blue Cockade*—hence the delay). I warned Maude about the problems of filming in limited daylight, but he needed the film as soon as possible and insisted we press ahead. I had insisted for my part on filming in Edinburgh. Location filming was then the latest fashion but I was prompted more by my own inclinations to authenticity. In the event, it took us almost eight weeks to film, approximately twice as long as planned owing to appalling weather, Harry Bliss coming down with pleurisy, and the holidays at Xmas and New Year. For Leo (we were on first name terms now) this was a bonus as his fee virtually doubled. As the frustrating weeks went on so his old confidence returned. As a cost-cutting exercise I was producer, director and cameraman, but I soon relinquished that first role to Leo. His experience of military logistics in the Service Corps proved highly useful. He managed to procure a small mobile generator which enabled us to deploy arc lamps while on location. He also bought three large sheets of mirrored glass which we used to bounce light back onto the actors on murky days. *Wee MacGregor*, I am the first to admit, is by no means an example of good lighting, but the fact that it was lit at all is something of a miracle—whose working was almost entirely due to Leo.

One other aspect of the film is worth recording here. At a key juncture in the story, Wee MacGregor, down on his luck, his last pennies spent in a consoling pub, shambles drunkenly out into the rain and weaves his way home to his dreadful lodging house. He spots on the ground a cardboard ticket—the eponymous sweepstake ticket—and unthinkingly pockets it. I wanted to shoot this moment from Wee MacGregor's point of view. Recalling my experiments with a hand-held camera in the field outside Elverdinghe I decided to try again. I broke apart a large alarm clock and removing the cranking handle on the camera rigged up the clockwork spring to the turning ratchet. Wound up and set going, this device gave me about 30 seconds of filming at the regular speed of 16 frames a second.

In the completed film, we cut from Wee MacGregor bouncing off the alleyway walls to what appears to be his uncertain gaze (nice work with the focus) wandering about the cobbled lane. The camera halts at the ticket, wavers, closes up and a hand comes into frame to lift it off the ground. I claim this as the first commercial use in Great Britain, possibly the world, of an independently powered camera. Later, when small portable dynamos and compressed air bottles were commonplace power sources, I still used my clockwork device for short bursts. I never like cranking cameras and was an early advocate of the power-drive. My only regret is that it was not available to me during the first war. I could have filmed the most sensational footage.

The delay in the film upset Sonia who was most annoyed when I told her I had to return to Scotland after the new year, and our marriage experienced its first truly bitter row. She was heavily pregnant and our child was due in January. I said I would try and get away. In fact I was filming in the Pentland hills when our son Vincent, named after his maternal grandfather, was born. I remember the cable.

SON BORN JAN 5 10.30 AM STOP MOTHER AND VINCENT DOING WELL STOP VINCENT

At first I thought Vincent Shorrold was making some kind of feeble joke. It was only when I returned home two weeks later that I learned the shocking truth and discovered my son was called Vincent Todd. He had been registered and I was told it was too late now for second thoughts. I was violently opposed to the name and fell out badly with old man Shorrold when he demanded to know what my objections were. I had to give way and have always regretted my weakness. I now had a son whose name I disliked. Every time I said 'Vincent' Vincent Shorrold's face came unpleasantly to mind. As I have said before names are important to me. This surrender on my part proved to be a serious error.

Wee MacGregor Wins the Sweepstake turned out to be a sizeable commercial success. Even the critics were kind. *The Daily Telegraph* described it as 'a delightful example of Caledonian folk-comedy'. The *Herald* said, 'Harry Bliss has never been so hilarious'. *Bioscope* commented, 'a limp comedy of shameful banality redeemed only by its technical excellence.' *Close-Up* remarked, 'if this is the best that the British cinema industry can produce we should shut up shop and go home.' But Superb-Imperial's audience loved it. The film made £21,000 at the box-office in its first two months of release (the trade show was in April 1923). Maude and Rosita were ecstatic. At Sonia's prompting I asked Rosita to be Vincent's godmother and she happily consented.

In fact the success came at an opportune time because Maude was having terrible problems with *The Blue Cockade*. Thanks to Faithfull's ineptitude it took over 16 weeks to film and the costs escalated to £29,000 not including Mary Mount's fee. Faithfull now cut me dead at the studios. Apparently he and Mary Mount hated each other. Originally, she had agreed to stay on and make another film for Superb-Imperial but she left the instant *Blue Cockade* was over. The film itself was a box-office disaster. Even starring Mary Mount, no American renter would touch it.

Maude sold the rights of *Wee MacGregor* to a film distributor, Ideal Film Renters, for £10,000 to make a quick profit. Ideal, so I learnt later, paid him another £15,000 to make two more Wee Mac-Gregor five-reelers, and these I was duly contracted to film. For the first time I was regarded as a director proper. Maude and I drew up an interim agreement. I would complete the two films before the end of 1923 for a fee of £4,000. Leo Druce was to be producer on them both.

It was not exactly what I wanted, but I could not ignore this good fortune. And, I suppose, this was a happy enough time, this summer of 1923. Leo had moved down to London and we both shared an office in the mews at Islington. Sonia and the baby were fine, and Sonia soon came up with the script for *Wee MacGregor's Holiday* and had a promising idea for the third film—*King Wee MacGregor!*

But I was somewhat unsettled and preoccupied. The *Wee Mac-Gregor* films were far from the ambitions that had been born with

Aftermath of Battle. I applied myself professionally to them but my mind was barely engaged. It was as if my imagination was away on patrol, scouting the countryside for a task that was equal to it. The garrison it left behind, as it were, kept the fort running, ticking over, but life there was drab and tedious. I felt myself oddly demeaned. I was an artist, I had grand plans, fabulous conceptions. The *Wee MacGregors* allowed me some licence to experiment technically but I was growing to loathe them, and myself for making them. A measure of my disquiet was the fact that I had a bitter stand-up row, over some matter or other, with the irrepressibly chirpy Harry Bliss— whom I could not separate from the character and consequently detested as much. We almost came to blows. Leo told me to bide my time—soon I would be able to do exactly as I wanted. But all I could see was an endless run of *Wee MacGregors.* Success can confine as easily as liberate. The appalling and interminable *Anna* and *Fido* series were dire warnings.

That summer Hamish passed briefly through London. He had just been awarded a research fellowship at Oxford. We went for a meal in a chop house on the Strand. I told him of my worries.

'I can see this rut stretching ahead of me,' I said. 'It gets deeper and deeper.'

He looked at me without speaking for a while. I have never forgotten the clear force of his expression.

'Make your own rut,' he said. 'It's the only way.'

He was right and it cheered me up. I resolved that *King Wee MacGregor!* would be my last compromise. 'Make you own rut' would become my motto.

Perhaps I should have seen the signs. Raymond Maude asked if he could pay me my fee in installments. I agreed and to my astonishment he handed me a banker's draft for only £100. In September, halfway through filming in Great Yarmouth, a pier-owner said that a cheque Leo had written had bounced. Leo wrote another for him. We finished the film in five weeks and returned to London to start editing. On October 3rd 1923 Maude announced to his assembled staff that Superb-Imperial films was bankrupt.

VILLA LUXE 16 June 1972

Something is in the air, these days, and it's not just the scent from the yucca flowers. A small electric charge crackles between Emilia and me. I can't put my finger on it. Something is different. The quality of the look she gives me. It's like that time with Oonagh. Superficially all is as it always was, but beneath the surface new currents are running. Something tacit now exists between us and while I don't know what it is it sets me on edge.

I spend the day fretting vaguely. I try to avoid her. When I hear her motorbike disappearing up the track I go into her WC. I peer at the shutter. I feel as though a billiard ball were jammed in my throat. My small drilled hole is neatly blocked with a pellet of lavatory paper.

8

Julie

The rain pelted down on Jager Strasse. I held the car door open with one hand, the other raised the large umbrella sheltering the fur clad old crone who was climbing with preposterous difficulty into her waiting taxi. Drips formed and fell from my cap's glossy peak. I could feel the damp seeping through to my shoulder blades. I kept the smile rigid as I shut the door on her. The window glass took an age to wind down. Her bejewelled hand presented me with a shamefully inadequate tip.

'*Vielen Dank,*' I said.

I backed gratefully under the canopy at the front of the Hotel Windsor. I was the doorman. It was February 1925. Berlin. I was making my own rut.

I have leapt a dismal year or so. 1924. All the wearisome frustrations of the Superb-Imperial bankruptcy and my own concomitant slump into insolvency preoccupied me for months. Raymond Maude was undeniably grief-stricken. It was the extravagant costs of *The Blue Cockade* and its total failure that had done for him. He sold everything the studio owned, including his remaining rights to *Wee MacGregor's Holiday*. It was truly galling to see the queues forming outside the cinemas, where it was playing as profitably as its predecessor and know that all the revenue it earned would benefit the Todd family not one penny. Finally, in the summer I joined the other litigants and sued Superb-Imperial for the outstanding £1,900 they owed me on the *Holiday* film. (I waived my claim on the still-born *King Wee MacGregor!*) In the eventual meagre share-out I received £187/18/6d. It was something I suppose. One other unhappy side-effect was that the Maude marriage broke up under the strain. Rosita took herself off back to Beira or Lisbon and Vincent never saw his godmother again.

About July or August I accepted the inevitable and started looking for another job but to my surprise and alarm found there was nothing forthcoming. Gainsborough Films offered me a week's work as a stand-in cameraman. Astro-Biocraft thought there might be an opening in their editing department in a few months' time. The film industry had entered one of its periodic slumps, true, but I soon began to suspect the malign hand of Harold Faithfull. It was my mistake, or bad luck, that I was almost unknown in the film community outside Superb-Imperial. I remembered Faithfull's absurd threat and dismissed it as sheer fantasy until I read in a trade paper that he was making a film called *The Sultan and the Temptress* for Talbot Instructional Films and UFA in Germany. A man who could get work so quickly after the almighty disaster of *The Blue Cockade* must have some power and influence. I became convinced that Faithfull had effectively blacklisted me. He was the first in a long line of enemies that have dogged and tried to destroy my career. I have no idea why, but I seem to attract malice in the way cattle attract flies. I am not belligerent but I always end up fighting someone. What had I done to Faithfull? How could my *Wee MacGregor* film have possibly discomfited him? It was his own inadequacies that compelled him to hate me. It has always been that way: the talentless envy the talented in the same way as the petty envy the strong.

I took the week's work at Gainsborough, around the corner from Superb-Imperial in Islington, as a stand-in assistant cameraman on a film called *Passionate Adventure*. And then, nothing. The year wore on and our savings dwindled. In August Sonia announced she was pregnant again. That was all I needed.

Leo Druce was similarly impoverished. He restarted his car-hire agency in London and from time to time I would do a job as chauffeur or bus driver on outings for a pound or two. It was hardly a living and Leo could not afford to take on a partner. And besides, I wanted to make moving pictures, not drive charabancs.

And then in October came my salvation. One morning a postcard arrived, forwarded from Edinburgh. The stamps were German. On one side was a picture of the Brandenburg Gate. And on the other:

Hello Johnny!
How are you doing? Well? I am in Berlin making lots of films and plays. Come and see me. Why not?
Kind best wishes from your old prison guard.
Karl-Heinz

He had given his address: 129b, Stralauer Allee, Berlin ... I remember that morning with perfect clarity. Sonia had gone out and left me with baby Vincent. I was sitting at the kitchen table in vest and trousers drinking a cup of strong tea. Vincent was crying lustily in his cot. I was faintly nauseous from the smell of old beer seeping up through the floorboards from the pub below. I needed a shave. I thought this tableau might have been done justice by some modern Hogarth: 'Jobless man,' perhaps; or, 'The Artist's Dream Frustrated.' I heard letters being pushed through the letter box and went down to the hall to collect them. There were two bills—one from my solicitor and one from a tailor—and Karl-Heinz's postcard. I read it as I trudged back upstairs towards Vincent's irritating screeching. And then I felt as if I had been punched in the chest—that sudden thump of exhilaration that is the physical corollary of a brilliant idea. Of course! Of course. How parochial and hide-bound of me! There were other film industries—America, France, Germany—far more audacious and inspirational than what was going on at home. Why stay put and marinate in one's own self-pity? I would go to Berlin, join Karl-Heinz. We would make films together ...

My mind began to work faster. I would leave as soon as possible— and alone. Whenever I was established I would send for Sonia and Vincent. I suddenly saw all the splendid potential in the idea. How vastly more intriguing to make one's name abroad in one of the real capitals of film. No more pap or trash. No more *Wee MacGregors*. I felt a stimulating sense of freedom. I was almost grateful to Raymond Maude for going broke and to Harold Faithfull for his vindictive spite.

*   *   *

I left home at the end of October, promising Sonia that I would send for her and Vincent before Christmas. I went by boat—cargo steamer—from London to Bremerhaven, and from there by train to Berlin. It was pouring with rain when we left the docks at London and I did not trouble to go up on deck. I sat in the small, dusty, panelled saloon drinking a warmish mug of unsweetened cocoa. I glanced once or twice through the portholes at the rainsmudged views of the disappearing city and savoured the excitement that ran like a tremor through my body. I had very little money, not quite £50 (I had been naturally obliged to leave the rest of what remained of our savings with Sonia, who as a further economy had quit the flat above the Salisbury and had moved in with her parents), but I felt much the same as I had that night I ran away from Minto Academy and caught the night train down to London. The future lay before me like an empty sheet of paper. All I had to do was make my mark on it.

I had written and cabled to Karl-Heinz about my impending arrival, but I had received no reply. The train from Bremerhaven arrived at Lehrter station in Berlin at 6.00 in the morning. It was just growing light and was decidedly cold. I bought a cup of coffee and two round bread rolls from a stall outside the entrance and wondered what to do—I thought it a little too early to turn up at Karl-Heinz's. So I left the station and walked along the Spree for a while (I had only one suitcase with me). The river water was dark, bottle green, sluggish. Barges were moored here and there. I crossed the river at the Marschall Bridge and wandered into the centre of the city.

Berlin ... First impressions. I will try to recall them, after all these years, after familiarity has worn down the images like old coins. Berlin that cold morning in October was very clean, extraordinarily clean. Wide, broad streets. Trees, statues—statues everywhere—and fountains. It felt modern, recent. It had a new feel, a busy feel. Above my head stretched a matrix of electric tram wires. Trams were everywhere, even at this hour. I wandered through the streets—Friedrich Strasse, Behren Strasse, Unter den Linden (with its disappointing spindly limes)—past the sombre palaces, the palatial stores and the fabulous hotels. It was like ... Take a prosperous British Victorian city centre—Bradford, Manchester, Glasgow. Buff up all the heavy over-decorated architecture, then push the buildings far apart to form clear prospects and broad avenues. Scatter young trees and white statues wherever space permits. Then add all the paraphernalia of the modern city: the motors, the tram and cable cars, the advertisement hoardings, the neon signs, the yellow autobuses, the green taxicabs with their white-hatted drivers, and an urgent hurrying smart population. That was the Berlin I saw that morning. Its newness was my abiding impression: a city that seemed only as old as its inhabitants, as if it possessed no past beyond the memory of the generations that lived and worked amongst its spic and spanness.

There were other Berlins, of course, that looked like Amsterdam, or medieval French towns, or cramped urban slums, or featureless industrial cityscapes, and I was to see them later that day, but I was inspired by its contemporaneity as I passed among its prosperous commuters and pedestrians. I could sense no dead hand of tradition about its open squares and immaculate boulevards. I knew I could achieve great things here.

It took me some time to find 129b, Stralauer Allee. Eventually, having obtained the necessary information from a helpful English-speaking clerk at a railway station, I took the Stadtbahn east to the Stralau-Rummelsberg stop. Stralauer Allee ran along the north bank of the Spree, and here the city faintly resembled stretches of London by the Thames at Chelsea before the Embankment was built. Old buildings with cellar shops and cafés, wooden jetties and unsteady rickety steps leading down to the slow river whose banks were crowded with barges lashed together.

Number 129 was a narrow five-storey house built around a small brick courtyard. The apartment where Karl-Heinz lived was on the first floor. I went through the main entrance, saw no concierge and mounted the central stone staircase to apartment 'b'. The name above the doorbell was Pfau.

I was about to ring for the third time when it opened to reveal a large untidy man in a collarless shirt. He had straight short grey hair and a large crude face with the sort of creases and dewlaps one associates with certain types of hound—a basset or a pug, say—rather than a human. He had damp lustreless eyes and a blunt nose with big hair-choked nostrils that needed clipping. He was smoking a cigar.

'Karl-Heinz Kornfeld?' I inquired.

The man, Herr Pfau, I assumed, shouted for Karl-Heinz who, after a short pause, came to the door wiping shaving soap from his face. His hair was longer but otherwise he was unchanged. Tall, thin, dark, vital.

'So, Johnny,' he said calmly. 'How wonderful to see you.'

I stepped over the threshold and we shook hands. He saw my suitcase.

'What brings you to Berlin?'

'Didn't you get my letter? My cable?'

'What letter?'

'You had no idea I was coming?'

'No, of course not. But it's a delightful surprise. Come in, come in.'

He introduced me to Pfau—Georg—who said hello and disappeared into another room. Karl-Heinz led me through a sitting room, dining room and kitchen and on into his own bedroom. The apartment was very badly designed. There was no hall or corridor. One room simply gave onto another as one moved around the central courtyard. The bathroom was at the end. I was so perturbed by the non-arrival of my letter that I did not really take in the simple décor and well-worn furniture. But I did notice that the walls of most rooms were lined with wooden boxes, like lockers, and stacks of fine wire mesh cages. The apartment was very warm as well. The air was filled with a faint electric hum, as if there were powerful dynamos in the basement.

The Hotel Windsor's doormen were obliged to wear typically preposterous uniforms. It was the usual comic operetta hussar get-up: gold buttons everywhere, bushy epaulettes, high peaked cap, yards of looped curtain cord with bell-pull tassels swagged over the shoulders, and the whole—in deference to the English note in the hotel's name—rendered in coruscating beefeater red and gold. I felt myself an unseemly shout of colour in the stolid grey streets, a human beacon that, I felt sure, must make most passers-by want to shade their eyes. My uniform was slightly too large as well. It belonged to Georg Pfau's nephew Ulrich, whose job it was and for whom I was standing in. Some unspecified family crisis had required his presence at home in Breslau for two months and I had had no hesitation in accepting the temporary post when Georg decently offered it to me.

It was an odd life being a doorman. I found it uncomfortable working in uniform—it reminded me vaguely of the army, but there is something pretentious about civilian uniforms that makes me uneasy. There were four of us working shifts at the Windsor and as I was the most junior I was always allocated the least lucrative—ten in the morning until four in the afternoon. I missed the crowd checking out in the morning and those checking in in the evening. The Windsor's restaurant was not highly regarded and the lunch trade was consequently slack. So I paced to and fro idly on Jager Strasse watching the traffic and the passers-by, trying to keep warm, trying to keep out of the rain and snow (the winter of '24–'25 was particularly raw). At four I went down to the basement to the staff canteen and had a meal—belly of pork with carrots, oxtail with turnips, something hearty, anyway. I had plenty of time to think and reflect.

Accommodation had proved no problem. Karl-Heinz encouraged Georg to rent me a room in his apartment for two pounds a month. But my other ambitions were harder to achieve. The 'lots of films and plays' Karl-Heinz had referred to in his postcard certainly existed, and Karl-Heinz was in them, all right, but usually as a non-speaking extra. He had profited from the post-war vogue for vast historical epics and he took me to see such films as *Anne Boleyn*, *Julius Caesar* and *The Trojan War* in which he felt I might be able to pick out his face in the swarming multitude. Currently, he was 'resting', he told me, ironing clothes and sewing on buttons in the costume department of the Schiller-Theater Nord.

I settled down quickly in the Pfau household. There were just the three of us. An old woman—Frau Mittenklott—came in the afternoon to clean and cook the enormous evening meal. What did I do? I wrote diligently to the studios and film companies. I wandered around the city. I drank beer and coffee, ate cake, sat in cold parks and listened to the bands. I received polite refusals from the studios and film companies, which Karl-Heinz translated for me. I started to learn German. After a month I cabled Sonia for more money. She sent £10 and a curt letter asking when she and Vincent would be sent for and reminding me that I had promised to be home for Xmas. The new baby was due, she added, in March and she would like—please—to be settled in her new home. I wrote back saying that things were going well and I was making progress but my plans were taking slightly longer to realise than I had expected. I sent all my love to her and little Vince and asked her to borrow another £10 off her father.

I must be honest. I felt as if I was on holiday. 1924 had been such a disappointing year—steady impecuniousness, Vincent teething, no work—that I was glad to be away. I liked living in Georg Pfau's inconvenient apartment. I enjoyed being abroad in a strange fascinating city. I strolled the clean wide streets, a happy alien among the incurious Berliners. I whiled away afternoons in shops and museums. I played at being a bohemian. I had a little money, I had a warm place to live and I had my entrancing fabulous dreams. Sonia, Vincent, the Shorrolds, Wee MacGregor, Faithfull, Superb-Imperial, poverty and frustration seemed to have nothing to do with me now.

And there was Karl-Heinz. The strong affection that had grown up between us in Weilberg quickly re-established itself. When he was not working he would take me to bars and cafés, to films and plays. He took me to the west of the city, to the Kurfürstendamm, we patronised the Bluebird and El Dorado, the Westens, Café Wien and the Romanisches Café. Here was the artistic lively heart of Berlin where I felt I truly belonged. The solid prosperous streets I had seen the morning I had arrived were for the older generation and the rich bourgeoisie. Real life was in the west. In actual fact Stralauer Allee was inconveniently placed for the west end. It was a longish trip on the elevated electric railway to the Kurfürstendamm and after the initial enthusiasm I decided to save money by staying at home. Karl-Heinz, however, went over three or four times a week bringing back—

through my bedroom on route for his own—a steady supply of Ottos, Klauses and Heinrichs. I kept a chamber pot beneath my bed to avoid disturbing him if I needed to go to the toilet and I soon became accustomed to new introductions at breakfast time. Georg himself did not seem to mind these transient visitors and after a while I began to suspect that he and Karl-Heinz were in some way 'involved'. I asked Karl-Heinz about this, delicately.

'Oh, for sure,' he said. 'Georg loves me. He lets me stay here for nothing. You know, one time a month, one time every six weeks, he asks me to give him a—what do you say?—a masturb.' He pumped one hand graphically.

'Ah.'

'Yes, it's a cheap rent.'

I actually found the idea somewhat revolting, not because of anything associated with the act so much, but because Georg himself rather disgusted me. I liked him, and was most grateful for his hospitality, but there was no getting away from the fact that he was a horrible looking person.

For example, I tried not to take breakfast at the same time as Georg since one morning when, buttering a fresh roll, I had looked across the table and my eye had been irresistibly caught by Georg's big dense hairy nostrils. Like two old caves, I found myself thinking, thick with brambles, moss and ferns ... Just at that moment he removed his cigar from his mouth and with smoke still curling and eddying around his face he had taken a huge cracking bite of salted cucumber. My gorge rose, my mouth flooded with saliva, I gagged and I had to run from the room.

His job, too, was unsettling and its associations were always with him, like a smell of onions. Georg was an insect breeder, hence all the boxes and mesh cages in his rooms; hence also the eerie buzzing of invisible dynamos and the high temperature in the flat (plump stoves and paraffin heaters constantly burning). He bred bait for fishermen (maggots), silk worms for the silk industry and butterflies for lepidopterists. He provided a steady stream of crunchy grass-hoppers for the reptile house and the snakepit in the zoological gardens. Recently, however, he had been in demand by the film industry. If you needed a shade-dappled clearing frothing with but-terflies, Georg Pfau was your man. If you wanted bumble bees visiting flowers in an alpine meadow, Georg would lay on hundreds of the fluffy little workers. He did most of his work for one particular studio called Realismus Films Verlag who specialised in grim low-life melodramas and who regularly required encrusted fly papers, humming heaps of ordure and infested hovels. In one Realismus film, Georg told me with pride, he could get through a thousand bluebottles. He was known in the industry as the 'Fly Man'—*der Fliegenmann*.

Georg was a taciturn but placid bloke who seemed entirely happy with his life. His profession occupied most of his time. His pleasures were cigars (he smoked from rising in the morning and stubbed out his last butt when he switched off his bedside light), food—Frau Mittenklott's gargantuan suppers—and his monthly masturb at the hand of Karl-Heinz. I worked with him for a while as his assistant when my funds began running low. I would parcel up dead butterflies and send them off to collectors, or take seething trays of maggots to fishing tackle shops. One day we went out to the vast UFA studios at Tempelhof. A scene was being shot where the heroine (played by Nita Jungman, I think) was to be awakened by a butterfly landing on her nose. Georg carried a large jam jar busy with cabbage whites while I lugged a hefty zinc-lined wooden box containing a block of ice wrapped in straw. One had to admire his technique. Georg encouraged his insects to act by chilling them, as it were, to the bone. The skill, the expertise lay in knowing just how cold a butterfly or bluebottle had to be before it would do what was required. Not cold enough and it would just take off and fly away; too cold and it would simply die or fall numbed to the ground.

I watched Georg at work with real fascination. Nita Jungman slept, the cameras turned three feet from her face. Georg reached into his ice box where he had been chilling a butterfly. The freezing befuddled insect sat on his blunt fingertips, wings opening and closing very slowly. Georg took a sip from his cigar, pursed his loose lips together and blew a thin gentle jet of smoke onto the butterfly. The creature, irritated, could just manage a groggy two-foot flight. One hoped, naturally, it would head for the alluring peak of Nita Jungman's pretty little retroussé nose. It was all a matter of nice calculations of correctly chilled, thus unenergetic butterfly, and direction and velocity of cigar smoke goad. On this particular day Georg got it right three times with five butterflies. The entire studio broke into applause. Georg himself was proudest of a scene which you will probably remember in Heinrich Bern's *Deception*. In it Georg persuaded a large house fly to visit every feature of the villain's face (Rex Ermeram in his greatest role) by using the ice trick and by laying on with a pin point a tiny path of honey from demonic eyebrows to hooked nose, from leering lips to sabre scar. Georg once told me, with passionate earnestness, that the single most important factor in any German

man's life was the freedom to smoke undisturbed in every corner of his house.

And so 1924 ended and I was still in Berlin, poorer and no further on with my career. In the New Year Sonia wrote begging me to return for the birth of our second child and informing me of the shocking news that her father had secured me a position in his old pharmaceutical supplies company as trainee salesman. It was just at this time that I started work at the Hotel Windsor. I sent most of my first week's pay home, said prospects were improving (I did not specify) and that the baby, if a boy, should be called Adam, and if a girl, Emmeline, after my mother.

I had not been entirely idle. Karl-Heinz and I had translated my script of *Love's Sacrifice* and so far it had received only two rejections. Karl-Heinz said he would like to play the hero and I instantly agreed. Thus simply a professional association was added to our friendship which was to survive the most hazardous traumas and ordeals.

Karl-Heinz, too, was knowing more success. He had acted in his first billed role as a shrewd detective investigating the disappearance of a lodger in a boarding house (I can recall nothing more of this film which is only remarkable as Karl-Heinz's début). On screen he had an enticing, eye-catching impact. There was something latently unruly about him, a sense of good behaviour only just being preserved with considerable effort. The *Jahrbuch der Filmindustrie 1925* described him as 'a most interesting find.' More offers of work came in. Karl-Heinz lent me money, some of which I sent on to Sonia.

Then, just before I finished my stint as Ulrich Pfau's replacement, events began to move and my life to change. It was March and I was impatient for spring. I had been in Berlin for over four months and was feeling oppressed by its new grey massiness. Karl-Heinz's modest success made me conscious of my own frustrated stasis. I was in a bad mood, further irritated by a letter from Sonia that morning informing me that my second son had been born ten days previously and that his name was to be Hereford. Apparently there had been Herefords in the Shorrold family 'for centuries' (I quote: 'You've heard of Hereford the Wake,' Vincent Shorrold proudly said to me later, 'we go right back to him'). As I paced up and down outside the Windsor I grew steadily more depressed. 'John James Todd,' I said to myself, 'accompanied by his two sons Vincent and Hereford.' No, really, it was too appalling! Again I suspected the sly influence of Vincent Shorrold.

Just before my shift was up, at about four o'clock, a taxi pulled up in front of the hotel. I opened the door and Karl-Heinz got out. He was wearing a fawn overcoat with a fur collar. He put on sunglasses and warmed his hands on my blazing coat.

'Most amusing,' I said.

'We have a drink when you finish,' he said. 'I've got a present for you. See you at the English bar.'

The English bar was on the Unter den Linden, in the passageway. It bore no resemblance at all to any hostelry in England but Karl-Heinz thought it was a treat for me. When I arrived he was in the middle of a meal. He was still wearing his coat. I ordered a half litre of pilsner.

'Like the coat,' I said.

'You want some?' He pointed at his plate. 'I pay?'

'What is it?'

'Smoked ham cooked in champagne. Delicious. With a radish sauce.'

'Tempting, but no thanks. What are we celebrating?'

'I got a job. Fantastic. Realismus Films. A. E. Groth directing. *Diary of a Prostitute*. I'm getting . . .' he considered it, '500 dollars.'

'Are you the prostitute?'

'And I got one present for you.' He smiled and handed over a book wrapped in brown paper. 'It's by the same fellow as in Weilberg. You know—Rousseau.'

*   *   *

I read *Julie, or the New Héloïse* in two days with an effort directly proportional to my mounting dismay and disappointment. The turgid rhetoric, the lachrymose posturing, the relentless rhapsodies were bitterly disillusioning after the never-to-be-forgotten exhilaration of *The Confessions*. For a landmark in the history of human artistic endeavour, and the signal for everything we know as Romanticism to begin, it was extraordinarily hard going.

I find it hard now to explain why I did certain things then. I was only twenty-six years old, but the war had provided me with several lifetimes of experience. I was constantly on the verge of brilliant ideas, or at least I felt I was, and that feeling can sometimes be as important as the ideas themselves. So why, after that reaction to the book, did I decide to adapt it as a film? I have no honest explanation. It simply seemed the right thing to do. So I did it.

I wrote the script of *Julie* in seventeen days. I updated it to the present but kept the essential simplicity of the story. Saint-Preux—sensitive, melancholy, heart-driven—is tutor to the beautiful young blonde Julie, who lives in an idyllic château. They fall in love.

Julie and Saint-Preux independently confide in Julie's friend Claire (sprightly, dark) and she makes sure that the two soon know of their mutual passion. Overwhelmed by their feelings Julie yields herself to Saint-Preux. They make love. Then Julie is stricken with remorse and guilt. She recoils from Saint-Preux and, distraught, marries an old codger called Baron Wolmar (her father's initial choice). Saint-Preux, suicidal, heads for the fleshpots of Paris. In despair, he decides against taking his life when he receives a letter from Julie saying that even though she is married Saint-Preux will always be close to her heart.

Wolmar—prudent, sagacious, a philosopher of the human spirit—who knows of Julie's past relationship with her former tutor invites him (Saint-Preux is on the verge of nervous collapse) to come and live in their household. It is a profound and tormenting trial but somehow Julie and Saint-Preux remain virtuous. Then Baron Wolmar announces he is going on a long journey and leaves the two behind. Julie and Saint-Preux suffer a terrible ordeal of temptation and frustration, but Julie does not succumb, she remains faithful. Then, tragically, she has a fatal accident. On her death-bed she informs Saint-Preux that she has always loved him. Cut to Saint-Preux's stricken face. Julie dies. The end.

It was, I think, a good piece of work and the story was no more impossible than any other drama currently being made. Karl-Heinz loved it and it was he who suggested we take it to Realismus. I thought this was frankly a waste of time but Karl-Heinz insisted there was some logic in his idea. He was currently filming *Diary of a Prostitute*; Realismus had a certain vested interest in his career and he had access to the head of the company, Duric Lodokian. I agreed to give it a try and he took the script off with him.

Duric Lodokian was a hugely wealthy Armenian who had fled from his native country to Russia in 1896 shortly after the first Turkish massacres and pogroms against the Armenian people had begun. He had fled again in 1918 after the Russian Revolution and was among the first of the thousands of Russian émigrés who found sanctuary in Berlin. Lodokian had made his fortune in nuts. He described himself to me as a 'nut-importer'. He spoke Russian, German, French and passable English. He had sold many nuts to England he said but of only one type: Brazil nuts. Hundreds of tons of Brazil nuts. 'What do they do with Brazil nuts?' he asked. I said I had no idea. I must say I find it hard to imagine a fortune founded on nuts but this was Lodokian's power base ('every time I open a pistachio I am saying thank you,' he said to me once). The nut business sustained him through the few ups and many downs of his passion for films. Realismus Films Verlag AG *was* Duric Lodokian and no film was made unless it conformed to the philosophy implicit in the name. His greatest success had been in 1920 with a movie about the horrors and dangers of venereal disease called *The Wages of Sin*, and Unsparing Social Comment would, I think, be a fair summary of the Lodokian and Realismus creed. True, it swam somewhat against the tide in the Berlin of the mid-Twenties, but for every three flops there was a modest Realismus success that confirmed him in his principles and he persevered. There was, in fact, a Realismus 'school' notionally in opposition to the UFA films, the Expressionists, the *Neue Sachlichkeit* movement and all the other various artistic 'isms' and groupings that flourished then. Two of Realismus's regular directors were Werner Hitzig and Egon Gast. Lodokian had just persuaded the celebrated Swedish director A. E. Groth to join him and *Diary of a Prostitute* was the result.

Lodokian was a small dapper brown man in his sixties. Brown as one of his nuts, I thought when I met him for the first time in the Realismus offices on the corner of the Französische Strasse and Friedrich Strasse. His face and hands were speckled with copious liver spots. He was smoking a Russian cigarette with a cardboard filter, the hand holding it trembling slightly. When he spoke it was through a kind of surf of wheezes and vascular gurglings as if he were crippled with emphysema. There was a wheelchair and an oxygen cylinder behind his desk. He introduced me first to his son Aram who stood beside him. Aram was as small and neat as his father, my age, and running to fat. He had dark slightly hooded eyes and a neat cleft in his chin. His plump cheeks gave a strange oblate look to his head. We shook hands and he smiled. It was a brilliant smile. Charm came off him like a perfume. He had the same immediate effect on me as Karl-Heinz had. Within seconds of meeting them both you liked them and, more importantly, you wanted them to like you back. The only difference with Aram Lodokian was a slight side-effect. A minute or so after yielding to the charm came a moment's doubt as to the wisdom of so doing. Just a fleeting moment, then it passed. Although Karl-Heinz was in many ways utterly disreputable this aftertaste never occurred.

I sat down.

'What do you know about my country?' Lodokian asked.

I decided on honesty. 'Absolutely nothing.'

With enormous effort he got to his feet, shuffled laboriously to the window and beckoned me over. We looked down on the crowds in Friedrich Strasse.

'Do you think they know about the two million? Of course not.'

'Two million what?'

'The two million Armenians the Turks killed in 1915. The biggest genocide in the history of the world.'

I did not know what to say.

'Nobody wants to know the truth. That's why I make these films.'

He clasped his mottled hands together and shook them at me in a curious gesture. He always did this to emphasise a point.

'Don't turn your back on reality,' he said fiercely to me. 'Don't let people dream too much. Is dangerous.'

A line from some modern poem came into my head. 'Human nature cannot stand too much reality,' I misquoted.

'It's the only medicine,' he said. 'The only medicine.'

I was wordless once more.

It took him two minutes to regain his seat where he lit another cigarette.

'This is why I like your film,' he said, mystifyingly. 'Very good philosophy, Jean-Jacques Rousseau. Now this *is* Realismus. You talk to Aram, he will make the contracts.'

I felt an effervescence in my body—my blood turned to seltzer. I shook the old man's hand and then Aram Lodokian showed me into another office. I think we talked vaguely of contracts. I remember Aram suggesting a fee of 10,000 dollars. He said they paid in dollars because of the last inflation. He smiled apologetically. I promised to acquire a lawyer that afternoon. He called for coffee and cake and offered me a Russian cigarette. His smiles and charm enfolded me like a shawl.

'Have you thought of a cast?' he said, leaning over to light my cigarette. His English was perfect, accentless, and somehow all the more foreign sounding because of that. He sat back and rubbed the knuckle of his forefinger up and down the cleft in his chin. It was a frequent gesture. I thought suddenly of it as a groove worn away by the constant motion.

'Well ... Karl-Heinz Kornfeld for Saint-Preux.'

'Excellent! What about Monika Alt for Julie?'

'Possibly ...'

'Or Lola Templin-Tavel?'

We nattered on, enjoying this the fantasy stage of a film project when absolutely everything and anything is possible. On my way out I asked if he could advance me 500 dollars against my fee. Without the slightest hesitation he wrote out a cheque. I went straight to a post-office and cabled Sonia: MONEY ON WAY STOP COME TO BERLIN SOONEST LOVE JOHN JAMES.

I still find it hard to explain why Duric Lodokian should have seen *Julie* as a fit subject for Realismus. I now think Aram had more influence than he acknowledged. He denied this at the time, stating that it was a combination of Rousseau's name, the extreme length of the book and the comparative brevity of my script. His father had been very impressed that I could have constructed a story out of such intractable material.

'There are some fools,' Aram said, 'who actually think that a story is unimportant. But a good story will satisfy *anybody*. Beautiful lightings, sets, costumes, fancy camerawork, intensity of style—this is for a coterie.' I half agreed with him. But, anyway, whatever the reasons for the selection of *Julie* I knew that I was now on my way. The path ahead was finally clear. And, also, I find it pointless to speculate on reasons too long. We can only do so much to influence events. The chain of cause and effect can be illusory and misleading. Why did that bullet shatter Somerville-Start's teeth and not mine? What made Karl-Heinz send me the postcard? And so on. A little reflection and the so-called 'pattern' of your life soon appears as little more than an aggregate of hazard and chance. We think we recognise good and bad luck when it affects us, but in reality there is nothing *but* luck. From that standpoint the Realismus contract did not seem fortuitous at all.

I acquired a lawyer, papers were drawn up and signed and half my fee was deposited in a newly opened bank account. I was suddenly wealthy again. I started looking for furnished accommodation for me and my family and moved into an office in the Realismus studios near the huge gasworks in Grunewald.

I found a furnished apartment not far from 129b on Rudolf Platz a few blocks away. I was oddly reluctant to change districts, so too was Karl-Heinz. The night before I left (Sonia and the children were due to arrive in a week or so) we had a final celebratory dinner. I gave Frau Mittenklott extra money and she cooked a gargantuan meal that made even Georg gasp. We had green corn soup, carp marinated in vinegar with horseradish sauce, stewed mutton with paprika and a hot chocolate pudding. It was a pleasant occasion in that warm fuggy flat, surrounded by the buzz of insects, and we all drank far too much. I promised Georg that no film would ever employ so many insects as *Julie* would. It was a fine evening. And prophetic. For the first time I registered how much Karl-Heinz drank—topped off on this occasion by three tumblers of brandy at the end of the meal. And then we talked about casting Julie. I said that at the moment Monika Alt was the prime contender. Karl-Heinz screwed up his face.

'I can see she might be good,' he said, 'but before you give her the job you should see one other person.'

'Who?'

'Doon Bogan.'

Doon Bogan, Doon Bogan. I can hardly write the name even to this day.

VILLA LUXE 18 June 1972

The old bus from town deposits us at the nunnery on the outskirts of the village. There was no mail for me today—something of a wasted journey. I walk through the village towards the track that leads to my villa. As I pass the church the German girl, Ulrike, steps out from the shadow of one of its crude buttresses.

'Mr Todd?'

'What! ... Hello. Sorry, you gave me a shock.'

'Can I offer you a drink?'

'Well, I'm in a bit of a—'

'Please, there's something I want to ask you.'

We go to Ernesto's bar. Amazingly, he is actually there, I can hear him shouting angrily at his mother in the kitchen. We sit on the terrace and Feliz brings us two beers. It is that pleasant time of the evening. The heat has gone from the sun, pink bathers plod by from the public beach, soon the early bats will be swooping between the pine trees. I raise my cool glass to Ulrike. Without her spectacles and with the even tan she has now acquired she really is quite pretty.

'Mr Todd, did you ever make movies?'

For an instant I thought about denying it. 'How do you know? Yes, I did.'

'I knew it!' She smiled broadly.

She explained: her boyfriend was a lecturer at the university in Munich. He was very involved with film studies.

'When you told me your name I thought I had heard it before. I wrote to him about you. Yesterday I got his letter.' She looked closely at me. 'He said you were very famous.'

'Well, I was, I suppose. Forty years ago.'

She went on to tell me about her boyfriend's work for some film festival in Berlin. A retrospective: Silent Films of the German Cinema. She unfolded a piece of paper.

'He has some questions he would like me to ask you. May I?'

'Fire away.'

'Good. Question one. Do you know the whereabouts of a film star called Doon Bogan?'

9

Passions

I knew who Karl-Heinz was talking about. Doon Bogan was an American, a film star with a huge following in Germany due to the improbable success of an improbable film called *Mephistophela*, made by Alexander Mavrocordato in 1922, a version of Faust in which—yes—Mephistopheles was a woman. Doon wore black throughout the film. Her face was chalk white with shadowed eyes and pale lips and always framed by a tight black cowl. She was the perfect embodiment of fate, sex and death, and the film itself, in a somewhat hamfisted Expressionist style, was dark and garish and untidily powerful. Doon Bogan became famous, married her director Alexander Mavrocordato, divorced him a year later and stayed on in Berlin where she made other successful films with the likes of Pabst, Murnau and Kluge. I asked Aram what he thought of Karl-Heinz's idea. He was intrigued and suggested that we meet her and sound her out. He warned only that the budget for *Julie* would rise considerably if she consented to play the part.

We sent her the script and a meeting was arranged for lunch in the Adlon or Metropole Hotel. Perhaps it was the Bristol ... I am not too clear on the details of that day. I remember feeling the sensation of softness of the pile on the maroon carpet in the hotel bar through the thin soles of my new expensive shoes. Inside, the bar was sumptuously gloomy. Outside, it was a dull noon, swagged pewter clouds over the city threatening rain, a fretful gusty wind tugging at the overcoats and skirts of passengers leaving the Friedrich Strasse station opposite (it must have been the Metropole Hotel, after all). I was early, having visited a travel agent on some matter arising over Sonia's and the children's tickets and encountered a mindless bureaucratic problem. The ensuing fruitless argument with the clerk had irritated me and I went straight into the hotel bar for a drink. I ordered a large gin and water and calmed down somewhat.

A blonde woman in a jade green dress sitting in a leather armchair across the room was scrutinising me. Her hair was pale blonde—

ivory coloured—bobbed, with a fiercely edged fringe cut short across the middle of her forehead. Wide, thin but well-shaped red lips. A narrow small nose with a perceptible hook. Where had I seen her before ...? She stood up. She was tall, tall as me, even wearing flat ballet-dancer style pumps on long, slightly splayed feet. She walked over towards me with an odd elegance, big strides, like a champion girl swimmer, say, muscled but lean, with a phocine grace.

'Mr Todd?'

I said Yes. I had to look up, just a little—a queer sensation.

'I'm Doon Bogan.'

We shook hands. My suddenly moist palm. Her dry fingers, the knuckly pressure of a big ring, just for an instant.

'I'm sorry. I didn't ... I thought you had dark,' I cleared my throat, suddenly clotted with phlegm. 'Dark hair.'

'I do. But Julie's blonde, isn't she?'

Aram Lodokian arrived at that moment. Alex Mavrocordato, her 'adviser', minutes later.

It took only the space of the subsequent luncheon for me to fall heedlessly, helplessly in love with her. The physical appeal glowed strongly, incandescent, but my emotional commitment followed fast. I think it was her laugh. She laughed easily in a low voice, a crescendo. In some people that facility is merely inane. But with Doon I felt it betokened a true generosity of spirit. Her laughter was a gift to others, you felt good when you heard it—or so I reasoned in my new fantastic state.

We drank. We lunched. I was a husk. I felt weightless on the chair. I picked at my food, but I drank so much Aram had to order two more bottles of wine.

Later, when they had gone, Aram and I sat over coffee and cigars in the Metropole's smoking room. I had a stinging dehydrated throat and a yammering headache.

'My God, you drank like a fish,' Aram said.

'She's Julie,' I said huskily. My cigar tasted of vomit.

'We can't pay twenty-five. It's crazy. Twenty, maybe. Just.'

'I can't do it with anybody else.'

Aram looked at me quizzically. He wore a blue suit with a metallic aquamarine shimmer to it. He had expensive bad taste in clothes.

'Take five thousand off my fee,' I said. 'Pay me it back as a bonus if we finish on time.'

'Are you all right?'

'I've never been so sure of anything in my life.'

'It's not such a bad idea.' He smiled. 'It'll be a good incentive for you.'

Aram liked me, but he was no fool. He saved five thousand and got Doon Bogan. He told me he was impressed by my artistic integrity. I accepted the compliment.

Do you know that feeling? When you meet someone and you *know*? The sudden hollowing out of your torso, as if your lungs, heart, viscera have gone and the ribs seem to creak like barrel staves under too much pressure. Glimmerings, intimations of the way I felt now had occurred before with Faye Hobhouse, Dagmar—even Huguette. It is, I think, to do with fear: a fear of impotence—not sexual, but of lacking the power or ability to capture the object of your vital passion. A haunting dread that you will never have the chance again, that the moment has passed you by forever.

I sat on with Aram, emptied out, made void by that fear.

'Relax,' Aram said, and patted my knee. 'Oh yes, I forgot. This arrived for you at the studio.'

It was a telegram from Sonia: she and the children would be arriving in four days' time ...

I felt a sudden nausea. A weariness of spirit, an almost complete despair.

I saw Doon again before Sonia arrived. In the Realismus offices where we met to sign the contracts. Karl-Heinz was there, and Mavrocordato also, to my annoyance. Mavrocordato had premature grey hair and was a handsome large jowly man with big shoulders and a big soft chest. Apparently, Doon still lived with him off and on, and used him as a kind of unofficial manager. Aram wheeled his father out from his office. Champagne was opened and we toasted the success of *Julie*. That day I had chronic indigestion and the champagne's acid bubbles seethed the length of my oesophagus. It was as if some physical colour had to attend my encounters with Doon: I suffered from a broth of confused sensations and emotions: heartburn, real and metaphorical; a sour hatred for the ursine Mavrocordato; fleeting elation and pride over *Julie*. And a dour worry about the impending arrival of my wife and children.

Amongst the chatter and the toasts Duric Lodokian beckoned me over to his wheelchair and shook my hand. Then he pulled me down, my ear to his smokey mouth.

'Fantastical girl,' he coughed. 'My God I like to have her once before I die.'

'Me too,' I said, punching my fiery chest. 'Me too.'

'I love Doon Bogan. I love Doon Bogan,' was the ill-timed refrain
pulsating through my head as I watched Sonia, Mrs Shorrold and
my two children advance along the platform towards me. I had not
counted on my mother-in-law, but it was reasonable to suppose that
Sonia could not have coped with the journey alone. I tried to expunge
the image of Doon from my mind as I kissed my wife. Sonia looked
as smart as ever, if a little tired, wearing a neat oyster-grey suit.
Vincent shied away from me, terrified, as if I were a threatening
stranger. Mrs Shorrold held Hereford. He looked fat and jolly and
shook his fist vigorously at me, in welcome, I hoped. He must have
been three months old.

I supervised the luggage and organised two taxis to transport it
and us to Rudolf Platz. It was a sunny day and I pointed out this and
that feature as we drove through the city centre. Sonia, I could see,
was excited and impressed. Berlin looked fresh and cosmopolitan.
However, Sonia's expression fell rather as we recrossed the Spree and
drove down Stralauer Strasse towards the apartment. Fine buildings
gave way to drab residential streets. From time to time we got
glimpses of the river to our right, with its untidy clusters of barges,
docks piled high with bricks and sand, sacks and boxes of vegetables.

'Why are we living here?' Sonia asked plaintively as we disembarked
at Rudolf Platz.

'It's very cheap,' I said.

'But I thought you said we were well off?'

'We are.' I tried to keep the irritation out of my voice. 'We'll move,
don't worry. We'll move tomorrow.'

'No need for sarcasm, Johnny.'

I could appreciate that seen through her eyes the apartment left
something to be desired. I was no interior decorator but at least I
had asked Frau Mittenklott to look in twice a week to do some
cleaning and cooking whenever her duties at Georg Pfau's permitted.
The unsatisfactory nature of our reunion was compounded by my
inability to make love to Sonia that night. Guilt about Doon made
me detumescent.

'What's wrong?' Sonia asked kindly. She was always thoughtful.

'I don't know ... I think I must be tired. Too much work, the
film—' I babbled on, seeking refuge in a monologue, and soon enough
Sonia fell asleep.

And soon enough a routine and ostensible family life was established at Rudolf Platz, facilitated and made tolerable—at least for
Sonia—by there being some money in the bank. A nurse was
employed to look after the boys and Sonia and her mother shopped

strenuously for curtains, carpets, furniture and all the odds and ends of a proper home that I had been unable to provide. At weekends we went to the beach at Wannsee, for a picnic in the Grunewald or took a steamer down to Potsdam. There was a sizeable British film presence in Berlin in those days, owing to the considerable number of Anglo-German co-productions, and Sonia discovered that she knew some of the girls working in the studios. Even Vincent Shorrold came over for a month's holiday. Suddenly, my life acquired its old context, something which—after the months of bachelorhood and freedom—I found unsettling. I concentrated on my film.

July and August went by as we waited for Karl-Heinz to finish *Diary of Prostitute* (A. E. Groth was notoriously pedantic—no-one could rush him). In the meantime all the innumerable logistical problems of film-making presented themselves and were laboriously overcome. We found our perfect château near Arneberg overlooking the Elbe and then lost it when the owner asked for double his fee. We found another. A large model of the Parisian skyline was constructed (the view from Saint-Preux's garret) and was destroyed in a medium-sized fire at the Grunewald studios. Monika Alt (Claire) had an abortion followed swiftly by a nervous breakdown and was replaced by Lola Templin-Tavel. And so on.

I found myself becoming steadily more harassed over the day-to-day aggravations. Aram Lodokian could only devote a portion of his time to *Julie* as he was preoccupied with running Realismus (old Duric seemed to be growing iller). I suggested we hire a co-producer and Aram agreed. I wrote to Leo Druce in London and offered him the job. Leo sold his car-hire business and was in Berlin by late August. Thus the old team was reunited.

Leo was almost embarrassingly grateful. 'You keep pulling me out of the fire,' he said. I told him he was doing *me* a favour, and sure enough his presence proved invaluable. I soon found myself with time on my hands and on the pretext of doing some rewrites on the script I went to see Doon Bogan.

She lived in the west end, on Schlüter Strasse, off the Kurfürstendamm and not far from the Palmenhaus Café. Her apartment was small and cluttered, no real attempt had been made to prettify or decorate it. Evidence of her wealth and fame—a walnut baby grand supporting a troop of silver framed photographs, a long rectangular chrome and leather sofa—contrasted strongly with her own untidiness. A bundle of half a dozen dresses was laid over the back of an armchair. In the hall was a large stack of what looked absurdly like political broadsheets.

She showed me into the sitting room. She had on a cobalt cardigan over a shirt and tie. The hem was coming down at the back of her crepe skirt. She wore—as I came to learn she always did—her leather dancing pumps. Doon was not an unconfident woman, but she was curiously self-conscious about her height. My abiding image of her entering a room is the relief with which she flung herself into chairs, as if she had been walking for hours. When compelled to stand, at a reception or a cocktail party, say, she always made straight for a pillar or wall to lean against. It was not a case of *politesse*, aware of shorter men; she did the same with Mavrocordato who was taller than her.

Now she sat promptly on the leather sofa and lit a cigarette. I made the usual insincere compliments about her flat. Above the fireplace was a blurry photograph of a strong-faced, dark-haired woman with an old-fashioned hairstyle.

'Your mother?' I asked.

'Rosa Luxemburg.'

'Rosa who?'

'My God.' She seemed surprised. 'Haven't you heard of her?'

'No. Who is she?'

'Those Free Corps bastards murdered her. 1919.'

'Oh ... Politics.' I remembered there had been an abortive communist revolution then. I took a cigarette from the inlaid box on the table.

'Can I borrow a light?'

'What do you mean "Oh ... Politics"? Aren't you interested in politics?'

'I should say not.' I pointed my lit cigarette at her. 'Politics is self-interest disguised by cant.' This was something Karl-Heinz had said once. I thought it had a good ring to it.

'Surely you don't mean that.' Her voice was flat and serious, her American accent strong all of a sudden. I sensed I was on the brink of something irrevocable.

'Of course I don't.' I tried a smile. 'Teasing. I tend to tease people—nerves.'

She was frowning at me, sceptically.

'I admit I'm a cynic,' I went on, more desperate than I hope I looked. 'But I do make exceptions.' I nodded at the photograph. 'The likes of Rosa, for one.'

I held my breath. She relaxed.

'Alex put you up to this. He said you'd get a rise out of me, right?'

'Alex who?'

'Mavrocordato. He can't stand that I'm a communist. The jerk.'

'No, honestly, it was me. My stupid idea of a joke.' I waved my hands about. I had to sit down, my entire left leg was trembling, for some reason. What the hell had got into me? Why had nobody warned me? The apartment was full of books, they now looked weighty, earnest, leftist . . .

I changed the subject and we talked about the script and the part of Julie. She said in all seriousness that she was keen on the role because she was interested in the concept of virtue and was tired of playing 'whores and bitches.' We talked on. She was bright and had thought hard about the film. The afternoon wore on and the apartment grew dim. Eventually she got up and switched on the light.

'Do you want a drink, John?' It was the first time she had mentioned my name. I felt the familiar clubbing start up in my chest.

'Do you like to be called John or James?'

'Whatever you like.'

'What about James. Jamie?'

'*Hrrrrm.* Hah! . . . mng. Sorry. Yes, fine.'

'Right, Jamie, what about that drink?'

'Gin and water. Please.'

'Good God.'

(Why did I drink that drink then? Pure affectation, but it was strong.) She went into another room to get it. Long strides, skirt swirling about her calves. The susurration of her leather pumps on the parquet flooring. I could see at the crown of her head a tiny rosette of dark hair, the blonde dye growing out. I knew suddenly why she was such a big star in Europe: she was different from European women, or at least was perceived to be so. She came from the New World and was not hide-bound or impressed by the Old. There was nothing specific about this, nothing you could put your finger on, but that sense of an entrancing alternative seemed to coil about her like ectoplasm.

She handed me the glass. I gulped at the drink. The single light shone orange on her ivory hair. Her small hooked nose cast a dark shadow across her face.

'You sure Alex didn't put you up to that Rosa jape?'

'Positive. I haven't seen him since the contracts were signed.'

'It'd be just like him . . .'

Pause.

'Are you and he . . . ? Not that it's any of my business. But I—'

It was my second mistake. She looked shrewdly at me. For the first time—and I believe this—she sensed the hot moist tentacles of my desire sneaking about her, dabbing at her skirt.

'Why? What's it to you?'

'Nothing ... or rather, energetic curiosity.'

She took this in.

'We blow hot and cold, Alex and me ... Alex and I? That's all.'

I left shortly after that. I felt a clawing ache in my chest. I walked up the Kurfürstendamm past the bright shops and gleaming cafés, the neon cinemas, the elegant overdecorated terraces of houses. The ache would not go away. It came, I know, from a mixture of intense longing and the saddened conviction that my life, or, rather, most of the things that pertained to me, were going to be altered, bruised or destroyed because of that very longing.

I went into a café, ordered a drink, then went into the WC and masturbated into my handkerchief. It had the desired effect of dispersing those querulous emotions and querulous fears. Now I felt merely depressed and seedy. I hailed a taxi and went home to my wife and family.

I strove intermittently and fairly valiantly to forget Doon. Or, more to the point as I would soon be seeing her every day I strove to direct the remorseless impulse of my emotions elsewhere. I was not successful. It is an insidious force that operates on you when you love and lust after someone impotently. It not only trammels up you, the agent, it bears down also on those innocent of its workings. Such as Sonia. All the real attraction I used to feel for her slowly evaporated, like a puddle in hot sun. Her neatness, her straight parting, her haunchy bottom-heaviness became irritants and flaws.

I remember one day in August we went swimming, to the huge beach at Wannsee. Me, Sonia, Vincent and Noreen Shorrold, Vincent junior and baby Hereford. The beach was full of pink and brown Berliners. I sat in my swimming costume and towelling robe steadily drinking cold hock from a bakelite cup. My son Vincent (he was dark like me, but looked Shorrold through and through) tottered between his grandparents. Sonia knelt over Hereford, a safety pin in her mouth, busying herself with some mopping up and cleansing operation (I have never known such a child for pissing and shitting himself: he had a vandal's urge to soil clean things, did Hereford). I felt, and almost welcomed, such was the state of my mind, the harbingers of a headache creeping up on me. Feebly, I tried to nestle into some warm congratulatory mood of self-satisfaction. Here was my happy family, I told myself; here was my wife, my sons. I was comparatively rich, with the prospect of further riches eminently realisable. And, as an artist, I was on the point of making my first real moving picture.

Why then did I feel the air around me electric with my own annoyance, crackling with static irritation? Why, when Hereford arched his back and squirmed his head round to look at me, did I not chuck the little fellow under his treble chin or rub his fat tum with a proud parental hand? Because ... Because I was thinking of Doon and wondering if she was spending the day with that bastard Mavrocordato. Why, that could be them in that white speedboat buzzing by, cutting across the lake heading for some rented birch-embowered villa on the far side of the Havel ... A girl swam strongly out to an anchored wooden raft and hauled herself up onto it in a fluent fluid motion. The cerise wool of her damp swimsuit clung to her breasts and belly. I tried to imagine Doon in a swimsuit. And even when the girl removed her rubber swimming cap and shook out her dark hair I thought of Doon, who cut her long dark hair and dyed it blonde for *Julie*. For me.

A tap on my forearm. Little Vince (as his grandparents called him, to my horror) offering me a tongue and cress sandwich to the loud applause of the other adults. His eyes were wide with alarm. Why did the boy fear me? Cruelly, I said no, thank you. He burst into tears, dropped the sandwich in the sand and fled to his mother's wide lap.

'Johnny, *really*.'

'I wasn't hungry.'

'Oh, but still ...'

'God almighty! I can't stuff myself just for his sake!'

I stood up and angrily threw off my robe. I strode down to the water and dived in. Cool shock, a silent glide, a sudden calm. I hated myself.

*   *   *

I will not bore you with the actual details of the filming of *Julie*. Suffice to say I knew from very early on it was going well. Karl-Heinz was superb. We whitened his face and hollowed his cheeks and eye-sockets to enhance his wracked, soul-tormented personality. The particular frisson in the film was the two types of delicious anticipation that operated in it. The first was before Julie and Saint-Preux's love was consummated. Then, second, there was more suspense over whether their sense of honour would allow their virtue to survive. It was given an added twist by Doon's loveliness and irresistible erotic allure. Her manner on screen was one of innocent carnal licence, which, in the second half when she was trying to be faithful to Wolmar, toyed with one's sense of frustration in the most agonising way. The two lovers desperately wanted each other. All that was physically keeping them apart were the abstract airy strictures of morality. Once old Baron Wolmar left them they had everything—place, occasion, inclination—but some higher code kept them at arm's length.

There was one scene towards the end of the film which, when we saw the rushes, had us all on the edge of our seats baying obscene encouragement at Karl-Heinz.

It is late one evening. An albescent moon shines on Baron Wolmar's château. On the terrace Saint-Preux wrestles with his conscience as he smokes a cigarette (remember, it has all been updated). Moths flutter round the lights (thank you, Georg). Then, further up the long terrace, Julie steps out through the French windows of her boudoir. She is wearing a luxuriant flimsy negligée which billows occasionally in the night breezes. She advances towards Saint-Preux, their eyes fast upon one another. She stops eighteen inches from him. Caption: '*I love this time of the evening. May I have a cigarette?*' With one movement Saint-Preux slides his silver cigarette case from his pocket. Close-up of Julie's fingers as she selects one—her lacquered nails on the slim white cylinder. Saint-Preux—cigarette in mouth—goes for his lighter in another pocket, but a slight hesitation on Julie's part halts him. She puts the cigarette in her mouth (close-up: those wide red lips, that white paper). She sways towards him. Tip of cigarette meets tip of cigarette. Ignition, burn, smoke wreaths. They move apart, gazing at each other. They draw on their cigarettes, exhale. Smoke, backlit by the moon, coils and swoops thickly about them ...

This scene has been much copied, at times blatantly, at times indirectly. It was the first use in a film, I believe, of the cigarette as an erotic symbol. The scene was mightily effective and so powerful that it was almost cut by the censor. Aram reported this dull bureaucrat's comments to me: 'He says they are fornicating on screen.' Our dumb literalness—'But they're only smoking. They're not even touching!'—won the day. Not a frame was removed.

Naturally, Doon was a triumph in the film also. Not that she required any elevation from the stellar heights she already occupied. Her last day of filming occurred two weeks before the end of the shoot. It was her death-bed scene where she declares she has been in love with Saint-Preux all along. Our final two weeks were to be occupied with Saint-Preux in Paris gamely resisting its temptations, sustained by Julie's faith.

I had champagne and flowers sent to Doon's dressing room. Aram Lodokian had arranged a formal farewell party for later that evening.

I felt calm. We had worked well together and there had been no disagreements. She could see I knew what I was doing (even if you do not know what you are doing the crucial talent required by a director, as far as actors are concerned, is to give the unchallengeable impression that you do) and, importantly, there had been no hint of intimacy between us. Certainly not from her and I had been prudent not to let my own desires be revealed again. It seemed to me that I was finally exerting some control over myself. Even when Mavrocordato visited the set a few times. Although, through my green eyes, it looked as if they were getting on uncommonly well for a divorced couple. So why did I go to her room alone? I wanted to say goodbye and I wanted, personally and privately, to set a seal on our relationship. Friendship with a tantalising hint of what-might-have-been. Or so I told myself.

Doon had not changed from her death-bed nightdress, a strappy satin thing with a low back. She had a long housecoat tied loosely over it. In an ante-room her dresser was ironing. Doon poured me a glass of champagne and we idly exchanged compliments about the film.

'Did you see Alex on your way in?'

'Alex who?' I always did this.

'God, Jamie! Mavrocordato. He's meant to be picking me up.'

'No. No sign.'

The dresser—a small, cross-looking woman—came out of the side room holding a short black jacket with diamante buttons.

'Fixed it?' Doon asked.

'You better try it on.'

Doon slipped off the housecoat and put the jacket on.

'It's fine. Thanks, Dora, you can go.'

Dora left. Doon checked the fit of the jacket, flexing, reaching, stretching, then she took it off and flung it over the arm of her chair. A wayward sleeve knocked her near-empty glass to the ground, shattering it.

'Shit!' she said. She knelt down to pick up the pieces.

Seeing Doon's slim tall body one might have thought her small-breasted. Not so. She had wide flat breasts, small-nippled, with almost no sag to them. A gentle convexity covering a largish area, like the lid of a soup tureen. I saw them now as she knelt on the ground before me, the drooping front of her nightdress affording me an unobstructed view.

My tongue seemed to swell to block my throat as I slipped off my chair to kneel before her, my fingers blindly searching for shards and fragments. The erotic archaeologist ... I caught a gust of her perfume, a kind of lavender. She looked up. My eyes snapped up just in time.

'Hey, don't bother, Dora'll get it in the—'

I kissed her with undue violence, crushing my nose painfully on her cheek, simultaneously clutching her shoulders and hauling us both to our feet. I pressed my taut bulging groin against her thigh and pushed her back and down onto the sofa. She flung her head back.

'I love you, Doon,' I said. 'I love—*MNEEAAGHHH!*'

The pain was infernal, not of this world. The hard apex of her knee mashed my testicles against the unyielding base of my pelvis. I felt as if I had been split from the perineum up to the top of my skull by an ice axe, or impaled, sitting, on a giant freezing horn. (Gentlemen, you surely know what I am talking about. Ladies, take my word for it, there is no more fiendish agony.) Everything went blue, black, purple, orange, white. I opened my eyes. An ultrasonic scream seemed to reverberate around the room as if it were a trapped demented presence. I was on the floor—balled up, well and truly, you might say—glass splinters sparkled before my eyes. My hands cupped the jangling fragments of my ruined groin.

I twisted my head around. Doon stood by the door, fully dressed (how much time had elapsed, for God's sake?). Through the scream in my head I seemed to hear her say calmly,

'I never want to see you again, asswipe.'

I felt the vomit—a prancing bolus—in my throat. I began to crawl to the bathroom. There was a knock on the door behind me, then Mavrocordato's voice saying, 'What is it?' Doon said, 'Nothing', and the door closed. I am sure I heard laughter.

I never made it to the toilet bowl. I vomited over the linoleum—maroon fleur-de-lys in a pretty pattern—a yard short. I left it for Dora to clean up in the morning.

*   *   *

Julie was an enormous hit. An international success. Realismus films made over a million dollars in Germany, France, Britain and America. Doon Bogan became for a year or two the most glamorous and celebrated actress in Europe. Karl-Heinz Kornfeld was acclaimed as the 'quintessentially *hoch-moderne* leading man'. But more of that later. My own life entered a strange troubled phase just as my personal fortunes were at their zenith.

I was, I think, actually driven a little insane by my 'falling out' with Doon—if that is not too absurd a euphemism. Even after such a brutal, unequivocal rejection I could not expunge or ignore my feelings for her. What can you do in such circumstances? If you are obsessed, you are obsessed. She telephoned me two days after the incident.

'Are you all right?'

'What? Yes. A slight limp, but otherwise . . . look, Doon, I—'

'I shouldn't have hit you so hard. But, I was mad. And not just at you. I was kind of upset that day.'

'God, I'm so sorry. Terribly sorry. I should never—'

'You're a fool John James Todd. A great big, grade 'A', ignorant fool.'

She hung up. I had no idea what she meant. Or rather, I had one idea but it seemed to me she was implying something else . . . In the event I grew none the wiser as I had to force my attention round to completing the film, which we did with little fuss and on time. Aram Lodokian paid me my 5,000 dollar bonus without demur. The film opened in the Kino-Palast on the Kurfürstendamm with a full symphony orchestra providing musical accompaniment on the 16th February 1926 and the rest is history.

We moved from Rudolf Platz, west, to a new villa in Charlottenburg. The area was being developed: on every corner new houses were being built and the streets were planted with frail lime tree saplings guarded by tight palisades of iron spikes. Mrs Shorrold left us and Sonia acquired an English nurse (Lily Maidbow, a plain efficient almost speechless girl) to look after the boys. Our house was fresh-smelling—of wax from the wooden floor, of paint, of leather and fabrics—it had a wide garden planted with birch and larch, and was surrounded by a white wicker fence. I never liked it. I felt like one of the lime tree saplings. I did not need such sturdy penning in. These were the accoutrements of prosperous middle age, of bourgeois plenitude. I found the place oppressive and minatory—but, conceivably, that would have been true of any home I lived in then. I was not of a mind to settle down, eat big dinners at my dining-room table, dandle my babes on my knee. Doon had knocked me off kilter, I was askew, like that first time I went over the top, drunk. Everything about Sonia was stable, placid and fixed. I was living in a different geometry.

I spent long hours over the autumn and winter of 1925 with Leo Druce editing *Julie*, writing and rewriting the captions. Sonia made no complaint about my protracted absence from the house. She kept herself busy and enjoyed the newfound Todd prosperity more than I did. Leo, I think, suspected that something was wrong but with his ineffable tact did not ask me anything about it. He was settling down rapidly in Berlin and was enjoying a diverting love affair with Lola Templin-Tavel. When I had had enough of work and could not bear the thought of going home I used to meet Karl-Heinz in a bar in Uhland Strasse, just off the Kurfürstendamm. There was nothing louche or depraved about this place although those were qualities its neighbourhood rivals strove earnestly to reproduce. Our bar, the Dix, consisted of two rooms: one, smaller, with a zinc-topped counter and a few tables and chairs; and the other, larger, with two billiard tables. Its very plainness ensured it was never over-busy. Karl-Heinz and I would sit and drink in the small room and from time to time play a game of billiards. I grew to love that place, warm and blurry with cigarsmoke, the air filled with the noise of subdued conversation, the rustle of newspapers (hung from the wall on sticks) and the solid reassuring click of the ivory billiard balls. It was anonymous, populated by transients. The owner and his large ginger-haired wife made no attempt to cutivate regulars. It suited me at that difficult time.

I told Karl-Heinz everything about Doon and he thoughtfully went through the motions of sympathising with me. He was not surprised, he said. He had been waiting for something to turn my life upside down. How come? I asked him, but he would not expand. Later he told me he could never understand why I had married Sonia. When I told him the honest reason—for sex—he was even more baffled. I think he regarded me—as a representative heterosexual— as being something of a chronic naïf when it came to sexual matters.

But he listened patiently, a true friend, to my protracted moans. I am ashamed to reflect now on these one-sided encounters. I never asked him about himself, never wondered how he did when I finally left him, or when he left me. I was up to my neck in a mire of my own selfishness. I thought of my drowning Ulsterman (I thought a lot about the war, then) as he sank in the mud of the Salient: 'I'm going doyne!' . . . No wonder. I could not escape Doon. My day was spent watching her images shimmer by me on the editing machines. Karl-Heinz knew that all I required was a listener and he provided it, selflessly. At least we could break off and play billiards (he was a terrible player, incapable of calculating the simplest angles. I always won.)

It was early in the new year. The film was finished and we were waiting for its release when his patience finally broke. As usual we were sitting in the bar Dix. Karl-Heinz was drinking beer with a schnapps chaser. I was drinking Moselle. I was a little drunk, typically brimful of self-pity, rhapsodising about Doon's beauty and how I longed for her. I paused. To my intense surprise Karl-Heinz took both my hands in his and stared fixedly at me. I looked into his dark eyes, hooded by his sharp circumflex brows. He squeezed my hands.

'Johnny,' he said. 'I tell you something very simple.' He smiled faintly, a suggestion of mischief. 'Boys are better than girls.'

'Look, Karl-Heinz, no.' I smiled apologetically back. 'I'm just not—you know—inclined that way.'

'But you never tried properly. I can show you. It's fun.'

'No, really—'

'But I like you, Johnny, I do.'

'No, really. I know you do. I like you too.' I was moved.

He let go of my hands.

'It's Doon,' I said. 'She's the only one ... I'm obsessed. I'm obsessed with her.'

'So. All right.' He sounded impatient. 'There's only one thing to do with such an obsession. You got to get another one.'

He was right. After he had gone I thought about what he had said. I would never forget Doon (in fact I had not seen her for months) but surely, I reasoned, there was room in my life for something more than this destructive unrequited longing? I had to face up to the facts. My life could not simply stand still with this rejection.

The lights were on in the house when I parked our new car—a Packard, Sonia's choice. Sonia was awake, in bed. Her face was scrubbed clean and her hair tucked behind her ears. She had put on some weight recently and the roundness of her face had increased, accentuating her small pointy chin. I thought she looked pretty. It was a good sign. Karl-Heinz may not have provided me with an answer but he seemed to have given me a jolt with his proposition—knocked the gramophone needle out of its groove. I switched off the light and snuggled up to Sonia, sliding a hand inside her nightdress to cup a girlish breast ... I am sure our third child was conceived that night.

Of course I had another obsession, but it was lying dormant, temporarily overshadowed by the Doon crisis. Myself. My development as an artist. My dreams, my ambitions. The next day I literally dusted them off.

In my office at Realismus's Grunewald studios I kept an old trunk containing certain precious possessions, such as my reels of *Aftermath of Battle*, my photo albums, my diaries (now temporarily abandoned), Hamish's letters and suchlike. It was superstitious of me, I suppose, but I did not want them in the house with me. Snow had fallen in the night and from my window I could see the three vast gasometers of the *Berliner Gas-Anstalt* capped with white, steel cakes with generous icing.

Idly, almost absentmindedly, I opened the trunk and contemplated these artefacts of my past, like a bored shaman looking at a scattered pile of bones, half-heartedly trying to devise the way ahead. These relics, precious totems of my youthful dreams ... I picked up a frayed bundle of paper tied with string. Pages from a book. I read:

'I am now entering on a task which is without precedent and which when achieved will have no imitator ...'

The fit passed in seconds. It *was* a fit. It is the only time I have ever experienced it so physically. Afflatus. Inspiration. The muse descending—call it what you will. It was a pentecostal confirmation of what I had to do. My task was clear to me now. I was going to make the greatest moving picture the world had ever seen. It would be unprecedented and have no imitator. I was going to make a film of Jean-Jacques Rousseau's *The Confessions*.

VILLA LUXE 20 June 1972

I am sitting at my 'lookout' with my binoculars trying to discern what's going on at the public beach. A police car has arrived and someone has been arrested, I think, but it is really just beyond my range. Perhaps a nudist? My hand shake is too pronounced. I consider buying a tripod.

Emilia shouts from the house that I have a visitor. I wander over. It's Ulrike. She wants permission to go down to my beach. I say, of course.

We stand on the pool terrace, in shade, looking at the hot empty pool.

'It's a shame about your pool.'

'It's that fig tree. Over there. The roots, they're pushing through the concrete searching for water. See the cracks?'

'From so far away, with such force. It's incredible.'

'Apparently they can get through a foot of concrete. It's always happening—cisterns, septic tanks.'

'Ah. Nature.' She said it with no cynicism. A sense of awe, rather.

I gestured at her bag.

'Off for specimens? I saw you the other day, in your boat.' I felt and attempted to ignore the beginnings of a blush. 'What are you working on?' I said quickly.

'Certain kinds of crab.'

'Really?' What more could one say about crabs? 'Plenty of crabs on those rocks.'

She frowned as if she could sense my indifference.

'I wrote a small thesis on the Fiddler crab. You know, the one with one oversized claw.' She paused. 'Do you know that before and after the male Fiddler crab mates he soothes the female by stroking her with his claw, very gently.'

'No. I—'

'And then—this is amazing—they make love face to face.'

'Really?'

'You see? I said "make love" as if they were humans. Apart from us they are the only animals to do this. Face to face, like so.' She held up her hands analogously. 'Just us and the Fiddler crab. Why should that be?'

'I don't know.'

A breeze shook the tree we were standing beneath. The dappled light spots shifted on her face and the air-blue towelling jerkin she wore. We were two feet apart.

'Extraordinary,' I said.

She picked up her bag.

'My boyfriend said they are showing your film—*Julie*. Maybe when we go back I can see it. He says it's very good.'

'It is. But he should see my—' I stopped just in time. 'I was very pleased with it. I'm delighted it's being shown. Doon ... Doon Bogan is marvellous.'

10

Comrades

I waited, wisely, prudently, until well after *Julie* was released before going to the Lodokians with my new plan. Aram had been pestering me for weeks to sign a new contract with Realismus but I had delayed, calculating that the audacity of my proposal would be easier to take if *Julie* was steadily earning money. So I was annoyingly evasive on the matter of what we should do next whenever Duric and Aram brought it up.

I was busy enough, anyway, with the success of *Julie*, attending gala premières in Munich, Hamburg and Frankfurt, consenting to innumerable press conferences and interviews. Long profiles appeared in *Ufa-Magazin*, *Film-Photos*, *Illustrierter Film-Courier* and *Kino*. It was the most successful and talked-about film in all Berlin until the première of *Potemkin* at the end of April. Aram sent Karl-Heinz and Doon on an international promotional tour, to Britain, France and Italy, but they both surprisingly refused to go with the film to the USA—Doon, I believe, out of some perverse sense that she was in exile, and Karl-Heinz for the odd but simple reason that—he claimed—it was not his sort of country.

For my part the success of *Julie* was highly gratifying. I felt calm, with a new deep self-assurance, which explains why in the many newspaper and magazine articles that appeared I was several times described as 'impassive' or 'brooding'. I *was* brooding—on what to do next—and was moving forward with steady determination. Karl-Heinz's advice had been astute: my new obsession had saved me. I had not forgotten Doon (we met from time to time at receptions, but there were always dozens of people there. Her attitude towards me is best described as 'pleasant') but I found her easier to cope with.

In June profits from *Julie* were such that Realismus paid me a bonus of 75,000 dollars, a vast sum in those days. Aram offered me another 50,000 to direct two films for the studio: *Frederick the Great* with Karl-Heinz and *Joan of Arc* with Doon. I asked for time to think it over.

I read and re-read the *Confessions* and my plans for it altered daily. The scale and grandeur of my project burgeoned in my mind. After blocking out a preliminary outline I calculated that the film would last eight or nine hours. For a week I was in despair, but then suddenly realised that its great length could in fact be its greatest asset. I would make not one but *three* three-hour films of the books— a truly epic moving picture, and fit monument to the man who inspired it.

In March Sonia announced that she was pregnant again and at the same time, though unconnected with this news, I rented for my own use a small wooden villa in the country, about an hour from Berlin in the woods of the Jungfernheide. There I spent weekdays alone, working secretly on the first draft of the *Confessions*, returning home at weekends. To my vague surprise on a Friday as I motored back to Charlottenburg I found myself actually looking forward to rejoining my family. Vincent had lost his terror of me and Hereford proved to be an engaging affectionate baby. I spent many hours teaching him to walk, during which he took the most appalling tumbles, crashing into tables, falling down steps, bouncing off walls. He would hit the ground—slap!—and looked stunned for a moment as if deciding what was the correct response to this misfortune. All one had to do was laugh ostentatiously—'Ha-ha-ha, Hereford, ho-ho-ho!'—and he would immediately join in, no matter how bruised or winded he was. He was a cute little fellow, still shitting himself at every opportunity.

I made one mistake that summer which was to have bitter consequences later. One Wednesday in June I drove into the city to attend Leo Druce's wedding. He was marrying Lola Templin-Tavel. The ceremony took place in the pretty English church (St George's) in the gardens of Schloss Montbijou, with a reception afterwards at the Palast Hotel. After the service Sonia felt ill and left me to go on to the reception myself. There was an impressive turn out at the Palast and I remember asking myself how Leo Druce, tyro co-producer, had managed to invite so many luminaries to his wedding—Pola Negri was there, Emil Jannings, Walter Rutman, Tilly de Garmo, Michael Bohnen, the baritone, Conrad Veidt, Lil Dagover and many more. It was a spontaneous reflection, I bore no ill-will to Leo, but I remember commenting on it—prophetically—and ironically complimenting him on his ability to get on in the world. He said, with typical modesty, that they had only come because of Lola. I might have added that that was precisely my point, but I refrained.

It was a hot day and not enough of the Palast's windows opened to provide any kind of breeze. I felt stifled in my morning suit and stiff collar and drank rather too much chilled fruit cup to compensate. I began to enjoy myself and the steady stream of compliments I received as a result of *Julie*'s success. That day I felt a kind of power emanating from me which was further generated by the secret that I owned.

I was talking to Leo when Aram approached. He was wearing a cornyellow-gold brocade waistcoat with matching spats. On anyone else they would have looked absurdly comical but somehow Aram could carry off the crassest vulgarity. We congratulated Leo all over again on his good fortune (a touch insincerely: Lola's famed vivacity had a distinct neurasthenic note to it) and congratulated ourselves on the news of *Julie*'s sale to RKO.

'I'm sailing to New York next week,' Aram said. 'They've gone mad for *Julie*. They want every new Realismus film.' He paused meaningfully. 'They're throwing money at me for *Frederick the Great*.'

'I'm busy,' I said.

'What are you doing in that cottage, for God's sake?'

'I'll tell you soon. Very soon.'

'But when are you going to make *Frederick*? We've got to start this summer.'

'I'll tell you what,' I said. 'Let Leo do it.'

They both looked at me in open amazement.

'You can do it, Leo,' I said. 'Of course you can.'

'But it's your film—earmarked—Karl-Heinz and—'

'It's my wedding present to you.' I put my arms around them both. I am not normally given to these sorts of gestures but I was a little drunk. 'Go on, Aram. Give it to Leo. He can do it.'

Aram looked shrewd: one eye closed slightly, bottom lip held between his teeth.

'Let's talk when you get back from the honeymoon.'

'Listen, John, are you sure you—?'

I gave him another impulsive hug. 'Course I am. Anyway, I've got something else on.'

There were more surprises to come. I took my punch glass to be refilled and as this was being done I heard myself greeted and looked round to see a small, perfectly bald young man with an idiot grin of pleasure on his face.

'Almyr Nelson,' he said. '"Baby". Remember?'

'Of course. How are you, Baby?'

He smoothed his imaginary hair on his gleaming pink pate. 'Bit thin on top, otherwise fine.' He smiled again. 'Well, you're certainly doing all right for yourself . . . Listen, Harold's here. Come over and meet him.'

'Delighted.'

Faithfull, fatter than ever, was standing too close to someone I knew, Monika Alt, who was fanning herself vigorously with a menu. She greeted me as if I was an old friend, though we were no more than acquaintances.

'Thank God,' she whispered as she kissed me. 'Terrible halitosis.'

'Look who I've dug up, Harry,' Nelson said, drawing me forward. 'Old Todd, the intrepid balloonist. Can you credit it?'

Faithfull managed a weak smile.

'Todd . . . Congratulations.' His face was moist with sweat. I smelt his rotting teeth as he spoke.

I accepted his good wishes. 'What are you doing over here?' I asked.

'Just started a film.'

'Called *The Tip-Top Twins go Sailing*,' Baby Nelson said cheerfully. 'Part of a series.'

'Sounds like fun,' I said. 'By the way, Faithfull, I should do something with your teeth. Your breath smells repulsive.'

I took Monika's arm and we turned away and strode off through the crowd, Monika's shoulders heaving with shocked silent laughter. It was childish of me, I know, but these opportunities are rare in life and must not be ignored. Cherish them, savour them, they provide some comfort in the dog days.

Monika and I had another drink and I told her about my past encounters with Harold Faithfull. We laughed some more. Monika Alt was in her mid-thirties, I think, maybe ten years older than me. She was a thin blonde sinewy woman who had been a celebrated theatrical actress but whose career had never fully restarted after the hiatus caused by the war. She had been married three or four times and drank rather too much. As we talked she leant against me occasionally, a breast flattening against my upper arm. It could have been accidental, but it is my opinion that a woman knows exactly when her breasts come into contact with anyone or anything, animate or inanimate. The warmth, the alcohol, my crude besting of Faithfull, and the new sense of confidence that irradiated me made me find her suddenly attractive. I felt a prickling and easing in my groin. However, I doubt very much if I would have gone to bed with her that afternoon if I had not just at that moment seen Doon and Mavrocordato across the room;

'Ouf! It's so hot in here,' Monika said, blowing discreetly down the front of her dress. 'Oh, look. There's your star.'

'Why don't we get out of here?' I said. 'Come and have a picnic at my villa.'

*   *   *

Monika visited me at my villa once or twice a week during the rest of that summer. We would make love and have lunch. After lunch she liked to sunbathe naked in the back garden, a policy I encouraged as this was the view overlooked by my study window. She returned to Berlin in the afternoon as the air cooled. That was as much as we ever did. Her thin hot oily brown body with small oddly deflated-looking breasts are inescapably associated with the genesis of my *Confessions* films. I grew to like her and I think she liked me, though we never spoke of our feelings. Perhaps that was why she came back. She had half a dozen scars, old and new, on her belly. I counted an appendectomy and a Caesarean section but I could not work out what the others were. I asked her how she got them.

'Too many men, darling,' she said. 'Too many men.'

One day Aram came round unexpectedly while she was there. He had returned from the USA and *Frederick the Great* was about to start. He did not seem particularly surprised to see Monika. We stood at my study window looking at her spread body, glossy with sun-oil.

'I've nothing against Monika,' he said thoughtfully. 'But for a man in your position I think it's a big mistake to get involved with an actress.'

'I'm not involved with her,' I said. 'Don't worry.'

I looked at him. He was wearing a powder blue seersucker suit—bought in America, I assumed—a red shirt and a big flat canvas golfing cap. He looked ridiculous.

'Anyway,' I said. 'What are you doing here? You know this is my secret refuge.'

'My father's dying. He wants to see you.'

The heat, that summer of '26 in Berlin, was immense. It slammed down out of a hazy sky the colour of Aram's suit, heavy as glass. One was glad of the city's clean wide streets then. At least in the broad avenues and boulevards the air could stir. It must have been some kind of public holiday that afternoon as I motored back with Aram, because the pavements seemed strangely deserted and the big shops in Leipziger Strasse were closed and dark. I remember hearing the sounds of half a dozen bands as we drove through the Tiergarten. I never learned what was going on.

I was cast down by Aram's news of his father. I had grown fond of old Duric, who had forgiven me my defection from the Realismus style once the money from *Julie* started to flow. He said he planned to use the funds to make a series of films about vermin in our cities. 'You mean child molesters, perverts, that sort of thing?' I asked. 'No, no!' he shouted. 'Rats and fleas! Rats and fleas!' I had only known him ill and foolishly had come to think of his gasps and wheezes, his snail's pace and omnipresent oxygen cylinder, as being as much part of him as his liver spots and grey hair. Suddenly features revealed themselves as afflictions, and that shocked and subdued me.

The Lodokians, father and son, lived in a thin grand house on Kronen Strasse. Inside it was dark, blinds and curtains drawn, and one was forcibly reminded of the summer heat once more. A butler let us in and a male nurse led us upstairs.

Duric Lodokian was sitting up—rather, lying up—on a soft ramp of pillows, his oxygen mask in one hand and a Russian cigarette in the other. He talked in breathless bursts of a few seconds, pausing to guzzle oxygen from the mask, or to drag weakly on his cigarette. His brown skin was damp and a greyish mud colour. His liver spots were more noticeable. He was the colour of a certain type of speckled egg (some kind of gull or game bird, I forget which now, but they used to be fashionable hors d'œuvres at parties in the Thirties. I could never touch them—they reminded me of Duric, dying.)

Aram and I sat down on either side of him. The blanket around the ashtray was covered in ash. He was too frail to tap his cigarettes accurately. After the usual bland enquiries I said carefully.

'Are you sure you should be smoking those, Duric?'

'Don't be idiot. Never did me any harm. Why should I stop now?'

'I agree, I agree. Don't deny yourself. May I have one?'

I lit one. Aram did too. We both smoked while Duric topped up on oxygen.

'Listen,' he said eventually. 'Come here.'

I leant further forward.

'What's this film you want to make? Why are you being so difficult?'

I glanced at Aram. He looked faintly surprised. I decided to tell him.

'I want to make a film of a book called *The Confessions*.'

'Who by?'

'Rousseau.'

'Rousseau again? That's *good*, good. I like it. Don't you Aram?'

'He won't tell me about it.'

They exchanged a few words of fast Armenian.

'Are you ready to start?' Duric asked.

'I'm working on the script.' I caught Aram's eye. 'It's, ah, very long.'

'I don't care. Realismus must do it.' He put his hand on my knee. 'This must be Realismus film, John. Aram will help you.'

'When I say "long",' I said cautiously, 'I mean very long. Extremely long.'

'What's "extremely"?' Aram said.

'I want to make three films. Three hours each.'

'*What!*'

'Is good idea,' Duric said. '*Phantastisch*. We do it at Realismus, of course. Promise me, Aram. I mean *promise*.'

Aram had the look of a man trying to control nausea.

'Yes, papa . . . if at all possible.'

'No "if". I want straight promise.'

'I promise.'

Duric lay back. He looked exhausted, his thin chest rising and falling at alarming speed. I felt I could punch a hole in it with my fist, as if his body were made out of balsa wood and paper, like a model aeroplane. As he breathed we could hear random treacly pops and gurglings from within the chest wall. His eyes shone with tears but it may only have been rheum. He drew me closer again.

'Promise me too, John.'

'Of course. Anything.'

'Don't let Aram sell the business. Watch him.'

'What business?' I looked at Aram. 'Realismus? He'd never sell it, don't worry.'

'No,' he was falling asleep. 'The nuts.'

'I'll watch him,' I said. 'I promise.'

Aram rang for the nurse and we stood up. The nurse came in and held the oxygen mask to his face. It seemed to rouse him and he beckoned us back. We crouched by his side. His eyes were barely open, just a slit revealing a brown limpid glimmer.

'Never give up the nuts,' he said. They were his last words. He went to sleep and died three days later.

At his funeral Aram and I shed copious tears. I had tried to hold them back but seeing Aram's example decided to let myself go. I had a 'right good greet' as Oonagh used to say. I felt surprisingly better for it too, and I think Aram was touched. It was odd seeing Aram cry. We walked away from the graveside sniffing, wiping our eyes and snorting into big handkerchiefs.

'He was a sly old fellow,' Aram said. 'A nine-hour film. My God.'

'It'll be amazing,' I said. 'Wait and see. There's been nothing like it.'

'I'd never do it normally,' Aram said. 'I think I should tell you that. I think it's crazy, disastrous.'

'But you promised.'

'I know, I know.'

'I promised too,' I said. 'Hang on to those nuts.'

Aram laughed. 'Too late, John, I'm afraid. I sold Lodokian Nussen four months ago.'

I felt mildly cheated by this but there was nothing I could do. Later, I used to wonder if Aram had lied, just to keep me out of his business deals ... I had no way of finding out. However, I blessed old Duric for extracting that death-bed promise from his son. I assumed that Armenian blood ties and dying oaths were inviolable, and in a sense they were. Aram was always true to the letter of his promise if not its spirit. A few days later contracts were signed. I was salaried at $1,000 a month while I wrote the script (back-dated) and Realismus paid me a $10,000 option on it against a fee for the world rights to be negotiated. In addition it was confirmed that I was to direct and participate in the profits. Bland announcements appeared in the trade press. I remember I cut one out and pinned it to the wall above my desk in the villa. 'Realismus Films announced yesterday that John James Todd is to film *The Confessions* by Jean-Jacques Rousseau in 1927 on location in Switzerland and France. K.-H. Kornfeld is to play the leading role.' These prompted some speculations by journalists. My replies, I thought, were teasingly oblique. There is nothing like refusing to be specific for arousing curiosity.

The first draft of *The Confessions: Part I* was over 600 pages long. After a month's effortful work I managed to reduce it by something over a hundred pages. I began work on part II in the autumn, but made bad progress. My mind was constantly on part I—the director in me had taken over from the writer. There were many technical problems to be solved or experimented with; logistical pitfalls multiplied in my mind. I wrote on for another two hundred pages or so before I decided to let part II rest for a while. In any event, winter was approaching and the wooden villa was not warm. Monika had stopped coming out too, now the opportunities for sunbathing were gone. We met once or twice in her apartment but it was not the same. Our curious affair went into hibernation, tacitly, with no hard feelings on either side, and waited for the return of more clement weather.

So I abandoned the villa in the Jungfernheide and returned to our

house in Charlottenburg. Sonia was heavily pregnant—the new baby
was due in December. I went to work in my Realismus office and by
the end of the year had produced a final draft of *The Confessions:
Part I* that was 350 pages long. Of course I knew it was almost twice
as long as it should have been but I was not concerned. Once we start
filming, I reassured Aram, you'll see how it will come down. He did
not seem unduly perturbed. He was planning another trip to the USA
in the new year where he expected to raise money for the film. Large
advances had been paid for Leo Druce's *Frederick the Great*; *Joan of
Arc* was generating similar excitement.

Aram was too calm, I now realise, and that tranquillity com-
municated itself to me. We drew up a schedule. Pre-production would
commence in January 1927, filming would start in June. I would
deliver a completed three-hour film in June 1928 for release in the
autumn of that year. It all seemed eminently realisable. These dates,
these plans conjured from the vaguest deliberations appeared utterly
fixed, like the movements of the stars in the heavens, or calendrical
predictions for high or low tides. We had created a timetable and
with it a kind of reality. It had no real existence beyond our determination, but we acted as if it had.

'We'll begin part II in '29,' I said to Aram. 'One year for each
part. The whole thing will be finished by 1931. We'll show them all
together. One nine-hour film.' I paused. 'It'll be magnificent,' I said
with absolute, utter confidence. 'Wait till you see what I can do.
Amazing things. There will never be a film like it again.'

'Excellent,' he said. 'But let's get part I finished first.'

Sonia gave birth to twins—girls—in early December. For the first
time I was near my wife when the event occurred. I was very surprised
at the news. Sonia said she had told me a month before her parturition,
but if so the idea had not registered. I swear. It is an unpleasant
reminder of just how preoccupied I had been with *The Confessions:
Part I*. My family life was no more than a backdrop. It claimed my
attention only when I wished it to. I was stunned. Suddenly I had
four children! I felt faint stirrings of panic. What on earth did I think
I was doing?

Our house that December was bedlam. Sonia and Lily were fully
occupied with the girls—Emmeline and Annabelle—and for a while
I had to oversee the two boys. For some reason Frau Mittenklott—
who had followed us from Rudolf Platz—had been given responsibility for the Christmas decorations. There was a vast green fir tree
in the drawing room burning real candles and hung with real cakes

and a kind of decorative shortbread. Small replicas stood in the hall and dining room. Furthermore boughs had been hewn from other conifers and were suspended wherever possible above doors, windows and staircases. The air was thick with resinous piny fumes that made my eyes sting and reminded me of my father's antiseptic experiments. Heavy swags of red velvet ribbon were draped above the fireplaces, and from every projecting ledge, picture frame and table corner the good woman had set or hung miniature presents—matchboxes wrapped in bright paper and filled with raisins or nuts to be unwrapped by the children whenever the anticipation proved too much or the wait too long. This was the whimsical custom, so Frau Mittenklott informed me, in the village where she was born and raised. Our house seemed the very paradigm of festivity, bright symbol of the Christmas season itself. The misery was capped, though my duties diminished, when Vincent and Noreen Shorrold arrived from London to share our joy.

On Christmas day 1926 we were all present in the sitting room. John James Todd, the film director, his wife Sonia, their four children—Vincent, Hereford, Emmeline and Annabelle—the nurse Lily Maidbow and the in-laws, Mr and Mrs Shorrold. In the kitchen Frau Mittenklott was cooking a goose, three rabbits, a suckling pig—a whole farmyard of animals as far as I know. I had just opened my present from Sonia. A pipe. A ghastly curved meerschaum with a carved yellow bowl the size of a coffee cup and—this is true—red and green tassles hanging from it.

'I can't smoke *this*,' I said, shocked, to Sonia.

'Course you can, Johnny,' Vincent Shorrold said. 'Nothing like a pipe for a man.'

'And what on earth does that mean? But—seriously—I can't put this thing in my mouth. I'd be a laughing stock.'

'Here, I'll get it going for you, boy,' Vincent Shorrold said, and took it from me. He proceeded to fill it with what looked like fistfuls of shag from his own pouch.

'That's a right big smoke, that's for sure,' he said as he tamped down the tobacco with his thumbs. 'There's a tin and a half of ready-rubbed in there.' He put it in his mouth. I saw his jaw muscles clench as they took the strain.

'Fair weight,' he commented. 'Give you a right stiff neck, this will.'

It took him five or six matches and as many minutes to ignite the compacted mass of tobacco. The room was soon blue with gently shifting strata of smoke. The twins began to cry, their pure new eyes stinging. I sat very still in my chair, my face fixed. The women looked on with admiration as Vincent Shorrold fumed and blew, thick smoke snorting, apparently, from every orifice in his head.

'Grand cool draw,' he said, coming over, sucking and blowing. 'It'll be going for a couple of hours yet.' He held the vile object out to me, its little tassles swinging, its stem gleaming with Shorrold saliva.

'Have a puff, John,' Sonia said.

'Go on, Johnny,' said her mother.

The telephone rang.

I threw myself from the chair and strode urgently into the hall to answer it (why did we—why did people—keep telephones in the hall then?). I snatched the receiver from its cradle.

'Yes?'

'Jamie?'

'Yes.' It was Doon. I felt my entire body tremble. I sat down very slowly.

'Did you ... ?' She paused. She sounded upset. 'Did you mean what you said that night?'

'What night?'

She hung up. I knew what night, of course. I swore at myself for not thinking faster. But how could I think at all in this farcical Xmas grotto of a house? I put on my overcoat and a hat and went back into the drawing room. Shorrold was relighting the pipe.

'John?' Sonia said, surprised at my appearance.

'I've got to go,' I said. 'Problems ... Karl-Heinz. He's ill.'

'But there's dinner.'

'Save some for me. I don't know when I'll be back.'

Exultantly, I went outside. There had been some snow earlier in the week but it had thawed. It was a cold dull afternoon as I drove towards the Kurfürstendamm. Schülter Strasse and Doon's apartment.

There was no reply. I knocked again. I pressed my ear to the cold door listening for signs of movement within.

A neat young man carrying a new briefcase came up the stairs.

'Are you looking for Miss Bogan?' he asked.

'Yes.'

'You've just missed her. I passed her in the street on my way here. You might catch her. She's heading north. Up towards the Knie.'

I spotted her as she crossed the busy intersection at Schiller and Grolman Strasse. She was wearing a leather coat and a small-brimmed brown felt hat pulled hard down on her head. I thought she must be going to the Schiller theatre but she passed that by. Why did I not

233

approach her in the street? Run up behind her, tap her on the shoulder? ... Because I felt suddenly weak and uncertain, now that I saw her tall figure again, striding so purposefully. Why had she telephoned me after months of silence? What had she meant by her question? I knew what I had said that night, so why now did she want the statement confirmed. I could provide no convincing answers to these questions apart from wishful ones, so I followed her discreetly as we walked through the cold quiet streets, even more deserted now as we moved further from the west end and into the industrial district of Lutzow. She turned right at the Landwehr-Kanal, with the sprawl of the Siemens electrical works opposite, and went through the doorway of what looked like a meeting hall or low-church chapel.

I paused. The granite afternoon light was fading. The canal looked solid and very cold, as if the water was viscous, at freezing point. I stood there dithering, getting colder by the minute. Some more people went into the hall. I had no gloves or scarf with me. Should I wait? She might be hours ... I went in.

At the far end of a thin vestibule a young man sat behind a table. He was wearing an overcoat, a roll neck sweater and a soft brown hat of quite good quality. There were some papers in front of him.

'Afternoon,' I said.

'Are you a member?' He had a square bulging jaw which needed shaving.

'I want to join,' I improvised. 'I came to meet Miss Bogan.'

He was impressed by the name. 'Oh, good. Excellent. There should be no problem.'

He rummaged in the desk drawer and produced a form. 'That'll be 200 marks,' he said. 'Fill that in. I can give you a temporary card now. We'll send the official one later.'

What kind of a club was this? I wondered as I handed in the money. I could hear indistinct conversation from the hall. The neighbourhood was so drab—too drab for pornography. I filled in half the form—name, address, profession—before I thought to ask what the letters at its head stood for.

The man looked suddenly wary.

'The Revolutionary Artists' Association,' he said. 'Of the KPD.'

The communist party. 'Of course.' I managed a laugh of sorts. 'What am I thinking about?'

He filled in my name on a square of cardboard and carefully stamped and initialled its reverse. He stood up and shook my hand.

'Welcome,' he said, then gestured at the door. 'The meeting's just starting.'

There must have been over two hundred people inside, mainly men, but with a fair representation of women. So many artists, I thought? I could see nothing of Doon. I edged diffidently in, pressed my back to a wall and waited. A thin man on a rostrum spoke passionately in clichés. I lost interest in seconds. In those days I was indifferent to politics, creeds and dogmas. Politics especially—I had not yet become one of its hapless victims. As Chekhov puts it, I wanted only to be a free artist. So as I scanned the faces of the audience, intent and earnest, impassive and immobile, I noted that some of them were well-to-do; these were not all workers or students. I wondered what it was about them or the occasion that drew Doon here.

Speakers changed but the tone of voice and diminished vocabulary remained the same. There was vehement applause at the end of every speech. And then Doon got up on the rostrum. I listened to what she had to say. She attacked the institituion of Christmas and, thinking of the travesty my own home had become, I found myself loudly applauding all the predictable ideological grievances. She wound up with a plea for donations to party funds. She would be passing among us, she said, taking a collection.

I waited for Doon to reach me. Four people were going through the audience with wooden boxes as the meeting's business was ponderously concluded by the thin man who had begun it all. I kept changing my position and thus made two donations before Doon and I finally met.

I felt a poignant helplessness suffuse my body as I stuffed notes into her box. To my credit, and my joy, she coloured. Admiring noises came from others at my party-spirited largesse.

'Thank you, comrade,' she said. Then, in a lower voice. 'What're you doing here?'

'I followed you. After you called. I had to see you.'

'Are you a member?'

'Yes.'

'How long? I thought you were a cynic.'

'Oh. Not so long . . . People are allowed to change their minds, you know.'

'Wait for me at the end.'

I was wrong about it finishing. That meeting ran on for three hours. By its conclusion I was overpoweringly hungry. My stomach was audible at three yards, my mouth awash with saliva as I thought helplessly of Frau Mittenklott's Christmas rum grog, her rabbit paprika and her *Schokoladenstrudel*.

It was night when Doon and I finally left. We walked back towards her flat, she talked overanimatedly of the cell, the cause, the struggle, the comrades. I let her natter on—she had slipped her hand through mind and I was close enough to smell her lavender perfume. Eventually I could stand it no longer and steered her into a small cellar café.

I ordered two coffees with kirsch and whipped cream and ate two large but rather solid slices of yesterday's date torte. Then I put my hand on hers.

'Doon,' I said. 'Why did you phone?'

'I shouldn't have.'

'But you did.'

'God . . . I don't know. I was feeling "blue". Fucking Christmas. I hate it . . . I left Alex. Two weeks ago. I was sitting waiting for the meeting and I thought I'd—shit. It was silly of me.'

My mouth was dry. 'I still mean it.'

She lit a cigarette. She seemed uneasy now.

'It's sweet of you to say that, Jamie.' She was trying to be composed. 'But you don't have to. Not on my account. Can I have another coffee?'

'But I *do*. I've known it since I saw you that first day in the Metropole.'

She looked down, blew of strong jet of smoke away to her left.

'But you're a married man. You've got two kids—'

'Four. Now.'

'*Jesus!* Four?'

'Sonia had twins three weeks ago.'

'My God. Well, there you are . . . It's useless. We shouldn't even be talking about it. I should never have called.'

She continued listing objections. I felt short of oxygen, like Duric Lodokian. I was breathing through mouth and nose but my lungs still felt starved of air. I had to divert her from the wife and children topic. She paused to take off her hat.

'See. I kept it blonde. Memories of *Julie*.'

The idea seemed to fly up in my face, like a game bird started from heather.

'I was going to get in touch anyway,' I said slowly. 'I want you to be in my new film. With Karl-Heinz again.'

'Oh, yes. I read about it. But what part is there for me?'

'Someone called Madame de Warens.'

'I don't know . . . '

'You'd be wonderful.'

'I don't think it's such a good idea. What's the film called again?'

'*The Confessions*.'

236

VILLA LUXE 22 June 1972

Emilia has been acting strangely, lately. It's all to do with that hole in the shutter, I'm sure. One day she was taciturn. Then yesterday she came wearing lipstick and some unattractive wooden earrings. I sense, too, that she doesn't like Ulrike. It's curious how women can become so proprietorial. I told her Ulrike had permission to use the beach. She was clearly irritated by this. I can't be bothered trying to work out what's going on. Could it be—however absurd it sounds—that she's jealous? My God ...

It's time I told you something of Jean-Jacques Rousseau, for those of you unfamiliar with him. First I will give you the public image, the official version, one we can swiftly forget. Unfortunately, my library here is impoverished. I can only quote from *A Student's Guide to European Philosophy* by one Dr Ida Milby-Low (MA, PhD, Oxon), published in 1934. I apologise, but this is the mere husk of the man we are interested in. Bear with me.

'*Jean-Jacques Rousseau* (1712–1778) was born in Geneva on the 28th of June 1712. His father was a watch-mender [a watch maker, in fact] and his mother died immediately after his birth. He received no regular education, but such as he had in the formative years of his life was augmented by a reading of French novels kept in his father's library. In Rousseau's infancy his father was obliged to quit Geneva as a consequence of a quarrel and the young Jean-Jacques was placed first in the care of a country parson and subsequently an uncle. After a turbulent adolescence he was apprenticed to an engraver, who attempted vainly to discipline him. Deeply unhappy, Rousseau made his escape from this employer and fled from Switzerland to Annecy in Savoy, where he shortly made the acquaintance of one Mme de Warens, a woman of facile morals [*this is the voice of Miss Milby-Low—spinster don, I predict, with a moustache, and whose sole vices are a rare cigarette and a secret tipple from that sherry bottle in her desk drawer*].

'Mme de Warens directed Rousseau to Turin where he was converted to Roman Catholicism and was employed as a domestic servant by two prosperous aristocratic families. He might have risen to become the steward of one of these households had not his perennial instability caused him to run away again. He fled his responsibilities once more, back to Annecy and Mme de Warens who became, in Rousseau's own parlance, his '*Maman*'.

'There now followed a succession of temporary employments and wanderings. Rousseau took up music as his main career and worked intermittently as a chorister. He even composed an opera during this uncertain period of fleeting attachments to adventurers which took him to Lausanne and Paris. Each time he returned inevitably to Mme de Warens with whom he had lived first at Chambéry and then at Les Charmettes, a charming country house nearby. Rousseau continued his education here, in a period of some tranquillity, through a self-imposed course of voracious indiscriminate reading. Emotionally, however, his life was less calm. Mme de Warens had introduced into her household a man named Witzenreid. Rousseau found himself unable to share his 'Maman' with another and left Les Charmettes to take up work as an itinerant tutor. He had written little by this stage of his life and was quite unconscious of his genius.

'In 1742 he decided to try and make his fortune in Paris on the strength of a new system of musical notation which he had devised. This was never popular and Rousseau remained ignored. In 1744 he took up with one Thérèse Levasseur, an ignorant girl of low class [*the voice of the senior common room again*] who became the mother of his children.

'Rousseau earned his living by copying music, secretarial work and the very limited success of his operatic comedies. In 1749, Diderot (q.v.) invited him to contribute to the *French Encyclopaedia* (q.v.), wherein Rousseau wrote the articles on Music and Political Economy. Thus he was drawn into the society of French intellectuals such as D'Alembert and F. M. Grimm, a German of gross impiety.

'The first thirty-eight years of Rousseau's life were passed in almost total obscurity. He occupied a succession of menial jobs and probably would have been content to remain with the *encyclopédistes'* claque (who contrived to find the amiable civilisation of monarchical France too despotic for their taste), had he not emerged as a figure of fame and renown with his *Discourse on the Arts and Sciences*. In this he asserted—with improbable eloquence obscuring the unlikely paradox—that man is happier in a savage natural state than in an advanced civilised one. He became the toast of Paris and his *Discourse* proved to be the passport he sought to high society. [*He did not* SEEK *this.*]

'In the meantime Thérèse Levasseur had borne him five children, all of whom, and with no qualms, Rousseau had abandoned in succession at the door of the foundling hospital in Paris.

'Fame and its trappings, however, consorted uneasily with the man who had enjoined the 'noble savage' as exemplary model for mankind. Rousseau returned to Geneva in 1754, promptly renounced his Catholicism and became a Calvinist and a citizen once more. His retreat did not last long. Society and its rich patrons proved to be too strong an allure and Rousseau accepted the offer of Mme d'Epinay to occupy the Hermitage, a pleasant cottage on her estate in the forest of Montmorency. The peace and quiet of the countryside delighted him but it was not to last. Mme d'Epinay desired his company; Diderot and Grimm besought him to return to the salons of Paris; and then Rousseau fell in love with Mme d'Epinay's sister, the comtesse d'Houdetot, who was mistress of the noble soldier-poet Saint Lambert. This led first to complications, then to tension and recrimination, concluding in bitter acrimony among the participants.

'With surprising ease Rousseau found another patron, the Maréchal de Luxembourg. Upon him now fell the honour of providing the philosopher and his doxy with a home [*this is academic bitchery at its worst*]. But new heights of celebrity awaited Rousseau. Within a period of eighteen months (1761–62) three large works were published: *The New Héloïse*, *Emile* and *The Social Contract*. They presented revolutionary views on all the topics most vital to humanity and society: government, education, religion, sexual morality, family life, the source of our deep emotions and love.

'This was Rousseau's *annus mirabilis* but, as so often with the man, it brought only disaster in its train. Unorthodox views of religion expounded in *Emile* (a treatise of education in the form of a novel) offended the authorities. The book was condemned and a warrant was issued for its author's arrest. Rousseau, however, was given every opportunity to escape and he proceeded quickly to Switzerland. But he was no longer welcome there and so moved to Neuchâtel, then in Prussian territory. He lived quietly there in rural seclusion, began writing his *Confessions* and received occasional visitors, amongst whom was the young Scotsman James Boswell, later biographer of Dr Samuel Johnson (q.v.).

'Conscious of the fragile nature of his state of exile in Neuchâtel Rousseau accepted the generous invitation of David Hume (q.v.), the philosopher, to come and live in England. He settled at Wootton Hall near Ashbourne. By this time the persecution complex from which he had always suffered took greater hold on him and degenerated to a chronic form of delusional insanity. He became convinced that Hume—his benefactor—was in fact plotting against him, and grew jealous of his fame. Rousseau accused him of intercepting his mail and a violent quarrel ensued with Rousseau and Mlle Levasseur returning to the continent. Then followed a nomadic period of brief sojourns in provincial France before Rousseau settled finally in Paris, tolerated and unmolested by an indulgent and forgiving government. He completed *The Confessions* (which was published posthumously) and composed the famous *Dialogues: Rousseau judge of Jean-Jacques* and the serene *Reveries of a Solitary Walker*.

'In *The Confessions* the bizarre compulsion to tell unsparingly the whole and entire truth about oneself was more original than edifying, but the more contemplative *Reveries* give rise to a sense of pity for a man who was, it must be admitted, his own worst enemy. He was a man in whom astonishing gifts were marred and undermined by serious defects of character and judgement. Selfishness and paranoia, vanity and reckless opportunism, base ingratitude, passion and prejudice ruled this simple, intermittently sagacious thinker. It is indeed true that Rousseau and his works irrevocably altered European thought and sensibility but it must be adjoined that it was not always for the better. He died on the 2nd July 1778 at Ermenonville, of an apoplectic fit.'

Apoplexy is the only adequate response to that final paragraph, which has to be the most contemptible and shameful epitaph ever bestowed on one of the great geniuses of modern history. I reproduce it merely as a small sample of what Jean-Jacques had—and has had—to endure from the small-minded throughout his tormented life and beyond. I will not dignify Dr Milby-Low's evil innuendoes, many inaccuracies and omissions by further comment. The rough shape of Jean-Jacques' difficult unique life is there—we will illumine it further, later. In the meantime only two observations need to be made.

One. Be sure of this, nothing Milby-Low recounts here is missing from *The Confessions*, as you might be forgiven for thinking from the note of smug revelation that she sometimes employs. Rousseau himself was and is the source of all slander directed against him by pedants and prudes. It is all down in fearless candour in that magnificent book and the companion volumes—*Rousseau juge de Jean-Jacques* and the *Reveries*. No misdemeanour escapes him from the great to the inconsequential: from abandoning his children to pissing secretly in a cantankerous neighbour's simmering soup pot when she wasn't looking. Rousseau is judged by Jean-Jacques, not the Milby-Lows of this world.

Two. Is it not curious that a life dogged with misfortune, riven with acrimony, disappointment and bitterness is somehow perceived by the rest of mankind to be the unhappy sufferer's own doing? True, there are people who are 'their own worst enemy', who pursue a helter-skelter ride to self-destruction. But at the same time why can't it be admitted that a man or woman can be cursed with filthy luck, can be denied opportunities available to others, can be surrounded by false friends and cozening flatterers? Why not? There is nothing in the scheme of things to say that this will never be the case—that it is always a result of one's misdirected Will. There is no guarantee of good fortune, no assurance that your allies will always be staunch, that unfairness and indifference will not always prevail. So why in these cases (Jean-Jacques' case) does the world howl paranoiac, lunatic, misanthrope, ingrate, egomaniac?

I will tell you why. Because it makes people feel better, more secure. They can live, grudgingly, with a *charmed* life—there's hope for us all, then—but a *cursed* life makes everyone uneasy. If they can lay all the blame on the victim it makes Fate seem to be somehow under control—we play as big a part in our own downfall. We are somehow agents, responsible. Chance, the random and haphazard, the contingent do not really dictate the way the world turns.

11

The Confessions: Part I

We began filming *The Confessions: Part I* in July 1927, a month later than we planned. Part I was to cover Rousseau's life from his birth in 1712 up to 1739 when, reluctantly and with heavy heart, he decides to leave his beloved 'maman', his lover and benefactress, with his rival, the detestable Witzenreid, and to seek his fortune elsewhere. Part II was to deal with his rise to fame and terminate with the scandal of Emile and flight to Switzerland. Part III—I had barely thought this out, I admit—was to deal with his last years: cold exile in England, the bitter quarrel with Hume, the return to Paris and the serene botanising of his last years. Thus, broadly, was the great scheme I had conceived. Part I was ready to film, most of part II was drafted and part III, I felt sure, would almost write itself when we reached that stage three years hence. I felt intoxicated, full of vigour and enthusiasm, on the brink of a great adventure.

Meanwhile, Doon and I . . . nothing happened that night after the meeting. We finished our coffees and kirsch and I walked her home. She allowed me to kiss her on the cheek at the door of her apartment. 'I think you'll like Mme de Warens,' I said. 'I hope so,' she said, sincerely.

After that meeting nothing could bring me to return directly home. I went first to Stralauer Allee to have Karl-Heinz confirm my excuse to Sonia but Georg's apartment was in darkness. Then for some reason I drove to the Tiergarten and walked down to gaze—superstitiously, I suppose—at the Rousseau-Insel, a small island planted with trees set in the middle of one of the lakes scattered through the enormous park. Karl-Heinz had told me about this island-monument. I had gone to visit it once or twice, more out of a sense of duty than inspiration. This evening it did not hold much of that last quality either. The trees were bare and patches of snow gleamed in the darkness like wind-scattered sheets of newspaper. I watched my breath condense around me, then evaporate, and tried to think seriously about the work that the next few years held for me, but my

mind returned—inevitably—to Doon ... The warm weight of her
hand in the crook of my elbow. The temporary moustache of whipped
cream on her upper lip as she drank her coffee-kirsch. How the quick
wet tip of her tongue had wiped it clean. Would she do Mme de
Warens? ... I had not thought of her in the role owing to the rift that
had developed since *Julie*, but now I wondered what had taken me
so long to see that possibility. She would only figure in part I, but it
would still mean months of proximity. I exhaled. Was I sure I knew
what I was doing, this Christmas night, with my wife and four
children waiting, no doubt impatiently, for me to return home? No.
Yes. Perhaps ... I turned and walked back to my car.

Throughout the first six months of 1927 I worked stenuously to set
the vast machine that would produce *The Confessions* in motion. My
key and crucial aim, my basic working maxim, was to reproduce the
facts of one man's life on film with an attention to detail that had
never before been witnessed. Just as for me, as reader, Rousseau had
presented himself in all candour for examination, so would I now
offer to millions of spectators around the world the portrait of a man
rendered in such intimacy, fidelity and verisimilitude that they would
come to know him as they knew themselves. Nothing would be
spared. It would be the story of the life of one extraordinary human
being, but one who was heroic in his humanity alone. The individual
spirit would have its great immortal document.

I had grandiose plans as to how this should be achieved and I
intended to employ every trick and technique available to the modern
film-maker—and a few more that I had devised myself. I was going
to extend the cinematic form to its very limits.

I was fortunate in that Aram had managed to supply the budget
that this dream demanded. Such had been the success of *Julie* that
large investments had been made in the film by a group of German
financiers, Pathé in France and Goldfilm, a cinema chain in the
USA. Not a penny was forthcoming from my own country. Aram,
meanwhile, had returned from the States with a hatful of investors
for Realismus films, and, most peculiarly, a new identity for himself.

This was really bizarre. I went to see him the first morning he was
back in the studio. The door to his office suite was open and a
workman was replacing the nameplate. I took no notice and walked
in. Lately, Aram had taken to wearing coloured shirts but kept his
collar white, regardless of what kind of suit he was wearing. Today
he was in a heavy brown tweed and red shirt. We shook hands. He
told me all the good news: Leo Druce had finished *Frederick the Great*

(it was not a first-rate job but it would do. Aram was giving *Joan of Arc* to Egon Gast) and he was ready to take over as producer on *The Confessions*. The money was all there, all one and a half million dollars of it ('But no more, John,' Aram said.) Doon Bogan was signed to play Mme de Warens. We talked on about some more details: the new studios that were being converted from warehouses just outside Spandau; how many weeks we would need to spend filming in Switzerland, and so on. When we finished, I stood up and said,

'Well, Aram, I—'

'Ah, yes, that's another thing.' He handed me a business card.

I looked at it. 'Eadweard A. L. Simmonette,' I read. 'Who's he?'

'Me.'

'I beg your pardon?'

'I've changed my name.'

'But you don't spell Edward like that.'

'Yes you can. It's recognised. But I want to be called 'Eddie'. Eddie Simmonette. From now on please, John. I won't answer to Aram Lodokian.'

'Aram, Jesus Christ! Are you—?'

His face went hard. He was the most even-tempered of men: to see such hurt and fury was disturbing.

'John, don't let this come between us, I implore you. I am Eddie now. You must never call me Aram.'

I decided to humour him. 'All right. Eddie. *Eddie*. But it's not easy.'

'I've told everyone else in the company. All my friends and associates.' He smiled. 'You'll see, in a day or two it'll seem the most natural thing in the world.'

Was he mad? 'But why?'

'I wanted to, for a long time. I had to wait for my father to die, of course. I don't want to be a Lodokian anymore.' He touched my elbow. 'Times are changing, John. Tomorrow's world is for the Eddie Simmonettes. You've never been to America ... that's where I got the idea.'

It made no sense to me, but it was his right, I suppose. So, no more Aram Lodokian. Enter Eddie Simmonette. And the funny thing about it all, Aram/Eddie was right.

*   *   *

In March I took the family back home for Thompson's wedding. It was inconvenient but I had been touched by a personal letter from him asking me to be there. We travelled first class and spent two days in London at Claridges. I booked two suites there, one for Sonia and myself, one for Lily and the children. I did the same at the North British Hotel in Edinburgh. At our window in the North British I stood silent for ten minutes or so looking out at the familiar view. The castle, the gardens, Princes Street. It was typically grey and wet. The castle loomed black over the damp windlashed gardens and the town, its cliffs slick and slimy with rain. I thought back to my last visit six or seven years before when we were making *Wee MacGregor Wins the Sweepstake*. Here I was now, twenty-eight years old, wealthy, celebrated, large family, servants . . . I should have felt pleased with myself, smug, full of I-told-you-so superiority. But the longer I stood there looking out at that uncompromising view the harder self-satisfaction was to achieve. I knew my father would be unimpressed.

We had not seen each other for six years. My eyes were smarting with emotion as he was shown into the suite with Thompson and his bride-to-be. Sonia had our family laid out as if for kit inspection. She was a little nervous too: it was her first encounter with her father-in-law. She had the boys spruce in neat golfing outfits—Norfolk jackets and plus-fours—and the girls were propped in the corners of a sofa—cherubs in lace—Lily sitting between them. My father was as he had always been: formal, polite, reserve encasing him like a relic in a glass cabinet.

'Hello, John,' he said. I shook his cool hand vigorously. 'And this'll be Sonia . . . You can let go now, John.'

The reunion was stiff, edgy. The conversation absurdly banal. My father was quite grey now, though he was as thin and upright as ever, impressively fit-looking for a man in his mid-sixties.

Thompson had settled into his portliness. It suited him. He was one of those stout men for whom weight loss would be something of an affront, almost indecent. He was rising steadily up the hierarchy of the bank and had, I think he told me, just been appointed to the board—hence his decision to get married. I envied him his young eager wife, Heather (who shyly told me how much she had loved *Julie*). She was pretty in an innocuous, pinkish way. She fussed nervously over the children, glad to have some diversion. Beside her, Sonia could almost have been described as 'matronly'. For a young woman the beam of Sonia's hips was unduly broad: her torso seemed to rest on it like an antique bust on a pedestal. She wore dark expensive clothes, sensibly cut, which to some extent disguised her bulk but she had a solid big-arsed presence these days that slim nervous Heather beside her accentuated. Heather was one of those girls, I could see, whose sunny temperament would not dim even when overshadowed by the grimmest clouds of adversity (she very charmingly rebuffed me some years later when I made a crude and shameful pass at her). I stood with my father and brother—we all stirred cups of tea, held at chest height—and watched the women marshal and drill the children. I think it was then that the last dregs of love I held for Sonia seeped away for ever. Why? Why do these things ever happen? ... I knew I had Doon now.

I glanced at father. His face was expressionless.

'Well, Innes,' I said. 'Grand to have the family back together.'

I saw him flinch as I used his Christian name. Thompson called him 'Daddy'—ridiculous in a grown man, I thought.

'Curious names you've chosen for your boys,' he said with a trace of a smile. The old bastard. 'That would be the Shorrold line, I take it?'

The wedding. It was all right—tolerable. Normally I detest weddings. All that false, timely sincerity nauseates me. Donald and Faye Verulam were there. Donald ever more courteous and patrician. Faye ageing with tact and charm. I was safe with Faye now, quite relaxed. Various burly Dale cousins showed up and I was surprised to see that old Sir Hector was still alive. If anything he was in slightly better condition than I remembered him from 1919, when I used to push him round the garden at Drumlarish House. He was swigging sherry and trying to eat crumbling wedding cake when I approached him.

'Grandfather!' I shouted. 'It's me, John James!'

He was appallingly badly shaved and cake crumbs were caught in the bristles. His moist eyes swivelled uncontrollably.

'Johnny. How are you, laddie?'

'Fine, fine.'

'Got a job yet?'

'Yes, yes.' I told myself to stop repeating my answers. I felt an immense sadness descend abruptly on me as I looked at this collapsed old man in his bath chair.

'Great day,' he said.

'It is, it is.'

'Get another of these wee sherries before my nurse comes back.'

I did and had a few whiskies to cheer myself up, which probably explains why I lost control so completely with Oonagh. She had of course been invited to the wedding but obediently filled her role as former family retainer, sitting on a hard chair at the farthest perimeter of the family group. She was drinking tea and had a plate of fancy cakes on her lap when I found her. She was stooped with arthritis and had given up working for my father, unable to climb the stairs any more. Two walking sticks hung over the back of her chair. She had softened and expanded with age, her hair prematurely wiry and grey. She wore a baggy white blouse, thick skirt and old-fashioned lace-up boots.

'Not too grand to speak to me, then?'

'Don't be silly, Oonagh.' I gave her a kiss. My voice was trembling. I felt my head bulging with a decade's unspilt tears, like a ripe melon about to burst. I sensed here, today, my youth and past life fading away for ever. The changes wrought in my six years' absence were too large and dramatic to be unconsciously assimilated. I had been away too long. The geography of my early life, its fixed points and certainties, were hopelessly out of date now. I was faced only with mutability and decay: to look back, to recall, only emphasised our awful fragility.

'That's a nice brooch,' I said hoarsely, pointing to a single cairngorm set in silver which Oonagh was wearing at her throat.

'You gave it to me, silly boy.'

My face wrinkled and the tears surged. Shoulders heaving, snorkelling back the rush of phlegm, I wrote out a cheque for £100 and pressed it into Oonagh's astonished hands.

Later, calmer, I had an awkward conversation with Thompson. I think he wanted to be affectionate but once again the years stood between us like chaperones and we exchanged only platitudes. It was the closest we ever got as adults, however, which is something. This hot fat man is my brother, I said to myself. We can't ignore these blood ties. I tried. We talked about money. He asked me if I had a lot of capital. I said yes. He looked around and lowered his voice.

'Get it out of Germany, John. Please.'

'Why? Things are doing better. I even get paid in American dollars.'

'That's something. But I'd still shift it. Back here. Or France or Switzerland. It's sound advice.'

'I'm filming in Switzerland later this year.'

He stepped closer. His hand hovered a moment as if he were going to place it on my shoulder. He let it touch my sleeve lightly, like a leaf.

'Will you do something for me, John?' he said. 'Get your money, in cash, and take it with you to Switzerland. I'll tell you where to take it.'

I obviously looked sceptical.

'Please,' he said. 'Let me set up everything.' He was excited. The smile he gave me was unlike his ordinary weak grin. For an instant

I sensed the almost carnal pleasure he took in his job, and why therefore he was such a good banker. For Thompson, nothing else was as much *fun* as money, and I daresay that included his new wife. I agreed. He promised to send me the details.

'You'll thank me for this,' he said. 'Believe me, John, I know what I'm saying.' He was right. It was the best and only favour he ever did me.

*   *   *

Aram Lodokian—sorry—Eddie Simmonette had leased the warehouses and workshops of an old military factory in Spandau on the Staaken which were readily converted into studios. They were devoted exclusively to *The Confessions: Part I*. There we had three stages of various sizes plus all the technical equipment and expertise we required.

Let me, without preamble, tell you of our first day's shooting as it unfolded to the members of the cast and crew. It will give you the best example of how I conceived *The Confessions* and how I planned to make it the most extraordinary film in the history of motion pictures. The following account appeared in the August 1927 edition of *Kino*. My translation.

'July 17th 1927. Realismus studios, Spandau. 7 a.m. Director John James Todd assembles the entire cast and crew of the film on the largest of the studio's three stages. Everyone is present whether he or she was required for that day or not. They number in all 167 men, women and children. Todd addresses the company, welcomes them to the film and demands total dedication. He stands above the crowd on a scaffolding platform, part of a set representing Mme de Warens' bedchamber in her château at Annecy. His voice is clear, his German simple yet full of errors. His curious accent demands extra concentration. He is a dark intense man of average height, somewhat thick set. His demeanour is one of almost uncontrollable energy and excitement. He tells his audience that they are immensely privileged to be working on what, he assures them with breathtaking confidence, will become the most celebrated film in the history of cinema. Such is his conviction, such the evident pride and exultation in his own face, that this short furious speech is greeted by loud cheering. Some people shed tears. Todd passes through the crowd, men and women press forward to shake his hand and clap him on the shoulders.

'7.30 a.m. On a smaller stage we find the interior of Isaac Rousseau's house in Geneva. Susanne Rousseau (Traudl Niemöller) is in the throes of giving birth to Jean-Jacques. At one side of the stage sits a

15-man orchestra playing Massenet's *Elégie*. Todd spends an hour filming close-ups for Susanne Rousseau's face as she is instructed to scream and scream again. His perfectionism reduces her to tears. Standing behind the camera is Karl-Heinz Kornfeld. Todd has asked him to be present during this scene, dressed in costume as if witnessing his own birth.

'At 9.00 a.m. an ambulance arrives containing a nursing mother and her male child born literally a few hours earlier. They are installed in a bed a few feet away from Susanne Rousseau's. As the moment of Jean-Jacques simulated birth arrives, the baby is removed from its real mother's breast, is smeared with olive oil and held aloft— screaming, dripping between the splayed legs of the actress. Todd spends another thirty minutes filming close-ups of the infant's face until the exhausted mother insists she and her child are returned to the maternity ward at the local hospital.

'At the end of the morning's filming there follows a one hour break for lunch. Karl-Heinz Kornfeld dines alone with Todd in a private room.

'1.30 p.m. Returning to stage 3 we notice that there are two cameras set up. One on Susanne Rousseau's death-bed and one facing Karl-Heinz Kornfeld who has been once again placed in a position where is afforded a clear view of the bed. The orchestra plays an adaptation of Fauré's *Requiem* as Susanne Rousseau dies, calling for her baby boy. Isaac Rousseau looks on, glycerine tears tracking his face. "Think of your own mothers!" Todd bellows at the actors as the cameras turn. "My son! My son!" Susanne Rousseau sobs pitifully. "Think of your mother dying!" Todd shouts. The music builds. Todd himself weeps uncontrollably. Some of the crew begin to cry. At the final sonorous chords Susanne Rousseau gasps, tries to raise herself from her pillow and falls back, dead. At that moment, at a sign from Todd, a door in the studio wall opens, and through it comes a bewildered old lady in a dowdy overcoat and black straw hat. Karl-Heinz Kornfeld looks on for a moment in total shock before collapsing sobbing on the ground. The old lady shuffles forward calling "Karl-Heinz! Karl-Heinz!" Todd cries 'Cut!' Pandemonium reigns.

'The old lady turns out to be Kornfeld's mother whom he has not seen in five years. Todd has secretly brought her to the studios for just this entrance, transporting her from Darmstadt where she has been living in impoverished widowhood.'

I have to tell you that Karl-Heinz very nearly did not forgive me for this little trick. But the emotion registered on his face was astonishing.

I did it because I wanted Karl-Heinz to be bound up in this film in a way which would be unparalleled. Which is why, so to speak, I wanted him to witness his own beginning; and why I enjoined everyone to substitute their own mothers for Susanne Rousseau. I knew Karl-Heinz's guilt over his neglect of his mother and I knew that, as his head filled with morbid images, her sudden appearance would be devastating. I was absolutely right. He was ruined, wordless, shivering with confusion and emotional fatigue. The music was excellent and essential too. I used the orchestra for all important scenes; they were kept permanently on hire and at hand. Everyone gave the performance of their lives, even the baby ... That was a brilliant stroke. Such a fragile, wrinkled thing, still red and squashed-looking. To see it held there screaming in the arc lights was enormously affecting. Unfortunately, and despite our best efforts, it developed a chill and nearly died. Some meddling relative persuaded the mother to sue (I had paid her handsomely) and we were obliged to settle out of court to avoid the adverse publicity she threatened. Aram/Eddie was mightily displeased at this unforeseen addition to the budget, but when I ran the film for him he had to concede the power in what otherwise might have been a hackneyed scene.

But it was the lasting effect on Karl-Heinz that most gratified me. He was typically blasé about the film during the run-up to the day's shooting. His brand of relaxed, lazy cynicism was the last thing I required from the man who was going to ignite the imaginations of the world as Jean-Jacques Rousseau. In one day he saw himself born, saw his mother die and then had her miraculously resurrected. It was a shock from which I never wanted him to recover, and from that day his dedication to *The Confessions* was second only to mine.

Consequently, he completely understood when I rescheduled the entire filming programme after we had been going for more than a month. The plan had been to shoot all our interiors before going to France and Switzerland to do our location work at Geneva and Annecy. But, I realised, as the day approached for Doon and Karl-Heinz to play their first scenes together that filming out of sequence—here and now—would have a disastrous effect on the intensity of mood we had been striving so diligently to achieve. It was quite obvious to me that the vital moment in this story of Jean-Jacques as a young man was his meeting and subsequent love affair with Mme de Warens. To film scenes *after* that meeting before it occurred (in film time) would be asking too much of the actors to reproduce the heights of feeling I required. Normally, chronological filming is something I am happy to dispense with, but here I knew it was essential. And Karl-

Heinz, who had his doubts anyway about producing a convincing heterosexual yearning (this was to be a different order from the melodrama of Saint-Preux and Julie), agreed. I spent three nights with Leo and our production manager working out a new schedule, then Leo went to Annecy to see if our locations could accomodate our early arrival. We wound up our first segment of filming at Spandau with the celebrated soup-pissing scene. We used real urine (mine) and did not tell the actress playing the quarrelsome crone. Her hawking and spitting when she tasted the soup was entirely authentic. I told her it was laced with vinegar (I had a half-empty bottle nearby) but she took some persuading and the prop was crucial.

We left for Annecy in September, a huge caravanserai of actors, technicians and equipment that occupied an entire train. I was exhilarated to see this troop assembled at my behest, but I was also troubled. When Rousseau went to meet Mme de Warens for the first time he envisaged the encounter as a 'terrifying audience'. Now, I felt something of that type of apprehension. I was leaving Berlin and my family behind me. Once that had happened, once those checks were removed, I knew it would be impossible for me to control my feelings for Doon any longer. Currently, a fragile equilibrium existed. Doon thought I was being loyal to Sonia, and interpreted my massive effort of self-control as a sign that I had realised we should only be friends. Apart from script conferences and costume fittings and the like I had only seen her socially three times since that Christmas night, in each case in response to an invitation from her to attend KPD meetings. I tolerated these interminable harangues only because they brought me physically close to her and because afterwards we would go for a drink or a bite to eat. But even then we had only managed to be alone once. Doon always tried to invite other comrades along, and because it was her they always accepted. My God, the deadly humourless earnestness of those young men and women! I would stare at Doon, enmeshed in passionate debate, and give the occasional nod or mutter the odd fatuous remark—'Now that's a fascinating concept', or 'I couldn't agree more', 'That's an outrage'— as token of my participation. But all that was behind us. For a month or more we would be living in the same building: the Imperial Palace Hotel on the lake shore at Annecy.

*   *   *

In those days—1927—Annecy was not the fashionable resort it was to become, but I found it a delightful place, with its spectacular view of the blue lake and its ring of mountains. I loved the old town with its canals and arcaded streets, and the way the castle dominated so many of one's images of the place reminded me vaguely of Edinburgh. I thought of Jean-Jacques here, aged sixteen, arriving at the crucial nexus of his life, walking these narrow lanes ... even the cathedral, which the guide-books describe as 'a poor Gothic building' held a precise and particular charm. Jean-Jacques had sung as a chorister here and his voice had echoed beneath this indifferent vaulting.

Somehow, Leo had managed to find accommodation for all of us but in separate hotels scattered about the town. We went to work straight away on establishing shots, clearing streets of modern accoutrements, hiring locals as extras. For two enchanting days we sailed the small lake in a jolly saloon steamer, with its own restaurant, filming the gently sloping orchards and meadows on the shore and the careless mountains above. The setting, the weather and the clean air all had a suitable Rousseauistic effect on us. That first visit to Annecy was the happiest filming experience in my life. We worked in harmony and with a curious serene efficiency. I was able to send reassuring cables to Aram/Eddie in Berlin. All was well—except for me.

Rousseau fled from his unhappy apprenticeship in Geneva (we were to film this later) and went to Savoy—then an independent duchy and a frequent sanctuary for exiles and apostates from Calvinism who were received with sacred glee by proselytising priests as political converts to Catholicism. Initially an old curé entertained the young Jean-Jacques for a few days and then sent him on to Annecy with a letter of introduction to a Swiss baroness, herself a recent convert, who often gave shelter and succour to Protestant refugees.

We had some trouble with Karl-Heinz who patently did not look sixteen. We provided him with a longish dark wig—shoulder length— with a rough fringe and this made him look strangely but suitably boyish. Annecy, in 1728, was a kind of convert-centre—busy and vital, well-populated by exiles and attendant nuns and priests. That street scene twenty minutes into the film is one of my best ever manipulations of a crowd and the first in which I used a mobile camera to its full effect. I had a camera and tripod bolted to a small wheeled cart which was pulled by a couple of strong lads. We start the scene in close-up on the clashing bells of a church tower, pull back and pan down to Jean-Jacques' face looking up at them. Then the camera begins to move away and we see him push uncertainly through the throng of urchins, citizens, priests, soldiers and nuns.

The camera appears to move effortlessly through the criss-crossing bodies, as if it were an invisible presence, then to weave sinuously through the arcades as Jean-Jacques, clutching his letter of introduction, makes his hesitant way towards the 'terrifying audience' with Mme de Warens.

It took me five days to shoot this scene. I admit I prolonged it unduly in order to delay and heighten Doon's first appearance in the film, but the crew were used by now to my near-fanatical desire for perfection and no-one guessed at my real motive. I had extras recostumed, buildings repainted. I even moved a line of six cypress trees fifty yards along the skyline to aid the composition of a single shot. But finally I could postpone it no longer—Doon herself was growing impatient. We had been two weeks in Annecy and she had done nothing but rehearse.

We had discovered an almost identical spot to the site of Mme de Warens' original house (later demolished, would you believe, to make room for a new police commissariat!). In *The Confessions* Jean-Jacques relates how he called on her there only to be informed that she had just left for mass. She had a private door into the nearby church which she reached by a small passage-way, bounded on one side by a garden wall, and on the other by a stream. It was here that Jean-Jacques caught up with her as she was about to enter the church. He called her name, she turned and—as he puts it—'in that moment I was hers'.

I did not sleep the night before we were due to film the scene. How to encapsulate that instant, those boiling, tremulous seconds when your love detonates for another person? I thought back, naturally, to that meeting in the Metropole bar in Berlin. How banal, how humdrum the setting—an empty cocktail bar in a fancy hotel! How doltishly inept my first words ... How could I invest the meeting of Jean-Jacques and his *Maman* with everything I felt for Doon? There was no possibility of doing so of course. Music would help; so would my editing of the images and the veracity of the expressions on the actor's faces. I even had my own lens: the Todd Soft-Focus Lens—a lanolin gel of exceptional clarity held between two plates of glass that did not cloud or blur so much as give faces a luminous powdery beauty. (I took the precaution of patenting this in both Europe and the USA: royalties from it later provided a vital financial mainstay.) With luck and hard work we would make it look wonderful, but I could never reproduce my emotions.

Baroness Mme de Warens. Louise Elénore. No authenticated portraits exist but she comes to life in Jean-Jacques' loving description.

She was twenty-eight years old when they met. He was sixteen. She had abandoned home and husband for the Catholic religion but in her life religious devotion and erotic yearnings often overlapped. She was an efficient proselytiser. Significantly, her converts were all young men who lived in her apartments as they underwent instruction. 'She had a caressing and tender air,' Jean-Jacques says, 'a very soft gaze, an angelic smile and plentiful ash-blonde hair of exceptional beauty worn in a casual unaffected negligence that increased her attraction. She was small in stature and a little plump, but it would be impossible to find a lovelier head or more beautiful bosom, or more graceful hands and arms.'

Doon's height was inaccurate but I felt the hair was a remarkable coincidence. Her hair was longer now than it had been in *Julie* but we had several wigs made in the casual style described by Rousseau and in them she looked incredibly beguiling. I dressed her in a jade-green gown, quite décolleté, with a transparent silk scarf thrown across her throat and cleavage. Whether anyone would have gone to church like that in 1728 I did not know or care—the realism I sought here was emotional and not to do with any pedantic accuracy of historical costume.

We filmed the meeting scene in the late afternoon when the light was soft and glowing and the shadows long. Technical problems managed to distract me from my own breathless emotions, though I still felt, throughout the entire day, that someone had wedged a matchbox down my throat. I kept massaging my windpipe, coughing and gulping air. At one moment I took the place of my cameraman— Horst Immelman—behind the camera. I reserved for myself the shooting of Doon's close-ups as she reacts to Jean-Jacques' call ... Doon's face as she turned to gaze into the lens: piety—shading to surprise, to stirring curiosity. It was almost too much for me to bear. The pure curve of her jaw, neck and throat set against the dark grain of the iron-studded church door is a masterful, tense counterposition. The sheen of translucent silk over her round shadowed breasts, their barely perceptible heave and subsidence as she breathed, the subtle shifts of their pale contours represented the very apex of discreet but fervent eroticism. And then I made her walk towards Jean-Jacques. Her full length was held in the frame of the lens as the camera retreated before her on its trundling dolly. I sat behind it—protected by it—and watched that particular stalking stride, and I was back that day in the Metropole Hotel as she came towards me across the thick carpets and the glossy parquet, though the groups of leather armchairs, her thighs brushing their round backs as she weaved by. Her long muscled swimmer's legs. Those curious, endearing, slightly splayed, slightly too large feet in their impossible dancer's shoes ...

Do I sound delirious? Do I sound overwhelmed, engrossed, utterly trammelled up? Do I sound in love? I called 'cut' somehow and gave orders to wrap up for the day, despite the fact we had scheduled Karl-Heinz's close-ups. The crew merely complied. I left the scene. I had to get away. Wordless, trembling, I went down to the lake, glorious in the evening light, and spontaneously boarded one of the neat steamers that left hourly for a tour of the small summer resorts on the lake shore. I got off at Menthon St Bernard and sat on the terrace of the Pension des Glaieuls staring emptily at the darkening view and, steadily over the next four hours, drank three bottles of wine and numerous cognacs. I paid a small fortune to a yokel who owned a motor brake to drive me back to Annecy. After numerous minor breakdowns and a wrong turning we arrived there well after midnight.

I went straight to Doon's suite and knocked several times before she answered the door. I had clearly woken her up.

'Jamie? What the hell's going on?'

'I had to say, that this afternoon you were ... it was stunning.'

'Well, thanks.'

She wore a child's flannel nightdress, white, printed with small blue flowers, ankle length. I swayed, she put a hand out to steady me. It was all the invitation I needed.

We made love that night, though I have only Doon's word for it. I remember nothing, a rank alcoholic amnesia depriving me of all memories beyond that image of her nightgown. Doon said later that I 'came in a second'. I suppose it was a fittingly impulsive coda to an impulsive day.

I woke early the next morning, naked, in Doon's big double bed. My head pulsed and hummed like a dynamo. I imagined my temples bulging and retracting horribly, like the throats on certain tropical frogs when they croak, or rut, or claim territorial precedence or whatever they do. Then Doon came in from the sitting room with a wide rattling, clinking tray of breakfast which she set down on the bed by my feet. Then she cruelly threw back the curtains and my eyeballs seemed to shrivel as if a jet of lemon juice had hit them. With my eyes shut I felt her open the windows. A breeze.

'Lovely day,' she said. 'Morning.'

She pecked me on the cheek. 'Who tied one on last night, then?' She smiled. She seemed to be in a good mood.

Slowly, very slowly, I was taking in the implications of our circumstances. She sat cross-legged at the foot of the bed. She still wore her nightgown (blue birds, not flowers), its skirt stretched, a drumskin, between her knees. She poured me coffee. I took the cup and noisily set it down on my chest, its comforting warmth soon penetrating the intervening sheet. She lit a cigarette for me and handed it over.

I took a few sips of my coffee, a cautious puff on my cigarette. I found my voice.

'Doon, I—'

'Don't talk,' she said. 'You don't need to say anything.' She shifted her position, rested her weight on one elbow, sipped at her own coffee or tea. A breast bulged heavily against the flannelette of her nightdress. Her ivory blonde hair was untidy. She looked at me across the small steaming crater of her cup.

'You were nice last night,' she said. 'You came in a second, but you were nice.'

Her lips were wet. She reached back behind her for a plate which she filled with toast, butter, a honey pot, a knife. Her breast shifted, flattened and fell with her movements. I gulped my coffee, felt its hot horizontal progress on my gut. I clenched my buttocks against the rumpled cotton of the sheet. I rubbed the back of my head very slowly to and fro on the pillow. Heard the hairs on my head grate against each other. Doon's knee—blunt, bony—appeared beneath the hem of her nightdress. Knife scrape on toast. Textures everywhere suddenly.

'You can't remember,' she said.

'I can. I meant—mean—every word.'

She bit. *Shkrnch*. Palp of a finger on a crumb at her lip's corner. She unscrewed the lid on the honey jar. Milled metal on milled glass. Clear honey. Liquid sun in this warm light. Sun glanced off her knife. That ray—photons Hamish called them—from sun across curved solar space to this angled blade to my phobic retina. Outside the blue lake and the mountains . . .

'What *did* you say, then?'

I felt my swelling cock roll across my thigh.

'Well?'

The tented sheet at my groin, sagged, rose.

'Come on.'

I lifted my coffee cup from my chest, a preliminary move to setting it down on the bedside table, but before I could do so Doon had reached forwards and flipped the sheet back.

'Mmm. What have we here?' Her grip closed firm about its base.

257

I was in the middle of the big bed. My right arm, extended, holding the coffee cup and saucer was six inches short of the right bedside table. My cigarette was in my left hand. I had to put that cup down. I transferred it, urgently, to my left hand with some rattling and slopping. Four inches short. I felt pinioned, immobilised. Arms spread, crucified, pegged down. Doon's hand on the stake that held me fast.

'Doon!' I said weakly. She was doing something with her knife. The honey was cool. Surprisingly—it always looks warm, like something molten, but it was cool. I watched her spread it. It ran thickly down the ridges of her knuckles and pooled, gleamy, in the hairs on my groin. My left leg twitched, my back arched.

'Doon, Christ . . .' feebly, as if succumbing to an anaesthetic. The coolness shifted quickly up through the heat spectrum, warming. She looked at me as she did it, cheeks hollowed, eyes candid and lively. Full of fun. I could not meet that gaze for long. I lay back. The pressure grew. The cigarette fell and rolled off the bed. Then, soon after, the coffee cup went with a clatter, spilling, soaking into the sheets.

*   *   *

God alone knows what the chambermaids thought when they saw that ruined bed later that morning, covered in honey trails, toast crumbs, coffee stains and a cigarette burn. My foot at the moment of climax kicked the tray awash with Doon's verbena *infusion*, sent knives sliding, tipped out plates' contents. It was only later, that evening, when I saw the immaculate plateau of the remade bed that I remarked on it to Doon. She laughed. 'God, you're a messy bastard,' she said. She reassured me. Chambermaids have seen it all, she said; they're like nurses, nothing shocks them.

During the filming at Annecy we slept together every night. When we moved to Chambéry in October Doon returned to Berlin for ten days. She was not required, she said, and I had a lot of work to catch up on. She was right—we were at least two weeks behind schedule. I asked her not to see Mavrocordato when she was in Berlin. She told me not to be stupid.

She left and the weather changed: squalling rain and snow showers which made us even slower. When she came back we managed some scenes at the Les Charmettes farmhouse and also shot the celebrated summer-house episode.

Time has passed and Rousseau is now twenty-one, earning his living as a music teacher in Chambéry, where Mme de Warens has moved her household. An attractive young man, he is proving rather too alluring to the mothers of the young girls he teaches. It can only be a matter of time before he is seduced. Mme de Warens decides to act herself. The moment occurs, or rather the option is mooted, in a summer-house set in a herb garden that Mme de Warens owned. Rousseau used to work in this summer-house regularly and in fine weather he and Mme de Warens dined there. One evening, after dinner, Mme de Warens suggests quite openly to him that it is time he lost his virginity and proposes that she be his partner in the enterprise. In a tone of high seriousness she gives him eight days to reflect on the proposition, which delay Rousseau, somewhat shocked, eagerly accepts. Eight days later in the little summer-house sexual congress takes place.

I had an identical summer-house built in a suitable walled garden. Some mornings we spent hours sweeping the fresh snow from the pathways and lawns, recreating sunlight with our powerful arc lights. It was an important scene—both bizarre and comic—and a key to Mme de Warens' own compromised sexual nature that would have special bearing on part I's conclusion.

I felt strange directing Karl-Heinz and Doon in a love scene. I intended to fade out on the first kiss to an exterior of the summer-house, the panes of glass suddenly opaque and golden with flashing sunlight. The caption I had written was taken directly from the book: 'Was I happy? No. I had tasted the pleasure but some invincible sadness poisoned its charm for me.'

How well I understood that emotion! I had never experienced the same natural abandon as I had that first morning with Doon. We made love with intense mutual pleasure and enthusiasm, but she always stopped me when I wanted to tell her how much I cared for her. But you've told me that before, she would say. You don't need to tell me again.

* * *

We were back in Berlin by mid-November, the weather having called a halt to filming. I was feeling unwell, I remember, a heavy cold and heavy heart. In Annecy and Chambéry I had felt free of my conscience and responsibilities. The banal truth is that physical distance is all that is required to make adultery safe and worry-free. Now back at home duplicity had necessarily to be enrolled as my co-partner. I found the strain of collating my lies and falsehoods with parts of the truth enervating and depressing. And the house seemed like a veritable zoo with the ubiquitous Shorrolds back again for two months over

Xmas and New Year. Had a year really gone by? I should have been celebrating: my film was being made; I was the lover of the one woman I had ever truly adored but these equations never work themselves out neatly. In our Charlottenburg villa there were nine of us: five adults and four children and only one bathroom. I started spending nights out at the studio in Spandau just to keep away.

There were huge problems with the film. We edited together a rough cut of the material filmed so far. It came to four hours and forty-five minutes. I did not know how I was going to break the news to Eddie (curiously, it was only now that I found his name easy on the tongue). Part I, furthermore, was nowhere near complete. We had still to shoot the Geneva scenes, and the bad weather we had endured at Annecy and Chambéry meant we would have to return there next year. At the same time there was no gainsaying that what we actually had in the can was superb. A story was unfolding here that was utterly enthralling and both Karl-Heinz and Doon glowed on the screen.

In early January I showed Eddie carefully chosen segments of our rough cut interposed with linking commentary from me. All my caution was needless: he said he was overwhelmed and deeply moved. But then he paused.

'Brilliant. Fantastic. But where's the film? That's six months' work?' He looked sad rather than angry.

'There's more,' I said. 'I haven't shown you the rest.'

We got down to business. We argued, we haggled. I was in a strong position: *Joan of Arc* had been a great success—not quite a *Julie*, but highly satisfying all the same. *Julie* was still playing in the USA. Eddie wanted Part I complete by July '28. I demanded the end of September. I won. Eddie stipulated that I must forfeit my $25,000 completion bonus if I was one day into October. We saved some money by actually closing down the film for two months—March and April. I add this note because I have read the wildest and most irresponsible accounts of the filming of *The Confessions*. It has even been written that I spent five years making a two hour film. For the record, then, the first phase of *The Confessions: Part I* lasted from July 1927 to February 1928. Phase two was to commence at Chambéry in May 1928.

Doon and I tried to meet as often as we could. She insisted, however, that if we made love we had to be together for a whole night. This not unreasonable demand made life extra difficult for me, as you might imagine. My lies to Sonia became less and less circumspect. I found the whole business of covering up increasingly effortful. And I was encouraged in my laxity my Sonia's astonishing naïvety. Or indifference.

I spent a whole weekend with Doon in February. Friday night, Saturday, Saturday night. I returned home on Sunday evening.

'Where were you?' Sonia said.

'I told you. At the studios, editing.'

'But they said you weren't there. That you'd left on Friday night.'

'That's nonsense. Of course I was.'

'I telephoned all day Saturday.'

'Well, I was in and out.'

'That would explain it.'

'What?'

'Someone told me they saw you in town on Saturday evening. In a restaurant. Kurfürstendamm.'

Mild panic symptoms. 'Yes ... Well, I had to meet Doon Bogan. Script—you know—decisions.'

'How is Doon?'

'What? ... Oh, fine, fine. Fine ... Why were you calling me?'

'Hereford was ill.'

'Is he all right?'

'Seems to be now. Just a bad cold.'

'There's no need to phone me just because a child's got a cold, Sonia.'

I found this conversation most disturbing. I looked at Sonia's expression closely (she was playing Patience) but she seemed entirely credulous. Yet she had virtually trapped me in a lie. More intelligent questioning, had she been truly suspicious, would surely have caught me out. *Had she been truly suspicious. . . ?* Why was she *not* suspicious? Over the next few days this question nagged at me. There were only two answers that I could come up with. One: that she was a trusting fool. Two: that my prolonged absences from the home suited her in some way.

I eventually asked Doon.

'Do you think Sonia could ever have an affair?'

'Why not? You are. Do you think you need a special talent?'

'I suppose so.'

'She's attractive.'

'*Sonia?*'

'Yeah. In a sort of comforting earth-mothery way.'

'Really?'

'Well, I just know Alex used to say she was sort of sexy. He liked English women.'

This did me no good at all. To me Sonia seemed unchanged. I had not felt a spasm of sexual attraction towards her since I had met Doon that Christmas night in 1926. But once the seed had been sown, suspicion began to flower. She was alone a lot; she was rich; she had servants, a car, and a driver if need be; the children were looked after ... What did she do all day?

It was during the lay-off months of March and April that these suspicions became intolerable. Doon asked me to come with her to a conference of International Socialism in Paris, but I excused myself on the grounds that phase two of part I required me in Berlin. I felt I had dedicated enough time and effort to the cause, with my generous donations, my signing of innumerable petitions and protesting letters to the newspapers. I had managed to cut down on the meetings, but along with Doon I had actually marched twice through the streets of Berlin on KPD rallies. It was enough, I felt. Much as I loved her I did not want to submit that love to the trials of a two week conference.

Thus, undistracted, I fell to brooding about Sonia and decided, reluctantly, to have her followed. I asked Eddie if he knew of a private investigator.

'Yes,' he said, 'what for?'

I lied. I said a friend of Sonia had asked to borrow money from her. I merely wanted the proposed 'scheme' investigated, discreetly.

Eddie looked shrewdly at me. 'We used to use a man called Eugen for chasing debts. I never met him but his success rate was high.'

'Sounds ideal,' I said. 'What's his address?'

I was relieved that E. P. Eugen lived in an unfashionable northern quarter of the city—Wedding—in a small street next to the infectious diseases hospital, and with a drab view of the Berlin ship canal at its southern end. I found it—and I am sure all Eugen's clients felt the same way—strangely reassuring to visit such an anonymous address. I travelled there by the *ringbahn*—it seemed more fitting—and got off at Putlitz Strasse station. I had never visited this district before: it was oddly spread out—warehouses, a new park which seemed not to have taken to its surroundings, the vast modern functional-looking hospital. I made my way quickly to Fehmarn Strasse.

On the door it said 'Eugen P. Eugen. Loan Repossession and Character References.' I knocked and was admitted by a young bespectacled girl. A small man, almost dainty, rested one haunch on what I took to be her desk. He turned and examined the dangling, gleaming toe of his boot.

'I have an appointment with Herr Eugen.' I said. 'I am Herr Braun.'

'Ah, Herr Braun.' The little man stood up. 'I am Eugen. Come in.'

I followed Eugen into his office. He really was very small, not much over five feet, and immaculately dressed. He had neatly parted blond hair with almost white eyelashes which gave him a look of childish openness. We sat down. Eugen took a long cigar out of a drawer in his desk and lit it. I imagined this was a reflex gesture. It seemed to say: I may be a small man but I have a big cock. I immediately disliked him.

He told me his terms and I told him my business. I told him that I wanted a woman followed with the utmost discretion. I gave no name, just my address and Sonia's description. I wanted to know where she went, who was there and what they did. It was simple, straightforward, and our discussion lasted less than five minutes. I paid in advance and he agreed to provide a full report in one month. I got up to leave but Eugen was round his desk like a cat and stopped me at the door.

'Would you oblige me with your autograph, Herr Todd? For my secretary. She's seen *Julie* five or ten times. Fifteen perhaps.'

I signed, grudgingly, but without comment.

'Too, I am a great admirer,' he said in English, in a soft confidential voice. Then as I left he added pointedly, 'Good day to you, Herr Braun.'

It was only two weeks before I heard from him. I was busy with the approaching re-start of the film. Leo was away in Switzerland supervising construction of a huge set near the small town of Grex which was doubling as eighteenth-century Geneva. I was working on a revolutionary technical device and was plotting its integration with the film when Eugen's phonecall was transferred to me in the photographic laboratories at Spandau.

'I wasn't expecting to hear from you,' I said.

'There is good and bad news,' he said. 'I must discuss them with you.'

We arranged to meet in a small café around the corner from his office in the late afternoon. It turned out to be a cellar café, a few uncomfortable doors away from the main entrance to the *Institut für Infektionskrankenhaus*. Eugen sat at the back of the café at a thin table, eating stuffed cucumbers. He had a bad fresh graze on his forehead and chin; apart from that he was as dapper as ever. He stopped eating as soon as he saw me and lit one of his stupid cigars.

'Can I offer you some beer? Some wine? There is excellent food here. Excellent—and at modest prices.'

'No thanks. What happened?'

'Your wife. She discovered me.'

Eugen told me that it was his practice to use a small motorbike to follow cars. In this manner he had followed Sonia undiscovered for ten days. The day before yesterday she had not used the driver but had taken the car herself. She took an unfamilar route and Eugen thought he was finally on to something. She motored out to the country. Somewhere near Dallgow, in a quiet lane, Eugen turned a corner and almost ran into the back of Sonia's car (our Packard) which was deliberately parked to bring about this result. Eugen had braked, skidded and fallen off his bike. He tore his clothes, grazed his face and has been momentarily stunned. Sonia confronted him, brandished a revolver (it must have been a child's—I had to admire her nerve and aplomb) and demanded to know why he was following her.

He looked down at his cucumber.

'I had to confess a powerful infatuation,' he said. 'I'm sorry, but it's the best excuse. It always works.' Sonia had gone through his wallet and had found his business cards (here I was thankful for Eugen's euphemistic job-description).

'But I must tell you,' he went on. 'Good news. She's an honest woman. There's nothing illicit in her life, nothing. She meets her friends, she takes her children to the park. She shops. She plays cards twice a week with other women. That's all.'

We haggled aimlessly for a while over his fee. He said the damage to his motorbike, clothes, face and self-esteem was barely covered by the unearned portion of his advance. I gave in and returned home somewhat relieved. Sonia never mentioned the incident to me. Why? Did she suspect me? Or was she flattered by Eugen's subterfuge? Although I was reassured I still harboured illogical worries, even though there was nothing in Sonia's demeanour or increasingly round placid face (Berlin was plumping her up) that could reasonably give me cause for alarm.

*   *   *

Is this the time for a brief tribute to Eddie Simmonette? I owe him so much (mind you, he owes me a fair bit, too) and I will never forget his generosity and tolerance, his help and understanding when I went to him in April 1928 and told him my plans to revise completely

certain aspects of *The Confessions* and reshoot some of the previous
year's scenes.

I was bold—I pushed my luck—only because of that death-bed
promise old Duric had extracted from him. I doubt if I would have
been so confident and audacious with another backer. But, sentimental
reasons aside, there were sound commercial reasons for backing a
John James Todd film in those days. Anyway, I made my bid because
I was fretting about certain sequences of the film and was seeking
some means of resolving them.

The plain fact is that by 1928 there was nothing much more to be
done with the camera. Every so-called trick and gimmick you see on
today's cinema screens had been discovered before three decades
of the century were up. Rapid cutting, multiple exposure, moving
cameras, angled shots, back lighting, matte screens, selective soft
focus, vignette masks, crane shots, lens diffusion etc. etc. were all at
the director's disposal. It was as if, to take an analogy, the history of
painting had moved from mud daubings on a cave wall to modern
abstract expressionism in twenty-five years. We were even experimenting with a kind of 3-D picture in those days and this was one
of the new techniques I wanted to employ. A firm in France was
producing a type of embossed film which when projected on a screen
gave the actors, if not a true three-dimensional effect, at least that of
a bas-relief. It was particularly effective in close-up. The film stock
was expensive but we had budgeted for it. I planned to use it in the
famous cherry-picking incident which we would film in Chambéry
that summer.

All film technique, I am convinced (and like many of my theories
I am probably alone in adhering to it), originates in dreaming. We
could dream slow motion before the moving camera was invented.
In our dreams we could cut between parallel actions, we assembled
montage shots long before some self-important Russian claimed to
show us how. This is where film derives its particular power. It
recreates on screen what has been going on in our unconscious. I met
a famous director once (he shall be nameless) who purported to be
the first man to launch a remote control camera down a stretched
wire and give us for the first time the sensation of flying like a bird.
But dreamers, I told him, have been flying this way since the birth
of consciousness. Many of my own inventions (the hand-held camera,
my soft-focus lens) originated in my dreams. This, then, was the
position I found myself in. Let us take another image—a still, burning
candle. It is beautiful, it illumines. Now, breath gently on the flame
and observe the flickering dancing transformation. As I saw it the

director's role in the film was to be the breath upon the candleflame. I had everything at my disposal in *The Confessions* to make that flame dance and sparkle—my vision, the actors, technical apparatus and the skills of my collaborators—but I still felt myself baulked and restricted by the confinement of the lens and what we could do with it, that fixed immutable rectangle that we had to fill. And then, that spring of '28, I dreamt about Rousseau and his walk from Geneva to Savoy. I saw him striding through the chilly landscape with the vast backdrop of the mountains behind him. It was as if I stood and watched him walk a mile in front of my eyes ... When I woke I knew that my task in *The Confessions* was somehow to escape the limitations of the frame.

The solution to this problem came so swiftly that I was baffled that it had not struck anyone before. If I could not extend the dimensions of the camera lens and thereby extend the dimensions of the screen, I would simply multiply the options available to me: I would use three cameras, five cameras, synchronise their images and project them on a corresponding number of adjacent screens. I had a sudden vision of my cinema of the future. We would sit the audience in a round amphitheatre, hemmed in by a circular screen. Jean-Jacques' walk could span 360 degrees ...

But this was far away. I sat down with my cameraman Horst Immelman to work out the practicalities (there is not much to say about Horst—in his forties, genial, efficient, an *artisan de luxe*). We quickly realised that the best we could achieve was the linking up of three cameras, otherwise synchronisation, image adjustment and continuity would prove nightmarishly complicated. Horst thought a prototype could be rigged up in a month. I went to Eddie to convince him we should use it. He at once saw the immense advantages the device would bring, but pointed out that we would have to adapt the world's cinemas too, if it was to be worthwhile. It was a fair point. In the end it was decided that I would shoot some scenes with the Tri-Kamera (as it was now known) and—this was Eddie's idea— Realismus would adapt key cinemas for premières, trade and publicity screenings. He enthused about my invention but for the wrong reason. He saw it as a spectacular publicity stunt and was indifferent to the aesthetic potential. We—Horst and I—went away with a revised budget and shooting schedule. I would re-film two scenes—Rousseau's walk to Savoy and his first meeting with Mme de Warens— and use the Tri-Kamera on two new ones: the cherry-picking incident and Rousseau's forlorn departure from Les Charmettes and arrival in Paris. If the device worked, and public response was favourable, we would look at expanding the Tri-Kamera sequences in parts II and III.

And so we were set to go again. The rest of the year lay before me, planned and funded. Spring and summer in Geneva, Annecy and Chambéry. The autumn taken up with shooting the Tri-Kamera scenes. Winter, back in Spandau for interiors. My new delivery date was 1st July 1929. Part II would commence in the autumn of that year.

*   *   *

Before we left for France I asked Doon to marry me but, typically, with my usual impulsive stupidity, chose entirely the wrong moment. I was at her apartment, we had just made love. I got dressed to go out and buy some cigarettes. As I took my coat and hat from the stand in the hall I saw an unfamiliar paisley-patterned fine-wool scarf hanging there. I picked it up and smelt it. Hair oil and cigars ... I replaced it and went out. Somehow I purchased cigarettes.

Mavrocordato.

Mavrocordato had been to the apartment. I could see the scarf round his thick neck. I issued a series of instructions to myself as I walked back from the tobacconist's kiosk all to do with calmness, logic, dispassion, self-respect but I promptly forgot them all as I stepped back inside.

Doon called: 'Hurry up with those cigarettes!'

I took Mavrocordato's scarf off the hook and put it in my pocket. I went into the bedroom and tossed a packet of cigarettes on the bed. Doon sat up to reach them, exposing her breasts as she leant forward. I dangled the scarf in front of her. She looked up.

'Mavrocordato's been here, hasn't he?'

'Yes.' She was candid, unshaken.

I felt my eyes heavy with tears. 'He forgot his scarf. You should be more careful.'

'No, it's not.'

'What?'

'Not his scarf. The plumber who came on Monday—no, Tuesday—left it.'

'The plumber ...'

'Well done.'

'But you did say Mavrocordato had been here.'

'Yes.'

I felt all my anger turn in mid-air like a boomerang and head back towards me.

'What the hell for?' I asked. 'I mean, what bloody right does he have...? What about my feelings, for God's sake?'

'We had a chat. Christ, I *was* married to him you know.'

I sat down on the bed and took her hand.

'Doon, I want you to marry me. I beg you. Let's get married.'

'No. I don't want to get married again. Once was enough. Not to anyone. Not even you.'

She freed her hand from mine, lit her cigarette and lay back in the bed.

'Why should we get married? Aren't you happy?'

'Of course I am. That's why.'

'Well, let's leave it at that.'

'I forbid you to see that ... that big hairy shit again.'

'No you don't. I like him. I'll see him if I want to. You don't need to be there. For God's sake don't be stupid, Jamie. Anyway, you're married already.'

Why can't we be content with the way things are? Is it a basic human failing, this constant need to improve your life? ... Is there a deep atavistic dream, which we all cherish, that however settled and content our life seems to be it can with more effort be a little bit better? Chimeras, mirages, illusions—not to be trusted. Why did I keep pushing Doon this way? Why did I keep pushing myself? Everything was fine until I unilaterally decided it could be better. That night I kept on at her, pleading the case for matrimony with keening insistence. It became very boring for her. We snapped at each other, we argued. Then I apologised and tried to calm down but the evening was ruined. My tone had been wheedling, selfish. Doon was right, damn her; my arguments could get no forensic purchase.

Shortly after that abortive proposal I came home one night at about half past eight. Sonia was in the kitchen talking to Lily. I went upstairs without greeting her. It must have been about half past nine. In the upstairs corridor I saw Vincent peering through the half-opened door to the boy's bedroom.

'Get to bed,' I warned.

'Daddy, Hereford won't talk to me.'

'He's a sensible boy. He's gone to sleep.'

I ushered Vincent back into the room and helped him into bed. Then I went over to Hereford's cot. He was lying on his back, one arm thrown high, two glistening streams of snot trailing from his nostrils. I took out my handkerchief to wipe his lip clean. The instant

I touched him I knew he was dead. He was barely warm. I picked him up and his head fell back. A curious gurgling sound came from his throat. I kissed his face, the tears running freely from my eyes, and laid him back down again. I went over to Vincent, got him out of bed and led him from the room.

Hereford's cold had lingered on, turned into a bad cough, gone away and returned again. He did not seem to mind. To him, I suppose, it was just another couple of orifices—nose and mouth— excreting in concert with his nether ones. He was three years old.

VILLA LUXE 23 June 1972

What can I say about Hereford? I think, I believe, I sincerely believe that everything might have been different had he lived. *But I can't be sure.* I can't be sure of anything. Hamish would agree with that conclusion. All I'm left with is a sentimental aggregate of fond recollection and wishful thinking. I know only that I loved that small boy in a different way from my other children. There was something in me that responded to his anarchic clumsy presence no matter how irritated and preoccupied I was. And then he was gone.

Is this the sort of occasion where a human life (mine) takes a quantum leap? One of those sudden jumps, an abrupt discontinuity that changes everything? Nothing was quite the same after Hereford died, the world had a different tinge and texture. From where do we get this funny idea that order, causality, sense and continuity should necessary prevail in the world in which we humans live and breathe? Yes, I thought, I can see how this place is governed by chance and random change, having just been the victim of a particularly brutal one. I can undertand now how visions of discontinuity and plurality fit my experience better than ideas of order and deliberateness. We don't know anything for certain. We can't determine anything. We function solely on terms of hopeful probability. It worked this way before, maybe it will again. But don't count on it.

I go into the main town, the port, to see Eddie's lawyer about getting the pool filled. The central square is shabbily elegant, paved with white stone and lined with mature fragrant oleanders. The yellowing stucco buildings around it have tall windows with shutters and wrought iron balconies. At one end there is an amusing baroque statue of two heavily armed, plumed soldiers wrestling with the flag of liberty.

Everywhere the tourists mill about. Inside his hot office the lawyer is diplomatic. He procrastinates. He apologises. What can he do? Perhaps at the end of the tourist season . . .

I leave and join the gaudy visitors to our island. I find my favourite café overlooking the harbour and after waiting no more than ten minutes I secure a seat. I eat some ice-cream—pistachio, always pistachio—and drink a coffee. I think about Ulrike. She's a charming girl. The tan she has now suits her. She exudes health and a settled happy confidence in her life or work. I try to picture her boyfriend, the cineaste. I see a beard, a check shirt, a name like Rudi or Rolf. Everything seems fine, Ulrike, but tread carefully. Remember the

Uncertainty Principle. It governs the molecules we're made of. A little of it is going to penetrate our human world. If a fig tree root can make it through a solid concrete wall what is going to stop the Uncertainty Principle? Look at my life—lived in unswerving devotion to its capricious edicts.

I stop. I'm getting depressed. I look up and at that moment a tourist bus goes by. And there at a window pointing at the attractions of our picturesque harbour is a man I know. An American. Reassurance is slow to fade. Relax, I say to myself, it could be a coincidence. It must be. It might not even be him at all. He never saw *you*, and anyway, nobody knows you are here.

12

End of an Era

In the summer of 1730 Mme de Warens quit Annecy temporarily for Paris leaving Jean-Jacques behind. He had a pleasant time in her absence dallying with young women, several of whom, or so he claimed in *The Confessions*, were in love with him. On one particularly beautiful day he went for a walk in the country. In a green valley beside a stream he came across two girls who were having difficulty leading their horses across. Rousseau had met one of the girls before— a Mlle de Graffenried—and was introduced by her to the other— Mlle Galley. They were both pretty, especially Mlle Galley who was 'both small and well developed at an age when a girl is most beautiful'. Rousseau helped them both across the stream and the girls insisted on his accompanying them for the rest of the day. They were going to the Château de la Tour at Thônes, a large farm house which belonged to Mlle Galley's family.

They duly arrived at the Château and enjoyed a late lunch in the kitchen. Saving their coffee and cream cakes for later they decided to round off their meal by going into the Château's cherry orchard to pick the ripe fruit. Rousseau climbed the trees and threw down cherries to the girls who teasingly threw the pits back up at him. A flirtatious game ensued. 'Mlle Galley, with her apron held forward and her head thrown back presented such a good target, and I threw so well, that a bunch of cherries fell between her breasts. What laughter! I said to myself, "If only my lips were cherries I would gladly throw them there."'

But nothing happened. It was an idyll, vibrant with sexual intimations and unrealised potential. As you can imagine, this particular episode had burned itself into my mind when I read it in my barren cell at Weilberg. And remember I read it as a virgin (my two girls were Huguette and Dagmar) and at the time it actually occurred Jean-Jacques was a virgin too. He never forgot that day in the cherry orchard. For him it was moment, he realised later, which proved that the erotic sensuality of innocence is often more powerful than the carnal pleasures of adulthood.

I filmed the entire day just as Rousseau had related it. I cast the two girls locally, searching touring theatre groups and music halls in Grenoble, Nice and Lyons. It was their appearance that was important, not their acting ability—I had no need for sophisticated, worldly actresses. All they had to do was look right, giggle and flirt. Karl-Heinz was a gauche monster of ardent frustration, positively deformed with the competing pressures of desire and shyness. In our orchard we cut out the centre of one tree and mounted a camera platform there. We used embossed film for the moment Mlle Galley's breasts 'catch' the bunch of cherries. It was during this week that I saw a further potential in the Tri-Kamera. I realised that it need not be employed solely for creating one single long stretched image—it could just as easily make three separate ones. Throughout one exhausting evening Horst and I worked out with the aid of diagrams a sequence of massive close-ups using the embossed film. The actors were baffled as we thrust the cameras to within inches of their faces from every possible angle, pausing between shots to consult sheaves of notes and scribbled drawings. The resulting sequence is breathtaking in its latent erotic power, as those who saw it on the three screens testified. Let me take you through it.

Everything in the episode, in terms of filming, proceeds orthodoxly. The encounter at the stream, the ride to the Château, the meal in the kitchen. Then, as the trio walk to the cherry orchard the curtains in the cinema draw back to reveal the two angled screens adjacent to the main one. The two auxiliary projectors start up and suddenly we have three separate images. Three heads in view: Jean-Jacques, flanked by Mlles Graffenried and Galley. We see covert glances pass between them. The two girls look up on either side as Jean-Jacques climbs the tree in centre screen. Then the contours shift and firm as the embossed film runs through the projector. The hanging clumps of cherries seem to take on the form of three-dimensional fruit. The perfect pallor of the girls' faces and shoulders seem cast in plaster relief against the leafy background. We look down with Jean-Jacques at the two delightful lasses gazing up at him. The girls eat the cherries, spit the stones into their hands and throw them back at Jean-Jacques, who ducks the gentle hail.

Then the centre screen is filled by Mlle Galley looking up, apron held out to catch more fruit. Jean-Jacques' face is on one side screen as he plots his revenge; on the other his hand plucking a bunch of cherries. Centre screen: we move in slowly on Mlle Galley's breasts, the low cut of her gown, the pressure, on either side, of her arms forcing them ever so slightly together. The swell and subsidence of her excited breathing, the soft deep shadow of her cleavage. Jean-Jacques' hand throws. Centre screen, the cherries land. Lips, cherries, lips. Eyes, cherries, eyes. Then three laughing mouths. We pull back. In the centre Jean-Jacques' laughter disguises his agonised face. The side screens dim, the curtains roll back to cover them.

It works magnificently. At the première the audience was in an uproar. The planning of it all was painstakingly difficult. (I must pay tribute to Mlle Sadrine Storri, a burlesque dancer from Lyons who disappeared back into obscurity after the film, who played Mlle Galley. She showed admirable patience and good humour as I, standing on a chair above her, dropped dozens of cherry-bunches onto her bosom, Horst's camera whirring twelve inches away.) Of course my delight and pride in this scene was delayed. We were working blind. I had to wait many months before I saw the sequence run on three full-sized screens. For myself, and I speak with total honesty and objectivity, I think it represents the most complete and effective blend of technique and content in the entire movie. Embossed film and the Tri-Kamera were the perfect devices to reincarnate the tender eroticism of that warm afternoon near Annecy. Add to that the audacious use of massive close-ups of lips and eyes, dark glossy cherries and pale heaving breasts . . . overpowering images. My close-ups in *The Confessions: Part I* were the largest ever witnessed on the screen up to that time (larger than Eisenstein's for sure) and, this is what makes me particularly proud, not a caption in sight.

And so we continued working throughout the summer beset by more than the usual delays and technical hitches. The embossed film stock was notoriously fragile and the Tri-Kamera presented us with understandable teething troubles. The list of problems was endless and of little interest now, but it will give you some idea of the conditions under which we had to work if I tell you that, after a day's filming, Horst, Leo and I drove to Geneva—where the nearest lab that could develop the embossed film was to be found—to examine the prints of previous days' shooting. More often than not we discovered some defect, some bubbling or flaking in a negative, that necessitated reshooting. The entire cherry-tree sequence, some two and a half minutes in length, took us most of July to film. By the end of that month I realised we were in serious difficulties. I received an angry cable from Eddie pointing out that the ratio of film shot to film used was running at approximately 80 to 1. In other words I was shooting eighty minutes of film to produce one minute of screen time.

A ratio of 30 to 1 is regarded as generous. 15 to 1 is not impossible. Somehow this news leaked out and it is from around this time that vicious stories began to circulate about my profligacy, extravagance, and manic perfectionism. After a particularly scurrilous and savage attack in the trashy *Das grosse Bilderbuch des Films* I even travelled back to Berlin to reassure Eddie, and calm him down.

We were now over budget. We were behind schedule. But what was being produced was extraordinary. It is true to say—and it is one of film's bizarre strengths—that the last category can always overrule the first two. There is no contest in the struggle between real Art and Accountancy. Audiences are indifferent to balance sheets. Eddie knew this but our other investors were less happy. *Julie* had been released in 1926. We were now approaching the last quarter of 1928 and no film was in sight. Unbeknownst to me Eddie had been obliged to buy out Goldfilm's interest and was renegotiating his deal with Pathé. *The Confessions* was fast becoming a Realismus project, pure and simple.

Delays meant we had to postpone our Les Charmettes filming yet again and we travelled to Grex in Switzerland to shoot the Geneva scenes. The huge set—the city walls of Geneva—had been standing unused for two months and Leo was contractually obliged to dismantle them by the end of September.

Doon had been with me all through this exciting but exhausting summer. I was immensely grateful. I think she sensed my grief over Hereford's death was deeper than I showed and, indeed, I doubt if I could have carried on if each evening I had not been able to return to her. At Annecy she was called upon to work from time to time (we spent a frustrating week trying to re-shoot her first encounter with Jean-Jacques but the Tri-Kamera kept breaking down); however at Grex there was nothing for her to do and I sensed boredom settling in. Curiously, I seemed to calm down once we reached Switzerland even though our problems in no way diminished. Perhaps it was the countryside. What I liked about the landscape was the way every possible bit of arable land was cultivated—some vineyards looked no more than twelve feet square, tucked in odd corners made by the angle between a barn and a cliff face or set on a largish ledge on a mountainside. It was this immaculate husbandry rather than the grandeur of the views that reassured me. It indicated, I thought, a determination and sense of purpose consonant with my own and I began to relax.

In this mood it was easier for me to take a weekend off when part of the Geneva city wall collapsed and filming had to be suspended while it was rebuilt. Grex was not far from Montreux so I suggested to Doon that we spend a couple of nights there. But she wanted to go up to the mountains so we drove up one of the valleys, ascending steadily from the lake shore, zig-zagging through the woods up into the thin air of the mountain plateaux. We spent the night in a small village (I forget the name) in a hotel made, it seemed, entirely from elaborately carved, densely knotted wood. We were even served a meal of ham, gherkins and potatoes on carved wooden plates. We both found it somewhat oppressive. Doon said it was like living in a sinister fairy tale. We decided to leave on the Saturday morning and return to the lake for lunch.

It was a sunny morning but cool. A level bank of cloud obscured the lake completely, as if we were shut off from the world below. We were happy as we motored easily down the tight bends, laughing about the monstrous wooden hotel.

Rounding one corner we passed a broken-down car and a man— the driver—tried to flag us down, but we were by him too quickly to pull up in time.

'He looks so cold,' Doon said. 'Stop for him.'

I braked, came to a halt some fifty yards further on and got out. I waved the man on down to us. A smallish fellow, he started jogging thankfully towards us. Then, suddenly, he stopped, glanced back at his car, and then leapt off the road and began to run down through a meadow towards a copse of fir trees. It was then that I recognised him. To Doon's astonishment I took off in pursuit.

I ran speedily down the slope through the thick dewy grass, arms windmilling backwards to keep my balance. I soon gained on my quarry, whose city shoes seemed to give him no purchase on the slippery ground. He fell several times and I caught up with him sprawled face down at the edge of the trees.

Eugen P. Eugen was soaked through and shivering. He stood up and plucked leaf mould and pine needles from his natty suit.

'Mr Todd,' he said. 'How pleasant to meet you again.'

'Why are you following me, Eugen?' I said. I was calm. I knew I could deal easily with whatever doltish blackmail was coming.

'Your wife hired me,' he said, with a mild grin. He looked down. 'My shoes are ruined.'

'But you can't work for *her*,' I said angrily. '*I* hired you.'

'Herr Todd,' he spread his hands apologetically. 'A fellow has to make a living.'

He told me that Sonia had contacted him a fortnight earlier (I have no idea what alerted her: it could have been one of a dozen inept cover-ups), he had come down to Annecy and followed us to Switzerland. He had already sent two long reports back to Sonia detailing her husband's infidelity. Eugen told me all this with perverse pride, as if it were evidence of his efficiency—a talent, so the implication seemed to run, to which I could also testify. As he elaborated on the contents of his reports I closed my eyes. Some kind of bird was singing noisily in the trees. I could feel the dew seeping up through the soles of my shoes as if searching for the sensation of fatigue and random remorse that was spreading downward through my body, its source—seemingly—some gland located in the crown of my head. Sonia had known for almost two weeks. What was waiting for me in Berlin?

I was roused by Doon's call from the road. Eugen and I looked round.

'Ah, Miss Bogan. Magnificent actress,' he said.

I thought I should feel more animosity than I did for Eugen. I tried to summon up a rage—unsuccessfully.

'Shut up, you little bastard,' I said with no conviction. Then I shouted 'Coming!' to Doon and set off back up through the damp lucent meadow towards the road.

'Herr Todd,' Eugen slipped and slithered behind me. 'Could you possibly ...? I'd be extremely grateful for a lift back down to the lake. These hired motors—'

'Sorry.' I strode on.

'Don't worry, Herr Todd. I quite understand.'

*   *   *

Sonia waited until I returned to Berlin in October. In the interim we did not communicate. The sun was shining and there were still some bright autumnal leaves on the birches in the garden at Charlottenburg. I got out of the car, a full cargo of guilt slowing my steps. The house was partially cleared. The carpets were gone but the pictures still hung upon the wall.

Sonia wore black. I suppose she was still in mourning for Hereford but the effect was suitably menacing and doom-laden. For some reason she suddenly seemed much older than me, and when I saw her face, pale but immaculately made up, I felt childishly frightened of her. I had done wrong. Even I could not rally any bravado. I had to face my punishment. Sonia confined herself to only one rebuke, but it was enough.

'Hereford dies. And then you do this to me.'

Lies and excuses filled my mouth but I ignored them. 'Sonia, I ... Where are the children?'

'In an hotel. We're going back to London tomorrow.'

I rubbed my face, as if I were washing it. I could see the long avenue of resentment and acrimony stretching ahead of me.

'I love Doon,' I said. 'I've loved her for years. I want to marry her.'

It was a mistake. My impulsive honesty ruined things for me again. I should have done nothing but apologise that day. I saw tears bulge in Sonia's hitherto conspicuously dry eyes.

'Oh, *really*,' she said with venomous cynicism. 'Well, you'll get no divorce from me.'

She took a letter from her handbag and gave it to me, said goodbye and left. I sat down and read the letter, from her lawyer, about the financial arrangements I was to provide for my wife and family; so much a month to be paid into this or that account, a trust fund to be established for the children, arrangements to be subject to an annual review, etc. etc.

I shed a few predictable tears of self-pity, and allowed my mind to travel back to those days just after the war at Superb-Imperial, days of Raymond Maude, the *Wee MacGregors*, beer and chops at the grill in Islington. Then, Sonia had been everything I desired, it was hardly her fault that I had fallen in love with Doon. I had been a late developer. In 1920 I was barely half-formed, now that I came to think about it. I had survived the Salient and prison camp but emotionally I was no more advanced than I had been at Minto Academy. I wandered around our house, revisiting chapters of my past. But the ghost of little Hereford seemed to haunt the rooms and passageways: I could hear echoes of his pratfalls and collisions at every step and corner, and soon the shawl of misery and regret that hung heavily over my shoulders drove me out of doors.

I never went back to that house. I had the contents packed up and sold it eventually for a small loss. I sent all the money to Sonia as it was going to take some time to get the funds I had deposited in Switzerland to London. Our separation proved a tedious depressing business; Sonia's lawyer was a particularly aggressive, solemn man and I used to dread the regular summonses I received to his office to iron out this or that hitch or petty grievance.

We were still filming, of course, throughout all this, and at a punishing pace too, in an attempt to make up for lost time. To my dismay, the rough cut of the film was now over seven hours long and we still had to shoot the departure from Les Charmettes and the arrival in Paris.

I asked Doon if I could move in with her but she said no. It was a perfectly reasonable refusal: she said we should wait a while. I was too disorientated to remonstrate for long and while I was waiting moved to Eddie's glum house on Kronen Strasse. Eddie was sympathetic, but he was more concerned about my professional rather than personal life.

'I told you not to get involved with actresses,' he said. 'Look at you now: money problems, no house, no family . . .'

'I'm not "involved",' I said earnestly. 'I *love* her, can't you understand that? I'm free now. I couldn't be happier. Really. Sonia'll give me a divorce eventually and then Doon and I will marry.'

'Has she said so? Doon?'

'Actually, she says she doesn't want to get married.'

'Wonderful.'

'But she will.'

'She'll never marry you, John. She knows herself. If she says she won't she won't.'

'She'll change her mind.'

'She's tough.'

'I'm tougher.'

'That's where you're wrong, my friend.'

He was right. I saw Doon a lot, we worked together, we spent most nights together, but once or twice a week I would spend a night or two away. It just seemed to happen. I would be working late, messages would miss one or the other person, meetings and appointments got in the way. When I rebuked her or acted petulantly she employed a brand of clear-minded logic I could not defeat.

'Will I see you tonight?' I would say.

'I've got a meeting, till late.'

'I'll stay up.'

'When do you start work tomorrow morning?'

'Six.'

'I'll be back around three.'

'Ah.'

'Wouldn't you rather get a good night's sleep? I'll come by at lunch time.'

What could I say? It made perfect sense. But there are times in your life when the sensible approach is exactly the one you do not require. I wanted to be irresponsible, as if that could somehow underline my love for her, erode my guilt over Hereford and Sonia. I wanted signs of grand passion. I wanted us both to declare that a moment apart was agony; that three hours sleep and a bleary-eyed start in the morning was a real proof of undying devotion. But I never got it.

*   *   *

Emotionally, I was in something of a bad way after Sonia had left me, but at least the work was going well for once. The Tri-Kamera was behaving impeccably on the reshoots and the first run-throughs of the cherry-picking sequence were a revelation.

We showed it to Eddie early in the new year, with an orchestral accompaniment. He was overwhelmed and embraced me, kissing me on both cheeks, the Lodokian in him breaking the Simmonette veneer for an instant. On his insistence we showed it again to some financiers to the same ecstatic effect. More funding came through. Rumours began to spread through the industry about the film, its revolutionary techniques, of a scale and size matched only by the ambition of its director. I suppose early 1929 saw me at the very apex of my fame. Impressive achievements behind me, limitless potential ahead. I was fêted, courted, flattered. Lubitsch wrote to me from Hollywood inviting me over. I gave interviews to newspapers from France, Italy, Britain, the USA. In Germany, in Berlin, I was for a few months a household name. I was approached in the street by strangers, offered drinks in bars, signed menus in restaurants. All the heady trappings of temporary renown. A publisher wanted to publish my auto-biography. A newspaper article about my war experiences was mooted as a possible movie. The whole world, it seemed, was agog with anticipation. *The Confessions,* as one newspaper put it, would be the film to end all films.

Was I happy? Yes and no. I find it hard to think of myself as I was then. I was thirty years old and on the brink of achieving everything I had dreamed of and more ... But I was unsettled as well. As some sort of exculpation I used to draw up a rough profit and loss column of my life. True, I was a rich and famous man—but my baby son had died. True, *The Confessions* was about to astonish the world—but my marriage was over, my wife and children estranged. True, I was in love with a celebrated and beautiful film actress—but she refused to marry me. And so on. Whenever I was alone this curious schizoid litany would enter my head to forestall any hasty conclusions about my good fortune.

I mention this because it is the only explanation I can find for what I did next. Or else I must have been a little mad ... But I think I unconsciously wanted to make life difficult for myself, simply to bolster the 'Loss' column. Does that seem perverse? I think we are inclined to do this more often than we realise.

Two aspects of *The Confessions* fatefully coincided in March 1929 to set me on this course of action.

In 1738 Rousseau had come into his inheritance and for the first time in his life was in the possession of a fair sum of money. However, he was not feeling well—'fading away' as he put it—and had diagnosed himself as suffering from a polyp on the heart. A certain doctor in Montpellier was reputed to have successfully treated such a case and Jean-Jacques went there to consult him.

This departure, significantly, coincided with the entry of his rival Witzenreid into Mme de Warens' household. The great love affair was nearing its end: things were no longer as they once had been between Rousseau and his beloved *Maman*.

On his way to Montpellier Rousseau encountered and fell in with a party of genteel travellers who included one Mme de Larnage and a Marquis de Toulignon. Mme de Larnage was attractive, heavily rouged, forty-four years old and mother of ten children, and the appearance of young Jean-Jacques on the scene proved much more enticing than her ostensible suitor, the old Marquis. For some reason, and this is what drew me to the episode, Rousseau seemed ashamed of his lowly background in this company and, quite astonishingly, claimed to be an Englishman called Dudding. By extreme good fortune no one asked 'Mr Dudding' to speak in his native language— of which he knew not one word. Mme de Larnage made her feelings evident and at one of their nightly stops in a coaching inn Jean-Jacques surrendered himself to this 'sensual and voluptuous' woman. They parted before they reached Montpellier, Jean-Jacques—phys-ically exhausted—promising a rendezvous a few weeks hence. This never occurred. Rousseau, having learnt a few English phrases in Montpellier to sustain the Mr Dudding disguise, and having regained some of his health, set off to meet up with Mme de Larnage at Bourg-St-Andeol. On his way there, however, his guilt at betraying *Maman* was so intense that he broke off his journey and returned immediately to Chambéry to rejoin her. He was received coolly. Witzenreid was still there. Jean-Jacques' place had been taken.

We filmed the coach journey in the state forest near Spandau and I cast Monika Alt as Mme de Larnage. I scrutinised the episode in *The Confessions* trying to understand Rousseau's motives in dallying with Mme de Larnage. Was it a pre-emptive revenge because he knew Witzenreid would edge him out of the nest? Or was there something in Mme de Larnage that he could not find in *Maman*? In the book he goes as far as to contrast the two experiences of sex. With

Maman, he says, sex is always accompanied by melancholy, but with Mme de Larnage he says, 'I was always proud to be a man. I surrendered myself to my senses with joy and with confidence.' What did he mean. What went on?

The Confessions is remarkable in its candour, not least about its author's sexual nature. From his earliest days Jean-Jacques liked to be dominated. When he was a child the sister of his guardian at Bossey, Mlle Lambercier, had to stop spanking him for his misdemeanours when she saw how much he was enjoying it. Later, in Nyon, a young girl—Mlle Goton—was to act out a fantasy of a strict governess and whip him. It was the only moment in his life, he implies, when a member of the opposite sex actually discerned *and* satisfied his deepest sexual cravings. Had Mme de Larnage, I wondered, done the same?

I must admit I was happy to see Monika again. We based ourselves up the road from Spandau in Falkenhagen for three or four days while we went out with the coaches and horses filming travelling scenes. Monika knew about Doon and me and was provocatively discreet about our past. 'It's all forgotten, Johnny,' she said on more than one occasion, miming sealed lips, which of course made me remember all the more vividly.

The last evening in the little *gasthaus* in Falkenhagen we had a ribald discussion about Rousseau and flagellation. Karl-Heinz said he found it very easy to sympathise with. Gunter Koll (he played the Marquis) said he thought it was depraved. Monika claimed to understand the feeling—even though she had no inclinations in that direction herself. She said that if a man asked her to beat him and it gave him real pleasure, she would not refuse.

I said, 'So if I asked you—"Monika, I want you to beat me," you wouldn't be shocked?'

'Not at all.'

We talked on. Karl-Heinz told us about a man he used to sleep with who liked having the juice of citrus fruit squeezed over his body. 'For some reason grapefruit was his favourite,' Karl-Heinz said. The tone of the evening's conversation degenerated further as we called for more drink.

Later, I came out of the *gasthaus*'s sole bathroom to find Monika waiting her turn.

'Ah. Monika,' I said stupidly. We were standing rather close together. I was wearing pyjamas and dressing gown. She looked at me, smiling.

'You want to try it?' she said.

'I'll come along in half an hour.'

She was still dressed when I went into her room. She seemed incapable of removing a knowing smile from her lips.

'Look, Monica ...' I began cautiously.

'This is just an experiment. Yes?'

'Yes.' I enjoyed the lie. 'Purely in the interests of research.' The pretence made my breathing quicken with excitement.

'What do you want me to use?' she said. 'I've got a newspaper. My father used to beat me with a rolled up newspaper. Or a brush.'

'What about a shoe? A slipper?'

We selected a fine suede slipper and stood and looked at each other.

'Do you think I should be naked?' I asked.

'Oh yes, I think so.'

I took my clothes off.

'See, you're excited already. Do you want me—'

'No, I think you should be clothed.' I could hear my blood like surf in my ears.

She sat down on the bed. I knelt beside her then bent over her knees. Her hands ran over my back and buttocks.

'Monika, please!'

'Sorry. I forgot. This is simply literary criticism. Shall I start?'

She gave me a good severe spanking. My buttocks reddened then stung. The erection I had had subsided utterly.

'Harder?'

'No. Stop, stop,' I said weakly. I stood up. 'Ouch,' I said rubbing my smarting arse. 'That's bloody *agony*!'

'And look, it's not working.' She got to her feet. 'Perhaps I should be naked too.'

I looked at her. She dropped the slipper and began unbuttoning her dress.

'Yes,' I said. 'Might be a good idea.'

*   *   *

I took up my journal again after a gap of several years.

Chambéry 15th May 1929. Filming at our version of Les Char-mettes. The house is ideal. Orchard very pretty in bloom. We have planted 400 mature vines in the field at the back and have terraced the garden in front. Now all we require is a sunny day.

I wrote that entry as we sat in a small tented village to one side of the farmhouse, listening to the rain rumble on the stretched canvas overhead. The Tri-Kamera was set up and ready to roll. The beehives were in position and Georg Pfau had five thousand bees ready to be loosed on the grassy meadows and orchard blossoms whenever the sun broke through the clouds. We had been waiting for sun—which the meteorological office in Grenoble had been assuring us was on its way—for four days. Everyone was numb with boredom. We had one scene left to shoot and *The Confessions: Part I* would be over.

I did not care what the weather was like for Rousseau's departure from Les Charmettes, and had already shot it in a dismal drizzle, but it was absolutely essential that when he arrived the gorgeous sunshine should, in the best traditions of the pathetic fallacy, reflect his mood. Remember, he has only recently betrayed *Maman* with Mme de Larnage, and conscience has now redirected his steps to Les Charmettes—his arrival unannounced and unexpected. I had changed things somewhat from the book. There, Jean-Jacques encounters Mme de Warens in her dressing room. In the film I wanted him to walk up the country road lined with bulging flowery hedgerows, his face animated with joyous expectation. He knocks at the farmhouse door. No reply. He hears a distant peal of female laughter. Slowly he walks down towards the orchard (we should recall the idyll of the cherry-picking sequence here) and comes across *Maman* and Witzenreid picnicking, Witzenreid stretched out on the grass, his head in *Maman*'s lap. (Witzenreid was dismissed by Rousseau as 'a hairdresser . . . tall, pale, with a flat face and dull wits, whose conversation betrayed all the affectation and bad taste of the hairdresser's trade'.) Jean-Jacques approaches them. We go to three screens—the three faces in close-up, each trying to disguise their respective emotions. It is the end of the affair. I wanted it to be a moment of bitter poignancy set in a scene of fragrant summer beauty. But all we had was rain.

I was prepared to wait it out. I had not let the weather spoil my film thus far and was not about to make compromises now. Doon sat in a deckchair beside me, in costume and makeup, reading a book. I glanced at her strong profile and felt a pleasant pang of love for her. My one night with Monika Alt at Falkenhagen had been a momentary aberration, a mere matter of circumstance and mood (and Monika) conspiring against me. I had no guilt about it because it had made no difference. Doon and I still saw each other virtually every day. I spent most nights at her apartment. I kept many of my clothes and possessions there. I talked from time to time of buying a new larger apartment for us both—Doon did not object and the implication was that we would both be living together before too long. My only worry was to do with future filming. Mme de Warens, at the end of part I, disappears completely from the story of *The Confessions*. We would be often separated over the coming three years as I filmed parts II and III.

Doon reached into her handbag and removed a cigarette case. I smiled, enjoying the oddly exciting anachronism of an eighteenth-century noblewoman smoking a Lucky Strike. She looked round and caught my eye.

'Bloody rain,' I said.

'Jamie, I was thinking, wouldn't the scene be better in rain. I mean, it's a low moment.'

'Absolutely not.' I reiterated my reasons. She was bored, idle. She knew she would never get me to compromise.

'Well, could I go down to the hotel? I've got some stuff to sort out.'

I looked up at the massed, packed grey clouds. If the sun appeared we would only have time to do Jean-Jacques' walk to the front door. I said yes. She went off with understandable relief.

What took me back down the valley early? What made me leave in advance of the cast and crew? I cannot remember. I think Leo brought a cable from Eddie querying some expense and I think I wanted to check my production notes before I dictated a reply. Anyway, whatever it was, I had myself driven down to the Hotel de France on the Quai Nezia (I can recommend it, if ever you find yourself in Chambéry). It was an agreeable drive, even in the rain. I remember that because my mood was so placid and settled. I had one scene left to film; *The Confessions: Part I* was everything I had dreamt it to be. I felt the benign confidence of a great artist—a da Vinci, a Rembrandt, a Monet—staring at his completed canvas, wondering only where to inscribe his signature.

Did I stop at my room before I went to Doon's suite? (The hotel only had one, rather pokey, on the top floor under the eaves, converted from servants' quarters.) I think so. I think I confirmed or refuted Eddie's inquiry. Then I sauntered along the corridor and up the steep stairs, and walked into Doon's sitting room.

Alexander Mavrocordato sat there, smoking, reading a script, my script. A briefcase rested against his chair leg. He was dressed casually—*à l'anglais*—sports coat, twills, a cream shirt and a cravat. He looked up as I came in. There was no surprise, no guilt, no welcome.

'Ah, Todd,' he said. 'I hear the weather is causing you problems.'

I thought for an instant I was going to have a heart attack so intense was the pain that seemed to zig-zag transversely across my chest from my left armpit. But it passed with gratifying suddenness. (Did I tell you Mavrocordato was Russian? Or so he claimed to be. He spoke English with a clotted central European accent. I am sure his name was assumed. Someone once told me his real name was Otto Blâc—the 'c' pronounced 'ch'.)

'Yes,' I managed to say, forcing my head to stay still and not swivel round to Doon's bedroom door. 'Minor problems. Minor. Very minor . . . Yes, entirely minor.'

He threw the script on the table. 'That's some film you're making.'

'Thank you.' I stood like a major-domo, unnaturally rigid in the middle of the room, canted forward ever so slightly, as if waiting to receive an order. I felt that if Doon did not come in soon I would shatter, so tensely was I holding myself.

She came through the door brushing her hair. I saw the bed for a second—flat, unrumpled. I relaxed, marginally.

'Hi, darling,' she said to me. 'Look who's here,' she said, indicating Mavrocordato.

'Yes,' I said, turning to him. 'What exactly do you want?'

'He's making a film,' Doon said. 'He wants me to be in it.'

'No,' I said.

'No what?' Mavrocordato said.

'No, she will not be in your film.'

'Jamie? Are you all right?'

Mavrocordato smiled wearily. 'I don't think that's your decision, Todd, with great respect.'

'Forget it,' I said. 'With great respect.'

Doon fixed me with a wide-eyed angry look. She turned to Mavrocordato. 'We'll talk later.'

He got up, picked up his briefcase, opened it and placed a script on the table. I picked it up and handed it to him. I smelt the sour reek of his cheroot.

'I leave you script, Doon,' he said setting it down again. I picked it up and handed it to him. We did this three times.

'Take it, Blâc,' I said.

He swore expansively at me in his tiny impoverished language, mangled munching sounds.

'Fuck off, cunt,' I said. Proud anglo-saxon brevity.

'Stop it, Jamie!' Doon was furious but I did not care. I felt cool, as if all my arteries and veins were ventilated suddenly with clear Alpine air. He stood there with his hands on his hips as if I were some irritating mendicant who would not take no for an answer.

'Is he always such a child?' he asked Doon.

It was the look he gave her that did it. Familiar, possessive, knowing.

Spontaneously I said to Doon, 'Have you ever slept with him? Since we—'

I left it unfinished. Her face was taut, stretched.

A hooting laugh from Mavrocordato. 'Ah, *yes!* Now we are there. So English!'

'Well?'

'Yes,' she said. 'Once or twice.'

'For old time sake,' Mavrocordato said.

I hit him with all my strength, a curved high right hook, catching him in front of his left ear. I heard, before I felt the pain—my knuckles break. He went crashing down and got up staggering almost at once, I swung two more wild hits at his face, a left and a right. The left squashed his nose, the right slammed into his shoulder. I bellowed in agony as my broken knuckles ground bone on bone.

Mavrocordato was swaying, snorting blood and mucus—nosejam—onto the carpet like a dying bull in a bullfight. Doon was cursing and yelling at us to stop. My right hand felt as if it had been plunged in a bucket of sharp knives. The hot pain had a jangling metallic quality to it.

His first punch caught me a glancing blow high on the head. Then he tried to knee me in the groin but, doubled over as I was, his knee drove into my ribs, blasting the air out of my lungs. I felt myself going down slowly and his second punch landed more like a club on the back of my head. He grabbed my collar, opened the door and dragged me through. I could see nothing but light meteors swarming like a shoal of darting fish in front of my eyes. I reached to grab something—I thought there was a wall in front of me—and I clutched air. Then I was launched into space with the vicious force of his boot in my arse. I took a header down the stairs.

*　　*　　*

I finished filming the final scene of *The Confessions* ten days later with two broken knuckles, a severe compound fracture of my right arm, three broken ribs and massive body-wide contusions. My torso was heavily strapped, my right arm and hand set in plaster and my brain fuddled with analgesics.

Doon could not stop laughing and we were obliged to shoot many takes. But it worked and was finally done exactly as I wanted.

I forgave Doon, with guilty magnanimity, when she apologised for not telling me about Mavrocordato. She was not ashamed, she said, using identical arguments to those I myself employed to ease my conscience about Monika. And she *was* going to appear in his film. Somehow that did not bother me so much now. But she was sweet to me while I convalesced for a week. She looked after me with merry, genuine care.

Eddie Simmonette came for the last days' filming. He seemed strangely subdued. He did not join in the great cheer that went up from the entire crew when I said for the last time, 'Cut! Print it!' My own elation was brief. I was exhausted from almost two years of creative struggle, yet was fully aware that the entire project was only one third complete.

We were jolly enough in the Hotel de France that night. Garrulous mutually admiring speeches were made, tokens were exchanged, much champagne was drunk. When the singing started, Eddie came over and asked if he could have a word with me outside.

We went out and strolled along the banks of the river Leysse towards the *jardin public*. It was a calm, balmy night with a clear sky. We talked inconsequentially about this or that. Eddie asked how my broken arms and ribs were. Eventually, I said,

'What's wrong, Eddie? Money problems?'

He chuckled. 'There are always money problems.'

'What is it then?'

He paused under a street lamp. Across the river I could see the gravel paths of the public gardens and the knobbled leprous boughs of the pollarded limes grotesque in the darkness.

'Whatever happens, John,' he began slowly, 'I want you to know that I will never be as proud of anything as I am of *The Confessions*. It's a masterpiece. A wonderful film.'

'Thank you, Eddie.' I felt my heart clog with affection for this neat dark man. 'But what do you mean, "whatever happens"?'

He looked at me. I could not swear to it—his voice gave nothing away—but I think his eyes were luminous with tears. He took a folded newspaper from his pocket. It was a trade paper, *Kino-Magazin*. Large type headlines dominated the front page:

END OF PATENTS WAR!!!

TOBIS-KLANGFILM SYNDICATE TRIUMPHS!!!

I had drunk too much. I was weary.

'What's it all about?' I asked.

'I think we're too late,' he said softly, desperately. '*The Confessions*, it's too late.'

'Late? Too late for what?'

'For sound.'

VILLA LUXE 24 June 1972

Sound. Sound . . . I had never worried about sound. I knew about it but it seemed to me then to be a fad. Moreover, it was a device that would take film back to its theatrical and literary origins that it had managed to shake off. I regarded it rather as a painter might take note of new developments in dry point etching. It seemed to have nothing to do with the purity of moving pictures. I, who despised captions so much, who had even invented the superimposed caption so that the screen never had to resemble a blackboard, what did *I* want—what did any film artist want—with dialogue, with the 'talkies'? How could words play any part in a purely visual medium?

Well, history proved me wrong. But we have lost as much as we gained. With sound it is too easy to *explain*, too easy to be precise. That dangerous edge of ambiguity had gone forever. The potent, multifarious suggestions of the visual image were subjugated to prattle. Articulate reasoning took over from the freedom the image had to operate below the level of conscious thought . . . I can go on. Technology stifled an art in 1927—or whenever it was that ghastly quacking blacked-up singer first articulated on film—and today, decades later, we are still fighting to regain that marvellous subversive quality of the mature silent film.

Anyway, I rehearse all these old arguments with Ulrike one evening at her parents' villa. She is a good audience—she agrees with every word I say.

Herr Gunter is tall and ruddy. He has red cheeks, as if he's spent the day striding through a chill gusty countryside. He looks like an English farmer. His entire family is gathered on the pool terrace and there are numerous other guests—strangers to me—from the new villas being erected around our bay. Most of the adults have forsaken the pool but the children still scream and shout in and around it. Ulrike has asked me if I want to swim, but I declined, saying I am not feeling too well. In fact I'm reluctant to display my old man's body amongst all this tanned youth and concupiscence. My flesh is slack and folded now. My flat chest has transformed itself into two soft drooping breasts. The virile furze that covered my body has grown long and mysteriously silky. My legs are thin, my buttocks half-deflated. All the usual signs. I might have swum with two or three present but not this loud, vital assembly.

Ulrike tells me her boyfriend is arriving tomorrow and that he's greatly looking forward to meeting me. She says he has requests from one or two film magazines to do interviews. Do I have any objections?

'No photographs,' I say quickly, thinking of the man on the bus. 'And he mustn't publish my address.'

'Of course not.'

We talk on. She is a keen student of film and I find I enjoy airing my views.

'But what about colour, Mr Todd. You can't object to that.'

'Oh yes I do, but not as strongly as sound.'

I tell her that colour makes the cinema film banal. It becomes exactly the same as seeing. We view the world in colour; black and white makes film quite different, an essential veil of artifice, like the two dimensions of an artist's canvas pretending to be three. With moving pictures—the great art form of the twentieth century—the addition of sound and the arrival of colour robbed it of its uniqueness.

'And besides,' I go on, warming up—Anneliese has arrived—'colour is modern so black and white becomes the past, the colour of history. Think of the Great War. You only know it in black and white. There are no colour photographs of the Great War yet I can assure you it was a very colourful event. Imagine it in colour—you'd have an entirely different impression of it. When I see newsreels I hardly recognise it—all that monochrome!'

Herr Gunter approaches and starts asking me about my First War experiences. I tell him something of them. People gather round, fascinated by an old man's memories. The sun dips below the crocodile headland and the first bats begin to dart between the pines.

13

The End of the Affair

It was some time between Adolf Hitler's appointment as Chancellor and the Reichstag fire that Doon told me she was moving to Paris. Her arguments were cogent. Eight of her colleagues in the Artists' Association had been killed in the last year. The Association itself was outlawed. She doubted if she would ever be able to work in a German film again. The country, she said, was ruined, she had no desire to live in it, and so on.

I encouraged her to go and said I would join her as soon as I finished work on the new sound version of *The Confessions*. Indeed by then, early 1933, half the German film industry seemed now to be living abroad. I went with her to Lehrter station to see her off. She had hardly any luggage. We kissed, we declared our love for each other and she left.

I walked gloomily out of the station. The unpleasantly bright flags—red, white and black—flew everywhere. Men in uniform hawked newspapers in loud confident voices. I hailed a taxi and thought about going to the Metropole for a symbolic drink but decided against it. I knew it would only make me more depressed and I had enough trouble on my hands as it was.

*   *   *

It was not only the arrival of the 'talkies' that had done for *The Confessions*. The Wall Street Crash had contributed too. As the repercussions of financial collapse in America struck the tottering edifice of German industry in 1930 Realismus films came alarmingly close to bankruptcy. The Spandau studios were closed and we moved back to our offices near the gasworks in Grunewald. The editing suites were cramped and uncomfortable and our machines were badly serviced. While I worked in these straitened circumstances on the miles of film we had shot, crowds stampeded to the cinemas to see and hear the babble of inane voices in *Die Nacht gehört Uns* and *Melodie des Herzens*. Perhaps if we had had more finance and better facilities *The Confessions* might still have made its mark, as talkies were rare and their quality lamentable. However, by the time it was finally ready—February 1931—the cinemas were full of insufferable operettas, dire homespun musicals cast with petit-bourgeois lads and lasses or blatant publicity vehicles for superannuated tenors like Kiepura and Neumark.

The Confessions: Part I in its final version ran 5 hours and 48 minutes. It had not been difficult to persuade Eddie that its only chance of success lay in emphasising its scale and extraordinary properties. We hired the enormous Gloria-Palast on the Kurfürstendamm and installed three vast screens. A 60-man orchestra was assembled (at the last minute Feuchtwanger denied us the Berlin Philharmonic—I never spoke to him again after that day). On 27th February there was a gala performance. The great auditorium was half empty; only a few hundred people saw *The Confessions* as it was intended to be. There was, consolingly, a rapturous reception from the press, but its tone was sad and valedictory. The *Illustrierter Film-Kunst* is representative:

> It is as if Todd had launched, in this the era of the motor car, the aeroplane and the transatlantic liner, a splendid three-masted clipper ship with billowing white sails, sumptuous saloons and the most elegant lines. Magnificent, but of another age than ours.

The film ran for a week in the Gloria-Palast to average houses before we had to close. The sole benefit was that the publicity revived Realismus's fortunes briefly. Leo Druce quickly made a musical comedy about three out-of-work window cleaners which enjoyed a modicum of success. Offers multiplied for me. I could have made any number of films in half a dozen countries had I so wished but I turned them all down. I will not dwell on my feelings but my despair at what had happened was so intense I half-seriously contemplated suicide, especially when—against my wishes—Doon went to Italy to make the film with Mavrocordato. Karl-Heinz was busy at UFA with a new contract. It is a measure of how low I was that I did not interfere when Eddie had cut and dubbed a ninety minute version of *The Confessions* with a partial soundtrack of execrable quality called *Jean-Jacques!* This was to appease Pathé and the French investors and I believe only played in France and Belgium. I have never seen it, I insisted my name was removed from the credits, I abjure it utterly.

I bought a modern apartment in the west end but Doon never moved in with me. I was so distracted that I soon gave up trying to persuade her. We continued to see each other as before, shuttling between the two addresses, as her work and political activities permitted, up to her departure for Paris. I suppose we led a social life but I remember little about those difficult months after the collapse of *The Confessions*. Amongst my papers I have a small engagement diary for 1932. I quote its entries in full.

> *Jan. 10: Eddie, KS, B von A at R.*
> *Jan. 25: Dinner, Leo. Feb. 2: Doon's b'day*
> *—café Berlin. Feb. 27: Heavy snow. Dentist.*

The rest is blank.

It was Eddie who encouraged me to think of adapting *The Confessions* for sound. His motives were not entirely altruistic. The film had cost the best part of two million dollars and virtually none of that had been recouped. Obviously we could do nothing with part I but he reminded me we still had parts II and III to go. Could we not commence filming these in sound and use some of the material of part I as flashback? Slowly, my enthusiasm began to regenerate itself. Over several weeks I ran the film again and again. Yes, there *were* episodes when voices could be synchronised to lip movements; there *were* sequences which could be saved by voice-over narration. New schemes and possibilities presented themselves to me and by the end of 1932 I started the overdubbing.

I had to do this piecemeal as both Doon and Karl-Heinz were busy on other films, and, moreover, it took many attempts to get the synchronisation perfect. But I was working again and in between these dubbing sessions I wrote a narrative monologue for Karl-Heinz's voice-over and we started recording music for key scenes.

Does it sound absurdly naïve, today, to relate that I was hardly concerned about the rise of the Nazi party? To be perfectly honest I thought they were a crowd of farcical jokers. I remember going—reluctantly and under duress—to an Association meeting with Doon in the spring of '32 where a scuffle broke out at the door and there was a distant sound of breaking glass. Afterwards I asked what all the fuss was about.

'Fucking Nazis,' Doon said.

'What are they after?'

She looked at me in hostile astonishment.

'Jesus, Jamie, where are you living?'

'In Chambéry,' I said.

Doon understood. But it was as close as the Nazis ever came to me.

Still, I am sure she told me in great detail what was happening in the country but I let it wash over me. It is quite easy to give an impression of intent listening even when your mind is somewhere else entirely. I remember in mid-'32, before the general elections, how Doon used vociferously to support the Communists' decision not to vote with the Social Democrats. And when the Nazis won all those seats she still maintained it had been the right course of action. ... Social Democrats, Communists, Nationalists, Nazis, Hindenburg, von Papen, von Schleicher, ban the SS and the SA, rescind the ban on the SS and the SA—around how many Berlin dinner parties did these names and topics hum? True, I did notice the uniforms on the streets, and there always seemed to be a march, a demonstration or a rally going on. But remember, it was not my country and as far as I was concerned there were more pressing affairs to be dealt with.

Georg Pfau, though, told me something which I do still recall. Poor Georg was attacked by party thugs with depressing regularity. 129b was near a hall frequently used by the KPD for their meetings, and Georg, who often walked home from work late, was set upon twice by Nazi gangs and was once even victim of a Communist ambush.

He turned up at the studios one day for a sound recording session (he had a basket of cicadas for me) with both eyes blackened and a large blue bruise on his forehead. I commiserated with him.

'At the root,' he said to me slowly, 'it's a Bavarian problem. You see, the Bavarians *hate* us Prussians. That's the danger. And they won't be happy until they have us under their control. That's what all this *verdammt* trouble's about. It's a German civil war. That's what we're living through.'

He was very gloomy about it. I used to repeat his remark at dinner parties whenever the conversation turned to politics and it always promoted serious debate—in which I took no part, content simply to have initiated it. But Georg's dark pessimism was somewhat unusual. Amongst our friends and acquaintances the mood was excited but one of patience too. 'Yes,' people would say, 'things are bad now but it's only a phase. It'll pass, you'll see.'

Even Doon thought this, although the phase she anticipated following this one sounded hopelessly unrealistic. I pointed out to her that the Association was a splinter group of a faction (The Artists' League) that had broken away from the KPD. It was hardly a firm base upon which to build a new society. She admitted that.

'But our principles are universal,' she would say.

'What do you mean?'

'Which side is your heart on?'

'The left.'

It was a neat debating trick, but I often used to recall it later when I became a victim of political ideologies myself.

But Adolf Hitler as Chancellor was too much for her to take. She began to plan to leave almost at once. And, it had to be said, her own career was not holding up that well. Doon spoke German, but not to a standard necessary for German talkies. The film she had made with Mavrocordato (*The Blonde Nightmare*, need I say more?) had, not surprisingly, flopped. Offers of work were now only forthcoming from British or American co-productions (hence the trip to Paris) but the parts were only cameos—the token American vamp or minx, tourist or heiress. Mavrocordato was already in Paris working with Pommer and Pabst. He had been trying to persuade Doon to move there for months. In the end Adolf Hitler provided the final push.

Why did I let her go? I was no longer worried about Mavrocordato, oddly enough. I guessed that if she felt like it Doon might sleep with him again, but no prohibition on my part would make any difference. In fact, I thought we could both do with a break from each other. Since Sonia had gone my life with Doon had not been the unalloyed bliss I had expected. We were like those gimmicky weather forecasters, where a man or a woman pops out of a little house to prophesy rain or shine. As luck would have it our fortunes and spirits rarely coincided during the early Thirties. While I was flattened by *The Confessions* disaster Doon was busy. When I picked up as I began to work on the sound version Doon could get no decent roles and the political situation made her miserable. I let her go, then, sadly but fairly confidently. I planned to be filming at Neuchâtel in the near future, we would not be far apart, Doon could join me there at weekends. After *The Confessions* I would happily move with her anywhere. In any event I did not see my tenure in Germany lasting much longer. Eddie had recently been summoned to the Propaganda Ministry by Goebbels himself and was asked to explain why he was making a film about the notorious French socialist J.-J. Rousseau. Eddie ducked the issue by saying the Rousseau he planned to film was in fact Swiss. But the dead hand of the official censor seemed poised. Paris might even be an admirable base from which to complete the film. Gently, I tried to persuade Eddie to transfer Realismus to another country. He said he would think about it.

*　　　*　　　*

The Confessions now existed in three versions. There was the worthless and appalling *Jean-Jacques!*, there was my six-hour definitive *Part I* and now we had about 50 minutes dubbed-sound episodes—fragments waiting to be linked by new sequences which we planned to film at the end of the year and into 1934.

Karl-Heinz would be free of his UFA contract in November, and then we would film the Neuchâtel episodes. We would link this new narrative to the flashbacks and then move on to film the years of triumph and fame in Paris. This part II would encapsulate part I and it would all be more or less in sound. At least, this was how Eddie and I worked it out. But Eddie was not all that sanguine. Realismus, while no longer in severe financial difficulties (so he assured me), was no longer the power it had been. A. E. Groth had returned to Sweden where he had had a stroke. Gast and Hitzig, the company's two most successful directors after me, had joined the ever increasing stream of exiles: Gast to Paris, Hitzig to London. Leo Druce was required as my producer and in any event his two films had not been particularly successful. Even the most charitable friend (i.e. me) would have to describe Leo's strength as 'workmanlike'. Also, he was preoccupied with personal affairs. Lola had divorced him, gone to Hollywood and returned, and was now suing him for some reason or other. Eddie could not afford to hire more established directors. The choice facing him as head of a small studio down on its luck was either make risky trash or else stick with his star. Eddie knew I could get work at UFA, Terra or Tobis at any time I wished. But I was loyal. He somehow managed to scrape up enough money and the filming of *The Confessions: Part II* was announced in small advertisements in the trade press.

*   *   *

From my diary:

> *17th Feb. 1934. Hotel du Lac et Bellevue, Neuchâtel. Successful day. Anny reacted marvellously when the stones came through the window. Real terror. Unfortunately she was slightly cut on one arm so I decided to save the English scenes 'til later. A scream is a scream in any language. No word yet from Doon. All my cables to Paris are unanswered. Good atmosphere amongst the crew. There is no doubt that sound has a limited role to play in the cinema. The noise of glass breaking and Anny's screams are genuinely frightening.*

We were late starting part II, true to form. We came down to
Neuchâtel in early January. The departure from Stettin station was
in strong contrast to that of 1928. Now our little troupe occupied
only one carriage and a baggage wagon. Still, it was stimulating to be
at work again. Despite the interruption I felt a strong sense of
continuity as we settled into the hotel. Here we are again in another
medium-class, medium-sized hotel on the banks of a lake surrounded
by mountains. Annecy, Geneva and now Neuchâtel. The pilgrimage
of *The Confessions* continued the tracing of Jean-Jacques' steps. And
here we all were: myself, Leo, Karl-Heinz, Horst Immelman, each
one dedicated to the task in hand. Only Doon was missing, but she
was not far away.

The first disaster struck before a foot of film had turned. Helene
Rednitz, who was playing Thérèse Levasseur, came down with bron-
chitis and after a week in bed went back to Berlin. Leo, Karl-Heinz
and I went to Geneva and spent two days patrolling bars, theatres
and variety shows looking for a replacement. We found our Thérèse
in the Théâtre de la Comédie, a young girl playing a chambermaid
in some tired farce. Her name was Anne-Louise Corsalettes. I decided
to call her Anny La Lance (after a small village on Lake Neuchâtel)
and, I would like to say, a star was born. I certainly enjoyed the
opportunity it afforded me of saying, 'I want you to be in my movie'
but Anny was no actress, she just looked perfect. Rousseau described
Thérèse as 'a girl of feeling, lacking in coquetry, with lustrous gentle
eyes.' Anny had large dark eyes and a blunt, quite pretty face. She
was a big girl with strong shoulders and hips and it had been her
clumping exits and entrances in the farce that had attracted our
attention and had taken us backstage. Naturally, she was overwhelmed
at our offer.

Anyway, that was Anny La Lance and she performed well under
my direction. She did everything I told her and bore me no ill will
when I set her up in order to get the right response (as in the incident
quoted in the diary above, when Jean-Jacques' house was stoned by
hostile suspicious villagers). Filming was going well and I was shooting German and English versions concurrently—such are the problems of sound. Karl-Heinz's English accent was strongly Germanic
and Anny spoke only French but I could over-dub later.

My one vague worry was the long silence from Doon. We had
spent a rather awkward Christmas in Paris—neither of us accustomed
to reunions. We were not at our best. Neither of us was a good letter
writer, either, and a month elapsed before I sent a cable to her Paris
address, but there was no reply. I was surprised, but assumed she

had gone off somewhere to make a film.

The day after I wrote that diary entry Eddie Simmonette turned up. It was in the evening and we had just finished dinner when he arrived. I knew there was something wrong because his clothes were dirty. He was unshaven and the cleft in his chin was dense with bristles. He had driven all the way from Berlin, via Austria, an arduous journey that had taken him five days. He brought the worst news. First, the luckless Georg Pfau had been arrested and incarcerated for some reason. His connection with Realismus Films had led to the studio being investigated. Shortly after that Eddie had apparently been declared a 'non-Aryan'. The scandal attaching to this had prompted the banks to foreclose on him and the creditors to rush in. The studios were shut down, the staff paid off, all Eddie's property was impounded.

'Everything?' I said. I felt a horrible cold nausea squirming in my body, like something trapped in a burrow.

'The lot.'

'What about *The Confessions*?' I could hardly get the word out. 'The negative.'

'Oh, I've got that in the back of my car. And that old trunk you kept there. No, I'm talking about my house, the studios—'

There and then I made him take me out to his car—a big Audi—and open it. I saw the flat gleaming aluminium boxes. I counted them—fourteen. I let my forehead touch the car's cold roof for a few seconds.

'Have you heard from Doon?' he said.

'No.'

'She made a long distance call, looking for you. I couldn't speak to her—the police were there.'

'When was that?'

'Ten days ago.'

It made no sense, I thought she knew where I was, but I had no time to ponder on it. We summoned the crew to a meeting in the hotel dining room and told them what had happened. Eddie said he would pay them off the next day. He speculated vaguely about setting himself up in Paris and reassembling everything at the end of that year once he had a secure base.

Later that evening Eddie and I talked alone. He told me that after paying off the crew and settling the film's debts he would have approximately two thousand dollars left in the world.

'It's over,' he said. 'I'm sorry, John.'

'For the time being,' I said bravely. 'It survived talkies and the

Wall Street crash. We'll just have to postpone it.' Half of me actually believed this, I suppose, the other half wanted to lie down and die.

'You have some money here, don't you?' he asked.

I had, in Geneva. My profits from *Julie* that Thompson had told me to transfer from Germany, minus certain payments to Sonia.

'Yes. Why?'

'I want to sell you the negative of *The Confessions*,' he said, 'for fifty thousand dollars.'

To this day I sometimes wonder if Eddie fooled me. Sometimes I am convinced he did, at others, absolutely not. He knew I had money in Switzerland because I had passed on to him Thompson's advice to me—which he had chosen to ignore.

At one dark stage in my life I was convinced he had set up *The Confessions: Part II* only to get me to Switzerland for the express purpose of selling me part I. He must have known I would buy it. In the end, though, I have to absolve him; the plot was far too complicated even for Eddie's byzantine mind. For example, he could not have known he would be investigated and declared a non-Aryan by the Nazis. But out of disaster the cards fell conveniently for him. I had something over 70,000 dollars in a bank in Geneva. Eddie had pitched his price just right.

It took a couple of days to sort out our affairs in Neuchâtel. We bade each other morose farewells. Karl-Heinz said he would go back to Berlin to see what he could do for Georg. I told him I would go straight to Paris and urged him to join Doon and me there. He said he would wait and see.

Anny La Lance contemplated the sudden demise of her short-lived film career and the resumption of her old identity with surprising calm. She said it had always seemed too good to be true and asked only for a lift back to Geneva, where both Eddie and I were going.

We spent a day with a lawyer. Fortuitously, Eddie had brought all the necessary documents with him. Now we had cause to bless the existence of *Jean-Jacques*! *The Confessions: Part I* belonged entirely to Realismus Films Verlag A.G. The film negative and everything that had been shot of part II were now purchased by John James Todd esq. for $50,000, less the legal fees the advocate demanded. I went to my bank and withdrew the money, in cash, all of which to my surprise Eddie managed to fit in his briefcase.

It was a mild wintry day, the sun shone on the lake as we sat in a café enjoying a farewell drink. Anny was still with us, holding on to her lost future until the final minute. Parked nearby on the kerb was Eddie's big Audi, which was now mine—he had generously included it in the deal.

'So,' I said. 'That's it. When are you off to Paris?'

'I'm not going,' he said. 'I'm going to America.' He patted his briefcase. 'See what I can do there.' He smiled. 'Why don't you join me? Eh, Johnny? That's where the future lies.'

'My future's sitting in that car,' I said. 'No, I'm going to Paris. Find Doon.'

I rang the doorbell on Doon's apartment door. She lived in a rather shabby building on the Rue de Grenelle. There was no answer. I went to look for the concierge. This turned out to be a beefy man in vest and braces who was watering the weeds in the damp courtyard with weedkiller. He told me Mlle Bogan had gone.

'When will she be back?' I asked.

No. I had not understood. She had gone away. She was not returning.

I felt a sadness infect me like a germ.

'Where has she gone? Did she say?'

'No,' he said. 'She just left. Monsieur Mavrocordato came and they went away together.'

14

Dog Days

I was back in London within a week. I sold the Audi in Paris and bought a large tin cabin trunk to take the contents of the old one and the reels of *The Confessions*. This I then deposited in the vault of a bank in Piccadilly. I rented a modest dusty flat in Islington not far from the site of the old Superb-Imperial studios and contemplated my future.

It was strange to be back in London after a gap of ten years. It was busier and dirtier than Berlin, apart from that, to my indifferent eyes, it seemed more or less unchanged. Sonia and the children now lived in a large house near Parson's Green. I deliberately chose a place to live as far away from Shorrold territory as possible.

I was depressed and often quite miserable during those initial weeks back in London. I had taken the demise of Realismus films and the end of my dreams about *The Confessions* extraordinarily well, or so I thought. I suppose it was because I never truly felt that the sound version was really feasible. Making it was a despairing effort rather than an enthusiastic one—an act of bravado, not conviction. I needed more time to generate that last emotion.

In fact, ambition had become almost extinct in me since 1929, hard though it may be to believe. I set up part II and did what filming I could manage powered by an energy that was derived more from dwindling momentum than from any self-generating creative source. Ambition had died, and now I needed a strong deep sentiment to fill the spaces it had vacated. That was why I drove to Paris with such joyous anticipation, and that was why Doon's betrayal was the most savage shock I had to take.

I could hardly believe that she had gone off with Mavrocordato. I could feel only hate and revulsion for what she had done to me. To try and forget I spent a couple of days getting drunk (we drank much more then, I think). Finally, sober, crapulous, fed up, I wondered what to do next. To go back to Berlin was out of the question. Eddie was going to America, so why not follow him there? For a while I was tempted. I even went to a shipping agency and inquired about booking a passage. But I was too hurt and sorrowful to take such a step straightaway. And so I turned for home with my films, my scripts and my bits and pieces to set about the task of putting my life back together in a mood not far off apathetic.

It was two weeks after my arrival in London before I got round to going to see Sonia and my family in the house I was renting for them. On Saturday, as a taxi-cab drove me up the King's Road, all the memories of the early years of my marriage passed through my mind. I allowed a wistful smile to accompany them. I thought of my younger self with affection. What an impulsive, sentimental idiot I was then!

I was shocked when Sonia came to the door. It was a considerable time since I had seen her and since then she must have lost at least three stone. Her clothes were as neat as ever, her central parting still ruthlessly defined but her once round plump face was gaunt and hard. She wore spectacles with pale caramel coloured frames and held a cigarette in her hand. She had never smoked in all the years I had known her.

'Hello, John,' she said. 'Nice of you to come by.'

I followed her in. Her round haunches had disappeared completely.

'Are you well?' I said, concerned.

'Fighting fit.'

'What's happened to your voice?'

The London accent had gone. The mild glottal stop that would have produced 'figh'ing' was now replaced by a positive 't'.

'What are you talking about?' Sonia, I realised, had gone radically genteel. She sounded like an actress.

'Nothing, nothing.'

We went into the sitting room where my children were waiting for me. Vincent, a bland brown-haired eleven year old, was a Shorrold to the dull roots of his hair. The girls—Emmeline and Annabelle—were absurdly dressed as if for a pantomime with satin bows in their hair and white silky dresses. They were plump like their mother used to be and shy. I kissed them all, strangers. In the corner a familiar figure hovered. Lily Maidbow. Loyal Lily.

'Hello, Mr Todd,' she said.

I looked uneasily at my family and retainer. Was I really something to do with all these people? I tried to ignore the pain of Hereford's absence.

'How nice to see you all,' I said like a headmaster, hands clasped behind my back.

'The girls have to go,' Sonia said.

'What a shame.'

'They've a dress rehearsal of their school play.'

'Ah. Good. Excellent.'

They went. Lily took Vincent out of the room. 'Goodbye, Daddy,' they said awkwardly as if it were a foreign word. Sonia and I sat down. Cigarettes were offered to me and declined.

'When did you start smoking?'

'Guess. Sherry?'

'Mmm. Please.' I felt soft vague guilts press upon me, like giant cushions. I was seized suddenly with a manic desire to flee this lugubrious house. 'The children look well,' I said with a thin flat smile.

'I need more money, John. Another thousand a year. Vincent goes to prep school—'

'Prep school!'

'And I'm going to board the girls too; place near Ascot.'

'Good God.' I did some quick calculations. I had approximately $20,000 and the apartment in Berlin to my name. I could not rely on a quick sale of the apartment and at six dollars to the pound that made something over £3,000. One to Sonia left me two to live on.

'I could manage a couple of hundred, I should think.'

I will not reproduce the profanity of the language Sonia employed after I explained how I had bought the negative of *The Confessions* from Eddie Simmonette. Impressively, the new accent never slipped. Abuse gave way to quiet, serious threats. The name of her lawyer— a Mr Devize—was frequently enjoined. Eventually I promised her the thousand and the proceeds from the apartment. This calmed her down somewhat.

'You'll just have to get another job,' she said. 'You can earn a lot as a director. I'm sorry, John, but I'm going to have to tell Mr Devize about you buying that film. That money wasn't yours to spend. It belonged to all of us.'

She left the room calling for Lily to show me out. I counted the cigarette butts in the ashtray—five. Lily edged in, head bowed.

In the hall, putting on my hat and coat, I asked a question.

'What does Mrs Todd do these days, Lily?'

'Well . . . plays cards, mostly. These three lady friends come round. They play cards for hours. Days. And smoke. Smoke something terrible. Cards, cigarettes, cups of coffee. Play right through the night sometimes. I get up in the morning and there they are, still at it.'

'Lord . . .' I felt very depressed.

'Oh, and she goes and visits that Mr Devize.'

I left after that. And, as events turned out, that was the last I ever saw of my family.

*   *   *

I looked, rather half-heartedly, for a job. I met some people and talked about *The Confessions: Part II* but it prompted little enthusiasm. Mr Devize summoned me to his office several times. He was a sleek burly man with thinning oiled hair who affected half-moon pince-nez spectacles. He was aggressive and unpleasant. I had him labelled *arriviste* at once, despite his banded institutional tie and the mellow professional fruitiness of his voice. I laid my documents and accounts before him including my notarised bill of sale from Eddie. He had this verified and reported to Sonia that I was indeed as impecunious as I claimed.

I was not bothered by this fiscal slump. Material prosperity has never meant much to me. I have always seen wealth and fame for the alluring shams they are.

In early June, for want of anything better to do, I went up to Edinburgh. The truth was that I was lonely in London, and, in that mood, sentimental notions about family and roots easily take hold. I sublet the flat for the summer and headed north.

I managed to last two days with my father before his unrelenting ironic inquiries drove me out. He had finally moved from his old apartment to an elegant Georgian house in India Street in the New Town. From there I booked in to the Scotia private hotel, a modest clean establishment in Bruntsfield. I took breakfast in my room, lunched in a public house and dined at 7.00 p.m. sharp with my fellow residents. They were all upstanding professional men, mainly engineers and surveyors working away from home, where they returned at weekends. During many weekends I was quite alone at the Scotia and was regarded by Mrs Darling, the widowed proprietrix, as a faintly louche and eccentric character, whom she blatantly patronised, introducing me to new guests as 'Mr Todd, our cinema producer'.

Now I look back on it I think I must have been suffering a mild but protracted nervous breakdown all that first half of 1934. I was listless and morose. I felt betrayed and let down by Doon. I saw myself as a hapless victim of technology. I idled my way through the long summer weeks going for long walks in the city or out in the country on the Pentland hills. Steadily, I found myself revisiting the haunts of my childhood: Anstruther, North Berwick, Cramond. I even revisited Minto Academy to find it had been converted to a youth hostel. It is an indicator of my mood and melancholy that my most frequent reverie was taken up with trying to imagine myself as an old man. I am sure this is an infallible sign of the end of youth. I had several popular versions. There was the sprightly old lecher with a grey goatee, a pink gin in one hand and a chorus girl's bottom in the other; or the dear bumbling eccentric whom everybody adored; or the spruce ascetic octogenarian steeped in calm sagacity. I never saw myself remotely like my father. I was thirty-five years old and I could not rid myself of the conviction that my life was over. My great work was as complete as it ever would be; my great love had abandoned me. I was half way towards my three score years and ten and the remaining portion stretched ahead featureless as a salt flat.

My God, I should have been so lucky . . .

I was roused from my torpid self-pity and introspection in August. Sonia wrote, announcing that she intended to divorce me. Mr Devize had everything under control. Sometime in the near future I would be contacted by a man named Orr. He would explain exactly what I had to do.

Orr arrived a week after Sonia's letter. Mrs Darling brought me my breakfast on a tray and said in tones of sorrowful disdain.

'There's a . . . man. By the name of Orr? To see you Mr Todd. We've put him in the smoking room. Out of harm's way.'

Orr was a small block of a man in a thick cheap suit. He sat to attention, smoking a cigarette as if he were testing it, examining the burning end after each draw. I noticed that the nail and first two joints of his forefinger were as brown as unmilked tea. He had shaved badly that morning, his jawbone was nicked and raw-looking. There was a small bright jewel of a scab on the volute of a nostril. He smelt powerfully of brilliantine.

'Ian Orr,' he said, standing up. He was about five feet two. I felt sure he had been a Bantam. He put his cigarette in his mouth to free his right hand. We shook hands. He had a strong grip. He then checked each pocket to his suit before discovering a used business card. 'Ian Orr,' it said. 'Orr's Private Detection Agency. Divorce and Debt Collection our Speciality.' After Eugen, Orr. I had a sudden doleful premonition that my life was going to be bedevilled by these sort of men.

'Shall we get down to business?' I saw no reason to be civil. However, Orr explained what we had to do with an enthusiasm that was almost infectious. We might have been organising a whist drive or scavenger hunt rather than orchestrating my culpability in a divorce case. Put simply, Sonia's divorce from me would be most swiftly and easily effected if I were caught *in flagrante* committing adultery. Smart Londoners spent an afternoon with a Mayfair tart in the Metropole Hotel in Brighton. Orr had booked two nights for me (for authenticity's sake, he explained) in the Harry Lauder Temperance Hotel in Joppa, the western extension of Portobello, scene of my first excursions to the seaside. At a pre-ordained point during the stay Orr would then 'surprise' me and the woman I was with and testify to that effect in court as chief witness for the plaintiff.

'Fine,' I said. 'All right. But do I really need to spend two nights?'

'I always find it's far more convincing, sir. You know, for real solid adultery. Not just a one-night fling.'

'Whatever you say.'

Orr had a strong stop-start Scottish accent, very nasal. He pronounced 'adultery'—'addle-tree'.

He smiled at me. He had small dark-cream teeth.

'We can get a whoor in town or at Joppa.'

'Let's get one here.'

That night Orr and I went down to Leith docks to a pub called the Linlithgow. The bar was full of mirrors, extravagantly etched and carved with prototypical Scottish scenes. The public room was well lit, to such a degree that I felt like shading my eyes. It was busy with men and sailors who seemed to be pointedly ignoring the 'girls'— only three of them—who sat behind a long table with their backs to the wall.

Orr paid for two pints of special (I was paying, in fact, his fee was two guineas a day plus 'sundries'). We stood at the bar, drinking, pondering who was going to be my companion.

'I don't care,' I said. 'I don't propose to do anything with her.'

'Might as well have *some* fun, Mr Todd. You're paying for it.'

He went over and spoke to the women and came back with one whom he introduced as Senga. She was young, rather heavy set with a slight squint. She wore a threadbare velvet coat over a grubby print dress. We made the arrangements swiftly. I would meet her under the clock at Portobello Station the next day at 4.30 in the afternoon. She would be paid £5 when the 'discovery' was complete.

Senga was waiting for me at the appointed time, wearing the same clothes and with no luggage. I asked her where she got her curious name.

'It's Agnes, backwards,' she said.

The Harry Lauder Temperance Hotel was not far from the station. It was a solid simple building of white-painted stone with brown mullions across the main road from the sea front. I had been told to use an assumed name so I signed ourselves in as Mr and Mrs Backwards. The proprietor, a small fat man with a dense sandy moustache, showed us to our room. There was something familiar about him. Once we were inside he introduced himself.

'Alexander Orr,' he said with a broad smile. 'Call me Eck. Ian's made all the arrangements. Don't worry about a thing, Mr Todd. I get all his clients.' He ignored Senga completely, as if she did not exist.

'Can I offer you a wee drink? I can send up a bottle. Rum or Whisky?'

'What would you like, Senga?'

'I'll take a rum.'

'Rum it shall be, Mr Todd.'

'I thought this was a temperance hotel?' I said.

'Oh, aye, it is. That way we get nae trouble fae the polis.'

After the bottle of rum had been delivered I unpacked my few clothes. Senga had a drink, a large rum diluted with water. I had not tasted the stuff since the war and its faint sickly aroma took me back to that day in the Salient when we went over the top for the first time. I touched the scar caused by Somerville-Start's tooth.

'Haven't you got any things with you?' I asked Senga.

'No.'

'Not even a toothbrush? A nightdress?'

'No.'

We went out to do some shopping. We caught a tram to Portobello and I bought Senga a toothbrush, a tin of toothpowder, a comb, a bar of soap, a flannel and a spongebag. Then we went for a walk on the long beach. Taciturn Senga made an ideal companion. We walked along the beach towards the pier and Restalrig. There was a cold stiff breeze coming off the firth and I had to pull my hat down firmly on my head. My mind was full of thoughts: picnics with Oonagh and Thompson, Donald Verulam taking photographs, Ralph the dog, the drowned men at Nieuport, Dagmar ... I fantasised briefly about Dagmar. Perhaps I would go to Norway, seek her ...

'Hey, mister!'

I looked round. Senga had fallen behind a good way. I retraced my steps.

'I cannae walk inna sond, wi' these shuze.'

'Take them off, then.'

'Whut? Oh, uh-huh. Silly me.'

She took her shoes off and we set off once more. We must have walked a couple of miles. I think Senga enjoyed herself. As we strolled along an idea for a film took shape in my head. On the way back to the hotel I bought a notebook to write it down.

Eck Orr had our meal sent up to the room—boiled mackerel and mashed potatoes. Senga sewed up the hem of her coat which was coming down and tightened a loose button on my jacket. When I commented how deftly she did this she explained that she had briefly been a housemaid in one of the Earl of Wemyss's homes. After our meal I wrote out my story idea. It was exactly my own situation: a man obliged to fabricate an adultery to obtain a divorce, the difference being that the man in my story falls passionately in love with the tart he hires, thereby complicating matters disastrously. I thought it might make a nice ironic melodrama. I wrote out a dozen pages while Senga sat silently, drinking rum and water. That evening as we waited to be discovered I felt a strange serenity come over me, and for the first time since my return to Britain sensed a stirring of my old energies. I glanced at Senga. There was in fact something oddly attractive about her astigmatism: it seemed to indicate a latent mischievousness, quite at odds with her true nature.

By eleven o'clock there had been no sign of Ian Orr. We undressed and prepared for bed with decorum. I changed into my pyjamas and dressing gown in the WC at the end of the corridor. Then, while I washed my face with water from the jug and ewer, Senga slipped out of her dress and in between the sheets. I asked her if she wanted to use her toothbrush but she said no.

She fell asleep almost instantly. I lay in the dark listening to her small snores wondering if Ian Orr would burst in at any moment. I could hear the noise of male conversation from a room below, which I took to be the temperance bar. Outside the summer night faded into darkness, I heard the rickety-tick of a train on the LNER railway line and a few motor cars passing on the coast road to Musselburgh.

The next morning was a Saturday and it was raining. Senga's bed was empty when I woke but her dress and coat were still in the wardrobe. I went to the window and looked out at the wet roofs of Joppa. Beyond the coast road the pewtery firth was calm and beyond that lay the rest of Scotland ... Rain seemed to be falling on the entire country from the solid low sky.

Senga came in, from the lavatory I assumed, wearing my dressing gown.

'Oh, yer up. Borrowed yer dressin'-goon.'

She took it off and handed it to me. She had slept in her underwear and cotton slip which was badly creased. I could see she had small sharp breasts and there was something provocative about the sight of her bare legs and battered high-heeled shoes. I saw a stubble of dark hair on her shins.

'Senga, I—'

The door was flung open and Ian Orr came in.

'Morning, Mr Todd, morning to youse all.'

I had to pay Eck Orr for the full two nights. I settled all my bills in the hotel's office, including Senga's. We drank to the successful conclusion of my divorce. Eck raised his glass.

'Here's tae us, wha's like us?'

'Damn few—and they're a' deed.' Ian Orr said.

Later, Eck slyly asked Senga to stay on but I was glad when she refused. We said goodbye to the Orr brothers and walked to the station.

'Where are you going?' I said as we waited for a train. 'Waverley?'

'I'll get the stopper to Bonnington.'

We sat on the station bench side by side. It was still raining. I felt obscurely cheated of my second night with her.

'Do you go to that pub—the Linlithgow—often?' It was the only reference I had made to her profession.

'Aye, sometimes.'

'Maybe I'll see you there.'

'Maybe, aye.'

Her train came in five minutes. She got up.

'Thanks for the spongebag, Mr Todd. Cheerio, now.'

*   *   *

My film *The Divorce* had its trade show in August 1935. *Close-up* described it as 'a powerful and at times shocking melodrama very much in the German style'. *Bioscope* said, 'a skilful and impressive film let down by mediocre performances'. In the film the impossible love affair ends with the hero murdering the uncaring prostitute and then killing himself. I shot it full of shadows; unrelievedly murky in every scene. It was a small inexpensive film compared to the scale I had become accustomed to in *The Confessions*, but I was pleased with it. It was infused with its own strange passion. On the whole *The Divorce* received a good press, though it did only average business. This was the result of the inept distribution deal negotiated by the film company I made it for—Astra-King. But I was pleased with the movie for a number of reasons, not the least of which was the fact that it was a memento of the bizarre twenty-four hours I had spent in

Joppa committing adultery with Senga. There were other advantages which accrued. The good notices had attracted interest from Gaumont, J. Arthur Rank and British Lion. *The Confessions: Part II* was being discussed once more.

My most ardent fan was the celebrated Courtney Young, variously known as 'Mr Film', 'Father of the British Cinema' and any number of flattering epithets. Young was a hugely wealthy man who had made his fortune in the ancillary trades of the film business. He started out hiring equipment—lamps and cameras—then he expanded into the costumier side. He bought a studio during the post-war slump, demolished it and then sold the land to the electricity board. The money he made from this purchased the second largest cinema chain in the north of England. And so on. He was one of those men who would have done well, and done it in the same way, no matter what industry he went into—he just happened to choose the cinema. Now he was making films. His company, Court Films, had produced two expensive flops: *Vanity Fair* and *Sir Walter Raleigh*, but this had not dissuaded him. He was mad for *The Confessions*.

Young was a large fleshy man with a handsome face spoilt by heavy bags under his eyes. He had thin blond-ginger hair which he brushed straight back from a pale freckleless face. He looked as if he should have been dark and saturnine. The fact that he was not was somewhat unsettling. For a while I used to wonder if his hair was dyed but I saw him naked once (showering in his golf-club) and his pubic hair was as pale as old thistle-down.

I did not like Young much, but I needed him. He was married to a still beautiful actress of the silent era, Meredith Pershing, and I spent quite a few weekends at their country house near High Wycombe. He paid me to rewrite my scripts so that Rousseau's English years were emphasised (he wanted Hector Seagoe to play David Hume) and I obliged. It took considerable persuasion to get him to accept Karl-Heinz as Rousseau, but I made it a condition of my directing. In the end he had to agree.

It was the spring of 1936, I think, March or April, when Leo Druce finally returned from Berlin. He was something of a wasted man, having been embroiled in a nasty court case after the death of his ex-wife, Lola Templin-Tavel. Her body had been found in a grove of trees near the Wannsee with a bullet hole in her head and a revolver lying nearby. However, in her room was a suicide note which stated that she and Leo were going to stage a double suicide exactly like Kleist and his mistress Henrietta Vogel (Lola had made her name in the role of Henrietta Vogel in a long-running play). Leo knew nothing of this and protested as much when he was arrested for murder. There was a lot of lurid publicity and it was only as a result of witnesses testifying to Lola's total craziness that the charges against him were dropped.

Since his window-cleaner film Leo had made three other low quality musical comedies and was now, I suppose, regarded as a director rather than a producer.

We met for lunch in an oyster bar off the strand. Leo looked thinner and needed a haircut. We shook hands with as much warmth as the gesture can generate.

'I came away with virtually nothing,' he said. 'I had to get out of the place. You should have seen those baboons that arrested me . . . and the jail! It's all the uniforms I can't take. Suddenly everybody's allowed to dress up. And flags. Flags everywhere. Never known a country so keen on flags.'

We ordered turtle soup and three dozen oysters. To my surprise I had developed a taste for them. In celebration of our reunion I called for champagne.

'Doing well, Johnny?'

I told him *The Confessions* was on the go again.

'Wonderful. Great news. Saw *The Divorce*. Splendid. The end shook me up a bit, I can tell you.' He lifted his chin and slid an oyster down his throat. 'You know—what with Lola topping herself like that.'

I asked him for news of Doon. He told me he had none. We talked on about the occupation of the Rhineland, life in Berlin and mutual friends. He told me that Georg Pfau had died in some kind of internment camp. Karl-Heinz was in a successful play at the Schiller Theatre but was still living in Georg's old apartment, which he now owned.

'Place is full of dead insects,' Leo said. 'Doesn't seem to care.'

'I must write to him. Get him over to meet Young.' I looked at Leo. 'What do you say to keeping *The Confessions* a Todd–Druce production? I'll talk to Young about it.'

He set down his coffee cup and looked solemn.

'I don't know what I'd do without you, John.' He held up his hand, palm outward. 'No, I mean it. I tell you that business with Lola almost finished me.'

'Don't give it a thought,' I said. 'What are friends for?'

Leo moved in with me for a week or so until he could find a place of his own. I introduced him to Young who quickly agreed to him producing *The Confessions*. In the meantime Young set him to work overseeing a musical version of *Major Barbara* while I got down to some serious revisions on my script. I was quite happy with the re-emphasis Young had proposed. I now saw part II as, in essence, a film about exile. It opened with Rousseau on a channel packet boat approaching Dover harbour on a wet squally day. He is alone (Thérèse Levasseur was following later escorted by Boswell).* His thoughts turn to the past, the fame and disgrace he has known, the celebration and vilification. He meets Hume and is soon settled in England. Then reunited with the faithless Thérèse he begins to write his *Confessions*. His mind goes back to his youth, Geneva, *Maman*, Paris and early fame ... In a series of fragmented memories we relive his past life (here I could employ some of the footage from part I). Gradually, however, his loneliness gets the better of him. He does not warm to England or the cold English. He begins to suspect Hume of inter-cepting his mail ... I worked on steadily and with growing satis-faction. For the first time since I had left Berlin I felt a modicum of contentment again. I even grew to enjoy my solitary bachelor's life— working in the morning, lunch in a local pub, a stroll round Islington's streets, perhaps some shopping, then another long session of work until seven or eight in the evening. Then I might go out to the theatre or the cinema and have a late supper. Often I'd meet up with Leo. He was dallying now with a chorus girl from *Major Barbara* (I rebuked him for this cliché) called Belinda and I would join them and assorted friends in restaurants or parties or wherever the 'fun' was to be had that night. I met a fair number of bright ambitious girls on these assignations but they must have found me disappointing company. My mind was full of Jean-Jacques again and I barely listened to the humorous chit-chat that flowed insatiably between the others. In the summer I went down to the Courtney Youngs for houseparties every second or third weekend. It was there one Saturday that I read in *The Times* of my divorce from Sonia on the grounds of adultery committed at the Harry Lauder Temperance Hotel, Joppa, Midlothian, with one Agnes Outram. ('Very Johnny Todd, somehow,' Young commented when he read it. This annoyed me.) I felt no grief or disappointment and smiled blandly through the sophisticated

---

*I discovered in 1955, on the publication of Boswell's diaries, that Boswell and Thérèse had taken this opportunity to have a brief affair. According to Boswell's log in his journal they fucked fourteen times in three days. Thérèse was insatiable and the young Scot utterly exhausted. The revelation came as a genuine shock to me. To this day I cannot forgive Boswell his vile betrayal of Jean-Jacques.

commiserations of my fellow guests. Instead I thought rather poign-
antly of that bizarre couple of days and the strange charade we had
played out—myself and Senga and the efficient Orr brothers ...

A few days later Sonia wrote to inform me that she was marrying
her lawyer, Devize, and that he proposed to adopt my three children
as his own. I gave them my blessing in the enterprise. There was
nothing for me there any more.

Then I received another letter that filled me with real joy.

'Hello Johnny!
My God you should be seeing Berlin now. We are in heavy
trouble. I am a great success in a bad play. Famous again, like
Julie. Good news about Jean-Jacques. I make a little more
money then I come to England. Poor Georg is dead, you know.
I tell you when I see you. Tell to your Mr Young that I want
£1,000 a week for your film. Hello to Leo.

Goodbye. A strong English handshake from your German
friend.

Karl-Heinz.'

It was a warm drizzly Wednesday in late July when I was telephoned by Courtney Young and asked to go and see him. I knew it
was Wednesday because I had gone out after lunch to buy some
bananas and found the shops all shut. I had forgotten it was half day
closing. I had returned home and was just beginning to write the
scene where Rousseau accuses Hume of plotting to defame him when
the phone rang. Young wanted to see me straight away.

During that summer of 1936, curious though it is to relate now, a
novel called *Great Alfred* by one Land Fothergill (an unlikely name
for a woman) had enjoyed a huge success both in Britain and the
USA. That afternoon in his office in Portland Square Young told me
he had just bought the film rights for £50,000, a vast sum, in
competition with MGM and Twentieth Century-Fox. The novel was
about Alfred the Great, preposterously romanticised (I had reached
page seven before I hurled it away), but Young said it would make
the English epic to rival anything the Americans would produce. The
cast would include Hartley Dale, Laurence Olivier, Merle Oberon,
Cecily Dart, Charles Laughton and Felicia Feast. He envisaged a
budget of around a million pounds. There was only one man who
could direct it—John James Todd.

'Don't say anything,' Young interrupted quickly. 'Think about it.
My committment to *The Confessions* is absolute, rock solid. But this
is an opportunity we have to take.'

'But what about *The Confessions*?' I said. 'Karl-Heinz is coming over.'

'Superb, wonderful. There must be a role for him in *Alfred*. We'll do *The Confessions* after.' He went to the window and spoke to the plane trees in the square. 'Think, John, think. After *Alfred* ... the whole world's talking about that book. Think what we'll be able to do with *The Confessions*.' He turned, his pale face was almost flushed. 'And you're the only man who can do it. You're the only English—sorry, British—director who's worked on this kind of huge scale. I saw what you did with *The Confessions*. You'll have a million quid for *Alfred* ...'

He went on sousing me in statistics, predictions and the grossest flattery. I went home and thought about it for hours. I telephoned Leo and said I needed his advice. We met that evening in a quiet restaurant in Bloomsbury.

'There's only one thing to do,' Leo said.

'What?'

'You have to stick with *The Confessions*.' He spoke with tense sincerity.

'I know.'

'Young's trying to sidetrack you. He's got this hot property. If he can persuade you to postpone *The Confessions* once he'll try again. You'll lose *his* commitment once he sees yours can be diverted.'

'You're right.' He was. 'I know.' I smiled at him. 'I think I just needed to hear it from someone else. Thanks, Leo.'

'Christ, we've waited long enough,' he said. 'Let's keep forging on, for God's sake. What about another bottle of rosé?'

This is how events went. I telephoned Young the next morning. I said I was deeply honoured to have been asked, but I had donated years of my life to *The Confessions* and that to set it aside now just as it was reaching fruition would be, in my opinion, disastrous. Alas, I had to say no to *Great Alfred*. It had been one of the hardest decisions of my life.

'Thank you, John,' he said. 'I'm sad, I wish you'd change your mind, but I think I can understand your position.'

We said goodbye. I said I was looking forward to seeing him and Meredith that weekend.

The next day in the *Manchester Guardian* I read that Land Fothergill's *Great Alfred* was to be filmed by Courtney Young's Court Films. The director was to be 'the internationally celebrated film director Mr Leo Druce.'

That afternoon I received a telegram. Regret *Confessions* no longer of interest to Court Films. They wished me luck.

That evening Leo Druce stood in the middle of my living room trying to lie his way out of a tight corner. He was agitated; he kept running his hands through his thick hair.

'You *must* believe me, John. I didn't know. I *swear*. I had no idea when we spoke. I never dreamt he would ask me.'

'You fucking liar.' I had said this about twenty times for far.

'He rang me out of the blue. We met. He said *The Confessions* was off. Finished. Did I want to direct *Great Alfred*. You'd turned it down flat, he said.'

'You should have told him where to stuff *Great Alfred*.'

'What good would that do? Look, I'm broke. I've got no job. This is the opportunity of a lifetime.'

'You stinking filthy scum.'

'I swear—' his voice cracked. 'I never knew. *The Confessions* is over, Johnny. Put yourself in my place.'

'No thanks.'

'Go back to him. Say you've changed your mind. I don't care. *You* do it.'

'You're vermin, Druce. I wouldn't piss on Young's grave, now. He's filth. You're a perfect match. I hope you'll be very happy.'

'John, I beg you.'

I felt my face harden, as if it were being slowly frozen.

'I made you, Druce. I've given you every break. When I think—'

'John, please—'

'When I think what I've done for you. How many times I've helped you. This is what you do to me.'

'I'll tell him I don't want it. Say you've changed your mind.'

'You disgust me. Get out.'

'John—'

'*GET OUT!*'

I actually screamed. The dam broke. I called him every vile name I could think of. He stood there and took it for a minute or so, then left. After he had gone I sat down and plotted murder. I was going to kill Young and his wife and their children. I was going to torture Druce in unspeakable ways until he died. Then I was going to seek out their families and relatives and spring on them from the darkness. I was going to conduct my own private pogrom, cleanse the world of this worthless contemptible human bacteria . . .

Well, this is the sort of thing you do—these are the words you say to yourself in such moments. It was the lowest point my life had reached. The darkest depths. The nadir. Only thoughts of vicious revenge kept me going. Eventually I began to calm down. The first thing I realised was that I had to get away. I had to leave London. So where did I go? I went back to Scotland.

*   *   *

I rented a small freezing cottage on old Sir Hector Dale's estate at Drumlarish. Somehow the old chap was still just in the land of the living. He was bedridden and quite gaga ninety percent of the time. A grandson, my cousin, Mungo Dale ran the increasingly decrepit estate. Mungo was a big, fair utterly stupid man in his early forties whose company I found oddly consoling. I never saw him wear anything but a kilt. From time to time he would come by the cottage and ask me if I wanted to participate in the life of the farm—repairing drystone dykes, feeding sheep and cattle, and so on—but I always politely declined. I have never sought solace in physical labour. My energies are purely mental.

Mungo was far too shy ever to marry and in fact was quite happy looking after the estate and his ancient grandfather. None of the other Dales enjoyed living at Drumlarish and were all firmly established in Glasgow and Edinburgh in various easy jobs. Mungo would inherit the house and land when old Sir Hector finally passed away. Mungo lived with him in the big house (colder than my cottage) and said with some pride that he had slept in the same bedroom for over forty years. An old couple saw to their food and tried to keep dust and all types of encroaching decay in hand. Somehow, with the occasional help of the sale of a few shares, a good picture or a piece of furniture, the leasing of pasture and moorland, the place just managed to keep going.

I went into a kind of mental hibernation during the winter of 1936–37. I grew a beard. I did some token work on my script and tried to keep warm. My social life consisted of visits to Mungo and Sir Hector and the occasional trip to Glenfinnan to stock up on provisions and draw money from the bank. My finances were about as healthy as Sir Hector. I spent Christmas at my father's with Thompson and Heather but returned to Drumlarish before Hogmanay. I avoided buying newspapers and listening to the radio. My only source of news was Mungo.

'There's a war going on in Spain,' he said to me in January, as we drove into Glenfinnan to buy paraffin.

'Oh yes? What's happening?'

'Well, to tell you the truth, John, I'm no very sure. But it's pretty bad, I believe.'

'I see.'

'Even been tae Spain, John?'

'No, can't say I have.'

'I hear tell it's an awfy beautiful country.'

'So I've heard.'

Thus we conversed. We could talk for hours like this, usually at night in the kitchen of the big house, a whisky bottle and two glasses in front of us. Slowly I healed. I shaved off my beard. In February I finished my script of *The Confessions: Part II* and then neatly retyped it.

Mungo came round one day with a load of peat for the fire. He saw the ream of fresh paper.

'Finished?' he asked. I said yes.

'I remember that film of yours, that *Julie*. I was in Perth, I'd gone there tae buy a dug. Grand film. Lovely girl that, eh? Gorgeous.'

I felt my guts knot as I thought suddenly of Doon. Mungo nattered on extolling her beauty. I felt light-headed with my loss. I breathed deeply.

'Can't wait to see the new one.'

To distance myself I explained something of my difficulties, of how Leo Druce and Courtney Young had betrayed me (Mungo had never asked why I had come to Drumlarish). He listened patiently, sometimes frowning as he concentrated.

'It seems to me,' he said, after I had elaborated on the role a producer played in film making, 'that you'd be a lot better off setting things up on your own. Why don't you go to a bank and borrow the money?'

A patronising smile was half formed on my lips when Mungo added, 'Why don't you go and ask that brother of yours, that Thompson?'

*   *   *

I was sorry to leave Drumlarish. I had achieved some measure of peace there and had grown attached to my icy cottage and the wild battered landscape, the mossy grass, the tough crouched trees, the meandering grey lines of the drystone walls climbing the big crude hills. Mungo drove me all the way to Glenfinnan in Sir Hector's ancient black Humber. He sat leaning forward, as if he had to peer out, his legs spread on either side of the wheel, his hairy scarred knees protruding from his kilt as unyielding as the granite boulders set into the hillside. Mungo honked the horn aggressively at the dirty shaggy sheep that cropped the road verges. I had a violent headache by the time we reached the station.

I cannot explain why but my attitude to Edinburgh had changed since my last visit. It was the usual filthy Scottish spring, that annual extension of winter. The city appeared unduly dark, almost black beneath low harassed clouds. It rained constantly, not hard, not a drizzle, just steadily without stopping. The wind scoured the streets. Perhaps it was because I needed something from the place; that I was coming as a supplicant, not a native son, but for the first time I shivered before the city's hefty formality and felt uneasy in the face of its unsmiling reserve.

I told no-one I was coming. I took a room in the Scotia hotel and resumed my old life with my anonymous fellow lodgers. Mrs Darling was not pleased to see me back.

I created and registered a private company. Alef-Null Films Ltd. Alef-Null, the name of the sign of infinity—it was an oblique homage to Hamish. There were ten one pound shares. I owned nine and gave one to Mungo out of gratitude. I had a letterhead designed and some stationery printed up: ALEF NULL. I liked it. Copies of the script were printed and bound. I drew up a preliminary budget and had it professionally typed at a typing agency. Only then did I go to Thompson with my proposal.

I should have said that since his wedding in 1927 Thompson Todd had borne issue. Innes arrived in 1933, Emmeline in 1935. Our father and mother's names of course (no matter that one of my daughters was already called Emmeline . . .). Thompson and Heather had moved some years previously to a large new house made of pale puce sandstone in Cramond with a fine view of the Forth and Cramond island. When I was ready I telephoned, then caught a motor bus out at Waverley bridge. Thompson met me at Cramond station and drove me to his house. My nephew and niece greeted me with polite enthusiasm. Heather was still fresh-faced and girlish-looking but a little fuller of figure, which suited her. Again, I wondered what such a nice pretty girl could have seen in Thompson, fat and sleek, his hair now prematurely grey. He had always been in a hurry to age, had Thompson, and his body was obliging him. He felt more like my uncle than my elder brother. Heather, I could see, was excited by my arrival. She said she hoped I didn't mind but she had invited some neighbours around for drinks that evening to meet me. She pressed me to stay as long as I wished. I realised that to her, if not Thompson, I was something of a celebrity. I was grateful to her. My self-esteem, as if it were an organ within me made of erectile tissue, swelled and grew. Heather's mild adoration acted as a catalyst. Yes, I told myself, yes— you are John James Todd. You were the toast of Berlin. You are the creator of one of the greatest silent movies ever made. So your career has taken something of a slide, but never forget what you have achieved and what lies ahead of you.

I accepted Heather's invitation and had my luggage sent on from the Scotia hotel. That afternoon I put my proposition to Thompson and asked him to suggest to his board at the bank that they invest in Alef-Null Films Ltd.

'I don't need all the budget,' I said. '£25,000 will be enough. With that I can go to Astra-King, Gainsborough, Gaumont-British, anybody for the rest.'

Thompson asked a few questions. He seemed quite impressed by my presentation.

'I'll put it to the board, John,' he said. 'It's the least I can do. But I have to warn you, don't get your hopes up.'

'Not at all,' I said. 'Fair and square. I just want them to look at it as an investment, pure and simple. Just like any other.'

Heather looked round Thompson's study door. Her thick short hair was freshly brushed, she had a touch of pink lipstick on and a blush of rouge. She really did look extraordinarily pretty from certain angles, I thought.

'Everyone's here, Thompson,' she said. 'They're all dying to meet John.'

I stood up and buttoned my jacket.

'Coming, coming,' I said. I did her proud.

During the following week I lunched with key directors of Thompson's bank. We ate bad food in hushed clubs and in empty overheated hotel dining rooms. I explained my film to solemn grey men who for some reason all reminded me of my father. Thompson remained strictly neutral, intervening only to clarify a point from time to time. Eventually I was told that a meeting was due two weeks hence when a decision would be made.

In spite of all the pragmatic cautious advice I gave myself during the subsequent days I could not prevent a sense of mounting excitement growing in me. I felt, too, a harder satisfaction, a cynical relish. I was glad Courtney Young had turned me down. Now I would have the pleasure of rubbing his nose in his own appalling judgement. I could not stop myself from indulging in longer term fantasies either. I saw Alef-Null establishing itself as a successful film company, negotiating deals with larger studios—nothing too ambitious, mind you, just three or four films a year. Perhaps I would invite Eddie Simmonette in as a partner. For the first time in years I began to contemplate what I would do after *The Confessions*. *After?* After *The Confessions*. It sounded unreal. My whole adult life it seemed had been mortgaged to the idea of this film, everything else had been peripheral, accidental. What would I do after *The Confessions*? I had no idea.

I suppose it was this newfound self-confidence that made me behave in the way I did. As you know I am a helpless victim of my own desires. I cannot resist temptation, especially when I generate it myself.

I liked Heather enormously. We became good friends in only a few days. She was an avid and intelligent film goer. She had seen *Julie* and *The Divorce* several times, and I am sure she found me a refreshing diversion from the stolid Thompson. While I waited for the bank's decision we spent a lot of time in each other's company. We talked endlessly. We went for walks with little Innes and Emmeline. I recounted anecdotes of my filming experiences, of the great directors and film stars I had known—A. E. Groth and Fritz Lang, Nazimova, Gast, Emil Jannings and Pola Negri and many others. She was entranced. I told her about myself, my dreams about *The Confessions*, my marriage to Sonia, my long affair with Doon. Heather learnt a lot about me very quickly. On many afternoons we would motor into Edinburgh and go to matinée shows of any film we could find and discuss them avidly in tea rooms filled with well-dressed old ladies in hats. Heather not only liked me but she was, I think, a little in awe of me. It is a dangerous impression to give any man, let alone a chronic impulsive like me with only minimal control over his emotions.

One morning, a Wednesday or Thursday towards the end of April, I was standing in Thompson's living room. There was a fire burning in the grate, the room was warm and I was alone in the house with Heather. Thompson was at work. The children were playing with friends nearby. There was an hour until lunch. A faint but delicious smell of roasting meat came from the kitchen where Heather was busy supervising the cook. I poured myself a schooner of dry sherry and drank two large mouthfuls from it. That first drink of the day...
I looked at myself in the mirror. I was wearing an old tweed suit, sand brown, a cream shirt with a soft collar and a bottle-green knitted silk tie. I thought, in that alcohol rush, that I looked astonishingly handsome. Dreamily, I pushed my dark hair around. With a finger I nudged a lock over my forehead. I tell you, I had a pleasant

narcissistic erection two full minutes before Heather came into the
room.

'Sherry?' she said hurrying in from the kitchen. 'Have another.'

'Thanks.' Sometimes you can get drunk on one mouthful. Normally I can hold my liquor but that morning I was already delightfully
bleary.

Heather refilled my glass. She wore a pale blue dress with a pseudo
sailor's collar. Its V neck stopped, I imagined, an inch above the
crease between her breasts.

'Gosh, I'm dying for this,' she said. 'That cook, really, it's just
mutton.'

She clinked her glass against mine.

'Here's how,' she said.

'Cheerio.'

We toasted. We drank. I was already moving in for the kiss as she
lowered her glass from her lips. I tasted sherry. Her lips were cool.
Her breasts flattened against my chest. Timidly, our tongues touched.
For a second I experienced that moment of unforgettable elation—a
stillness, a deep calm at the centre of everything.

Then she was pushing me away. Fiercely. She stepped back. She
looked frightened, as if I was threatening her with something awful.

'I wish you hadn't done that,' she said in a sad resentful voice. 'It
wasn't kind of you.'

'Heather . . .' I put my hand on her shoulder. She knocked it away.

'You've spoilt everything now.' She seemed calm, there were no
tears. 'Why didn't you think, John? Why didn't you think?'

I almost wished she was weeping. I was profoundly unsettled by
her solemn gloom.

'Because I never do,' I said honestly.

'You should have chosen *not* to,' she said. 'I had. Couldn't you see
I'd made that choice? Sometimes to choose *not* to do something is as
important as . . .'

She faltered, but I had the gist of her reasoning. The left turning
or the right? Down which avenue of possibilities will you travel? We
want to do the best but there is always a course of action that gives
you the worst of all possible worlds. I seemed to have a knack for
picking it out.

We never kissed or touched again. And we lost what we had before
I embarked ourselves on those impulsive seconds. My kissing Heather
opened no door for us; it merely cancelled the alternatives and left
us both impoverished. What I envy most in people is their ability to
use restraint and denial in a positive way. To live and be happy with

the negative, the route not chosen. In the scale of my life's enormous disappointments my three-second kiss with Heather has to be regarded as insignificant, but it proved to be a small and lasting regret, like a grumbling appendix, nagging, nagging.

My next blunder was not of that order. It cost me dearly, its ramifications were massive, but I forgave myself immediately. Any man in my position would have done the same.

I went to the dentist, Thompson's dentist, a nice man in Barnton, to have a tooth filled. This was two days after my—what?—my brush with Heather and three or four days before the crucial meeting at the bank. I sat down in the waiting room and picked up a copy of *The Daily Herald* that was lying there. The paper, along with every other publication in Britain, was full of news about the impending coronation. I flicked through it. I stopped abruptly on one page because I thought I saw a photograph of Sonia, but it turned out to be of Mrs Wallis Simpson. Then, down below, my eye was caught by a headline:

20th Anniversary of the Third Battle of Ypres

Now, here *was* a face I recognised. I read on.

> As part of our series commemorating this great battle we invite old soldiers to share their memories. This week the distinguished film director Mr Leo Druce, currently at work on Court Films' *Great Alfred*, recounts his part in the battle.

The piece was headed *Bombing the Ridge at Frezenberg*. I read on.

> We went over the top at dawn. Our objective was the first German trench-line on the notorious and deadly Frezenburg Ridge. I was leader of the bombing section in 'D' coy. 13th (public school) service battalion of the South Oxfordshire Light Infantry. The Hun machine-guns did not open up until we were half way across the perilous quagmire that was no-man's-land. All hell broke loose. Bullets buzzed through the air like maddened bees, only these insects carried a fatal sting. I saw our platoon commander go down, shot through the heart, as he stopped to aid a wounded comrade. Before he died he waved us on and shouted 'on you go, lads!' We struggled on through the merciless hail of bullets. Then, on my right, there was an enormous explosion as my close friend the Hon. Maitland Bookbinder literally disintegrated as his sack of bombs exploded. The fields of Flanders had become a charnel house flowing with

English blood. We pressed on gallantly, men falling like flies all around. Fortunately the tremendous barrage from our guns had cleared enormous gaps in the Hun wire ...

Leo Druce duly threw all his bombs. Modestly, he 'did not pause to see what dread effect those mighty detonations had.' Then on his way back—to re-arm himself, naturally—he was flattened by an explosion and came round with a 'searing pain' in his left leg. Somehow he managed to crawl back to the lines where he fell unconscious from pain and loss of blood. When he woke up in a casualty clearing station he knew,

> the battle was over for me. But I was proud to have played my part in one of the bitterest, bravest conflicts that the modern world has seen.

There were further banalities about 'our men who fought like lions' and not allowing the gallant fallen to go unremembered. At that point I was summoned into the surgery. I never felt a thing. I was in the grip of a frying, sputtering rage. As the dentist pumped away on his drill I was composing my letter to the editor of *The Daily Herald*. I wrote it that evening and posted it the next day. Unfortunately I have lost the original clipping but have preserved a draft amongst my papers.

> Sir,
> Mr Leo Druce writes with vivid authority about his dramatic experiences during the attack on Frezenburg Ridge by the 13th (PS) service btn. of the SOLI. This is most curious. I was a member of that same bombing section led by lance-corporal Druce and saw nothing of him during the entire action. The only member of our section who successfully bombed the German lines was Mr Julian Teague, for which gallantry he was later decorated, I believe.
>
> When I next saw Mr Druce he explained his absence from the battlefield in this way. He told me he had been shot through the calf seconds after leaving our trench. He asked me to relate the events of that day (in which our section took appalling casualties) as, and I believe I quote him accurately, 'I never saw a thing.'
>
> It is bad enough when self-appointed heroes like Mr Druce turn up at battalion reunions wearing medals to which they are not entitled, but it really is a disagreeable if not intolerable slur on the memory of those men who perished in this most futile

of battles when a newspaper such as your own allows charlatans fraudulently to boost their own non-existent reputations as 'gallant soldiers'.

I remain, sir, your obedient servant,
John James Todd (ex-pvte. 13th (PS) btn. SOLI.)

I think I toned down the frothing outrage in the last sentence and changed the odd word (I think I called Druce a 'toiling cliché-monger') but this is essentially the same letter that was published three days later. I have no regrets. It was a sublime opportunity for revenge—I imagined it being read in horrible embarrassed silence at Young's mansion near High Wycombe. But I wrote also out of principle. No-one in that benighted squad had the right to the airs of fortitude and derring-do that Druce bestowed upon himself, apart possibly from Teague—and look how he ended up. It was a matter of pure principle first and foremost but I have to admit I enjoyed picturing Druce's hideous shame when the letter was read by his friends and colleagues. I waited for his retraction with glee. What denial would he, could he possibly offer up? I pondered getting in touch with Teague and Noel Kite to see if they would like to join in but I was distracted from this, and indeed forgot all about it, when the day of the bank's decision arrived.

I walked into that bank (a vast Greek temple of a building on George Street) as if I were coming before a Heavenly tribunal. The marble chill of its many halls and corridors, the busts and dark oil portraits, the uniformed doormen and porters, the studied absence of any light or human touch (not even a flower display, for God's sake!) seemed to portend that the denizens of this lair took their business very seriously. I sat in an airless ante-room whistling stupidly through my teeth. Alef-Null lived or died today and suddenly I saw through all the silly optimism of my plans.

Then Thompson came out. His smile gave nothing away, the professional mask was admirable. But as I walked past him into the board room he whispered in my ear.

'Relax. Good news.'

In the room was a long table behind which sat three of the bank's directors whom I had lunched with. I delayed events slightly and irritated everyone by accepting the Chairman's purely formal offer of tea or coffee. While Thompson went in search of someone who could provide me with one or other of these libations (I had not made a choice; either would do, I had said, nervously, whatever was easiest) we made awkward small talk until a little woman in a green overall brought me a juddering cup of coffee, well skinned, and a cracked rich tea biscuit on a china plate. I did not touch either of them.

One man spoke and the other two nodded. Thompson stared expressionlessly at his steepled fingers poised on the table in front of him.

'We were very impressed with your ... your "film" proposal. All of us, I think.' Nods, grunts of accord. 'You will understand, Mr Todd, that the "cinema" industry is not one in which the bank normally invests.' I nodded. This man had a deep super-polite Scottish accent. He pronounced 'bank', 'benk'. 'But I'm glad to say that in your case it was felt that this was an area which was well worth entering.'

I felt relief ooze through me, warm and comfortable, almost as if I had wet myself.

The senior man (I think his name was McIndoe) consulted his notes. 'Consequently the Investment Division has decided to advance your company £1,500 at current rates of interest. But at your brother's insistence and he, ha ha, put the case most eloquently—we have raised the loan to £2,500.'

McIndoe stood up and stretched his hand across the table.

'Delighted to be doing business with you, Mr Todd.'

I managed—how, I will never know—I managed to control myself. I produced some sort of smile and shook Thompson's hand as he escorted me to the main door.

'It's not as much as you hoped, I know,' Thompson said. 'But it's a start.' He smiled. 'You can have no idea how heretical it seems to the board—some members of our board—to lend money to a film company.' He chuckled. 'It wasn't exactly a unanimous decision, I can tell you—in confidence of course—cries of "nepotism" and all that.'

'I'm very grateful to you.'

'Remember, John, great oaks and little acorns ...' He clapped me on the shoulder. 'Good Lord, is that the rain on again?'

I think it was my impotence that really distressed me. I was not quite able to rage and shout against injustice. I could hardly berate Thompson for not standing up for me, either. I honestly think I would have been happier if they had got their flunkeys to throw me out on the street. What earthly good was £2,500? What film studio was going to be convinced by this munificence? I had to get out of Thompson's house at once. It was bad enough with Heather's frozen good manners, but Thompson was *so* pleased with himself. His smug pleasure in his good deed was intolerable. I think he had always felt guilty about me and somehow this loan cancelled out all his childhood indifference. He was really upset when I said I had to go. I moved temporarily back in with my father which proved a ghastly error. He was there to witness the final indignity.

I was sitting in his drawing room half-reading *The Scotsman*. Father was in his study across the hall. It must have been four or five days after my meeting at the bank. I had an account there now, credited with £2,500. From time to time I wondered what to do with it. I was coming to the conclusion that I should just give it back—I was not sure I could manage to pay the interest for more than a couple of months.

I heard the doorbell. Joan, my father's housekeeper, answered it. Some conversation ensued, then I heard my father emerge from his study. More chat. I paid it no further attention until my father came into the room.

'John, there's a gentleman here to see you.'

Ian Orr entered. He wore his old shiny suit and carried his hat in his hand, hollow crown facing me so I could see clearly the effect of years of Orr sweat and brilliantine on the lining. I stood up. What could the man want?

'Hello, Orr. What can I do for you?'

'Are you John James Todd?'

I looked closely at him. Was he mad? He seemed slightly embarrassed. His face was as badly shaved as ever, red and sore-looking. He had sticking plaster on an ear lobe.

'What are you talking about?' I said.

'Yes, of course he is,' my father said eagerly.

Orr gave me a buff envelope. I opened it. 'Dreadful sorry about this, Mr Todd. I wish I could have said no. But there you are.'

It was a writ. Leo Druce was suing me for defamation of character.

My father took it from my hand.

'Could I have a wee look? Thanks, John.'

Three days later in London my solicitor explained the problem to me. He was a pale young man with long wrists, or at least that was the curious effect his hands gave as they extended from his starched cuffs. He was called Cordwainer and was a partner in the firm of Devize, Broome and Cordwainer. I had phoned Sonia to see if Devize would represent me. He declined but passed me on to Cordwainer.

Cordwainer's white clean hands needlessly smoothed the blotless blotting paper in the pad on his desk as I considered the news he had just given me. My crucial error did not lie in the fact that I had accused Druce of fabricating his role in the attack on Frezenburg Ridge. It was the allegation that he wore medals to which he was not entitled that had provoked litigation. I felt suddenly helpless. My brain emptied. All I was aware of was noises: distant traffic, someone talking down the corridor, the dry susurration of Cordwainer's white hands on his blotter.

'Can you prove,' he said softly, 'that Druce ever wore medals to which he was not entitled?'

'Well, morally he's ... No,' I said.

'We have no choice then,' he continued. 'You must pay for a printed advertisement in the *Herald* retracting the statements in your letter and apologising.'

'Jesus Christ ...'

'And Mr Druce's lawyer informs me that an out-of-court settlement of 2,000 guineas will be acceptable.'

'*2,000 guineas!*'

'That's correct.'

'But, God Almighty, I just don't have ... that ... kind ... of money ...'

So Thompson's loan placated Leo Druce. Once I had paid for the advertisement (as loaded with ambiguity as I could make it), my legal fees—Devize charitably arranged a 10 per cent discount—I was left with some £325. I felt with powerful certainty that the only course of action available to me was to flee the country. But where could I go?

VILLA LUXE 25 *June* 1972

Something odd is happening to Emilia. Today she came to work wearing a new dress, scarlet with white polka dots and strappy shoes with wedge-shaped cork heels. Her broad horny feet looked most inappropriate in them. She's being very friendly and solicitous.

I compliment her on her dress. A terrible mistake. She simpers like an ingénue. The horrible suspicion strengthens: she is responding to what she sees as my own carnal interest in her ... But then, I rebuke myself. Her life isn't circumscribed by her domestic duties at the Villa Luxe. God alone knows what she gets up to when she's left this place.

As she serves lunch she says.

'Oh, yes. My friend told me a man was looking for you in town.'

'In town? Not the village?'

'No, in town. You know my friend who works at the post office. This man was asking there.'

I drank some water. My throat was suddenly parched.

'What was he like?'

'She didn't say. She just said a man. An American.'

'Did she tell him anything?'

'Of course not. This information is confidential. You want some more melon?'

'No thanks.'

'I brought it specially for you.'

'No, no. I'm not hungry, thank you.'

I felt the Past again, like a fog creeping in from the sea, curling round the house, seeping through its rooms. A damp, old, saline smell.

15

Pacific Palisades

The day war began in Europe was the day my temporary resident's visa ran out. As Adolf Hitler invaded Poland on September 3rd 1939 I left my home in Pacific Palisades, Los Angeles, California to drive south across the border to Tijuana, Mexico. I had an old grey Mercury in those days, 1935 model. It got me down to Tijuana with no problem.

I drove on to Rincon, a small village outside Tijuana on the road to Tecate, on the other side of the mesa where the airport is. In those days it was just about preserving its status as an independent township. There was a main street with a small square at one end, a couple of hotels and a court house, nothing too attractive but far more pleasant than Tijuana and much cheaper than the scandalously inflated prices you find there. Saving money was the only reason you stayed in Rincon while you waited for your resident's visa to be renewed. I say 'you' but I mean the Europeans, the Exiles. There was a fairly constant shifting population of between two to four dozen Europeans—Germans, Austrians, Czechs, Poles—from Los Angeles. The odd composer, artist, musician or novelist, but mainly made up of people from the film world. The two hotels were the Vera Cruz and the Imperador Maximilian. The Max, as it was called, had a very small swimming pool and a restaurant. The Vera Cruz was cheaper. At the back were six clapboard cottages for long-term residents. The last time I had been here was a year previously. It had taken only a week to arrange a new permit. Once we had that document we could drive back to Los Angeles and pick up our lives for another year.

I checked into the Max. It had been a long drive. I had some ground steak, fried potatoes and frigoles with a glass of beer and then went up to my room. I hadn't recognised any of the other faces in the restaurant. I stood at my hotel window looking down on the main street—the Avenida Emilio Carraza—lined with dusty nutant trees. It was getting dark. The streetlights all worked but they were irregularly spaced. Two together brightly illumined the forecourt of a gas station.

A little mall of shops and a doctor's surgery stood in inconvenient darkness. Overhead a twin-engined aeroplane came in to land at Tijuana airport. Further down the street multi-coloured fairy lights were strung in the two large fresno trees that shaded the terrace of the Cerveceria Americana. Some Mexican youths lounged outside a cinema that was showing *Los Manos de Orlac*. I saw an elderly German novelist and his wife return from their morose constitutional. A dog urinated against the white-wall tyres of an old Ford. It was a warm night.

*　　*　　*

When I arrived in Los Angeles in 1937—I flew from New York, fifteen hours, a UAL 'Sky Lounge' Mainliner via Chicago—it had almost been like returning home. Half of Berlin seemed to be there— Wilder, Reitlinger, Thomas Mann, Lang, many others. I stayed with Werner and Hanni Hitzig for the first month. Egon Gast lived three houses away. Most of the German émigrés had settled in the cheaper districts around the Santa Monica canyon, mainly in Brentwood and Pacific Palisades. On our reduced budgets we socialised as energetically as we could in each others' small houses. I joined the Hollywood anti-Nazi League and some days spoke more German than English. Most of my fellow émigrés were dejected and cast down—with good reason. Their country had rejected them, or vice versa, and all the fame and renown they had known there counted for little in their new home. They were employed—apart from a few—in dead-end charity jobs in various studios. Most spoke the language badly or not at all. The future was dark with dwindling prospects. But I, on the contrary, was excited. For a start I liked the sunshine and the proximity of the huge ocean. And I was relieved to be out of Britain. Remember, unlike the others, I was coming to Los Angeles from a position of no great advantage. And I had no language problems. I was not leaving some sumptuous villa in the Grunewald to live in a small frame house tucked up a steep road in a canyon suburb. To me Pacific Palisades was a more than fair exchange for the Scotia private hotel, my father's house and my flat in Islington. To me at that time Britain represented bad faith, broken promises, my ruined marriage, thwarted ambition and unjust legal persecution. I was perfectly happy to convalesce in California.

Stirrings of liberal conscience prompted many of the studios to offer jobs to émigrés. However, this usually involved little more than paying them a modest salary to stay away. Egon Gast was on contract to Twentieth Century Fox. He had been in Los Angeles a year and

a half and was still waiting to make his first film. He got me a job as
a writer there on a salary of $100 a week. In those days I suppose
that was a living wage—just. Some writers, I heard, earned as
much as $3,500 per week. Aldous Huxley once told me he got $15,000
for two months' work. The studios were being thoughtful but not
generous.

The first day I went to my office on the Fox lot the name above
my door read 'J. J. Todt'. The other four offices on that floor were
all occupied by Germans—directors and writers. It felt like something
of a ghetto, or like a quarantine ward in a hospital. Perhaps it wasn't
so surprising that we tended to cling together. At lunch we would eat
in a group in the corner of the canteen and the others would moan
and bitch about the venality and crassness of the work they were
expected to do—the debased standards under which they were obliged
to operate. They had all the highbrow disdain of the chronically
insecure. Men—I will mention no names—who had produced vulgar
musical comedies and mindless historical epics now became thorough-
bred intellectuals and *artistes,* grand arbiters of good taste.

I did not complain. It is extraordinary, but true, but in the months
that I was at Fox I was paid thousands of dollars and did not a stroke
of work. On the strength of the new salary I left the Hitzigs' and
rented a small apartment—$361\frac{1}{2}$ Encanto Drive—off Chatauqua Boulevard. It was half a house, the top half, which I sublet from an
illustrator called Ernst Kupfer. A lugubrious solemn man, he was
now known as Ernest Cooper and had a steady job working as an
animator for Walt Disney. He and his wife Utta had four children
who all lived with them downstairs. Utta was small, dark and of stout
peasant build with a huge sagging shelf of bosom. She worked
indefatigably about the house, controlling her children (three boys
and a little girl) with swift vicious punishments, usually powerful
stinging slaps to the back of legs, just like Oonagh administered.

Upstairs, I had a bedroom, a bathroom, a small sitting room
dominated by a horsehide davenport and, off that, a kitchenette with
a three burner stove, an electric icebox and a woodstone sink. I used
to feel guilty about all my space when I heard the six Coopers crashing
about below.

From the kitchenette window you could see the Pacific, always
grey, it never looked blue even on the sunniest days. The house itself
was wooden, set in a plot hacked out of a scrubby hill, and it had
three flights of steps leading down to the road from a screen porch.
Ernest cut the steep lawn from time to time, but it would have
smartened the place up unduly to do it regularly and made it stand

out from its neighbours. Encanto Drive had a shabby well-worn look. And there seemed to be kids everywhere. Some evenings when I parked my car after work and looked at the lounging adolescents, the toddlers, the shouting brats on their bicycles, I felt like a solitary adult in a school playground.

I settled in at Fox easily and quickly. My salary cheque too was made out to J. J. Todt but I never thought of complaining. It was generally understood that I was working on my own project which I would eventually show to the script editor (I never met this man after the first day). Weeks passed pleasantly. What did I do? I learnt how to play tennis, I acquired a suntan and put on some weight. I went swimming in the sea with Ernest's two older boys, Clancy and Elroy ('They Yamericans now,' Ernest would say. 'Europe finish.') I tinkered with my script of *The Confessions: Part II*. I felt oddly unreflecting and unbothered about things. One reason for this is that Europe might as well have vanished from the map of the world as far as life out here on the Pacific littoral was concerned. At our dinner parties, on beach picnics and in anti-Nazi League meetings we energetically debated political events in Europe but emerged from these sessions into sunny, prosperous, disinterested and indifferent realms. Soon, inexorably, Hitler, Mussolini, Chamberlain, Czechoslovakia, Anschluss came to have the status of arguments in a balloon-debate: abstract posits, forensic positions. Somehow, or so it seemed to me, these distant agitations just weren't my problem anymore.

The second reason was that I lost all sense of urgency. This was new, and harder to explain. Lethargy as far as I am now concerned is to do with spirit of place rather than state of mind. I simply find it impossible to work in some milieux. Perhaps in Los Angeles it was something to do with the absence of real seasons. The thermometer shifted down a few degrees, you put on a sweater, it was overcast and rainy—that described an average day in an English summer, not *winter*. And the trees were always green. Passing time lost its common demarcations. The sap never rose in spring, the days never shrunk, the nights never grew longer ... I was approaching my fortieth birthday, half my life had gone and yet I looked younger than ever. Those extra pounds I gained smoothed out the mature angles and declivities of my face. I tried to generate some energy but to little avail. In compensation I told myself I was biding my time.

But then perhaps, like a field, every life needs its fallow period. As it turned out mine lasted two years and ended with the invasion of Poland. But I am jumping ahead.

I did three things almost immediately on arriving in Los Angeles.

I wrote to Thompson and I tried to find Doon and Eddie Simmonette. I had left England without informing anyone. Thompson, as he put it, was 'devastated'. To his eyes the whole affair looked like the worst sort of fraud and betrayal. He contemplated repaying the loan himself but decided in the end to let me take the consequences of my actions. I quote a portion of his letter to me:

> ... Your behaviour, after the initial shock, did not seem on reflection to be all that surprising. You have always been far and away the most selfish member of our family, the most wayward and irresponsible. This sort of cavalier attitude to one's most serious obligations may be regarded as the norm in your 'world', but I assure you that it is anathema to the banking community. I consider your defaulting on the bank's loan a gross personal insult as well as an act of criminality. I cannot forgive you for the distress and embarrassment you have caused both me and Heather ...

And on and on. I could see that there had been a massive loss of face on his part and I was genuinely sorry. But what else could I have done? I wrote back briefly, apologised again and said I would send $100 a month, and more if circumstances permitted, until my debt had been cleared. While I worked at Fox I was as good as my word.

Very surprisingly, and somewhat worryingly, there was no news or sign of Doon. Few people seemed even to remember her. 'Didn't she go to Europe in the Twenties?' was the best I could come up with. I came to the reluctant conclusion that she was still in France. Willi Gast, Egon's brother, arrived in Los Angeles and told me there was a sizeable community of émigrés in Sanary, in the south of France, amongst whom he had noticed Mavrocordato. I assumed that was where I could find Doon—if I wanted to.

Eddie Simmonette, I discovered, was in New York, where he was making films in Yiddish. I wrote to him and he—typically—offered me a job, but I declined. I had settled in by then and the effort of moving east seemed too much. The Californian lethargy was already in my blood, coagulating it, slowing me down. Besides, I couldn't speak Yiddish ... but neither could Eddie as far as I knew. I stayed put.

I earned some extra money on top of my Fox wage from a man named Smee, Monroe Smee, whom I met at the anti-Nazi League meetings. Smee was an unfortunate looking fellow with receding hair and chin and yellow equine teeth with large gaps between them. He said he ran a small production company and I acted as a freelance script reader for him at $25 a script. I read seven before I asked to be relieved of the job. The scripts were absurdly bad, quite appalling. I had been expecting earnest, liberal-minded tracts but what he sent me was the worst sort of trash—turgid thrillers with creaking conspiracy theories and cloying romances with a strain of positively nauseating sentimentality, as far as I recall. Smee had great hopes for these scripts and I was reluctant to dash them as wholeheartedly as I felt they deserved, but I did. He was paying me for my honest professional opinion, I reminded him.

For a few weeks we saw a fair amount of each other. I didn't dislike Smee, but he just wasn't my type. He had only one joke which he employed endlessly. If, as you left a coffee shop, say, you asked 'Are you coming?' he would respond, 'As the Actress said to the Bishop.' If you said 'Shall I stay inside?' he would pipe up with 'As the Bishop said to the Actress.' I became almost maddened by this jocular tic. It was astonishing how the most innocuous question could be turned in Smee's mind into a Bishop/Actress gag.

I handed the last—the seventh—script back to him one night after a league meeting and told him I was quitting. I apologised.

'I just can't do it anymore,' I said.

'As the Bishop said to the Actress.'

'No, seriously, Monroe, wherever you're getting these screen-writers from I'd dump them. They're useless, worse than useless. You must be able to find some better ones. Ask the first person you meet outside ... I mean this is crap. Really. And that *Promises, Promises,* I think that's probably the worst script I've ever read. The guy should be locked up. What was his name?'

'*Promises, Promises*? That was, ah, Edgar Douglas.'

'Well he ought to have his brain examined. There was something actually rather disgusting about that story.'

Smee grinned. 'Well, anyway, I'm grateful to you, John. At least you're honest.' His face was damp. Smee sweated easily. 'But I should level with you now you're quitting. I'm Edgar Douglas. I wrote *Promises, Promises.* I wrote them all.'

'*Jesus Christ!* Monroe! God, why didn't you—'

'No, no. Don't worry. I'm grateful.' His grin was now distinctly cheesy. 'I'd never have known. I can't judge my own stuff. I needed an honest opinion.'

'Jesus ... I've got to give you your money back.'

'Nonsense, you earned it.'

'But I feel such a prick.'

336

'As the Actress said to the Bishop ... No, really, John, I needed to hear it. I respect your honesty. So I'm not cut out to be a screen writer. Now I know. Once a location manager always a location manager.'

'Monroe, I—'

'No hard feelings.'

We shook hands. 'I owe you one,' he said. 'I mean it.'

I felt bad about it and continued to apologise when we met at league meetings. He kept telling me to forget it and eventually I did. I held on to the money he had paid me, though. He was right, I *had* earned it.

And so I drifted through 1938 and into '39. On the day of my fortieth birthday (I looked ten years younger) I was invited to a tennis lunch-party at the Bel-Air home of an English director called Cyril Norman. Norman was a north-country homosexual who took his sport seriously and the day was mapped out with a series of round-robin competitions of singles and doubles. I was scheduled to start proceedings off with a doubles match: me and Clive Brook against Ronald Coleman and Richard Barthelmass. I had left my racket in the office and drove there to pick it up before going on to the party.

I parked in the nearest vacant space and ran upstairs. I came out two minutes later to find a large Chrysler coupé partially blocking me in. Its driver, a small red-faced man in a light grey suit with a yellow silk display handkerchief stood beside it. I was in white flannels, white shirt, dark navy cotton jersey. I was carrying my tennis racket. It was Wednesday, 11.00 a.m.

'Sorry,' I said. 'Won't be a second.'

'You work here?' The man said.

'Yes.'

He looked me up and down. 'Could have fooled me. What do you do?'

'I'm a writer,' I said. I didn't like his tone.

'Oh yeah? Chances are you can read, then.'

I looked at him, then at my watch. 'Look, I'd love to stay and chat but I'm pressed for time.'

He pointed. 'What the fuck you think that sign says? "Please park here"?'

There was a sign. PRIVATE. RESERVED and a name I couldn't read from that distance.

'If you move your car,' I said patiently, 'you can have your space back. I was in a hurry.'

'I don't give the steam off my shit if you're in a hurry. You're not meant to be there in the first place, dork.'

I got into my car.

'Hey! Jerk off. You English?'

'Scottish.'

'What's your name?'

'Todd.' I started the engine.

'Todd? Todd? . . .' he thought. Then his eyes widened. 'J. J. Todt! You're the fuckin *German* writer. What do you mean you're *Scottish*? We don't hire *Scottish* writers here! There are no fuckin Scottish refugees!'

'You'd better move your car, you little prick, or I'll hit it.'

'You're fired, asshole! I'm going to sue you for fraud.'

'So sue me!' I contemplated getting out and laying into him with my tennis racket. But instead I backed out fast and took the front fender neatly off his new car. For good measure I ran over it as I drove off.

I *was* fired. The very next day. I don't know who the man was, some self-important vice-president, I suspect, but somehow word got around that it was Darryl Zanuck himself. I'm sure it wasn't, but the rumour circulated anyway, and even made some gossip columns. 'Hapless German writer J. J. Todt clipped D. F. Zanuck's fender on the Fox lot last week and promptly got himself fired.' 'Writer J. J. Todt left his car at the kerb in the Fox lot and popped into the office to collect his tennis racket. But the rookie writer had parked in the Prez's place and got himself blasted out of court with a Zanuck ace! *Nein, Nein,* J. J.!'

In the way these things happen I even started dining out on it myself. It may have made a good story at a cocktail party but it also meant it proved almost impossible to get another job.

'God. So you're the guy Zanuck fired.'

'No.' I would say, 'It wasn't him. I've never met him.'

'But I read about it. Didn't I read about it? Jeez, what did you say to him, for God's sake?'

My remonstrations had no effect. None of the major studios would hire me. I was not only burdened with the Zanuck misapprehension but I was now irrevocably associated with the émigrés. People would often congratulate me on my excellent English, and there were too many Europeans looking for too few jobs. I realised then the extra-ordinary tenacity of first impressions. From then on I ceased putting such trust in my own.

I was out of work for two or three months. Of the two hundred or so émigrés in Los Angeles I suppose thirty or forty were regularly employed. Amongst the others there was fierce competition for the available jobs. I had to take my chances with everyone else.

I supplemented my rent by coaching Elroy Cooper with his maths—or math, as I was now instructed to call it. Elroy was a bright kid, but lazy. I kept him hard at it and found I rather enjoyed myself. I enjoyed the mathematics too; it took me back to the early days with Hamish at Minto Academy.

But I soon ran low on funds and I ended up accepting the first job I was offered. The Associated Motion Picture Releasing Corporation sounded quite grand. In reality it was one of the 'Poverty Row' film companies producing B-movie horror films and, this was its speciality, westerns. The man who offered me the job was called Brodie McMaster. He came from Illinois but was deeply proud of his heritage. The ethnic connection worked to my advantage for once.

The only difficulty was that AMPR paid its writers $50 a week. As a result they tended to be very old, very poor or heavily dependent on narcotics. In my time at AMPR I worked with two morphine addicts, a cocaine junkie and half a dozen soaks. I received shared writing credits on several AMPR films but I have no recollection now of which ones.

So my life restarted but on more reduced terms than before. I had virtually no savings by now and had stopped repaying my loan from Thompson's bank. Apart from my salary, I earned only a trickle of royalties from my films (*Jean-Jacques!* was currently playing in Francophone Africa) and from my patents. The graphline of my fortunes was still heading downwards.

But I was happy enough. Those two years in Hollywood before the Second World War now seem to me to be amongst the most placid and carefree of my life. It was similar, I imagine, to the experience of going to university: a finite period of independence with few responsibilities and limited funds. The sun shone, I had work, a little money, friends, a social life, a place to live. What more did I want?

Sex. Sex was something of a problem until Monika Alt arrived in town. It may sound strange but I had been practically celibate since Doon had left me. I had had one unsatisfactory visit to a prostitute in Paris during my sorrow-drowning binge after *The Confessions: Part II* had ended, and a heartless fortnight's affair with the head of make-up during filming of *The Divorce* (it ended the day we wrapped—her decision). Otherwise, I swear, nothing. After Doon left I felt sexually dessicated. From time to time the old urges returned, with Senga for example, and, for a hot week at Drumlarish, a sort of rutting season, I suppose. I asked Mungo what there was available locally and he told me about an old woman who lived in a filthy bothy on the road to Glenfinnan with whom you could have your way for a tumbler of whisky, but I was not tempted. Doon's betrayal had left me emotionally mawkish. I returned to the solace and 100 percent reliability of adolescent methods.

However, America had stimulated me once again and shortly after I moved into 361½ Encanto Drive I courted and won the manageress of a coffee shop on the Pacific Coast Highway. Her name was Lorelei, Lorelei Madrazon. I think she was half Turkish and Lorelei an approximation to her Turkish name. She was in her forties, a divorcee with three young children—Hall, Chauncy and Nora-Lee. Lori's, her coffee shop, was a pleasant ten minute saunter from Encanto Drive. Her ex-husband was a Filipino who ran a garden maintenance service. He had set her up in the coffee shop and they remained good friends. I met him several times. Anyway, Lori was solid, fleshy with wiry blonde hair—she was a victim of the permanent wave—and a pretty face, always bright with make-up. I think it was a combination of the olive skin and primary colours set against the improbable Nordic blondeness of her hair that attracted me. We enjoyed efficient, uncomplicated, fairly regular sex, twice a week on average, usually in the early evenings after she'd closed and after which we would go out for a meal or take in a movie.

I was glad to see Monika again. She had left Berlin in 1934 and had come straight to Hollywood where she enjoyed brief and modest success in two or three sub-Marlene Dietrich thrillers. This trip had the bonus of securing her an American husband and citizenship. For a year she had been content to be Mrs Geraldo Berasconi but then came divorce and another attempt to return to the screen. Monika however was now in her fifties, astonishing though that fact seemed when I stopped to consider it, and the flood of émigrés had provided a glut of sensual foreign vamps. She still looked good I must say— hair shorter, as thin as ever but more groomed. Unfortunately, her new consort was Harold Faithfull.

Faithfull was still a successful second rater—they never truly succeed, these types, but they never seem to truly fail, either. He was in Hollywood under contract to Warners and, like most of the European directors in the place, was engaged in serving up a trashy version of 'Old Europe' for American consumption.

I met Monika and Faithfull at a cricket match in Bel-Air (once again organised by the indefatigable Cyril Norman, a ghastly annual occasion for all the has-been, bit-parters and lounge-lizards to parade their stage Englishness). Faithfull ignored me except to comment, 'Hard times, Todd? Hard luck,' and wander away. He was very fat but still annoyingly handsome in his sleek prosperous way with his thick grey hair brushed straight back from his forehead. Every time I saw him I felt a bizarre cannibalistic urge to carve a steak of his plump haunches. I have a feeling Faithfull would have tasted good— porkish, with crackling, served up with roast potatoes, sprouts and apple sauce. He had a superb tailor. His immaculately cut dark suits made him look tapered rather than bulky.

Monika wouldn't leave him for me (she said he'd had his teeth fixed) and they made a stylish couple. However, she would motor down from Mulholland Drive to see me occasionally in my little apartment. I always liked Monika and we got on well. The sex was not the sole reason for the continued association. She was no snob. Faithfull wouldn't be seen with me because I was a $50-a-week writer on Poverty Row. Monika had a European egalitarianism which the British don't possess. Hard Times? ... Hard luck. No-one from Berlin would have said that in 1939.

*   *   *

The next day I drove to Tijuana to the American consulate to renew my resident's visa. I waited for an hour to see the consul, a Mr Lexter, a quiet elderly man and a lay Baptist minister, so he told me later. He had a big shock of unruly grey hair that kept falling into an unlikely boyish fringe. He looked over my form, and me, and said he would get it processed right away. Then, dropping his functionary's guard for a moment he said, 'I think your country is doing a fine and noble thing, Mr Todd. I pray for an end to this evil.' It was only then (he obligingly fetched an American newspaper) that I learnt war had been declared.

I left the consulate and went round the corner to the Hotel Cuatro Naciones. I sat in the bar and read the news. I drank several beers and wondered what to do next. How did I feel? ... First, oddly divided. Then emotionally and tearfully patriotic. Then irritated and frustrated. I thought of my years in Berlin and of all my German friends. Then I thought of those mad bastards with their uniforms and their flags. I wasn't at all surprised by the news. Our Santa Monica chapter of the anti-Nazi League had been predicting war in Europe for years. Now it had come and abstract arguments were suddenly concrete facts. I thought, for some reason, about my father, Hamish and Mungo before I considered my three children. These misplaced loyalties upset me. I felt a rush of self-hatred for so easily abandoning Vincent, Emmeline and Annabelle to Devize. I ate a solitary lunch of chorizos, goat's cheese and a bottle of sweet wine, growing steadily more depressed as the particular fears—destruction of country, death of loved ones—elided into the generally maudlin.

My mind went back to 1914. I thought of the Salient, the bombers, that day with Teague. It was just my luck to fit *two* European wars into my four decades. How could all this be happening *again*? and so soon? ... Then, *Christ!* Karl-Heinz! What about Karl-Heinz? Then I felt bitterly sorry for myself, alone in this noisy, noisome border town. What the hell was I doing here? I grew angry. I strode back round to the consulate but it was shut. I had a vicious argument with an impassive concierge. I left a note urging Lexter to process my application with the greatest speed as I wished to return to Britain at once.

It was a curious day. I drove back to Rincon and packed my suitcases. Then I unpacked them. That evening I went down to the Cerveceria Americana. The place was full of glum Germans. As I sat on the terrace and talked with them I suddenly realised that notionally we were enemies. To cope with this absurdity I drank too much tequila añeja and took a $100 bet with an affable man called Ramon Dusenberry that the USA would declare war on Germany before the end of November. When I left the Cerveceria at 2.00 a.m. it was still loud with the noise of morose disputation.

I confess the events of the next week or so are hard for me to untangle. My journal entries are undated.

Wednesday. To Tijuana. Lexter says he will do everything he can to expedite matters. Back to Rincon. Cerveceria at night. F. says Hitler will sue for peace once he has Poland ...
Friday. To Tijuana. Lexter—no news. Cable father for money. Telephone Lori to pass on message to the Coopers and Monika— no reply from AMPR ...
Tuesday. Herr and Frau K. return LA
Saturday. Americana—Dusenberry.
Sunday. Pack up. Settle bill—330 pesos ...
Monday. Cable AMPR for advance on salary
No news, Lexter. Cannot understand delay. Return Rincon. New room. Unpack ...
Wednesday. Dusenberry bets me that Russia will ally with Germany against Britain and France—$50 ... [Here there is an unexplained gap of one week.]

Wednesday. Lexter says my request for visa renewal has been turned down.

This was an astonishing blow. I had been in Mexico for getting on for three weeks and despite the unprecedented delay I had never once suspected that I would not be allowed to return to the United States. Lexter was apologetic but formal. He declined to explain why I had been refused entry. His sympathy for me, his decent pro-European liberal sentiments disappeared behind apparatchik reserve. As symbol of my plight he naturally became my enemy. Suddenly I found his mop of hair an offensive affectation. Shouldn't a man of his age, I suggested to him, stop pretending to be a college kid? He called a marine in to throw me out. I apologised, said I was over-wrought, my country was at war, I just wasn't myself. We sat down again. It must be a simple mistake, he said. He would investigate further. He advised me to do what every frustrated emigrant did: be patient and reapply.

I took his advice. There was one other course of action I could have followed: I could catch a boat to England from a Mexican port. But I was now running into the other eternal problem—money. Brodie McMaster's chauvinistic loyalty to a fellow Scot had its limits. He sent me one week's salary in lieu of notice. I was unemployed. The Coopers wrote and said that without the rent they could only hold my apartment until the end of October. Soon I would be homeless. I left the hotel and moved into a clapboard cottage behind the Vera Cruz. It cost 16 pesos a day, cheaper than a double room at the Max. After a week there and more fiscal calculations I transferred to a single room in the main hotel that bore an unfortunate resemblance to my cell at Weilberg, but it only cost 11 pesos a day.

My life took on a strange routine. I ate a modest breakfast at the Vera Cruz—*pan dulce* and coffee. I wrote letters in the morning. I lunched in a cheap restaurant (surrounded by suspicious monoglot locals. What was this *gringo* with his old newspaper doing here every day eating *refritos*, eggs and rice with a bottle of Garci-Crespo mineral water?) After lunch I took a long siesta. In the evening I bought a couple of lardy quesadillas—hash and cheese—from a roadside stall on my way down the Avenida towards the Americana. There, I tried, and usually succeeded, in getting mildly drunk on white tequila with beer chasers. I became a regular. There were always new émigrés to engage in conversation but I am afraid people tended to avoid me after a couple of nights of my company. I could only talk about one subject and at length—the conspiracy to prevent me entering the US.

343

I had become a bore. Even Monroe Smee (whom the anti-Nazi League had sent down with some money) stayed only twenty-four hours.

Three times a week, then once a week to economise on petrol I drove into Tijuana. I visited the consulate where I enquired about the progress of my re-application, and changed the books I was generously allowed to borrow from the small eclectic library they had there. Lexter was a thoughtful decent man, but even he admitted that this delay was more than bureaucratic ineptitude. But he couldn't clarify matters any further. After that I went to the post office to post letters and collect mail, bought whatever English language newspaper was available and drove back to Rincon and my drear accommodation at the Vera Cruz.

On Christmas day 1939 I motored up to Tecate, parked the car in some scrub and walked several miles across the border to Portrero where sanity returned and I retraced my steps. So many official inquiries had been instigated on my behalf, my particulars had been forwarded to so many government agencies that I realised I must be the best documented would-be immigrant the USA had ever seen. I would be lucky to last a week before being deposited back in Tijuana with all hopes gone. And Lexter would never forgive me. He was my only hope. I simply had to be patient.

My begging letters kept me alive, hovering above the poverty line. Lori, the Coopers, Monika, the Hitzigs, the Gasts and the anti-Nazi League subsidised me in my exile. All my Californian gloss disappeared. I grew thin again, my hair was cut rarely and my clothes were grubby. My friends corresponded regularly, sent me food, newspapers and magazines. Even my father wrote. I had cabled him for £50. He replied, saying he would see what he could do—then, silence. My letters to Eddie Simmonette were marked 'return to sender'. To my eyes it looked suspiciously like Eddie's handwriting on the envelope, but I couldn't swear to it.

I felt as if I was in quarantine. A dog suspected of rabies. I was free, but I was not free. Free in Mexico to do what I pleased as long as it was not the one thing I desired—leave. I caught something very nasty from a charming whore in Tijuana that cost me a precious twenty Yankee dollars to have put right. I didn't visit Lexter for two weeks out of pure shame. Those pale Baptist eyes of his saw everything, I knew.

My diary:

Rincon. 1 February 1940. The Fiesta of El Rescante, in honour of

344

our Lord of the Rescue. I lit a candle in the church of Our Lady of Los Dolores. It is all too horribly apt. The battery on my car has gone flat and I can't afford a new one. Assets: one immobile 1935 Mercury. Two suitcases of worn clothes. One camera. 27 dollars, 55 cents. The frightening thought strikes me that I could keep going like this indefinitely. Years may pass. Enough money to hang on in Rincon, but not enough to escape. If only Thompson would help. I hate that fat sanctimonious bastard! I think I understand the poverty trap. You have to have a little money, a little self-esteem, a little respect for authority. That way you don't starve, beg or steal. And that way you never do anything.

That evening I went down to the Americana to sell my camera, an expensive Leica I had bought in Berlin in '32 (I still took photographs from time to time, mainly portrait shots of people I worked with). Juan, the patron of the Americana, had offered me 200 pesos for it.

The fiesta was more or less over. It was a bluey warm dusk. A band was playing and some people were dancing in the Playa Zaragoza at the end of the main street. Mercifully, all the fireworks seemed to have stopped. For once the Avenida Emilio Carraza was empty of cars. Beneath the nutant trees—strung with bunting—two exhausted policemen collected the *No Estacionarse* signs. It was hard to imagine that all Europe was at war. For the first time I realised how easy it was to be neutral.

The Americana terrace was crowded with families. I made my way through the tables into the dark bar and asked for Juan.

'Mr Todd, at last!'

I turned round. It was Dusenberry, smiling in a friendly way. I hadn't seen him for weeks. Ramon Dusenberry was half Mexican, half American. He lived in San Diego, California but kept a large house outside Rincon where his mother stayed. He was a slim fine-boned man with a neat goatee. He was in the newspaper business. He owned a chain of local papers on both sides of the border. He was brown skinned and dark haired, but spoke English like an American.

'Hello,' I said without enthusiasm. The fiesta had depressed me.

'Still here?'

'For my sins.'

'You owe me a hundred dollars. The US remains stubbornly neutral.'

I laughed and then felt sick. Briefly, with passionate terseness, I outlined my position to him. One of his slim hands lightly tapped the marble surface of the bar. It looked like an elegant woman's hand—light brown, hairless, shiny nailed, very clean.

'Well, what are we going to do with you, Mr Todd?'

I sighed. 'Don't tell me this is an affair of honour ... Look, I'm broke. Flat, stony. Skint. *No tener un centavo*, mate.'

He ignored my aggression. I apologised.

'I am, really. I'm even trying to flog this camera to Juan.'

'You a photographer?'

'Yes of course. I'm a motion-picture director, for heaven's sake.'

'Ever worked for newspapers?'

'I was a newsreel cameraman in the Great War.' I suddenly felt old. I muttered, 'you know—'14–'18.'

'Got a car?'

'What is this? Yes.'

He smiled. He was handsome in a faintly sinister, over-refined way. 'You're just the man I'm looking for.'

*   *   *

That was how I became a photographer for the Tijuana, Tecate, Rumorosa and Mexicali *Clarions*. During the weeks I was employed I presided at a dozen weddings, four fiestas, two mayoral inaugurations, several livestock shows, a warehouse fire at Mexicali, the arrest of a rapist in the village of La Hechicera, the Miss Baja California 1940 beauty pageant and, my scoop, the collision of a freight train with a lorry full of oranges on the railway between Mexicali and Nuevo Leon. My shot of the body of the lorry driver lying on a bed of spilled oranges was syndicated throughout Mexico and even, so I was told, made the pages of some American magazines.

Ramon Dusenberry paid me $25 a week plus bonuses. I stayed on at the Vera Cruz partly out of affection for the place (seediness has its own allure for the seedy) and partly to save money. I abandoned my plan of returning to Los Angeles, someone or something was blocking that route far too effectively. I decided instead, when I had some money saved, to make for Tampico and try to book a passage on a merchant ship heading for Britain. If that proved unsuccessful I would head down to British Honduras or cross over to the West Indies and make my way home from there.

It was curious, however, how a job relieved a lot of my anxiety. I had the Mercury repaired and drove up and down the border to whatever assignment one of my four editors deemed worthy of photographing. I took a strange pleasure in these trips, motoring through the dusty arid landscape along the badly paved highway parallel to the border. I had some coarse linen suits run up for me in Mexicali, I acquired a taste for Mescal. I became a well-known figure in Rincon and opened a bank account in the Tijuana branch of the Banco Nacional de Mexico where my savings steadily accumulated. I was told that it was something of a social cachet in the border towns to have the gringo photographer turn up to cover your wedding. In short, I began to settle in.

Then, one evening in the middle of April I turned down the Avenida Emilio Carraza and parked my car in front of the Vera Cruz. I had just returned from photographing the winner of the 5,000 peso prize in the Federal District Lottery. The hotel owner's daughter, Elisa, who acted as receptionist, handed me a message.

'Meet me in the bar at the Max. 7.00. Monika.'

I shaved, changed my shirt and went to meet her. She was waiting in the bar. She looked hot. A combination of the day's lingering warmth and the Max's ceiling fans contrived to dishevel her carefully waved hair. The little vertical creases in her upper lip gleamed with perspiration. We embraced, my palms on her damp bare shoulders.

'My God, what's happened to you?'

I looked at myself in the bar mirror. 'Nothing.'

'You don't look . . . We were worried about you.'

It was a measure of my new contentment that I had stopped writing letters to my friends. No-one had heard a word for weeks.

We went to the Americana and had a cold beer beneath the coloured lights in the fresno trees. Monika's hair was backlit with blue, green, red. I felt a surge of affection for her. I never expect to inspire friendship let alone loyalty. These moments, these gestures disarm me. I took her hand.

'It was sweet of you to come looking for me. But I'm fine. Well, I am now.'

'Eddie Simmonette's in town. He wants to see you.'

'Eddie? Where's he been? I must have written him a dozen letters.'

'Nobody knows. But he's rich. He's bought a film company. Werner's already working for him.'

'What does he want?'

'He wants you to make a film.'

'Jesus Christ.'

Over dinner in the Max I explained my new travel plans to Monika. Vain months of trying to get a visa rendered other attempts futile. I was somehow going to make my way back to Britain.

'What's the latest war news?' I asked. 'We're a bit behind here.'

'Oh God, I can't remember . . . Nothing much. Something's going on in Norway, I think.' She took my hand. 'You must come back. Eddie has plans.'

347

'Wonderful. But how?'
She smiled.
'Simple,' she said. 'We'll get married.'

*   *   *

I married Monika Alt on the 23rd April 1940 in the offices of the US Consul at Tijuana. Mr Lexter officiated. My best man was Ramon Dusenberry. The other witness was Miss Raffaella Placacos Diaz, Lexter's secretary. Two hours later we drove across the border into the United States. As the spouse of one of its citizens I was passed through immigration with no delay.

*   *   *

VILLA LUXE 26 June 1972

I remember today, for some reason, a conversation that took place when I was teaching Elroy Cooper.

Apropos of nothing he said.

'Can God hear everything we say?'

'No,' I said without thinking.

'Why?'

'Because I don't believe there is a God.'

'Yeah? So what do you believe in?'

He was a bright boy, Elroy, not one to let things go by him. He was waiting for an answer and I realised I had never thought that deeply about it. I thought of something Hamish always said—'Anyone who can't explain his work to a fourteen-year-old is a charlatan.'

I tapped the cover of Elroy's maths book. Coincidentally, we were working on prime factors and how to factorialise. I had a go.

'Well, I'm inclined to believe in this,' I said. 'In science—maths and physics. I prefer to believe what they tell us about the world.' I paused. 'They say that the world is a highly complex place but at its root, at its basic elementary level, it is a realm of random events governed by chance and uncertainty. It doesn't make sense, any logical sense that we can understand. It can't be figured out by what you and I would regard as common sense ideas. This is what lies at the bottom, at the foundation of everything.

'But what we do, as human beings, in our everyday life, is go around pretending it *does* make sense, that there is a meaning and solid foundation to everything which we will discover one day.' I smiled. 'Mind you, I think in our heart of hearts we have to believe whatever the mathematicians and physicians are telling us. People have various ways of pretending the world makes sense and believing in God—or a God, or Gods—just happens to be one of them.'

Elroy was sceptical. 'But couldn't God have made the world to look like that? You know, to fool us?'

'I suppose that's a theory, but it's a bit feeble. There wouldn't be much point in believing in God, then. You see, people like to think there's a meaning in life and a hidden order in the universe. It would be a pretty strange God who made his presence known by arranging things so it looked like there was no meaning, and making the universe random and unpredictable.'

'I don't know. He can do what he likes.'

'A very famous mathematician said, "God may be devious but he doesn't play dice"—or something like that. I don't think you can have a dice-rolling God. There wouldn't be any point. In fact I think they're mutually exclusive as ideas, dice and God. You see if—'

'Can we get on with these prime factors?'

Another thing I forgot to tell you is that while I was in town the other day I went into a bookshop. In the English language section I found a book called *The Movie Encyclopaedia*. There was an entry under my name. I copied it out.

TODD, JOHN JAMES. b. 1899, d. 1960? English director of the silent era (Julie, Jean-Jacques!) *reappeared briefly in Hollywood during WWII where he made a number of indifferent B-feature westerns.*

16

The Kid

Between 1940 and 1943 I made eleven westerns, all but one of them under an hour long. Among the titles I can recall are *Gun Justice, Four Guns for Texas* and *Stampede!* As always the names tell you much about their quality. I shot them quickly, efficiently and wholly without passion. I might have been making deck chairs. All they had to do was work.

Eddie Simmonette had arrived in Hollywood in early 1940 with a considerable amount of money. I never knew how he became such a rich man again—it certainly wasn't his Yiddish films. I think it was something to do with wartime currency restrictions and gold bullion. From time to time he made trips to South America. Once he went to the Bahamas. I asked him why.

'To see the Duke of Windsor.'

'Oh yes, *sure*, Eddie.'

'It's the truth. You don't have to believe me.'

I laughed and told him of course I didn't. I think if I had pressed him he would have told me then. But I thought he was having me on. Anyway, he bought a small company called Lone Star Films and doubled its output. We made cheap westerns and a few thrillers. I have a feeling that Lone Star was part of this wider financial manipulation but I could never figure out just how and where it fitted in.

I was glad to be working, albeit on such a reduced level. It was pleasant, also, to be prosperous again. I stayed on in Pacific Palisades, I liked the ocean. I bought a larger house on Chatauqua Boulevard itself and Monika and I settled down to some sort of domestic routine.

We were divorced, quite amicably, six months later. We were tolerable lovers but lamentable spouses. We needed our liaison to be illicit for it to flourish. I think we rather bored each other, married. I started sneaking off to Lori's again and Monika took up with some young man she met. It soon became apparent that we should separate.

However she told me one fact that clarified the recent past somewhat. Evidently, during a drunken argument with Faithfull she had taunted him with our affair and its more intimate details—size of Todd organ *via à vis* the Faithfull member, ingenuity of position, stamina reserves and so on. Faithfull threw Monika out and went blustering round to my house to confront me and 'teach me a lesson' only to find I was away in Rincon awaiting my residency renewal. He got straight on to a crony at the British consulate and had him warn the US Immigration about me. Fuller investigation on their part revealed that I was a registered debtor in Scotland. It was enough to keep me in Rincon all those months.

One effect of this was to salve my patriotic conscience. If the British Diplomatic Service could connive at my being dubbed an undesirable alien then I certainly wasn't about to hurry back to serve my country. In any case, Hollywood was full of British actors, directors and producers—Korda was here, Wilcox, Olivier, Spenser Bellamy, Norman and many others. I did not stand out.

I didn't mix with the British community; I stayed with the émigrés, my Berlin friends. By now it was clear who was going to flourish in Hollywood and who was going to just make do. Eddie, I must say, was loyal to the Realismus boys. Hitzig, Gast and I were kept busy on the Lone Star B-features. Our fortunes had levelled out—at least they weren't declining—while others' ascended. Lang, Glucksman, Wilder, Strauss, Brecht—these were the fêted and the high flyers. We wished them well. Honestly.

I had another reason for avoiding the British. In 1942 Leo Druce arrived with Courtney Young to film *A Close Run Thing*, a torpid epic about the Duke of Wellington and the Battle of Waterloo, thinly disguised British propaganda to be directed at American audiences. I was walking along the beach one Sunday at Malibu and passed in front of the jutting deck of a beach house. A loud lunch party was going on and with a cold, spine-jolting shock of recognition I saw Druce's face in the crowd. Someone leant over the rail and shouted down to me to come and join them. I saw Druce's head swivel round at the mention of my name. I made sure our eyes did not meet. For an instant I was tempted by the thought of reconciliation—we had been friends for close on twenty years, after all—but my charity was snuffed out by memories of that day he so earnestly and altruistically advised me to turn down *Great Alfred* (a half success like all his films). I knew I could never forgive him. His own greed and ambition had lost me *The Confessions* and effectively driven me from my own country. There was no possibility of ever recovering our old warm friendship. I waved, shouted an excuse and walked on.

Around this time there was another arrival in Los Angeles whom

I was, paradoxically, happier to see. Alex Mavrocordato turned up in the émigré community impoverished and jobless. He didn't look well: his weight and bulk seemed a burden to him now, a slack load. He was still a big man but he had lost his big man aura, if you know what I mean. Before, he seemed to fill a room, as if his personality emitted some kind of force field. That was all but gone. A difficult journey through Vichy France and Spain, followed by a long wait in Lisbon for a boat west, seemed to have dispirited him, to have decanted his bullishness. He was staying with the Coopers and I went round to see him shortly after he had arrived. We walked down to Lori's and I bought him a 14-ounce steak with two fried eggs, french fries and a green salad on the side.

We sat down in the bright diner. Young people laughed and chattered in the booths. Lori and her smiling waitresses patrolled the aisles. The merry lights of Malibu pier stretched out languidly into the darkness. Mavrocordato chewed vigorously on his steak. I ordered him another beer.

'My God,' he said with some bitterness. 'War is hell.' He looked around him incredulously. 'You should see Europe.'

I felt an itch of guilt. 'You'll get used to it,' I said a little ruefully. 'It's quite easy.'

'Always in the right place at the right time,' he said. 'You find your feet, eh, Todd?'

'That's not how it looks from my angle,' I said, and added pleasantly, 'you can't possibly know what you're talking about.'

'Nobody knows the troubles I've seen?' He had a sense of humour, had Mavrocordato.

'Something like that.'

'Well I have to thank you for the meal. What do you want?'

'Where's Doon? What happened to Doon?'

'I haven't seen Doon for ...' he thought. 'My God, eight, nearly nine years. 1934, Paris.'

I felt the strangest sensation in my body, an odd mixture of alarm and elation.

'But she was in Sanary with you.'

'For one week. Then she left. She went to Neuchâtel to look for you.'

'But we'd left ...'

Bafflement clogged my brain. I felt thick, dull, like a man with a heavy cold.

Mavrocordato told me that he had seen Doon for a week in Paris in January '34, after our unhappy Christmas together. She seemed very depressed, he said. She was drunk most of the time. They left Paris for Sanary together; he thought the Riviera would do her good. But all they did was fight. She talked all the time about going to America. She left for Neuchâtel to tell you her decision, he said. That was the last he had seen of her.

We walked slowly back up the road towards the Cooper house. My mind was squirming with the revelations I had heard.

'So she must have gone . . . come here?'

'Yes. I always thought so.'

'I thought . . .' I was suddenly close to adolescent tears. 'I thought she had gone off with you.'

'I asked her,' Mavrocordato said, with some of his old vehemence. 'You know, I even asked her to marry me again.' He shrugged. 'You know Doon. I always think she's a little bit mad.' He tapped his head.

I was still thinking. 'But if she came here, where is she?'

'If she's drinking like Paris she's got to be dead. Or very sick.'

We stopped at the three flights of steps that led up to the Cooper house. Mavrocordato was sharing $361\frac{1}{2}$ with two other destitute émigrés.

'I'd better try and find her,' I said vaguely.

'Say hello from me.'

We shook hands.

'Listen, Todd, if you are needing assistant on your film . . . Bygones can be easily bygones.'

'Of course,' I said. 'I'll bear it in mind.' I felt only an immense gratitude towards Mavrocordato. I derived no pleasure from this triumph.

I went home and drank half a bottle of VAT 69 as I thought about Doon and this news. She hadn't betrayed me. She had simply run away. I felt peculiar: I should have been elated, my heart big with joy. But I wasn't. If she had been in America since 1934 why was there no sign of her? No trace at all? All her old friends from Berlin were in Hollywood, why had she not once made contact?

Eddie said I should get in touch with the Bureau of Missing Persons.

'Where was she from?' he said. 'You know, her "home town"?'

'I've no idea. My God.'

'Very useful.'

Eddie was married now, to a small shy dark woman called Artemisia Parke. It struck me that in all the years I had known him this was the first time I had ever associated him with a woman. Somehow a love-life, even a sex-life had seemed inappropriate for him, superfluous to his needs. He was like one of those worms or amoeba, hermaphroditic, that can service themselves (and I don't mean that unkindly). Like most facets of his life these days Eddie's marriage seemed a means to some mysterious end. He appeared unconcerned and incurious about the Doon mystery.

'She was a strange girl, Johnny, I told you so years ago. She could have suicided.' He snapped his fingers. 'They break, these types, like that.'

'Not Doon.'

'You should know.'

He sighed. He was on his way to play golf, wearing an outfit patterned with lozenges of lemon yellow, burnt sienna and maroon. I had a slight headache resulting from my attack on the VAT 69—and the colours seemed to press against my eyeballs painfully. I took a pair of green sunglasses out of my jacket pocket and put them on. We were sitting in his vast Beverly Hills home.

'Anyway,' he said, 'don't go running off. I've got a new project for you. The biggest yet.'

'Oh yes? What?'

'A film about Billy the Kid. But listen, in colour.'

I drove down to San Diego to see Ramon Dusenberry. Since he had been best man at my wedding we had become quite close friends. We would meet up from time to time when he was in Los Angeles on business. He was a great admirer of my westerns. 'Any time you're tired of movies, you can have your old job back,' he would joke. I liked Ramon and not just for his gratifying enthusiasm. He was older than me and I had unilaterally appointed him as surrogate older brother, now Thompson had abandoned the role. I asked him what to do about finding Doon. He said he had a friend in the San Diego police force who might be able to help.

We sat in Ramon's yacht club overlooking the marina. It was a clear day, the sky empty of clouds. A flying boat—a Catalina—flew past at low level on the way to the naval base. Over in Europe the Red Army captured Kharkov on their advance to the Dnieper. The RAF bombed Cologne. The USAF bombed St Nazaire.

'So what's the next movie?' Ramon asked.

'What? Oh, Billy the Kid,' I said.

'My God! Well, you've got to meet Garfield Barry.'

'I have?'

'Yes, old Garfield *knew* him, for God's sake.'

After lunch Ramon drove me up the coast to Cardiff-on-the-Sea, to a retiral home called Bella Vista across the coast highway from the public beach. It was a series of attenuated bungalows in the English style linked by covered walkways. Here and there were palms and ancient pepper trees with wooden benches set beneath them. We found Garfield Barry sitting outside in a wheelchair rather too close to a lawn sprinkler. The back of his head and shoulders were quite damp from the spray. We wheeled him out of range.

Barry was a lively old geezer but physically incapacitated by a recent stroke. He had a big nose and bright watery eyes; an uneven skull beneath a thin floss of white hair. One of Ramon's newspapers had run a long interview with him on his eighty-fifth birthday a couple of months previously called 'The last man who knew Billy the Kid' (this was quite true, I believe. There were a couple of old ladies still living who remembered the Kid, but Barry was definitely the last male.)

Barry had been born in 1857. His father kept a saloon in Fort Sumner, New Mexico. Barry himself had been postmaster there for forty years. In 1880, the year the Kid died there, Barry had been 22, a year older than the desperado. It was strange talking to the old man. I realised that Billy the Kid himself could have lived as long had circumstances been different. I felt an odd melancholy. Here I was, 44, born nineteen years after Pat Garrett killed the Kid, talking to their contemporary. Meanwhile the sun shone on San Diego and the Red Army pressed on towards the Dnieper. I felt a swooning disorientation of space and time, the present and the past. The objective and subjective worlds I occupied seemed to swirl and dance around me. I forced myself to concentrate on the old man.

'What was he like?' I said. 'Billy the Kid?'

'Well, for a start his name wasn't Billy the Kid. It was Henry McCarty and I would say ...' The old man paused for breath. A breeze stirred his fine hair and the branches of the pepper tree above him. I thought suddenly of old Duric Lodokian in his Berlin death-bed.

'... I would say he was one of the meanest, shortassed, buckteethed, foxy little fuckers I've ever met.'

With the help of Barry's reminiscences I rewrote Eddie's rotten script. Out went the American Robin Hood and in came something more sinister. The way I told it, my Henry McCarty was an evil runt who shot charming William Bonney and stole his name. Sheriff Pat Garrett, immensely tall (six feet four inches according to Barry) became a moralistic, lugubrious avenging angel. I took plenty of liberties with the story but the facts were accurate. It was the eighteenth Billy the Kid film, but the first one to portray him as he really was.

'He wasn't even left-handed,' Garfield Barry told me. We were examining the only known photograph of the Kid, where he stands with a rifle by his side. 'Some fool reversed the picture first time it was used and now everybody thinks he was a left-handed gun,' Barry said, chuckled and coughed.

I looked closely at the photo. 'My God. He's got three-inch heels on his boots,' I said.

'Told you he was a stunted little bastard.'

I think that was one of my most brilliant ideas in the film. Sonny Pyle, an astonishing young actor (whose tragic death in 1944 was a huge loss to the cinema) played the Kid throughout the film in four-inch cuban heels. It had the most bizarre effect on every posture and movement. Pyle was thin faced with staring eyes and we gave him a plate of false teeth so we could get the famous jackrabbit smile. Many people have subsequently analysed his performance without being able to say precisely why it was so mesmerising. Quite simply, it is the high heels. My Billy the Kid teeters; he has to go upstairs carefully; he jumps down from his horse with uncharacteristic caution. He walks with a curious bent-kneed gait. For the first time since *The Divorce* I worked with some enthusiasm on a motion picture.

I think this is what Eddie responded to. I had little trouble in convincing him that we had to shoot the film in New Mexico. The budget doubled, then trebled.

'Yes, Johnny,' he said patiently. 'I know. Location authenticity. I've heard it all before, remember?'

Towards the end of the year I flew down to Albuquerque to do a location scout. We based ourselves in Roswell and motored out across the Pecos flats searching for small villages that could stand in for nineteenth-century Lincoln and Fort Sumner. For the first time too I became excited about the possibilities of colour. Around me were the red and purple mountains, the pink and blue adobe houses, the hay meadows and the rolling alfalfa pastures, the canyon walls stippled with piñon and oak bush. This would be the backdrop for my morality play in which Sheriff Pat Garrett was the hero and the Kid the villain.

I was going to call the film *Alias Billy the Kid* but I decided in the end that I would use the name the cowboys gave to their six-guns, *The Equaliser*.

I am proud of *The Equaliser*. It doesn't rank with *The Confessions: Part I* but it was made—fast—with a kind of angry fervour which allowed me to invest a tired genre with a rare intensity. We filmed in the spring of '44. Padiko was Lincoln; Little Black was Fort Sumner. There was still snow on the El Capitan mountains and I kept them in the background of every exterior shot possible. Cold and remote, they are a continual presence in the film. We filmed also in a fruit ranch near the Ruidoso river. Acres of peach, plum, apple and pear orchards were in bloom. Their blossoms hung like a low-lying pink and white smoke across the landscape. (You will remember that scene when Pat Garrett—Nash McLure—stalks the Kid through the candied pink of the peach orchard.) I used colour like a painter: I literally daubed it on. It was my first colour film and I had every tone I could heightened. I repainted the adobe houses in Padiko. The Kid smoked cigarettes wrapped in bright yellow paper. I ran blue dye down canyon streams. And everything in the landscape had a vernal freshness—the chaparral thickets, the cottonwoods, the bunchgrass and greasewood. The whole film glowed.

Where did this urgency and angry fervour I referred to come from? Why, I hear you ask, was it not present in *Gun Justice, Four Guns for Texas* and *Stampede!*? The answer lies in the fact that I ran across Leo Druce a week before I started filming—the encounter acted as a powerful goad.

We met in the Los Angeles airport departure lounge. I was flying a Transcontinental and Western 'Sky Chief' to El Paso and then flying on up to Albuquerque. Druce was travelling to New York. Both our planes were delayed. Druce was with an elegant woman (his wife?) and two other men. I was alone. It was the first time we had met face to face in six years. He was grey haired now and stouter. He looked well off. I decided to ignore him and carried on reading my newspaper, but he came over. He was smoking a cigar and I suspect he'd been drinking. He stopped about six feet away from me. I looked up.

'Hello, Todd. Still here?' he said.

I ignored the implied insult. 'So are you, I see.'

'Ah, but I'm on my way home. To England.'

'*Bon voyage.*' I returned to my newspaper. It was full of speculation about a second front.

'Any message for the folks back home?'

'Just go away, Druce,' I said. I am sure it was my indifference that galled him most.

'Been a long time in your funk-hole now.'

I stood up and advanced on him. He stepped back quickly, then recovered himself.

'Listen, Druce,' I said quietly but full of venom. 'I don't need to prove myself to you or anybody. I was three months in that fucking Salient and six months in a prison camp while you were convalescing and totting up figures in the quartermaster's store. So just go away and leave me alone.'

'The next time you go up in a balloon make sure the wind's blowing in the right direction.'

'The next time you shoot yourself in the leg cut the powder burns out of your trousers.'

I swear until that moment I had never regarded the bullet that had passed through Druce's leg as anything other than German. The shock in his eyes confirmed the accuracy of my gibe.

He slapped my face.

'You bloody coward!'

I am told that my yell as I leapt on him was quite inhuman. I was hauled off him quickly enough by some TWA officials but not before my flailing clubbing fists had connected with that self-satisfied, dishonest, craven face. I had shut one of his eyes and split his top lip. I felt a silent howl of atavistic triumph echo through me as I saw his party lead him away to the washrooms groaning, doubled over.

'Madman!' he shouted weakly at me. 'You'll pay for this!'

'Can't you think of anything more original to say!' I yelled back. I'm delighted to report that the entire departure lounge burst into laughter.

I was in Albuquerque and Roswell when the story broke in the newspapers and so saw nothing of it. I believe it was all reported with clumsy irony: the 'Britishers' fighting each other in LA while the real enemy lay overseas. At any rate that, plus the Zanuck incident was enough to get me branded as a 'hellraiser'. For a good while afterwards people greeting me would recoil with gestures of mock terror and hostesses would whimsically entreat me at parties not to rough up the guests. Never believe anything you read in newspapers.

*   *   *

We were within a week of completing the film when I received the message. The crew were in Padilla shooting a scene under the shade trees in the square when the runner from the production office in Roswell arrived with a telegram:

DOON BOGAN LIVING IN MONTEZUMA ARIZONA STOP NEAR WINSLOW
STOP GOOD LUCK RAMON

When the film ended I hired a car and drove up to Albuquerque and on through the mountains into Arizona. It took me two full days but I have no recollection of the splendid scenery through which I travelled. I have no recollection of my mood: I was moodless, I think. It had been so long; I didn't want either pessimism or optimism to prejudice me. I would find what I would find.

I turned off the highway before Winslow and found Montezuma, a small town on the edge of the Navaho reservation. Distant mountains ringed the wide mesa. It was hot and dry.

I drove down the main street. There was a gas station, a used car lot, a Piggly-Wiggly supermarket and a cut-rate clothes emporium. I parked outside a funeral parlour and strolled down the cracked sidewalk to a small street market. At the market the stalls—fruit and vegetable—were manned mainly by Navaho Indians. If you wanted to hide away Montezuma seemed like a fair choice. I asked one fellow selling cheap trinkets and bright woven rugs if he knew where Doon Bogan lived.

'Miss Bogan? Sure. Go back to the gas station and take a right. There's an old ranch house two miles down the road—"The Colony". Can't miss it.'

I followed his instructions. The road ran through a dusty scrub of sagebrush and manzanita bushes. 'The Colony' announced itself with a freshly painted sign. It was a low wooden ranch house with rusted screens on the windows and a tumbledown corral. Three cars were pulled up outside. Two had California plates. My mouth was quite dry. My movements were slow and studied, as if I were recovering from a grave illness.

I knocked on the door and got no answer. I went round the side of the house. In a kitchen a thin bald shirtless man in chino shorts washed up dishes in a tin basin.

'I'm looking for Miss Bogan,' I said.

'Hi. You must be Wally Garalaga. Pleased to meet you, Wally. I'm Morris Drexel.'

He wiped his hands on a towel and offered me his right one to shake. I shook it.

'We kinda figured you wouldn't get here 'till late,' Drexel said. He had a thin chest with grey hairs grouped round the nipples.

'My name's Todd. I'm not expected. I'm an old friend of Doon.'

'Oh ... I'm sorry. We were expecting a Mr Garalaga.' He led me to the door and pointed. 'See that arroyo. Just follow it down a ways. Doon's there.'

I set off. My God, had Doon set up home with Morris Drexel? ...

I couldn't imagine it. I walked down the sandy bed of the arroyo contemplating this notion further. I began to perspire. The heat seemed trapped in the gully. I took off my tie. I had left my jacket in the car.

Then I saw Doon and stopped. She stood with her back towards me in front of an easel. She was wearing a denim shirt over white duck slacks. She had a widebrimmed straw hat on her head. I felt faint. My mouth was still as dry as the arroyo bed.

'Doon,' I said and advanced a few steps.

She turned. She was wearing dark sunglasses.

'Morris?'

'No, for Christ's sake it's *me*!'

She took off her sunglasses and put on spectacles.

'My sweet Lord,' she said. 'If it isn't John James Todd.'

I sat in the main sitting room of 'The Colony' trying to bring under control the competing emotions of profound shock and mounting irritation. The comfortable plain room was lined with abstract paintings that might just have passed for landscapes. Doon's work. To my eyes they seemed entirely without merit. Doon was in the kitchen making a pitcher of iced tea. She came back in.

'Sorry,' she said. 'Rita hasn't been into town for the ice. Will fairly cold tea do?'

'Fine. Perfect. Don't you have an icebox?'

'We don't have electricity.'

I forced a smile, trying to come to terms with the transformation in her. Doon was thinner and deeply tanned. Her hair was long, dry, dark brown streaked with grey. I had lived with her bobbed blonde fringe for so long it was as if the person I was now conversing with was an older sister, or an aunt. She put on her spectacles, searched for her cigarettes, found them and lit one. Her voice was deeper— raggedy—from smoking.

'You want one?'

'No thanks. I'm trying to stop.'

'Don't snap, Jamie ... So what happened after Mexico?'

I finished the brief sketch of the intervening years leaving out my marriage to Monika. Doon had already told me her story. She had left Sanary, gone to Neuchâtel to tell me her decision to return to America. She had found no trace of us, only news that the film had collapsed. She went back to America and Hollywood. She stayed there for a month and found she was lonely, miserable and forgotten. She hated it and so, as she put it, she 'resigned'. She bought this ranch house and took up painting. When her funds began running low, she established it as an artists' retreat. She made ends meet with no great difficulty, she said.

'But why,' I had said carefully on hearing this, 'Why in God's name didn't you contact me?'

'I tried. I tried to ring you in Berlin, I got some policeman on the line. I went to Neuchâtel, you were all gone. It was over Jamie, you know that. I couldn't go chasing round Europe looking for you.'

I had let that one go.

'I'm happy now,' she said. 'Really, I wasn't happy in Paris.'

So I told her what had happened to me. I felt glum, suddenly immensely tired. I could sleep for a week.

'So you're making westerns? For Eddie Simmonette? Isn't that a bit degrading?'

'I make ends meet with no great difficulty.'

'See. We're arguing already ... Sorry,' she said. 'Have some more tea.'

She stood up to fetch the pitcher. I went over to her.

'Doon, I saw Alex Mavrocordato—'

'Alex? How is he?'

'*Stop it!* Stop being so fucking hardboiled!'

Morris Drexel glanced into the room. I calmed down.

'Don't you see? I thought you had gone off with *him*. I thought you had chosen him instead of me ... That's why I never tried to get in touch. I was trying to get over it, do you see? Trying to forget you.'

'Well, of course. You had to do that.'

'But then he told me what really happened.' I looked out of the window and saw two ladies walk by with canvases under their arms. Two 'artists', like Morris, paying guests.

I shut my eyes. My head seemed to hum with a high, keening melancholic whine. I had been driving too long. The huge needless frustrations of the years without Doon were almost insupportable. Only my irritation with her own calm was preventing me from weeping. I was exhausted too from my weeks' work on the film. What had I expected to find here? The Doon I had known in Berlin in the Twenties? In her green dress and her short blonde fringe? Dully, I started calling myself names: fool, idiot, hopeless romantic ... I opened my eyes. Doon had sat down and was looking at me. She had hooked a leg over the arm of the soft chair she was sitting in. She still had that lean dancer's grace I always associated with her. Perhaps, in time, we could re-establish old intimacies ... But too much history bulked between us. My Doon was a blonde, smooth skinned, provocative beauty full of crazy enthusiasms. This thin, tanned deep-voiced cynic was someone else entirely.

'You've hardly changed at all, Jamie,' she said, as if reading my thoughts. 'You're not so slim, maybe. A few grey hairs. You look a bit tired.' She smiled. 'Why did you come?'

'I've missed you,' I said hopelessly. 'Nothing's been the same. I wanted to see you. I can't tell you—'

'I hope you weren't too shocked.' She got up and moved to the door. Clearly, she didn't want to talk. 'Staying for lunch?'

'Yes,' I said. I couldn't simply leave. 'Please.'

So I stayed, and chatted effortlessly with dull Morris and Rita and Elaine, the two spry lesbians, and tried not to think about Doon and the past.

When I left that afternoon she removed her spectacles to let me kiss her cheek. I looked into her myopic eyes and tried to conjure up that day in the Metropole Hotel in Berlin twenty years before.

'Don't fret about it,' she said softly. 'I remember you told me once—"Make your own rut". I'm happy, I told you. Now, *you* be happy. Come back and see us, soon.'

I drove off in blackest despair. I was convinced we would never meet again. I was wrong.

*   *   *

I could not shake off my depression. I could measure it in millibars. You know these moods? I'm sure you do. I saw my life as a catalogue of wasted opportunities, of intemperate decisions, of blind, crazy impulsiveness and, of course, heedless circumstance and filthy luck. It seemed to me to be the most desperate tragedy that Doon and I, of all people, had ended up almost strangers. I looked back over the last decade and saw it as a fruitless wasteland shadowed by clouds of disappointment, betrayal, flight and persecution. Perhaps, I thought, my individual life was merely acting as a conduit for the *zeitgeist* of that low dishonest decade ... but now we were four years into the Forties—I was four years into *my* forties. I was as old as the century and yet entirely out of step with it. The world was at war and what was I doing? Undermining the Billy the Kid myth and making a forlorn and futile visit to my old love. I was stuck in my Thirties' mood—failure and disillusionment. It was time for a change.

There were two baffling letters waiting for me on my return from Montezuma, both a fortnight old. One was from Hamish ... It announced merely that he had recently arrived in the States and was working for a US government department called the National Research Institute in Zion, New Jersey, not far from Princeton. He said he hoped that we might meet up soon, then he added,

> I can't tell you how sorry I was to see you vilified in that despicable way. I wrote several letters in your defence but none were printed. I suspect you have become the scapegoat for more eminent appeasers.

What vilification? What appeasement was he talking about? The second letter was from my father and even more perplexing.

> My dear John,
>
> I am prompted to write because I know the distress you must be suffering at these scandalous allegations. The fine letter in your defence from a Mr Julian Teague published in Wednesday's *Times* came a little too late I fear to undo the damage or halt the momentum. I merely wanted you to know that your family (and that includes Thompson) is standing by you during this difficult and unpleasant time.
>
> I am surprisingly fit for an old man. Please convey my respects to your new wife Monika, and I hope we will all meet soon in more happy circumstances.
>
> Yours aye,
> Dad.

It was the 'Dad' that shook me. He had never signed himself so affectionately before. But what was going on? Clearly, some vile slander on me had been perpetrated in the British press. I wrote to my father and Hamish immediately asking for more information.

I didn't have long to wait. I was in an editing suite at Lone Star working on *The Equaliser* when I received a call from a reporter on the *LA Times*. He would like to talk to me, he said. I assumed it was about the new film.

I met him in a bar round the corner. It was a sunny fresh morning and the place was quiet. Rumba music played gently on the radio. I ordered a Four Roses with ice and ginger ale in a tall glass. I munched some pretzels from the bartop bowl. The journalist arrived and introduced himself as Karl Shumway. He fanned out a series of newspaper clippings on the bar.

'What do you say to this?' he asked.

Let me summarise briefly the history of this particularly sordid campaign of character assassination. It had begun in a small circulation British film magazine called *Cinema Monthly* in an article entitled 'Fun in the Sun: our absent industry'. This purported to criticise the large number of British actors, producers, writers and directors who were living the high life in Hollywood while war was being waged at home. In fact, over three-quarters of its length was given over to a sustained attack on me. Amongst the lies were these: I had been pro-Nazi before the war when I had made my name in Berlin during the Twenties; I had stayed on long after Hitler came to power. I had been unable to further my career in Britain and had left for the USA when war clouds (predictably) 'loomed' over Europe. In Hollywood I consorted with Germans, married a German actress— one Matilda Halte—and when the war began had fled to Mexico for several months before sneaking back to Hollywood when I thought the coast was clear. Now I whiled away my time making worthless films and living in a loud and ostentatious style.

This might have travelled no further except for the fact that some cineaste in the editorial department of *The Times* read it, and on a quiet day wrote a third leader 'deploring the example set by English artists and intellectuals who sat out the war in the Lotusland of the USA, far from the hardship and suffering being endured by Europe.' Furthermore, 'the example of John James Todd, an English director, is particularly unedifying,' the leader said and went on to adumbrate *Cinema Monthly*'s allegations, concluding with an exhortation that the government seize and impound all the said artists' assets in this country until 'they deigned to return to our beleaguered shores and defend themselves.'

This was the signal for the rest of the press to join in. Stories were run about me, photographs were printed of starlets and swimming pools, supermarkets and sunny beaches. Here and there an old photograph of myself, dark and grinning, looked out as if to say 'too bad, suckers!' One caption read,

> *John James Todd, a notorious hellraiser at Hollywood parties, drives a luxury car and lives in an eight-bedroomed house overlooking the Pacific Ocean. Another English film director, who visited Hollywood recently on a war-bond fund raising drive, said, 'Todd seems very much at home. Quite frankly, he's not the sort we want back here. We're better off without him.'*

I felt first warm with shame, then this was replaced by a more general state of nausea. This must be Druce's revenge. I went back to the original *Cinema Monthly* piece. The byline was 'From our special Hollywood correspondent.' Old familiar feelings of helpless impotence returned. Dutifully I rebutted all the points to Shumway. I had left Berlin in '33. I was and had always been anti-Nazi. I had been in an anti-Nazi organisation in Berlin in the Twenties and I was a member of the Hollywood anti-Nazi League. I explained about Mexico and detailed the modest size of my house and the temperance of my life.

'What about this fight you had at LA airport?'

'That was a personal matter.'

'Didn't Zanuck throw you off the Fox lot?'

I refuted that one too. Druce's features came to mind. I very nearly told Shumway about the self-inflicted wound but wisely decided against it. Shumway wrote everything down in a notebook. Two days later on page 4 of the *LA Times* a small two column piece appeared, headed 'Director Todd slams British smears'.

Nobody read it, or at least nobody commented on it. But the lies had their effect on me. Coupled with the complete failure of my reunion with Doon I went into something of a nervous decline. I imagined people I knew reading these stories and believing them. I wrote to my family—even Sonia—asking them to spread the truth. I saw the way the world's perception of a person could change so easily. Who would now recall the triumphs of *Julie* and *The Confessions: Part I*? What was Julian Teague's letter against this huge tide of calumny and innuendo. I felt my life had been wasted, both as an artist and as a human being. All my films were forgotten. The emotional centre of my life—Doon—had disappeared and abandoned me. The world and the future seemed dull, hostile, uninviting. I began to drink more than was good for me, not venturing out of my house for days at a time. I knew I had to do something soon or I would go under. Eddie, who was delighted with *The Equaliser,* was offering me a script about Jesse James. But the unfair stories about my craven absence from the war unsettled me. I began to feel guilty. Guilt infected me. I, of all people ... But that sort of accusation is insidious—it touches the very core of our self-esteem. I forgot about the Salient, the horrors I had endured in the Great War. Fool that I was, only one course of action seemed open to me: I began to plan my return to Europe.

But in what capacity? I was too old to enlist. And besides, I had no desire to kill anyone—except Leo Druce. Ramon Dusenberry solved my problem when I confided in him. I became an accredited war correspondent for the Dusenberry Press syndicate. I would report the latest news from the European battlefronts for the Chula-Vista *Herald-Post,* the El Cajon *Sentinel,* the Imperial County *Gazette* and the Calexico *Argus*. I had my old job back. I packed my Leica, bought a portable typewriter and headed east to New York to embark for London.

VILLA LUXE 26 June 1972

For some reason Emilia didn't come today. At lunchtime I went into the village to buy some oranges but no-one knew if she was ill or not. I cleaned up the kitchen and washed the dirty dishes, partly to please her, partly to make her feel guilty. I'm alarmed at the rapid growth in the complexity of my feelings for her. She's been working here for at least three years and until recently I never gave her more than a passing thought.

This evening I take my drink out to the seat on the cliff edge and watch the sun set. I notice that although the hill on the crocodile promontory casts a shadow onto the villa my small beach on the bay below still gets the sun for another half hour or so. Perhaps I will go down tomorrow. I feel like a bathe.

And so I took myself off to a war once again for just as idiotic motives as led me off to the first. However, before I left for Europe I paid a visit to Hamish in Zion.

I had some spare days in New York before I embarked and decided to spend one of them visiting Hamish. I telephoned him and made the arrangements. I caught a train to Princeton and from there took a taxi over to Zion. It took several inquiries before we discovered where the National Research Institute was. We found it eventually, situated in an old school on the outskirts of the small town. It was a pleasant red brick single-storied building around a grassy quadrangle. I waited in a sort of porter's lodge until Hamish came to collect me.

He hadn't changed a great deal. He was even wearing the same clothes I'd last seen him in: grey flannels, stout shoes, a tweed jacket—still pervaded by his musty bachelor smell. I noticed he had some teeth missing. Hamish was not a man overburdened with vanity. His only concession to the warmth and American taste was the absence of a tie. His collar was open exposing his white throat. We shook hands with some nervousness.

'I thought you'd be in uniform,' he said.

'Well, I've got one but I'm not comfortable wearing it, yet.'

'Same here. I've got one too. It seems silly, somehow.'

We chatted a little awkwardly as we walked through the wide quadrangle. On the other side of the building were playing fields and tennis courts, but the courts were now covered by neat rows of new Quonset huts. Power lines looped from the main building. Some of the huts had whitewashed windows. Here and there were incomprehensible signs: NRI/77/Dec.1/2 55th.

'We've doubled our staff,' Hamish said. 'Hence these rabbit hut-
ches.'

'What do you do here?'

'Oh, government stuff. Mainly maths.'

He led me to his hut which was raised on brick piles on the edge
of the football field. On the door it said 'NRI Major H. Malahide.'

'Are you a major?' I said, astonished.

Hamish laughed. 'It seems they had to make me one, because of
my work. It doesn't make the slightest bit of difference, they just pay
me more money.'

Inside the hut was an orthodox desk, a couple of old leather
armchairs, a sink and a cooker. Beyond them were row upon row of
automatic electronic calculators. A small bespectacled man was bent
over one of them reading the numbers it had printed out.

'Fancy a dry martini?' Hamish said. 'The most wonderful invention
known to man.'

'Yes, please,' I said.

'Not for me, Hamish,' said the little man. 'I must be going.' He
had a strong mid-European accent.

'By the way,' Hamish said, 'this is Kurt.' I shook hands with him.
'Kurt, this is John—the friend I was telling you about.'

'*My God!* My good heavens! John James Todd.' My hand was
reshaken vigorously by Kurt. 'I am honoured to meet you, Mr Todd.
Truly honoured.' He shook hands with delighted incredulity.

He had a high voice. He was very warmly dressed with a thick
jersey under his grey suit and had an unwrapped woollen scarf around
his neck. His dark hair had dramatic broad streaks of grey and was
brushed straight back off his forehead. There was a marked intensity
in his gaze: friendly but profoundly curious.

'I never forget that evening in Berlin. Never,' he said. '1932. Your
film, *Die Konfessionen*.'

'You saw it?'

'Yes. Three times in one week. Gloria-Palast ... Mr Todd, I tell
you. The most extraordinary film. A work of genius.'

'Thank you very much.'

He tied his scarf and took a tweed overcoat off the back of the
door. The sun shone strongly on the green of the playing fields. He
buttoned the coat.

'My only regret is I never saw parts II and III.'

'They were never made. I started part II—we had to abandon it.'

'That's a shame ... But you must finish it, Mr Todd, you must.
It is most extraordinary work. You mustn't leave it incomplete.' At

this he glanced at Hamish and gave an odd, high yelping laugh. Hamish joined in.

'Good one, Kurt,' he said.

Kurt shook my hand for the third time. 'I mean it, Mr Todd. I've never seen a movie like it. Finish it. It would be the most terrible waste.' He folded up the collar of his overcoat and turned to Hamish. 'It looks fine, Hamish. I think you're on the right track. Goodbye, Mr Todd. It has been a most memorable meeting.' He left.

I looked at Hamish. 'Who the hell was that?'

'Probably the most brilliant mathematician in the world.'

'Really? ... Amazing that he saw *The Confessions*. What a coincidence ... What's so brilliant about him?'

Hamish put some ice in his cocktail shaker. 'He produced this theorem, the Incompleteness Theorem—that's why we laughed. It was quite devastating.' He shook the shaker. 'Changed the face of mathematics for all time.' He poured out two drinks and looked at me. 'In fact I was going to write to you about it, try and explain Kurt's theorem to you. It's quite uncanny how it all fits together. Now you're here I can tell you about it.'

'Super,' I said.

Hamish handed me a glass.

'Good to see you, John.'

'Cheers.'

That night we had dinner in one of Zion's better restaurants. I think we ate a kind of pot roast followed by ice-cream. I can barely remember eating. Hamish talked constantly, and with the single-minded intensity of all lonely people, of Quantum Mechanics and its bizarre world of chance and supposition. He mentioned names: Einstein, Bohr, the Copenhagen Statement, De Broglie, thought experiments, Schrodinger's cat. But he kept coming back to Werner Heisenberg and his Uncertainty Principle and how everything linked up with Kurt's Incompleteness Theorem. Absolute truth, he said at one juncture, had been finally exposed as a chimera, an utterly vain ambition. In the sum of human knowledge there would always be crucial uncertainties. And Kurt had shown how even in the most abstract formal systems there would be holes, gaps and inconsistencies that could never be overcome.

Eventually we paid our bill and went outside. I felt stupid, my head stuffed with strange concepts. It was a warm night. I breathed slowly, deeply, as we walked back to the Institute.

'Shifting sands, John. Shifting sands.'

'Yes?'

'We live in extraordinary times. They'll call this the Age of Uncertainty. The Age of Incompleteness.'

'Yes,' I said again, simply.

'Strong stuff, isn't it?' He paused. 'Limits. Limits everywhere.'

'It's rather depressing, in a way.'

'Why?' He seemed astonished at me. 'There may be uncertainties but don't you think it's better to live in the full knowledge of this than go on looking for illusory "truths" that can never exist?'

I left Hamish at Zion the next day. It had been a disquieting visit. We went back to his Quonset for a last drink and he had gone on talking for two more hours about Kurt and Heisenberg, Schrodinger and all that crowd. I felt slightly alarmed also: I was worried that he was becoming obsessed and he wanted me to share his obsession with him. I looked at his rows of calculating machines and asked him what he did with them all. He told me he was still working on prime numbers.

'Very, very big ones,' he said. 'Enormous ones.' He thought he had found a way of devising an unbreakable cipher using these vast prime numbers. That explained why he was working for the government and why he had the rank of major.

He tapped out a number on a machine. It printed 2,146,319,807.

'That's the largest prime number known to man,' he said. 'I'm trying to find one half as big again.' He waved at the calculators. 'With the help of these chaps. Once I've found that I can make the code.'

He spent another hour explaining how the cipher would work but it was all over my head.

I continued thinking about Kurt and his Incompleteness Theorem and its implications on the train back to New York. I was intrigued that the little man who loved my film had removed the foundations of certainty from the entire world of mathematics. How remarkable, too, that he had seen my film and how gratifying that it should have affected such an extraordinary man so. I felt a warm glowing surge of self-esteem within me. He was right, as well. *The Confessions: Part I* was a work of genius. It took one to recognise it. I knew its worth and I owed it to myself and to the world not to let it languish unfinished.

I looked out of the window at the new Jersey swamps. But first there was a war to get through.

17

The Invasion of St Tropez

Dateline St Tropez. 16 August 1944. Yesterday, the South of France was invaded by 300,000 men from the US and French armies. Operation Dragoon had begun. A vast armada of over 1,200 vessels, the largest invasion fleet the Mediterranean had ever seen, assembled secretly off the golden beaches of the Riviera. Thousands of parachutists were dropped inland before dawn. 959 aircraft pounded the coastal defences on an invasion front that stretched from Cavalaire to Fréjus . . .

I paused. I thought I had the tone just about right. I imagined it being read in an urgent 'March of Time' voice, which I felt was just the sort of voice required. I did not find journalism at all easy.

I was sitting typing on the terrace of a ruined café situated on the quay at St Tropez harbour. The Germans had blown up and largely demolished the port installations and had badly damaged most of the quayside buildings. The rest of the small ancient town was more or less untouched. The big white hotel—the Hotel Sube et Continental—seemed to pulse with brightness in the midday sun. The old walls and fortifications of the citadel were sharp and distinct against the washed out blue of the sky. I drained the last of my beer, brought to me by the cheerful patron of the demolished café. Yesterday, had been a very curious twenty-four hours.

The invasion force—General Patch's 7th Army—had been attacking three sectors of the coastline. Alpha force was assaulting beaches at Cavalaire and St Tropez. Delta force was concentrating on St Maxime, and Camel force was divided between Fréjus and St Raphael. I was assigned to a company of the 17th RCT (Regimental Combat Team) which was going in on Alpha Yellow beach, the long strip of sand on the Baie de Pampelonne.

There was a heavy mist on the 15th August, so heavy it looked artificial. As I peered over the gunwale of the chugging LCI as we

cruised steadily in towards Pampelonne beach I was reminded of that
day at Nieuport when I had raised the false gas alarm. I wasn't sure
if that thick line of white smog was mist or the dust raised by the
bombers and the naval barrage. I suspected that whoever was at the
helm was similarly inconvenienced because we landed somewhat off
target, to the right of the beach in a small rocky shingled cove. I kept
my eyes on Captain Loomis as he led the company off the front of
the LCI into the water. It was eerily quiet for an invasion. No-one
was shooting at us.

I jumped in. The water was cool, thigh deep. I wore an olive drab
combat uniform, webbing with a water bottle attached and a tin
helmet. I had painted PRESS across the front of this in six-inch-
high white letters. A huge, envelope-sized Stars and Stripes had been
badly stitched onto my left sleeve. I held aloft the pack containing
my camera, film and rations. As I waded ashore I sensed the water
was strangely viscous and unyielding against my thighs. I looked
down. Dead fish. Inches thick. Red mullet, grey mullet, monkfish,
whitebait, thousands of what looked like sardines formed a thick
piscatorial crust on the water. I sloshed out of the water and clambered
across the rocks, following a furious Loomis to where we should have
landed. Loomis was a young man, ludicrously proud of his role as a
leader of men. He had a snub nose and soft fleshy lips which made
him look strangely effeminate and sat oddly with the constant martial
frown which knitted his brows.

Along the length of the wrecked, smoking beach to our left we
could see the other LCIs depositing their men amongst the mess of
tangled metal anti-invasion fortifications placed just above the tide
mark. Now, from somewhere distant I could hear the pop-pop of
small-arms' fire. Loomis assembled his company and waited for the
engineers with their mine detectors to lead us off the beaches. I
wandered off through a gap in a screen of umbrella pines to urinate.
The cold water had stimulated my bladder and now the fear of
opposed landings seemed groundless I had to relieve myself.

Beyond the pines was a clear patch of sand and some old yellow
beach cabanas, rather knocked about by the pre-invasion barrage. A
sign read '*Tahiti Plage*'. I pissed up against this and was just buttoning
up my flies when a handsome man in a beret, white shirt and blue
shorts emerged from behind one of the cabanas. He carried a German
submachine-gun.

'*Hey-oh, Americain,*' he said. 'What's new?'

He shook me by the hand and told me in French that his name
was Luc, that he was with the resistance and he was going to guide

us to St Tropez. Then I heard Loomis, shouting.

'Todd! Where the fuck are you?'

I led Luc back through the pines to Loomis. He was enraged.

'There's fuckin mines everywhere, asswipe!' he shouted at me.

Luc shook his hand and said, 'What's new?'

Later I took a photograph of Luc, the cabanas and the *'Tahiti Plage'* sign. I liked to think that I had personally liberated this tranquil bathing beach from the German army.

Eventually, after taped pathways had been marked through the minefields the 17th RCT left the beachhead and moved across the scrub and pine copses of the St Tropez peninsula in the direction of the town. The day became very hot. Overhead a Piper Cub spotter plane buzzed annoyingly. By 10.15 all firing seemed to have died away. In the woods the air was shrill with the sound of cicadas. From time to time a break in the trees or a rise in the ground afforded a view of the gulf of St Tropez with the Monts des Maures in the background. In the bay sat the vast fleet, the still grey ships with the sun dancing prettily off the silver barrage balloons tethered above them. The rumble of artillery duels came across the gulf from Fréjus and St Maxime. Thin clouds of smoke rose into the air from burning buildings. I thought that it may not have been the most exciting invasion of the war but it was certainly the most agreeable. Perhaps I had been lucky after all.

*   *   *

I had never got to London, you see. At the offices of the North American News Association in New York I had requested that I be sent to Normandy. I was initially dismayed when I found that I was instructed to proceed to Ajaccio, Corsica, via Casablanca and Palermo to join the US 7th Army. I travelled there on a boat filled with dynamite accompanied by two other NANA journalists, Sam M. Goodforth—so his card informed me—chief reporter of the Fort Worth *Bugle* and Elmore Pico from the Hearst newspaper chain. Pico, thin and neurotic, later died on the beach at St Raphael. Camel force, to which he was assigned, saw the fiercest fighting of Operation Dragoon. Pico told me why we were going to Corsica.

'Because we don't write for friggin *Life*, or *Collier's* or *McCalls*. We're not famous, we're not fuckin novelists. We don't have important friends. All the big guys get to go to Normandy. They go by air. Us schmucks wind up in stinkin Corsica!'

He moaned all the way to Casablanca where he caught dysentry. Goodforth and I reached Corsica in July. Pico caught up with us at the beginning of August. I filed reports for the Dusenberry papers regularly from Casablanca and Salerno but later I learnt they had all been spiked as too boring.

My disappointment over being assigned to the Mediterranean theatre was short-lived. As I had hoped my new job provided me with the peace of mind I had been seeking. It was enough to wear a uniform, to own a tin helmet again. I felt, in a strange way, that the step I had taken had the effect of voluntarily submitting myself to the contingencies of the universe once more. I had stopped trying to steer a course; I was content to be carried by the current. Even dark embittered Pico with his relentless bitching did not irritate me unduly.

*   *   *

By mid-afternoon of the 15th August St Tropez was cleared of Germans, most of whom had either fled or surrendered. I stood in the ruined port with Luc and a rather attractive girl wearing a revolver in her belt called Nadine and watched the prisoners being assembled ready to be marched off to the beach. In front of us was a large group of about one hundred and twenty men. They were in Wehrmacht uniforms but they looked more Arabic than German. I asked Nadine who they were.

'From the *Ost Legion*,' she said. 'Armenia, Azerbaijan, Georgia. They don't even speak German.'

'We've got plenty Poles here too,' Luc said. He offered me a cigarette, a French one. I lit it and the sour tobacco reminded me suddenly of Annecy and the first days of my affair with Doon. All at once I was very happy to be back in France, in Europe. We went to a bar and drank pastis. Luc and Nadine were intrigued to learn I was a film director. We took our drinks and sat outside. The bar was in one of the narrow streets back from the port. We sat in shade but the late afternoon sun burned strongly on the faded pink, tiled roofs of the buildings. I took big gulps at the aniseed liquor. Nadine had thick curly hair held back from her face with tortoiseshell clips. She was dark-skinned and wore a blue and white print dress with neat canvas shoes on her feet. I wondered if she and Luc were lovers. I felt suddenly very sexually attracted towards her, perhaps because she had a gun. I looked at her hand that held her cigarette. Her nails were short and dirty. The way she was sitting caused her right breast to bulge gently over the butt of the revolver thrust in her belt. I at once saw these images as if they were projected on a cinema screen. Her dark mobile face as she pouted scepticism to some point Luc had raised. The careless way she drew on her cigarette; how she raised her chin and kept her eyes fixed on Luc to blow smoke sideways. The pale yellow paper of the cigarette. The pale yellow drink. Her breast. The gun. Just for a second or two—the slightest movement of the camera—so much hinted, so much implicit. I remembered Hamish's friend, Kurt, and what he had said to me. I knew then that *The Confessions* was not over.

I took a photograph of them both and then left them to return to Loomis at company HQ which was now established in an old villa on the outskirts of town. My kit was there and my typewriter. Loomis had allowed his frown to relax and passed on new instructions, namely that I was to motor up to a place called Le Muy, some miles inland, to cover the effects of the air and gliderborne landings.

'Seems there's some colonel in the 509th from San Diego,' Loomis said. 'He's heard you're here and wants a lot of local coverage back home.' He looked at me curiously. I continually had to remind myself that I was twenty years older than Loomis.

'Where're you from, Todd?'

'Edinburgh, Scotland.'

'Yeah? What's your paper called?'

'The Chula-Vista *Herald-Post*. That's the biggest one I work for.'

'Good God.' He shook his head. 'You got a driver and a jeep outside. Why don't you check with him about tomorrow?'

I went out into the garden. It was overgrown with mimosa, tamarind and lavender bushes. The night was very warm. Across the bay I could see some fires still burning in St Maxime. The flames looked pretty on the water.

I found my jeep but there was no sign of the driver. I looked around and saw someone crouched over a lavender bush.

'Are you all right?' I asked.

'Oh yes, sir.'

He stood up. He was tall and well built. I could not make out his features in the dark. His voice sounded educated. He inhaled ostentatiously.

'Have you smelt the air here, sir?' We inhaled deeply together. 'Pines, eucalyptus, lavender . . . Intoxicating.'

He handed me a small bunch of lavender.

'Smell that.'

I did. The scent was so strong it seemed as if I had inhaled a fine powder. I sneezed.

'Excuse me, but are you my driver?'

'If you're John James Todd of the Chula-Vista *Herald* I am.'

'I am indeed. What's your name?'

'Private Brown, sir.'

'What's your first name? And there's no need to call me "sir". I'm a civilian.'

'It's Two Dogs Running.'

'I beg your pardon?'

'Two Dogs Running. I'm a Cherokee. A Cherokee Indian to you. A "redskin" in case you were wondering.' His tone was pleasantly, inoffensively ironic.

I didn't get a proper look at Two Dogs Running until the next day. We rendezvoused at the company HQ villa after I had written and filed my invasion report for the Dusenberry papers. Two Dogs, as I came to call him, was young—in his early twenties—tall and solid looking. He had a classic hooked nose and thin eyes. His black hair had been shaved to a stubbly crew cut.

'Morning, Mr Todd,' he said. 'Another beautiful day.'

We drove off overtaking long columns of trucks and marching men that were moving inland from the beachhead. Shortly after lunch we were in Plan de la Tour where a lieutenant in the 157th RCT assured us that the road to Le Muy was clear. There had been a link-up that morning with patrols from the 509th Airborne.

We motored off. It was a badly paved road with dusty verges. The hills around us were covered in scrub and new plantations of pine trees. On either side we could see huddled dun and orange-pink villages, small farms and olive groves. The blue sky above was scarred with thin salty contrails of the Marauders and Liberators flying in from their bases in Corsica and Sardinia.

'You see that air raid last night?' Two Dogs asked. 'Spectacular, wasn't it?'

There had been an air attack on the ships lying off St Tropez. The sky had been hot with searchlights and tracer for a good five minutes. Two Dogs told me a plane had been shot down but I had seen nothing. We bumped along the road. An old lady in black sat beneath an olive tree tending some goats. She waved as we passed. Everything was tranquil and calm; I reflected on how easy it was for the world to swallow up a war.

'You'd pay a lot for a vacation like this,' Two Dogs said.

'Aren't we lucky.'

'Where are you from, Mr Todd?'

'Edinburgh. Edinburgh, Scotland.'

'How come you're working for the Chula-Vista *Herald-Post*?'

'It's an incredibly long story.' I changed the subject.

'Where are you from?'

'New Mexico. Little town called Platt.'

'Really? I made a film in New Mexico earlier this year.'

'You're kidding. What's it called?'

'*The Equaliser.*'

Two Dogs stopped the jeep. 'You made *The Equaliser?*'

'Yes.'

'I saw it! Christ. Just before I came overseas. It's playing every-where, congratulations.'

'Is it?' I thought for a moment. I left New York for Casablanca in mid-June. Eddie must have opened it earlier than he had planned. I felt vague alarm. How come I had to find out about this travelling in a jeep in the South of France?

Two Dogs restarted the engine and we set off again. I listened to him recount various episodes in my film. He had a good grasp of its implications.

'What did you do before you enlisted?' I asked.

'Travelling salesman. Perfumes and cosmetics.'

'Hence the lavender.'

We talked some more: about films, about scents, about Two Dogs' ambitions for his career. He was a college graduate and the unspoken question hedged itself in between us.

'How come you're—'

'In the motor pool? They don't give commissions to "pesky red varmits", Mr Todd.'

'Well, there's nothing wrong with being a private. I was one too.'

'No shit? When?'

'The Great War. 1914–18.' My God, I thought, that was only twenty-six years ago! I felt my age clamber onto my shoulders like the old man of the sea. Two Dogs was twenty-two ... We carried on talking as we drove through the hot shimmering landscape. I liked the big dark man with his wry educated views. We discussed *The Equaliser* further. The invasion. The Riviera. Two Dogs had just asked me if I had read Ernest Hemingway when the jeep broke down.

We had come down out of the hills and were in a small wooded valley with a dried-up river bed running through it. The Argan valley, I guessed, consulting my map. I calculated that we were about seven miles from Le Muy. The next bend in the road was obscured by a wood of corkoak trees, their stripped trunks a fresh ochre. Two Dogs checked the engine and said there was something wrong with the fuel pump. I looked at the map once more.

'There's a small village up the road. If we are where we think we are.'

Two Dogs took his carbine out of the back of the jeep and we set off. It was mid-afternoon and now, deprived of the early cooling breeze of the jeep's progress, we felt the full heat of the sun. After half a mile I wished I had left my helmet behind. I carried it dangling from its strap like a tureen and thought seriously about throwing it away. It was very quiet. The metallic sawing of the cicadas only emphasised the stillness.

The hamlet—Castel-Dion—consisted of a few houses, some barns and a semi-derelict church. There was no prospect of getting our fuel pump repaired here. We walked down the main street. A small patient crowd was gathered at the far end around an overturned lorry. As we approached an old man advanced to meet us.

'*Ecossais?*' he said.

I looked at him in frank astonishment. 'What?'

'*Americains,*' Two Dogs said, pointing to the flag on my shoulder. The old man led us over to the lorry. The crowd of villagers parted to reveal several dead bodies, some badly scorched. They wore German uniforms but they were swarthy dark-skinned Arabs of the *Ost Legion*. They had been dead for hours, since the morning, probably. The spilt blood was black, coagulated like treacle. Flies were everywhere. The few inhabitants of Castel-Dion seemed incapable of doing anything about this morbid visitation but stare.

'Who did this?' I said to the old man.

'*Sept Ecossais,*' he said. '*Les paras.*' Then he proceeded to describe the incident with many French gestures and sound effects. '*Paf!*', '*Pan-pan-pan!*' '*Boum!*', '*Clack! Finis. Bof!*' He dusted his palms.

I knew from the pre-invasion briefing that the only British troops taking part in Operation Dragoon *were* paratroopers, of the 2nd Independent Paratroop Brigade. I assumed some roving unit had been responsible for this ambush ... But were they Scottish paratroopers?... And I had no idea what to do about the dead men. I consulted Two Dogs who suggested we get the jeep fixed first. I explained the problem to the old man who led us back into the village and pointed to a road that led through some vineyards. Ask at the villa, he said. Two Dogs and I set off. Beyond the vineyards was an avenue of cypress trees and at the end of this two stone gateposts— no gate—with a name carved on them: Villa Gladys.

'Villa Gladys,' Two Dogs read. 'Jesus. Does everything feel normal to you?' He looked at his carbine. 'I mean, I'm a terrible shot ... suppose it's a trap?' He handed me the gun. 'Why don't you take this?'

'No, no. Absolutely not. I'm never touching guns again. I swore, after the last war—things that happened, you know.' I smiled uneasily. 'Look, we're miles from the fighting. I'm sure everything's fine.' I was trying not to think of the last time I had fired a gun. 1917. The Salient. My drowning Ulsterman.

We walked cautiously through the gates and down the drive. Here and there discarded parachutes hung in the trees like huge limp flowers, or were draped over the rubble-retaining walls of the vineyards like giant dying fungi. Then in a field we saw the splintered wreckage of half a dozen plywood Waco gliders. We turned a corner and there was the Villa Gladys, a small stone château with a roofless round tower. Laid out neatly on the edge of the gravelled forecourt were five bodies covered in blankets. An old man holding a rake and an old woman looked aimlessly at them. When she saw us coming she ran into the house and emerged with another old man. Tall and erect, he wore a linen jacket, a shirt with a collar and tie and baggy canvas trousers and sandals. A fine tracery of burst capillaries reddened his nose and cheeks. Wiry grey hair was badly combed over his bald head. If I hadn't known better I would have assumed he was English.

'*Nous sommes Americains*—' I began.

'Thank Christ for that,' he said. 'You come to take these chaps away? One of the gliders broke up pretty badly.'

'You're English,' I said. 'Good God.'

He looked at me shrewdly. 'And you're no Yank, I'll wager. Not with that accent.'

'No,' I said. 'No. I'm ... I'm Scottish.' I don't know why but I felt there was something baleful about my nationality that day. Six years in America hadn't seen so many enquiries about it.

'We had some Scottish paras land on us the night before last,' he said. He gestured at the bodies. 'One of them's there. Fell right into my cucumber frames. Cut his throat. The other chappies cleared off before the gliders arrived.' He contemplated the wrecked machines. 'Made a *fucking* awful mess of my vineyards.' He smiled. 'Still, glad to see you. Perhaps you can help me with another problem.'

We wandered round the side of the château past an empty swimming pool. The old man told me his name was Peter Cavenaugh-Crabbe (two 'bs' and an 'e'). He had bought Villa Gladys in 1902 and had lived there ever since.

'Didn't you have any trouble with the Germans?'

'Not a jot. Not until this fellow turned up.'

We had stopped outside a small stone lean-to at the end of a barn.

The door was bolted on the outside. From inside came a clucking of hens.

'There's a Gerry inside,' Cavenaugh-Crabbe said, then, with a glance at Two Dogs, he lowered his voice and added, 'though he looks more like an A-rab to me. He crept in early this morning— after the eggs no doubt. Old Lucien there,' he gestured at the rake-toting gardener, 'spotted him and locked him in. I don't think he's got a gun but you can't be too careful.'

'What do you want us to do?'

'Take the bugger off my hands, of course. You *are* soldiers.'

'I'm not. I'm a journalist.'

'Well, what about this fellow? He's got a gun.'

'Yes, well ... You see our jeep's broken down.'

'Don't worry about transport. I've got an old Citröen you can commandeer. Give me a chit, then just leave it in Le Muy.'

I looked at Two Dogs. He shrugged.

'All right, then,' I said. I went up to the door of the lean-to and shouted through it in German.

'We are American soldiers. Come out with your hands up!'

A voice came from inside. '*Kamerad!*'

I unbolted the door and stepped back. Two Dogs covered the doorway with his carbine. A couple of hens sidled cautiously out into the sunlight. Then the soldier appeared. He was helmetless in an ill-fitting, lumpy, bloodstained uniform. Egg albumen glistened thickly on the bristles of his chin. He was a small thick-set man, dark-skinned, with a narrow forehead. He blinked stupidly in the sunshine.

'*Hände hoch,*' I said. He complied instantly.

'Bastard's been at my eggs,' Cavenaugh-Crabbe said. 'I knew it.'

He went off and drove a very dusty black car with wide running boards out of a barn into the yard. I wrote him out a receipt for the car and signed it on behalf of General Patch, c.o. of the 7th Army.

'I'll drive,' I said to Two Dogs. 'You cover him in the back.'

Two Dogs prodded the soldier—Azerbaijani, I guessed—into the back of the car.

'If you follow that track there between the fields,' Cavenaugh-Crabbe pointed out the route, 'you'll hit the Le Muy—Fréjus road after five minutes or so. Then turn left.'

'Fine,' I said.

'Thanks very much,' Cavenaugh-Crabbe said. 'And could you tell the medicos to come and pick up the dead chappies. They've been out in the sun a couple of days now and they're beginning to hum a bit.'

'Certainly.'

'Much obliged,' he said. 'By the way, what's your name? Very grateful.'

'Todd,' I said. 'John James Todd.'

He looked enquiringly at Two Dogs.

'Two Dogs Running.'

'Say again?'

'Two Dogs Running.'

'Oh yes? . . . Well, jolly good.'

I got into the front of the car. Two Dogs slid in the back beside the Azerbaijani. There was a powerful smell of chicken shit.

I waved goodbye to our host and bumped off down the cart track in the direction he had indicated.

'You'd pay a lot for a vacation like this,' I said to Two Dogs.

It took twenty minutes to reach the Le Muy–Fréjus road, much longer than Cavenaugh-Crabbe had estimated. I stopped the car thirty yards short of the junction. I was worried that we had got lost somehow. I got out and looked around. It was still very hot. The dust that had risen behind us hung in the air. I looked at my watch—4.15—it had been a long day.

There was a scuffle in the back seat. Two Dogs shoved the Azerbaijani out of the car.

'Look at this guy's pockets, Mr Todd. Something's bothering me.'

The soldier stood there, his hands half raised. The two hip pockets of his tunic were dark with old blood. They were buttoned down and bulging.

'Is he wounded?'

'No. Look at his wrists.'

The man wore two wrist watches on each wrist. I told him in German to empty his pockets. He didn't seem to understand. I reached to undo the flap on one and to my astonishment he slapped my hands away.

'*Nein,*' he said, taking a pace backward. He looked nervous, worried. Then, suddenly, he turned and ran into the vineyard.

With a shout Two Dogs was after him. I followed. Two Dogs ran down the aisle of vines gaining on the soldier easily. He caught up with him on the edge of a small copse of corkoaks and, holding the barrel, he swung his carbine like a club in a wide arc. The butt glanced heavily off the soldier's head. When I arrived Two Dogs stood over him, gun levelled. The soldier was trying to get up on his knees but kept falling over like a concussed boxer. Two Dogs pushed him down with a boot. This time the soldier gave up and lay there, flat.

'Check his pockets, Mr Todd.'

I was out of breath. Dusty sunbeams slanted through the leaves of the corkoaks. The Azerbaijani had a bad gash above his right ear. His eyes were shut, his face was covered in dust and he was moaning slightly. Carefully, with bilious foreboding, I unbuttoned his pocket and reached in. My fingers felt something.

I thought: saveloys, thin German sausages, Azerbaijani biltong.

I pulled out five severed fingers, women's fingers, old and young fingers, all with rings on them.

I did not scream. I gave a kind of audible shudder, as one does when shocked by sudden cold.

'Jesus Christ,' Two Dogs said.

The man had fourteen ring fingers in his hip pockets. His breast pockets were full of jewellery and more watches. By now I was feeling sick. He was still lying down, moaning slightly.

'What'll we do?' I said.

'I don't know,' Two Dogs said.

'Maybe we should—'

Two Dogs put the muzzle of his carbine in the man's left ear and pulled the trigger. The man's head gave a little jump and then seemed to half deflate. Then Two Dogs stepped back and fired three shots into his body. Puffs of dust rose from his tunic.

'We'll say he tried to escape, OK Mr Todd?'

'What? Yes, fine. Absolutely.'

We didn't touch anything. We left the fingers—a small pile of human kindling—beside the body. We walked silently back through the vineyard towards the car. Two of its doors stood wide open. All around us were woods, hills, small fields, vineyards. Some birds soared above in the pale blue sky. Cicadas screeched in the grass at our feet.

Two Dogs patted me on the shoulder.

'Best thing to do. I think we had to do that.'

'What a day,' I said.

'Shall I drive?'

'No, no. Let me. It'll take my mind off things.'

We got into the car and I started the engine. We bumped down onto what we hoped was the Le Muy–Fréjus road and turned left as instructed. We had gone, I suppose, about four hundred yards when the first bullet shattered the windscreen and there was a metallic punching sound down the side of the car. I felt as though I had been kicked in the thigh and my right foot instinctively drove the accelerator down to the floor. We swerved, plunged off the road into an irrigation ditch. I banged my head and lost focus. My brain was a mist. I felt Two Dogs helping me out.

I stood on the road somehow. Two Dogs kept saying, 'Are you all right? Are you all right?' I was aware of a damp heat about my torso. Before I fell over I saw the paratroopers advancing on us and I heard the clear accents of my native country.

'Sorry, Yank. We thought youse was Gerries inna fuckin Merc. Onyboady hurt?'

VILLA LUXE 27 June 1972

I set off for the beach today longing for a swim. But I turned back after five minutes. My leg was aching slightly.

If we hadn't shot the Azerbaijani ... If I hadn't volunteered to drive ...

Two Dogs bruised his elbow. I took a bullet through my chest, high up on the right side. It smashed a rib, passed through my right lung and ricocheted off my shoulder blade. The big rectus femoris muscle on my left thigh was almost severed, as if by a butcher's knife. The two lasting consequences of this accident were a limp, when I was tired, and the ruination of my fine first serve at tennis.

Anyway, that sort of 'if only' digression is futile. To indulge in it is to place a blind obeisance in the laws of cause and effect. The cause of my bullet wounds was a trigger-happy Scottish para. Any attempt to trace the line further back is doomed. Could we say that my being shot was the result of Leo Druce's smear campaign in the English press? In one sense that would be entirely accurate. In another it's patently absurd. It was bad luck. Happenstance. The Quantum state breaking into one human life. I bear that soldier no grudge.

I convalesced in a large naval hospital near Washington DC. I was well looked after—Eddie saw to that. Fresh flowers every day, the best food. *The Equaliser,* as Two Dogs had told me, had been a considerable success. I had made some money. Lone Star was buoyant, as was its owner. Eddie had great plans, he told me: next we would make Jesse James, then Kit Carson. We could run the gamut of western folk heroes. When I left hospital he invited me to come and stay with him in Los Angeles, but I saw out the rest of the war in Ramon Dusenberry's San Diego home, slowly and steadily regaining my health. I seemed to function surprisingly well on one lung. I wondered why nature had bothered to double up that organ— perhaps in case you got a bullet through the first.

I was as fully recovered as I would ever be by the end of 1945. Eddie was still urging me to have a look at his script on Jesse James. I pleaded ill-health for as long as I could, but then a letter arrived that changed everything and set me on a different course of action.

The envelope that contained it was a curious looking object, almost obliterated with official stamps and chinagraph markings. It had been sent first to my father's house and had eventually found its way to me. It was from Karl-Heinz and was dated October 1945.

My dear Johnny

So sorry to have to ask you for this but would you lend me some money? 100 dollars is all that I need and I will be in your debt for ever and ever. I know it seems like a fortune to ask for but I'm told that over there in Hollywood USA dollar bills grow on trees in your gardens. Pick me one bunch please and send it to me at the Dandy Bar, 574 Kurfürstendamm, British Zone, Berlin.

How are things with me? Don't ask my old friend, don't ask.

A warm English handshake from your old prison guard.

Karl-Heinz

Karl-Heinz was alive. This was the best news. How? By what unlikely chance? Suddenly the lethargy of my convalescent's life fell away. I knew what I had to do now. I was going back to work for the Chula-Vista *Herald-Post*.

18

Berlin. Year Zero

I was full of astonishing optimism during my journey to Berlin. I felt, hard though it may be to credit, that my life was beginning again. Karl-Heinz was alive. Somehow, I knew we would finish *The Confessions* now, and though I had no idea what form it would take, I was sure it would come about. Too much lying around in hospital beds. Too many hours staring at the Pacific Ocean with nothing to occupy my mind, I hear you say. I had sent Karl-Heinz the money he had asked for, now all I had to do was find him.

However, that elation—that old exhilarating sense of potential— began to seep away as we flew over the city on our approach to Tempelhof. I had been prepared for an image of destruction but the vision that confronted me that afternoon in March 1946 was not so much shocking as unreal in a bizarre, sinister way. Berlin was gone, its skyline vanished. When you stand in a city and look casually about you, you see towers, roofs, steeples, gables, chimneys, treetops. Light comes at you through angles and over inclines, sometimes squeezing in through alleyways, sometimes basting the general view in wide boulevards and parks. Berlin was not razed, the shells of buildings still stood, but it had lost all those idiosyncrasies that made it par- ticular—that made it 'Berlin'. Only the Funkturm stood tall and untouched above the devastated streets. Everything else was uni- formly grey and everything had been battered.

How can I explain it? If you have ever seen a rugby team troop off the pitch at the end of a game played in exceptionally muddy con- ditions you can bring to mind an analogy. The tired, tousled, dirty men seem suddenly the same size and thickness all covered and clotted in mud. The slim, speedy winger is indistinguishable from the balding hooker with the beer belly. Their ordeal, their exhaustion and dishevelment have homogenised them. And this is what had happened to Berlin. It was one large ruin. The city had fused.

I was billeted in a villa in Zehlendorf-West in the American sector. It was designated by the press bureau of the military government

PRS-4, for some reason. There were half a dozen journalists staying there and it was run by a pale silent woman called Frau Hanf. She was tall and rather beautiful in an exhausted strained sort of way, but she was the very paradigm of formality. I never dared ask her a personal question.

The next day we were taken on a tour of the city. My depression deepened. What overwhelmed me was the mess. It seemed impossible that it could ever be cleaned up. I could not imagine how a new city could ever emerge from this devastation. We drove up the Kurfürstendamm towards the Gedächtniskirche. The houses on either side were scorched shells, uneasy façades, set between vast rubble mounds. To my amazement, however, I saw bright signs and fresh paint, even neon. Shops, cafés, *localen* were open and making a brave show of plying for trade. The streets were full of people, stooped and intent and walking uncharacteristically slowly for Berliners. Everywhere were gangs of grubby trousered women sorting through bricks. Opposite the church, the Gloria-Palast—where *The Confessions: Part I* had played for a week—was a tumbled crater of stone and concrete.

We drove on. Another tremendous shock. The Tiergarten had gone! Gone completely, not a tree left. In its place were thousands of tatty allotments. I was overwhelmed by this transformation. I tried to imagine Hyde Park, the Bois de Boulogne, Central Park as vast vegetable gardens, all the trees cut down for fuel . . .

On the Brandenburg Gate were red flags and pictures of Lenin. The stark white of the memorial to the Unknown Russian Soldier seemed almost obscene set against the miserable incinerated black of the buildings all around. The Dome, the Schloss, the Chancellery . . . The Aldon Hotel, Wilhelm Strasse . . . everything shattered or demolished. I looked out of the windows at the drear view, the gangs of women and POWs sifting through the debris, my mind a confusing sequence of 'before' and 'after'. Where was the Bristol, the Eden, the Esplanade? Where were the embassies, the theatres, the department stores? That pile of bricks was the bar where I would have a drink after my stint as doorman at the Windsor. This space used to be Duric Lodokian's house. That rubble mountain was the hotel where Leo Druce had had his wedding reception. Monika Alt used to live behind this cauterised façade . . . And so on. It's pointless to rehearse the conflict of emotions, the sweet and sour memories that day provoked. They lessened subsequently and with some speed. You can get used to anything. Normality is like some tenacious wasteground weed: it will establish itself in the most unlikely places. But

I never got used to what had happened to the river Spree. Perhaps because that first day I had arrived in Berlin in '24, in the early morning before the city was up and about, I had walked along its banks from the Lehrter station through a cold misty dawn. Now it was the city's sewer, clogged and polluted, rimed with scum and thick with effluent and excreta. Its strong ornamented bridges were all destroyed and makeshift wooden spans replaced the shattered arches. It seemed almost too solid to flow, but if you could bear to stand long enough (you could hang a hat on the smell off it, as the Berliners used to say) you could see its surface shift and eddy after a fashion, as if it were a prototype river not yet perfected, an early design model now superseded and antiquated.

My diary. A typical day.

Berlin. 25 March 1946. Woke early after a bad night's sleep. Frau Hanf obligingly provided me with an early breakfast of stewed fruit and porridge before the other journalists were up. I got her to sit and have some coffee with me by offering her a cigarette. I asked her what her husband had done before the war—she said he was a washing-machine manufacturer. She has no idea where he is now. We talked about how one might set about finding a missing person. You can leave notices around the city she said. There were even agencies who will track down relatives for a fee. The Military Government and the Control Commission were no use at all. She said this without resentment or bitterness.

Driven to the Kommandatura for a briefing on the next four-powers meeting. Dull stuff. Talked to an American staff captain who said the Russians had not raped excessively. They were more interested in looting, he said. Given that most of the Russian troops were Asiatics he thought that the amount of raping in Berlin had been 'about average'. He became very bitter, however, about the question of silk stockings. 'More women in Berlin wear silk stockings than in Paris or London,' he insisted. Must see if I can confirm this.

Lunch at the WarCorrMess in the Hotel Am Zoo. Windsor soup, brisket of beef, dressed cabbage. Floated the silk stockings theory. Several people agreed. Wrote a small article for the Herald-Post on the matter. Later in afternoon took some photographs in a burnt-out-tank park—v. dramatic.

Saw DIE SPUR DES FALKEN. *Not bad. Bogart excellent. Cinema freezing. Looked in at Dandy bar. No sign of Henni. Home.*

The Dandy bar was in a small street just off the Kurfürstendamm. It was in the ground floor and basement of a ruined apartment block. In the vestibule there was a reception desk and a cloakroom. Stairs led to the basement where there was a bar and tables and chairs set around a small stage and dance floor. The place had pretensions. Some of the walls were panelled, the wood salvaged from grander buildings, and there was a lot of red plush about. The tables had white cloths and the waiters wore uniforms. It was patronised almost exclusively by American soldiers—who had more easy-going fraternisation laws—and girls.

I went there the evening after my tour round the city. The bar was open but empty. A three-piece band of emaciated men in loose Hawaiian shirts played *Don't Fence Me In* rather well. I showed the barman a photograph of Karl-Heinz. Yes, he said, he used to come here when it was the 'old' Dandy Bar, before the management upgraded it. In the old days it was for homosexuals, 'men and women', he added liberally. Karl-Heinz hadn't been seen since. 'How long ago was that?' I asked. 'Four, five months,' he said. And no, no letter for him had been delivered or collected. I left a message just in case and took to dropping in there most nights. It seemed the only thing I could do. A bottle of wine cost £10 and I once ate a meat dish there that someone later told me was 'spaniel'.

During those first weeks in Berlin I did my job reasonably dutifully and associated with other journalists. I found myself very quickly caught up in the apathy and aimlessness that seemed to brew in the air above the ruined city. In a curious way it was a bit like Los Angeles, only here the constant climate was destitution and deprivation. Those of us exempt from these afflictions were still contaminated by the prevailing mood, like an air-borne virus. The tone employed in conversation was one of bitchery and complaint. We sat in our basement nightclubs, drinking and eating our fill, moaning about our work and living conditions. Outside, the rest of the city went to hell.

It wasn't that my zeal to find Karl-Heinz had diminished, it was that I couldn't think of any other way of channelling it apart from sitting at the bar in the Dandy, drinking and listening to the band and hoping vaguely that he might look in. Sometimes I went to other clubs—Rio Rita's, Femina, Tabasco—with their lesbians and stunning transvestites, the racketeers, the cigarette and chocolate smugglers with their expensive women. In spite of evidence to the contrary one could live very well in Berlin in those days, if you could afford it. But I found, quite apart from its association with Karl-Heinz, that I preferred the Dandy's shabby pretensions and its ever changing multitude of whores.

One evening I chatted to one of these girls. Henni. I had no sexual interest in her but the American press was desperate for vice-stories from occupied Germany—how victorious GIs were being corrupted by conquered Fräuleins—and as she was alone I thought I might get some 'Human interest' from her. Henni was a tall girl, very pale with almost a subterranean pallor. She had thick fair hair which needed a wash. Her upper lip was long and it gave her a faintly doleful expression. She was drinking coloured water and smoking a cigarette. She said she was waiting for a major in the 82nd Airborne but he never turned up. She told me that she had been in the chorus of the Deutsches Opernhaus. I offered her another cigarette and ordered a bottle of wine. After we had talked for half an hour she gestured towards my pack of cigarettes and said, in English and without much enthusiasm, 'you give me that, we go ficken'.

She took me back to the room she shared with her mother just off Savigny Platz. Her father, a music teacher, had poisoned himself in '45 when the Russians entered the city. Her mother, an old lady, smiled politely at me and left the room when we arrived. The room was small, very cold and neat. There were many pictures of cats on the walls. There was only one glass pane in the window that looked over a rubble-filled courtyard, the other holes were filled with cardboard.

Henni made a thin tea which we drank without sugar and milk. She put my cigarettes away in a cupboard.

'My mother will be delighted,' she said. 'We can sell them tomorrow.' She gestured at the bed. 'Shall we? Hunger is a great incentive for prostitution.'

I liked Henni. I found her intelligent dry efficacy entertaining and quite inoffensive. I went to the Dandy most nights and when she was there returned home with her. I brought food and chocolate but what she really wanted were cigarettes, the only hard currency in Berlin in those days. When I bought a carton of 200 Lucky Strikes at the big Post Exchange in the American sector I used to say to myself, 'ten nights with Henni'. Henni's mother would take them down to the black market site in the Tiergarten and exchange them for food. Berlin was full of prostitutes in 1946, nearly all amateur ones. 300,000 at least, one journalist said. It was moreover a city of women, three to every man. It was difficult for Henni to get regular clients, such was the competition, and there was something about her faintly doleful, faintly disdainful expression that put men off. Apart from

393

me, she said, she averaged three or four customers a week, and she never went with Russians.

I liked to lie in bed with her, chatting (her mother went down the hall to a neighbour's room). It was warm in bed and we would lie there smoking Lucky Strikes and drinking whisky. I told her about my days in Berlin (she found it strange to think that we had shared the city before—that I might even have seen her as a little girl. 'And look at us now,' she added). She would tell me about her singing career and how she was looking forward to renewing it. One evening I asked her to sing me something and, straight away, lying on her back, cigarette burning between her fingers, she sang in a pure clean voice *Wohin Sint die Goldenen Zeiten*. The haunting loveliness of the tune reduced me to tears.

10 April 1946. Managed to get a car and driver to myself and went to a beach on the Havel for a picnic with Henni. We motored through the Grunewald which is more or less untouched. A bright day with watery sun. Yachts and motor boats on the lake. Henni went swimming, I declined. She wore a dark blue two-piece swimsuit and a red and white rubber bathing cap. She splashed energetically in the water then rushed out and flung herself on the sand to sunbathe. Beneath the wool of her costume I could see her nipples were hard and erect and the fair hair in her armpits was dark and sleek from the water.

I felt unaccountably depressed. If it hadn't been for the khaki Chevrolets and the sprinkling of uniforms on the beach we might have been back in the 1930s. What was I doing here prostituting this bright intriguing girl? I felt heavy with guilt. To expiate it I spent an hour telling her about myself as if sheer weight of information could transform me from a client to a person in her eyes. I told her about Karl-Heinz and my search for him, my dream of finishing THE CONFESSIONS. *She suggested matter of factly that I leave a poster outside Karl-Heinz's former apartment saying I was looking for him. Everyone in Berlin used this method to trace missing friends and relatives. (Why hadn't I thought of this?)*

As we drove back into the city I sensed my guilt and awkwardness receding. I went back to her room for sex. The ruined city, I can see, is the true context of our relationship. But why do I want her to be at least fond of me?

I took the U-bahn back to PRS-4. It started to rain as I walked the few blocks to the house and I smelt the corpses. Most of the dead beneath the rubble have decomposed completely by now but a shower of rain seems to call forth a final ghostly reek of putrefaction.

Back at Frau H's a man I knew vaguely from Reuters—just arrived—asked me if I know a Monroe Smee. I had forgotten all about Smee. I said I knew him in Hollywood before the war. Why? 'I was in LA' this man said, 'and I met him. He was very curious to hear what had become of you.'

Tomorrow I go to Stralauer Allee. Frau H. serves up an interesting dinner. Two small carp and a sauce made from black bread, beer, onions, carrots and gingerbread seasoning.

Berlin in those days was one huge noticeboard. On every available surface were nailed, pinned or stuck printed notices and handbills. Most sought news of people who had at one time occupied the now ruined houses, but there were also want ads and for sale signs. Someone in our street, for example, wanted to buy a pair of skis. I wrote out my own notice in red ink asking for information about the whereabouts of Karl-Heinz Kornfeld, former occupant of 129b and, armed with hammer and nails, set off.

The block was almost completely destroyed and the nearby Spree smelt particularly purulent. I hammered the notice on the door jamb and stood back. What could make Karl-Heinz want to return to this ruin? Sentiment? Very unlikely ... Spring was well advanced and the piles of masonry were green with weeds. I felt a sudden helplessness. Henni had told me that 25,000 refugees arrived in Berlin each day at the moment. How was I going to find Karl-Heinz amongst all these people? I realised I should have gone at once to the missing persons agencies that Frau Hanf had told me about. I was irritated by my procrastination. My Berlin aimlessness had cost me several weeks. I looked at my notice stuck to the door. The street had several of these requests for information. Did anybody ever read these things or was it just a typical Berliner illusion of getting something done? I went back to PRS-4 without much confidence.

However I resolved to make one final effort. With Frau Hanf's help I discovered the names and addresses of two agencies and approached them with Karl-Heinz's details. They were not sanguine. They hinted that he might not even be in Berlin anymore. Four million German refugees, they told me, had fled westward or had been expelled from Russian occupied countries since the war had ended. Perhaps Herr Kornfeld had gone with them? They would see what they could do.

About a week after these visits I went to see *Meine Frau die Hexe* at the cinema. I'm not sure what stimulated my memory—I think

one of the extras reminded me of his secretary—but I thought
suddenly of Eugen P. Eugen. Was he still alive? He might be worth
trying. I thought of our earlier encounters. The man was tenacious,
there was no denying that, and unscrupulous. Conceivably, he might
be more efficient than the harassed agencies.

The building which had contained Eugen's offices had been completely destroyed along with the rest of Fehmarn Strasse. Indeed the
street had not yet been cleared, only a meandering path ran through
the rubble hills. I knew I was in the right place because I could see
the burnt and shattered blocks of the Infectious Diseases Hospital a
few hundred yards away. Then as I walked back to Putlitz Strasse
station I had an idea. Ten minutes further searching uncovered the
small café where Eugen used to lunch. What had he been eating that
day when he told me Sonia had beaten him up? Cucumbers? Cabbage?
Sausage? ... Yes, it was cabbage—I remembered the smell.

The cellar café still existed and was open. Above it teetered the
façade of a house, shored up with wooden buttresses. Somehow I
knew Eugen would be there.

Of course, he wasn't. Life is rarely that accommodating, but the
proprietor said there was a good chance he would be in that evening.

When I returned at seven, half a dozen people sat in silence staring
at watery beers in front of them and trying not to look at a small man
eating avidly and noisily in a corner. I knew it was Eugen, though I
would scarcely have recognised him. He was gaunt and his blond hair
was gone. He wore a collarless grey flannel shirt and a green uniform
jacket. On his bald pate were three large scabs. I sat down opposite
him.

'Herr Eugen?'

He looked up.

'My name is Todd. You did a job for me, a long time ago. 1928 ...'

He stared at me and frowned.

'My God,' he said. 'My God, yes. And then we met again in
Switzerland. With Miss Bogan.'

We shook hands.

'How is Miss Bogan?'

'She's fine.'

'Good, good. I am a great admirer.'

Neither of us seemed to want to reminisce about our last encounter.
I told him what I required of him. He screwed up his face.

'Difficult. Almost impossible.' He paused. 'Have you got a cigarette? You're sure he's in Berlin?'

We discussed the problems, then his fee. We settled on 500 cigarettes. Somehow the transaction seemed to rejuvenate him. I could see the tiny dapper blond man in him again, like his soul.

'Can I offer you some food? They say these are rabbit rissoles. It may not be rabbit but there is certainly a minimum of sawdust.'

I declined politely. We were awkward with each other. Two decades intervened.

'It's strange to meet again,' he said. 'I can't tell you how distressed I was—the last time. I felt most embarrassed.' He laughed. 'Which is most unusual in my trade. Not like me at all.'

He then embarked upon a long angry complaint about a burnt-out tank which still hadn't been removed from the end of the street where he lived. I commiserated with him.

'What do you think of our wonderful city?' he said with sudden bitterness.

'It's terrible,' I said. 'I couldn't believe it, at first.'

'Can you imagine London, Paris so totally destroyed?'

I thought about it. Buckingham Palace razed, Nelson's column toppled, Sacré-Cœur a heap of white rubble, all the bridges gone across the Thames and the Seine, the Grand Palais open to the sky …

'It's hard,' I admitted. I was about to remind him who had started the destruction business off but I changed the subject. I asked him where he would start looking for Karl-Heinz.

'Berlin is full of gangs,' he said, 'deserters, displaced persons, refugees. They live in holes in the ground. I'll make some enquiries with the police.' He smiled proudly. 'I still have my contacts there.'

23 April 1946. Interminable press conference at Lancaster House—British HQ—announcing the failure of discussions for pooling food supplies in the four sectors. Talk to a British soldier who says the officers 'are living like Gods' in Berlin while the other ranks are confined to barracks. Everywhere is out of bounds to the British enlisted man. 'We are an army of gentlemen and floor-wipers,' he says. It is not like this in the American sector.

To the Dandy bar. Henni tells me she has the chance of a job in Hamburg teaching music in a school. She thinks she should get her mother out of Berlin. I encourage her. To her room for one hour then back to PRS-4 in time for a late supper. I think Frau Hanf has developed a soft spot for me, she remembers seeing JULIE. *I tell her what has become of Doon.*

*24 April 1946. Saw a film poster today—*DER AUSGLEICHER, *a western. I almost walked past it until I translated the title and saw* EIN FILM VON J. J. TODD. *Word soon got out in the WarCorrMess and I find I am something of a celebrity. Two of my colleagues interview me. Curious to have a film playing in Berlin again.*

A message from Eugen. We are to meet tomorrow in the Dandy bar at midday.

Eugen wasn't actually allowed in the bar because he was too badly dressed. I arrived to find him arguing with the doorman. I led him away and calmed him down. He was close to tears.

'My God! In the old days I wouldn't even have *looked* into a stinking dive like that!' he said. 'I belonged to five clubs. Five. Very select. The most exclusive places.'

'Have you found him?'

'What? Yes. Yes, I think so.'

He calmed down when I gave him his cigarettes.

He took me to somewhere in the French sector. There were tricolours everywhere. I think the French were enjoying occupying Berlin just as much as the Russians. We abandoned the car and walked through a partially cleared street. Tremendous fires had raged here and the buildings were quite black with soot. It was a cool cloudy day with occasional drizzle. From time to time the fresh wind unpeeled a patch of encrusted soot from the walls and sent it dancing through the air like a stiff black handkerchief. We turned a corner and came to an open space, once a small square, perhaps. Beyond it, the houses had been completely flattened and we found we were in a brick wasteland, big as a football pitch, pretty with copious weeds and wild flowers. Here and there people seemed to be camping in hollows burrowed in the rubble. A crowd of about thirty gathered round a blazing bonfire.

With some difficulty Eugen and I made our way across the uneven ground towards a half demolished church. I felt most peculiar. I could hardly believe I was going to meet Karl-Heinz. I felt childishly tearful and full of trepidation. I stumbled badly and my leg began to ache.

The roof of the church had gone and so had all the pews and furniture—for firewood I assumed. Many people seemed to be living there, sitting docilely against the wall guarding bundles of possessions or crouched over tiny fires cooking food in steaming pots. We went down into the crypt. It was lit by electric light to my surprise and was very smoky. Eugen spoke to a young woman with one arm. I looked around, the place was full of young people—boys and girls. She pointed her stump towards the back of the room.

We walked towards the rear past a row of makeshift rickety tables. Half a dozen people sat at them, they seemed to be rolling cigarettes but I couldn't be sure, I only glanced at them.

Then I saw Karl-Heinz.

He was cooking something over a large woodburning stove that was responsible for all the smoke. He wore a thick crudely cut greatcoat that came down to his ankles. His hair had recently been shaved off and was now a patchy prickly furze. It was mostly grey. He was very thin and his grizzled neck and jaw looked like that of an old man, slack flesh and stretched sinew, no firmness. He looked up and turned. His eyebrows were the same dark circumflexes. He smiled. A few teeth had gone.

'Hello, Johnny,' he said, simply. We embraced. He stank. But it reminded me of that day in 1924 in 129b Stralauer Allee.

I don't mind telling you that I wept. I blubbed. I was happy to see him and at the same time unbearably sad. He was only a couple of years older than me but he looked like my father. We sat down around the stove and he insisted on serving up a miserable lunch. A soup of breadcrumbs and salt in hot water and potatoes fried in old coffee grounds scavenged from US army messes.

'At least it gives them a taste,' he said.

While we ate Karl-Heinz told me briefly about his war. He had been declared unfit for military service because of his ulcer which, owing to wartime deprivations and the crudity of the liquor he consumed, flared up in 1942. He carried on working in the theatres while they were open. He was in Hamburg for a while and then Munich. However, as the war neared its end he had been drafted into a special battalion of men all suffering from stomach disorders. They were sent east of Berlin to face the Russians as they advanced.

'It was a very strange unit, Johnny. We talked about nothing except our health, our doctors. 95 percent of us had ulcers.' I tried without success to imagine this unit.

By the time they had retreated from the Ringbahn to Potsdamer Platz Karl-Heinz decided that this was the moment to desert and go to ground. For three months he pretended to be insane.

'Best performance of my life,' he said with a thin smile.

'What did you do?'

'Not while we're eating, Johnny, please.'

I looked around at the disabled youngsters. 'What's going on here?'

'Well, I had to live. I became a *kippensammler*. I collected cigarette butts. Then I decided to become an entrepreneur. There were all these young people living in the ruins. I got them to collect cigarette ends for me. It takes about seven butts to make a new cigarette. We sell them for two marks each. I pay them some money and we buy food on the black market. For a while we did well, but then everybody started doing it. Life has got hard again. But then you arrive . . .' He smiled. 'My God, Johnny, you remember the day we met in Weilberg? 1918?' He stopped suddenly. The thought of all that time in between seemed to unsettle him. His smile faded. It unsettled me too. It is one of the least happy consequences of ageing. All that 'past' seems to mass behind the present moment, rendering it insignificant and nugatory. I thought of our two lives. All that effort, all those years to end up eating coffee flavoured potatoes in the crypt of a bombed out church. Around us the ruins of the third largest city in the world. And there was still the future to come.

'I want you to come away with me,' I said to him. 'We must get you to America.'

'Very nice idea,' he said. 'What for?'

'We're going to finish *The Confessions*.'

I think for the first time in the twenty-eight years we had known each other Karl-Heinz looked at me with unalloyed admiration.

*   *   *

I found Karl-Heinz a place to stay not far from Henni's building. I read a notice in the street that there was a room to let in a basement apartment. The young family who owned it were delighted to welcome him. The wife had seen him on stage many times. I bought him some clothes, gave him money for food, had him deloused and medically examined and secured some false teeth and a new set of papers for him. All that was comparatively easy; getting him out of the country seemed impossible.

Finally, I learnt of a special Home Office scheme that was created to allow German nationals the opportunity to rejoin members of their family in Britain. I applied on Karl-Heinz's behalf, saying that he was a half brother of Mungo Dale and that there was accommodation and a job for him at Drumlarish. This claim was met with some scepticism. Proof was called for. I had conspired with Mungo and he obligingly wrote to the authorities saying that Karl-Heinz was the offspring of his mother's second marriage and that he had spent many summers with the family before the Great War. They had rather lost contact with him since Mrs Dale had died but would be delighted to welcome him back to the Dale household once more.

In Berlin a search was instigated for documents to verify the story. It would take time, I was told, and in the end might be futile—so much had been destroyed. By this stage we were almost into June.

In the end I solved my problem by blackmailing a wing-commander in the RAF (later Air Marshall Lord D——) who was suitably placed in the hierarchy of the Military Government to give the authorisation. He was making a fortune by flying stolen antiques back to London dealers in RAF planes (an open secret in WarCorrMess). He was not alone. I could give the names of half a dozen high-ranking British officers who secured a comfortable post-war income for themselves based on German loot. This particular man was completely unperturbed when I put the deal to him. He said no editor of a British newspaper would dare print the story. I pointed out that I worked for an American newspaper and was not similarly constrained. He signed and had Karl-Heinz's papers drawn up and authorised while I waited. As I left, he said, 'It's little shits like you who voted Winston out of office.'

Karl-Heinz left Berlin before me but his journey took longer. As a low priority passenger he was held up, reprocessed, delayed and misdirected. His papers were in order, that was the main thing. In the end that fact alone made it inevitable that he reach his destination.

I said goodbye to Henni with much regret and real sadness. Her job in Hamburg had fallen through. But she had heard from Karl-Heinz's landlady that I had secured him passage out of Berlin and asked if I could do the same for her and her mother. I had to say no. I told her to be patient. Life in Berlin couldn't be like this for ever. On our last night together we lay in her thin bed, smoking and drinking as usual—both of us, I think, trying to pretend that we would be doing this again the next evening.

'Are you married?' Henni asked.

'No.'

'Will you marry me?'

'*What?*'

'Marry *me*.'

'Good God.'

'Don't you like me?'

'Of course I do.'

'Well then ... We can get divorced as soon as we're in England.'

'I'm not going to England, I'm going to America.'

'Even better.'

'I'm not American, though. I have to apply for a permit.'

'But if they let you in surely they'll let your wife in too. And your mother-in-law.'

I wanted to say that I'd already been married to a German and it had only lasted six months.

'Look,' I said. 'I'm an old man. I'm forty-seven years old. Twenty-five years older than you. You can't marry me. It would be a terrible mistake.'

'Oh, all right,' she said. 'My mother said I should try. She likes you—much better than Major Arbogast.'

'Who the hell's he?'

'He's my other man who comes here.'

I felt hurt, then foolish. 'You'll be all right,' I said reassuringly. I'm sure she was.

I left the city on a mild June day, the usual cocktail of emotions bubbled in my brain. This was the city that had made my career and reputation. It had brought me Doon. It had also undone me, in a way, too. And now it was undone itself. I had a funny feeling I would be seeing it again so I didn't bother to look out of the window when the USAF DC3 took off from Tempelhof. I was wrong. It was a shame. I never came back.

VILLA LUXE 28 June 1972

A gorgeous, stifling, unbearably hot day. I wonder if I might try the path down to the beach today. I can get down there not too badly, it's the coming back that does for me. There is a small row of stone sheds in the cove where the fishermen keep their boats. I watch these old codgers as they come back up the path after a day's work. They certainly don't stride but their plod never falters. A couple of them even look older than me. How come they can do it and I can't. Perhaps I should ask Ulrike to take me round by boat ...

It was a hot day in 1946 when Karl-Heinz and I travelled up by train to Scotland. We sat in the thick warm air of the compartment looking at the English countryside bright in its summer clichés. We stopped, inexplicably, for two hours outside Doncaster—or was it Peter-borough? I remember vaguely that Karl-Heinz and I talked about the war and its terrible consequences. I recall one thing he said.

'Why did you let him, it, happen?' I asked him. 'Couldn't you see?'

'Well, I tell you, John,' he said. 'One thing about the German people—we're very like the British in this. We have no *social* courage. That's why we make good soldiers and bad citizens.'

'Haven't you? Haven't *we*?'

'No. Not really. Don't you think it's true? We never complain. Neither do you. It's always a bad sign in a population.'

We spent a couple of days in Edinburgh in a hotel in Princes Street. I took Karl-Heinz to meet my father, an encounter I'd long relished. Innes—Dad—had sold his house and now lived in an old folks home in Peebles, twenty miles from Edinburgh in the Tweed valley and not far from Minto Academy. My father was eighty-four. I can see him now, his big arthritic knuckles trembling ever so slightly on his two walking sticks. We took tea with him on the terrace of the rather grand house he lived in (it's a hotel now) on a hill overlooking the town and the fresh green park beside the fast brown river. We talked about this and that.

'So. What're you going to do now, John?'

'Well, I'm going back to America. Karl-Heinz and I are going to finish a film we started a while ago.'

'God Almighty!' He had grown more profane as he had aged. 'Finish? When did you start it?'

'1926.'

He shook his head sadly.

'Your son is a great artist, Mr Todd,' Karl-Heinz said. 'Truly.'

My father looked at Karl-Heinz as if to say '*Him? That* joker?'

'He is,' Karl-Heinz said.

'There's no need to be polite on my account, Mr Kornfeld. I know my son well enough. Full of daft schemes from the day he was born.' His face darkened a moment. I knew he was thinking about my mother—my birth and her death inseparable. 'I knew he'd never amount to much.'

We laughed politely.

Then he took one of his hands off a stick and patted me on the knee. He left his hand there, lightly, light as a napkin.

'Not like his brother, now. Done very well for himself has Thompson. Rich man, successful, lovely family. Grandmaster of the Lodge.'

I wasn't upset. I looked at the old man. He wouldn't give an inch. Eighty-four and as intractable as ever.

'You're a difficult bugger, aren't you, Innes?' I said. 'Here—have another cup of tea and shut up.'

He laughed. Quite long and hard. Then he took his hand off my knee.

It was only after we left him that I realised his touch on my knee had been the only affectionate physical contact between us since I was a child. It brings tears to my eyes as I sit here and think about it now. That gesture carries a heavy cargo.

I never saw my father again. He died peacefully in his sleep one night in the winter of 1948.

19

The Hollywood One

I was back in Los Angeles when I got the news of my father's death, wrangling with Eddie Simmonette over the start of pre-production on what I regarded as *The Confessions: Part III*—but which was known to everyone else as *Father of Liberty*. I was dreadfully upset by the news, much more than I had ever expected to be. In the midst of all the grief, the guilt and remorse for things unsaid and undone, one obsession came to dominate my mind—perhaps, I can now see, as a way of allowing myself to cope. What distressed me most was the sudden realisation that my father might have died without ever seeing one of my films. I telegraphed Thompson immediately.

DID FATHER EVER SEE MY FILMS STOP
URGENT I KNOW SOONEST JOHN

Thompson himself replied:

YOUR QUESTION IN WORST POSSIBLE TASTE
STOP SUGGEST YOU SEEK PROFESSIONAL
MEDICAL ADVICE STOP THOMPSON TODD

I wrote to Oonagh, then a very old lady living in Musselburgh, with the same enquiry, and received a shaky scrawl in reply, written by a neighbour.

Dear Johnny,
    Terrible sad news about your father. He was a fine good man and we will all miss him 'something dreadful'. I do not know if he ever saw your 'films' (I have seen them many times), but I do remember him saying on frequent occasions that he 'abominated the kinema'. But I am sure he would have changed his mind if only he had seen your own 'pictures'. I do know he was very proud of those 'photos' you took when you were a 'wee laddie' ...

And so on for another breathless couple of pages clotted with arch 'colloquialisms' all about the 'funeral' and the 'family'.

I think it was that finality in her message (I could hear quite clearly, as if from beyond the grave, the sound of his voice 'abominating', and could sense his intense pleasure in the archaic pronounciation of kinema). Even if he had been an avid cinemagoer I was sure that he would have contrived to ignore my own work. I told myself to forget it. Why was it so important that one cantankerous old man had seen my films? I felt ashamed of my abject filial needs—as if all sons worked only for paternal approbation. Grotesque idea!

Father of Liberty was on the surface little more than a conventional biopic of the sort manufactured by any Hollywood studio—usual subjects being kings and queens, philanthropists and bandleaders. You will be familiar with the genre. Eddie had insisted we follow this format if Lone Star were to finance it. Consequently I had rewritten the 1934 script with this stricture in mind. His second condition was that I must make the Jesse James western afterwards. *The Equaliser* had been Lone Star's top grossing film of 1944 and '45. Eddie was hungry for more. There was also the now pressing problem of Karl-Heinz's age. I decided that convention would allow us to use him from the affair with Mme de Warens onwards, although even that was straining credibility somewhat. I bent the truth slightly by allowing the implication to surface that the affair began later in his life than it really had. The much vaunted verisimilitude of part I was being compromised, but under the circumstances what else could I do? I expanded the adolescent and childhood years considerably. Then heavy make-up, a thick wig and careful lighting should just about see us through, or so I argued to Eddie who was keen not to employ Karl-Heinz.

Karl-Heinz looked much better than he had in Berlin. He enjoyed California. He sunbathed a lot and his tan smoothed out the shadows and taunt angularities of his face. His health improved too: his ulcers—he had several, apparently—responded to treatment. The studio rented an apartment for him in the Hotel Cythera on the ocean front at Santa Monica, not far from my house, and I used to look in on him most days. Getting him over from Scotland had proved straightforward. *Father of Liberty* was slated to start and Karl-Heinz was cast as lead. His entry visa and resident's permit were rubber-stamped by the relevant authorities.

Karl-Heinz's attitude to life was now even more one of placid resignation. He accepted his transformation from troglodyte *kip-*

pensammler to Hollywood movie star with nothing more than a shrug and a faint smile. I recognised the condition: he had surrendered himself to the current. In Santa Monica he affected the dress style of a slightly down-on-his-luck artist—faded shirts, baggy trousers and neckerchiefs—and settled easily into the community as if he had only been away on vacation for a while. One day when we were strolling along the beach a boy abandoned his surfboard and loped up to him calling, 'Hey! Hey Karl, man, how are you!' We were introduced (I forget this lad's improbable name—Chet, Brett or Rhett, I think) and he and Karl-Heinz discussed where they would meet later that evening. We strolled on.

'Ah, the boys...' he said wistfully.

'Having fun?'

'I wish they all could be Californian.'

I stopped worrying about him after that.

*   *   *

Pause, Reflect. Consider. Here we are in November 1948. I am going to be fifty years old in a few months. I am about to start filming a medium-budget biopic on the life of Jean-Jacques Rousseau for Lone Star Films called *Father of Liberty*. It will feature my oldest friend in the lead role and will be produced and financed by another old friend and long-time collaborator. I live alone in my own house in Pacific Palisades, Los Angeles, California. I am not rich but I am by no means poor. *Father of Liberty* will be my eighteenth completed film. I have two ex-wives and three children. I have a few close friends: Karl-Heinz, Eddie, Hamish, Ramon, Monika, the Coopers, the Gasts, the Hitzigs (Lori Madrazon was killed in a car accident in 1945). I have a few enemies. I have survived two world wars and serious injury. I have one lung, a strong heart, a weak left leg, and my right shoulder stiffens up easily. I am carrying a little too much weight, my hair is greying but I am told I still possess a certain vital dark attractiveness which is unusual in a man of my age.

My disappointments are profound but not numerous. I was unreconciled with my father when he died. My brother will not speak to me. I am estranged from my children. My second son, whom I adored, died when a baby. Worst of all, the woman I truly loved, and who could have transformed my life, abandoned me.

My moment of greatest triumph came early in my career. I have known fame, great wealth and have suffered poverty, neglect and obloquy. My most commercially successful films have not been my best. My best work, the true expression of my particular genius is

407

unknown or unrecognised.

This seems an honest, not unreasonable summary. A half century with more than enough excitements and disasters, you might say, to fill several lives. And now with a pleasing structural neatness I am about to embark on a project which will complete an endeavour begun twenty years previously. Yes indeed, you might judge—with all objectivity—all things considered, given the absurd capriciousness of fortune, *ceteris paribus*, John James Todd has been a fortunate man.

I thought so too. I thought so too.

Then one day I got a call from Eddie Simmonette. Would I meet him in a certain drugstore on La Cienaga boulevard. And would I please make sure I was not followed. What are you talking about, I demanded? He wouldn't say. I assumed he was going to tell me he was getting divorced. Rumour had it he and Artemisia were no longer happy together. I braced myself for a bout of Eddie's self-pity, a rare event but an enervating one. Of course I made no checks to see if I was being followed.

It was a fine day, I recall, with only a faint haze. I stopped and bought a bottle of Coke from a sidewalk dispenser and drank it as I drove to meet Eddie. I looked at the tall spindly palm trees, the neat houses and immaculate gardens, the big chrome-heavy cars. The Coke was sweet in my mouth. The long nightmare that was to be the rest of my life was about to begin.

It was nearly four o'clock in the afternoon when I arrived at the drugstore. I could see no sign of Eddie's car outside but when I went in he was there, pretending to browse at a revolving stand of crime novels. We sat down in a booth. He took off his sunglasses and mopped his face with a handkerchief. We exchanged pleasantries. Eddie was trying to lose some weight. He had grown really quite fat in the last two years. The cleft on his chin was half an inch deeper.

'How's the diet?' I said.

'Great, great,' he said. The waitress approached.

'You want something?' Eddie asked me.

'I'll have a black tea with lemon.' My teeth felt furry, faintly neuralgic.

'I'll have a cheese burger with slaw. Banana milkshake. No fries.' He smiled at me. 'No fries. No booze. Why do I live?'

'What's this all about, Eddie?'

He became serious. 'I think we have some problems.' He took a magazine out of his pocket and handed it over, open at a page. I looked at the cover. It was called *Red Connections*.

'Look at that list of names.'

My eyes ran down the list. I recognised most of them. Herbert Biberman, Edward Dmytryk, Ring Lardner jnr., Dalton Trumbo, Humphrey Bogart, Danny Kaye, Eddie Cantor and many more.

'You know who they are?' Eddie said.

'The Hollywood Ten. And the people who signed that petition.'

'Right.'

'What's it got to do with me?'

'Keep reading.'

I went on down the list. Groucho Marx, Bertolt Brecht, Frank Sinatra, John James Todd...

'What the hell is this?' I looked at the list's heading: 'Joe Stalin's Hollywood buddies.' The magazine was cheap—bad colour reproduction, poor quality paper. I scrutinised the contents. There seemed to be a lot of exclamation marks.

'What does this mean?'

'You've been listed.'

'I can see that, for Christ's sake, but so what?'

'Did you sign that petition, any petition, for the Hollywood Ten?'

'No. I mean I would have if I'd been asked. But I wasn't. I wasn't here at the time. I was in New York meeting Karl-Heinz.'

'Thank Christ he's not on it.'

'Why should he be? Why should *I* be?'

'That's what I want to know.'

'I haven't the faintest.'

'Must be some mistake, then.' He smiled. He was the old Eddie again, relaxed and in control of his destiny.

'I don't know why, John, but this Red shit has really got me spooked. Those bastards—McCarthy, Parnell Thomas—they've really started something. Now everyone gets to hunt Reds.' He gestured at the magazine. 'And now this garbage.' He sighed. 'Why do we do this to ourselves?'

I liked the 'we'—good old Aram Lodokian.

'I can see why you're worried,' I said, guilelessly. 'I mean, God, you were even *born* in Russia.'

He gripped my arm fiercely. 'Never. *Never* say that to anyone, John, never again.'

'Christ! All right. Let go ... Don't worry Eddie. Jesus...'

He relaxed again. I had never seen him like this. I watched him eat his hamburger. Like everyone else in Los Angeles I had heard of the Hollywood Ten, the Senate Permanent Subcommittee on Investigations and the House Committee on Un-American Activities.

It reminded me a little of Berlin in the Twenties. I paid it little heed, I was busy with *Father of Liberty*.

I drove home, somewhat perturbed. Eddie had told me that *Red Connections* was published by an organisation called Alert Inc. which gave a mailing address on Sunset Boulevard. As I pulled up near my house I saw two men in dark suits standing on the sidewalk opposite. As I approached one of them—who for some reason seemed vaguely familiar—jumped into a car and drove off. The other man stood his ground.

'Can I help you?'

'Are you John James Todd?'

Why did I hear the voice of Ian Orr? I wish I had had the presence of mind to say 'Who wants to know?' but I only managed a docile admission. He handed me a manilla envelope and walked away.

I waited until I was inside before I opened it. I poured myself a beer from the fridge and switched on the air conditioning. I killed two flies in the kitchen. Then I turned to my envelope. There was something immediately unpleasant about the sheet of pink paper it contained. Something ironic about it too: that the House Committee on Un-American Activities should issue its subpoenas on paper of such a politically suspect shade. I, John James Todd, was to present myself before the Brayfield subcommittee of HUAC (we'll call it HUAC, everyone else did) at room 1121 of the Hollywood Roosevelt Hotel where I would be questioned in 'executive session'.

I phoned Eddie.

'*Oh no!* Oh no Jesus fuck no!' He went on in this vein for a while. 'When is it?'

'Next week.'

'Sweet suffering Christ. Have you got a lawyer?'

'No.'

'I'll get you one. There's a young guy works for us—very sharp. Don't worry, John, I'm sure it's just some terrible mistake. But listen, you'd better stay home for a while. Work from home.'

'All right. But we were going to start casting.'

'Let's get this hearing out of the way.'

I went along with what he said. I spoke confidentially with a few people who reassured me. All HUAC activities, they said, were in theory suspended pending the appeal of the Hollywood Ten. No-one could understand why this subcommittee had been instigated. Even my lawyer, Page Farrier, was mystified.

Farrier was a junior partner in a firm that did a lot of business with

Lone Star. He was a young man, in his late twenties, and his looks inspired confidence. He was big, over six feet, with a strong bulging jaw and thick curly hair which he forced into a parting. He wore bow ties, something I approve of in professional men: it hints at human qualities—vanity, self-esteem—behind the impassive expertise. But after talking to him for half an hour, I found him less reassuring. He was soft-voiced and diffident, with mobile eyes that met your gaze only for split seconds. He gave me one of the worst pieces of advice I've ever received.

'I think you should take the Fifth.'

'The Fifth what?'

'The Fifth Amendment to the American Constitution.'

'What's that?'

'It means that you can't be asked to bear witness against yourself. If you're asked a question that might incriminate you, you can refuse to answer it—on the grounds of the Fifth Amendment.'

'But I haven't done anything.'

'I would take it just in case, Mr Todd. It's safer than taking the First. The Hollywood Ten took the First and look what happened to them. You take the First, you get cited for contempt of Congress. That could mean jail.'

'Jesus . . . Right. But when do I take it?'

'Whenever it seems like something you'll say will incriminate you.'

'Fine. You'll tip me the wink if it looks like a tricky question.'

'Ah . . . I won't be there, I'm sorry to say.'

'But you're my bloody lawyer!'

Page coloured. He took a pen out of his jacket pocket and replaced it carefully.

'Mr Todd. May I be frank with you?'

'Please.'

'Ordinarily, I'd really prefer *not* to be associated with your case. I'm only a junior partner. But because of the Lone Star connection I've been told—been assigned to it.' He gave me a weak smile. 'I'm sorry. We don't even have your name on a file in the office.' I seemed to feel a sort of transparency invade my body as if I was half way to disappearing. I was around, *here*, but fewer and fewer people were acknowledging my presence. Page cleared his throat and touched the tips of his bow-tie.

'May I ask you a personal question, sir?'

'Yes.'

'Are you in point of fact a communist? In the party?'

'I'll take the Fifth . . . No, of course not. I'm a film director.'

He beamed with relief. 'God, that's good news.' He lowered his voice. 'I'm sort of a liberal-minded person but I don't think my conscience could let me represent a real communist. If my fiancée found out . . .' He swallowed. 'Holy shit.'

'Your conscience can rest easy. Listen, do you want a drink?' We were in my house.

'No . . . No, Sir, thank you. I've got to run. Is there a back way out of here?'

*   *   *

Three days later I walked along the corridor of the Hollywood Roosevelt Hotel towards room 1121. I knocked. It was opened by the man who had served the subpoena on me. I was shown in.

Room 1121 was a suite. The sitting room had been cleared and a long desk set up at one end with three chairs behind it. Another solitary chair was set opposite some six feet away in the middle of the room. A man in a pale blue suit was standing by the window smoking a cigarette. He came out and shook my hand.

'Mr Todd? I'm an investigator for the Committee. Paul Seager. This is Investigator Bonty.'

Seager had a fat kind face with thin brown hair. Bonty—the man with the subpoena—was dark and sallow with a harelip scar like MacKanness, the Bantam who'd threatened to kill me.

'Congressman Brayfield will be with us in a moment.'

From the bedroom I could hear the buzz of an electric razor. We stood around in awkward silence. Our roles were about to be defined, until then we didn't know whether to be pleasant or formal.

'Some fog today,' Bonty offered.

'Yes,' I said.

'We get bad fog in Washington,' Seager said.

'Really?'

Brayfield came in, pulling on his jacket. Representative Byron Brayfield was a fat man who thought tight three-piece suits might disguise this condition. Naturally, it had the opposite effect, as well as making him needlessly hot and uncomfortable. His waistcoat was tight as a corset, a small fan of creases, like crow's-feet, on either side of the row of buttons. He had a pale fleshy face, with an eave of fat overhanging his collar all round, small alert eyes and balding crinkly black hair combed straight back. He did not offer to shake my hand. We took our places. I felt a sudden urge to go to the lavatory. Seager made a telephone call and a minute later a stenographer came in. She sat down behind me.

Bonty uttered some preamble about the Brayfield subcommittee of the House Committee on Un-American Activities being in executive session. Then proceedings were interrupted for a long moment as Brayfield blew his nose with astounding ferocity. His face went quite red and he examined his handkerchief diligently as if he expected to see particles of brain there. Eventually, Seager swore me in and the hearing began.

BRAYFIELD: You understand, Mr Todd, this is a special sub-committee of one instigated as a result of a confidential dossier we, ah, that came into our possession, alleging subversive activities undertaken by you over a number of years.

TODD: May I know who supplied you with this dossier?

BRAYFIELD: That is classified information. However, such was the seriousness of these allegations it was decided that this committee be set up ... You have lived and worked in Berlin, Germany, I believe?

TODD: Yes. And in Scotland, England, France, Switzerland, and the United States.

BRAYFIELD: You are about to start production on a film called *Father of Liberty*?

TODD: Yes.

BRAYFIELD: And this film is about a [checking notes] man called Rousseau? A French socialist?

TODD: For Heaven's sake!

BRAYFIELD: Who is producing this film?

TODD: That is a matter of public record, I suggest you get Investigator Seager on to it.

SEAGER: I would remind you, Mr Todd, this is an official sub-committee. We have powers to cite you for contempt.

TODD: Thank you for reminding me. I will not answer any of your questions until you tell me who gave you that dossier.

BRAYFIELD: I've told you—

TODD: Was it someone called Leo Druce?

SEAGER: Who?

BRAYFIELD: Seager!

TODD: Courtney Young? Harold Faithfull? Alexander Mavro-cordato? [blank faces]

BRAYFIELD: Who are these people? Can we get back to business? ... We believe, Mr Todd, based on information we have in this dossier, that you may be well placed to inform the committee of known subversive and communistic elements in the

Hollywood film community. Any such information you provide us with will remain confidential, of course ... I would like to remind you we are in executive session. Ah, in the light of your providing us with names and information the committee will be predisposed to look favourably on any ... any indiscretions in the past that you may have, ah, that you may have done. Perpetrated.

TODD: [gets up and takes newspaper from nearby table]: why are you people wasting your time? Why? Catch some real criminals. Look, look, at random from today's paper [quotes] 'Two men, Kemp P. Heald (25) and Coren Schlag (52) were today accused of breaking into Brewer Poultry Farm at Tujunga on the 14th November and committing there acts of sexual indecency with 54 Christmas turkeys, leaving over twenty of the birds for dead...' Good God! There are your criminals. Why aren't you out catching them instead of wasting all our time and—

BONTY: May I see that newspaper please?

SEAGER: Mr Todd, will you please resume your seat?

BRAYFIELD: Can you establish that these two men are Soviet agents? Or members of the communist party?

TODD: What?

BRAYFIELD: Only then are we empowered to act.

BONTY: Five'll get you ten they were commies.

SEAGER: Who?

BONTY: The men who boffed the turkeys. They do that sort of thing in Russia, I read about it. Yeah.

BRAYFIELD: Mr Bonty, please?

BONTY: Sorry, sir.

BRAYFIELD: Mr Todd, are you or have you ever been a member of the communist party?

TODD: I'd like to plead the Fifth Amendment.* I will not answer that question on the grounds that I may incriminate myself— in your eyes.

When I saw the smile momentarily expand in Brayfield's eyes and across his plump cheeks I knew I had made a mistake. We wrangled over whether I was entitled to take the Fifth for a while, and Brayfield's threats became more and more explicit. At one stage he shouted

---

* To add to my list of firsts: I was the first person to take the Fifth in Hollywood. There was little publicity. Ramon Dusenberry tried to run a campaign in his papers but no-one else took it up. Only in Southern California was I referred to as 'The Hollywood One'.

at me 'You are a resident alien! We can deport scum like you!' All this was excised from the transcript. I realised later I should have taken Bertolt Brecht's route: lie badly and then run for it. If Brecht hadn't followed that course of action it would have been the Hollywood Eleven. But old Bert lit out. When he was asked in 1947 if he had ever applied to join the communist party he said, and I quote, 'No, no, no, no, no, never,' and left at once for France. As I sat in my sitting room later that afternoon waiting for Page Farrier to turn up I felt foreboding infest the house like vermin. Had I done the right thing?

'Yes,' Page said. 'Without doubt.'

'Oh *yes*,' said Eddie Simmonette. This was two days after the hearing. We were sitting in what used to be Lori's diner. It was now called 'Chauncy's' after her eldest son. I hadn't been there since I had returned from Berlin. News of Lori's death had distressed me greatly and I couldn't imagine the diner without her. In fact few memories lingered. Chauncy had redone everything in plasti-pine and melamine—it was altogether more nasty-looking, cheaper and dirtier. But when Page had telephoned to say that Eddie wanted a rendezvous 'somewhere very discreet' Chauncy's had seemed the most convenient.

Eddie wore dark glasses and a snap-brim hat. Page kept looking over his shoulder.

'Look, would you mind relaxing?' I said angrily. 'Nobody's going to know you here ... Have you heard anything? Are they going to cite me for contempt?'

Page told me he thought I would be all right, at least until the Supreme Court had heard the Hollywood Ten appeal.

'Well, thank God for that.'

'Ah, unfortunately, Mr Todd, you're on two more lists.'

'Jesus. But I haven't done anything. Whose lists?'

'The *American Legion Magazine* and the AMPOPAWL list.'

'The what?'

'The American Motion Picture Organisation for the Preservation of the American Way of Life.'

'But at least you're not on the MPAPAI list,' Eddie said. 'Thank the Lord.'

'?'

'The Motion Picture Alliance for the Preservation of American Ideals.'

'Great. Wonderful.'

The waitress came over to our table. Eddie and Page ordered

coffee. I looked up. 'Nothing for me,' I said. She was a dark faintly oriental girl with a grubby apron on over a check dress. Slim and pretty in an acceptably sleazy way.

'Hey, *John*,' she said. 'God, how are you?' She leant over and kissed me on the cheek. 'Nora-Lee,' she said. 'Nora-Lee Madrazon.'

'Good God. Of course.' I'd last seen her four years ago, a sulky lanky teenager with cropped hair and braces on her teeth.

'Catch you later,' she said. 'Great to see you again.'

'You know her?' Page said, his voice high with incredulous WASP lust.

'I knew her mother.'

'Page,' Eddie said, 'would you leave us for a moment? I need to talk with John.'

Page left for another booth. Nora-Lee delivered Eddie's coffee. As he stirred it we sat in silence. I looked out of the window at the beach and the Pacific. There had been some rain that morning and the roads were shiny. The ocean looked cold.

'John, that's three lists you're on now: *Red Connections*, the Legion and AMPOPAWL.'

'Someone sent a dossier on me to that committee. That's the only reason this fucking ... *farce* is happening at all. Someone's setting me up. I'm being informed on. Framed.'

'Who?'

'I wish I knew.'

'Which still leaves us with our problem.'

'What problem?'

Eddie took a sip of coffee and made a disgusted face.

'Jesus! This stuff would make a billy goat puke!' He pushed it aside. He sighed, inhaled, touched his nose, tugged at an earlobe.

'After the Ten were cited for contempt of Congress last year there was a meeting in New York at the Waldorf-Astoria of the MPA ... the Motion Picture Association—'

'Yes, yes.'

'Fifty of us. All the top executives. I was there. We said, we agreed that no communists or subversives would knowingly be employed in the film industry.'

'So?'

'You heard Brayfield. He thinks you're a subversive; he thinks *Father of Liberty* is a subversive film. We've had calls from the Legion, the Catholic Veterans, *Red Connections*, ODCAD—you name it. They think you and Rousseau are a couple of foreign Bolshevists.'

'You're not going to worry about what that arsehole Brayfield says?'

'John ... I'm party to the MPA decision. Don't you see? I can't afford not to.'

It was at this moment that any residual humour—of the black ironical variety—left the discussion.

'So what are you saying?'

'The film's off. Until this blows over.'

'Wonderful.' I felt the tears squeeze into my eyes. 'Well, I'll do Jesse James then, fill in some time.'

'I'm sorry, John.'

'Come *on*.'

'I'm going to have to let you go. I have to be seen to fire you. You're greylisted now.'

'Looks pretty black to me.'

He leant forward. 'I've just signed a fifteen million dollar, twenty picture deal with Loew's. I can't jeopardise the company for you and *Father of Liberty*. What would you do in my place? The same, I know. I've got to distance myself from you. But I'll stick by you, John. You won't go without.'

'Fuck you.'

'All I ask from you is your discretion. Just don't name me. Don't ever mention what you mentioned the other day.'

'Well, after all you're doing for me, how can I refuse?'

'For the sake of our friendship. You'll be all right.'

'I can go somewhere else.'

'You can try ... But they've got you, John. They've got us. By the balls. Sit it out.'

'Thanks, Eddie.'

'Don't be cynical, John. It doesn't suit you.'

'You sound like my father.'

'Don't ring me at the office or at home whatever you do. I'll keep in touch through Page.'

'Why not?'

'Your phone is probably tapped.'

'Christ! ...'

He leant over and kissed me on both cheeks, the Armenian in him surfacing briefly, and then said something like, '*Cesaretini toplamak*'. I found this phrase in Lori's Turkish–English dictionary. It meant 'take courage'.

I sat on alone in the diner for a while after Page and Eddie had left. I felt a kind of draining of my spirit, as when a runner knows he's used up his last reserves of stamina. I felt like sobbing with self-pity and frustration, but two competing trains of thought prevented a whole-hearted surrender. First, I marvelled at Eddie's utterly decent ruthlessness. I suppose it was the same attitude that had got Duric Lodokian through pogroms and revolutions and now it was coming to the aid of his son. I wanted to rail at him and accuse him of treachery and disloyalty but I could not fault his logic ... I even rather respected him for it.

The other pressing question was to do with the identity of the informer. Who? Why? I knew who my enemies were but I found it hard to credit them with something so thoroughgoing. There was a fanatic diligence about this plan that seemed to speak of vast resources of perversity—all committed to bring me down. Faithfull? Druce? ... It seemed far-fetched.

I sighed, contemplating once more the ruin of *The Confessions*. How many scripts had been written, how many false starts and premature conclusions had there been? The concept, the work, seemed almost alive, animal-like in its capacity to live on, evolve and adapt itself to the multitude of obstacles the century placed in its way. *The Confessions* had a life of sorts, that was true. It had been born, grown up, suffered setbacks, struggled on, changed, adapted itself ... I felt urgently that I needed to round it off, let it mature and die. I had hoped that *Father of Liberty* would have been that final hybrid. How long would I have to wait? Sit it out, Eddie had said. Be patient.

I got up, planning to wander along the beach and tell Karl-Heinz the bad news. Nora-Lee came over. I saw she was a tall girl wearing flat shoes like dancing pumps. I thought suddenly, painfully, of Doon.

'Do you want to come upstairs for a moment, John? We kept some things of Mom's. Maybe you'd like to have something, like a sort of souvenir. No, I don't mean that. What's the word?'

'Memento.'

'Yeah.'

'I'd like that.'

We went upstairs to the apartment. I chose Lori's Turkish–English dictionary.

*　　　*　　　*

I sat it out for four years. For four years I waited for things to blow over. It may sound strange to you, it may even sound unlikely, but it was during those years that I missed my children the most. I have not spoken of them but I had not forgotten them. I missed them

keenly, desperately—or rather I missed a private fanciful version of
them. I used to think about them often—Vincent and the twins, a
young man and two young women now, total strangers to me, and
vice versa. I had corresponded with them, dutifully, desultorily, but
their letters were banal and disappointing—and I dare say mine were
too. It was the change of surname that distressed and distanced me:
this Vincent Devize didn't seem to be my son any more (it can happen
so easily, believe me). At times I was wracked with the loss of
Hereford. Hereford, dead all these years, was closer and more real to
me than my three children living. I had an ideal Platonic love for
them of sorts, but its concrete manifestations were mere tokens,
mutual obligations half-heartedly and effortfully fulfilled.

My life bottomed out, as they say, until 1953—when it got worse.
But let me take you through this unsatisfactory interlude.

The Hollywood Ten were not so lucky either. They had pleaded
the First Amendment—the constitutional right to freedom of thought
and opinion—and were cited for contempt of Congress. This was
foreseen and planned for. In the Supreme Court there was a majority
of liberal judges who, it was calculated, would overturn the verdict.
Unfortunately, in the summer of 1949 two of the judges died and
were replaced by hardline reactionaries. The Ten went to prison and
the HUAC hearings on Hollywood subversives resumed with new
spiteful vigour in 1951.

That was a fretful year of genuine worry for me. I felt sure that
Brayfield and his subcommittee would release its findings or the
dossier itself. But nothing happened. Slowly, I began to relax. Perhaps
the dossier had been a crude trick to try and panic an admission out
of me? Perhaps it had never existed? Sometimes I saw the open
sessions in Washington on television and I would contemplate Brayfield's fat sweaty face amongst the others on the committee with a
mixture of loathing and acute trepidation. But I seemed to have
been forgotten. Others were subpoenaed, took the Fifth and were
blacklisted, or named names and were cleared. Then I realised that
I was forgotten because the damage had already been done. I was
greylisted. I approached other studios for work—Fox, RKO,
Warners—but as Eddie predicted they had me by the balls.

In 1950 I was dropped from the Legion's list but *Red Connections*
and AMPOPAWL never left me out. Briefly, in 1952 I appeared on
the MPAPAI list and got a call from a man in Alert Inc. offering to
get my name cleared for a cost of one thousand dollars. I didn't have
the money then so I asked him to call back but he never did. As I
hadn't made a film since 1944 I assumed that Alert Inc. concluded

that it was hardly worth clearing someone so evidently unemployable as me.

I had some savings, profits from *The Equaliser*, some money I'd inherited from my father, and I was soon reduced to living off my capital. I did three versions of the Jesse James script for Eddie until I realised he had no intentions of making the film and it was merely a way of giving me money. Eventually I told him I wouldn't go on. So I wrote another script, a story of adolescent love loosely based on my own entanglement with Donald Verulam and Faye Hobhouse. I embellished my experiences in World War II with Two Dogs Running and produced a war adventure called *Alpha Beach, St Tropez*. Eddie paid me for them out of charity.

I sublet the ground floor of my house. I rented a room to Nora-Lee Madrazon and the rest to an Austrian couple, the Linds, friends of the Coopers. When funds ran lower still I took up teaching again, some maths, but increasingly English lessons, mainly to Japanese immigrants and some Filipino relatives of Nora-Lee. Ends met with some difficulty.

When I told Karl-Heinz what had happened he seemed more concerned for me than for his own prospects. Curiously, from that point on his own career advanced. He acted under the name K. H. Cornfield and he soon had a steady supply of small roles—usually playing shady or dandified foreigners—in films and on television. He never moved from his two-room apartment in the Hotel Cythera on the sea front. The hotel became another 129b Stralauer Allee: its unpretentious decrepitude was the sort of environment he flourished in, and besides, as he put it, the beach was so very handy. He would reassure me when, in my low moments, I used to bemoan my wretched luck. Don't worry, Johnny, he would say. I know we'll finish *The Confessions*. He saw something talismanic in our encounter in Weilberg in 1918. Over thirty years ago, he would remind me. Who could have guessed then that the two of us would be living in Los Angeles? There had to be some reason for it? I wished I could have shared his confidence.

Outbreaks of war always affected my life in surprising ways. At the end of June 1950, the day after the North Koreans crossed the 38th parallel, my affair with Nora-Lee Madrazon began. She came upstairs with a cousin to arrange an English lesson for him and stayed on for a coffee after he had left. Lori, though hefty, had had a pretty face. Nora-Lee had inherited this, modified somewhat by her half-Filipino blood. She looked Eastern—dark skin, slanted eyes, straight black

hair—but she was in fact unregenerate American. It was this jux-
taposition that particularly attracted me. I admit that the fact she was
nineteen years old had something to do with it as well. She had a
slim brown body with perfectly round almost black nipples. She was
tired of boys, she said, that's why she liked me. She had been renting
the room from me for almost a year before we became lovers and
couldn't understand what had taken me so long.

'Chauncy and Hall figure we've been balling since I moved in.'

'They do?' I didn't go to the diner very often but that explained
the leering familiarity with which they greeted me. 'Don't they mind?'

'Why should they? They know about you and Mom. You're practically one of the family.'

And so my life progressed on this somewhat reduced level. I still
had my small circle of friends—Karl-Heinz, the Gasts, the Coopers,
the Hitzigs and Monika. Monika's career too had taken a leap forward.
Now that she conceded she was a mature woman she began to get
more work, particularly on television. She urged me to try the
television and then the radio companies, which I did, only to find
that the greylist made me if anything even more of a pariah. As long
as I appeared on lists I would get no work. I thought vaguely about
paying to have my name 'cleared', but when I rang Alert Inc. they
told me it would cost between five and ten thousand dollars. The
longer I left it the harder it became.

I had plenty of time on my hands. One bonus of my new leisure
was that I discovered California north of Los Angeles. Karl-Heinz and
I spent two long holidays near Carmel and the Monterey peninsula in
'51 and '52. I liked the coast up there. It reminded me vaguely of
Scotland—the pines, the cliffs, the small beaches in coves—and of
holidays I had taken as a child with Oonagh, Donald, Thompson and
my father.

However it was on that second trip in '52 that I noticed the
surveillance had begun again. I spotted a maroon Dodge behind us
on the highway from Ventura to San Luis Opisbo where we stopped
for lunch. I saw it again two days later when we made a trip to the
hot springs at Tassajara. I didn't tell Karl-Heinz because I didn't
want to spoil his vacation. I wasn't that perturbed. Since the day I
had been called before the Brayfield subcommittee I knew I had been
watched. As Eddie had predicted, my phone was tapped for two
years. My mail was intercepted regularly (everything from Britain
was opened). I was often aware of being followed, though I could
never identify the men doing it. Once or twice I had seen a figure in
the crowd that looked oddly familiar. He reminded me of the man I

had seen jump in his car the day I was subpoenaed. I never saw his face. It was something about his posture that nagged at me: the set of his shoulders, the rake of his hat ... I couldn't place it.

The year turned, my fifty-fourth birthday came around, and for the first time I began contemplating giving it all up. One evening with Karl-Heinz, drinking Scotch in his rooms at the Cythera, he began talking about the five months he'd spent at Drumlarish with Mungo Dale—old Sir Hector had passed away in '39. (In fact Karl-Heinz talked very fondly of Mungo and from time to time prurient speculations flitted across my mind ...) Anyway, I felt a sudden urge to abandon everything, to go back home to Scotland and settle down. I confided this to Karl-Heinz. He laughed at me. You'd go mad, he said. Wait 'till you're sixty, and besides we have to finish *The Confessions*. I was moved by his faith. It was much stronger than mine. Don't worry, he said, this crazy witchhunt can't last forever.

He was wrong. A few weeks later I was round at Ernest Cooper's house having Sunday lunch when a US marshall knocked on his door and served him with the dreaded pink subpoena. Ernest looked as if he had been shot. I tried to calm him down.

'They can't do anything to you, Ernest. It's not like it was in Germany. They can't lock you up. Just plead the Fifth like I did.'

'Then they blacklist you. You haven't worked for three years.'

'Well, not properly, that's true. But ... Why don't you lie? Look at Bertolt.'

I could make no headway. He was terrified.

The next day Monika Alt phoned me. She had been subpoenaed too. Werner Hitzig as well.

'Have you been subpoenaed?' she asked.

'No. Why? I was subpoenaed in '48.'

'Well, why are they calling us and not you? They've been watching you for years, you said.'

I didn't like the implication in her tone of voice.

'It's got nothing to do with me, if that's what you're trying to say.'

'I'm sorry, Johnny. No, it's just that I'm worried. Everything's going so well for me now. I got a film at Fox. Eddie promised me something at Lone Star. I can't go on those filthy lists, I just can't.'

'They call masses of people. Hundreds. It doesn't necessarily mean anything.'

I saw Monika's appearance on television. It looked like an enormous press conference: microphones, TV cameras, lights, a crowd of about 400 people. Monika looked marvellous. She denied everything and seemed to have an easy time. Ernest admitted that he had been in the

communist party in Germany before World War II but insisted that
since then had utterly repudiated everything it stood for and was now
staunchly and proudly American. Werner Hitzig took the Fifth.

Two days later I was lugging groceries from a supermarket to my car
when I heard a hoarse stage whisper.

'*Mr Todd.*'

I looked round. It was Page Farrier, crouched behind a Chrysler.
He pointed at an open-air hot-dog stand a couple of hundred yards
away.

'*See you there. Ten minutes.*'

Page arrived eventually, with a caution that would have done credit
to a commando behind enemy lines. I had seen him regularly over
the intervening years. He picked up my scripts for Eddie and delivered
payment in cash. I knew him well. He sat down. I had ordered him
a Dr Pepper and a chili-dog. I knew he liked them.

'Ah, no thanks, Mr Todd. Really, I can't eat.'

'How's Brooke [his wife]? Rockwell and Stockyard [his children]?'

'Stockard. Fine, fine. Yes. Fine, all fine.'

'Good. What's up?'

'You've been named. In executive session.'

'*What*? Who by, for Christ's sake.'

'Some people called Monika Alt and Ernest Cooper.'

I felt a stretching feeling in my head, as if small claws were tugging
fiercely at my scalp.

'What did they say?'

He opened a notebook. 'That you were a member of a revolutionary
communist cell in Berlin in the Twenties. That you were a member
of the Santa Monica chapter of the Hollywood anti-Nazi League in
the Thirties. That you consorted with subversives in Mexico in 1939.'
Page looked shocked, shriven. 'This is much worse than last time,'
he said. 'They're going to subpoena you again. This time it will be
Washington, the full committee, open session. The works.'

'God.' I felt very tired. 'What should I do?'

Page cleared his throat. 'Well with these sessions you've got three
choices. Plead the First and go to prison for contempt. Plead the
Fifth and effectively admit your guilt. And you get on the MPA
blacklist. Or, three, name names. Tell them all the communists and
ex-communists you know. You get cleared and you stay in work.' He
paused, and popped a gherkin from his plate into his mouth. 'You
see,' he said munching, 'the ultimate test of a witness is not whether
he lies or tells the truth. It's the extent to which you co-operate with

the committee. And the only way to do that is inform.'

'So what do you suggest I do?'

'Well ... Name names. Everyone's doing it. Look, even your friends have named you.' He gave a puzzled smile. 'I tell you, people are naming their family, their friends, their colleagues. Anything to get off the list.' He looked at me worriedly. 'But in your case, Mr Todd ...'

'Take the Fifth?'

'Yes.'

'What do I risk?'

'They might deport you. But I doubt it, because you're British.'

I sat in silence for a while. Page began to nibble at his chili-dog.

'Terrible times we live in, Mr Todd,' he said. 'I know there's going to be a nuclear war—an atomic bomb war—for sure. In the next two, three years. There has to be.'

'Surely not.'

'Yes. Oh yes. Without any doubt. I'm absolutely certain.'

'But you can't be worrying about that?'

'But what about these camps they've got ready for subversives? They're getting ready for a war.'

'Nonsense.'

'No. The McArras Act. All subversives are going to be held in concentration camps. Why pass the Act if nothing's going to happen?'

'Me included, no doubt. Relax, Page, for God's sake. Do yourself a favour. And listen, you don't need to come with me to Washington. I can plead the Fifth on my own.' I stood up. 'Send me your bill.' I held out my hand. 'See you soon, Page.'

'*Don't shake my hand. Don't.* Just sorta wave casually ...' He gave me a wry smile.

I waved casually and left.

*   *   *

BRAYFIELD: Todd, you got your nose against the penitentiary gates! I warn you!

TODD: The Fifth Amendment allows—

BRAYFIELD: This is a communist party card issued to John James Todd in Berlin, Germany, 1926—

TODD: It is a patent forgery.

BRAYFIELD: *The next time you refuse I'm going to call a marshall and have you sent to jail!*

CHAIRMAN: Representative Brayfield, please.

BRAYFIELD: I apologise ... I put it to you Mr Todd, that your last film *The Equaliser* was Un-American.

TODD: It's pro-American.

BRAYFIELD: You denigrate one of America's folk heroes, Billy the Kid.

TODD: Billy the Kid was a thief and a murderer. The hero of my film is a law enforcer, like Mr Hoover, Sheriff Pat Garrett.

[muttering amongst the Representatives]

TODD: May I ask if Representative Brayfield has seen the film?

BRAYFIELD: No I have not ... I don't need to see pornography to know what it is. What nationality are you, Mr Todd?

TODD: I'm British.

BRAYFIELD: How long have you lived in the United States?

TODD: Since 1937, off and on. I made two visits to Europe. One in World War II when I was a war correspondent for America—

BRAYFIELD: Why have you never applied for citizenship? You were married to an American, were you not?

TODD: Yes, but I'm British. There was no need—

BRAYFIELD: Well, Mr Todd, I'm going to do everything in my power to get you sent back there!

The Klieglights for the TV cameras made Brayfield sweat more than ever. On the desk in front of me were seven microphones. Three TV cameras were ranged to survey the scene. From time to time flash bulbs flared from the press gallery. We were in the Caucus Room of the Old House Office Building, Washington, DC. It could sit four hundred people. Today it was almost empty. I noticed investigators Seager and Bonty up at the back. Bonty gave me a wave. It had to be said that the interrogation of John James Todd did not draw the crowds. I was no star. Brayfield was no Torquemada.

I had been before the committee for forty minutes. Ninety percent of the questions had come from Brayfield. I had stonewalled with blunt persistence, taking the Fifth Amendment whenever I felt like it. We paused now, while Brayfield blew his nose with his customary ferocity, as if he were trying to make his eyeballs bounce onto the desk in front of him. True to form he scrutinised his handkerchief for bits of expressed brain. The other Representatives on the committee (I forget their names, an undistinguished bunch of second-rate opportunists eager for the limelight) looked at each other with evident distaste. I had felt nervous, but now I was possessed by an angry calm. Brayfield was astonishingly well informed about me, and this— paradoxically—abated my concern. I was not a 'subversive', I was the victim of a vengeful and elaborate plot, and Brayfield, I was sure, was in it up to his neck.

REPRESENTATIVE EAMES: Mr Todd, ah ... Do you know the names of any members of the communist party, and if so are you prepared to, would you volunteer them to this committee? In executive session, of course.

TODD: Well, I volunteer to name one dangerous fanatic who is desperately trying to pervert the course of justice and undermine the US constitution. And I'm prepared to name him in open court.

EAMES: I don't think we—

CHAIRMAN: Really? And who is that?

TODD: Representative Byron Brayfield! That man is waging a personal vendetta against me!

Uproar. Brayfield swore vilely at me. I was fined five hundred dollars for contempt. The session resumed after a recess. Brayfield was armed with more questions of astonishing accuracy.

BRAYFIELD: Did you attend a meeting of the Hollywood anti-Nazi League on the night of November 14th 1940 in the home of Stefan Dressler?

TODD: I decline to answer that question on the grounds—

BRAYFIELD: You lived in Rincon, Mexico for a period during 1939?

TODD: Yes.

BRAYFIELD: And at that time you were friendly with Hans Eisler who appeared before this committee last year, were you not?

TODD: I can't remember. Lots of people passed through Rincon.

The committee got nowhere. I was dismissed before lunch, Brayfield still threatening deportation. In the corridor outside the Caucus Room a journalist from the *Hollywood Reporter* stopped me. He asked me if I had any evidence of a blacklist.

'Oh there's a list, all right,' I said. 'Only no-one will admit it.'

He asked me what I was doing now.

'Teaching maths and English and minding my own business.'

'Is that all?'

He looked disappointed and walked away. I watched him go. As he passed through an open door leading through to an ante-room. I saw Doon sitting inside. She wore a blue dress with white polka dots, white shoes and gloves. Her hair was up. Her tan was as deep as ever.

She looked lean, old and tough. She saw me, stood up and walked towards me.

My heart ... My guts ... I kissed her cheek.

'Hello, Jamie.'

'What're you doing here?'

'I was subpoenaed. I think they want to nail you.'

We sat down on a bench in the corridor.

'They seem to know everything about me,' I said.

'There was a guy came down to the ranch, asked me a whole lot of questions about you. About us.'

'What was he like?'

'Sort of unpleasant looking. Big gaps between his teeth. Said his name was Brown. Worked for the FBI, he said.'

'Gaps in his teeth?' ... Who could it be? Brown. Gap teeth. I looked at Doon. 'Can I see you tonight?'

She told me the name of her motel. We arranged to meet at eight.

Doon perjured herself for me. She lied to the committee with flair and aplomb. She swore I had never been in the communist party and declared that the membership card was an inept forgery.

Later that evening we sat in a small restaurant on 14th street, west, talking about old times. Doon chain-smoked. Nobody paid us any attention. I thought: this used to be the most famous beauty in Europe. Women strove to emulate her. She was the object of a million male fantasies. Thirty years ago the world was at her feet. I felt the universe's huge indifference to our fates. It made me cold.

'What're you thinking?'

'Nothing ... When are you going back?'

'Tomorrow. Got three new guests coming this week. I only hope they didn't see me on TV.'

I looked at her. I thought about sex with Doon, what it would be like now. Our old bodies.

'Doon. I love you. I've never loved anybody else. It's as simple as that. You're the only—'

'Jamie. Please. That was ages ago.'

'No, I mean it. When I saw you this morning. It all came back. It was like that day in the Metropole ...'

She smiled. 'It takes two you know. We fouled up. Nobody's fault, but it would never have worked.' She patted my fist. 'You're my oldest friend. That's all.'

My mouth was dry. I forced a smile. At least I had told her.

'I suppose you're right.'

I walked her back to her hotel.

'Why don't you go home, Jamie? You don't need all this HUAC shit. Just leave.'

'What about Karl-Heinz? I brought him here.'

'God, he'll be all right.'

'What about my film?'

'*The Confessions*? For Christ's sake.'

'I've got to finish it. Bloody hell, I'm fifty-four. I haven't made a film in nine years. And I was *so* close ... Anyway, Eddie owes it to me.'

She kissed my cheek. 'OK, honey. You do what you want. Like you used to say to me—make your own rut.'

I hugged her. Felt her thin body against mine. Smelt the tobacco in her wiry hair. She had none of my regrets. My massive regrets. I felt desperately sad—not because nothing was going to happen but because I suddenly had a glimpse of an alternative life in a different world. Do you know those moments? I saw myself in Paris, 1934, knocking on her apartment door and this time Doon would answer it. It was another edition of my life, our lives, and these two people standing outside a Washington hotel weren't allowed to participate in it.

'Look after yourself,' she said cheerfully. 'And come and visit. Keep in touch.'

We said goodbye to each other.

*   *   *

After my appearance before the committee in Washington I achieved a small notoriety. There were articles and a photograph in *Variety* and *Hollywood Reporter*. In the latter the headline ran: 'Ex-wife names Todd in HUAC session.' The old lady of the Italian fruit stall just round the corner from my house, spat at me and called me a Red 'stooge'. Eddie Simmonette was interviewed in *Variety* under the headline 'Lone Star Prez says nix to Reds.'

> Chief Exec. Eadweard Simmonette admitted hiring Todd in the '40s to direct B-feature westerns. 'I knew him vaguely in Berlin, but I never guessed he was a commie. He hasn't worked for me in ten years—since *The Equaliser* in '44. I respect his expertise but deplore his values.'

A late night show of *The Equaliser* was picketed by an organisation called ODCAD and the film was withdrawn from circulation. Another trickle of income dried up. I increased my teaching to six hours a day. Nora-Lee moved into my rooms and I rented hers to a student at UCLA. Foolishly, I lent Chauncy and Hall $1000 to redecorate the diner and never saw any of it again. My poverty level descended to Berlin 1924 standards.

I went to see Monika but she had moved to New York to do television there. I spoke to her on the phone.

'I'm sorry, Johnny, but I had to do it. I had no choice.'

'But for God's sake we were married once! Man and wife.'

'Don't give me that. Eddie Simmonette paid me five thousand dollars to marry you. It was strictly business.'

Another revelation I did not need. I went round to the Coopers shortly after my return from Washington but found the front door locked. I returned several times to the same rebuff. Then one day Elroy answered.

'Hi, Elroy,' I said. 'Is your Dad in?'

'My dad days he's sorry and will you please stop coming here.'

I pushed past him into the hall. I heard a lock turn on the dining room door. I hammered on it.

'Ernest! Come on! This is stupid. Come on out!'

When I stopped shouting I could hear him sobbing behind the door,

'Stop it, Ernest. For Christ's sake, I don't care, honestly.'

'I'm sorry, John. I'm sorry. Forgive me, please. But go away. Don't come here again. They're still watching me.'

Elroy stood behind me, his face contorted with shame and indignation.

'Will you please go away and leave him alone.'

*   *   *

For several weeks nothing depressed me more than this new status I had achieved as a one-man leper colony. Even Werner Hitzig, who had taken the Fifth, didn't want to associate with me because he was now paying Alert Inc. to clear his name. (He eventually named me as a communist in 1954. The problem was that once you were named it was open season. Between 1953 and '55 I was named twenty-seven times, mostly by total strangers.) I lost all my friends, apart from Karl-Heinz, and all connection with the film community.

But what surprised me was that I was still under surveillance. My phone made strange clicking noises when I picked it up. My mail was still being intercepted a year after the hearings. Someone was watching me too, I was sure, though I had no evidence. In late 1955 a local paper called the *Ventura Bee* ran a scurrilous story that had me as a communist agent poisoning the minds of immigrants with Soviet ideology while purporting to teach them English. I asked Page to sue for libel but he advised energetically against it. Ramon Dusenberry discovered that the *Ventura Bee* was owned by ODCAD—the Organisation of Decent Citizens of America for Democracy—which in turn was run by the American Business Union, whose address on Sunset Boulevard was the same as that of *Red Connections*.

It was Toshiro Saimaru who finally helped me out. Toshiro was a portly Japanese businessman who wanted some work done on his English accent. He had been greatly impressed by Laurence Olivier in 'Henry Vee', as he called it, and chose him as his model. We read a lot of Shakespeare and English poets to each other. His accent never improved, but he seemed to enjoy himself and it was an easy $5 an hour for me. We were reading Shelley's *Mont Blanc* one day.

'And what were thou,' I repeated, 'and earth, and stars, and sea, if to the human mind's imagining silence and solitude were vacancy? . . . '

'Sirence an' soritude were vacancy.'

'Great, Toshiro. Much better. Let's try *Ode to the West Wind*.'

He leafed through his anthology.

'Toshiro, do you ever use a private detective in your business?'

'Oh yes. Very good. Very good man. Mr Sean O'Hara.' He wrote down his name and number. I phoned and a secretary said Mr O'Hara would call round to see me.

The next Saturday morning there was a knock at the door. A small thick-set Japanese man was there, wearing a beige suit and a pork pie hat.

'No teaching on Saturday,' I said. He looked blank. 'We no teach on Saturday . . . No teachee . . . Nevah teachee. We close. Close. Shuttee.'

'You got the wrong guy, bub.' He handed me a card. SEAN O'HARA. PRIVATE DETECTIVE. I apologised and asked him in. He spoke with a perfect American accent. I felt a headache coming on. Eugen, Orr and now O'Hara.

'I'm so sorry,' I said. 'Your name. I had this image of . . . Silly me. Just goes to show.'

'Relax,' he said. 'My real moniker is Yatsuhashi Ohara. For a whole year I got no work. Absolutely zilch, *nada*. Couldn't figure out why. It's amazing what one of those apostrophes will do. Call me Sean.' He lit a Kool. 'What's the problem, Mr Todd?'

I told him my story. 'I think someone's behind the whole thing. I just want to know who.'

'Twenty-five dollars a day plus expenses.'

'Fine.' I would have to borrow some money off Nora-Lee. 'How long do you think it'll take?'

'Who knows? A week—a month? Don't worry, Mr Todd, I'll find out who it is.'

I hadn't actually set eyes on Eddie for over two years. Shortly after O'Hara's visit in the summer of '56 Karl-Heinz spent two weeks in hospital with a ruptured stomach ulcer. He recovered, but all the rejuvenation of his Californian years disappeared. He looked old and grey beneath his tan. I went to see him in hospital after the operation.

'My God, Johnny,' he said. 'Let's do this fucking film soon. Else I'm in a wheelchair.'

I was filled with a sudden nervous panic. I went round to Page's office, unannounced, to set up a meeting with Eddie. His secretary buzzed him.

'A Mr Todd to see you? He says it's urgent?'

Page flung himself through his office doors.

'Mr *Smith*. What a surprise.'

He marched me out of his office.

'For God's sweet sake, John!' he wailed once we were outside. We were on first name terms now. 'I don't know you, remember?' We found a coffee shop. 'Someone rang the other day asking if I represented you. I think the office may be bugged. I only use pay phones now.'

'Christ, you're worse than me . . . Look, I want to see Eddie.'

'I'll see what I can do. Only promise me you won't call round like that again.'

Eddie stood at the surf-edge in front of his beach house. The spent waves crept up to his feet and crept away again. He wore cerise and mustard bathing shorts and smoked a cigar. His neat round belly hung like a medicine ball beneath his plump girlish breasts. From the sun-deck of his beach house smoke curled from a barbecue.

'Hey, John!' he shouted as he saw me approach. It was as if absolutely nothing had happened. We stood for a while and watched the waves curl in, smash and spread themselves on the sand.

'I'm sorry about that piece in *Variety*,' he said. 'But I knew you'd understand.' He looked at me and at my clothes. 'Is everything all right, John? You don't look so good.'

'I'm fine. I just need to make a film.'

'Soon, John, soon. Come on up, have a bite of lunch.'

'Lunch? Good God, you're sure?'

'Everything's beginning to change. Ike's got a second term. People are relaxing. Even Trumbo got the Academy Award.'

'He did?'

'Yeah. For *The Brave One*.'

'He wrote that?'

'He's "Robert Rich". Didn't you know?'

'No. Remember I'm rather out of touch these days.'

We climbed the steps up to his deck. A petite dark woman was sunbathing in a two-piece swimsuit, the same colour as Eddie's.

'This is my wife Bonnie. Bonnie, say hi to my oldest friend John James Todd. John, why don't you take some clothes off?'

Later we talked about my plans. I told him about Karl-Heinz's state of health and that I had a new idea for a film, not *Father of Liberty*. Something much smaller scale, much cheaper. But we had to do it soon.

'I don't know, John. It's a question of timing. I'm sure I can do you a pseudonymous script now. But directing a film ... Let's wait awhile.'

I took a deep breath. 'Eddie, I've done a lot for you, these last years ...'

'And I've done a lot for you John.' It was obviously one of those days for using christian names. But I think he sensed my seriousness.

'Yes,' I said, thinking about Monika. 'But look where we are today.'

'Johnny, Johnny ...' He put his hand on my shoulder. 'My father told me something I've never forgotten. You've got two forces in life that control everything. Just two. The Profit Motive and Human Values. Sometimes they run together but mostly it's war. Pick your side early, my father said, and stick with it. And by the way, my father said, remember this: the Profit Motive always wins.' He spread his hands.

I looked out to sea. 'It's not as simple as that.'

Sean O'Hara called round.

'Well, I got him,' he said. 'This guy turns out to be a vice-president of AMPOPAWL. He's a special investigator for ODCAD and HUAC. He's been an FBI informant since 1934. He owns 50 percent of *Red Connections*, which has a monthly circulation of 24,000 copies at five bucks a copy. Know how much money that is? 120,000 dollars a *month*. This bozo hates commies and it's making him a stack of mazoola. He's a professional blacklister who advises radio and TV stations and sponsors about the OK-ness of the people they hire. Quite a guy. What I can't figure out is what he's got against you.'

'What's his name?'

'Monroe Smee. Mean anything?'

*   *   *

I sat beside O'Hara in the front of his Buick Roadmaster. He had a cardboard cup of Pepsi-Cola on the dashboard shelf, a shrimp and pastrami sandwich in one hand a Kool in the other. He stubbed out his cigarette and took a bite of his sandwich. It was half past eight in the morning.

'This gumshoe life is bad for your health. You gotta eat proper.' He offered me a cigarette. 'That's why I smoke menthol.'

'No thanks,' I said. 'I'm trying to give up. I've only got one lung.'

'No shit? What happened?'

'I got shot in the war.'

'No shit? God ... I respect you for that, Mr Todd, I really do. Was it the Krauts or us lot?'

'Actually I was shot by my own side ... I'll tell you about it later.'

We were on Sunset Boulevard, not far from where Beverly Hills becomes West Hollywood, parked outside the building that contained the *Red Connection* offices. Waiting for Smee.

'Every second Wednesday he comes, my man says,' O'Hara said. Then he started to sing quietly to himself. He always got the lyrics slightly wrong. Today it was, 'A kiss on the lips may be quite sentimental.' Yesterday, when we had arranged this stake out, it had been, 'Petting in the dark, sad boy. Petting in the dark, sad girl.' He unwound his window and threw the wax paper wrapper of his sandwich outside.

'Here he comes,' he said.

Smee had left his car in the building parking lot and strode briskly along the sidewalk. He wore a dark suit and carried a briefcase. I saw again the pale face, the gap teeth, the large uneven nose and the slightly weak chin. He looked thin and wiry. But the balding brown hair had gone. He wore a neatly combed, short-haired dark wig.

'He used to be bald,' I said.

'Yeah, that's quite a toop,' O'Hara said.

I watched Smee as he went inside. What did I ever do to you, I wondered? I couldn't believe that Monroe Smee was responsible. There must have been some terrible error or confusion.

He emerged at half past three. O'Hara had lunched on a box of ribs, root beer and popcorn and was well into his second pack of Kools. We followed Smee's car, a Cadillac Fleetwood, to some offices on Wilshire Boulevard and then on to his dentist in Highland Park. When he left there he drove all the way down Almeda Street to Long Beach and picked up the Pacific Coast Highway south. We motored past the oil pumps, Huntington Beach, down to Newport, and followed him off the highway into the smart beachside suburb of Balboa.

'No wonder he only comes in every second Wednesday,' I said. I felt like we had been driving for hours. 'I'm exhausted.'

'You'd never make a shamus.' O'Hara laughed. 'I spent eighteen days living in this car on one case.'

That was the source, I realised, of the Buick's particular moist frowsty smell.

Smee's house was a big low stucco bungalow with an orange tiled roof. At the back there was a long garden and beyond that what seemed to be a private dock with two boats inside it. As Smee's Cadillac pulled into the carport a teenage boy dressed in tennis whites left the front door. He waved at Smee and jogged off. Smee got out of his car and went inside.

'What now?' O'Hara said.

'I've got to talk to him.'

'Yeah, well, be careful.'

I got out and buttoned my jacket. I felt crumpled and dirty after a day in O'Hara's car. I rubbed my chin—I needed a shave. I wished somehow I looked smarter, more prosperous.

I went up to the front door and rang the bell. A Hispanic maid answered. Right behind her was a thin, rather sharp faced woman with hard blonde hair.

'It's all right, Caridad,' she said. Then to me: 'Yes?'

'I'd like to speak to Mr Smee. It's a Committee matter.'

'Oh . . .' she frowned. 'Come in.'

I stepped into the hall, and as I did so my fear returned. Mrs Smee went into a room and I heard her say, 'Monroe? It's a man from the Committee.'

Smee came out. He wore black braces over a white nylon shirt.

'Hello, Monroe,' I said. 'I think we need to talk.'

He looked deeply and profoundly shocked. Then his nose wrinkled in a curious way.

'Get out,' he said. 'Get out of my house you filth! You commie filth.'

'For God's sake, Smee—'

'You evil Red Bastard! How dare you contaminate my house! How dare you!'

'Very impressive,' I said. 'Academy Award stuff. Now, we've—'

'*Get out! Get out!*'

I grabbed his shirt front with both hands and slammed him up against the wall.

'Call the police!' He bellowed at his wife.

'*Why?* Why me? Just leave me *alone*!' I felt a homicidal anger distort my voice unpleasantly. Years of frustration boiling over.

Mrs Smee screamed behind me. I felt her fists pound my back. I let him go.

'You can't do anything more to me,' I said. 'Just leave me alone.'

He rummaged in the drawer of a hall table and took out a small revolver.

'I could kill you, Todd!' he screamed. 'I could kill you here and now and they'd give me a medal for killing a Red scum—'

'You're fucking *mad*!'

'—but I don't want the stink in my house!'

'I'll kill *you*!' I yelled back unthinkingly. 'Leave me alone or I'll kill *you*, so help me!'

'Get out, you commie shit! Get out of my house!' He levelled the gun at me.

'You're a lunatic. Madman ... I warn you!' I backed off all the same. Mrs Smee had sunk to her knees and was sobbing loudly.

'You've had it, Todd! I'll get you!'

'And I'll break your fucking neck!'

We shouted insults at each other as I opened the door. My last image was of Mrs Smee hauling herself up his body, clutching imploringly for the gun.

As I strode across the front lawn the sprinklers came on—automatically, I assume—and soaked my trousers from the knee down. I danced over the grass to O'Hara's car.

'Did he do that?' O'Hara asked as I got in beside him. 'Want me to knock him about some? Little roughhouse stuff?'

'No. Let's go.'

O'Hara pulled away.

'He pulled a gun on me,' I said, delayed shock setting in. 'Jesus, he pointed a fucking gun at me.'

'Bastard,' O'Hara said. 'Want me to break his legs? His arms?'

'Some other time, Sean.'

He lowered his voice. 'I can do that sort of thing for you, Mr Todd. Anything. Not too expensive, for certain clients. Get my drift?'

I wasn't listening.

'He's mad,' I said, my arms and body beginning to tremble. I rubbed my face. 'As simple as that. Stark, staring, grade "A" nutcase.'

VILLA LUXE 29 June 1972

Why did Smee hate me with such vehement passion? I don't know. It couldn't have been simply that incident with the scripts? But it must have started then, as a basic irrational dislike that over the years his anti-communist mania had turned into something righteous and patriotically American. He was indisputably mad, Smee, beneath the perfect humdrum sanity of his life. Perhaps one shouldn't look any further. He was a manic force operating in Los Angeles and I just happened to come into range.

And yet ... admit it, we have all met people whom we have instinctively disliked. It doesn't take much irritation to turn that emotion into something altogether more venomous. I presume Smee must have felt something like this where I was concerned, especially after I had so guilelessly rubbished his work. When I did that I turned the knife in his vanity—and there are few people vainer than the deluded, talentless ones amongst us. But also he was an FBI informer when he met me and possibly he saw me as even more of a traitor ... Anyway, one can't speculate much beyond this. The motivating factors in a psyche like Smee's are too dark and baffling to be elucidated. He hated me; he was convinced I was a communist. It was his bounded duty to bring me down. Smee was a given—call it another brute contingency that my life had thrown up. And I had never guessed, not for a moment. And that made the experience even more alarming. Monroe Smee, G-man, HUAC investigator, Red scourge, anti-communist entrepreneur. My appointed nemesis.

Emilia has done something appalling to her hair. She has dyed it black—a gunmetal blue-black—and has had it set in hard waves around her head. She wears a pungent scent that today at lunchtime I thought I could even taste in my food. On two occasions this morning she found opportunities to brush against me. And I sense her looking at me, covertly, as if weighing me up all the time. The atmosphere in the house is charged, tremulous, on the brink of something drastic.

Her new hairstyle is not flattering, but as the day wears on I find my thoughts returning to her more frequently than I would have imagined possible. There has been no-one in my life for years, you see. Perhaps, like Jean-Jacques, I could do worse than take up with someone like Emilia, faithful and efficient. Just as he had his Thérèse, so I would have my Emilia ... I project myself into this putative future and—do you know?—it has its own real attraction. There's a lot of life left in Emilia. She is attractive in a crude, faintly primitive way.

I go looking for her. I find her in the living room which is shuttered against the afternoon sun. She was dusting the books on the bookshelves, something I had never seen her do before. Suddenly, I knew I could find a sort of happiness with her, and that's not something to be spurned.

'Oh, Mr Todd,' she says. 'That man was looking for you again. I forgot to tell you. In the village. The American.'

Jesus Christ. 'Did you see him?'

'No, Ernesto told me, at the bar.' She sees the look of worry in my face. 'Is there a problem, Mr Todd? Is something wrong? You can tell me. If you like.'

She comes over, heralded by her perfume. I go to meet her. She stops.

'I don't know, Emilia ... Something happened a long time ago.'

Unthinkingly, I put my hands on her shoulders. For the first time my fingers on her flesh. Her new hair gleams with dull blue highlights. She twists the duster in her hands.

'Mr Todd, are you in trouble?'

'I don't know.'

She pushes me away with astonishing strength. I stumble, catch the back of my leg painfully on a coffee table. Emilia seems to be shivering slightly. She has one hand up to her mouth.

'No,' she says. 'No. We must wait. We must wait.'

She turns and runs out of the room. Wait for what? A minute later I hear her motorbike start up. I sit down. What was that all about, I wonder? Shock, shame, second thoughts? Head in hands time ...

Then I remember what she told me and I feel the fear creep back. It's like a smell, my nostrils flare, my mouth feels pasty, dry. I decide to ask Ernesto for more information.

I walk up the track towards the village. Gunter's driveway is clogged with cars and jeeps. Children's shouts and conversation rise up from the swimming pool. It's hot. I should have brought my hat. I slow down. On either side of the track the pinewoods seem to bake in their dusty silence.

I arrive at Ernesto's, parched and overheated. The terrace is deserted apart from a couple in their swimming costumes. I look again: Ulrike and a young man. I wave limply to them.

'Mr Todd. A moment.'

They come over. I step into shade and lean against a pillar. Ulrike wears a bikini. Despite my exhaustion I note the muscled plane of her stomach, the swell and cleavage of her breasts, the flick and contraction of her thighs as she comes over. Certain women, walking towards me ... My stomach dips. I think of Doon. I would weep if I wasn't so tired. But what's happened to me today? I seem to be in the grasp of some geriatric satyriasis.

They sense my vague distress. Soon I am seated, a cool beer is in front of me, offers of food have been declined. I am an old man, over seventy. I keep forgetting. Sometimes I feel a coltish eighteen, hard though it may be to credit.

'Is Ernesto here?' I ask.

'No. Just Concepcion.'

'Never mind.'

'Mr Todd, I'd like you to meet Tobias, my boyfriend.'

I look at the young man. Dark hair, receding temples. He is thin with broad shoulders. He takes my hand.

'Mr Todd,' he says. He speaks good English. 'This is a real honour for me. I couldn't believe it when Ulrike told me about you.' More plaudits followed. I begin to relax and order another beer. Tobias tells me of the new plans he and his colleagues have made since Ulrike's discovery of me. From the way he talks you'd think I was a new continent. I barely listen. I hear him mention old names from the past: *Julie*, Doon Bogan, Karl-Heinz, Duric and Aram Lodokian, UFA, Realismus, *The Confessions* ...

I interrupt. 'Have either of you, by any chance, heard of a man in the village looking for me? An American?'

'An American? No.'

'I heard this man was asking for me. Asking Ernesto.'

More negatives. Tobias leans forward.

'The great mystery, Mr Todd, this is what we all want to know: *The Confessions: Part I*—what happened to that film? We can find no print in all Germany. No negative. It hasn't been seen for forty years. Do you know where there is a copy?'

'Alas, no,' I spread my hands, 'sorry.'

'Think hard,' Tobias implored. 'Imagine, if we could discover it.' For a moment he allowed his own ambitions to overrun his altruism. 'Think what a discovery it would be. A lost masterpiece restored. The greatest film of the silent era. Astonishing news.'

'I wish I could help you,' I said. 'But everything must have been destroyed in the war.'

20

The Last Walk of Jean-Jacques Rousseau

I believe that *The Last Walk of Jean-Jacques Rousseau* has something of a cult following on the university film club circuit. I saw a poll in a magazine once where it came third equal with *Juliet of the Spirits*, after *Un Chien Andalou* and *Last Year in Marienbad*, in the category 'Off-Beat and Avant Garde.' It was the last film I made and far and away the strangest.

It was shot in three weeks, cost $128,000 and lasts one hour and ten minutes. Eddie financed it ('No more than one hundred grand for an art movie') on the condition that I used a pseudonym and that I directed a low budget epic called *Hercules and the Sirens* afterwards. I agreed at once. I knew that *Last Walk* would be my last film.

The final years of Jean-Jacques' life were spent in Paris, in a tranquil enough state, apart from his occasional bouts of acute paranoia. He was famous and sought after but made no attempt to capitalise on his renown. He received many visitors, encouraging young people in particular to come and see him, and took up his old career as a music copyist. His great hobby was botanising, or herborising as he called it, and he knew no greater pleasure than to take long solitary walks through the countryside around Paris. In the last two years of his life—1777 and '78—he wrote his final piece of autobiography, the *Rêveries d'un Promeneur Solitaire*. It is unfinished, but in the course of these ten promenades he surveys his life from the serene vantage point of old age. *The Confessions* is passionate and vital. The *Rêveries* is elegiac and sagacious. In the summer of 1778, feeling unwell, he and Thérèse went to live in a pavilion on the estate of the Marquis de Girardin at Ermenonville, north-west of Paris near Senlis. There, he worked on the *Rêveries*, herborised and seemed to be regaining his strength.

On the 1st of July 1778 it was a warm day. Rousseau went for a long walk with the Marquis' son in the meadows of the park of Ermenonville. That night he dined extremely well in the company of the Marquis and his family. He seemed amiable and vivacious. The next day, however, he felt ill. Thérèse assumed he had eaten too much. At ten o'clock, staring out of the windows at the gardens he had a severe apoplectic fit. He fell to the ground, breathless and in agony, striking his head against the floor causing a bad wound. He died almost immediately.

*   *   *

The Last Walk of Jean-Jacques Rousseau opens with a shot of the dining room in the pavilion. Jean-Jacques (Karl-Heinz) sits at the table eating his breakfast. The young Girardin comes to collect him and they set off on their walk. The pavilion, we then observe, is set in a meadow on the Monterey Peninsula near Big Sur. The sense of reality that the opening scene seemed to present so faithfully begins to fall away, never to be recovered.

When Jean-Jacques had collected and examined a plant he used to tie a red or gold ribbon around one of the same type so he would know it was documented. On leaving the pavilion, he and Girardin find themselves on a prairie alive with red and gold ribbons. They enter a copse of trees and descend into a little wooded canyon through which runs a fast shallow river (the Little Sur river, in fact). Two girls are sitting beside it, one combing the other's hair. In the background their horses graze. Jean-Jacques watches them mount up and ford the river. We cut to the prelude to the cherry orchard idyll in *The Confessions: Part I*. Colour gives way to black and white. We see a young Jean-Jacques help the girls across a similar river. Then we intercut the orchard sequence with the curious faces of old Jean-Jacques and the baffled Girardin. Later, they botanise, Jean-Jacques diligently tying red and gold ribbons on plants as they go. They come upon a hermitage. The monks offer them lunch. A lesson is read during the meal about how futile it is for man to complain about his lot. 'God has brought man nothing. He oweth him nothing.'

After lunch they go into the garden of the hermitage. A group of contemporary Californians sit before a screen watching scenes from *The Confessions: Part I*. Old Jean-Jacques observes his young self arriving in Annecy on his way to the house of Mme de Warens.

Jean-Jacques and Girardin leave for home. On their way back they cross the Pacific Coast Highway (completely unperturbed by the automobiles). They stop at a roadside diner which is full of garish tourists. The owner recognises Jean-Jacques, sets up a table for him outside underneath a redwood and provides him with bread, wine and cheese.

GIRARDIN: He seems to know you well.
JEAN-JACQUES: In fine weather my wife and I used to come here and eat a cutlet of an evening.

As they approach the pavilion they notice a huge Great Dane loping and bounding about the meadows. The dog sees Jean-Jacques and races towards him. It leaps up and knocks him heavily to the ground. Unconscious, Jean-Jacques has a vision of Mme de Warens, her back towards him, about to enter the door of the church at Annecy. Then he sees a view of the Lake at Annecy which merges with the Pacific Ocean off Big Sur. He hears the monk's voice saying: 'All flesh is as grass. It withereth and the flower thereof falleth away.' We see the meadow with its fluttering ribbons through which they passed that morning dissolve into a smoking ashfield (a National Guardsman with a flamethrower was responsible for the transformation, supervised by the Carmel fire department).

Jean-Jacques recovers himself and they make their way back home. We cut to the dinner scene, with the Marquis, the Marquise and their family present. Candles flicker, their gleam is reflected in the silverware. Jean-Jacques talks with almost manic animation. Later, when everyone has gone, and Thérèse is upstairs in bed, he stands alone in the dark room looking out through the windows at the moonlit garden. For an instant we see the Great Dane lope across the lawns. Then the windows become white screens and upon them is projected the vision he saw earlier: Mme de Warens about to enter the church.

'Julie,' he whispers.

She turns. And there is Doon.

Suddenly the image is shattered by a stone. Then dozens of stones are hurled through the panes. Glass breaks. Shards fly. We are back in Motiers, the mob is stoning his house. A rock catches Jean-Jacques on his forehead, blood flows. He clutches his chest in monstrous agony and falls to the floor.

Thérèse comes in. The room is exactly as it was. Exquisite moonlight floods the tranquil room. Jean-Jacques lies on the floor, dead. End. Credits.

My sources for the film were the *Rêveries*, a description of a walk taken with Rousseau, written by Barnardin de Saint-Pierre, my own memories (which no doubt you will have spotted) and inspired pilfering of my subconscious. I assembled my sources and the narrative seemed to flow from my pen with an ease I had never before encountered. The one critic of any repute who noticed the film wrote, '*The Last Walk* exerts a beguiling grip on the viewer but remains in the end a maze of impenetrable symbols.' Ah, but remember there is always a way out of a maze.

We shot the film in the late summer of 1958. For the three years previously Academy Awards for the best screenplay had gone to blacklisted screenwriters using pseudonyms. Eddie was sure that 1959 would see the MPA rescind its by-laws against those who had refused to co-operate with the HUAC. The time was right, he said, but he still wanted my director's credit to be pseudonymous. I chose the name John Witzenreid.

I enjoyed making that small film as much as I relished the scale of *The Confessions: Part I.* Our cast was composed of amateurs and bit-part players. We had a small crew, based ourselves in San Francisco and travelled out to whatever location took our fancy.

For a fortnight Karl-Heinz and I rented the small shack that we had used on our previous holidays. It had been refurbished somewhat; it had a shower now and the kitchen had been modernised. Karl-Heinz wasn't well, after filming he was due to go into hospital for another operation on his ulcer, but our time in that cottage seemed briefly to revive him. We reminisced a lot about the past, the forty years we had known each other. The fogs would come in from the sea in the evening, shrouding the spectacular sunsets like a Todd soft-focus lens.

It was here I perfected the dry martini—John James Todd style. One: chill everything to just above freezing point—gin, Noilly Prat, lemon, glass and shaker. Two: fill a saucer with Noilly Prat and up-end the cocktail glass in it. About half an inch of the rim should be submerged. Three: fill the shaker with ice and then add the gin. Do not shake, rotate gently a couple of times. Four: take the glass from the saucer. Five: fill with gin. Six: cut a piece of lemon peel and allow a few spots of zest to spray onto the surface of the gin. Seven: drink. This method is infallible. It is the only way to (a) guarantee the minutest addition of Noilly Prat to the gin, and (b) to taste it. Otherwise you might as well drink neat gin. The vermouth is a crucial ingredient. Those people who say, 'show the gin the Noilly Prat' don't know what they are talking about. It is a *cocktail*, not a draught of neat alcohol.

So I drank these dry martinis and Karl-Heinz swigged some white chalky liquid to line his stomach and we watched the earth tilt into darkness. Although I had to ignore it there was a valedictory note in these evenings. Karl-Heinz began, idly, ironically, to speculate about his death. For my part I was aware that my *Confessions* film was about to be as complete as it ever would be. Without Karl-Heinz there would be no point in persevering further.

While I was editing the film Karl-Heinz went into hospital. The operation apparently was a success, and he was soon back at the hotel. I visited him often. He said he felt well but he looked frail and elderly. We would take slow strolls along the concrete boardwalk, taking half an hour to cover a few hundred yards.

One day I was called from the editing suite of Lone Star to go down to reception. It was an urgent and confidential matter they said. A tall man in leisure clothes stood looking out at the sunlit car park. He turned around.

'My God,' I said. 'Two Dogs Running.'

'Mr Todd. You're looking good.'

We shook hands. I was pleased to see him.

'What're you doing?' I asked him.

'Still selling,' he said. 'But I've moved into shoes.'

We caught up quickly on the past. The last time he'd seen me was at St Tropez, 1944, my stretchered body being carried aboard an LCT at Tahiti Plage ... I asked him if he had time for a drink or a meal but he pointed to an old convertible outside containing a young woman and three children.

'Vacation,' he said. 'We're going on up to Yosemite. I just wanted to talk to you about something, something strange.'

'What's that?'

'Well, about a month ago a man looked me up. Said he was from a veteran's organisation. Started asking me all about the invasion. Then he got more specific. He started asking me about you. And then, wait for this, he started asking about that German ...'

'The one you—'

'Yeah.'

'Jesus. How did he know?'

'That's what I wondered at first. But you see, I told these guys, those paratroopers, afterwards. They picked up his body and the dead guys at the villa. I guess, somewhere, some kind of report was written up. Some man from the Provost Marshall's office interviewed me. You were badly wounded and they wanted to know what we'd been doing in that car. And I guess that old man at the villa—what was his name?'

'Can't remember.'

'Well, I guess he would have been brought into it. I think he was pretty ticked off that his car had been totalled. You gave him that receipt and he turned up at Le Muy looking for his car. He wanted compensation. It's got to be all on the record somewhere.'

'Cavenaugh-Crabbe, that was his name.'

'Yeah. Well, this guy—from the vets organisation—said the case was being reopened and that you were suspected of executing that German. Murder of a POW, he said.'

'But that's crazy.'

'That's what I told him.' Two Dogs lowered his voice. 'I told him I had done it. The guy had made a run for it. I shot him and then we found the fingers . . . Like we said.'

'Exactly. Christ, I didn't even have a gun.'

'He said he was going to Europe to make further investigations. He got nasty when I said I had done it. Said there was no need for me to cover up for you.'

'What did he look like?'

'He had this kind of black wig on. Gaps in his teeth.'

I walked out to the car with Two Dogs and met his family. His wife looked Mexican, quite pretty. His eldest boy was ten. I was introduced as 'Mr Todd, the film director, the man I was in the war with.' I shook everybody's hand. I felt very old, like a grandfather.

The eldest boy said, 'Sir? Is it true you were shot by your own side?'

'Yes,' I said. I wished I could have bragged that I'd stormed a machine-gun nest or two. 'It was bad luck. Sometimes it turns out that way.'

We said goodbye. I thanked Two Dogs and we made polite plans to stay in touch.

Back in the office I phoned O'Hara straight away.

'I think Smee's going or has been to Europe,' I said to him. 'Can you check on that?'

'Pleasure, Mr Todd. I should tell you, though, that since we last did business my rates have gone up to $35 a day.'

A week later O'Hara called to tell me Smee had recently flown to London on HUAC business. I hung up. I felt a mad frustration knot my brain. My head ached. What was going on? What was the man after? Why wouldn't he leave me alone. The phone rang.

'Yes?'

'Mr Todd? This is Mr Ashplanter from the Hotel Cythera. We're a bit worried about Mr Kornfeld. His door's locked and we can't get any answer from him.'

There was no expression on Karl-Heinz's face. His eyes were

slightly open, as was his mouth. I tried to read a peaceful passing in his countenance and almost made it. I touched his hand. It was stiff and cold. I wished I hadn't seen him ... But how many dead people had I seen in my life? Hundreds upon hundreds. Most anonymous: the drowned men at Nieuport, the burst mattresses and battered furniture of no-man's-land. A few were acquaintances. But only two had made me quake and cower internally. Only two had led me down the cul-de-sac of my own mortality. My dead son Hereford and my dead friend Karl-Heinz ...

A weeping Mrs Ashplanter called a doctor and the morticians. I wandered out onto the beach. From somewhere came a noise of tinny thumping music. A group of young men played volleyball whooping and shouting with heroic energy. The waves creamed in, all the way from Japan, somebody had once told me. Some journey ... Maybe I'd go to Japan, next year. Who gave a damn, anyway.

*   *   *

We planned to open *The Last Walk of Jean-Jacques Rousseau* at a small arthouse cinema called the Rio in Westwood. The day we chose was July 2nd 1960, one hundred and eighty-two years to the day since Jean-Jacques had died. Eddie approved the plan. He hated the film but he thought the anniversary might just attract some press coverage.

As I approached the cinema on opening night I was gratified to see a large crowd—over a hundred people—gathered outside. It was a warm smoggy evening, a smell of tomcat in the air. Then I saw they were carrying large banners. PASADENA WOMEN'S TEMPERANCE ASSOCIATION, I read, and, BURBANK DIVISION: SECOND DEGREE KNIGHT COMMANDERS OF THE GOLDEN CIRCLE.

Just my luck, I thought, we've got a convention in the next door hotel. But as I drew nearer I saw they were clustered in front of the cinema entrance. I noticed some of the actors standing forlornly about in their evening dress. I tried to push my way through. A sharp-faced young man stopped me.

'This is an official picket, sir. This film is communist propaganda made by a subversive.

'Excuse me, please.'

'The director of this film has been named and listed as a member of the communist party.

I felt suddenly weak. I backed off.

Eddie got out of an enormous limousine. 'What's going on, John?'

'Some sort of maniac picket. Real esoteric weirdos tonight.'

'*Jesus!*' Eddie leapt back in his car. Through an inch of open window

447

he said. 'Let me know how it goes. Good luck.' As he drove off the crowd cheered. A man in a tuxedo came up to me.

'Mr Todd? I'm the manager.'

'Sorry about this. Can we delay everything an hour or so? They'll get bored and go away soon.' I noticed that the man's face was taut and pale.

'I've been threatened, sir. He said they're going to torch the place if we show the film.'

'Just some crank. Call a cop.'

'I think he was a cop. He showed me a badge. I think it was FBI.'

'Who was it?'

The manager scanned the crowd. 'That's him, in the back. Just going round the corner.'

I saw a close cropped black wig above the heads of the crowd.

'*Smee*!'

I started to run. I skirted the picketers and ran down the side of the cinema. Fifty yards away I saw a car pull out and drive off. A Cadillac Fleetwood.*

*   *   *

I drove north. Back to our convict shack near Big Sur. I turned off the coast highway and drove down the narrow lane that led to the house. The shack had a new tarpaper roof and the hedge around it was full of dog roses and morning glory, the garden lush with lupin and poppies. I left the car parked in the lane and made several trips down the steps to the house with my luggage and provisions. Almost as soon as I arrived I felt a calm descend on me. The fog over the sea was clearing but shreds of it still clung to the headland, like muslin snagged on the rocks.

I spent a pleasant four days alone pondering my future. Three times a week the mailman called. He honked his horn up on the highway and you clambered up to collect your mail and buy provisions from him. Like a steamer on an African river his arrival attracted the others living round and about and we would gather like a tribe by his van and chat. This was my fourth visit to the cabin over the years and I was beginning to recognise the denizens: the solitude freaks, the failed artists, the cheerful bullshitters. When they asked me what I did and I said 'film director' I could see them relax. 'One of us,' I

---

* *Last Walk* finally opened in New York in 1961. It was unpicketed. A few months earlier President Kennedy had crossed an American Legion picket to watch a screening of *Spartacus*, script by ex-Hollywood Ten Dalton Trumbo. I owe JKF a vote of thanks.

could hear them thinking, 'another fantasist.'

I resumed my old habit of walking the two miles down to the mouth of the Little Sur river for an evening swim. I changed in the rocky dunes and dashed out, naked, into the modest surf.

I think it was my fifth evening on the beach. I waited for a rare car to pass on the highway before I made my nude run to the waves. I looked down at the grey wiry pelt that covered my body and beat out a short rhythm on my firm little pot belly. I checked the road—all clear—and trotted out into the sea.

Gasping and snorting I thrashed around in the waves for a while. I never went out far, I was happy to cavort oafishly in the breakers. I stood in the foamy water, waist deep, and let the waves surge and batter away at me. A particularly strong one knocked me over, and as I went down beneath the surface I saw a flash of light from the hillside. I stood up, spluttering. The next roller was heaving itself towards me and I stood in a patch of temporarily calm water, latticed with spume. About a quarter of a mile away I saw a small figure of a man run from behind a rock and vanish into a copse of birch trees.

I went under. I swam out, kicked sideways and surfaced for a second, guzzling air. I saw no more movement on the hillside. I swam vigorously north, trying to keep warm, before doubling back. The sun seemed to hang on the horizon forever.

When it was dark enough I crept out and found my clothes and towel. When I had dressed I waited an hour before going up the highway. I hitchhiked for ten minutes before a car stopped. I got the driver to drop me at a roadside diner some miles away. I ordered coffee and some food and wondered what to do.

I thought first about ringing the police. But Smee was a G-man, or had been. He had some kind of badge, that was for sure. I knew Smee would be waiting for me at the shack. I called Sean O'Hara.

'Come up there now?' he said. 'It's got to be 250 miles. You crazy?'

'I don't care,' I said. 'Smee's here ... Hello, hello?'

The line was very bad.

'... expect me to do about it?' I heard O'Hara say.

'I don't care,' I shouted. 'Just get him off my back. The man's ruined my life as it is.'

'Your back is ruined? He shot you?'

'*Off* my back. Get him *off* my back. Off. *Off.*'

There was a long pause full of fizz and crackle.

'Hello?'

'OK, Mr Todd. I'll do it for you. But it'll cost you ... Hello? ... An out of town job like this.'

'I don't care how much it costs. *I don't care*. Just do it.'

'For you one thousand dollars. But five hundred down or I don't move.'

I thought that was a bit steep for a special favour, but I was happy to pay anything to put the frighteners on Smee.

I told O'Hara to go to Eddie. Eddie would pay him the five hundred. I felt exhausted from my massive swim. I gave O'Hara the precise directions to my cabin. 'He's bound to be there,' I said, 'staking it out. Waiting for me.'

'Don't worry, Mr Todd, I'm on my way. Soon as I get the money. It's as good as done.'

I told him where Eddie lived, and hung up. I offered up a prayer or two and phoned Eddie. He was in.

'Five hundred bucks? Are you in trouble? ... What the fuck's wrong with this line? Hello? ... '

'I just need a job done quickly. This guy's the only one who can do it. I'll explain later.'

'OK, John, What's his name?'

'Sean O'Hara.'

'Who?'

'*Sean O'Hara!*'

'How will I know him?'

'He's Japanese.'

'Jesus Christ!'

He eventually agreed. I stayed in the diner until it closed. I bought a fifth of bourbon from the owner and began the long walk back to my cabin, ten or twelve miles south on the switchback, hairpin highway.

I reached home at about five in the morning. It was cool and there was a dense milky fog over the ocean, flat like a snowfield. I moved very cautiously down the lane. O'Hara was sitting on the bonnet of my car smoking.

'Sean,' I said softly. 'It's me.'

'Hi, Mr Todd,' he said. 'Just like you predicted. He was waiting for you. I got here about an hour ago. I come down the road real slow, real quiet. I hear him taking a leak. End of problem.'

'Is he still here?'

'Sure. Up here a ways.'

I had walked right past him. Smee had been hiding in the bushes on the edge of the lane where he could overlook all approaches to the house. He lay quite still, a large pair of army-issue binoculars beside him. His wig was dislodged, tilted forwards almost to his eyebrows. He looked stupid and ugly.

'He's not dead is he?'

'I should fuckin' well hope so. For one thousand dollars Sean O'Hara gives you dead.'

'What? . . . Jesus Christ! Why the hell did you do that?'

'Because you said you wanted the guy offed.'

'I said I wanted him *off my back*.'

'Uh-uh. No. No, Mr Todd. You said offed. I ast you to repeat it.'

'I said "off my back". I didn't want you to *kill* him. Bloody hell!'

'You said you didn't care how I did it. Money no object. Get rid of him.'

O'Hara jabbered on, proudly justifying himself. I knelt shakily beside Smee. He seemed quite unmarked. I felt vainly for a pulse. I held a wet finger beneath his nostrils. No cooling breath.

'What did you do?'

'I crep up behind him. He couldn't hear me, 'cause of his pissing, like, and I did this.'

I felt O'Hara's hard blunt index fingers press gently in the cavities behind the lobes of my ears. I shivered.

'You press hard, they're unconscious in twenty seconds. Then they die in a couple of minutes. Not a scratch.'

So that was that. For another $500 Sean agreed to help me dispose of the body. We loaded him into his car and I drove it south, O'Hara following, to a point where the highway ran along the edge of a cliff, high above the ocean. I couldn't see the rocks or the surf, below me all was mist, swirling, dense, shifting. Smee's car had been hired under a false name. O'Hara removed all other documents from his body and volunteered to dispose of them for $25. I agreed. We positioned Smee in the driving seat, released the handbrake and ran the car over the edge. I saw it cartwheel into the whiteness. Then I heard a splash. Sean ran me back to the cabin. I had $600 dollars there which I gave him. I said I would send him the remainder. He left. I went to bed. I slept until midday. Then I got into my car and drove to Los Angeles, to Eddie, and my salvation.

VILLA LUXE 2 July 1972

Last night I woke at about 3 a.m. I heard footsteps outside. At first I paid them no attention. Fishermen often walk past the house at all hours on their way to the beach. But then, as I lay there, I realised that this person was walking *around* the villa. I lay stiff and still in bed, mentally re-bolting and re-shuttering every door and window. Yes, I was sure. I am compulsive about locking up everything at night.

I got out of bed trying to catch sight of this night visitor. I crouched in the hall. I could hear him outside on the gravelled forecourt. Then his footsteps walking away. A few minutes later the sound of a car starting.

In the morning I go outstide. The sun shines down. The sky is pale blue. I can't make out any footprints. Half way up the track I find a cigarette butt. Lucky Strike. Does it mean anything in this day of the ubiquitous international brand?

The fact remains ... The fact remains and I have to face up to it. Smee's body was never found. The car was discovered some two weeks after O'Hara had pushed it over the cliff (all this was related to me by Eddie. I was already in Europe). It was assumed that the driver had been thrown out as the vehicle tumbled through the air before it hit the water. A search was made but no body ever turned up. Because Smee had hired the car under a false name it was several weeks before he was identified as the missing man. His wife had reported his absence shortly after my departure. She thought he was away on HUAC business in Chicago. As far as Eddie was aware no link had been established between him and me. He said no-one from the FBI had come to question him. That part of the coastline was scattered with holiday cabins and campsites. It would be impossible to establish who had been there at the time of the accident. And it was still regarded as an accident. The only hint of foul play was Smee's alibi. He had told everyone he was going to Chicago. The FBI denied he was working on a case for them. As I had thought, Smee was pursuing his own warped vendetta by this stage. I supposed that Smee thought there was only one way to get me before I was rehabilitated. The offices of Alert Inc. gave no clues, either. Their files were full of 'communists' and 'subversives' whose lives they had ruined. Smee had thousands of enemies. At the inquest no verdict was returned. The case was left open.

I had gone straight to Eddie and told him everything. He said I should have come earlier. 'I could have handled this, John,' he said sadly. 'So much more neatly.' He was annoyed with me for my thoughtlessness. I realised that even after forty years there were aspects of Eddie Simmonette that remained completely opaque to me. And what was worse was that I had inadvertently implicated him too, by asking him to pay O'Hara. O'Hara had been to his house, had seen him and received money from him. He was not too concerned about O'Hara, however. His silence could be relied on. I was the problem.

Eddie sent me home and told me to settle my affairs in an orderly way with no unseemly urgency. I sold the house. I said goodbye to Nora-Lee (a real retrospective regret, this, but at the time I could think of nothing but my safety). Ten days after Smee's death I was on the plane to London.

I followed Eddie's instructions faithfully. I travelled to Paris where I hired a car and drove across several borders (ostensibly scouting for locations). Ultimately, after further trail covering I arrived on this island and moved into Eddie's villa. He gave me a selection of three houses he owned in the Mediterranean basin where I could hide up. I chose this island (the others were in Turkey and Beirut). It was almost unknown then, it had none of the vague notoriety it nowadays possesses. And so my exile began. Only Eddie knew where I was. He kept distantly, discreetly in touch; kept me reassured about the continuing absence of suspicion. Some months after I had arrived Mrs Smee went to the police, her memory jogged about my fight with her husband and our mutual threat (something tells me Mrs Smee was not too unhappy to lose Monroe). A mediocre description was issued of me but as Mrs Smee claimed not to remember my name the investigation did not get very far. Eddie told me to give it a couple of years. Let everything blow over. I stayed put, quite happy in a strange sort of way. Eddie visited me sometimes on his yacht. He was my only contact with my old life. He tried to persuade me to come back. But I said no.

So why did I stay on and on? Guilt, fear, peace, seclusion, indolence, old age, apathy, the strange contentment I spoke of. All of these are true. But at the back of my mind I was profoundly frightened of being found out. Also, I have to say this. I was never wholly convinced that Smee had died. O'Hara's killing technique seemed dubious to me. What if it had only sent him into some kind of deep unconsciousness, a coma? And what if he had been thrown clear of the tumbling car and the shock of hitting the water had revived him? You may laugh at my fears, I did too, most of the time. But these thoughts come back to haunt you. You lie alone in your bed at night and your mind is prey to stranger fantasies than these. I stayed because I felt safe. I was far away. Enough was enough.

I catch the bus into the main town and, once there, I start to visit all the tourist hotels. At the third hotel the register yields the man I am looking for. A receptionist directs me to the swimming pool.

I stand looking over the vast crowded terrace, thick with half naked people. Beyond the pool is a strip of dirty brown beach, and beyond that a ruined tower on a small rocky island. I pass slowly among the tables, chairs and rows of sunloungers looking for the face I had seen on the bus that day. Eventually, I find him among four hefty middle-aged American couples. The remains of lunch litter the table. Blue smoke of cigars rises in the sunlight. Laughter. Bellies. Straw hats.

'Hello, Investigator Bonty,' I say.

Bonty looks around. No recognition at all.

'Sorry, fella? ...' His funny lip. His half-lisp.

'Todd. John James Todd.' I can see his brain turning over.

'Mr Todd? ... Yeah. *Yeah*! Got it. Mr *Todd*. Good to see you, my God. This is incredible! After all these years.'

It's convincing. He stands up.

'Listen. Hey, guys. Hold on. I want you to meet John James Todd. The movie director ... Martha, you remember ... John ... ah, he and I met on a HUAC investigation. When did we subpoena you, John? '54?'

''48, the first time.'

'Great days. Great days.'

I was introduced to everybody. I shake seven hands. Smile at smiling faces. Bonty really quite proud.

'God, I remember your case. Brayfield—Christ, you got to that asshole like no other subversive. It was fantastic.' He starts telling his friends about me and Brayfield.

' ... and then he says, this is in open court, Washington DC for Christ's sake!—"Sure, I'll name a dangerous lunatic who is trying to destroy the constitution of the USA." "Who?" says the chairman. "Representative Brayfield," says John here.' Wild laughter and applause. 'I tell you Brayfield practically shit himself, he was so mad ... John, sit down please. What are you drinking? Can you believe this for a coincidence? I'd never have recognised you. Gone native, eh, John?'

'Could I have a word, in private. Just a moment.'

'Excuse us, folks. Be right back.'

We walk to the low wall that seperates us from the thin beach.

I say, 'Very good. You can drop the act now. Where's Smee?'

'Who?'

'Smee. The man who gave you the dossier. HUAC investigator Smee, you know.'

'Smee ... Oh yeah. He's dead.'

'He's here. On this island.'

'John, are you feeling OK? Smee's dead. He drove off a cliff in Carmel somewhere, years ago.'

'He's here, and you know it. You're after me, working with him.'

'John, come and have a drink. You been away too long. That HUAC shit's over now.'

'Don't lie to me Bonty. Was it you or Smee asking questions about me?'

'John, this ain't so amusing.' He frowns. 'In fact you're getting to be a pain inna ass.'

'But I *know*. There's no point in pretending.'

'What are you? Crazy? Some kind of paranoid nut?'

I back off. 'Forget it. Sorry to bother you. Say goodbye for me.' I leave him standing there looking at me, hands on his hips.

It's four in the afternoon by the time I arrive back at the village. I feel grubby and exhausted. But what's worse is the confusion squirming inside me. I feel uneasy, frightened. I feel old. I can't cope with what's going on. Bonty's right. Eddie's right. Smee must be dead, surely ... I can't even ratiocinate. Who, what, where, when?

I try the café. Ernesto isn't there as usual. Lazy bastard! I walk down the track to my villa. Outside the main door three men are waiting. I sigh audibly with relief when I see they are locals, old men. Oddly, they are all dressed in dusty black suits.

'Gentlemen, can I help you?' I say.

They hem me in. Brown, grey moustachioed, seamed faces. They start shouting. Pointing fingers. They talk in some fast glottal patois that I cannot understand. I feel a spray of spittle from their angry mouths. I can understand nothing except one word:

'Emilia ... Emilia ... Emilia ... '

Jesus Christ! Her husband and his brothers. I never expected them to be so ancient. No wonder Emilia was interested in me. Then one of the old codgers spits in my face. Another thwacks me heavily across the shoulders with his walking stick. I swing a punch at the spitter. He has grey greasy hair. I hope it's her husband. I catch him in the throat. He falls back, hawking and gagging. I'm always game for a fight. Then my legs are kicked from under me. I fall down.

'*Bastards!*' I yell, suddenly frightened. These old fellows wear prodigious boots.

I hear a woman's scream. Cries of '*Police! Stop it!*' Emilia, I think. Bless you.

The old men back off. I shake my head and look up. Ulrike. She switches to German. Those harsh relentless consonants work like a whip. Suddenly cowed, the cuckold and his sidekicks shuffle off. Greasy hair turns and shouts at me. Revenge, no doubt.

Ulrike helps me up. I tell her it's an absurd misunderstanding. She takes me into the house and looks after me. A cup of coffee. Some sticking plaster on a grazed knuckle.

'You shouldn't be fighting at your age,' she says. She's right. I feel terrible, jumpy, as if all my organs are overheating and malfunctioning. Lung popping. Heart shudder. Stomach heave. Like an old banger about to break down once and for all.

I stand up and take her hand.

'Here,' I say. 'Come and see this.' I take her into my study. There, I pull the cardboard boxes filled with papers and documents aside and reveal the stack of dull silver canisters.

'You can have it,' I say. 'You and Tobias. Take it away, show it, do what you like.'

'What is it?'

'*The Confessions.*'

*   *   *

What takes me down to the beach that evening? I don't know. I felt like a swim. Naked, I thought, in the sea, just like Big Sur. My back and legs were hurting where those old buggers had hit me. I imagined floating, my weight suspended in salty water. Cool, relief.

I feel something has ended, or is about to end. Or else something new is about to begin. I go carefully through the pine trees. The path to the beach, although well worn, is narrow and meanders perilously close to the cliff edge on some occasions.

As I go I think about something I read once, about a certain kind of ant—a stink ant that lives on the floor of the West African forests. This ant goes about its ant business on the ground in an unremarkable way. It does not know the curious and bizarre fate nature has in store for it. For in these forests there is a particular type of arboreal fungus that flourishes at the top of the great forest trees. At certain times this fungus releases its millions of spores into the air. They blow here and there, driven by softest breezes, eventually coming to rest somewhere on the ground. Some of these spores fall, by the law of averages, onto animals and reptiles and some on crawling insects. They are quite harmless except for one species: our stink ant. This one minute fungus spore falls on the stink ant and is absorbed into its ant system. It drives the ant mad. Remember the stink ant's habitat is the ground, but the lethal poison of the fungus spore engenders in it the sudden desire to climb. So the stink ant, for the first and last time in its life, leaves the ground and begins to ascend. It climbs up and up, higher and higher, until it can climb no more. There, at the very top of the tree. It sinks its mandibles into the ultimate twig—fast, immovable—and abruptly dies. Inside the dead ant the fungus peacefully grows, nourished by ant meat, warmed by the top of the tree. The ant is consumed and a new fungus is born.

Sometimes I look back on my life and I feel like a maddened stink ant driven on by my one random fungus spore. Today, I sense, the time has come to sink my mandibles into the bark at the top of the tree.

21

John James Todd on the Beach

The sun shines warmly on the beach. The rush and roar of the little Mediterranean breakers is ideally soothing. I abandon thoughts of swimming. I sit down in the sun (easy, boy, easy now) and try to relax.

Hamish died last week of throat cancer. Mercifully swiftly. I forgot to tell you—in fact I chose not to, it might have spoilt this story. His solicitor wrote to me, saying that Hamish's last wishes were that I should be sent some papers he had written on prime number theory and an unfinished monograph on Werner Heisenberg's Uncertainty Principle and Kurt Gödel's Incompleteness Theorem. Poor Hamish, I suppose he went a little mad before he died. It can happen easily, I know. I walk up and down the beach and shed a few tears for him. Hamish and his Quantum Mechanics. Hamish and his maths. I had been recalcitrant material for him; he had been trying to make me 'see' things clearly for decades—since we were at school together—and I had blundered along, heedless, saying 'yes' and at once forgetting.

I look back at my life, my three score years and ten, and think—yes, I would like there to be an underlying order to these seven decades of reality. I would like some sense, some meaning. But if I understand Hamish correctly, everything has changed this century. The search for 'truth' can never be the same. Science, which used to attempt to ennumerate all the cogs in the Great Machine, has abandoned that endeavour now. Life at its basic level, the quantum physicists tell us, is deeply paradoxical and fundamentally uncertain. There are no hidden variables, there is no secret agenda for the universe ...

I stop, sniff and look out to sea. This is a mite depressing. Poor old Hamish. God, they're all dead or dying now. Karl-Heinz, my father, Oonagh, Donald Verulam, Faye, Mungo ... on and on. Or lost. Sonia and my children. I haven't seen them for decades. They stopped writing, steadily. I stopped replying, steadily. Then I used to fantasise that one of them would be curious about me and come and seek me out. Emmeline perhaps ... a lean serious girl, I imagined, with a distinct look of my mother. She would have grown suspicious of her mother's crabbed anti-paternal propaganda, unhappy with the name 'Devize', determined to see the truth for herself, to attempt her own reconciliation ... But why should she? Why should Vincent fill the role I wishfully assigned to him? If only Hereford ... Well, it's pointless now. My loss lingers, a haunting, hurtful regret. But I'm replete with 'if onlys'. We're stuck fast in this being-human game. First prize: mortality. I kick a faded plastic container. It rattles dryly on the pebbles. Like bones ... At least it's cooler now. Perhaps I could attempt the climb back up.

Then I hear the clatter of stones from the path in the pine woods and look up, alarmed. I see a momentary flash of white through the trees and then nothing. Quite far off yet. Silence. Stillness. Suddenly—crazily—I think: *SMEE*. It *is* Smee. Then: what nonsense! Deranged fantasies. For God's sake get a grip on yourself! It must be Emilia. Or more likely Ulrike and Tobias come to look for me, to thank me for my gift to them. I won't call out. I'll just wait and see. Whoever it is they'll be here in ten minutes.

I walk up and down the small beach, more composed now. A few midges darn the air. I think of Hamish again and watch the mild waves come in, unfold and collapse. I step down from the dry bank of seaweed onto the strip of sand and pebbles. I look around me. I look at the pebbles at my feet. I plan to select one stone and skim it over the water. Which pebble shall I choose? The beach brims with astonishing potential, each stone teeming with all the possibilities of being a pebble on this particular beach. Rocked and rolled by the waves, rubbed up against its neighbours, draped in glossy seaweed, covered for a while by rank flotsam and jetsam. ... I stop and choose. Now this flat pebble will be hurled out to sea.

I throw, west, towards the setting sun. Skipskipskip—skip, skip. Sink. Rather beautiful. The arc of the throw was strong and flat. The stone partook easily of the air and danced briefly on the water.

There are more noises from the path in the pinewoods. I stand my ground. Up above I hear the human cry of the gulls as they beat their way homeward. I turn and face the sea and watch the waves roll in. I wonder which way my life is going to go now? I have a sudden vision of it as a wave. The little motion in the waters that was my birth, the gradual swelling and building as trough and crest developed, the roar of the breaker as I trundled through the decades. And now here I am on the beach and someone is coming towards me. I consider the possibilities. It couldn't be Smee, could it? Is it just an old man's guilt and paranoia? More likely to be a lovelorn Emilia. Or perhaps it's her greasy husband and his brothers? Then there's Ulrike, come with news about my retrospective. Or even, the happy fancy strikes me, the American private detective, the one who's been asking so many questions about me in the neighbourhood, sent by Doon to seek me out? Or, less exciting but more plausible, it might simply be one of the island's lean spectral dogs, picking its way down to the shore to mooch for scraps of food. Six possibilities, then. Six roads my life could take. I pause. The moment coagulates, a sense of stasis thickens almost palpably around me. This is my reality, absolute, steady, poised.

What will become of me? Death at the vengeful hand of Monroe Smee? A fraught encounter with a passionate Emilia? Battered again by her husband and his decrepit thugs? Fame and renown with Ulrike and her film buff? Reunited with my enigmatic Doon? Or left here, as I am, with a pie-dog for company.

I don't know. I care, I know what I'd like to happen, but in the end we never know. I am uncertain, and so is my fate. Well, I'll go along with that, I think as I stand on the beach, waiting. The world and its people spin along with me, an infinite aggregate of atoms, all obeying Werner Heisenberg's Uncertainty Principle. I look back at my life in this gravid tensed moment and I see it clearly now. Above me, two gulls ride high on the thermals heading home. It has been deeply paradoxical and fundamentally uncertain. That's how I would sum the whole business up, my time on this small planet—deeply paradoxical and fundamentally uncertain . . .

I ponder all the possibilities that come with being human. Good and evil, happiness and misery, achievement and failure, love and isolation—everything that goes into being the particular person you are in your particular social and historical setting. That's a lot, isn't it? My God, that's some menu! I smile to myself, with faint pride, I suppose, but with some wry resignation too. Yes, I've done that human-being business pretty thoroughly, thank you very much. I've participated in the human drama, all right. You—yes, you—can testify on my behalf that I've hunkered down in the mulch of the phenomenal world. Boy, haven't I just! . . . But then, so have you, I dare say. We all do that, don't we—all of us. Like it or not.

As I stand here on my modest beach, waiting for my future,

watching the waves roll in, I feel a strange, light-headed elation. After all, this is the Age of Uncertainty and Incompleteness. John James Todd, I say to myself, at last you are in tune with the universe.